About the Authors

Elle James spent twenty years in South Texas, ranching horses, cattle, goats, ostriches and emus. A former IT professional, Elle now writes full-time, penning intrigues and paranormal adventures that keep her readers on the edge of their seats. Now living in northwest Arkansas, she isn't wrangling cattle, she's wrangling her malti-poo and yorkie. When she's not at her computer, she's snow-skiing, travelling or riding her ATV, dreaming up new stories.

Ever since **Lisa Childs** read her first romance novel (a Mills & Boon of course) at age eleven, all she ever wanted to be was a romance writer. Now an award winning, best-selling author of nearly fifty novels for Mills & Boon, Lisa is living the dream. Lisa loves to hear from readers who can contact her on Facebook, through her website www.lisachilds.com or snail mail address PO Box 139, Marne, MI 49435.

USA TODAY bestselling author **Cassie Miles** lives in Colorado. After raising two daughters and cooking tons of macaroni and cheese for her family, Cassie is trying to be more adventurous in her culinary efforts. She's discovered that almost anything tastes better with wine. When she's not plotting Mills & Boon Intrigue books, Cassie likes to hang out at the Denver Botanical Gardens near her high-rise home.

Tempted

COLLECTION

Tempted by the Bodyguard

ELLE JAMES

LISA CHILDS

CASSIE MILES

MILLS & BOON

First Published in Great Britain 2020
By Mills & Boon, an imprint of HarperCollins*Publishers*
1 London Bridge Street, London, SE1 9GF

TEMPTED BY THE BODYGUARD © 2020 Harlequin Books S.A.

Secret Service Rescue © 2014 Harlequin Books S.A.
Bodyguard's Baby Surprise © 2016 Lisa Childs
Mountain Bodyguard © 2016 Kay Bergstrom

Special thanks and acknowledgement to Elle James for her contribution to *The Adair Legacy* series.

ISBN: 978-0-263-28109-5

MIX
Paper from
responsible sources
FSC™ C007454

FSC
www.fsc.org

This book is produced from independently certified FSC™ paper to ensure responsible forest management.

For more information visit: www.harpercollins.co.uk/green

Printed and bound in Spain
by CPI, Barcelona

SECRET SERVICE
RESCUE

ELLE JAMES

This book is dedicated to my husband who made the trip out to the Outer Banks and captured the essence of the area for me to include in this story, while I attended Writer's Police Academy. Gotta love a man who sacrifices his time to visit the beach for my research!

Chapter 1

Daniel Henderson stood with his hand on the butt of the HK40 pistol resting in the shoulder holster beneath his suit jacket, his gaze locked on the man standing in the middle of the room.

"I repeat, your granddaughter has been missing for two weeks," Patrick O'Hara insisted, worry lines etched deep into his weathered face. "I've pursued all other options. I've filed a missing persons report, but the police have no leads. I'm at my wit's end. That's why I came to you."

"What do you mean, I have a granddaughter?" Former vice president Kate Winston stood straight, her shoulders squared, her lips tight. The only indication that the man in front of her had disturbed her normal calm was how pale her face had become. She glanced around the room at her three sons, Trey, Thaddeus and Samuel. "Is there something you three haven't told me?"

The three men shook their heads as one.

O'Hara, who'd made the shocking statement, shook his head. "Not the child of one of your sons, the child of your daughter. *Our* daughter."

"What the hell are you talking about?" Trey, the oldest son, demanded.

Patrick O'Hara's eyes narrowed. "Maybe you should ask your mother."

Kate closed her eyes and pressed a hand to her chest.

"You're upsetting her." Thad slipped an arm around Kate's shoulders. "Perhaps you should leave, before we have you escorted out."

"No." O'Hara stood firm, his gaze locked on Kate. "I need help finding my granddaughter and you are my last hope. Unless you're going to throw her away like you did our daughter."

Samuel lunged forward. "Get the hell out."

Kate's arm shot out. "No, wait. Let him speak."

Patrick glanced from Trey to Samuel and back to Kate. "Shelby was at the university library Tuesday night two weeks ago, working on some research paper for her graduate program. She said she'd be home by midnight. At two in the morning, I closed the bar and went home. She wasn't there. Her car wasn't parked out front. I got worried and drove all the way into Beth City, to the university. I found her car in the library parking lot, but not Shelby." He scrubbed a hand down his haggard face. "I don't know what else to do."

Daniel's heartstrings were tugged by the desperation in the man's tone and eyes. Two weeks might as well be forever. A woman missing for that long had little chance of being alive.

"How old is she?" Kate pressed her fingers to the bridge of her nose.

"Twenty-three. She's never late for anything." Patrick stepped forward.

Daniel walked between Patrick and Kate, holding his gun out. "That's far enough."

Patrick's glance shifted to Daniel. "I just wanted to show her the picture of Shelby." He looked back at Kate. "She looks just like her mother. And Carrie looked just like you. Brown hair, bright blue eyes." He smiled, then the smile quickly faded. "We have to find her. She's all I have."

Daniel took the photo from the man's hands and held it out to Kate.

Trey intercepted it. "The man is crazy. You're not really going to help him, are you? He's preying on your weakness—" Trey shot a glance at the picture, his eyes widening. "Damn."

Kate held out her hand. "Give me the photo."

Trey handed it across. "It has to be a forgery. You can do almost anything with computer graphics these days."

Patrick's lips turned up. "She's her mother's daughter."

Kate stared at the picture for a long time, tears welling in her eyes. "This could be me as a young woman." She stared across at him. "I don't understand."

"What's to understand? You gave up your daughter. I raised Carrie, and she had a daughter, Shelby. Whom I also raised." He jabbed a finger at the photo. "Shelby Raye O'Hara. A beautiful, smart young lady with a full life ahead of her. *If* I can find her before something awful happens to her." He swallowed hard. "If it hasn't already."

If she had been missing for two weeks, Daniel predicted bad things had, indeed, happened to the girl. And nothing anyone could do would bring her back.

"I didn't give up my daughter. She died," Kate whispered, a single tear slipping down her cheek. She lifted her head, her chin trembling.

"Is that what you told yourself?" Patrick laughed, the sound completely without humor. He stepped closer. "I don't care if lying to yourself helped you throw away your own flesh and blood. I can't believe I ever loved you. You're selfish, heartless and deserved the man you married."

Daniel laid a hand on the man's chest. "Back off."

Patrick stared at Daniel as if it was the first time he'd seen him and his gun. "Kate, I don't give a damn about you or your high-society family. What I do care about is getting my granddaughter back. Alive. If you have any sense of decency, you'll help. She's your family, too."

"Mother," Sam said. "Say the word and I'll throw him out."

Daniel braced himself for a fight with Patrick O'Hara. He didn't want to use his gun; it would leave a big mess in the Winstons' house. And as far as he could tell, O'Hara wasn't armed.

"No." Kate shook her head. "If someone thinks Shelby O'Hara is related to me in any way, she's in danger."

"I've never told anyone about her bloodline. Shelby doesn't even know her mother was your daughter."

"Stop." Kate held up her hand. "Until I verify your story, I promise to help. And if Shelby has been kidnapped because of me, we will do our best to help find her." Kate turned to Thad. "Our only link to the Cartel at this time is Robert D'Angelis. Can we check and see if he knows anything about the missing woman?"

Thad, who was on the Raleigh Police crime scene investigation team, nodded. "He's in a holding cell at Wake County Jail. I'm on my way."

"I'm going with you," Kate insisted. She turned to her personal secretary, Debra Winston, Trey's wife. "Debra, cancel all my afternoon appointments."

"Yes, ma'am." Debra, eight-and-a-half-months pregnant, but just as on the ball as ever, waddled out of the room, tapping the touch screen on her cell phone to make the necessary calls.

Kate turned to Daniel. "Mr. Henderson, please notify the director of the Secret Service about this new development. If Shelby's kidnapping has anything to do with me and the Cartel's attempts on my life, I want the Secret Service involved in finding her, as well. The more people looking, the better chance we have of finding her. Now let's get to the county jail." Kate passed Daniel, heading for the door, her heels clicking determinedly on the white marble tiles of the foyer.

"I'm going with you," Patrick said as he fell into step with Kate.

"Of course you are." Kate didn't display any emotion in her announcement. "If you're lying to me, we won't have far to go to have you arrested for trespassing and attempted assault."

As Kate's personal bodyguard, Daniel insinuated

himself between her and Patrick, limping along as fast as he could, ignoring the pain in his knee.

If O'Hara had a knife, he'd have to go through Daniel to get to Kate Winston. It wouldn't be the first time he'd taken a hit for the woman. His scars had barely healed over from the bullets he'd absorbed by throwing himself in front of her at a rally. And if he hadn't torn a ligament, he'd be investigating instead of performing bodyguard duties.

Debra must have alerted the chauffeur. One of the two Winston limousines stood out front in the curved drive, the second one coming to a halt behind it.

"Daniel and Thad, I want you two in my vehicle. Mr. O'Hara can ride with the others in the second."

Patrick stepped away from the Winston family. "I'll take my own car."

Trey slipped an arm around his pregnant wife. "Debra, Sam and I will follow in my car. No need to take the other limousine. Besides, it's hard for Debra to get in and out of it."

"Suit yourself." Kate slid into the limo, tucking in her long legs. Thad sat on one side of her and Daniel on the other. He didn't like that Patrick was leaving alone. But Daniel refused to leave Kate's side. As long as he was assigned as her bodyguard, he would provide the best protection he could. Normally, he hated playing bodyguard to politicians. But Kate Winston wasn't a normal politician. She was smart, down-to-earth and personable.

Still, Daniel would rather be investigating the case than babysitting the target. Given his latest injury, he was lucky to be working at all. A torn ligament meant being relegated to the sidelines, gimping along until he could return to investigations.

By the time they'd arrived at the Wake County Jail, Daniel had contacted the director of the Secret Service and relayed the information about Shelby O'Hara's disappearance. Director Kincannon agreed to meet them there.

"What's going on, Mother?" Thad asked on the drive across town. "Why did O'Hara say you had a granddaughter?"

"It's a long story." Kate looked straight ahead. "I'd rather not talk about it just yet. The most important thing to focus on is finding the girl."

Daniel suspected that, like most high-powered politicians, even Kate Winston had a few skeletons in her closet. Skeletons not even her sons knew about.

Once inside the building, Kate insisted Daniel go with Thad to interrogate the prisoner. "If Robert D'Angelis has any information concerning the missing girl, the sooner we get it out of him, the better for Shelby." A sheriff's deputy led her to small room where she could watch the interview through a two-way mirror.

As promised, Director Kincannon met them outside the interrogation room. "Agent Henderson, Detective Winston." He nodded to each of them. "They've moved the suspect into the interrogation room. Do you want me to question him?"

Daniel paused outside the interview room his hand on the doorknob. "I've had more recent experience interrogating suspects."

Director Kincannon nodded. "Then, by all means, question him."

Daniel turned to Thad.

"Go for it." Thad held up his hands. "I'll stand back and listen."

"While you two conduct the interview, I'll watch from the observation room." Director Kincannon moved back toward the room where Kate Winston waited.

Daniel gathered his thoughts and entered the interrogation room, Thad close behind him.

Former Secret Service agent Robert D'Angelis sat in a metal chair with his hands cuffed and resting on the table in front of him. His face was pale with a slightly green tint. A half-empty paper cup of water sat on the table within his reach.

The tall man was hunched over, his fit body seeming to sag with the weight of his muscles. A fine sheen of sweat covered his face, and his eyes were yellow and bloodshot.

"Why am I here?" he said. "I'm not talking to anyone without my lawyer."

"Agent D'Angelis, we have a few questions for you," Daniel said.

D'Angelis blinked and squeezed his eyes tight, then opened them, squinting. "Light is so damned bright." He shook his head and blinked again.

"Are you all right? Do you need a glass of water?" Daniel asked.

"Just had one." He lifted his cuffed hands and tugged at the collar of the bright orange jumpsuit supplied by the Wake County Jail. "So damn hot in here. Don't they have an air conditioner?" He rolled his head around on his neck and stopped to stare across the table as Daniel took the seat opposite him. "I got nothing for you." He spit in Daniel's face.

Daniel removed an old-fashioned handkerchief from his back pocket, wiped the spit from his cheek and folded the handkerchief neatly before returning it to his pocket, maintaining his silence until he was finished. Then he leaned close until his face was within inches of D'Angelis's. He didn't blink, staring straight into the suspect's eyes. In a firm, direct voice, he asked, "Where's the girl?"

D'Angelis sat back in his chair. "I don't know what you're talking about."

"Do you know what they do to police officers and Secret Service agents in jail?"

"I have more years of experience than you do, Henderson. I know exactly what they do," D'Angelis ground out, his voice raspy. He coughed into his sleeve. When he pulled his mouth away from the crook of his elbow, blood stained the orange fabric. "I don't feel well. I want a doctor."

"You'll get a doctor as soon as you tell us where the girl is."

"I don't know about a damned girl." D'Angelis coughed again, more blood staining his sleeve and dribbling from the corner of his mouth.

Daniel nodded toward the mirror. "Get a doctor," he said, then turned back to D'Angelis. "I'm getting that doctor for you. Give me something on the girl."

D'Angelis raised his hands and slammed them, cuffs and all, on the wooden table. "What's it matter, anyway? They're gonna use her to get to Kate. Then they'll kill her."

"She's still alive?" Daniel's pulse raced through his veins. "Where is she?"

"It's hot in here." The man slumped across the table. "I feel awful."

"Damn it, where is she?" Daniel grabbed D'Angelis's shoulders and forced him to look up.

The man's eyes were completely bloodshot and watery.

"Basement."

"Basement of what?" He shook D'Angelis, trying to get him to focus and tell him the rest of the address.

"House on East Cabbarus Street," the man said.

"Which house? What address?" Daniel demanded.

"Sixty-two fifty." D'Angelis's head lolled and his eyes rolled to the back of his head. His body went limp and he slid out of his chair onto the floor.

"Damn." Thad ran for the door. "Get a medic in here!"

Daniel pushed the chair away from the fallen man and squatted beside him on the floor, loosening the zipper on the orange jumpsuit.

D'Angelis's hand grabbed his wrist and he raised his head long enough to say, "Don't trust—" He choked on the phlegm in his throat and blood trickled out of the corner of his mouth, then he coughed again and passed out.

The door burst open. Two paramedics raced in and bent over D'Angelis. Daniel and Thad left the room, moving to the side of the hallway to get out of the way of the emergency staff.

They entered the room where Kate, Trey, Sam, Patrick and Jed Kincannon, the director of the Secret Service, stood watching the staff work on Robert D'Angelis's inert form.

"What happened?" Kate's hand rested on her throat. "One minute he was all cocky, the next he seemed to fail in front of us."

"I don't know," Thad said.

"I do." Daniel nodded to Thad. "We're going to Cabarrus Street to find Shelby O'Hara."

Daniel led the way out of the county jail.

Thad followed, dialing for assistance from the Raleigh Police Department dispatch.

When they got outside, Daniel remembered they'd come in Kate Winston's limousine. "We can't go in that, and Mrs. Winston can't go with us."

"Take my vehicle." Trey tossed the keys. "I'll stay with Mother to make sure nothing happens to her."

"Thanks." Daniel caught the keys and ran for Trey's car, Thad on his heels.

"Shouldn't we wait for backup?" Thad asked.

"If Shelby's captors get wind that we're on the way, they might kill her before backup arrives."

"Give me the keys." Thad held up his hand.

Daniel hesitated only a moment. As a member of the Raleigh Police Department, Thad would know the streets better than Daniel, who'd only been in Raleigh a couple months since he'd been assigned to protect Kate Winston. He hopped into the passenger seat as Thad twisted the key in the ignition.

In seconds, they'd pulled out of the parking lot and raced away from the jail. "It's only half a mile from here. We'll be there before the police can get a patrol car there."

Daniel removed his gun from his holster, checked to

ensure a bullet had been chambered and braced himself for arrival at their destination.

Shelby Raye O'Hara rubbed the plastic zip tie that bound her wrists on the ragged edge of a broken brace she'd ripped from the wooden chair she sat on. Her wrists chafed and bled where she'd scraped them across the splintered wood. For fourteen days she'd been confined in the dark room, tallied by the number of meals she'd been granted and what was provided. Mornings were stale bagels and bottled water. In the late afternoons, she was given a bologna sandwich and more water.

The men wearing masks who'd grabbed her on her way out of the Beth City University Library hadn't spoken a word to her. They hadn't explained why she'd been kidnapped and hadn't given her a chance to change their minds.

From what she could tell, she was being held in a basement, the concrete brick walls as solid as they came and no windows to let sunshine in. One light shone down on her when the men fed her or allowed her to use the facilities in a small corner bathroom. There, she'd managed to finger brush her teeth, wash her face with the single bar of soap and duck her head under the faucet to scrub her hair every other day. Spit baths were a blessing, but she'd give anything for a real soak in a hot tub.

So far, they hadn't used any violence against her, but the conditions were far from the Ritz and she was tired of being kept in the dark physically and mentally. And if she didn't see another bologna sandwich in her lifetime, it would be too soon.

What bothered her almost as much was knowing how frantic her grandfather would be by now. She'd promised to be home by midnight. Two weeks ago, she'd been researching case studies for a paper she was writing for her graduate degree in counseling.

God, she'd be so far behind on her coursework if she got back.

When she got back.

She worked the plastic tie harder, refusing to give up, her skin slippery with her own blood. By the rumbling in her belly, it was close to dinnertime. One of her guards would be down with her meal soon. If she could get loose before he came…

The zip tie snapped and her wrists flew apart, the pressure and pain lessening immediately.

Hope surged, along with adrenaline.

The lock on the door jiggled, heralding another visit from her silent jailors who would undoubtedly be bringing her the bottled water and bologna sandwich.

Shelby hid the broken brace beneath her thigh and sat in the chair, slumped over, as if she'd fallen asleep.

The door opened, and light shone down the stairs, the beam stopping short of where she waited. If she could get past one guard, she'd have a chance of getting out of the basement. The other guard would be waiting at the top of the stairs.

She'd cross that bridge when she came to it. First, she'd take care of the bologna man.

He wore his requisite mask and carried a flashlight in one hand and the sandwich and water in the other.

When he reached the bottom of the stairs, he crossed to her, shining the bright beam across her face.

Shelby feigned sleep, her head drooping low, her

hair sweeping over her cheeks, shadowing her eyes. Her muscles tensed as she prepared to strike.

Her guard bent to place the water bottle and sandwich on the floor by her feet.

With all the force she could muster, she kicked her feet up, caught the guard on the chin and sent him tumbling backward onto his backside.

The flashlight flew out of his hand toward the stairs.

Shelby leaped over the man's flailing legs, snatched the light and raced up the stairs.

Bologna man shouted, "Get her!"

By the time the second guard reached the doorway at the top of the stairs, Shelby was there. She swung the heavy metal flashlight with all her might, clipping the man in the temple. He staggered backward.

Shelby ducked past him and ran for a door. She ripped it open and found a broom closet. Footsteps running up the stairs and muttered curses from the man behind her sent her scurrying to the next door. She pulled it open and ran down a long hallway into a kitchen.

As she reached what looked like a heavy wooden exterior door, she was hit from behind with a flying tackle. She crashed to the floor, her head making contact with the hardwood planks and stars danced before her eyes. She fought not to give in to the gray fog creeping in on her peripheral vision. She couldn't stop now. She'd come too far.

The door opened in front of her and a man in a mask stared down at her. "Time to leave," he said, his voice low and gruff.

The man lying across her legs scrambled to his feet,

pressing a foot into the middle of her back. "What about her?"

"Leave her. And hurry. D'Angelis sang."

Shelby's head ached, her vision blurred, but she held on, trying to grasp what they were talking about.

"Torch the place," said the man who'd given the order to leave.

Her heart pounded, sending blood rushing through her system, chasing back the fog. Shelby forced herself to lie still, pretending to be out cold.

"Good, the bitch deserves to die after what she did to me."

"And me." A hand grabbed the back of her hair, jerked her head back and slammed her forehead into the floor. "That's for kicking me in the teeth."

Pain knifed through her head, bringing with it a rush of darkness. As she fought to stay awake, her temples throbbing, she heard the man at the door say, "Come on, I hear sirens."

The door opened, and a fresh draft of air washed over her.

The scent of gasoline filtered through the open door as the other two men exited. They closed the door. Seconds later, smoke sifted in through the cracks.

Shelby knew she had to get out before she was burned alive. She pushed to her hands and knees and crawled several steps before the pain drained her strength and she fell to the floor.

Lying against the cool hardwood flooring, she prayed death would come quickly. Smoke filled the room and burned her lungs. With her eyes closed tight, she accepted her fate and welcomed oblivion.

As she drifted in and out of consciousness, she felt

a cool breeze stir across her, then strong arms curl around her, lifting her from the floor and floating her through the clouds to cool, clean night air.

Shelby's eyes fluttered open and she stared up into the face of her guardian angel, a man with dark blond hair and green eyes. "Am I in heaven?" she whispered.

A deep chuckle rumbled against her side and a voice as smooth as melted chocolate filled her ears. "Not hardly. But at least you're no longer in hell."

Chapter 2

Daniel had taken the back of the building and Thad had gone through the front. The entire house had lit up like a bonfire, thanks to the gasoline used as an accelerant. Worried they wouldn't find her in the burning structure in time to save her, Daniel had practically fallen over Shelby when he'd raced through the back door into what appeared to be a kitchen. She'd been out cold, lying facedown, smoke filling the room over her head.

Without stopping to think, he'd gathered her into his arms and run out of the inferno into the fresh air. The woman was light, petite and curvy.

Ambulances, police cars and fire trucks, all with their sirens wailing, converged at the location.

Not wanting to put her down on the damp grass, Daniel held her until a paramedic rolled a stretcher

out of the back of the ambulance and urged him to lay
her on the clean white sheet.

Only then did he let go. Despite her tangled and
dirty hair, and a bruise the size of a goose egg rising
on her forehead, her pale face was beautiful. Her dark
brows arched delicately, and high cheekbones and soft,
pink lips tugged at something in Daniel's heart. Something he thought long suppressed in his determined
march down his chosen career path.

"We'll take care of her." The medic stepped between him and the girl to position an oxygen mask
over her face.

Daniel didn't want to leave her side. "I'm staying
with her." Based on the photograph Patrick O'Hara had
shown Kate, this was Shelby O'Hara, granddaughter
to the former vice president of the United States. He
turned to a cop and told him to let Thad know he'd
found Shelby.

"Anyone else in the house?" the cop asked.

"I don't know."

Firemen went inside, checking the rooms one by
one until they all came out, declaring the house was
clear. Whoever had kidnapped Ms. O'Hara had gone,
leaving her to burn to death.

Daniel's hands clenched into fists. If this kidnapping
and attempted murder were in any way related to Kate
Winston, one attempt on Shelby might not be the last,
given the rash of attempts over the past few months.

Thad joined him at the back of the ambulance as the
paramedics loaded the stretcher with the pale woman
strapped down. "She gonna be all right?"

The paramedic paused with his foot on the back
step. "You a relative?"

Thad shoved a hand through his smoky hair, a half grin on his face. "I think I'm her uncle."

The paramedic frowned. "You think, or you know?"

Thad stared down at the woman. "She has dark hair like our mother's. Yeah, I'm an uncle."

The paramedic rolled his eyes and gave him the news. "She has some nasty bumps on her head and possible concussion and smoke inhalation, but she should be fine."

"Where are you taking her?" Thad asked.

"WakeMed. Now, if you'll excuse us." The paramedic climbed in and started to close the door behind him.

Daniel grabbed the door. "I'm going with you."

"Are you a relative?"

"No. I'm Secret Service, responsible for the safety of this woman." Daniel flashed his credentials.

"Guess you get a free ride to the hospital." The paramedic jerked his head toward the front. "You can ride shotgun." Then he closed the door and twisted the handle, locking it in place.

Daniel rounded to the front and climbed into the passenger seat.

"I'll notify the family and meet you there." Thad closed the door, shutting Daniel in the ambulance.

Daniel twisted in his seat, peering through the window into the back of the ambulance, watching every move made by the paramedics as they checked Shelby's vital signs.

At the hospital, she was taken to radiology for X-rays of her head and lungs. By the time she was moved to a room on the third floor, the entire Winston family had arrived, along with Patrick O'Hara.

When Patrick spotted Daniel and Thad at the nurses' station, he hurried forward. "Where is she?"

"They just moved her into a private room and are getting her settled," Thad told him.

"I want to see her." Patrick pushed past the two men.

Daniel hooked his arm. "The nurses are settling her in. They said they'd let us know when she's ready for visitors."

Patrick slumped. "Two weeks. She's been missing for two weeks. What did those bastards do to her?"

A nurse emerged from a room down the hallway and strode toward the group of Winstons. "Who is Ms. O'Hara's closest relative?"

Patrick and Kate both spoke at once. "I am."

Patrick glared at Kate and stated, "I'm her grandfather."

The nurse addressed him. "Ms. O'Hara is still unconscious, but the doctor administered a mild sedative and pain medication. He'll be by to give you her diagnosis shortly."

"Can I see her?" Patrick asked.

The nurse stared around at the others. "Just you, for now. The rest of you should stay in the waiting room and leave the hallway clear for the staff."

The relief in the man's face was palpable. The nurse led him into the room, the door closing behind them.

Daniel wanted to follow them, but remained back. Part of the job of a Secret Service agent was to maintain a low profile, only stepping forward to defend those he is assigned to protect. He moved with the rest of the group to the waiting room on the same floor.

Kate, Trey and Samuel circled Thad.

"Did you see her?" Kate asked.

Thad nodded. "I did."

"What did she look like?"

Thad shrugged. "The paramedic had already slipped the oxygen mask over her face. I couldn't tell what she looked like, but she has light brown hair."

"She looked a lot like you, Mrs. Winston," Daniel offered. "Light brown hair, slight build. When she opened her eyes briefly, I could tell they were blue."

"So it could be true." Kate stared at the door leading into the hallway. "My baby didn't die like my mother told me."

"Mom, what baby?" Trey held her hand. "Who is Patrick O'Hara? How do you know him?"

Kate's gaze shifted to the window, looking out into the night. "We were teenagers when we met on the Outer Banks. I was vacationing at the family beach house. He was the bar owner's son." She smiled. "We spent the whole summer together. Young, in love and foolish." Her smile faded. "When I returned home, I found out I was pregnant. My father was livid. He'd been grooming me to marry rich. I didn't want to. I wanted Patrick."

"What happened?" Trey asked.

"My father threatened to hit Patrick with charges of statutory rape if I didn't go away to New Hampshire to live with my aunt until the baby was born." Kate's hands covered her belly as if she was seventeen and pregnant all over again. "I wanted to keep the baby. I was going to run away with it and find Patrick. He'd said he loved me. I was certain once he saw his baby, he'd want us to be together as a family.

"When my due date arrived, I was scared. My mother was there with me, but no one prepared me for what it would be like. The delivery was difficult because the baby was breech. The doctor gave me something to knock me out. When I came to the next day, my mother was crying. She told me the baby was dead."

Daniel's chest tightened at the anguish evident in Kate Winston's face. It was a lot for a young girl to handle.

"My mother told me the baby was dead." She pressed her fist to her mouth. "I was so sad, I wanted to die."

Trey hugged his mother. "But you didn't, and we're glad you didn't." He pressed a kiss to the top of her head. "We love you."

Samuel and Thad gathered around their mother, hugging her.

Trey was the first to step back. "Actually, your story would explain some of Grandma Eunice's dementia."

"What do you mean?" Kate glanced at her oldest son.

"Last time I paid a visit in the nursing home, she was babbling on about a baby girl, and giving her to her father to care for. She was really upset. The staff nurse calmed her with a sedative. I didn't think anything of it." He looked at his mother's face. "Until now. I bet it was deep-seated guilt gnawing at her."

"Why would she do it?" Kate swayed, pressing her hand to her chest. "I had a daughter and I didn't know it. All these years…"

Trey slipped an arm around his mother's shoulders and drew her close.

"How could she?" Kate pressed her cheek into her

son's chest. "My mother loved me. Why would she give my baby away?"

"Could she have done it to protect you and the baby?" Thad asked. "Grandpa Adair was a mean old bastard."

Daniel stood back, trying not to eavesdrop on the family's business, but was nevertheless shocked at Kate's story. Was this how the rich and famous lived? Stealing babies, threatening loved ones?

If it was, then he wanted nothing to do with it. He'd grown up in an average family where they had their arguments, but they loved each other. His father was as much a part of his life as his brothers. It sounded as though Kate's childhood had been less beautiful than her family had let on to the public.

Daniel made a note to himself to call home the next quiet moment he had to himself.

"Where is she?" Jed Kincannon entered the waiting room. "Has she spoken yet?"

"She's still unconscious." Daniel pulled his boss aside and told him what he knew, which wasn't much. "The kidnappers escaped and burned any evidence they might have left behind in the house."

Jed let out a deep breath. "I want to be there when Ms. O'Hara wakes up. We need to know what she knows. The sooner she identifies her kidnappers, the better. I want them off the streets before they cause any more grief."

"You and me both."

Kate stepped up to Jed. "Do you think they'll try to take her again?"

"They took her once," he said.

"But they didn't present a ransom note or any demands," Samuel argued.

"Maybe they were waiting for proof of her lineage," Thad said. "Now that we're involved, it could mean even greater danger for her."

"We can't let anything happen to her or her father." Kate faced him. "Daniel, I want you to provide Shelby's security. I trust you the most of any agent." She smiled, laying a hand on his arm. "I know you'll do everything in your power to protect Shelby, even take a bullet for her."

"I'd say he's good for it," Samuel nodded. "He took three for you."

"Exactly." Kate's hand was warm on Daniel's arm. "Take care of my granddaughter. I want the opportunity to get to know her."

Patrick O'Hara stepped through the door, his face haggard. "They chased me out." He scrubbed a hand through his hair. "She never woke up. The doctor said it's to be expected with head trauma. They're keeping an eye on her tonight, but expect she'll wake up in the morning. The good news is that they didn't detect any brain swelling or hemorrhaging."

Lucy Sinclair, Thad's fiancée, followed Patrick into the room, crossed to Thad and slipped an arm around his waist. "I got here as quickly as I could and checked in with the nurse in charge of the floor. It's like Mr. O'Hara said, she's sleeping. Other than being a little dehydrated, her vital signs are good. She should be up and talking by morning."

Trey glanced down at his watch and across to his wife. Despite her attempt to look in control, Debra was sagging under the weight of the baby. "There's no use all of us waiting for her to wake up. We should go home and get some rest. Tomorrow will be stressful in itself."

"Trey, you need to get Debra home and off her feet." Kate turned to Patrick. "You and Shelby will be staying at the Winston Estate."

Patrick crossed his arms over his chest. "You can't order me around like you do the rest of the world. I have a business to run on the Outer Banks."

Kate nodded. "I know. But we almost lost Shelby tonight. If there's any possibility her kidnappers will try to take her again, she needs protection. Can you provide that for her at your bar?"

Patrick's lips pressed into a thin line. After a long pause, he answered, "No."

"Then I implore you to bring Shelby to the Winston Estate where she can have 24/7 protection by the most trusted man the Secret Service has to offer." She nodded toward Daniel. "I've just tasked Daniel Henderson with the duty of providing protection for Shelby."

Daniel bit down hard on his lip to keep from reminding her that he hadn't agreed to play babysitter to a twenty-three-year-old woman. He'd rather be out investigating this case, finding the men responsible for the attempts on Kate's life and kidnapping her granddaughter. But discussing that in front of the rest of the family was not professional.

He'd wait and get her alone to discuss his duties in private.

For the time being, if the former vice president wanted him to provide security for her granddaughter, he'd protect her granddaughter.

"Okay," Patrick said finally. "I'll get my assistant

manager to run the bar for the next few days. And I'm only doing this for Shelby. If I had any other choices, I wouldn't have come to you."

"Patrick." Kate stared into his eyes. "I thought my baby was dead."

"Her name was Carrie," Patrick bit out. "She was beautiful, just like you."

"Was?" Tears welled in Kate's eyes.

"She died in an auto accident when she was only twenty-four. Shelby is all I have left and I'll be damned if I lose her, too." Patrick walked out of the room, leaving a stricken Kate in his wake.

Daniel turned away, unable to watch as tears slipped silently down Kate's face.

"I never knew my own daughter." Kate's voice shook.

"We had a sister." Samuel stared after Patrick's retreating figure.

"And we'll never know her." Thad hugged Lucy close.

Daniel wanted to storm through the room and yell at all of them, "You have Shelby. Don't screw it up with her."

"Mother," Trey said. "Go home. Get some sleep. I'll stay."

"No need," Daniel said. "I'll keep watch through the night. If she wakes, I'll call."

"She should be surrounded by familiar faces when she comes to," Kate said.

Patrick stood at the doorway. "Which isn't even one of you. I'm staying."

"Fair enough." Kate hooked Trey's arm and leaned

on him as they walked out of the waiting room. As she passed Daniel, she paused. "Keep her safe."

Daniel nodded. "I will."

Then the Winstons stepped into the elevator that whisked them to the ground floor. All the tension left the floor with them and Daniel let himself take a deep breath.

Patrick stood beside him, his gaze on the closed elevator doors. "She's as beautiful today as she was when we first met. If not more so."

Daniel didn't comment. He saw a lot of Kate in her granddaughter's features. If Shelby had half the gumption of her grandmother, she'd be a formidable foe and a dedicated friend.

"I'm going to sit with Shelby. There's a chair in the room that reclines." Patrick stuck out his hand. "I understand you were the one who pulled her from the burning home. Thank you."

"You're welcome." Daniel clasped the man's hand and shook it. This was a man he could relate to. He had a firm handshake, the calloused hands of a working man and an open, friendly face. "I'll stay outside her room and make sure no unauthorized personnel enter."

"I owe you a debt I can never repay."

"No payment necessary. It's part of my job."

Patrick returned to Shelby's room, entering quietly, closing the door behind him.

Daniel's leg ached, and he was tired but still wound up by the events of the evening. He found a chair and propped it against the wall beside Shelby's room. Too preoccupied to sit, he paced, dreading the boredom of being a bodyguard at the same time as he embraced the job, knowing he was protecting a woman who'd done nothing to become a target other than being born into the wrong family.

After a while, Daniel sat to relieve the strain on his leg.

Several hours passed, the clock hands spinning around the dial to six in the morning. Patrick O'Hara emerged from Shelby's room, eyes bloodshot, clothes wrinkled and chin stubbled with a day's growth of beard. "I'm going to hit the hay and then find a cup of coffee and a meal if such exists at this hour. Can I get you anything?"

"No, thank you." Daniel stood and stretched the kinks out of his sore muscles. "You might as well take your time. I'll be here."

Patrick left, shuffling down the long hallway to the elevator.

A nurse made her rounds, checking on the patients. When she came to Shelby's door, Daniel entered behind her. She checked the position of the IV needle, the bag of fluid and the monitors and shone a light into Shelby's eyes. When she finished, she left the room and Daniel stayed.

Someone had wiped the dirt and soot from Shelby's face. Clean and free of makeup, she looked younger than her twenty-three years.

She stirred, her hand clenching and her lips twitching. Behind her eyelids, her eyes moved, but she didn't open them. Daniel wondered what she was dreaming about.

She raised a hand to her chest and moaned, the sound so sad and mournful, Daniel couldn't help himself. He lifted her hand and held it, hoping his touch would ease her nightmares and allow her to sleep.

She curled into him, tucking his hand beneath her cheek, and moaned again.

His chest tightened and he leaned over her, wrapping his arms around her, shielding her from the bad guys in her dreams.

Shelby walked to her car, carrying the satchel with all her notes, the copies of the pages she had yet to read and the half-eaten sandwich she'd set aside as she'd dug deeper into the shelves of case studies and books.

Time had slipped away before she realized she should have left the library an hour before. Now she hurried, knowing her grandfather would be checking on her to see that she got back to the house by midnight.

Her car was the only one left in the parking lot, parked near a large tree. When she'd arrived, the sun had been bright and hot, the tree providing blessed shade on an unusually sultry spring day. Now the tree loomed over her two-door economy car, casting darker shadows in the light from a million stars overhead.

A trickle of apprehension skittered across her skin, making her walk faster, keys in her hand, ready to pop the locks and jump inside. Not that there was anything to worry about. She'd left the library this late on many occasions and had no trouble.

She neared her vehicle and hit the lock button on her key fob; the locks clicked open. As she reached for the door handle, a shadow detached from the base of the tree and lunged forward.

Too shocked to scream, Shelby swung her satchel

containing her notes, laptop and wallet, hitting her attacker in the temple.

He grunted and staggered to the side, bringing a hand to his head.

Before Shelby could run, a second attacker, also wearing dark clothes and a ski mask, shot out of the shadows, grabbed her and clamped a gloved hand over her mouth.

She fought, kicking and twisting, but the man was much stronger and bigger than her five feet two inches. He lifted her off her feet.

A van drove up, her captor leaped in, still carrying her, and the man she'd hit dived in beside them.

"No," she moaned. This was not happening. She couldn't let it happen. Wasn't she smarter than this? Shelby struggled, but the arms holding her tightened, the hand over her mouth cutting off her air. The shadowed interior of the van faded. The next thing she was aware of was smoke. She lay on a floor, the smoke growing thicker around her, filling her lungs, blocking her view of the door, her only escape.

A figure materialized out of the drifting smoke, a tall, broad-shouldered man. He scooped her up into his arms and ran out of the house. She nestled against his chest, her fingers digging into the fabric of his shirt. She breathed in and out, the acrid smell of smoke still burning her nostrils. She was afraid to open her eyes, afraid that when she did she'd still be in that basement, locked in the dark. A captive.

Shelby moaned, her fingers curling around fabric. No.

"Hey, Shelby. You're having a bad dream. Wake up."

"No. I don't want to go back in the dark."

"It's okay. You're free."

The soothing sound of a man's voice lured her out of the basement and into the light. She opened her eyes and looked up at a long fluorescent light mounted on a white ceiling in a clean room.

"I'm not in the basement?"

The man chuckled. "No, you're not."

She glanced up into the green eyes of a stranger and jerked back, fighting to be free of his hold on her.

"It's okay. I'm not going to hurt you. I'm the Secret Service agent assigned to protect—"

She scrambled over the bed and would have fallen off if he hadn't grabbed her wrist and stopped her.

Shelby winced. "Ouch."

He frowned, glancing down at where his hand clasped her raw skin. "What the hell?"

"Let me go."

"I will when you promise you won't throw yourself off the bed."

She stared at him, not sure if he was friend or foe and not willing to give up her freedom again so soon. "I promise," she whispered, tensing, ready to move fast once he let go.

"I'm going to release you and step away from the bed. You don't have to be afraid of me. I'm here to protect you, not harm you."

"How do I know that? I don't even know you."

"I'm letting go to reach for my credentials." He raised his free hand. "Honest."

"Okay, let go, already."

He did and she dropped to the ground on the opposite side of the bed, dragging the tubes in her arms with her. The heart monitor wires ripped loose and the machine set off an alarm. Her knees refused to hold her, shaking so badly they buckled, and she felt herself falling, her head swimming as she went down. The IV stand tilted and crashed to the floor.

The man flung himself across the bed and caught her beneath her arms before she hit the tile.

"You've suffered a head injury," he said softly. "You really should take it easy for a couple days."

"I'm fine." She leaned into him despite her desire to be free of him. His muscles were solid beneath her fingertips and his breath warmed the side of her neck. "I can stand on my own."

"Prove it."

She fought the fog threatening to engulf her and willed her legs to straighten, all the while leaning into the man and his broad shoulders. "I've got it now." Shelby planted both hands on the side of the bed, sagging against it. "I can stand on my own."

"You're a stubborn woman."

"Stubborn is better than dead."

Slowly, he released his hold and rolled off the bed, reaching for his wallet in his back pocket.

The door opened and a nurse rushed in. "What's going on? Why is she out of bed?" She glared at the man and cast a worried look at Shelby. "Ms. O'Hara, you shouldn't be up yet. Please, let me help you back into the bed."

"I don't want to go back to bed. And who is this man?"

"Why, he's your bodyguard, Ms. O'Hara. Your grandmother left word that he was allowed to be in your room and we were to do whatever he said in order to protect you." The nurse planted a hand on her hip and pointed to the bed. "Now, are you going to get back in the bed or will I have to call an orderly to help me put you there?"

"It's not necessary to call an orderly." Her stranger was there by her side, scooping her wobbly legs out from under her. Shelby squealed and wrapped her arms around his neck to keep from falling as he set her down on the mattress, the strength of his arms and the solid wall of his chest oddly reassuring and comforting.

"You really should stay in bed until they bring you something less revealing. You can see everything through the gap in the back of your gown." He grinned and stepped away, missing the hand she swung at his face.

"You're no gentleman."

"Never said I was."

"You never said *what* you were."

The nurse tsked. "Please hold still, Ms. O'Hara, while I reconnect the IV and monitors."

"I don't want the IV. I'd rather have a steak or lobster."

"There are no restrictions on your diet. Would you like me to call the kitchen and have them prepare a sandwich?"

"No! No sandwiches. No bologna!" Shelby clapped a hand over her lips. "I'm sorry." Tears welled in her eyes, clouding her vision. "I don't know what's going on, where I am and who *he* is. And I don't have a grandmother, just my grandfather. Could someone please tell me what the hell's going on?"

Chapter 3

"I'll let your family explain all that when they get here." Daniel dialed the number for Kate Winston's secretary.

"Debra speaking." Her voice was clear and cheerful, with no indication she'd been up late the night before. She'd probably been awake since five or five-thirty, preparing Mrs. Winston's schedule for the day.

"Debra, please inform Mrs. Winston her granddaughter is conscious."

"I will. Right away. Thank you."

Daniel had no doubt she would. Debra Winston was the most efficient personal assistant a person could have. He wasn't sure how Kate could operate without the other woman's help.

Shelby jabbed at the controls on the bed, making the feet rise, then the head of the bed lower. "I don't have a grandmother and I don't need a bodyguard. Damn this thing. How do I get it to sit me up?"

Daniel fought to keep from smiling, took the controls from her hand and adjusted the settings, raising the head of the bed until Shelby sat up. "Thank you," she said, her tone reluctant. "I could have figured it out myself."

"I can't have you falling out of bed. What kind of bodyguard would I be if I let you fall twice?"

"Someone else's, I would hope. I don't need a bodyguard."

"Your grandmother and your uncles think you need one. And I agree. Now, whether or not it's me is an entirely different concern."

"I don't have a grandmother, and I don't have any uncles. It's just my grandfather, Patrick, and me. You must have the wrong woman."

"No, sweetie, he doesn't." Patrick entered the room carrying two cups of steaming coffee. He set them on the rolling table and engulfed his granddaughter in a long, heartfelt hug. "Thank God you're all right. I was so scared. I thought I'd lost you."

"Believe me, I was pretty scared, too." She hugged him again and pushed him to arm's length, tears running down her cheeks. She brushed them aside and studied her grandfather. "You look like you haven't eaten in days. Have you been taking your vitamins?"

He chuckled. "God, I've missed you."

Her brow wrinkled. "I take that as a no." The next minute she was smiling, her bright blue eyes dancing, making Daniel's heartbeat stutter then race. "That's okay. I'll have you back on track in no time," she assured him.

"That's my girl." Patrick hugged her again and perched on the edge of the bed.

Shelby rolled her eyes at Daniel. "And who is this man? I have to say, after being bound and kept in the dark for two weeks, to wake up in the arms of a stranger wasn't reassuring."

"Oh, baby, what did those animals do to you?" Patrick hugged her again.

"Thankfully not much more than keeping me tied up in the dark and feeding me the nastiest bologna sandwiches and water."

Daniel's lips twitched. That would explain why she'd gone over the edge at the nurse's mention of a sandwich.

Patrick sighed. "At least they didn't hurt you more than that." He cast a glance at Daniel. "This is Daniel Henderson, an agent with the Secret Service. He saved your life."

Daniel almost laughed at the skeptical look she threw his way.

"It's okay, you don't have to thank me," he said, his voice deceptively even, the undertones dripping with sarcasm.

"Thank you for pulling me out of there," she said and turned toward her grandfather. "But why do I need a Secret Service agent watching over me? And what's all this about a grandmother and uncles? Does the hospital staff have me in the wrong room?"

"Shelby, about that." Patrick stared down at where he patted her hands in his. "There's something I should have told you a long time ago."

Shelby's lips tightened and her face blanched, but she held her tongue.

Daniel had the sudden urge to pull her into his arms and shield her from what was coming next. She was so small and pale against the hospital sheets.

Her grandfather continued, delivering the news straight and free of any sugarcoating. "You have a grandmother and three uncles."

She breathed in and out several times, pinching the bridge of her nose.

Daniel admired her for her calm and ability to take it all in without falling apart. After two weeks of captivity in a dark basement, and waking up in a hospital with the news she had more relatives and a bodyguard, Shelby had earned the right to come apart.

She asked quietly, "Since when, and why haven't I heard of them before?"

"I didn't think it was important before," her grandfather said. "But when you went missing, I had to get help. The only person I knew who had enough clout and influence was Kate Winston."

Those bright blue eyes blinked and she laughed out loud. "Kate Winston? Former vice president of the United States?"

Patrick nodded. "She's your mother's mother."

Shelby's face lost all color, and she pressed a hand to her temple. "How?"

Her grandfather chuckled. "The usual way. It happened one summer when we were teenagers, both young and stupid. Your grandmother was on vacation on the Outer Banks when we met. By the end of that summer, we thought we were in love." He stared out the window. "Your mother was born nine months later."

"What happened? I take it you didn't make an honest woman out of her or I'd have known sooner about her."

Her grandfather flinched, his jaw hardening. "I wanted to marry Kate, but she wanted nothing to do with me."

"Why?" Shelby leaned forward and cupped her grandfather's face. "What's not to love?"

He covered her hand with his and pressed it against his cheek. "It was complicated."

"Try me."

Feeling like an outsider in a personal, family discussion, Daniel moved toward the door. "I'll just leave you two alone."

"No," Patrick said at the same time Shelby said, "Please."

A knock on the door had all three of them changing focus.

Before anyone could respond, the door slowly opened and a nurse peeked in. "Hi, I'm Lucy. Is Shelby up?" She smiled across the room. "Oh, thank goodness, you're awake." Still, she hesitated. "Are you up to receiving a few visitors? There are people out here who want to meet you."

Shelby shot a glance at Daniel, her eyes wide, her fingers gripping the sheets.

Her grandfather patted her hands. "You don't have to if you don't want to."

"No." She sat up straighter. "I want to meet the woman who wanted nothing to do with you."

"Uh, okay. I'll let them know." Lucy popped back out into the hallway, the door shutting behind her.

"Now, Shelby, be nice," Patrick warned. "What happened forty years ago is in the past."

"Yeah, but what kind of woman throws away her own child? And to think, I used to admire Kate Winston." Shelby crossed her arms over her chest, some color returning to her pale cheeks.

Daniel knew he should leave, but his protective instinct kicked in. Having four Winstons in the same small room at one time was overwhelming, even for a healthy person. Their egos and their combined charisma could be intimidating.

Lucy opened the door and stood to the side, holding the door wide as Kate and her three sons entered.

As Daniel expected, the three towering men filled the room with their broad shoulders.

Kate walked forward, tiny in comparison. She wore a light gray skirt suit and a pale pink blouse, appearing every bit the poised politician. But when her gaze fell on Shelby, her eyes filled. "Oh, my God. I could be looking at myself as a young woman." Tears slid silently down her cheeks. "All this time, I didn't know."

"If I'd had any doubts before, I don't now. She looks just like you." One of the men with dark brown hair and eyes the same color as his mother's and Shelby's pulled Kate into the crook of his arm. "Shelby, this is your grandmother, Kathleen Winston. Most people call her Kate." He walked with Kate to the other side of the bed from where Patrick stood holding Shelby's hand.

Shelby held out her hand. "Nice to meet you, Mrs. Winston."

Kate ignored the hand and engulfed Shelby in a hug. "I'm so sorry. I didn't know."

The stricken look in Shelby's eyes made Daniel move forward. "Perhaps we should give Ms. O'Hara some room to breathe. This is a lot for her to take in."

Shelby muttered a soft, "Thank you." She brushed moisture from her eyes and sniffed.

Kate straightened, tugging at the hem of her suit jacket. "This is Trey," she said, her voice shaking. "He's the oldest of my sons—your uncles." Kate laughed. "I'm sorry, this is all surreal to me." Her voice caught on a sob.

"You're telling me." Shelby held out a hand to the first of the men. "Nice to meet you."

Another one of the men stepped forward. "Hi, I'm Samuel, but you can call me Sam."

"Sam." Shelby took his hand. "You're all so tall."

"We take after our father," he said.

The next man stepped forward and held out his hand. Shelby shook it. "Name's Thad. I work with the Raleigh Police Department. I'd like to ask you some questions about the men who held you captive."

Shelby's face paled and she snatched her hand away.

"Thad," his mother touched his arm. "Can't it wait just a few minutes?"

Thad frowned. "We need to catch the men who did this. Shelby's the only witness we have." One look at his mother's face and he nodded. "Okay, just a few minutes."

Sam shook his head. "You look so much like Mother."

Her face pale, her eyes wide, Shelby chewed on her bottom lip. "I'm sorry. It's going to take some time getting used to all this."

The door opened again and the doctor entered. "Good grief, are we having a family reunion?"

"We're going." Trey nodded to his brothers. "Let's give our niece some room."

"I have questions," Thad insisted.

"They can wait until we get to the estate," Kate said softly.

The doctor stepped past the people standing around and shone a light into Shelby's eyes, then pressed his stethoscope against her chest.

"What estate?" Shelby leaned around the doctor. "I'm going home as soon as I get the okay from the doctor."

The doctor straightened and tucked the stethoscope in his pocket. "That will be as soon as we can get your discharge papers."

"She's okay?" Kate asked.

The doctor nodded and stared down at Shelby. "Drink plenty of liquids and take it easy for a few days."

"I can go?" she asked.

"Yes, ma'am."

"Good." Shelby tossed the sheet aside and swung her legs over the side of the bed. "Come on, Grand-dad, let's go home."

Patrick O'Hara shook his head.

Daniel braced himself for the coming storm.

"Honey, we're not going home yet. Not until the police find the ones responsible for kidnapping and almost murdering you."

"If we're not going home, then where are we going?" Her eyes narrowed and her arms crossed.

"You'll stay with us at the Winston Estate," Kate said, her tone brooking no argument. "You'll have round-the-clock security. Daniel Henderson will be your bodyguard."

Daniel almost laughed at the shock on Shelby's

face. He wasn't sure what she found most disturbing—staying at the Winston Estate or having him as a bodyguard.

He leaned close and whispered in her ear. "If it's any consolation, it's not my idea of a good time, either."

Shelby stood on shaky legs, wearing slim-cut, cream-colored trousers, a short-sleeved cashmere sweater, sandals and undergarments thoughtfully provided by her supposed grandmother. The clothing she'd been wearing for the past two weeks had probably been condemned and thrown away as unfit for the granddaughter of the former vice president.

Though her knees wobbled and the pain meds she'd been given hadn't quite worn off and left her feeling a little fuzzy headed, Shelby refused to show even the slightest weakness to the Winstons or the odious man who'd been assigned as her bodyguard. That he was no happier about the arrangement than she was did little to appease her. Strangely, it made her more angry and disgruntled about the entire arrangement.

"I have assignments to complete. I can't do them without going to the library in Beth City," she muttered.

Daniel Henderson stood beside her, his face impassive, wearing mirrored sunglasses that completely hid any expression in his eyes, frustrating Shelby even more.

"You can't leave the estate until we find your kidnappers."

"Like hell," she stated. "I'm not giving up one prison for another."

"Trust me, the Winston Estate is far from a prison."

"It's a prison if I'm not allowed to leave."

"Perhaps *allowed* is too strong a word. But it would certainly be *ill-advised*."

She snorted. "No difference." They stood in the lobby at the hospital's entrance, waiting for her grandfather to complete the paperwork to release her. Kate and her personal secretary waited close by.

Did he have to stand so close? Shelby shifted away from Daniel. He shifted with her. His bulk was doing funny things to her insides. She'd tried to blame it on the breakfast she'd been served by the hospital staff, but it had been pretty darned good after the bologna sandwiches and bagels she'd been given for the past two weeks. She'd eaten every last bite and wanted to lick the plate, but just managed to refrain with Daniel, Kate and her grandfather looking on.

The food had given her the strength to make it this far, and a lighter dose of pain medication didn't make her head fuzzy. She almost felt normal. Almost as if her world hadn't been upended and thrown her off-kilter.

A grandmother and three uncles. And all this time she'd thought it was just her and her grandfather against the world.

Patrick signed one last form and turned toward the exit, his gaze zeroing in on Kate. She stood looking cool, calm and confident in her gray suit, her hair short and stylish with just a hint of frost at the temples. No dyes and highlights for her. And she didn't need them. She was beautiful, even in her late fifties, the lines by her eyes adding character.

Shelby didn't want to like the woman, didn't want to believe a word she said. Not when she'd abandoned her own daughter and then claimed she hadn't known she was alive. How does a mother not know her baby was alive?

Patrick's face gave him away. He might have said he was over Kate a long time ago, but the way he looked at her at that moment said the opposite.

"Oh, dear." Her heart aching for her grandfather, Shelby pressed a hand to her chest.

"What?"

"This isn't right."

"What isn't right?" Daniel asked.

She tried to think of something to say that would make it better. "We don't belong with the Winstons. My grandfather and I should just go home. We can manage on our own."

"Don't be ridiculous." Daniel captured her arm. "You were almost killed. Those men who kidnapped you are experienced thugs. What training do you have to defend yourself against them?"

Her back stiffened. "I took a self-defense class one semester during my undergraduate degree."

Daniel snorted. "And how'd that work for you?"

Shelby opened her mouth to give him a sharp retort, but she didn't have one. The reality of the past two weeks sitting in the dark wasn't something she wanted to happen ever again. "I'll be more aware."

"When you're outnumbered, outweighed and outgunned, being aware may not be enough."

"It will have to be." She smiled at her grandfather as he closed the distance between them.

"Ready?" he asked.

"I am. But I think we should go home."

Her grandfather's brows drew together. "Shelby,

honey, after what happened, I don't think it's safe. I can't provide the kind of protection Kate can."

Staying at the Winston Estate would be as hard on him as it was on her. They didn't belong with these people. The Winstons traveled in an entirely different circle from the folks at the O'Hara Bar and Grill on the Outer Banks where she and her grandfather lived and worked.

The worried look on her grandfather's face made her reconsider for the moment. She stepped outside the hospital where two long black limousines stood waiting at the curb.

"Tell me we're not going in those," she said.

Daniel's mouth twitched into a grin, although his eyes were invisible behind his mirrored sunglasses. "Then I won't tell you."

Thad walked up behind them. "If we could move it along, the cars have been waiting for thirty minutes in a no-parking zone. The hospital security staff would like us to get going."

Her father hooked her arm and led her toward the limo. The chauffeur opened the back door for her.

The closer she got to the dark interior, the faster her heart raced. "No." She braced her hands on the roof of the car and refused to step inside.

"Is there something wrong?" Kate asked.

"I can't get in. It's too…"

"Too what, dear?" Kate laid a hand on her arm.

"Too dark," Shelby whispered.

Kate's hand gently smoothed over her arm. "It's okay. You don't have to ride in the limousine." She turned to the driver. "Take it back to the estate. Miss O'Hara will ride with Trey in his vehicle."

The driver nodded, rounded the front of the vehicle and got in.

Kate's brows rose as she directed a glance at her oldest son. "You don't mind bringing the O'Haras and Mr. Henderson, do you?"

"Not at all, Mother." Trey turned away from the hospital. "If you'll follow me to the parking lot—"

The limousine engine revved and died. The driver cranked it again and the same thing happened.

"What do you suppose is wrong with the limousine?" Debra frowned, making a note on her smartphone. "I have it serviced regularly."

"Not good." Daniel gripped Kate and Shelby's arm. "Get down!"

Trey spun Debra around, shoved her behind the open door of the Jeep and shielded her with his body.

Before Shelby could react, Daniel pushed her to the concrete. Kate dropped to her stomach beside her and Daniel threw himself on top of both of them.

Shelby struggled to get up. "What the hell—"

An explosion rocked the ground beneath her, blasting her eardrums. She fought to breathe beneath the weight of Daniel lying across her as metal shards fell on her legs and arms.

Chapter 4

His ears ringing and pain knifing through his leg, Daniel rolled off Shelby and Kate and leaped to his feet.

Smoke poured from the limousine's engine. The hood had been blown off and had landed several yards away in the middle of the driveway. The windshield was completely shattered and the driver was slumped against the door.

Daniel limped to the limousine and tried to open the driver's door to get him out. It wouldn't open, and the acrid scent of gasoline and smoke made him pull harder.

Bracing his foot on the side of the vehicle, he pulled on the door handle but it wouldn't budge.

Shelby helped Kate up on the other side of the vehicle.

"Get the hell away!" Daniel called out. "There's gas leaking out, it could go up anytime."

Shelby hooked Kate's elbow and tried to hurry her toward the building.

Kate pushed her hands away. "No, that's Carlo. We have to get him out."

Thad ran toward Daniel, carrying a tire iron. He yelled back at Sam, "Call 911!" Thad wedged the pointed end of the tire iron between the door and the frame and leaned back. The door metal bent, but the door didn't budge.

Daniel grabbed the iron below Thad's hands and put his back into it. Together they pulled. Trey rounded to the opposite side of the car and tried the door. "This side is locked, too."

Daniel glanced at the puddle of fuel pooling around their feet and the smoke still rising from the engine. "We have to get him out." He took the tire iron from Thad and smashed it against the broken glass of the window behind the driver. The first strike wasn't enough. He swung again and the safety glass caved in. He ran the bar along the edges of the long side window, breaking out enough of a hole to get inside.

By then, nurses and orderlies were running out of the hospital.

Sam stood between them and the limousine. "Stay back! It's too dangerous."

A siren wailed in the distance.

Daniel shrugged out of his suit jacket, laid it over the broken window and dived into the back of the limousine. He crawled over the back of the leather seat and shoved open the window between the back and the front. Pushing his bulky shoulders through the narrow opening, he reached through and checked the driver for a pulse. For a moment, he could feel nothing, then a faint throb bumped against his fingertips. "He's still alive!"

Shimmying through the window, Daniel dragged his body into the front seat and hit the switch to unlock the doors. Nothing happened. "Take the tire iron to the other side!" he yelled, the smoke making him cough and his eyes fill with tears.

Thad rounded the vehicle and jammed the bar between the door and frame. Sam joined him with another tire iron. With the three Winston brothers on the outside pulling, Daniel kicked as hard as he could.

A scream rent the air and Daniel glanced up long enough to see flames shoot toward the sky. If he didn't get the door open, he'd cook inside the limousine with the driver.

Flames engulfed the engine and driver's side of the vehicle. Shelby screamed and pushed forward. If her grandfather had not been beside her, she would have joined the men at the door. "Don't! You'll be hurt," he said, his arm catching her around her waist.

Her heart lodged in her throat, Shelby stood by helpless as the drama unfolded. "Where is the fire truck? Why isn't it here yet?"

"They're coming as fast as they can," her grandfather assured her.

"They're not going to get here in time. If my boys don't get out of there…" Kate started to walk forward.

Patrick snagged her arm. "The best thing you can do is stay safe and away. If they're worrying about you, they won't be concentrating on their own safety."

Kate pressed her hands to her face. "I can't stand by and do nothing."

Shelby pushed her grandfather's arm away. "I have to help." Before she could take one more step, the door to the limousine flew open. Smoke billowed up into the air as fire devoured the fuel.

Get out, get out, get out! Shelby screamed inside, but Daniel didn't appear. Her chest squeezed tight and her breath caught and held in her throat as fire consumed the vehicle.

Then a leg came out, followed by another, and Daniel backed out of the limousine, dragging the limp body of the driver.

Trey and Thad took over, dragging him the rest of the way out and as far away from the burning vehicle as they could before they laid him on the ground.

A fire engine, lights and sirens blaring, pulled up next to the hospital.

Firemen leaped to the ground and dragged hoses from the side of the truck. A rescue vehicle stopped behind it, along with four police cruisers. Soon the bystanders were herded back into the hospital.

Trey ushered Debra inside, but Shelby, Patrick and Kate refused.

"Those are my sons," Kate insisted. "I'm not going anywhere."

The firemen extinguished the blaze and the hospital's medical staff carried the injured driver into the hospital on a gurney.

Once the driver was taken care of and the flames doused, the Winston sons and Daniel joined Patrick, Shelby and Kate.

While the Winstons checked out their mother, Daniel touched Shelby's chin. "You should have that cut looked at. Are you okay?"

With his fingers warm on her face, Shelby couldn't think straight. "I think so." Shelby pressed her palms to her ears and flexed her jaw. "But you sound like you're in a tunnel."

"Concussion from the blast." Daniel's hand dropped to his side. "It'll take a while before your hearing returns to normal." He faced Shelby's grandfather. "Maybe we should get everyone back inside the hospital to be treated."

Patrick nodded. "I agree. Starting with you." He turned Daniel around. "Looks like you collected some shrapnel from the explosion.

Shelby looked at Daniel's back and gasped. "You're coming with me." She grabbed his arm and dragged him toward the door.

He pulled free of her grip. "I'm okay. I'd rather get everyone back to the Winston Estate and out of range of anyone else targeting you or Mrs. Winston."

Kate and her three sons gathered around them. "What the hell happened?" Kate looked at the destroyed limousine.

"It appears someone got to the limousine and planted a bomb in it," Daniel said.

"How? I thought the drivers were with them at all times."

Thad wrapped an arm around his mother's shoulders. "I'll have security camera footage checked. Maybe it'll shed light on whoever did this. Main thing now is to get you and Shelby home."

Kate shook her head. "I can't leave now. I have to stay and see to the well-being of my driver."

"No." Sam took his mother's hand. "You have to get home. If someone is willing to bomb a vehicle at a hospital, he's not concerned with collateral damage. By being here, you're putting others in danger."

Shelby watched as Kate's brows pulled together. "I'm so damned tired of my family being terrorized. Who is doing this?"

"We don't know, but I'd prefer to get you out of here before someone tries again." Sam nodded toward Shelby. "And Shelby could use some recuperation time after what she's been through."

Kate reached toward her. "I'm so sorry. This is all my fault."

Shelby stepped away from the woman's hands, not yet willing to accept her as anything other than the person who was going to host her and her grandfather for the next few days. "I don't understand why I'm a target, or why it's because of you. But I agree standing around here isn't going to solve our problems." And she didn't want to let on that she had a splitting headache. Not when Daniel was cut and bleeding and willing to forgo medical attention to get Kate and her to safety.

"I can take a total of five in my SUV," Trey said. "I'll bring it around."

"Sam can take the rest in mine," Thad offered. "I'm staying to help gather evidence. This is now a crime scene."

Daniel stepped in front of the women. "We need to search the vehicles before anyone gets in."

"Daniel and I will handle that," Thad said. "Patrick, could you take Mother and Shelby into the hospital and have the staff give them a once-over?"

Kate shook her head. "I'm fine."

"As am I," Shelby assured him.

Thad shrugged. "Hardheaded women."

Kate's lips quirked and Shelby couldn't help but think the men were tough and hardheaded like their mother. Not an entirely bad thing in this case.

A few minutes later, Shelby was in the backseat of an SUV with Daniel riding shotgun, her grandfather at her side and Trey Winston at the wheel. Kate rode in Thad's SUV with Sam driving and Debra sitting beside her in the backseat. They'd decided to leave the second limo behind in case it was similarly rigged to explode.

Once they were away from the hospital, Shelby noticed Daniel didn't sit all the way back in his seat.

She leaned forward. "You should have had your back seen to."

"Don't worry about me. I'll be fine until I get to the Winston Estate."

"You can barely sit in this vehicle." Shelby tapped Trey on his shoulder. "Take us back to the hospital. This man needs medical attention."

Trey shot her a glance in the rearview mirror. "Thad's fiancée is on her way. She's a nurse and can remove the shrapnel and clean the wounds."

Not completely satisfied with Trey's response, Shelby sat back in her seat, chewing on her bottom lip.

Her grandfather patted her knee. "I'm sorry I didn't tell you about your grandmother."

Shelby covered her grandfather's hand. "It's okay. I guess I understand why you didn't. A woman willing to give up her baby isn't worth knowing."

"My mother didn't give up her baby knowingly," Trey said, his jaw set in a hard line, his fingers tight on the wheel.

"I didn't know she was lied to. All I knew was I had a baby to raise by myself. What did I know about raising a kid?"

Shelby's fingers squeezed around her grandfather's. "Apparently you knew enough to raise my mother and me."

"Not enough to keep Carrie safe."

"You did the best you could. You couldn't have known she would die in a car wreck."

Patrick lifted Shelby's hand and kissed her knuckles. "Not a day goes by that I don't think of her. How can I forget when you look just like her?" He smiled, then his lips turned down at the corners. "When I thought I'd lost you as well, I had to get help."

"I'm glad you did." Memories of being abducted washed over her, and she relived the terror of being so helpless. "I'm sorry I didn't come home on time that night."

"You think I could be mad about that?" Her grandfather laughed, choking on a sob. "You couldn't have known someone would target you."

"Yeah, but if I had left when there were more people out, I might not have been captured and imprisoned in that horrible basement."

"Well, it's all over now. We have to count our blessings and make sure it doesn't happen again."

And that was where Daniel came into the picture. If he was to be her bodyguard, he'd be around all the time.

Shelby's insides quivered, her core heated and her palms grew clammy. "I don't like living in someone else's house. I'd rather go home to my own home, with my own bed to sleep in and the people I know and love around me."

Patrick nodded. "I'd like nothing better. But it's clear someone wants to get to Kate through her family. And like it or not, you're part of Kate's family."

At that moment, they pulled up to a gate. Trey pressed a remote-control button on the sun visor and the gate opened. They wound along a driveway and through parklike manicured lawns and gardens, and finally stopped in front of a huge white-painted brick mansion with black shutters and red accents.

Shelby gulped, her pulse quickening, feeling more uncomfortable by the minute. "For the record, I don't like it. I don't know the woman, other than that she's the former vice president. I don't like putting my life on hold because someone doesn't like her. I've already missed enough time at school. I have no idea how I'm going to catch up. And holy smokes, who lives in a house this big?"

"You will." Daniel climbed out of the SUV and opened Shelby's door for her, his face grim, his jaw hard. "Perhaps you need to understand a few things." He held out his hand, pulled her out of the vehicle and stood her in front of him.

"Don't get all he-man on me," she said, pushing his hands away before the feel of him made her do something truly foolish. "You're just the bodyguard."

"I might only be the hired help, but Kate Winston was a good vice president and she's an even better person. She didn't have to come to your rescue, but she did. And she doesn't have to provide you protection. But she will." He gripped her arms and glared down at her. "I suggest you be grateful you're alive, thank Kate for making that happen and stop whining about school."

Shelby opened her mouth to tell the man she wasn't whining, but he stood so close she could feel the heat from his body and the intensity in his gaze. All the words she could have shouted back at him died on her lips and she shut her mouth with a snap. It wasn't in her nature to be so angry. And, damn it, Daniel was right.

She should quit worrying about school. Free from her kidnappers, no longer confined to the darkness, she had a lot to be thankful for. And she had yet to thank this man for saving her from the burning house.

Her grandfather chuckled as he rounded the vehicle. "Shelby has a mind of her own, but I do believe she's met her match." He glanced up at the house in front of him, his smile fading. "Kate sure has done well for herself," he stated.

Shelby stepped back from Daniel, her voice caught in her throat as a surge of emotion welled up in her. She was lucky to be here, and she should accept a night's protection from the woman who'd been someone special to her grandfather forty years ago.

Slipping her arm through her grandfather's, she leaned into him. "In case I haven't told you yet, I'm glad you didn't give up on me."

He pressed her arm to his side. "Never."

Shelby stared up at the house and shook her head. "Pretty impressive, isn't it?" Shelby glanced at her grandfather.

For a man who didn't know a stranger and always had a smile on his face, he looked pretty grim. "I could never have given her all this."

A thread of anger shot up her back, stiffening her spine. "You'd have given her everything she needed."

His lips twisted. "But not this."

"Funny, I grew up in your house, and I never longed for anything."

"There were a few times I was hard-pressed to put food on the table."

"We always had plenty of love."

"Remember the time after the hurricane that almost destroyed the bar? I didn't know how I'd get back on my feet."

Shelby hugged him to her side "Everyone on the Outer Bank helped us rebuild."

"When you didn't come home…" His face blanched and his throat worked as he swallowed hard. "Hell, Shelby, I could replace a bar, but I could never replace you."

Shelby blinked to keep tears from welling in her eyes. All the time she'd been held in captivity, she'd worried about her grandfather. He didn't have anyone else in the world. And neither did she. At least, she'd thought she didn't have anyone else. Things were changing.

The other SUV pulled to a halt behind Trey's. Kate, Debra and Thad stepped out.

"I hope you weren't waiting on us." Kate hurried forward. "Please, come inside. I'll have Maddie make tea and coffee and find something for lunch. Lucy's on the way. She'll help Daniel and anyone else with injuries from the explosion." Though her knees were scuffed, her pretty gray suit was wrinkled and dirty and her hair was mussed, Kate marched up the steps like a force to be reckoned with.

Shelby and Patrick both drew in long breaths and followed her up the steps into the house. Shelby told herself it would only be for a day. Maybe two, then she was going back home. She didn't belong in this big old mansion.

Most of all, she wanted to get away from the bodyguard who had such a low opinion of her and who got her stomach all tied in knots every time she glanced his way.

Before Kate reached the top of the steps, Trey and Sam got there and threw open the doors. She smiled at them and stepped inside, then turned to welcome her guests.

Beneath the smudges, her cheeks glowed a soft pink as Patrick stepped past her. Her eyelashes dipped down and her gaze followed him like a shy teenager.

Shelby was shocked by the change. From confident former vice president to shy young woman, Kate Winston was an enigma. Which was the woman who'd abandoned her baby girl and broken her grandfather's heart?

The wide front doors opened into a spacious foyer tiled in black-and-white marble. A grand, sweeping staircase curved upward to the second floor, trimmed in glistening rich mahogany. To one side of the entryway was a large, formal living room with shining wood floors and white furniture. In sharp contrast, a black grand piano filled one corner, ready to provide an elite guest list with subtle entertainment.

An older woman, slightly plump with red hair, hurried forward, her arms opening to Kate. "Oh, Mrs. Winston, I'm so glad you're not harmed." She engulfed

the former vice president in a hug and then stepped
back, raising an apron to dry her eyes.

"I'm quite all right, Maddie." Kate patted the older
woman's back. "Just a little shaken up by the explosion."

Maddie shook her head. "When Debra called ahead
to warn me about what happened, I nearly had a heart
attack." She pressed a hand to her chest and took a deep
breath. "I had to see with my own eyes."

"Well, now that you know I'm fine, let me intro-
duce my granddaughter, Shelby O'Hara." Kate swept
her hand toward Shelby. "And this is her grandfather,
Patrick O'Hara." Her voice dropped and her eyelashes swept down over her eyes, her cheeks flush-
ing. "They'll be staying with us until we sort all of
this out. Shelby, Patrick, this is Maddie Fitzgerald, our
housekeeper, the rock in our household. If you need
anything, she's the one you should ask."

Sam hugged the older woman. "She's so much
more than a housekeeper. She's like a surrogate grandmother." He kissed the top of her cap of short red hair.
"She's really part of the family. She takes good care
of us all."

Maddie smiled and held out her hand to Patrick,
her gaze going from Patrick to Kate, a slight wrinkle
in her brow. "You both are welcome here." She turned
to Shelby, her smile widening, her hand reaching for
Shelby's. "My goodness, girl, you're the spittin' image
of your grandmother."

"And my mother, so I'm told," Shelby added.

Kate stiffened beside her, her face paling. "I'd better
clean up. I have a meeting with the press in an hour.

I'm sure they'll want to know all about what happened this morning." She inhaled deeply and let it out.

Debra leaned close to Kate and whispered, "You might want to tell her what to expect."

With a nod, Kate's gaze captured Shelby's. "If word gets out that I have a granddaughter, be prepared to be inundated by the press." Her lips twisted. "I apologize for that, but I can't change what is." She glanced over Shelby's shoulder to Daniel. "Daniel will help to keep them at bay, but you won't be able to go anywhere without someone snapping pictures of you."

"We should be going," Debra prompted Kate. She smiled at Patrick and Shelby. "Maddie will help you two get settled." Then she ushered Kate toward the staircase, the two women walking with quick, purposeful steps as they climbed to the second floor.

"Press?" Shelby's head spun with the thought. "Why me?"

Trey scrubbed a hand over his face and grimaced. "With so much happening, I hadn't thought about that." He stared at Shelby. "Brace yourself."

Shelby's belly tightened. So much was changing around her, she was having a hard time grasping it all.

Sam touched her arm reassuringly. "The fact our mother had an illicit love affair before marrying our father will have the tabloids screaming for all the details. You'll be a celebrity by association."

"Sam Winston, don't you have something better to do than scare this poor child?" Maddie waved her hands toward the big Winston man as if she was shooing a fly. She took Shelby's hand and tugged her toward the stairs. "Come with me. I'll show you two to your rooms."

Shelby was swept away by the woman and herded up the stairs, her grandfather following and Daniel bringing up the rear.

Everything was happening too fast. From a nameless college student to the granddaughter of the former vice president of the United States all in the span of a day. Or rather, in the span of the two weeks she'd been held prisoner.

Shelby shivered, wishing she could go back to being the faceless college student who had nothing more to worry about than the next exam or the next paper due.

Daniel followed Shelby up the stairs. The consummate professional, he shouldn't have been focusing on the sway of her hips as she took one step at a time. In the tailored slacks and cashmere short-sleeved sweater, she looked more like one of the Winstons than the soot-covered waif he'd found passed out on the kitchen floor of a burning house.

Even in the new clothes, she still conveyed a sense of vulnerability, no matter how fiercely she valued her independence. The kidnapping had to have taken its toll on her and made her aware of just how helpless one woman could be against two strong men. Hell, a grown man would be equally helpless in the same circumstances. Especially if he wasn't expecting an attack.

His back stung where shards of metal and glass had impaled him, but he refused to tend to himself until he was certain Shelby was secure. After he'd taken a bullet for Kate Winston, he knew the threats to the Winstons were real and not only in the outside world, but behind their supposedly secure gates.

Shrugging his shoulders, he winced and continued

up the stairs, concentrating on Shelby's sweet derriere. Each of her movements took his mind off the pain in his back and his bum knee.

At the first opportunity, he'd seek out Mrs. Winston and ask her to remove him from the responsibility of watching out for Shelby. She was young, opinionated and didn't want the added aggravation of someone following her around. He couldn't blame her. He'd grown up in a large family and he valued his privacy. But there was inconvenience and there was danger. She needed to understand the difference.

Shelby had to figure out really quickly which was more important. But Daniel didn't want to be the man to play babysitter to the college coed. Let someone else be.

Still, she was pretty, slim, athletic, and when she smiled, as she had when he'd pulled her from the fire, it did funny things to his insides. Apparently, she'd gone through hell being kept in the dark for two weeks, not knowing why she'd been targeted, who was keeping her, or if they'd eventually kill her. Poor kid.

She reached up to push the hair back from her forehead, the motion emphasizing her narrow waist, the swell of her hips and the sexy way she moved. His groin tightened and he had to retract his previous thought. She wasn't a kid. At twenty-three, she was six years younger than he was. He told himself that she might as well be a baby. While he performed the role of her bodyguard, he had to get his mind and his gaze off those hips. The woman was his job, not a conquest.

Chapter 5

Maddie climbed the steps as quickly and with as much agility as a woman half her age.

Tired and still recuperating from her ordeal in the basement, Shelby wasn't going to complain about the stairs. She held on to the railing and climbed, wishing she could find a nice soft bed to fall into.

"You'll have the blue guest room," Maddie was saying. "On account of it's the most feminine of the rooms. Your grandfather will be staying in the brown room." She stopped and threw open the door to a room decorated in creams and browns. The bed was made from intricately carved burled wood. The mattress was covered with a cream duvet and pillows in various shades from cream to a rich, dark chocolate. In one corner stood a deep brown leather wing-back chair and a burled wood table with a wrought iron and stained glass reading lamp. Wide windows gave them a view out of the back of the house.

Directly below was a swimming pool, the water rippling in the breeze, sun sparkling off its surface.

Shelby blinked her eyes at the intensity of the sunlight. After days spent in complete darkness, it would take time before she got used to light again.

Beyond the pool lay an expansive garden and neatly trimmed grass. Trees shaded the edges of the lawn and made Shelby long to walk among them. She had to stop herself from exclaiming over the beauty of the room, the house and the surrounding grounds. O'Hara's Bar and Grill on the Outer Banks was nothing to compare with the elegance and luxury of the Winston Estate.

Her grandfather stood beside her, his lips pressed into a thin line, the dark circles beneath his eyes more pronounced.

Maddie chattered on, "There's a private bathroom through this door and it's fully equipped with towels and toiletries. If you should need anything that isn't provided, let me know." She faced Patrick, her smile fading. "Is something wrong?"

Patrick forced a smile. "Nothing at all. This will be fine."

Shelby could tell by the tightness of his jaw that everything was not fine. She could bet what was going through his mind. He was probably comparing their home over the bar to the Winston Estate and coming up short. She slipped her arm around him and squeezed. "Think of it as a fancy hotel. We won't be here long," she whispered.

He nodded and squared his shoulders. "The main

thing is to keep you safe. Come on, let's see your digs."
He winked and stepped out of the beautiful room.

Maddie crossed the hallway and opened another
room. "This is the blue room where you will be staying, Miss O'Hara." She led the way in and crossed to
another door. "You have your own walk-in closet and
bathroom. Mrs. Winston is having additional clothing
delivered this afternoon. If there's anything in particular you'd like her to include, just let me or Debra know
and we'll add it to the order."

Shelby raised her hand. "Wait. What's this about
clothes?" She shook her head. "I don't need clothes. I
have my own."

"Mrs. Winston wanted you to have anything you
might need brought here."

Shelby glanced around at the soft blue-gray painted
walls, the gauzy white curtains and the beautiful
driftwood-style white headboard. The room was too
beautiful. Too pristine. All light and clean. Almost
sterile. Had she traded a dark hell of a prison in a basement for a lighter, beautiful cage so foreign to everything she'd known and grown up with? "I'd rather have
my own clothing. Please thank Mrs. Winston. But as
soon as I can, I'll go get my own."

Maddie smiled and nodded. "I completely understand. I'll have someone sent out to collect whatever
you want from your home."

Shelby bit down on her tongue, wanting to tell the
woman what she thought of someone else digging
through her drawers in her tiny bedroom above the
bar. But to do so would be attacking an older woman
with an open, honest, welcoming face who was only
doing what she was ordered to do.

Shelby squeezed out a smile. "Thank you, Maddie. If you don't mind, I'd like to take a shower."

"Oh, dear. After all you've gone through, you should soak in the whirlpool bathtub." Maddie opened the door to the bathroom and stepped inside with more purpose than Shelby expected from a seventysomething-year-old woman.

Before she could say anything different, the woman had the water running into the tub, bath salts and bubbles sprinkled in the water and towels laid along the polished granite edge.

"Do you need help out of those clothes?" Maddie asked as she advanced toward Shelby.

Shelby backed away. "No, no. I'm quite capable of undressing myself."

A chuckle sounded from behind her. She turned to see where it had come from.

Her grandfather stood beside Daniel, a grin spread across his face.

Daniel's face gave no indication of what he was thinking. But was that a twitch she saw at the corner of his mouth, and were his eyes twinkling? The man's face lit, making her insides flip. He was too good-looking for her own good.

Shelby squared her shoulders. "If everyone doesn't mind, I'd like a little privacy."

"Certainly, Miss O'Hara."

Not at all used to the formality and slightly irritated by it, Shelby insisted, "Please, call me Shelby."

The older woman smiled. "Shelby." Maddie waved Patrick and Daniel toward the door. "Now, you two shoo. Give the girl some space."

Patrick hugged Shelby. "I'm going to take a shower

and then I want to speak with Kate. Don't worry about coming down. Take a nap or a long soak in the bath. After all you've been through, I'm sure it'll feel great."

When she didn't let go right away, he pushed her gently to arm's length. "Don't worry. I'm not going anywhere. I'll be downstairs should you need me for anything."

She let go of her grandfather, not wanting him out of her sight for even a second. "I missed you," she whispered.

He nodded. "I know. And I missed you, too." He turned and left, his eyes suspiciously bright.

Daniel stood inside the room. "I'm not leaving until I check out the room."

Maddie frowned. "Oh, yes. Of course. One cannot be too careful."

Shelby watched as Daniel checked the huge walk-in closet and the bathroom where the water ran in the bathtub and bubbles formed on its surface. Back in the bedroom, he dropped to his haunches and checked beneath the bed.

"Looking for the boogeyman?" Shelby taunted.

He straightened, his broad shoulders making the room seem so much smaller. "It's my job."

A twang of regret tugged at her belly. She was just a job to him. Not that she cared. When she left the Winston Estate, she'd forget about him before she drove off the grounds.

Liar.

How could she forget looking into his face when he'd carried her from the burning home? She'd thought he was her guardian angel.

Now he was just another reminder of the threat to

her and of her need to be aware and ready should some-one try to kidnap her again.

"Are you finished?" she asked.

"No." He nodded toward the door on the other side of her room. "You need to leave that door unlocked."

Shelby frowned. "I would think you'd want me to lock all doors. Why not this one?" She walked toward it. "Is it another closet? Because if it is, I don't have enough shoes in my entire collection to fill it."

She jerked open the door to another bedroom. The walls were painted a rich cream with white crown molding. A king-size bed stood on one side of the room with a simple ebony headboard and matching night-stand. In a corner near a floor-to-ceiling window, a black lounge chair sat beneath a wrought iron floor lamp. The artwork on the walls showed black-and-white images of river and lake scenes.

Shelby frowned and turned back toward Maddie. "I don't need two rooms, you know. There's only one of me."

Daniel's lips twitched unmistakably this time. "That's not another room for you."

"Then who is it for?" Even as she said the words, a warm shiver rippled across Shelby's body and her pulse beat a rapid staccato against her eardrums.

Maddie answered, "Mrs. Winston asked Daniel to move his things from the guest house into the main house to be closer to you. He'll be staying in the room adjoining yours."

Shelby's heart flipped and slammed into her ribs. How could she sleep knowing Daniel would be in the room next to her? The man exuded testosterone the way flowers gave off fragrance.

She opened her mouth to protest, but Maddie had turned her back and was headed out the door. "If you'll excuse me, I need to check on supper." Maddie left the room, hurrying down the hallway.

Shelby was left alone with her bodyguard.

Daniel fought the grin threatening to overtake his entire face. He found that he liked tormenting the young woman. The color rising in her cheeks and her flashing blue eyes made him want to grab her and kiss her before she walked away.

Shelby's mouth sagged open and then snapped shut. "I'm sorry, but this arrangement is not acceptable."

"I normally stay in the guest house at night. Mrs. Winston thinks it would be better for me to stay closer, especially since the bombing this afternoon." Daniel crossed his arms over his chest. "Trust me, I'm no happier about the arrangement than you are. I much prefer solving crimes than babysitting spoiled heiresses."

The pink in her cheeks deepened and she glared at him. "I'm not an heiress, and I'm not spoiled."

Daniel raised his eyebrows challengingly without saying a word.

"I'm not." Shelby stamped her foot and stared down at it, her eyes widening. "I'm not," she repeated. This time, she didn't stamp her foot. "I work hard, I support myself financially and I'm trying to further my education so that I can improve my skillset and my life."

With her shoulders thrown back and her chest pushed out, she was a fiery goddess and far too attractive. Straightening his spine, he dismissed her with a soft snort. "Nice speech." He turned away. "There are no monsters under your bed at this time. Please, enjoy your bath." He walked to the connecting door and turned in the threshold. "If you need me, all you have to do is call out my name." His lips quirked up at the corners as he pulled the door closed behind him.

"Jerk," she said to the closed door.

"I heard that," came his muffled response.

"I'd say it to your face," she said, louder.

"I know."

Alone and fuming over the bodyguard's low opinion of her, Shelby considered throwing something at the door. One glance around frustrated her even more. She'd feel guilty if she broke any of the fine porcelain statues or if she ruined the pretty white lacy pillows.

The sound of running water reminded her of the bath. Shelby turned away from the connecting door and hurried to shut off the water before it overflowed the enormous gleaming white bathtub. For the moment, she ignored the bath, stripped out of her clothing and stepped into the granite-lined shower that was big enough for two people.

As soon as that thought crossed her mind, she envisioned a naked Daniel standing beside her under the second showerhead, water running over broad muscles and down tight abs. Her body heated and she switched the handle back toward cold.

What was it about him that made her feel off-balance and out of whack? Then again, everything about her current situation did that. But Daniel's insistence on being close had her more on edge than anything else. She could put up with living in the mansion for the short-term, and even wanted to get to know her uncles. But the bodyguard made her skin twitch and places low in her belly ache for something she had never ached for in the past.

Sure, she'd had her share of experimenting with sex with men her own age, but none of them seemed as raw and dangerous as Daniel.

After she'd cleaned her body with scented soap, she scrubbed her hair with herbal-scented shampoo, applied conditioner, rinsed and climbed out of the shower.

The tub full of water and bubbles called to her, the soft-scented bath salts filling the air with subtle fragrance. What would it hurt to soak for a while? After being tied to a chair for the better part of the past two weeks, stretching out in warm, perfumed water sounded like pure heaven.

Wrapping her hair in a large fluffy towel, she pressed the button on the side of the tub that activated the jets lining the sides. The water roiled, creating more bubbles. Shelby slid into the warm water and stretched her legs along the bottom of the tub, positioning herself in front of strategic jets and redistributing the bubbles to cover herself should anyone walk in uninvited.

Again, her core tightened and throbbed.

If she called out from the bathroom, would Daniel hear her through two doors? Her nipples peaked through the bubbles. Why couldn't she get the man off her mind? Daniel had told her he wasn't thrilled with his assignment. He obviously wasn't interested in her or the fact that she was naked in the room beside his.

Shelby lay still, letting the jets and warm water do their thing to relax her and let the soreness of two weeks of captivity leach from her muscles. With her eyes closed, she pushed all thoughts out of her head except for the amazing way her body felt. She leaned back and let go of a long sigh.

Moments later, sleep claimed her and she slipped into the nightmare.

She was back in the parking lot at the college, juggling her books to get her key out. Dark figures floated out of the trees and surrounded her, shoving her into the dark interior of a van.

A hand clamped over her mouth, stifling her scream. She struggled, but couldn't break the hold on her arms. Shelby kicked out, but only hit air and water.

Her mouth and nose covered by meaty fingers, she couldn't breathe, couldn't get air to her lungs and felt herself blacking out.

A moan rose up her throat. One of the men backhanded her cheek. Another moan escaped and she thrashed, trying to break the hold on her.

Then strong arms scooped her up and carried her away from the van.

She fought the arms, kicking, struggling, desperate to get away and back to her grandfather.

"Shh…it's okay," a deep male voice whispered into her ear. "Open your eyes, Shelby."

"It won't help. It's dark," she muttered.

The arms lowered her into a bed so soft, she felt as if she floated on clouds. It wrapped around her, warming her wet body.

"Shelby, open your eyes." A hand smoothed across her cheek.

She winced, afraid of being hit again. "My eyes are open," she insisted.

"No, they're not," the voice said. A thumb brushed gently across her eyelid. "Look at me."

Shelby blinked, her eyelids fluttering. Light filtered through her lashes as she focused on the face leaning over her. She wasn't in the parking lot of the university, but in a bed. She'd fallen asleep.

A glow from behind illuminated the highlights in his dark blond hair. Moss-green eyes stared down at her and he wore a gentle smile on his face. "See? You're safe. You were having a bad dream."

She leaned her face into his shoulder, breathing in the clean scent of his shirt. Her hands pressed into the solid wall of his chest and she felt safe and protected.

He held her, his warm hand stroking her back, skin against skin. After a while he stiffened and set her away from him. "This isn't a good idea."

Without his warm chest to lean against, a cool air-conditioned breeze brushed across her skin and she glanced down. The remaining fog of sleep whipped away and she pushed to a sitting position. "Holy hell, I'm naked!" She grabbed the comforter and pulled it up over her body. "Explain yourself," she demanded in the commanding tone she only used when she had to evict a rowdy customer from the bar.

The bodyguard chuckled, straightened and stood. "Let's get something straight, little girl—I never explain myself." He trailed a finger along the curve of her shoulder. "You might want to dry off with a towel. And next time you take a bath while recovering from a concussion, don't fall asleep. I'll do my best to protect you from bad guys, but unless you want me to be with you in your bathtub, I can't always protect you from drowning."

* * *

Daniel retreated to his room. As soon as he closed the door between them, he heard a soft *whomp* against the door. Probably a thrown pillow. He smiled.

"I'm not a little girl!" she shouted, the sound muffled by the door.

No, she wasn't a little girl. When he'd carried her wet, sexy body to the bed, he'd been more than aware of that fact. And he was glad he'd left her mad instead of terrified, as she'd been when he'd found her, thrashing in the tub, splashing water over the sides, deep in a nightmare.

She must have been reliving her kidnapping and captivity. Kept in a basement in the dark for two weeks had to have played hell with her mind, not knowing who was holding her, what they had planned for her or if she'd ever see her family again.

Lucy, Thad's nurse fiancée, had been to his room, removed the pieces of shrapnel lodged in his back and applied antiseptic ointment.

He'd just dressed after showering off the stench of smoke from the day before, when he'd heard her soft moans. At first, he'd thought the sound was the wind in the trees. When the moans continued and grew louder, he'd pushed through the connecting door, afraid she was under attack again and that he wouldn't get to her in time to save her.

He'd run into the bathroom and found her caught in a terrifying dream after having fallen asleep in the bath. He'd reached in and scooped her out, holding her naked body against his.

She'd fought, kicking and wiggling, her breasts rubbing against his knuckles, her thighs straining against his hold, and he'd been so turned on by the sight of her body he could barely walk with her into the bedroom and lay her on the bed.

When he should have set her down and walked away, he couldn't. He'd stayed, holding her, his pants growing tighter by the minute.

Then she'd leaned into his chest, pressing her breasts against his shirt, her fingers curling into the fabric, holding him hostage.

Hell, he'd wanted to strip down and climb onto the bed with her.

Daniel paced the length of his room, his leg aching, the walls seeming to close in around him. He wasn't cut out to be a bodyguard to a woman like Shelby. The Secret Service was his life. He'd been all about the job, training hard, putting his life on the line daily. But this... Being with her constantly would only create more problems. He had to get Kate to see reason, assign someone else. Anyone but him.

His mind made up, Daniel unbuttoned the damp white dress shirt and ripped it from his shoulders, the scent of Shelby still clinging to him. How could he protect a woman he wanted to kiss, hold and make love to? She'd keep him distracted every moment of every day.

He pulled a black polo shirt over his head and tucked it into his pants. Then he marched toward the door and threw it open.

Patrick O'Hara walked toward him, his face drawn and haggard. When he spied Daniel, he smiled. "Mr. Henderson."

"Daniel," he said. "Call me Daniel."

Patrick held out his hand. "I want to thank you again for saving my granddaughter from that burning house."

He shook his head, tears welling in his eyes. "That girl means more to me than anything. I don't know what I would have done if I'd lost her."

Daniel took his hand, prepared to shake it, but was pulled into a firm hug.

"Thank you," Patrick said over his shoulder. "Thank you for everything you've done for her and for taking care of her now."

Guilt rose up in Daniel's chest. "You're welcome, but you don't have to thank me. I'd have done it for anyone in the same situation."

Patrick gripped his arms and held him at arm's length. "But it was Shelby, and for that, I'll be forever in your debt." The older man dropped his hands and stepped back. "I'm sorry, but for two weeks, I thought she was gone for good." He scrubbed his hand through his graying hair. "You've given her back to me." Patrick straightened. "Thank you."

Made uncomfortable by all the emotion in the man's face, Daniel cleared his throat. "If you'll excuse me, I need to check on something." Leaving Shelby's grandfather in the hallway, he hurried down the stairs to the main level and went in search of Kate. She had to find someone else to be Shelby's bodyguard.

His chest tightened when he stepped through the open door of Kate's office.

Kate sat at her desk. Debra sat in a chair to the side with a computer tablet resting on her big belly, writing on it with a stylus.

"I rescheduled your appearance at North Carolina State, apologizing for the inconvenience. They were understanding and concerned about today's bombing."

Kate looked as smooth and together as she normally

did. "I want you to cancel all my meetings for today. I want to spend time getting to know my granddaughter." She glanced up. "Daniel, good. I wanted to speak with you." She turned to Debra. "Do you mind?"

Debra rose with a smile. "I'll go make those calls." She left the room, closing the door behind her.

"Please, Daniel, have a seat."

He crossed the floor, but veered toward the window instead of the chair. "If you don't mind, I'd rather stand."

Kate nodded and pushed back, rising to stand beside him.

For a long moment, neither said a word.

Kate sighed. "It never ceases to amaze me that while our lives are so chaotic and stressful, the world around us continues on. The trees produce leaves, the sun shines and the birds sing." She laid a hand on his arm. "What's troubling you, Daniel?"

"I want you to find another bodyguard for your granddaughter." He hadn't planned on blurting it out like that, but there it was.

Kate's hand dropped to her side and she faced him. "Are you worried you might take another bullet?" She stared at him. "I will understand. You've put yourself on the line for me already and have the injuries to prove it. I know it's wrong of me to ask you to do it again."

Daniel shook his head. "It's not that. I'm not afraid of being shot at."

"Are you afraid you aren't recovered enough to do the job?"

"No." He pushed his hand through his hair. "I'm

not afraid of the job. I just don't think I'm the right man to protect her."

Kate snorted softly. "You're the only man I trust to protect her. You threw yourself in front of a shooter to save my life. Your dedication to duty and your selfless disregard for your own life make you the only person I know of who could protect Shelby the way she needs to be protected." Kate touched his arm again. "Please, Daniel. If she truly is my daughter's daughter, I owe her and her mother, God rest her soul, my promise to protect her."

"Do you have any doubt she's your granddaughter?" Daniel asked, staring down into the bright blue eyes so like Shelby's.

The former vice president's eyes misted. "I thought my daughter was dead. I never would have given her up willingly." She hung her head and turned away, her voice thick. "That was the darkest moment of my life. I didn't want to live."

Daniel's heart squeezed at the raw emotion.

Kate spun back toward him, tears trembling on her lashes. "I'll do anything to protect her. I want her to know how much I loved her mother, how much I could love *her* and how much I want to be a part of her life." She reached out to him, taking his hand. "Daniel, please help me to keep her safe. I've only just found her. I don't want to lose her."

Daniel didn't want to be affected by her plea, but he was. This woman was strong, gutsy and willing to take on any political battle to right a wrong. And when it came to her family, she'd lay down her own life to protect them. She was a real, genuine, good person and it seemed there were too few of those to go around. Especially in the world of politics.

Kate let go of his hand. "Of course, if you feel that strongly, I'll find someone else. But I won't feel as confident that he'll protect her like I know you will."

Daniel turned back to the window. The trees were still green, the sun was shining and nothing out there had changed. As Kate had said, the world would continue on despite their problems.

If he left Kate to find another bodyguard, she'd worry that her granddaughter wouldn't have the protection she needed. Whether or not that was true, Daniel couldn't disappoint Kate. And now that he'd saved her from a burning building and possibly from drowning in her bath, he had a responsibility to keep Shelby alive.

Would he trust someone else to be there when she needed him? And the thought of another bodyguard rushing in to save her when she lay naked in a bath didn't sit right with him.

"Daniel?"

He drew in a deep breath and turned. "Don't worry. I'll do the job."

Chapter 6

Shelby dressed in the same outfit she'd worn from the hospital, provided by her grandmother. The feel of luxurious cashmere beat the heck out of the blouse she'd worn for two weeks straight, but it still made her uncomfortable, knowing someone else had purchased the garments for her.

She was not a charity case, and she refused to be treated as such. More determined than ever to reclaim the life that had been interrupted so brutally, Shelby stepped out of the room and went in search of her grandfather.

She knocked on the door across the hall. After a moment, when there was no answer, she turned toward the staircase.

Before she took one step, a low sexy voice asked, "Going somewhere?"

Shelby gasped as a shadow detached itself from the wall beside the staircase and Daniel stepped into the light.

"Don't do that," she exclaimed, pressing a hand to her racing heart.

He spread his arms wide, all innocence. "Do what?"

"Scare me like that." She braced herself as she faced the man who'd upended her self-control and left her head spinning and desire rising like molten lava through the vent of a volcano. Heat rose up her cheeks as she recalled his hand stroking along her naked back and clamped around her rib cage and thighs as he'd carried her to her bed. The man had seen more of her than a bodyguard should ever see, and it made her hot all over knowing it. Why did he have to be so darned handsome and aggravating at the same time?

She pushed past him and marched toward the stairs. "I'm looking for my grandfather."

"He was headed into Mrs. Winston's office a moment ago. I'm sure he's still there. Is there something I can help you with?"

"No. I'm quite capable of helping myself."

"Good enough." He fell in step behind her.

She could feel the heat of his gaze burning into the back of her neck. Halfway down the stairs, she stopped and turned. "Do you have to follow me everywhere?"

"Yup," he said with too much cheer in his voice. "It's my job."

"Really? Inside this big ol' house I would think I'd be safe enough to walk around on my own."

"As you mentioned, it's a big house. I have to stay with you, just in case."

Shelby blew a sharp burst of air through her nose

like a bull in a fighting ring. "Are you always this irritating?"

"No." He grinned. "Sometimes I can be even more
irritating...when I try."

She turned and walked two more steps down.

He followed.

She stopped, then he stopped.

Giving up, she hurried down the steps. When she
reached the bottom, she heard voices coming from one
side of the open entryway. One of them sounded like
her grandfather. She headed that direction, slowing
when she came close to the half-closed door.

Shelby paused, her hand reaching out but not pushing the door open.

"I told you, I didn't know our daughter was alive,"
Kate Winston was saying. "If I had known, I'd have
gone after her. I loved her, and I was devastated when
I was told she'd died."

"So devastated you didn't bother to verify that she
really was dead?" Her grandfather sounded angry, disappointed and sad.

Shelby wanted to go to him and wrap her arms
around him. The man had given her so much love and
understanding all her life. She loved him so much and
couldn't stand to see him sad or angry.

Shelby started to open the door when Kate's voice
said softly, "My mother told me she'd died when she
was born. I had no reason to think she'd lie. Whatever
you might think, my mother loved me."

"You didn't bother to see the body for yourself?"

"I was in no condition to. I was heartbroken. After
carrying her for nine months, to lose her like that...

The doctors gave me a sedative. I don't remember much of anything the first week after she...was born."

"I find it very hard to believe."

"Believe what you want," Kate said, her voice growing more firm. "The fact is, I didn't get the chance to know my daughter and I'd give anything to have had that time with her. Now that I've found Shelby, I won't give up the chance to get to know my granddaughter."

"And you'll have time in your busy political schedule to get to know her? Rumor has it you are being groomed to run for president."

"It's true. But my family is more important than anything else. That includes Shelby."

"What if she doesn't want to get to know you?" her grandfather asked.

"Whatever our differences, I hope you will give her the choice."

"Shelby has a mind of her own. It will be up to her. I trust you will abide by her wishes."

Kate hesitated, then answered softly, "I will."

"You're eavesdropping." Daniel's warm breath stirred the hairs along the side of Shelby's neck.

A delicious shiver rippled down her spine and she squeezed her eyes shut. Then she stiffened her back, opened her eyes and knocked on the door.

"Come in," Kate called.

Shelby pushed the door open and entered.

Shelby's grandfather stood in the middle of the room. Kate stood behind her desk, as if using it as a shield. The air sizzled with their energy.

"Ah, Shelby, we were just discussing you." Kate rounded the desk and crossed to her, holding out her hands. "Are you feeling better? I can have a doctor stop by and check you over, if you'd like."

Shelby ignored the woman's outstretched hands. "I don't need a doctor."

Kate's arms fell to her sides and she smiled, though the effort looked forced. "I had Debra order clothes for you, but Maddie said you refused and wanted me to cancel. Is something wrong?"

"Yes. I'm not used to people ordering for me, doing things for me or otherwise running my life."

"I'm sorry, darling. I just wanted you to feel welcome and comfortable after what you've been through." Kate turned to Shelby's grandfather. "I can't imagine what you *both* went through."

Shelby closed her eyes and opened them again when they reminded her of being in the dark for so long. "I'm not fragile and I'm not going to fall apart, so, please, don't treat me like I will. I want to put it behind me and get on with my life."

"Of course." Kate's smile grew, becoming more natural. "Your grandfather was telling me you had a mind of your own. You remind me of him when he was eighteen." Her gaze softened and she cast a glance at Patrick. He didn't look away, their gazes seeming to connect as if with a shared memory. For a moment, they both appeared much younger than they were. It struck a chord in Shelby. Could it be there was still a spark left between them after forty years?

Pushing the thought aside, Shelby said, "I'd like to get back into my life, starting today."

Kate's brows rose. "So soon?"

Shelby's grandfather stepped forward. "Don't you want to take another day to recuperate?"

Shelby shook her head. "I can't sit around and do nothing. I'm two weeks behind in my schoolwork and I need to talk with my instructors to see what I can do to catch up."

"I know how important school is to you, Shelby." Her grandfather touched her arm. "But you've been through a lot."

Shelby held up her hand. "Enough. If one more person says I've been through a lot, I'll explode. The only way I can put this all behind me is to move forward, get back into my life and live it." She glanced at her grandfather. "You know me. I'm no good at sitting around."

Her grandfather smiled. "No, you're not."

"I need my books, class notes, assignments and my own clothes."

"I'll have someone sent out right away," Kate said.

"No. I'm going myself. I need to check on my car and talk to my instructors. If I hurry, I might catch them before they leave for the day."

"But is it safe for you to go?" Kate looked to Daniel.

His lips pressed into a straight line. "I can be with her every step of the way."

"You can take one of the cars," Kate offered.

Shelby put her foot down, determined to do it her way. "No, I won't be chauffeured around in a limousine."

"I need to go out to the bar and check on things there," Patrick said. "We can go in my vehicle."

"How long will you be staying?" Daniel asked.

Patrick scratched his chin. "I'm not sure."

"Then I'll take her in my vehicle. She needs to be at the Winston Estate at night. The security is tighter here."

Patrick nodded. "Fair enough." He stared at Shelby. "Do you want me to follow you to the university?"

"No, Granddad. I'll be fine with Daniel." Much as she hated admitting it, she felt protected with her bodyguard around. "You need to check on things back home."

His bar was his livelihood. He needed to be there to manage and keep it running as smoothly as possible. Shelby wondered how much time he'd spent away from it while she'd been missing. Probably more than the staff could handle on their own.

As if reading her mind, her grandfather reassured her, "The staff has been taking care of things fine without me, but I want to make sure they don't need any more supplies."

"Go on." She squeezed his hand. "I'll be okay."

Her grandfather hugged her. "Don't go disappearing on me again. I can't lose you twice. My old heart can't go through that again."

"Like you're old." Shelby snorted. "You were a kid when my mother was born, and my mother was a kid when I was born. That makes you pretty young for a grandfather."

And Kate Winston looked too young to be a grandmother. Perhaps if she'd been old and gray, Shelby would have been more accepting of her. But she was too darned young and looked every bit the formidable political candidate.

Before she'd learned Mrs. Winston was her grandmother, she'd admired her as the former vice president and had hoped she'd run for president. Now...

Shelby sighed. She had a hard time believing the woman hadn't known her daughter was alive. What mother didn't go to her daughter's funeral or ask to see her daughter, even if she was dead?

The jury was still out on Grandma Winston. The thought of calling her Grandma nearly made Shelby laugh out loud at the absurdity. "Come on. It's quite a way to go to get to Beth City and I want to get there before all the professors go home."

Daniel frowned. "Beth City?"

"You didn't think I was going to school here in Raleigh, did you?" She smiled at his disapproval. "I live on the Outer Banks. Beth City was the nearest school with the master's program I needed."

"Do be careful," Kate said. "We still don't know who is responsible for taking you in the first place."

"That's why we'll be taking the big guns, right?" Shelby rolled her eyes toward Daniel and then relented. "I'll be okay. It's broad daylight. I was abducted after dark in an empty parking lot. There will be students and faculty still milling about. If we get there before they all leave." She headed for the door. "Come on, Granddad. Mr. Henderson and I will walk you to your truck."

"I don't know. I think I'd like it better if you stayed here and let someone else do your running around for you," her grandfather said, second-guessing himself.

Shelby stopped in the middle of the room and propped her hands on her hips. "Let's all get one thing straight." Her gaze moved from one person to the next. "I did not escape one prison to be trapped in another. This estate is pretty and tastefully decorated, but if I can't come and go, I might as well be in that basement in the dark, tied to a chair." Her body shook with the force of a harsh tremor. "I can't live like that."

"But—" her grandfather started.

"Patrick," Kate cut in. "Let her go. Daniel will take good care of her."

Her grandfather glared at Kate. "You have three sons. Shelby is my only family. If I lose her…"

Shelby's eyes stung at the anguish in her grandfather's voice. She went to him and hugged him close. "You're not going to lose me. I promise." She turned back to Daniel. "And so does Daniel."

Daniel's brows furrowed and he stood tense, his hands balling into fists.

"Don't you?" Shelby pleaded with her eyes.

Finally he relaxed his hands and he nodded. "I'll do the best I can to keep her out of trouble."

Shelby's grandfather laughed. "You'll have your hands full. That girl is as sweet as they come, but trouble seems to follow her wherever she goes." He kissed Shelby's forehead. "Okay, then. Go to school, though what good it will do you at the bar, I don't know."

"Granddad, you were the one who told me a good bartender is an underpaid psychiatrist."

"Yeah, and you don't have to have a fancy degree to be a bartender."

"I know, but the bar might not always be there. I have to be able to support myself." She narrowed her eyes at him. "And you were the one who told me to get a degree."

"You'd have done it without me telling you to. Besides, you already have one."

"I could never have done it without your love and support and the tip money I make at O'Hara's. But a psychology degree won't buy me much. I have to go further and get my master's."

"I know. I know. I just like to yank your chain." Her grandfather smiled.

Maddie poked her head in the office door. "Mr. Kincannon is here to see you, Kate."

"Send him in, please," Kate said.

A tall brown-haired man with tinges of gray entered. "Ah, I see the young Ms. O'Hara is getting around. I trust you didn't receive any injuries from the explosion earlier?"

Shelby frowned at the man. "No, I did not." Her eyes narrowed. "Should I know you?"

Daniel stepped forward. "This is my boss, Jed Kincannon, director of the Secret Service."

The older man held out his hand.

Shelby took the hand, but she didn't get a good feeling when she shook it. She wondered how long it would be before she trusted a stranger again.

"Jed, do you have anything to tell me about the men who abducted my granddaughter?" Kate asked.

"Nothing yet," he replied.

"I have the feeling this is Cartel related. They use dirty tactics like this." She gave the man a direct stare. "Don't you have any undercover agents who have infiltrated the Cartel?"

"We don't have any leads at this moment."

"Nothing? Not even a motive? Why would someone want to hurt my granddaughter? Who would have dug deep enough to learn something even I didn't know?"

"I don't know." Kincannon shook his head. "And we have nothing."

"What about Richard Nelson?" Kate asked.

The director tilted his head. "What about him?"

"He's made several statements about eliminating the

opposition. I'm his competition in his campaign to secure the party nomination for the presidential election."

Kincannon seemed to consider her words. "That's
a possibility. He wants to position."

"We've had this discussion before. I've toyed with
the idea of backing out of the race, but I haven't made
up my mind. And I don't want word of my decision,
or indecision, to leave this room, is that understood?"

Shelby could see how the woman had built her reputation as a strong political candidate and opponent.
She didn't mince words and she thought through everything.

Kincannon nodded. "My lips are sealed."

"As are mine," Daniel said.

Shelby almost smiled.

Kate didn't mess around. She demanded loyalty
from the people around her, and they seemed willing
and almost happy to give it to her.

Kate turned to Patrick and Shelby. "If someone is
after me and my family because of my run for president of the United States, can you imagine if I were to
actually go through with it?"

She shook her head. "Sometimes I wish I was that
eighteen-year-old girl back on the Outer Banks. Before I was forced to marry the man my father chose
for me, before I entered politics. My family wouldn't
be under attack and I wouldn't have to worry about
having a target painted on my back every time I step
out my front door."

Patrick stared at her. "It was the life you chose."

Kate nodded. "Not really, but that's water under the
bridge." She turned to Kincannon. "I've asked Daniel
to provide for Shelby's security."

"What about you?" Kincannon asked.

"If this is an attack on my family because of my former position or my current politics, I want my family protected. After D'Angelis turned, Daniel's the only man from your agency I trust at this time."

"I have more trustworthy agents. Let me assign one to Ms. O'Hara."

Kate's lips pursed. "No. I want Daniel."

Kincannon stared from Kate to Daniel. "You're on board with the change in assignment?"

Daniel nodded.

A little thrill rippled through Shelby. Watching Kate Winston in action gave her a strange sense of pride. And then for Daniel to agree that he was okay with taking on the responsibility of being her bodyguard…

It shouldn't have given her that rush of heat through her body. But it did, and she couldn't fight what she couldn't control. "If you all have finished deciding what's best for me, I'd like to get out of here."

Kincannon frowned. "Where's she going?"

"To gather her school assignments and clothes," Kate said. "Then she's coming back to stay here with us until we get this figured out."

Kincannon seemed to digest that. "Okay, then. Daniel's on it. Do you want me to assign another bodyguard to you, Kate?"

"I'll hire my own, thank you." Kate faced Shelby. "I'll see you back here later tonight?"

"Yes, ma'am." Shelby turned and left before they started talking about her again as if she wasn't in the same room with them. As she left the front door of the mansion to climb into Daniel's SUV, she was struck again by how bright the sun shone and how green and colorful everything was. Being in the dark so long was like being blind. When she could finally see again, she couldn't seem to get enough.

Locked inside a mansion, no matter how beautiful, was not where she wanted to be. If Daniel was going to be her bodyguard, he'd have to get used to following her around or be left behind.

Daniel drove the SUV down the driveway and out onto the highway heading toward Beth City, wondering what the hell he'd done by agreeing to watch over the independent, young Shelby O'Hara. He'd have his hands full keeping up with her.

"I'll take you to the university and then we head back to the Winston Estate."

"What if I'm not ready to go straight back?" she countered.

"I want to be back by dark. It's hard enough watching out for bad guys in the daylight."

He noted Shelby didn't agree or disagree with his idea of heading right back to the estate where he could keep her in a defined area that was rigged with security cameras.

Out in the open, he had no way of knowing who might hit and when. His hands gripped the steering wheel as he navigated Raleigh traffic and finally made it out to the highway leading east to Beth City. He checked his rearview mirror periodically to make certain they weren't being followed. So far, so good.

Shelby pressed a button and lowered the window, letting the breeze blow through the car. She leaned her head toward the wind, her dark hair flying out behind her, her blue eyes gleaming in the sunlight.

Daniel could imagine Kate looking like this when she'd been the same age. He could see why the young Patrick O'Hara had fallen for her. Too bad their affair had gone so wrong. Both had been too young, too impetuous.

He'd seen the anguish in Kate's eyes when she'd learned her daughter hadn't died, but had lived to die before she got to meet her. No one could fake that. To have missed knowing your child, missed watching her grow up, her first steps, her first day at school, her first crush on a boy…

Daniel's mother had celebrated all his and his siblings' firsts, loving every minute of their lives and loving them unconditionally.

Had Kate's mother been that cruel, to tell her that her child had died? Why would she do that?

"Do you mind if I play some music?" Shelby asked.

Daniel shook his head. "Have at it."

She fiddled with the tuner until she found an oldies station.

"Really?" Daniel laughed. "I'd have pegged you for pop/rock."

She shook her head and smiled. "I live on a beach. This is my comfort music. It reminds me of home."

He could relate. His family home was on a beach much farther north and rockier than those found on the Outer Banks of North Carolina, but still, the music reminded him of home, as well.

"It was so dark and quiet where I was, all I had were the songs I remembered to keep me company." She glanced out the window, her mouth turning down, her eyes darkening. "I only sang the happy ones."

His chest tightened, imagining her tied up in a basement, alone and scared. His fists curled around the steering wheel. He wanted to be on the investigation team searching for the bastards who'd kidnapped her. When he found them, he'd be hard-pressed to control his anger and resist the desire to kill them for what they'd done.

"Are you angry at me?" Shelby asked.

Daniel glanced her way, shaking out of his thoughts. "No, why?"

"You looked like you wanted to kill someone."

"I was thinking about the men who kidnapped you."

"And you want to kill them?"

"Yes," he said through gritted teeth.

"What good would that do?"

"They'd be off the street and unable to hurt anyone else, for one."

She stared at him a moment, then said, "Despite what they did to me, I don't wish them dead."

"You're much nicer than I am."

Shelby sat back in her seat and gazed out the window at the road in front of them. "I'd want to know why they kidnapped me."

"You're related to a very influential and wealthy woman."

"But that's her. I'm not influential or wealthy."

"Yeah, but she's known for taking care of her family."

"Who would have known I was her granddaughter?" She laughed humorlessly. "*I* didn't know I was her granddaughter. I still find it hard to believe. Did they demand a ransom?"

"No." Daniel shook his head. "That's what has us

all stumped. They never demanded anything. Did your captors say anything to you?"

"Not a word. It was as if I was a dog at the pound, to be fed and locked up until it was time to euthanize me." She sighed. "Well, that was one of the thoughts I had at the time."

"Not a particularly good one."

"I know. Thus the beach songs."

"You were lying on the floor in the kitchen when I found you. How did you get there?"

She straightened, her lips curling. "I broke a brace off my chair and used it to break the zip tie binding my wrists." She glanced down as she rubbed the sores there. "I would have made it out if I'd run a little faster. But after sitting still for so long, my legs weren't cooperating." She smiled. "But I kicked one of my captors in the face and hit the other with a heavy flashlight."

Daniel's stomach tensed. She'd been kept in the dark both physically and mentally. It had to have been tough. But she'd been tougher. To have the inner strength to figure a way out of her predicament was a testament to her resilience.

Shelby wasn't what he'd thought the granddaughter of Kate Winston would be like. But then she'd been raised by her grandfather and thus she was much more down-to-earth. He found himself drawn even more to her, and not just because of her physical attributes—all of which he'd seen and admired, and many of which he'd touched and wouldn't mind touching again.

Shelby's head swiveled as they passed a road. "That was our turn."

Damn. He'd missed his turn off the highway just thinking about her. Being a bodyguard to Shelby was a mistake when all he could think about was getting his hands back on her delectable body.

Once again, he wondered why he'd agreed to continue on as her bodyguard. To be a good bodyguard, he needed to be impartial, focused and free of distraction. Shelby O'Hara had distraction in every ounce of her gorgeous body.

Chapter 7

Shelby sat on the other side of the SUV, her mind on the man driving instead of the assignments and classes she'd missed. When she should have been planning ahead on the catch-up work she'd have to hustle to complete, she was thinking about how thick Daniel's thighs were and wondering what they looked like beneath the denim of his jeans.

Hell, he'd seen her naked. She ought to have the same privilege. Not that she should be thinking about him that way at all, but she couldn't help it.

Her core heated and she squirmed in her seat, inches away from his big hands gripping the steering wheel. The same hands that had carried her from the bath to her bed, naked.

"So how did you become a bodyguard?"

"I work for the Secret Service. I was detailed out

to provide protection to former vice president Kate Winston."

"Secret Service. Sounds impressive." She tapped her fingers on the armrest. "And interesting. Are all Secret Service agents glorified bodyguards?"

His jaw tightened and his fingers curled around the steering wheel turned white around the knuckles.

She must have bruised his ego. She smiled inwardly, glad she'd gotten beneath his skin.

"Some of us work on investigations into threats against the president and vice president."

"Why aren't you working on the investigation? Did you make someone mad?"

His fingers loosened and he sighed. "I was injured when someone shot at Mrs. Winston. I've been sidelined from the investigation."

"You were injured? Is that why you limp?" Now she felt bad for poking fun at the man.

He nodded. "I took the bullets meant to kill your grandmother."

Shelby sat for a moment in silence, the full extent of what he was saying hitting hard. "Who would have it in for her and why?"

"If we had the answers, wouldn't we have caught him by now?"

"I suppose." She glanced out the window as they passed houses and businesses. "I don't understand why people have to be so callous and angry all the time."

"Being a part of the Winston family, with all their wealth and property, has its perks."

"And apparently its price." Shelby pushed a hand through her hair and stared forward. "I didn't ask for it."

"No, you didn't. But you can't deny it. You look just

like a younger version of Kate. Anyone with a pair of eyes could see it."

As they drove onto the university campus, Shelby stared at her reflection in the side mirror. She did look a little like her grandmother and a lot like the pictures of the younger Kate Winston.

Campus looked the same as it did the day she'd entered the library to research information for her paper. The sun was just as bright, the trees weren't much different and the buildings were all still there.

The only thing that had changed was her. Two weeks ago, the most important thing in her life was getting a good education.

Her grandfather had done everything in his power to give her all the opportunities to improve her life. Despite his argument earlier that day about not needing an education to be a bartender, he'd been the first one to kick her butt and remind her of how important it was to get a degree that would provide a livable income. He'd drilled it into her head that she had to be able to support herself and anyone else who might come along. That *anyone else* being any children she might bring into the world.

Her grandfather worried that she wouldn't be able to support herself when he was gone. He'd admitted he'd spoiled her mother and she'd been less than responsible when she'd been growing up, as evidenced by her pregnancy at age eighteen.

He'd raised Shelby to be more responsible. She'd helped out at the grill from a young age, earning her own spending money. Nothing was free in life, he'd told her. And she alone was responsible for her own actions.

She didn't mind working, and she loved her grand-father more than anyone in the world because deep inside she knew he loved her, too. And she'd almost lost him. Or rather, they'd almost lost each other. With her life back in her own hands, she vowed never to be so vulnerable again.

She pointed to a brick structure, "Pull up beside that building. I'll just run in and see if my professor is there."

When she reached for the door handle, his hand snaked out and grabbed her arm. "*We* will go inside the building together."

His unrelenting grip on her arm left her no choice.

"Seriously? Look around you. There are students everywhere, and faculty and staff. I can make it to my professor's office and back with no problem."

"If it's all the same to you, I'd rather go with you."

"It's not all the same to me. I don't need a body-guard to lead me around on a leash." Shelby yanked her arm free and pushed the door open, jumping out. She set off at a good pace, hoping to reach the building and duck inside before he could catch up.

She hadn't gone five steps before Daniel was out of the car and at her side, matching her pace. Students passed on each side of her.

Each time one walked by, Daniel glared and moved closer to Shelby.

Finally Shelby stopped and faced him. "You can't do this. You're scaring the other students."

"Do you realize how close they are getting? Anyone that close could jam a knife into you and you wouldn't see it coming."

"They're students, damn it, not terrorists." Shelby

stomped away from him and pushed through the door into the building.

Once inside, she mounted the stairs in the stairwell to the third floor and hurried toward her professor's office.

Daniel dogged her footsteps, never more than a few steps behind, his limp more pronounced after climbing the stairs.

When they reached the office, Shelby faced Daniel. "I'm going inside. Alone."

He frowned. "I'd rather check it out before you go in."

"Too bad. I'll take my chances. You're staying out here."

"But—"

She poked a finger into his chest. "Stay."

His frown deepened. "I'm not a dog."

"I know. A dog would have a much more obedient disposition." Shelby slipped through the wood-paneled door into the professor's office and closed it behind her. She waited on the other side, fully expecting Daniel to jerk the door open and follow her inside. When he didn't, she was almost disappointed, then she shook her head and turned.

The professor wasn't in, but his teaching assistant was.

Shelby wrote down all the assignments and promised the assistant she'd email the professor with her excuse.

She was sure most professors had heard every excuse in the books, but being kidnapped and held for two weeks had to be new, ranking right up there with being taken by aliens. And they might not believe her, since Kate's team had kept the abduction below the radar from news and media sources.

Once she had a list of the assigned work, she braced herself for her next encounter with Daniel.

When she stepped out into the hallway, Daniel stood surrounded by several young, college coeds. And the jerk was smiling at them.

One batted her eyes and took his hand, penning her phone number on his palm. When she'd replaced her pen in her purse, she lifted her thumb to her ear and her pinky to her mouth and mouthed the words *call me*.

Shelby's fingers curled into tight fists, her fingernails digging into her skin. She walked away without looking back. It wasn't as if he was her boyfriend. She was the job to him.

So what if he'd seen her naked? As a Secret Service agent he'd probably seen lots of naked women. A girl on every job, like James Bond.

She heard him behind her say, "Sorry, ladies, I have to go."

He had a job to do.

Her.

Shelby's teeth ground together. As she passed the elevator the doors were closing. She ducked in before they closed all the way. Daniel ran the last couple steps, but didn't make it in time to jam his hand between the doors and stop its progress.

Thankfully, the elevator was going down. But it stopped at the second floor. Damn.

If she gauged it right, Daniel would assume she would get off on the ground floor. What he didn't realize was that there was a walkway across to the next building on campus from the second floor. And the entrances to that building led to the parking lot where she'd left her car.

Her grandfather had left it there, more worried about her return than bringing her car home. She kept a spare key in a magnetic box on the undercarriage of the vehicle. If she could get there before Daniel, she would take herself to the Outer Banks and collect her own clothing. Maybe she could help her grandfather out for a few hours at O'Hara's Bar and Grill.

She stepped off the elevator and crossed the glassed-in walkway to the next building and took the stairs to the exit, all the while glancing over her shoulder for Daniel. Once outside the building, she hurried toward her car, sitting where it had been the night she'd been attacked.

The closer she got to the car, the faster her heart beat. She told herself there was nothing to worry about. The sun shone down on her, there were other people in the parking lot and she wasn't a lone student asking to be abducted in an empty parking lot.

A white SUV backed out of a parking space, blocking her path to her car.

Shelby stopped and waited for the vehicle to move on.

The longer it took to complete the reverse, the more impatient she became. She glanced behind her, worried Daniel would figure it out and come after her before she reached her car.

The SUV turned, still backing toward her. Then when the driver should have shifted into drive, it continued backward, sliding up alongside the position where Shelby stood.

A door swung open.

Something clicked inside her, her heart rate sky-rocketed and her senses jumped to full alert. Shelby backed up a step, turned and ran, daring only one glance over her shoulder.

A man in a black ski mask leaped out of the vehicle and gave chase.

Heart racing, she ran for her life, the nightmare happening all over again. "Help!" she cried.

Students stopped and stared, too shocked by what was happening to be of any use.

"Help!" Shelby cried, adrenaline the only fuel powering her legs. She refused to be caught; she couldn't go back to a dark cellar where all she'd had were her thoughts to keep her from going insane.

She ran around a vehicle and headed for the building she'd just exited. Pushing through the glass doorway, she ran into a solid wall of muscle.

Shelby screamed and fought, every instinct geared for survival.

"Shelby, it's me!" Daniel yelled. "Stop fighting."

When she realized it was Daniel, she fell against him, wrapping her arms around his waist. "Don't let them take me."

"Shh...it's okay." His arms circled her, drawing her close. His hands ran down her back, stroking her to calm. "Now, tell me what you're talking about." He pushed her to arm's length and stared into her face.

"A man in a ski mask." She pointed toward the door as the white SUV raced past. "He came out of that SUV."

Daniel shoved her to the side and sprinted out the door. Shelby followed behind him, refusing to let him out of her sight.

He didn't go far before he stopped. "Damn. No license plate." Daniel pulled his cell phone out of his pocket and hit one of his contact numbers. "Why the hell did you run from me?" He glared at her as he put the phone to his ear. "How can I protect you if you don't cooperate?"

"I didn't think it would happen in broad daylight." Shelby stood like a recalcitrant child, her head hanging low. "Why is this happening to me?"

He shook his head, the anger melting from his face. He gathered her against him with one arm, while he held the phone to his ear. "Do us both a favor and don't run from me. I might not find you in time if it happens again."

Shelby nodded, thankful for his arm around her and completely terrified by the thought that it *could* happen.

Again.

When Jed Kincannon picked up on the other end, Daniel didn't waste time on pleasantries. "Henderson here. There's been another attempt to kidnap Kate Winston's granddaughter." He gave the details and a description of the white SUV. "It didn't have a license plate."

"I'll get on the horn with the local police immediately. Stay with the girl," Kincannon said. "You're headed back to the Winston Estate?"

He could feel Shelby trembling against him and his arm tightened around her. "Yes, sir." Damn right he was taking her back where there were pretty stiff security measures in place, and not only would it be difficult for someone to get in, it would be almost impossible for someone to leave unnoticed.

"Good," Kincannon said. "Keep her there as much as possible."

Daniel wanted to laugh at the man. That would be like caging a wild cat. She'd eventually find her way out and he'd be running to keep up with her. His bum knee throbbed in anticipation. Daniel clicked the off button and pocketed the phone. "Come on. We should be getting back to the estate."

"I'm not going back," she said into his shirt, the tremors subsiding. She pushed back and stared up into his eyes. "I'm going home."

"Like hell you are. It's not safe."

Her lips pressed into a thin line. "I'm going home to get my own clothes. Then you can take me back to the Winston Estate."

He didn't like the idea of driving all the way over to the Outer Banks. It would take a couple of hours to get there from where they were and even longer to get back to Raleigh. "It'll put us getting back after dark."

"I'm not going back without my own clothes. I'll take my own car if I have to."

Anger and frustration mixed and boiled over. "You were almost kidnapped again. Don't you get it?"

She stared up at him. "Yes, I get it. I was stupid to run away from you."

"Then why did you do it?"

She looked away. "You're pushy, and I'm not used to someone telling me what to do and following me around like I'm a child to be coddled."

"Then stop acting like a child." He gripped her chin in his fingers and tipped her head up. "I can't help you if you don't let me." With her face turned up to him and her lips only inches from his, he realized his error too late. All the anger at having been duped, followed by the surge of emotion he'd experienced when he'd seen her running toward him with fear and desperation in her eyes welled up in him and he took it out on her. He pressed his lips to hers in a searing kiss, one that took his breath away and left him dizzy with the intensity.

When he broke away, he whispered against her lips, "Don't run from me."

She braced her hands on his chest, curling her fingers into his shirt, clinging to him.

"Promise." His hands slid over her shoulders to grip her arms. "Promise you won't run from me," he said through gritted teeth.

"I promise," she whispered. Then her hands circled the back of his neck, bringing his lips back to hers. She gave as good as she got, her tongue pushing past his lips to take his in a long, slow glide. Her hips pressed against his as she moved closer, her calf curling around the back of his leg.

They could have been anywhere, but he felt as though they were alone on a deserted island, only him and Shelby.

A horn honked, shaking him out of the dream he'd been in, waking him to reality. They were standing in a parking lot. People were moving around them and anyone could have run them over and they would never have seen it coming.

"Come on." He grabbed her hand and dragged her back to the other building's parking lot.

She ran to keep up, her fingers wrapped in his. When they reached his SUV, he gave it a quick once-over, checking for bombs, before he allowed her to get in. Given her track record, a bomb could happen again, just like a kidnapping had almost succeeded.

He shivered at the thought. Even more than his promise to Patrick to keep her safe, he couldn't live with himself if he lost her.

"Where are we going?" she asked as she buckled her seat belt across her lap and settled back against the leather seats.

He shifted into Reverse, backed out of the parking space and drove toward the exit, his focus on the road, the vehicles around him and everything else but that kiss. "We're going to the Outer Banks, damn it."

Ah, who was he kidding? He couldn't think of anything *but* the kiss.

Chapter 8

Shelby leaned forward as they crossed the Washington Baum Bridge onto the strip of land known as the Outer Banks. With her window lowered, she breathed in the salty tang of the air, her chest swelling with love for the island, love for the long stretches of beach and this crazy touristy piece of heaven.

The sun was low in the western sky, making the sky orange and the water glisten like a thousand black, sparkling diamonds.

"I love this place," she said out loud, not expecting any response from Daniel. "It's home to me."

Daniel had driven all the way from the university without uttering a single word.

Shelby had been hesitant to break the silence, figuring he was still mad about her attempt to escape him. She wanted to be mad back. After all, she was more or less on a short leash with the bodyguard, unable to take a step without his approval or clearance.

Mad as she should have been, she couldn't wipe that kiss out of her mind. When she'd been thinking about him naked, she hadn't imagined how just a kiss would fry every brain cell in her head and leave her lips tingling for the next hour. Hell, they still tingled.

Sure, she'd dated guys, had sex with a couple of them, but none of them had kissed her like that and left her wanting so much more.

She sat as far away from him as possible in the confines of his SUV, running her tongue over her lips, tasting him there, and as she wondered what had triggered the kiss, one thing became perfectly clear. As much as she'd been thinking about him, he'd also been thinking about her.

Heat filled her insides, surging into places that shouldn't be feeling warm while stuck in a car with a surly bodyguard for the next few hours.

When they crossed the bridge and she could see the Atlantic Ocean ahead, she felt a sense of relief, of coming home and excitement.

"There were a couple of times I didn't think I'd see this place again," she said, her fingers gripping the armrest, emotion swelling in her throat.

Daniel glanced her way. "Seems like you did your best to make it happen."

She nodded. "I couldn't give up. I knew my grandfather would be beside himself with worry. If for no other reason, I had to make it back for him." She smiled. "But now that I'm here, I'm glad I made it back for me, too. I love the smell of salt, the beautiful sunrises you can only get here on the edge of the ocean."

Daniel turned south along the long stretch of land that made up the Outer Banks, passing tourist shops, restaurants, hotels, cottages and all the places Shelby knew by heart. She'd ridden her bicycle past them when she was too young to drive and driven past them every day she went to school or on those rare occasions when she went to Raleigh to do some shopping at the big department stores.

She loved this place where people came to relax and vacation away from the stress of the bigger cities.

When she spotted the roofline of O'Hara's Bar and Grill, excitement filled her and she could hardly wait for Daniel to park the SUV before she threw open the door and jumped out.

"Shelby," Daniel said, his voice stern, brooking no argument.

She stopped and waited for him to join her, aware he'd saved her twice in the past two days, and she owed him something for that.

When she stepped into the bar, the waitresses and bus boys stopped what they were doing and rushed over to her, exclaiming and hugging.

"Shelby, oh, dear, sweet Jesus," Lana Innman cried. "We were all so worried about you. You grandfather has been beside himself. How are you? Are you okay?"

Shelby's heart swelled at the welcome and she blinked back ready tears. "I'm fine, just glad to be back."

Marisa Webber joined the group hug. "Patrick said you'd been found, but I couldn't believe it without seeing you with my own eyes." She sniffed and brushed tears from her cheek. "We'd almost given up hope."

"Yes, we had. Almost. But I knew you were tough

and you wouldn't let anyone keep you down long." Lana hugged her again and glanced across at Daniel. "Wow. Who's the hunk?"

Shelby bristled. "This is Daniel. He's my…" she struggled with calling him her bodyguard, not wanting to sound like she was all that important.

"I'm her friend," he finished for her, saving her the embarrassment.

With a grateful smile at him, she repeated, "That's right, he's my friend."

"Just a friend?" Marisa asked. "If that's all, can I have his number?"

Normally Shelby couldn't be mad at Marisa; she flirted with all the male customers. She was kindhearted and fun loving and didn't have a mean bone in her body. But after Daniel's kiss, Shelby had a hard time taking Marisa's flirting lightly.

Patrick O'Hara came out of the back office, grinning from ear to ear. "I told you she was okay. Now move, so I can get a hug in there."

The staff stepped back and let Patrick in. He engulfed her in a bear hug. "I can't seem to get enough of these." He kissed the top of her head, the way he had when she'd been a little girl. "I'm so glad you're back."

"We only came in to collect her things," Daniel said.

"I'm glad. I was about to go through your bedroom and would probably have gotten the wrong items."

"Don't worry. I'm here now, and I can get what I need." Shelby kissed her grandfather's cheek. "Don't forget you need to be back at the Winston Estate sooner rather than later."

"I will, as soon as I put together the order list for tomorrow."

"Don't take too long." Shelby hugged a couple of the others, then broke free and headed for the back exit and the staircase that led up to their apartment above the bar.

Daniel grabbed her arm before she put her foot on the first step. "Let me go first."

"Fair enough." She handed him her key and followed him up the stairs. "The lock can stick a little. You have to wiggle the door when you put the key in it."

He inserted the key and attempted to twist it in the lock. As she'd predicted, it didn't work.

"Like this," Shelby reached around him and wrapped one hand around his holding the doorknob and the other over his fingers and turned the key, wiggling the handle at the same time.

When she touched him, a jolt of electric awareness burned through her.

As soon as the handle turned and the door opened, she jerked her hands away and moved back. In her hurry, she forgot she was so near to the edge of the landing. She teetered on the steps and nearly fell.

Daniel slipped an arm around her waist and crushed her to his chest. "Steady there," he whispered into her hair, his mouth touching her temple.

Her pulse slammed against her veins, shooting red-hot blood through her body.

Though she'd gotten her feet under her, he didn't let go, holding her longer than was necessary, and she was glad. Had he let go, her knees would have given way and she'd have melted like a puddle of goo at his feet.

"Are you okay?" he asked, his lips brushing against her earlobe.

Hell, no, she wasn't okay. The man made her turn to mush whenever they touched.

Digging deep, she summoned enough willpower to pull herself together and look up at him. "I'm..."

That was her second mistake. In the fading light, she stared into his smoldering green eyes and lost herself all over again. She leaned up on her toes and pressed her lips to his.

He cupped the back of her head and sealed the kiss with one of his own, his mouth consuming her, his tongue thrusting between her teeth to caress hers.

When at last he lifted his head, he dragged in a deep breath and stepped through the door, pulling her behind him. "Wait here," he commanded.

Wait? Her body on fire, she stood rooted to the spot, afraid if she moved, she'd collapse.

In the span of a few minutes, Daniel had searched the entire two-bedroom apartment.

But those few minutes were barely enough for her to come back to earth and get a grip on her rioting emotions.

"Get your things," he said, his voice stern. "We're going back to Raleigh."

She'd been ready to march into her room and do just that, but having him come back at her as though what they'd shared hadn't happened was a slap in the face. Anger rocketed up inside her.

"What just happened here?" she demanded.

His gaze met hers briefly and he looked away. "Nothing."

"Are you telling me that kiss meant nothing?"

He faced her, and for a long moment, he stared down at her, a muscle ticking in his jaw. "Really, Miss

O'Hara, I'm just doing my job." He turned and walked toward the door, where he stopped and glanced down at his watch then back up to her. "Five minutes."

Daniel waited outside the apartment door, sucking in fresh air and sanity. The kiss had rocked him deeply and he had been far too tempted to drag her into the apartment and take it ten steps further. And, damn it, that was the worst thing he could do.

He was on the job, not on vacation. He wasn't supposed to kiss the woman he should be protecting. It violated every ethic in his books. As a bodyguard, he was supposed to remain detached and observant. When he'd kissed Shelby, he'd lost track of everything. If someone had decided to shoot at them, they'd have had plenty of opportunity to kill.

The best way to end this was to make a clean, if ugly, break. Piss her off and she'd never get close enough for him to be tempted to kiss her again.

By the sound of drawers and doors slamming and the curse words coming from inside the apartment, he'd accomplished his mission.

That didn't do anything to lessen his desire for her. He'd have to deal with it. No more kissing the girl.

After five minutes on the nose, she emerged from her bedroom, a duffel bag slung over her shoulder. She breezed past him and clomped down the stairs, her eyes blazing and her back ramrod straight.

Oh, yeah. She was mad. And damn if she wasn't even sexier.

Swallowing a groan, he followed her down the stairs.

A few steps ahead of him, she entered the back door, the spring slamming it shut between them.

He had his hand on the handle to open the door when he heard a piercing scream.

Daniel ripped open the door and ran in. At first, he didn't see Shelby. She couldn't have gotten that far ahead of him. He rounded the corner into the kitchen and found a group of the staff gathered in a tight circle.

Daniel pushed through, zeroing in on Shelby's light brown hair. "Shelby, are you okay?"

She shot him an irritated glance. "I'm fine, but Lana isn't." Shelby held the woman's hands tight, bright red blood dripped from both of them.

Patrick O'Hara hurried through from another door, his face pale, the lines around his eyes and mouth deeper. "Here's the first-aid kit."

"Someone give me the gauze and surgical tape. I can't let up on the pressure until we can apply more."

Lana's face was pale and tears streaked down her cheeks. "I can't believe I was so stupid. I knew there was a broken glass in the dishwater, but I wasn't careful."

"We'll get you fixed up enough to stop the bleeding," Shelby reassured her. "But you're going to need stitches."

Lana swayed. "I'm feeling kind of dizzy."

"Get her a chair."

One of the busboys ran out to the dining area and returned with a chair. Daniel seated Lana, then took the first-aid kit from Patrick. He pulled out a roll of gauze and medical adhesive tape. He made a tight pad of gauze and applied tape on two sides. "Can you stand long enough to dip your hand under clean water?"

Lana nodded. "I think so."

He eased them toward the sink.

Marisa turned on the cold water and Shelby held Lana's hand beneath the steady stream. "I'm going to let go. Look at me, not your hand. I don't want to pick you up off the floor." She smiled. "Come on, Lana, you're tough. You can do this."

"Okay, Shelby, just do it." She stared at Shelby as they pushed her hand beneath the water.

Once Shelby let go, the blood flowed heavily.

Daniel pulled her hand from the water and clamped the wad of gauze over the cut and taped it down. He added another wad of gauze and more tape. "She needs those stitches."

Shelby washed the blood from her hands and found a clean dish towel for Lana to hold under her hand. "We can take her."

"No, let me. As the owner, I should take her." Patrick hooked Lana's arm and guided her toward the exit. He paused and turned back to Shelby. "I just let Kayla go home sick and we have a group scheduled to come in. They're going to be shorthanded."

"I'll stay and help out." Shelby shot a glance at Daniel, daring him to argue.

He washed the blood off his hands, shaking his head. "We're not staying."

"I'm not leaving. Unless you plan to hog-tie me and throw me in the back of your car, I'm not going anywhere."

Marisa whooped. "Yeah, baby. I gotta see this."

Daniel's adrenaline spiked and he fought to control the urge to do just what she'd said. With a deep breath, he resisted and played on her father's fears. "Mr. O'Hara?"

Patrick shook his head. "No, sweetheart, you need to go with Daniel." Her grandfather frowned. "I don't want to leave you, knowing you could disappear again."

"Go, Granddad." Shelby touched his arm and Lana's. "I'm fine, and I'll be here when you get back. Take care of Lana. She needs you now."

Patrick's gaze went to Daniel. "Don't let anything happen to my girl, will ya?"

Short of dragging Shelby out of the bar, Daniel wasn't convincing her to leave until her grandfather returned. Resigning himself to waiting this one out, he nodded at Patrick. "I'll do my best."

The older man's eyes narrowed. "Do better. She's the only family I have left."

"Yes, sir."

"Come on, Lana, let's get you sewn up before you bleed all over the place." He winked at her and led her out of the bar.

Ignoring Daniel, Shelby clapped her hands together. "Come on, people. We have a party arriving in twenty minutes. Let's get this place cleaned up and ready."

The waitresses, busboys and bartender hurried back to their duties. Shelby snagged a mop and a bucket of cleaner and headed for the kitchen.

Daniel followed.

"If you're going to hang around, you might as well help." She shoved the mop into his hands, stepped over the puddle of blood on the floor and, using a strainer, scooped the broken glass out of the sink and deposited it in the trash.

While she cleaned the dishes, Daniel mopped the floor, thinking there was no glory in being a Secret Service agent. Once again, he wondered what he'd been thinking when he'd agreed to be Shelby's bodyguard.

Trouble. With a capital *T.*

As expected, a group of thirty men from a rowing team out of D.C. converged on O'Hara's, shouting, laughing and raising good-natured hell.

Daniel helped by bussing tables while keeping a close eye on Shelby. He studied all the men, searching each face for a clue as to his intention.

Most of them wore polo shirts with their club logo on them. They were healthy, muscular men with innocent faces out to have a good time. For the most part.

Daniel wished Shelby was serving behind the bar. As she wove her way between the tables, any one of the men could attack and he'd be too late to help her.

He tried following her around, but that only made her mad, and she told him to back off.

At one table, she smiled and chatted with several of the rowers while serving fresh drinks and collecting the empties. When she turned back toward the bar, she tripped and would have fallen, but one man reached out and yanked her onto his lap, saving her, but not the contents of her tray.

Bottles and mugs toppled to the floor. Only one broke; the rest remained intact. Rubber tub in hand, Daniel hurried to her side.

"Oops." Shelby laughed. "Thanks for the save, but you can let me up now."

The man who'd pulled her into his lap laughed and refused to let go of her, his buddies egging him on.

Shelby retained her ever-present smile. "You really should let me up." With a glance at Daniel, she looked back at the man. "My boyfriend doesn't like it when other guys touch me."

The man immediately let go. "Sorry, dude. Didn't mean to poach."

Daniel's fingers clenched around the tub he'd been about to throw at the man. He still wanted to throw it, but he held back with a considerable amount of effort.

Shelby's lips twisted into a crooked smile. "See? He gets all hot and bothered when other guys so much as look at me, don't you, baby?" She kissed his cheek and slid a hand along his shoulder as she passed by him.

The guy in chair held up his hands, apparently seeing the danger in Daniel's eyes. "Like I said, man, I didn't know."

After a moment, Daniel shrugged. "No harm, no foul." He bent to clean up the bottles and mugs. When he had the mess cleared, he went to find Shelby.

She wasn't in the bar.

His pulse ratcheting upward, he hurried for the kitchen. Not there either, nor was the cook or anyone else.

The back door stood open as if someone had gone out in a hurry.

Daniel slammed the tub of bottles and mugs on a counter and ran for the back door.

Outside, the cook was tossing a heavy bag of trash into the Dumpster.

"Where's Shelby?" Daniel demanded.

The young man lost control of the bag he'd been hefting up into the trash container and it crashed back behind him, breaking open. "Well, damn." He glared at Daniel over the mess. "Don't sneak up on me like that."

"Shelby? Where is she?"

"How should I know? You're the one who's been following her around all night."

Daniel glanced left then right. Nothing moved in back of the building and there was no sign of Shelby. He ran back into the building and down the hallway toward the bar. A door opened immediately to his right and someone stepped out of the ladies' room and smacked into him. Reaching out, he grabbed the woman to keep her from falling.

His hands wrapped around Shelby's arms. As soon as he realized it was her, he crushed her against his chest. "Where the hell have you been?"

"To the bathroom," she said breezily.

"You just about gave me a freakin' heart attack."

"I didn't go far," she whispered, her mouth close to his, her breath warming his skin.

With her body pressed to his, his adrenaline still running high, he couldn't hold back. "Woman, you're making me crazy." He crushed her lips with his in a brutal kiss. His fingers knotted in her hair and he tugged, tipping her head back more so that he could trail his mouth along her jawline and down the side of her throat to that place where her pulse raced beneath her delicate skin.

Shelby's hands circled the back of his neck, drawing him closer, her calf rising up the side of his leg, curling around. "Missed me, huh?"

Chapter 9

Shelby could have kicked herself.

From hot and fiery to cold and distant, Daniel pushed Shelby away and stepped back. "That shouldn't have happened."

"But it did and you can't take it back." Her lips curled upward in a smirk. "You wanted to kiss me. Admit it."

He stared at her for a long time. Then he pushed his hand through his hair and turned his back to her. "We'd better get back to work."

She grabbed his arm. "Would it hurt so much to admit you find me attractive?"

He whipped around, his eyes blazing. "It wouldn't matter. You're in a different stratosphere entirely. I'm your bodyguard, not your lover. Don't get the two confused."

"What do you mean, I'm in a different stratosphere? We're both human. What's so different about you versus me?"

"You're the granddaughter of the former vice president of the United States, for the love of God."

Shelby's eyes widened. "Really? That's what's got your shorts in a twist?" She shook her head. "I'm the granddaughter of a man who owns a bar. I don't live in a mansion, I'm not a debutante with a purse for every outfit and a room full of shoes. I'm Shelby O'Hara."

"And I'm your bodyguard. Nothing else."

"Damn right it's nothing else. And I thought you were down-to-earth and a straight shooter. But I believe you're something of a snob." She pushed past him and marched back into the bar. "Just stay out of my way. I have work to do."

Much as he'd like to stay out of her way, he couldn't. Not when the danger was real. If the first kidnapping hadn't convinced her, the second attempt sure as hell had convinced him.

He spent the rest of the evening jumping at every loud noise, dogging every one of Shelby's footsteps and hating that all the guys in the bar were falling in love with the petite brunette with the perpetual smile for everyone but him.

The more he frowned, the brighter her smile grew, to the point he wanted to throw her over his shoulder like a caveman and take her back to the Winston Estate just to put an end to his agony.

Near eleven o'clock, Patrick O'Hara returned to the bar, having taken Lana to a twenty-four-hour clinic for the stitches and dropped her off at her house on the way back.

Patrick hugged his granddaughter as soon as he walked through the door. "I was worried sick the entire time I was gone, thinking I'd get back to find you had disappeared again." He kissed her forehead and she hugged him again.

"I'm not going anywhere. We had a good night and nothing out of the ordinary happened."

Daniel noted that Shelby hadn't bothered to tell her grandfather what had happened at the university. Had she informed him of the near miss, he'd have been even more determined to stick to her like glue, something Daniel had discovered Shelby didn't like. She was an independent young woman, sometimes too independent for her own good. His job was hard enough keeping her safe without worrying about her taking off because she was mad at him for something.

Thankfully, the rowing team had to be up at the crack of dawn to work out. One by one, they filed out of the bar, leaving it nearly empty.

"You two can head back to the Winston Estate now. I'll be right behind you as soon as I give the order list to Marisa."

"Are you sure?" Shelby wiped her hands on a towel and tossed it on the bar. "I can stay and help clean up."

"No, the staff handled it fine while you were gone. I'm sure they can do it again."

Her brows furrowed. "Don't think you're going to get rid of me altogether. This arrangement is only temporary."

"I hope so, dear. The sooner they figure out who was responsible and lock him up, the sooner you won't have to have a bodyguard and the better I'll feel. Now get going so I can finish up."

When Patrick put it that way, Daniel didn't know how he felt. On one hand, he'd be free of babysitting duties. On the other, he'd have no need to be around Shelby. They'd part ways and that would be the end of it. A Secret Service agent's life wasn't geared toward long-term relationships. "You heard your grandfather. You're slowing him down." Daniel hooked Shelby's arm and guided her to the exit and his vehicle.

Shelby jerked her arm free. "You don't have to be so pushy, bodyguard."

He prayed she'd stay mad. After the fiery kiss in the hallway, he wasn't sure he could keep his distance. "I do if I want to get you back to the Winstons' place before dawn. As it is, it'll be nearly one in the morning before we arrive."

"Well, then, let's get crackin'." She led the way out the door to Daniel's SUV.

When she placed her hand on the door handle, he stopped her. "Let me check first."

Shelby stood back while Daniel shone a pocket flashlight under the car. He opened the hood and checked inside the engine compartment for anything that didn't belong. When he was satisfied there weren't any explosive devices attached to the vehicle, he waved a hand toward the passenger seat. "Your chariot awaits, princess."

Her lips thinned. "I'm not a princess. I'm a waitress." She got in and slammed the door shut.

Daniel hid a grin as he slid into the driver's seat and buckled his seat belt.

The long drive back to Raleigh was completed in silence. Shelby fell asleep against the window, the shadows beneath her eyes more pronounced.

Daniel had to remind himself she'd only been free from her captors for a little more than a day. A lot had happened in that time frame. She was exhausted. When she wasn't mad, her face softened and her lips relaxed, full and pink and completely kissable.

Daniel forced himself to concentrate on the road ahead. If he wasn't careful, he'd drive into the ditch. He stayed alert by going over everything that had happened. D'Angelis had told them enough to save the girl before he died. But he'd died in custody. Someone at the police station had to have poisoned him.

D'Angelis had been a Secret Service agent like Daniel, with one huge difference: he'd gone bad. Sold out to the highest bidder, and it was suspected he'd worked for the Cartel. If there were dirty agents in the Secret Service, there could be dirty cops at the police station. But who had access to the man? Who could have slipped him the poison between the time he was brought from his cell and the time he died?

Daniel's grip tightened on the steering wheel. He didn't know who to trust anymore. Anyone could be after Shelby. If he asked Kate to find a different agent to provide for her safety, he couldn't be certain that agent was a good agent.

The only reason he could come up with that would make someone target Shelby was her connection to Kate Winston. And who would have known Kate's daughter had survived? For all these years, Kate had presumed her child was dead. The only others who knew about her pregnancy were her mother, father and the hospital staff who helped deliver the baby. And, of course, her grandfather.

Daniel pulled up to the gate of the Winston Estate,

no closer to the truth than when he'd left and a whole lot more frustrated by a couple of incredibly hot kisses.

He parked at the front of the house. As late as it was, he didn't want to make Shelby walk any farther than she had to. She was still asleep when he rounded the car, grabbed her duffel bag out of the backseat, looped it over his shoulder, then opened her door.

She tipped slightly until her seat belt caught her and kept her from falling out.

Daniel reached across her lap and unbuckled her belt, then gathered her in his arms and carried her up the steps to the big house.

The door opened as soon as he stopped in front of it and Kate Winston stood there in her bathrobe, her face clean of makeup. "I was beginning to worry, until Patrick texted me to say you were on your way back. Any mishaps?"

"Not on the trip back. Let me get her up the stairs and then we'll talk."

"I can get there myself." Shelby's eyes blinked open and she stared up at him. "Put me down."

"Are you sure, dear?" Kate asked. "You look so very tired."

"I can walk." Shelby pushed at Daniel and he set her on her feet, keeping one of his arms behind her back to steady her.

"Let me check your room before you go up," Daniel insisted.

"I'm sure it's the same as I left it. You and Mrs. Winston need to talk, and I need a shower. I can manage on my own."

Daniel hesitated. "I'd rather not leave it up to chance."

"And I'd rather be alone," she said. "I'll be sure to scream if there's a monster under my bed."

Kate touched Daniel's arm. "Thad was here earlier. I had him check things in Shelby's room. I'm sure she'll be fine."

Shelby cocked an eyebrow. "See? Even the lady of the house thinks it's safe here. If it isn't, I might as well go back to *my* home."

With a smile, Kate took Daniel's arm. "Let her have her peace. Shelby, honey, do you need help getting up the stairs?"

"No." Shelby took the duffel bag from Daniel and set off across the foyer toward the stairs, her gait more wobbly than Daniel liked. She made it to the stairs and gripped the rail all the way up, half carrying, half dragging the duffel bag. The whole time Daniel watched, wanting to go after her and carry her and that damned bag up to her room.

"Come, Daniel," Kate said. "I want to know everything that happened today."

Daniel followed Kate into her study, determined to tell her only the things pertinent to the case. Kate didn't need to know he'd kissed her granddaughter.

What would she do if she did know? Have him reassigned?

Without knowing who to trust, he couldn't leave Shelby in someone else's hands.

Shelby had to drag herself up the stairs. The nap she'd had in the car had done little to banish the exhaustion she was feeling. Working at the bar had been a stretch after two weeks in hell with no exercise. Though it had felt good to be back to normal, she'd been tense and jumpy all night. Partly because she wasn't sure who to trust in the crowd at the bar and partly because of Daniel watching her.

Her lips still tingled from the kiss on the landing outside her apartment and the kiss in the hallway outside the bathroom in the bar. She'd kissed a few boys in her life, but nothing had compared to what she'd experienced with Daniel. Not only had it been good, it had sparked desire so strong, she'd almost forgotten where she was.

She moaned softly. The thought of kissing Daniel heated her blood and pushed her exhaustion aside. Now that she was awake, her body recalled the way it felt pressed against his. He'd been hard with desire, of that she was certain, and it made her hot and bothered all over.

A cool shower and her own nightgown would help her settle in for a good night's sleep.

Dropping her bag on the floor, she rummaged inside until she found clean panties and her favorite baby-doll nightie. She'd bought it on a whim and hardly wore it. Living in the apartment over the bar, she'd always worn an old T-shirt and stretchy shorts to bed.

Living in the Winstons' mansion made her more conscious of everything she wore, including her nightclothes. At home, instead of grabbing the ratty T-shirt she normally wore to bed, she'd dug the pretty teal nightgown out of her drawer. Now she almost changed her mind and scrounged for a T-shirt, but one glance at the connecting door made her hold on to the gown.

The man had some serious commitment issues and prejudices against people with a lot of money, not that she was one of them. Shelby had served all kinds at the bar and they all put their pants on the same way. Her connection to Kate Winston was an accident of birth. She was not connected to Kate's bank account and wouldn't want to be, even if she was asked.

Shelby had inherited her grandfather's sense of responsibility and drive. If she made it in this world, it would be because of hard work and her intelligence, not because she'd been born into wealth.

Gown in hand, she entered the bathroom and shut the door behind her. The bathroom was bigger than her bedroom back home and almost as big as the living room. The counters and shower were made of a beautiful white granite with brown and black speckles. The floor was covered in white marble tile and the fixtures were a shiny gold.

She glanced at the bathtub she'd used the day before and her cheeks heated. That was the first time Daniel had seen her naked.

And the last time he would, she decided. He'd have to beg her to make love to him after he'd been so callous earlier. Even then, she'd tell him where he could get off.

She stripped out of the clothing Kate had given her, now rumpled and stained from waiting tables at the bar. She glanced down at the sweater with regret. It was nice and she'd hate it if the stains wouldn't come out.

She filled the sink with water, applied some of the hand soap to the spots and then let it soak.

Stripping off her undergarments, she couldn't help but think of Daniel sleeping in the room on the other side of her bedroom. All she had to do was walk over there, open the door and let herself in.

Her core tightened, electric tingles spreading through

her body, angling downward. She jerked the handle on the shower, setting it on cool and stepped beneath the spray. The chill of the water made her catch her breath, and her wrists stung when the water hit the sores she'd created scraping the zip tie off. Both shocked her back to sanity.

Daniel was off-limits. He was her bodyguard, a Secret Service agent and a damned good kisser. But that was all. He wasn't the stuff relationships were made of. He'd told her that in no uncertain terms.

Knowing him only a day was not long enough to form an attachment to her guardian angel, the man who'd pulled her from a burning building. Hell, a fireman could have done the same and she wouldn't be drooling over him or wishing he'd kiss her again.

She should be worrying more about catching up on homework or about who was trying to kidnap her and less about getting in bed with the government agent. She squirted a little of the beautifully scented shampoo on her hand and applied it to her hair, scrubbing hard, as if she could scrub the images and thoughts about Daniel out of her head.

Not likely.

With quick efficiency, Shelby washed her body and rinsed her hair and skin, careful to avoid touching the bump on her forehead. Then she shut off the water. The towel she wrapped herself in was thick and luxurious, like everything else in the mansion. All the towels they had back home on the Outer Banks had been well worn and washed. They were thin, some threadbare. It wasn't that she and her grandfather were poor, they just hadn't found a need to replace things that worked just fine.

Shelby tossed the towel over the rack and slipped into her nightgown and bikini panties.

A sound in the bedroom made her jump.

"Daniel?" she called out.

No answer.

She grabbed the metal toothbrush holder and eased toward the door. "Daniel?" she called out, louder this time, her heart lodged in her throat.

As the bathroom doorknob turned, she remembered that she hadn't locked it and dived for the handle and the locking mechanism, twisting hard.

She got it locked. With her pulse slamming against her veins, she stood in her nightgown, holding the toothbrush holder and wondered what the hell to do next.

Chapter 10

Daniel paced in front of Kate's desk. "I don't like what's happening. The attack at the school made it clear that Shelby is still a target. Whoever is after her won't stop until they've caught her and used her for whatever they hope to accomplish."

Kate sat in the leather chair in her robe, looking no less regal than if she wore one of her tailored gray suits. "I don't know what else to do. She's at risk because of me. Until I know who they are or what they want, I can't do anything about it." She rested her face in her hands. "All I can do is pray that you're always there to keep her safe."

"She's got a mind of her own and she's not afraid to use it."

Kate smiled. "She's like her grandfather. Stubborn man."

"The point is, she doesn't take kindly to being followed around and putting her life in someone else's hands."

"For the time being, she'll have to get used to it. She's not safe." Kate stood and cinched the robe at her waist. "It's late, Daniel. Even a good bodyguard needs his rest. Go to bed. We can worry about this again in the morning."

He was ready. The few minutes he'd been talking to Kate, he'd been farther from Shelby than he'd been since he was assigned to protect her. His instincts were to go to her and make sure she was all right. Not that much could happen to her in the relative security of the Winston Estate. Still, he didn't trust anyone but himself to ensure her safety.

Kate drifted off toward the kitchen for a cup of tea while Daniel hurried up the curving staircase and along the landing to the door to Shelby's bedroom. He leaned his ear against the thick wood paneling and heard nothing. He tested the door. It was unlocked, and he debated whether or not to knock or barge in and demand she lock the door. Instead, he opened the door, reached in and twisted the lock, then closed the door again. No use alarming her. She was probably already asleep. Daniel went to his own room to get ready for bed.

As he closed his door behind him, he heard a noise from Shelby's room.

He crossed to the connecting door and listened.

The noise sounded again...and he could swear he heard Shelby calling his name. He could be mistaken; the sound was so soft he could have imagined it.

Then the noise sounded again and Shelby's voice called out, louder this time.

He tried the door and discovered it was locked and cursed himself for locking the other door before checking to see if Shelby was okay. Pulling his weapon from the holster beneath his jacket, he performed a hard side kick with his heel close to the locking mechanism. The door frame splintered, but the door didn't give. He kicked again and the door flew open, the frame shattering.

"Daniel?" Shelby called out from inside the bathroom. "Please tell me that was you," she said, her voice breaking as if it caught on a sob.

"It's me," he responded, arriving at the door to the bathroom as she opened it and threw herself into his arms. He caught her and held her against his body with his free hand, his gaze panning the room. Nothing moved; the room was empty except for the two of them.

"What happened?" he asked.

"I'd just gotten out of the shower when I heard a noise in my room. Then the doorknob twisted. I got to it in time to lock it." She looked up, her eyes wide, her fingers digging into his shirt. "Please tell me it was you."

He shook his head. "Sorry, sweetheart, it wasn't."

Shelby closed her eyes and pressed her forehead to his shirt. "I could have been imagining it. With all that's happened, my mind could be playing tricks on me."

He didn't believe it for a minute. "Had you locked your bedroom door?"

She nodded. "I'm pretty sure I did."

"Wait here."

Her fingers tightened on his shirt. "I'd rather not."

With her tucked in the curve of his arm, he led her through the connecting doorway to his bedroom door. He gripped her arms and moved her to the side of the door. "Lock this behind me and don't open it until I tell you to."

Opening the door, he pointed his weapon out into the hallway, then poked his head out, glancing in one direction and then the other. The hallway came to a dead end to the left, and the right led toward the staircase. No one stirred; nothing moved.

Carefully turning the knobs on the other doors in the hallway, he checked inside. Two of the rooms were empty. The room Patrick was to stay in was empty, as well. Daniel hurried down the hallway to the staircase and stared down at the floor below.

Kate Winston walked toward the stairs, carrying a cup. She glanced up and gasped. "Daniel? Is something wrong? I thought I heard a crashing sound."

"I don't know."

"There must be, or you wouldn't be carrying a gun." She looked around her and back up to him. "Is Shelby all right?"

"Yes. If you don't mind, I'll do a security check of the house."

"Please, by all means." She waited at the bottom of the stairs as he checked the other rooms on the second floor. When he returned, she met him halfway up the stairs. "Anything I can do?"

He shook his head. "No. I'll finish my check. You can go to bed. Your room is clear."

"Thank you, Daniel."

The sound of a key scraping in the lock on the front door echoed across the foyer, Daniel turned toward the sound.

The ornate door opened and Patrick O'Hara entered, closing the door quietly behind him. When he turned, he started. "Oh. I'm sorry, did I wake you?" His gaze went to Kate, his look one of longing.

"No, we were up." Kate held up her cup, descending the stairs. "Can I interest you in a cup of tea? Daniel was doing a last-minute check of the house."

"Shelby?" Patrick asked.

"In my bedroom for the moment. She's okay." Daniel descended to the first floor. "I'll only be a few minutes." He left Kate and Patrick in the foyer and checked all the rooms on the main floor, testing the windows and door locks to ensure they were secure. When he passed the kitchen on his way back to the stairs, he saw that Patrick and Kate sat at the bar, talking softly, mugs of steaming tea in front of them.

Daniel hurried back up the stairs and knocked softly on his bedroom door. "Shelby, it's me, Daniel."

She opened the door.

He stepped inside and closed the door behind him, then opened his arms.

Shelby went to him, burying her face against his chest, her body fitting close to his. She wore nothing but a sheer nightgown that barely covered her bottom, and he could see teasing shadows of her breasts beneath the thin fabric.

Holy hell. If he'd thought he could resist her, he was

sorely mistaken. Once he had his arms around her, there was no going back.

She ran her hands across his chest and around his middle, hugging him closer, her hips pressed against his.

His groin tightened, blood rushing to his head and lower to his throbbing member. The warmth of her skin beneath the sheer nightgown burned through, igniting flames inside him.

He lifted a hand to the back of her head, twisting his fingers in her hair, tugging her head back. "I didn't want this to happen."

"So why are you letting it?" She lifted her full, plump lips toward his.

"I can't help myself." He took her mouth, crashing down on her, thrusting through her teeth to caress her tongue with his. She tasted minty and fresh, warm and wet.

He reached down, cupped her bottom and lifted with one hand, the other still holding his pistol.

Her legs curled naturally around his waist and her arms went around his neck.

Her silky panties and his denim pants were all that stood between them.

Without breaking their kiss, he walked her to the bed and let her slide down his front to her feet.

Shelby pulled the weapon from his hand. "Can we set this aside?"

"I don't know. I think I'm in dangerous territory."

"Damn right you are." She shoved his jacket over his shoulders and he let it drop to the floor. When she reached for the buckles on his shoulder holster, he shoved her hands aside and worked them himself.

Meanwhile, she unbuttoned his trousers and ran the zipper downward, releasing his member into her palm.

Daniel jerked the holster off and tossed it onto a nearby chair. Then his hands slipped beneath her night-gown, cupping the full roundness of both breasts—so warm, soft and tipped with the tightest buds. He pushed the gown upward and claimed one of the rounded orbs, sucking it between his lips and tongu-ing the intriguing tip.

Her back arched, her hand pressing against the back of his head, urging him to suck the nipple deeper into his mouth.

He complied, licking the areola, nibbling the bud with the edges of his teeth while his hands roved over her waist and down to the elastic on her panties. Slid-ing his fingers beneath the fabric, he cupped her bot-tom, tracing the line between her cheeks.

Her hands grew restless, shoving his trousers down his legs.

He stopped her long enough to unearth his wal-let from his back pocket and toss it on the bed. Then Daniel toed off his shoes and stepped out of the pants, kicking them to the side. He yanked his shirt up over his head and threw it across the end of the bed. Im-patient to reveal all of her, he grabbed the hem of her nightgown and tugged it up over her head.

The gown flew across the room and he stepped back, his hungry gaze raking over her naked body, the panties the only thing in the way of him feasting on her.

The longer he stared, the brighter the pink in her cheeks became. She raised her hands to cover herself.

He caught her wrists. "Don't."

"Then quit staring and do something."

He laughed, dragged her into his arms and reveled in the feel of her breasts pressing against his chest. "Bossy much?"

"Don't make me wait. I'm on fire." She slipped out of his embrace and scooted up onto the bed.

Staring down at her delectable body, Daniel knew he was doomed. "This goes against all the rules."

"I'm betting you follow all the rules."

"I do." This woman had him so tied in knots, he couldn't back away.

Rules be damned.

The fire in his eyes had Shelby's body burning. She caught the elastic of her panties, slipping them down her legs in a long, sensuous move designed to leave Daniel panting. "In this case, I think you can break them." She let her knees fall to the sides.

Her entrance was slick and drenched with her juices. All she needed was him inside her, filling her.

He crawled up between her legs and kissed a path along the inside of her thigh to the center, the feathery-soft touches of his lips sending tingling electric shocks throughout her body.

Shelby ran her fingers down through the curls covering her mons, sliding a finger between her folds. She wanted him there.

Daniel tongued the tips of her fingers, pushing them aside to access the tiny strip of flesh packed with a plethora of nerves.

On the first flick, she moaned, her back arching off the mattress.

The second one had her grabbing his hair, her fingers digging into his scalp. "Oh, my," she whispered, her voice choked with desire.

Daniel slid two fingers into her and tongued her nubbin at the same time, catapulting her to the edge. "Yes! Oh, my, yes!"

He focused on that spot, flicking and tonguing until she hurtled over the edge, her body growing rigid, her insides a cascade of sensations, rippling over and over one another. Just when she thought she could die like this and be happy, Daniel moved away. "No!" she moaned.

"I'm not going anywhere." He reached for his wallet, extracted a foil packet and tore it open. In seconds he'd rolled the condom down over himself and slid up between her legs, his shaft poised at her opening. "Here's to breaking all the rules." He thrust deep, her channel stretching to accommodate his girth.

Shelby pushed up, meeting his thrust and urging him deeper, the sensations exploding throughout her. She gripped his hips, guiding him out, then back in. Soon he settled into a smooth, steady rhythm, pumping in and out, increasing in speed with the tension in his body.

One final thrust and he held still, his member throbbing inside her.

Shelby wrapped her legs around him, her heels digging into his buttocks, holding him as close as he could possibly get. At that moment, they were one, connected in the most beautiful way.

After a while, he rolled her onto her side and fell to the mattress beside her, maintaining their intimate bond.

Lying in the crook of his arms, she couldn't think of a place she'd rather be. The lack of sleep and the strain of being kidnapped and targeted again, not to mention the two weeks in captivity, pulled at her eye-lids and she gave in, feeling safe and protected in her bodyguard's arms. If only real life didn't intrude, she'd be happy to stay like this forever.

Daniel held Shelby, her body pressed against his side. She fit perfectly in his arms, her soft brown hair brushing against his skin, her breath warming him.

For a long time, he refused to think, to let the logical side of his brain spoil the moment. But as Shelby's breathing grew steady and deep, he had to face the facts—he'd screwed up. He'd had sex with the woman he was assigned to protect. It went against every rule in the books. He'd lost perspective, lost his self-control and, if he didn't get back on track, he'd lose his focus.

And if he lost focus, Shelby's life would be at risk.

Daniel extricated himself from the bed, sliding his arm out from under Shelby's head. Bending over her, he brushed his mouth across her swollen lips, tasting her one last time before he steeled his resolve and got his head back on straight.

At twenty-three, she was tough, independent and completely irresistible.

And she was the former vice president's grand-daughter. Out of his social league.

And the most important detail was that she was Daniel's job.

He lifted her in his arms, careful not to wake her, and carried her into her room, laying her on her bed.

She snuggled into the sheets without opening her eyes.

Daniel wanted to crawl in bed with her. Instead

he stepped away, ensured her door was locked and checked that the latch on her window was secure and then left.

When he reached the connecting door to his room, he heard a soft knock. He tensed, his body on full alert.

"Shelby?" Patrick O'Hara's voice called out.

Shelby stirred, her eyelids flickering open. "Grand-dad?"

"Are you all right in there?"

She sat up, the sheet falling down around her waist. Her eyes widened as she came fully awake. Her glance shot to the pillow beside her and then around the room, landing on Daniel where he stood in the doorway.

"Shelby?" her grandfather called out again. "I was just heading to bed and I thought I heard a noise or something. Are you all right?"

"I'm all right, Granddad, just tired."

"Oh, okay. Goodnight, sweetheart. I'll see you in the morning."

Her gaze never strayed from Daniel, her eyes narrowing in confusion.

He felt pinned to the wall, but he couldn't reassure her when he needed to put distance between them. Without a word of explanation, and using every ounce of resistance he could muster, he pulled the door closed between them. He couldn't lock it since the frame had been destroyed.

Walking away was the right thing to do, but it didn't make it any easier. Shelby would be mad, and she had a right to be. He'd been a jerk to take advantage of her. But he'd be more of a jerk if he continued down that same path. Ultimately, the job would end and he'd move on to his next assignment. Leaving Shelby behind.

As much as he'd resisted being her bodyguard in the first place, he didn't relish leaving her in the end.

Chapter 11

Daniel tried to sleep, but knowing Shelby was only a few short steps away left him wide-awake, and full-on frustrated.

When the early light of dawn crept through his window, he knew he had to get out, breathe fresh air and clear his foggy brain.

He pulled on shorts and running shoes and headed downstairs and out of the house. He slipped through the gate, making certain it closed securely behind him. Only those with a need to know had the security code to enter, but anyone could get out with a single push of a button. He made a note to talk to Kate about other options that were more secure.

Ignoring the ever-present pain in his leg, he half jogged and half walked a mile before turning back. He didn't want to be too far away from the estate should anything happen. With Shelby asleep in her locked bedroom, she should be all right for a while. And he needed the exercise, or his injuries from that fateful day of protecting Kate would never heal.

The sun had yet to rise on his return. When he was within a hundred yards of the gate, he stopped to tie a shoelace that had come undone.

Leaning against a tree, he bent, tied his shoe and happened to look up just as someone exited the Winston Estate on foot, wearing shorts, a T-shirt and a baseball cap. Despite the hat, Daniel knew who it was and anger spiked in him.

Did she *want* to be kidnapped again?

Shelby turned away from him and set off at a jog.

Adrenaline spiked and Daniel took off after her.

At a crossroad, she turned right and disappeared around the corner.

Still a good fifty yards behind her, Daniel ignored the pain in his knee and sped up, concerned. Shelby was out on her own, now on a busier street and no one around to keep her from being taken.

Daniel raced for the corner. Before he reached it, a large white SUV like the one that had been at the university the day before sped by, heading the same direction as Shelby.

Sprinting as fast as he could go, Daniel rounded the corner without slowing, in time to see SUV's brake lights flash and the vehicle slow next to Shelby.

His heart thundering, Daniel yelled, "Shelby, run!"

Shelby had already noticed the danger and stopped on the sidewalk.

Move, Daniel willed her, still running to reach her in time.

As the vehicle slowed beside her, Shelby spun and ran back toward Daniel.

Without a gun or any other type of weapon, Daniel would only be able to shield her with his body. But he'd throw himself in the line of fire before he'd let a single bullet hit Shelby.

The SUV whipped into Reverse and backed up after Shelby's running figure.

Daniel reached her before the SUV, grabbed her hand and ran with her, dragging her faster and faster.

The SUV swerved in an attempt to hit them.

Daniel veered away from the road and headed through a stand of trees between two large houses. As he and Shelby emerged on the other side of the trees, the SUV was there, heading directly for Daniel.

Daniel had to let go of Shelby or risk her getting hit along with him.

Pushing her one way, Daniel dived in the opposite direction, narrowly missing the crush of the SUV's tires.

Shelby staggered and fell to the ground.

As Daniel picked himself up off the pavement, a man wearing a ski mask leaped down from the SUV and ran toward Shelby.

She lay on the ground, motionless.

When the man reached out to grab her, she exploded from the ground, kicked the man in the face and rolled out of reach.

About the time the man reached for her again, the back door opened and another man with a ski mask leaped out. Daniel arrived at the SUV at that moment and slammed the man into the side of the vehicle.

Startled by the attack, the man swung, his fist connecting with Daniel's jaw. Daniel's head whipped back, but he balled his fists and aimed for the man's belly, landing a hard one to the guy's breadbasket. He doubled over.

A scream behind him gave Daniel the necessary incentive to end the argument sooner. He raised his knee with a hard jerk, hitting the man in the nose. He went down, holding on to his face, blood streaming from beneath the dark ski mask.

Daniel spun toward the other guy.

He had Shelby in a headlock.

"One step closer and I'll break her neck," the guy growled.

"I'll give you one chance to let her go," Daniel bluffed, wondering how the hell he'd get Shelby away from the gorilla.

Shelby's face was red and she clawed at the meaty arm wrapped tightly around her throat.

At a standoff, Daniel edged closer.

Shelby went limp and collapsed in her captor's arms. She'd done nothing to deserve this. She was an innocent pawn in a game of politics and deception.

His heart in his throat, Daniel lunged for the man, rage driving him forward.

As he reached them, Shelby jabbed her elbow into her captor's groin. The man let her go and grabbed for his crotch. Daniel slammed his knee into the man's face and shoved him backward; he tripped over the curb and fell on his backside.

Daniel gripped Shelby's hand and ran back the way he'd come, dragging her along with him, praying she had the strength to keep up. If the men who'd threatened them followed, he wasn't sure he'd be so lucky to get her away the next time.

Shelby ran next to Daniel, gulping air into her lungs and shooting glances over her shoulder to gauge whether or not the bad guys were still following. The man she'd bested helped the one with the broken nose into the SUV. The driver sent the vehicle up over the curb in his effort to get away.

Daniel didn't let her stop until they'd reached the entrance to the Winston Estate. He punched the code into the keypad and the gate opened. Once he'd shoved her through, he hit the close button and the gate slammed shut behind them.

Shelby collapsed on the ground and lay there for a full two minutes until her breathing returned to normal. The adrenaline still spiking through her veins made her sit up. "Thank you," she said.

Daniel paced away, the color high in his cheeks. His eyes blazed and he breathed through his nose like an angry bull. He stopped in front of her, towering over her. "I don't know what was going through your head. I'm not here to make sure you have a good time. I'm not here to make love to you. My primary goal in this assignment is to keep you safe. If you insist on pulling stupid stunts like that, you can find yourself another damn bodyguard." He stalked away, leaving her on the ground by the gate.

She rolled to her feet and went after him. "Really? You think I *asked* to be grabbed off the street? You think I *planned* on having a secret identity connected to the former vice president of the freakin' United

States?" She grabbed his arm, forcing him to stop, though he refused to face her.

She marched around in front him and stood with her arms crossed over her chest. "I didn't want a body-guard in the first place." Jabbing a finger into his chest, she went on, "And I sure as hell don't want one who has a problem with sticking around. You couldn't get up and get out of my bed fast enough." He stood rock solid, his face poker straight, his flashing green eyes the only indication she was making him angrier.

"What's wrong with you? Are you afraid you might like me? Afraid you're not good enough for me? 'Cause let me tell you, bubba, you aren't. I need a man who doesn't judge anyone based on their lineage. A man who will love me no matter who my parents or grand-parents are or what they did." On a roll, unable to stop her tirade now that she'd started, she poked him again. "You know what you are? A scaredy cat. A big ol' scaredy cat."

He grabbed her finger and yanked her hard, slam-ming her against his chest. He caught her lips with his in a crushing kiss that stole her breath away and made her head spin.

When he shoved her away from him, she reeled backward.

He poked a finger into her chest. "For the record, I didn't ask for this assignment. I was stuck with it. For the record, I don't like babysitting little girls who don't know what's best for them. And for the record, I didn't run away from you. Did you ever think I might have left because I didn't want to make love to you again?"

That hurt like a punch to the gut. Shelby fought to keep from doubling over at the slam. "Good. Because

I don't want you touching me." Damn. She tried to stop it, but her eyes teared up and her bottom lip trembled. "Ever again."

Daniel stared at her, his jaw hard, his face impassive. Finally he eased her back into his arms and pressed his cheek against her hair. "You scared the crap out of me."

"I thought you didn't care."

"I don't want to." He stroked her soft brown hair, twisting his fingers in the silken strands.

"But you do."

"Yes." He sighed and took her hand in his. "Let's get you back to the house."

With her hand tucked in his big, warm one, Shelby leaned against him as they walked back to the mansion.

Kate met them in the foyer, her brows coming together in a worried frown. "What's wrong?" She glanced at Shelby's legs. "Why are your knees skinned?"

Shelby hadn't realized she'd been hurt. The adrenaline rush and near miss had blocked the pain. "I fell."

"The hell she did. She was attacked again," Daniel said.

"Dear God." Kate wrapped her arms around Shelby. "Are you okay? Should I call the doctor?"

Shelby hadn't been hugged by a female relative since her mother died and she'd been almost too young to remember. Kate's hug was warm, welcoming and seemed genuinely heartfelt.

After nearly being taken again, Shelby let the woman hug her. She liked the way Kate Winston smelled of honeysuckle, and she was warm and soft. She could see how a man from the Outer Banks could have fallen for the pretty socialite.

"Shelby?" Her grandfather hurried down the stairs, dressed in jeans and a polo shirt. "What's going on?"

The front door opened and Thad entered, followed by Jed Kincannon.

Thad smiled. "Looks like I'm just in time for the party. What's going on?"

Everyone started talking at once. Shelby's head began to ache and her skinned knees stung.

Daniel whistled to get everyone's attention. "We aren't accomplishing a thing." He curved his arm around Shelby's waist. "We're going to clean up."

"Yes, yes. Of course. Shelby's injuries need tending to." Kate waved toward the hallway. "Let's take this discussion into the kitchen while Daniel takes care of Shelby. I'll make breakfast, and we can talk about what we want to do."

"Are you sure you don't need me to help?" Patrick asked.

Shelby smiled. "You patched up all of my skinned knees as a kid, but I think I can handle this on my own." She leaned close and kissed her grandfather's cheek. "I love you, Granddad."

"Not as much as I love you, little girl." He patted her shoulder and followed Kate toward the kitchen.

Shelby had always been the only woman in her grandfather's life, and he'd never dated anyone that she knew of. She'd assumed he hadn't dated because he'd been too busy raising his daughter and then his granddaughter. Could it be that he had never gotten over his first love?

Shelby stared after her grandfather's retreating figure. A little nip of jealousy was quickly overridden by the thought that her grandfather might still be in love with the beautiful and powerful Kate Winston. How sad. With her in her mansion and him in his bar on the Outer Banks, they couldn't be farther apart.

Her heart aching for her grandfather, Shelby turned to follow Daniel.

"Wait," Thad said. "You'll need the first-aid kit." Thad ran to the kitchen and returned with a red-and-white box.

"Thank you." Shelby reached for it, but Daniel got there first. She frowned. "I'm not an invalid, you know."

"I know, but I'd rather you concentrated on getting up the stairs unscathed."

"Again, I think I can handle climbing and carrying a little box."

Daniel gave her lopsided smile. "Are you always this argumentative?"

Patrick snorted from the hallway. "She can be a pill sometimes."

"You're not helping, Granddad," Shelby shot back, crossing her arms as she turned on Daniel. "Are you always this domineering?"

"Let's agree you're argumentative and I'm domineering and maybe we'll get cleaned up sometime today. We have bigger fish to fry, and arguing down here isn't getting the oil hot."

Shelby started to give him a scathing reply, thought better of it and clamped her lips shut.

Daniel led the way to her room where she sat on the edge of the big tub in the bathroom while he cleaned the gravel from her skinned knees and applied ointment and bandages. His hand lingered on her thigh and she held her breath, waiting for him to lean close and claim a kiss.

When he didn't, she wanted to scream with frustration. Instead, she turned the tables on him. "My turn." She took the kit and stood. "Sit."

"I can manage on my own."

She gave him a meaningful stare and pointed to the edge of the tub. "Sit."

With that gorgeous lopsided grin that made her go weak at the knees, he sat.

She wet a clean washcloth and dabbed at a gash on his cheek where he'd been punched. "You're going to have a bruise."

"I'll live," he said, his smile slipping as she leaned closer. "You don't have to get so close."

"Yes, I do." She straddled his lap and sat with a smile. "I haven't properly thanked you for saving me." Shelby applied ointment to his cheek.

He caught her wrist in his hand and stared at her hard. "Don't make this any harder than it has to be."

"What do you mean?"

"When the threat is gone, you won't need my protection. I'll be reassigned."

Her heart fluttered. She'd already come to that conclusion, but hearing him say it drove it home. Forcing a smile, she shook her hand free. "I know that. In the meantime, let me take care of you for once."

His lips tightened, but he let go of her wrist. She applied a butterfly bandage to pull the edges of wound together and taped a gauze pad over it. "There. That shouldn't leave much of a scar." With her thighs rubbing against his, she could tell her position in his lap was having the desired effect. She patted his bandage softly and shifted her gaze to his mouth, tilting forward until her lips hovered over his. "Thank you for coming to my rescue." She swept her mouth across his, her lips barely skimming his.

He sat like stone for an excruciatingly long moment, his hands bunching into fists.

Shelby thought he'd mastered his self-control and that she'd overstepped her bounds.

Then he cupped the back of her head and kissed her hard, his tongue sweeping into her mouth, claiming her in a dizzyingly powerful connection.

As quickly as he'd taken her, he stood and set her on her feet. "They're waiting on us." Daniel collected the items of the first-aid kit, threw them in the box, closed it and left the bathroom in record time.

Disappointment fused with raging desire. Shelby wanted to stand in Daniel's way and demand he stay and face up to what they were feeling. The stony expression on his face made her step aside and allow him to pass.

"Get dressed and meet us in the kitchen in five minutes." He didn't ask, he *demanded*.

Shelby bristled, but clamped her teeth down on her tongue as Daniel crossed her bedroom and passed through the connecting door to his own. Once the door was shut behind him, she was tempted to rip it back open. He couldn't lock it because the door frame was splintered. Instead, she marched to the bed, lifted a pillow and cocked her arm to throw it.

The door opened and Daniel poked his head through and he pointed at the pillow. "Don't do it."

Shelby launched the pillow and it hit the door as he closed it quickly.

Throwing the pillow didn't fix the fact that the man was exasperating, but it made her feel better.

"Five minutes," he reminded her through the closed door.

Part of her wanted to drag her feet and arrive in the kitchen in ten minutes just to spite him. How could he kiss her like that and then practically dump her off his lap and go about business as usual?

She dressed in her jeans and one of her better pull-over blouses. The outfit was not nearly as nice as the slacks and cashmere sweater Kate had given her to wear, but they felt more like her and she felt more normal in them. Running a brush through her hair, she washed her face and applied a little blush to her pale cheeks and a bit of mascara to her eyes. Not that she wanted to look better for anyone but herself.

Slipping into her favorite sandals, she let herself out of her room, betting Mr. Bossypants was already in kitchen making plans for her without her input. She hurried down the stairs and found the kitchen by following the sound of voices.

"Well, the fact is she's not safe in Raleigh."

"The house is wired for security and the gate should help keep people out."

"How does that explain someone being in her room last night?"

"We don't know that for sure." Shelby stepped into the room. "I could have been imagining things."

"There have been too many attempts already. I'm afraid you're not safe here," Daniel said.

"Then I can go home?" she asked with a bright smile.

"No!" Kate and her grandfather both said at once.

They smiled at each other, and then her grandfather faced her. "It's not safe at the bar."

"I had no problems there last night."

"But you had problems yesterday afternoon and this morning," Daniel pointed out.

Shelby glared at Daniel, sitting quietly in a chair across the table, drinking coffee. "So I made a bad choice in going out without my watchdog. I won't do that again."

"And what about school?" Kate asked.

Daniel's jaw tightened. "She's not going."

"The hell I'm not."

"You got your assignments, you can work on them and turn them in when we get this thing resolved. Your instructors will work with you."

"Maybe and maybe not." Shelby crossed her arms over her chest. "Did anyone even bother to ask what I want to do?"

Her grandfather reached for her hand. "Honey, you need to listen to what these people are saying."

"I can't live like this. I'm just as much a prisoner in this house as I was in that basement."

Daniel stood and waved his hand toward the door. "If you don't like it, go."

Her back straightened. "I just might."

"No, either you will or you won't, but stop straddling the fence." He pinned her with his stare.

No one else said a word, each waiting expectantly for her response. "It's my life."

"Yes, it is. And if you step out of this house, off this property by yourself, you'll end up in the hellhole you were in before, and maybe for longer than two weeks this time. And they might not be as nice to you. You might not even get bologna sandwiches. They could decide it would be fun to assault and torture you."

The blood rushed from Shelby's face and a cold shiver shook her. Her grandfather's face paled and he shook his head, his eyes pleading with her.

"Daniel," Kate warned.

"No, Kate. If she wants to go out on her own, she needs to know the truth. No sugarcoating." Daniel stepped up to her. "If you leave, you might die this time."

Shelby sucked in a breath, finding it harder to breathe than moments before, her hands growing clammy. She rubbed her palms on her jeans and stared down at the scabs just beginning to heal.

"Is that what you want?" Daniel asked softly.

She shook her head, her eyes blurring. "No."

Kate stood and came to her side, laying a hand on her arm. "Then let us protect you. Let Daniel keep you safe until we can figure this out."

"How to your propose to keep her safe if she's not even safe in this house?" Thad asked.

"I could assign another agent to the detail," Jed offered.

"Thank you, Jed," Kate patted his hand. "I appreciate the offer, but after D'Angelis proved to be a traitor and his death took place in a public facility surrounded by law enforcement officers, I don't know who to trust except my children and Daniel."

"I would be willing to offer my own services," Kincannon said.

Kate frowned. "You're the director. You have another job to do. Finding who's doing this to my family is as important as protecting my granddaughter."

Thad leaned forward. "We could hire an independent bodyguard."

Kate shook her head. "That goes back to my original point. I don't trust anyone but my family and Daniel."

Thad tapped his fingers on the table, his eyebrows dipping low. "I'm leading the investigation from the local law enforcement side. Though I wish I could be here, if we want to catch the person responsible, I can't do both."

Kate nodded. "I know you can't and I won't ask it of you. Which leaves us only one option." She faced Daniel.

Shelby inched closer to him, despite his effort to frighten her.

"What choice is that?" Daniel asked.

"You have to get Shelby out of here."

"And where do you want me to take her?"

"Away." Kate waved her hand in the air. "Someplace no will think to look for her."

Chapter 12

Daniel frowned. "Far enough away she won't be found? That would be the moon."

"We would be the only ones who know where she's going. If the media and everyone else is in the dark about her location, whoever is determined to take her will not be privy to that information."

"I don't know, Mom. If she's far away, Daniel will have no backup in case they get in trouble."

An idea began forming in Daniel's mind. Kate might be on to a plan that held merit. "I know of a place."

Shelby looked at him, her eyes widening. "I can't leave. I have school."

"Like I said, you can bring your work with you and turn it in later when we resolve this case."

"I'm glad you're able to speak for my instructors."

"It's stay here and risk your life or go with Daniel and be safe." Her grandfather reached for her hand. "Please, Shelby. Be reasonable. I love you and I want to be around for great-grandchildren someday."

"Granddad!"

"I'm serious, Shelby. I'm not going to be around forever."

"Don't go pulling the age card on me. You're in better shape than I am and will probably outlive me when I die of natural causes."

"Enough talk about dying." Patrick O'Hara straightened to his full, intimidating height. "You'll go with Daniel, or else."

Shelby laughed out loud. "Granddad, your blustery bull didn't scare me when I was a child and it surely isn't scaring me now. But since you feel so strongly, and I have no desire to spend more time in a dark basement, I'll consider going with Daniel."

Kate let out a heartfelt sigh. "Thank goodness. I really didn't want to order him to kidnap you to keep you safe." Kate smiled.

"It's okay, I'll go peacefully." Shelby turned to Daniel. "And where, pray tell, are we going?"

He smiled. "Maine."

She nodded. "That's pretty far. And do you have a specific place in Maine in mind?"

His grin broadened, the idea solidifying and taking root. "I do."

She waited for him to continue.

His decision made, he stated, "My folks' house."

Shelby backed away. "I can't stay at your parents' house. I don't know them. Can't we hole up in a hotel?"

"That would be too public. If we stay with my family, I'll have built-in backup. My brothers are police officers in the small town where I'm from. One of them lives with my folks, the other comes by often. No one but the people sitting at this table will know where you are."

"Maine?" Shelby shivered. "Isn't it cold up there?"

"Not during the day at this time of year. The nights get chilly. My parents live along the coast in a small fishing town."

"Sounds perfect," Kate said. "How soon can you leave?"

Shelby shot a glance at her grandmother. Did she *want* to get rid of her?

Kate gave her soft smile. "I'd love to keep you here and get to know you better, but as long as you're threatened, I'd rather have you safe."

Daniel nodded. "I can be out of here as soon as we can rent a decoy car and get out of town." He glanced down at Shelby. "Can you be packed in five minutes?"

"I can do better than that," she said. "I can be ready in three minutes."

Patrick pulled Shelby into his arms and stroked her hair. "I just got you back and I'm going to lose you again."

"This time you'll know where I am, Granddad." Shelby kissed his cheek. "And Daniel will keep me safe."

"I know. He's a good man." Patrick stepped back and offered Daniel his hand.

Daniel shook it, feeling like a fraud, knowing he'd betrayed this man's trust by bedding his granddaughter. "I'll take care of her, sir." He owed them all his promise to keep her safe. Her life was his responsibility.

"I'll be back in two shakes." Shelby hurried toward the stairs.

Daniel's gaze followed her.

Kate touched his arm. "You can't let anyone else know where she is."

"I know that." He fished his cell phone out of his pocket and handed it to Kate. "I don't want to take anything that could be tracked. Keep this. If I need to reach you, I'll call from a public phone. For the most part, I'll keep communication to a minimum."

Kate took the phone. "Understood."

"If anything happens, or you suspect you've been discovered, bring her back here," Patrick said. "I don't like having my girl so far away, especially when she's in trouble."

"Yes, sir." Daniel backed away. "If you'll excuse me, I'll get my things."

He took the stairs two at a time and hurried down the hallway, past the room where he and Shelby had made love. Soon, they'd be alone on the road. He prayed he wasn't making a mistake. What if the men trying to take her found her in Maine? They didn't have a handy informant to question about her whereabouts. D'Angelis was inconveniently dead.

Daniel jammed his things into a duffel, checked his weapon, ensuring the clip was fully loaded, and knocked on the connecting door.

"Why bother knocking? The lock's broken," she called out.

He pushed through the door and entered her room.

She had her duffel bag slung over her shoulder. "I'm ready when you are."

"Then let's hit the road."

She nodded. "Do you think this will work?"

"I hope so."

Shelby glanced around the room. "I've never been so far away from home."

"My family is pretty welcoming. They'll do their best to make you feel at home."

"I worry about my grandfather."

"He's on board with this and ready to do anything to keep you safe."

"I'd feel better if I knew someone was looking out for *him*."

"I'll leave word for someone to keep tabs on him."

She glanced up with a small smile, her eyes suspiciously moist. "Then I guess there's nothing else. Let's get going."

Daniel's heart pinched in his chest. He dropped his duffel and held open his arms.

Shelby walked into them. "Why is all this happening to me?"

"You know why."

"I know. But it doesn't make sense. I'm nobody."

"Not to a lot of people, including your grandmother," he said softly. Crooking his finger, he angled her chin up so that he could stare down into blue eyes awash with tears. "It's going to be okay."

"Promise?" she whispered.

He bent to brush a soft kiss across her mouth.

Shelby dropped her duffel, leaned up on her toes and deepened the kiss.

Daniel couldn't back away and didn't want to.

She was like an addiction he was having a difficult time shaking. He crushed her against him, his fingers threading through her silky brown hair. If he could, he'd hold her like this forever.

He broke the kiss and he stepped back to keep from doing it again. "We need to go."

"I suppose."

When she reached for her bag, he got there first. Carrying both bags, he waved her forward.

Shelby descended the stairs first and ran to her grandfather.

He hugged her and kissed her forehead. "Be safe, Shelby. I kinda like having your around." His eyes glistened.

"I'll miss you." She hugged him tight and then stood back.

Kate Winston stepped forward and took Shelby's hands. "I know we haven't had a chance to get to know each other yet, but if you're anything like your grandfather, you're smart and pretty tough. Between you two—" she nodded toward Daniel "—you'll be okay." The older woman leaned forward and kissed Shelby's cheek. "I look forward to spending more time with you in the near future. If you'll let me." Her smile was shaky when she let go of Shelby's hands.

One of Kate's cars had been brought around for them to take. Daniel threw their bags in the backseat and held the door for Shelby.

She slipped in and turned to wave as he shut the door.

Once they left the security of the Winston Estate, Daniel zigzagged through neighborhoods and out onto the main road toward the airport. He parked the car at one of the car rental places, grabbed his bag and Shelby's and walked with her to the neighboring rental lot.

"Why didn't we rent a car at the last one?" Shelby asked.

"If the car we drove was bugged with GPS, they could then find record of our rental there."

"Oh." She waited while Daniel secured a vehicle and then quietly climbed into the four-wheel-drive SUV he'd rented without saying a word.

Once they were on the road headed north, Shelby fell asleep leaning against the window, her dark eyelashes fanned across her cheeks. Daniel had to continually remind himself to keep his focus on what was ahead of him and what might be behind him. But he couldn't help glancing over at her. She looked like a dark angel sent to Earth to torment him and make him question his dedication to the job.

When they found out who was trying to kidnap her and why, Daniel would ask to be assigned somewhere far, far away from the temptation that was Shelby. A career Secret Service agent didn't have time for family or relationships.

Then why the hell couldn't he get her out of his mind?

Shelby didn't wake until the vehicle slowed. When she opened her eyes, it was to a congested six-lane expressway.

"Where are we?"

"Washington, D.C."

"That means we only have nine more hours on the road."

"Roughly."

"Do you want me to drive so that you can stretch?"

"I'm doing okay for now."

"Good, because I'm not good driving in traffic, but I could use a bathroom break when you get past all this."

Once they got past the heaviest of traffic, Daniel pulled into a gas station and topped off the gas tank while Shelby went inside to find a bathroom. The door was locked and there were two women in line to use the facilities.

Shelby roamed the aisles, watching the door to the bathroom, waiting for her turn.

A man in the row with all the snack foods, one over from her, stared, his eyes narrowing so slightly, she wasn't sure if she'd imagined it.

Shelby moved the opposite direction, glancing back over her shoulder.

The man was still watching her, his brows narrowing.

A cold tingle slithered down her spine. The last woman in line at the bathroom exited and Shelby made a dash for it.

Once inside, she took care of her needs and washed her hands. When she came out of the bathroom, she looked down the hallway toward the front of the store, wondering if Daniel had finished filling the tank.

The shuffle of feet behind her made her jump.

"Good, I was getting worried about you."

Daniel moved in front of her, his brow furrowed.

Shelby slipped her hand in his. "Sorry. There was a line."

Daniel curled an arm around her waist and guided her toward the door.

Shelby glanced back at the hallway to the bathrooms. A man turned his back to her and lifted a case of soft drinks. If Shelby wasn't mistaken, it was the same man who'd been staring at her earlier. He glanced over his shoulder, his gaze following her yet again.

A shiver rippled across her skin. Reasoning with herself, she figured the man worked there stocking shelves, and she was getting too paranoid for her own good.

Shelby didn't say anything to Daniel, not sure what she'd actually say if she did. She settled back against the leather seat and tried to let it go. For the next hour, she looked behind them every five minutes for someone following their vehicle, a creepy feeling following her.

By the time they reached the outskirts of New York City, Shelby was ready to be there. Daniel hadn't said much and he hadn't made a move to touch or reassure her in any way.

"Do you want me to drive the rest of the way?" she asked.

"I'm used to making this trip. Why don't you find something on the radio?"

She settled on an old Beach Boys song that reminded her of home, her father and the beaches she grew up on. After a minute of that, she was so homesick she switched the radio off.

"Why'd you do that? I like The Beach Boys. They remind me of home."

"Same here," she said.

He glanced at her and nodded. "I know you miss your home and grandfather, but you'll be back soon enough."

"Are you sure?" She stared out the window, wondering when this nightmare would ever end. When he didn't respond, she glanced his way. "What if whoever is trying to grab me follows me to Maine? Won't we be placing your family in danger?"

"No one will know where you are. And if they do happen to find us, the members of my family can take care of themselves."

"I would hate to bring trouble to your hometown. What if someone is hurt? I'd never forgive myself."

"As my mother would say, 'Don't borrow trouble.'"

Shelby's mouth twisted into a wry grin. "And as my father would say, 'Go with your gut.'"

"And what is your gut telling you?"

"There's a storm rising out to sea, and things will get worse before they get better."

Daniel pulled into the driveway of the house his parents owned on the beach in Bar Harbor, Maine. The sun had set and the stars and streetlights were shining brightly.

No sooner had he parked the SUV than the front door opened and his mother and father stood framed in the doorway, squinting at the strange car parked in their driveway.

Daniel stepped out of the vehicle and walked around to the front of it. "Mom, Dad, it's me, Daniel."

"Daniel!" His mother exclaimed, flying down the steps. "It's Daniel, James."

"I can see that." His father chuckled, following his wife at a more sedate pace.

Daniel smiled. "I hope you don't mind company on short notice."

His mother reached him and enveloped him in a

warm hug. "Oh, honey, you know you're always welcome here. This is your home."

Daniel hugged her back and then pulled back to face her. "Mom, I'm not alone." He walked back to the car, pulled open the passenger door and held out his hand. "This is Shelby O'Hara."

Shelby took his hand and let him help her to her feet. She smiled tentatively at his parents. "Mr. and Mrs. Henderson, we're sorry to be arriving so late and without warning."

Daniel cringed at the way his mother's face lit up. She'd think he and Shelby were together. Nothing would make his mother happier than to see all her sons settled with wives and a couple of kids she could spoil.

"Oh, honey, we're *delighted* to see Daniel. We came down to be with him when he was in the hospital after the shooting, but having him home is so much better." She turned to her husband. "What's it been, almost a year since he's been back to visit?"

Daniel's father nodded. "Thereabout."

Daniel's mother hugged Shelby as though she was a long-lost family member, then turned back to her husband. "Please, call me Lea, and this is James."

Daniel's father reached a hand out to Shelby. When she took it, he pulled her into a hug. "Any friend of Daniel's is welcome."

Her cheeks blushing pink, Shelby hugged James Henderson. "Thank you."

"You know we had the extra bedroom converted into an office. Which leaves Daniel's old bedroom. One of you is welcome to sleep on the couch…." His mother gave them a knowing look. "Unless, of course, you're…together."

"Lea," his dad warned.

"We might be older, but we know what happens between young folk." She leaned close to Shelby and whispered conspiratorially, "We weren't married when Daniel was conceived."

"Now is not the time to confess." Daniel hugged his mother and father. "Shelby can have my room, I'll sleep on the couch." He grabbed their bags out of the backseat to avoid further questioning, but his mother wasn't quite done.

"But since you two are together, that shouldn't matter right?"

Daniel enjoyed the way Shelby squirmed. "We're not…together. We've only known each other a couple of days."

His mother waved a hand. "It only takes a moment to know someone's the one. I fell in love with Daniel's father the day I met him." She took Shelby's hand. "Come inside. I have some leftover clam chowder I can heat up. Do you like hot tea or the iced tea they love so much in the South?"

"I'd love some hot tea. But I don't want to be a bother."

"Be a bother," Daniel said. "My mother loves to bother."

"Mothers *like* to bother." His mother squeezed her arm. "Don't they, Shelby?"

Shelby stiffened.

"Mom, Shelby's mother passed away when she was a little girl."

"Oh, honey, I'm so sorry. How awful to grow up without her."

"My grandfather raised me." Shelby glanced at Daniel. "I think he did a good job."

"I'm sure he did." Daniel's mother patted her arm and led her to the kitchen. "Now, you sit down there while I fix that cup of tea."

"If you don't mind, I'd like to find a bathroom."

"Of course. Let me show you."

Daniel's father touched his wife's arm. "Let Daniel. You and I can fix the tea. Personally, I'd rather have a cup of coffee."

"You know you shouldn't drink coffee at night. It keeps you awake."

"If I want a cup of coffee, I'll have coffee."

"Don't you take that tone with me, James. I have to sleep with you."

Daniel tipped his head to the side and Shelby preceded him from the room, glancing back over her shoulder.

"Are they mad at each other?" she asked when they were halfway down the hall.

The sound of his parents arguing carried into the hallway. "No. That's just the way they are. Mom takes care of Dad and he takes care of her."

Her brow furrowed. "Kind of like me and my grandfather." She sighed. "Good. I didn't want to be the cause of a fight."

"No, you're not the cause of a fight. They love each other very much. Mom needs someone to need her, and my father lets her fuss over him."

Daniel opened a door off the hall. "This is my old bedroom." He entered and dropped her bag on the bed. "The bathroom is right across the hall." He stepped back out into the hallway. "Make yourself at home, and if you need anything just ask. I'll be in the kitchen." He left her standing in the hallway to avoid the temptation of kissing her again. The last thing he needed was to get his mother's hopes up. Being with Shelby was temporary.

He hurried away. He couldn't keep Shelby's situation to himself. His parents had to know what they were up against, should someone find Shelby here.

When he entered the kitchen his mother turned from the stove where a kettle of water had just worked up a steam. "Shelby seems very nice. How did you two meet?"

"Lea, that's none of our business."

"I'm his mother. I have every right to pry." She raised her brows and directed a questioning look toward Daniel.

"I'm on assignment to protect her."

His mother's brows dipped. "Protect her from what?"

"She's already been kidnapped and held captive once, and there have been other attempts made."

"Oh, dear." His mother set the kettle on a cool burner and turned. "Why?"

Daniel smiled. "She's the granddaughter of Kate Winston."

"*The* Kate Winston? The former vice president?" his father asked.

Daniel nodded.

"Oh, dear." His mother pressed her hand to her chest. "Practically a celebrity."

"Is there anything we can do to help?" Daniel's father asked, slipping his arm around his wife's waist.

"Help me keep an eye out for anything suspicious."

"Like what?" His mother leaned into his father's embrace.

"Strange cars driving by on the street, strangers hanging around. If anyone calls to ask for Shelby, you don't have any idea who she is. Let me know if anything is out of the ordinary."

"We can do that."

"And if at any time you feel unsafe or uncomfortable with us being here, let me know. We'll leave. Shelby and I don't want anything bad to happen to you two."

Shelby entered the room at that time. "Seriously, I don't want to be here if it's going to put you in danger."

"Don't be absurd." His mother opened the cabinet and retrieved four ceramic cups. "We're a family of law enforcement officers. James just retired after thirty years as a police officer and police chief. Daniel's brothers are both on the Bar Harbor police force."

James nodded. "We'll look out for you."

"Thank you," Shelby said.

Daniel's chest swelled. He'd known he could count on his family to help him keep Shelby safe. He just hoped and prayed they wouldn't need the help.

Chapter 13

Shelby sat at the table while Lea bustled around the kitchen scooping chowder into bowls and warming them in the microwave. Playful banter and shared stories about life on the police force filled the air and gave her the impression of the warmth between them and the love for their son.

When the front door opened and slammed shut, she jumped.

"That will be Daniel's brother," Lea reassured her. "He just got off his shift." She filled another bowl full of chowder and popped it into the microwave. "You two will have to fill him in on what's going on."

Daniel stood.

"Whose car is that?" A man looking a lot like Daniel entered the room and grinned, then pulled Daniel into a bear hug. "Well, you ol' son of a—"

"Robert." Daniel's mother nodded toward Shelby. "Keep it clean. We have company."

Robert's grin broadened. "As I was saying, you ol' son of a—"

"Robert!" Lea Henderson glared at her son. "Be nice and say hello to Shelby."

Shelby stood and held out our hand. "Nice to meet you."

"Well, hello." He gripped her hand, and his green-eyed gaze, so much like his brother's, roved her from head to toe. "The pleasure is all mine."

Daniel stepped forward. "Back off, Rob."

"Don't tell me, you're with him?" Robert rolled his eyes toward Daniel. "I don't know what you did to deserve her, but if she's got a sister, I got dibs." Robert winked. "Seriously, what do you see in that broken-down secret agent?"

Shelby didn't know how to answer that, so she kept her comments to herself.

Daniel's father saved her from answering. "Quit harassing your brother, son, and sit." He pulled out a chair and pointed. "We have serious matters to discuss."

At the tone of his father's voice, Robert sat, wiping the smile off his face. "What's going on?"

By the time Daniel filled him in, it was getting late and the stress of the past couple of weeks weighed heavily on Shelby's eyelids.

Robert shook his head. "Damn, Shelby, who'd you make mad?"

"I don't know." She covered her mouth as she yawned.

"Oh, honey, you need to get some rest." Mrs. Henderson slipped an arm around her and led her out of the kitchen. "We get up early around here, but don't feel like you have to, as well. Sleep as long as you need to."

"I'm okay, just tired."

His mother patted her arm. "Don't you worry. My men will make sure you're well protected."

"I don't want to be a burden," Shelby said.

Mrs. Henderson stopped in front of Daniel's bedroom door. "Honey, you're not a burden. I'm just sorry this is happening to you. I can't imagine how terrified you must have been." Her eyes misted and she pulled Shelby into a tight hug. "Two weeks held captive is awful. Your grandfather must have been beside himself."

Shelby's own eyes filled with tears. The warmth of Mrs. Henderson's hug reminded her of her grandfather. It made her feel homesick and wish everything could go back to the way it used to be. Before she'd been kidnapped. Before she'd learned who her grandmother was. But if she'd never been kidnapped, and if she wasn't Kate Winston's granddaughter, she'd never have met Daniel.

Lea held Shelby at arm's length and forced a watery smile. "Now, you get some rest and don't worry. We'll take good care of you." She cupped her face. "Such a pretty girl and so brave. Daniel would be smart not to let you slip through his fingers." She winked. "Speaking of Daniel, I'd better get him a blanket." Mrs. Henderson kissed Shelby's cheek. "Good night, dear."

Shelby entered Daniel's bedroom and closed the door behind her at the same time she flipped the light switch on.

The room was decorated in black, gold and white. Mrs. Henderson must have upgraded the decorations since her son had left the nest. The comforter, curtains and matching area rug looked new. But it was the photographs on the wall that drew Shelby.

Some of the pictures were of a miniature Daniel with laughter in his eyes and a smile on his face. Others were of the grown-up Daniel, hanging with his brothers or standing on the beach, looking out over the ocean. All of the pictures had been enlarged and printed in black-and-white to match the decor. Tastefully done, the photos personalized the room without making it a child's room. Obviously, the Hendersons loved their sons.

Having grown up an only child with one parental figure, Shelby had known a different life. There had been times, when she'd been at a sleepover with friends, that she'd observed families with a mom, dad and siblings and had wondered what it would be like growing up in the chaos.

Since she was a little girl, she'd sworn she'd have at least two kids so they'd never be lonely. They'd always have each other to play with.

Shelby roamed around the bedroom, feeling as if she was getting a glimpse into the boy who'd become Daniel. What a happy childhood he must have had. Not that hers had been unhappy. She paused at the French doors looking out over the ocean. The moon was full, shining brightly on the water and the silvery sands of the beach. After being cooped up in the car for the past thirteen hours, she needed to stretch her legs.

Pushing aside her exhaustion, she opened the door and stepped out onto the porch, inhaling the salty tang in the air, so much like home. A light, cool breeze lifted her hair off her face. She crossed the wooden planks and kicked off her shoes, then hurried down the steps, the sea calling to her.

Once her feet hit the sand, she couldn't stop. She walked out to where the tide slipped in and out, wetting the sand, packing it firmly.

With the moonlight lighting her way, Shelby set off, walking down the beach, her face to the wind, beach houses on one side, the ocean on the other. For the first time in weeks, she felt free. Free of captivity, free of confining walls and fences, free from potential exposure to the public as the granddaughter of a wealthy and politically connected woman.

On the beach, Shelby could be who she was. A child born and raised by a selfless grandfather who'd done the best he could with a little girl.

Caught up in the beauty and the feeling she'd come home, Shelby didn't hear the footsteps slapping against the sand behind her until they were almost upon her. Startled, she spun around to see a dark figure hell-bent on catching her.

Her heart slamming into her ribs, she took off running.

"Shelby!" A familiar voice called out. "Shelby, wait. It's me, Daniel."

She stopped at once and looked back at him as he raced to catch up with her.

Even in the dark, she could tell he favored his left leg. When he ground to a halt, he bent over, catching his breath while rubbing his leg. When he had his breathing under control, he straightened and glared at her. "Where the hell do you think you're going?"

"For a walk." She stared at his leg. "Is that where you were shot?"

"One of the places," he said. "You can't just go walking off without telling me. What if someone had attacked you? What if those jerks who'd taken you the first time somehow found out where you were and were waiting for you to take one step alone?"

Shelby touched a finger to his lips. "What if you would be quiet, take a deep breath of the salty air and enjoy the moonlight? Hmm? Think you can do that?" She crossed her legs and sank to the sand, catching his hand as she went down. "Come on, give that leg a break."

"It's fine."

"No, it's not." She pointed at the sand beside her. "Sit." With a smile, she added, "Please."

"I don't even have my gun on me."

"Good. Hopefully, we'll have this one night without bad guys and without guns to remind us there are bad guys. We can enjoy a beautiful night brought to you by a delightful moon." She held on to his hand until he sighed and lowered himself to the ground, stretching his sore leg out in front of him.

"See? That wasn't so hard, was it?" She lay back on the sand, crossing her arms behind her head. "Whenever school, friends, boyfriends or Granddad got me down, I'd sneak out at night and walk along the shore. The sound of the surf and the smell of salt in the air grounded me, reminding me that no matter how bad things were, the beach was only a few yards away."

Daniel lay down beside her, his hand behind his head. "Until you were kidnapped?"

"Yeah." Then she hadn't had the luxury of thinking the beach was only a few yards away. She'd been trapped in a dark, dingy place with no access to a beach or a window to look out on her beloved shoreline. Though it was dark out, the moonlight gave her hope, dispelling some of the blackness she'd experienced in that basement.

Daniel leaned up on one elbow and stared down at her. "You're safe now."

"I know." Her stomach fluttered and her pulse raced. Suddenly, she didn't feel so safe. From the bad guys, maybe. But from Daniel? Not so much. She realized she was in danger of falling for this man who'd told her more than once he wasn't in it for the long haul.

He smoothed his hand through her hair, brushing it back from her cheek. "Did you know that your hair looks like blue-black ink in the moonlight?"

"Did you know you could kiss me and I wouldn't object?" she whispered. She reached up and curled her fingers around the back of his neck. "Need a little help with that decision?"

"My head is telling me not to go there…but for some reason, I can't resist." He swept low, taking her lips in a crushing kiss, his tongue lancing out to caress hers in long slow thrusts.

Her core ached and her belly tightened with a need to be lying naked with this man or running into the waves, making love with him. When he let her up for air, she asked, "How cold is the water here?"

He kissed her forehead and the tip of her nose. "Around sixty degrees. Why?"

She laughed. "I've always wanted to go skinny-dipping, but never mind."

He pushed to his feet and reached toward her. "Come on." He captured her hand, dragging her up with him and started walking back toward the house.

Disappointment made her lag behind him. Why had she opened her big mouth? Maybe he didn't want to get naked in the water with her. Maybe he'd kissed her and had second thoughts.

She should have just gone to bed instead of venturing out on the beach and filling her head with sexy ideas about things she wanted to do to his body.

They mounted the porch steps, entered through the open French doors into his room and closed the door behind them. When Shelby thought he'd let go of her hand and leave her alone, she was wrong.

Daniel held on to her hand and continued through the bedroom to the door leading out into the hallway. It was dark and quiet, and the bathroom door stood open, the light off. Without pausing, Daniel crossed the hall, pulling her into the bathroom behind him. Not until he shut the door and twisted the lock did he turn and face her. Then he was kissing her, pressing her back against the wooden door.

She'd barely had time to catch her breath when he cupped her bottom and lifted. She wrapped her legs around his waist, feeling the hard ridge of him beneath his jeans pressing against her center.

"The ocean is too cold for skinny-dipping, but in case you didn't notice, there is a bathtub big enough for two."

Shelby glanced at the tub as Daniel trailed kisses along the side of her neck and down to where the pulse beat at the base of her throat. "Why would your parents install a tub this size in the guest bathroom?"

"You're looking a gift horse in the mouth?"

"No, no. I'm glad they did." She reached for the buttons on her shirt. "Is it hot in here?"

"Extremely." He set her on the floor, pushed her fingers aside and finished unbuttoning her shirt, then slid it off her shoulders, exposing her lacy bra. He bent to bite her nipple through the fabric.

Shelby yanked his T-shirt from his waistband, shoved it up over his head and tossed it to the floor. "Won't your parents hear us...you know...making noise?"

"Probably." He reached behind him and turned the handle on the bathtub faucet, adjusting it to the right temperature before returning his focus to her.

With her hands on the button of his jeans, she paused. "We really shouldn't."

"You're right. We shouldn't." He covered her hands with his and ripped open his jeans. "But we are."

She took over, dragging his zipper down. "Just say the word and I'll stop."

"Don't tease." He unclipped her bra in the back and flung it to the side.

"I feel guilty, doing this in your parents' hou—"

Daniel pressed his mouth to hers. "Anyone tell you that you talk too much?" He bit her bottom lip and tugged on it, then let go.

Shelby ran her tongue across the lip. "Just you."

"Then stop talking and get in the water." He quickly unbuttoned and unzipped her jeans and dragged them down over her legs. She stepped out of them and climbed into the tub, the water rising up to her ankles.

Moonlight shone through the glass-brick window over the tub, turning Daniel's body dark blue and silvery.

Shelby's breath caught and held as he stepped into the tub with her.

"Ever been skinny-dipping in a bathtub?" He eased into the water and pulled her down to lay across him, the displaced water rising around them.

"Not until now." She lay against the side of his chest, her hands smoothing over taut muscles, sliding lower, across rock-solid abs to the jutting evidence of his desire.

When her fingers curled around him, he thrust upward, sliding through her wet grip.

"You make me crazy," he whispered.

"Good." She moved over him, bracing her knees on either side of his hips, her entrance poised to receive him. "That makes two of us." It took every ounce of restraint to keep from taking him into her.

He cupped her cheek, brushing his thumb over her lip. "What are we going to do about it?"

Shelby kissed his thumb. "We're going to start with protection." She leaned over the side of the tub and reached for his jeans.

He caressed her bottom, his hand gliding across her skin, his fingers curving around to tickle the inside of her thigh.

She tensed, her search for his wallet focused, almost desperate. When she found it, she almost cried out in relief. "Please tell me you have one."

"And if I don't?" He chuckled, his finger finding her center and sliding into her channel.

Shelby gasped and breathed, "Then this night would be over. When I'm ready to have a baby, I'll forgo contraception." She flipped open the wallet and fished inside for the foil packet she'd known would be there. "You must have made top scores in agent school for being prepared." She held up the condom in triumph and tore it open. Scooting back, she rolled it down over him.

"I learned something else in agent school." He gripped her hips and held her up over him, nudging her, teasing her.

"Oh, yeah? Are you like James Bond and you kiss every girl involved in your case?"

"That's a good idea." He leaned up and kissed her lips. "But no. I learned that for every action, there's a reaction." He eased her down.

"I'm beginning to see your point," she said, her channel sliding around his shaft. "Perhaps you can drive it home?"

"Impatient?" He slowed her descent, guiding her down, one agonizing inch at a time.

"I'm a quick learner, are you a quick teacher?" She tried to speed up the process, but he held her at bay.

"Some things take a more delicate approach."

"Damn the delicate approach, I want you." She leaned down and took his lips as he started thrusting up into her, hard and fast.

"That's more like it," she said against his lips. She pushed against his chest, her back arching as she rode him, water splashing up around them.

All too soon, Daniel thrust hard and held her hips as his member throbbed inside her. He gave it a minute, then stood her on her feet and rose, water running down over his torso.

He soaped her body, she soaped his and together, they splashed each other free of suds. Then Daniel scooped her up and stepped out of the tub, setting her on the bath mat then grabbing two towels.

Shelby worked on drying him off, memorizing every inch of him as she worked over his body.

When she was done, Daniel dried her. He dropped to his knees and started at her feet, sliding the soft terry cloth up her calves and over her thighs, spreading her legs as he went. He dried the mound of hair at the apex of her thighs, then parted her folds and bent to touch that sliver of flesh nestled between with his tongue.

Shelby moaned and threaded her fingers through his short hair, urging him to give her more. "Please."

"Like that?" He tongued her again, sliding across her in a smooth, wet stroke.

She came up on her toes, her fingers digging into his scalp, aching to her very core. "Oh, yes!"

"Well, there might be more of that later." He rose and dried her bottom, her waist and upward to her breasts. There he paused to taste a nipple, sucking it into his mouth, rolling the bud between his teeth.

Shelby's body was on fire, craving anything and everything he could do to her. She cupped the back of his head and pressed her breast deeper into his mouth, her other hand sliding down his back to caress his tight ass.

When she thought she couldn't stand another moment of excruciating pleasure, he swept her into his arms, kicked open the bathroom door and strode across the hall.

Shelby clung to him, trying to cover her nakedness in case his family happened to be roaming the house and caught them on display.

A door opened at the other end of the hallway just as Daniel stepped across the threshold into his old bedroom. He kicked the door shut behind them.

"Are you insane? What if your mother or father had witnessed that?"

"I'm pretty sure I've seen them do something similar before. I didn't learn *everything* in agent school." He kissed her and tossed her on the bed.

Shelby liked it when he played rough and disregarded the rules. But in his parents' house?

Then he climbed over her, leaning up on his arms. "I didn't sign on to this job to make love to you."

She caressed his face, smiling up at him. "Consider it a perk."

"What happens when this is case is cleared?"

"I guess it's up to us."

"I'm an agent—"

She pressed a finger to his lips. "I know. Relationships aren't in the job description. So we take what we can get and part ways when you move on to your next assignment."

He frowned down at her. "You're okay with that?"

No, she wasn't, but she didn't have any other choice. Shelby forced a smile. "I'd rather have you for a little while than not at all." She slid her calf up the side of his thigh. "Now, are we going talk all night or are we going to make good use of the time we have together?" She cupped the back of his neck and brought his face close to hers. "Because I can think of a lot better things to do than talk."

"You know, I don't know what I did without you."

"Yeah, well, you'll find out soon enough. Now shut up and kiss me."

Daniel complied, kissing her deeply, taking her breath away with his tender caresses.

If she wished they could be together for longer than

the night, for a lifetime, she pushed the thought to the back of her mind and focused on what they had in that moment. Tomorrow the case might be solved, Daniel might move on and she'd be left to forget about him. Then again, tomorrow might never come and tonight might be all they had together.

Chapter 14

Daniel woke to the sun shining in through a window and the sound of voices coming from another room. When he tried to move, his arm was weighted down and something warm and soft snuggled up against his side.

Shelby's hand rested across his belly and her head lay in the crook of his shoulder, her cheek pressed against his chest. Her warm breath feathered across his skin, stirring him to back to life.

Part of him didn't want to wake her. He wanted to drink his fill, memorizing every contour of her face, her shoulder, breasts and hips to store the images in his mind for when she was no longer part of his life.

She stirred, her hand drifting lower until her knuckles bumped against his rapidly growing erection. He wanted her, but figured she needed her sleep after being up all night.

If he was a gentleman and very careful, he could slip out from under her, dress, go to the kitchen and let her sleep.

When her fingers curled around his shaft, all gentlemanly thoughts flew out the window and he thrust upward.

Shelby's eyes remained closed, but her breathing grew faster and her hand moved up and down, pumping him as he rocked his hips.

Within a few seconds, he rocketed over the edge, sensations exploding inside. Her movement continued until he captured her wrist and held it. "I take it you're awake."

"No," she said, her eyes still closed.

"Perhaps you need someone to wake you?"

"Perhaps," she whispered.

He leaned up on his elbow and touched a finger to her mouth, following it with his lips.

She was beautiful, her face kissed by sleep, her body perfectly proportioned and her skin as smooth to the touch as the finest silk.

Moving to her neck, he traced a path with his finger that his lips followed. As he worked his way downward, he tweaked a nipple until it budded into a tight little bead, then captured it with his lips, sucking it into his mouth.

Shelby's back arched and she moaned, her eyes still closed, a smile curling the corners of her lips.

His fingers slipped over her ribs and into her belly button, lower still to the puff of curls at the apex of her thighs.

She eased her legs apart, offering herself to his ministrations.

He accepted, parting her folds to stroke a finger across that narrow strip of flesh between.

Her breath caught and her eyes opened, their blue depths dark with desire.

His gaze captured hers, and he stroked again, sliding deeper to her slick entrance, damp with the dew of her arousal.

Daniel's member throbbed at the remembered feel of her tight, drenched channel encasing him in her heat.

Wanting her to experience that sense of utter ecstasy, he slipped down her body and lay between her legs, draping her thighs over his shoulders. He kissed the tender inner flesh and trailed his tongue and lips toward her center.

He hovered, blowing a warm stream of air over her dampness, then he flicked her nubbin with the tip of his tongue.

"There," she said. Digging her heels into the mattress, she lifted her hips up.

He tasted her again, licking, tweaking and flicking her until she twisted her fingers in his hair and gasped. "Stop."

"Am I hurting you?" he asked, concerned.

"Yes. No. In the most wonderful way." She remained tight, tense, her hips rocking even though he wasn't touching her at this point. A few moments later, she lowered herself to rest on the mattress, her arm flung over her head, her breathing slowing. "Wow."

Daniel grinned, smacked her thigh and rose to his feet.

"Wait." She grabbed his hand. "Where are you going? You're not done yet. I want you inside me."

"It'll have to wait. I'm out of condoms." He winked

and bent over her, kissing her lips. "Besides, my mother will be knocking on the door any min—"

A soft tapping sound interrupted him.

Shelby yanked the sheet up over her body, her eyes round, her cheeks flushed a bright pink.

"Good morning, Shelby. I hope that rowdy son of mine let you sleep. How do you like your eggs?" Mrs. Henderson asked from the other side of the door.

"Uh…scrambled, please."

"Do you two need the clothes you left in the bathroom? Or can I run them through the wash for you?"

Daniel laughed out loud while Shelby glared at him.

"Wash them, if you don't mind," Daniel responded.

"In the meantime, I have your duffel bag. I'll leave it here by the door. Breakfast will be ready in five minutes."

"Thank you, Mrs. Henderson."

Footsteps led away from the door.

Daniel opened it, grabbed the duffel and closed it again and was promptly hit by a flying pillow.

"I've never been so embarrassed in my life." Shelby threw the sheet back and stood, naked, angry and more beautiful than any woman he'd ever been with. Her blue eyes flashing, she advanced on him. "Why didn't you warn me sooner?"

He pulled her into his arms. "I didn't want to spoil the moment." With her naked body pressed to his, he wanted nothing more than to go back to bed and take her with him. "Why don't we skip breakfast?"

She leaned into him, her pelvis nudging his member. For a moment, she hesitated, then she leaned back. "We'd better get going. I refuse to show up to breakfast naked or give your mother the opportunity to come storming in to demand we make an appearance."

He kissed her. "Mom doesn't storm." He kissed her again. "Not much, anyway."

Three loud knocks pounded on the door.

"Hey, you two, break it up in there. Mom's got breakfast waiting. Humph! Not together, my royal hind end."

"Beat it, Robert!" Daniel yelled over his shoulder. "I guess we'd better show up."

Shelby dressed then crossed the hall to the bathroom.

Daniel slipped on his jeans and joined her to splash water over his face, then he ran a comb through his hair. Standing beside her at the sink felt natural and good. He could imagine what it would be like to live with her on a permanent basis.

The thought caught him by surprise, and he nearly bolted for the door. "I'll see you in the kitchen. Take your time."

She ran the brush through her hair one last time and smiled. "I'm ready." No makeup, her hair falling straight and shiny to her shoulders, she was everything a man could ask for.

A man who wasn't an agent, disappearing for weeks at a time on assignment.

If he wasn't careful, he'd fall for Shelby, and what would that accomplish? Nothing but heartache.

Keep it simple. This is only a fling, he tried to remind himself.

Shelby entered the kitchen behind Daniel, her face burning and almost afraid to face Daniel's parents.

"Shelby, you look refreshed, I hope you slept well. Sit." Mrs. Henderson smiled and waved a spatula toward the table. "Robert beat you to the scrambled eggs, but I'll have yours ready in just a minute. "Daniel, get the juice from the refrigerator and pour your guest a glass."

Daniel leaned close to Shelby and said in a loud whisper, "Our mother doesn't ask, she orders and we obey."

"Damn right we do," Robert said, taking a deep bite out of a piece of toast slathered in jelly. "Do as she says or miss out on her great cooking."

Shelby sat the table, enjoying the teasing between the brothers.

"All I have to say is, yes, ma'am!" Daniel yanked open the refrigerator and grabbed the jug of orange juice. "Where's Dad?"

"He's down at the marina, buying up enough lobster for a lobster bake this afternoon."

"Is there a festival or something?"

"No, but we had invited a few friends over before we knew you two were coming." Mrs. Henderson frowned. "We can cancel if want us to."

"No, no. We're the ones intruding on your plans," Shelby said. "Besides, I have to admit, though I've lived on the beach all my life, I've never been to a lobster bake."

"Then you're in for a real treat." Robert grinned. "I'm in charge of setting up the pit."

"You?" Daniel's brow wrinkled. "I remember you almost burned down a tent the last time you were in charge of the pit."

"That was eight years ago. I've had more success since then."

"Since he joined the police department, he's become a model citizen." Mrs. Henderson's chest swelled. "I'm so proud of my boys."

"Speaking of boys, where's Marcus?" Daniel asked.

"He and Stacey will join us this afternoon." Mrs. Henderson laid a plate full of fluffy yellow eggs in front of Shelby, along with a smaller plate of toast and bacon. "Eat up. I need you two to pick up some extra tablecloths at the store in town. It's not very far and you can show Shelby around. Take her down on Main to the yogurt shop."

"Mom, we're not here on vacation."

"Good grief, son, you can't hold her prisoner. Get out and show her a good time." Lea winked at Shelby. "Daniel can be too serious sometimes."

"I've noticed," Shelby said.

"All right, then, a day in Bar Harbor it is." He dug into his scrambled eggs. "If we don't, my mother will nag me until I do something to entertain our guest."

"He's got that right," Lea said.

Shelby felt more at home in the Henderson house than she'd ever thought she would. She genuinely liked Daniel's parents and even though his brother teased him, she could tell they loved each other.

Ten minutes later, she and Daniel were on their way to Bar Harbor in his father's truck.

"Don't be late. The party starts at five!" his mother called out as the truck pulled out of the driveway.

Once they were out of sight of his home, Daniel glanced her way. "Sorry, my mother loves to organize our lives."

Shelby smiled. "I think she's sweet."

"My father puts up with her. She has to have a project or *he* becomes her project."

Shelby's smile lasted all the way into town. She liked his parents and the way he and his brother acted together. If she ever had a family, she wanted a husband who cared and definitely more than one child. As an only child, she hadn't known what she was missing. Her grandfather had tried to fill all the gaps by being her father, mother and best friend when she needed a shoulder to cry on. It wasn't the same as having siblings, but she wouldn't trade her grandfather for anything. He'd been the center of her universe for so long.

Daniel parked just off Main Street and they walked along the sidewalks, window-shopping. Daniel held her hand and she pretended they were a couple, there to relax and enjoy the small tourist town.

What did it hurt to imagine? She knew this wasn't real. As directed, they stopped at the yogurt shop and got a double-dip waffle cone that melted as they stood outside the store, licking as fast as they could. Shelby caught a glimpse of them reflected in the window and a lump formed in her throat.

They looked like a couple. As if they belonged together. Her heart fluttered and her gut knotted. If only...

Another reflection caught her attention. A man passed behind them, his dark head down, his gaze shooting to the side, capturing hers for a brief second.

Maybe her imagination was overactive, but she could swear it was the same man she'd seen on the trip up from North Carolina. The one who'd been in the convenience store when she'd come out of the bathroom.

Shelby's head whipped around. "I swear I've seen that man before, in North Carolina."

"What man?"

A crowd of teenagers chose that moment to walk by, crowding the sidewalk, jostling each other and bumping into her and Daniel.

She craned her neck and stood on her toes. "I don't see him now." With a shrug, she dropped down on her feet. "I'm probably just paranoid."

"You're dripping." Daniel handed her a napkin.

Shelby had been searching for the stranger so long, her frozen yogurt had leaked through the hole in the bottom of the cone. She quickly licked the drips and sucked on the tip. When she'd eaten all she could, she tossed the rest into a nearby trash can and wiped her hands and mouth with the tattered napkin.

Daniel stuffed the last bite into his mouth and licked his lips. "Nothing better than frozen yogurt on a sunny day."

"Missed a spot."

"Where?" He tipped his face from side to side.

Shelby caught his cheeks between her palms and bent his head toward her. "Here." She kissed the tip of his nose and then took his lips in a sweet, creamy kiss.

When she stepped back, he grabbed her around the middle and pulled her against him. "You missed a spot, too." His mouth brushed across hers, then his tongue swept along her lips and pushed between her teeth. When he came up, he grinned. "I think I got it." He grabbed her hand. "Come on, there's something I want to show you. We can get there and back if we hurry."

"Where?"

"You'll see."

He led her back to the truck and drove around the point to park along the side of the road next to other vehicles.

Daniel got out and helped Shelby down. Then he grabbed her hand. "We'll have to hurry."

"Why?"

"We have to beat the tide."

Not sure what he was talking about, she half ran and half walked down a road toward the water.

When she reached the end of the road, it turned into a gravel sandbar that led across the bay to an island.

"That's Bar Island. While the tide is out, you can get there and back on foot. Come on." He hustled her across the long bar to the small island with lush green trees and giant boulders peppering the shore.

By the time they reached the island, Shelby was panting.

"Now you can have the best view of Bar Harbor. Turn around."

She turned and stared back at the point where the grand hotels lined the shores and a huge sailing ship with four tall masts lay anchored off the shore. Sailboats and yachts skimmed through the water around them.

A few other hikers were walking back across the land bridge to Bar Harbor, leaving Daniel and Shelby alone on the island.

Shelby could almost imagine how it would be if she and Daniel were marooned on a deserted island. After all the drama of the past few days, it sounded like heaven.

Daniel slipped an arm around her waist and hugged

her close against him. "I almost wish we didn't have to go back."

Her stomach fluttered. It was as if he'd read her mind.

"We have a date with some lobster tonight and it gets pretty cold out here, otherwise I'd say to hell with it." He carried her hand to his lips and kissed her palm. "We'd better get back. The tide is coming in. If we don't hurry, we'll be stranded."

She sighed and held tightly to Daniel's hand as they hurried back across the land bridge, the water rapidly inching up the sides. At one point, they had to leap to get over a spot where the water completely covered the sandbar. They ran the rest of the way, the water rising to cover their feet as they reached shore.

Shelby ran up the bank and turned, looking back, her heart hammering against her ribs. The land bridge had completely disappeared and only water stretched between the mainland and Bar Island.

Shelby laughed and leaned into Daniel. "That was amazing."

"Bar Harbor has its attractions. My brothers and I got caught on the island more than once. Mom and Dad grounded us from going there until we could prove we had enough sense to get off before the tide came in."

"You and your brothers sound as if you have given your parents many a gray hair."

He turned and started up the road toward the street where they'd parked the truck. "My parents were both gifted with healthy heads of hair that haven't turned gray even as they entered their fifties. I hope to inherit that particular trait from them."

Shelby tilted her head. "I hadn't pegged you for a vain man."

"Isn't it always said that to be successful in life, you have to keep a full head of hair and stand over six feet tall?" He stood straighter, far exceeding the height limit for success. "So far, I meet the criteria."

"Success is relative. There's the extremely rich, like my grandmother, who have enough money to own a car in a color to match every outfit." Shelby looked ahead at the passing cars, picturing her grandfather waiting on customers, a smile on his face. "And there's the small-business owner just trying to make a living. I consider my grandfather successful. When he took over the bar from his father, he brought it back to life. It doesn't make a ton of money, but it employs a number of people, provides decent food and drinks and generates enough profit that I was able to go to college."

"He is a successful man. And his greatest success of all was raising you to be an amazing woman."

She shrugged. "I'm not that amazing yet. But I hope to be. My grandfather gave up a lot to raise my mother and then me. He deserves an easier life."

They arrived at the street and turned toward the truck. "Do you think your grandfather would want an easier life?"

Shelby snorted. "No. Sitting around watching television would drive him nuts. He thrives on being with people."

Daniel held the door to the truck open for Shelby and helped her up into it. "Your grandfather is a special man."

Her heart squeezing in her chest, her gaze met his. "He is, and I miss him already."

Daniel leaned in and kissed her lips. "We'll get you home soon."

"I hope so."

After closing her door, Daniel rounded the front of the truck and stepped out into the street to open his own door.

Shelby's gaze followed him, admiring how tall and straight he stood, like a man with military training—strong, proud and determined to do what was right.

She glanced over her shoulder, gauging the traffic flow as Daniel opened his door.

A dark SUV barreled toward the truck, faster than the posted speed limit.

Daniel had his hand on the steering wheel and was about to step up into the truck.

Shelby reached across the seat, grabbed his hand and pulled as hard as she could. "Get in!"

Daniel sprawled across the seat and pulled his feet into the truck's cab right before the SUV slammed into the open door of the truck, ripping it right off its hinges and sending it flying across the pavement into oncoming traffic. The truck rocked violently, skidded forward and slid to a stop.

A car coming from the other direction swerved out of the SUV's way and ran up on the opposite sidewalk, scattering pedestrians.

The SUV never slowed as it continued down the street, burning a layer of rubber off the tires as it accelerated.

Daniel jumped out of the truck and raced after the speeding vehicle. He ground to a halt and turned back, asking a man on the side of the road, "Did you see a license plate?"

The man shook his head.

When Daniel reached the truck, he leaned in. "You okay?"

Shelby nodded. "I should be asking you that. It was your side that was hit."

"I am now. Stay put while I clean up the mess."

"But I can help."

"I'd feel better if you stayed where you are. Please." He reached in and squeezed her hand and then circled the truck to check the damage.

A couple stopped to ask if he was okay or needed help.

Shelby debated getting out, but figured she'd cause him less worry by staying where she was.

Daniel retrieved the damaged door from the middle of the road and tossed it into the truck bed. Then he climbed into the doorless side of the pickup and buckled his seat belt. "I don't like it."

"You think it was just an accident?"

He shook his head. "I hope the hell it wasn't something to do with you."

Shelby's gut was knotted, her hands shaking. Daniel had almost been hit. "It looked as if he was aiming for you."

Daniel turned the key in the ignition and the engine fired up. "You sure it wasn't some kid texting?"

"I didn't see the driver."

He rested his hand on the gearshift. "Did you happen to catch a license plate number?"

Shelby shook her head. "It all happened too fast."

Daniel shifted into Drive and pulled out onto the street. "When we get to my parent's home, I'll call my brother on the police force and have him submit the hit-and-run as an anonymous report. They can be on the lookout for the SUV."

Shelby shivered. "That man nearly killed you."

"But he didn't. Let's get back to the house. I have to break it to my father that I wrecked his favorite truck." Daniel's mouth twisted. "I haven't had to do that for over ten years."

Shelby sat in the seat beside him, her hands clasped together to keep them from shaking. She'd almost lost Daniel and she was shocked at how much she cared.

Chapter 15

When Daniel pulled into his parents' driveway, the street was lined with cars. People he vaguely remembered were climbing out, carrying beach blankets and tote bags, and wearing large beach hats.

"We're just in time for the party."

"I don't feel much like partying," Shelby said.

"Look, we can't dwell on what happened. It'll solve nothing. Dad's insurance will cover the damage and fix up the truck like new." He unbuckled his seat belt and slipped out of his side of the truck.

"I could care less about the truck. It's *you* I worry about."

"I'm okay." He helped her out of the truck. "Put it all behind you. We're here and my parents have planned an epic lobster bake that my brother is cooking." He held out a hand for her and she placed her more delicate one in it. "All we have to do is play on the beach, maybe take the WaveRunners out and enjoy this beautiful, sunny day." He grinned and slipped an arm around her waist. "See? I'm fine, you're fine. We're gonna have a good time."

Shelby stepped down from the truck, still holding on after she was safely on the ground.

He wished he felt as confident as he was pretending to be. The earlier wreck had shaken him almost as much as it had Shelby. Especially since he'd only recently returned to duty after being in the hospital for gunshot wounds.

"You go inside, find your skimpiest bikini and get ready for a party."

"How do you know I have a skimpy bikini?"

He raised his hand. "I admit, I noticed your tan line last night. You, my dear, have a teeny-weeny bikini that I'm betting will make all the other girls green with envy."

"Fine. I'll get changed, but don't disappear for long." She walked ahead of him into the house.

"I'll be there in a minute. I need to report the accident and then find my father and pull him aside to break the news."

"You want me to be with you?"

"No, thanks, I've got this."

He sent Shelby down the hallway and he ducked into the kitchen where he found his mother at the center island butcher block chopping lettuce and tomatoes for a salad.

"Where's Dad?"

She glanced up, her keen-eyed gaze piercing through him. "Something wrong?"

He never could lie to his mother, she saw through him and his brothers every time. "Yeah, but I need to tell him."

She wiped her hands on her apron and turned to peer out the back window over the kitchen sink. "He's out on the porch talking with the neighbor."

"Daniel!" Marcus, the youngest of the Henderson boys entered the kitchen, a pretty blonde holding on to his arm wearing a bright red bikini and a sheer wrap over the revealing scraps of material. "Stacey, this is my oldest brother, Daniel. Daniel, this is Stacey."

"Nice to meet you." He shook Stacey's hand, then enveloped his baby brother in a bear hug. "How are you?"

"Good. I'm working the graveyard shift for the next two weeks, but other than my nights and days being confused, I'm fine."

"I might need your assistance in a minute. First, I need to find Dad."

"I'll help your mother. You go on." Stacey smiled and gave Marcus a shove toward the door.

Daniel pushed through the back door and stepped out onto the porch.

James Henderson stood on the porch with a group of men, talking as he looked out over the expanse of beach a hundred feet from his yard.

"Dad," Daniel said. "I need you for a few minutes."

Just then, Robert climbed the porch steps. "The coals are getting hot. We'll be ready for the lobster and fixings soon."

"Your brother needs my attention." Daniel's father said. "I'll be right back."

Daniel nodded to Robert. "If you've got a minute, I could use your advice, as well."

"Sounds serious." Robert wiped his hands on the apron he had tied around his neck.

Daniel led the way around to the other side of the house and out to the damaged pickup.

"Wow, Daniel!" Marcus stood back, his eyes wide. "I put a dent in Dad's old truck back in the day, but never ripped a door off."

"I didn't rip it off. Someone sideswiped me on one of the main roads. From what Shelby witnessed, it appeared he was aiming straight for me."

His father ran his hand over the ragged edges of the hinges. "Damn." He looked up. "You sure you're okay? That SUV hit hard enough to rip the door clean off the hinges. If it had hit you... Damn. Don't tell your mother. Let her think it happened while you were clear of the vehicle."

"Tell me what?" His mother walked out of the house, wiping her hands on her apron.

"Nothing, dear."

"Oh, dear lord, what happened to your truck?"

"An accident. The insurance will cover it. We have a lobster bake about to kick off—we don't have time to worry about a dumb old truck." Daniel's father wrapped his arm around his wife and guided her back in the house.

"Do you think this had anything to do with Shelby's situation?" his mother asked.

"I don't know, but I could use some extra eyes watching out for her at the lobster bake."

"You got it."

Daniel entered the house and went in search of

Shelby. When he opened the door to his bedroom, he stopped, his breath stolen away by the beauty standing in front of him.

"Too much?" Shelby turned left then right, displaying a lot of her beautiful skin in a tiny powder-blue bikini that matched her eyes perfectly.

"Too little."

"I thought you liked tiny bikinis."

"I do, but in private. Every male eye will be on you at the lobster bake."

"I doubt that."

"Really?" He turned her to look into the mirror over the dresser. "Look at yourself. You're amazing." His hands rested on her hips, and he pulled her back against him, nuzzling her neck.

"I believe we're expected."

"Let them all wait."

"Daniel!" His mother called out. "Could you help Marcus get the WaveRunners started?"

Daniel drew in a deep breath and let it out slowly. "Duty calls. And you're coming with me." He glanced down. "Do you have a T-shirt or some kind of cover-up?"

"I thought you wanted me in a bikini."

"Oh, you'll need the bikini where we're going."

"I thought you said the ocean temp was around sixty degrees."

"It is, but the idea is not to stay in it for long." He nodded toward her duffel. "Get that T-shirt and I'll grab some towels."

Daniel found the beach towels in the hall closet.

Shelby emerged from the bedroom wearing a Hawaiian patterned skirt over her bikini bottoms.

He groaned. The cover-up did little to detract from her shapely curves, if not enhancing them exponentially. He'd be fighting off the local guys before the end of the evening.

He hurried out to the beach where Robert had dug a pit in the gravelly sand, and the smell of roasting lobster filled the air.

Marcus waved to him from the water's edge where two WaveRunners stood.

Shelby followed Daniel to his brother. Marcus had the engine compartment open and he fiddled with the wires inside.

He glanced up, his gaze traveling over Shelby's exquisite body and the blue bikini. Marcus gave a slow, sexy wolf whistle and got punched in the shoulder by his older brother for it.

"Keep your tongue in your head, little brother. You have a girlfriend."

"So I have a girlfriend. Does it hurt to recognize beauty when you see it?"

"I don't know. You tell me." Daniel punched his brother's arm again.

Marcus rubbed the shoulder, frowning. "I guess it does." Then he looked down at the WaveRunner. "I've tried all the easy solutions."

Daniel looked at the engine, spotted the problem and had it running in less than five minutes. He turned to Shelby. "This is why you needed the bikini."

"We're going to ride those?" Her blue eyes lit up and she grinned, stripping her skirt down over her legs. "I've only ridden something like this twice, so I'll need a little instruction."

"You can ride with me, and Marcus will take the other."

"Good." She gripped the handles and, with Daniel's help, pushed the machine out into deeper water. He helped her mount the WaveRunner, then he climbed up behind her, straddling her hips.

With a few short instructions, he guided her in how to start, give it gas and stop. "It really is simple. And don't be afraid of speed. Going too slow makes it unstable."

"Ready?" she asked, her fingers curled tightly around the handgrips.

"Ready."

She gave it the gas and the WaveRunner shot forward, almost unseating him.

He grabbed her around the waist and held on as she plowed through the waves closest to shore, riding up then sinking down. Once she'd cleared the waves, she gave it all it would take, zooming across the bay, her hair flying out behind her.

Shelby let out an excited whoop and turned sharply, the tail end of the machine swinging out behind them. The centrifugal force nearly threw Daniel off on the next turn. He braced his feet on the running boards and held on tightly.

After a moment, she slowed to a halt. "Are you okay back there?"

"Doing fine," he said, enjoying the look of rapture on her face. "Are you sure you've only driven one of these two times?"

She shrugged. "Only two," she confirmed.

Marcus blew past them, headed along the shoreline toward the point.

"Hold on!" Shelby shouted and gunned the throttle, shooting forward.

Daniel's feet left the running boards. He held on tightly around Shelby's waist as she raced after Marcus. Marcus pulled sharply around and headed back in the opposite direction.

Not to be outdone, Shelby followed suit.

As Shelby made a sweeping turn, Daniel held on to her.

Before she got all the way around, a motorboat came out of nowhere, aimed straight for her.

"Turn!" Daniel shouted.

Shelby jerked the handlebar to the right and gunned it.

Daniel clung to her waist, gripping the seat of the WaveRunner with his thighs.

At first, he thought the driver of the boat wasn't paying attention. Daniel looked over his shoulder. The boat turned around and headed straight for them again.

"He's coming back!" he yelled.

"What should I do?" Shelby cried.

"Go straight until I tell you to turn." Daniel prayed he could judge the speed of both watercraft.

The boat sped toward them, full-on, as fast as it could go.

Shelby gave the little WaveRunner all it had.

"Slow down."

"What?"

"You heard me, slow down," he insisted.

The boat was almost on them when Daniel yelled, "Turn right!" He reached around her and laid his hands over hers, yanking the handlebar to the right at the same time as he gunned the throttle. He could feel the blast of air and spray from the wake churned up by the motor.

When the boat turned and aimed for them yet again, Marcus raced in front of them, kicking up a rooster tail that splashed into the driver's face. The craft slowed, then sped up again.

Daniel aimed for the shore, giving the WaveRunner all it had. They couldn't keep up the fight with the motorboat; their best chance was to run ashore and get out of the water altogether.

His focus on the shore, Daniel steered to one side of where the people who had gathered for the lobster bake were now crowded, witnessing their fight for survival.

When they realized he was heading straight for them, the mass of people dodged to the side. Daniel ran the WaveRunner all the way up on dry land before he killed the engine, jumped off and pulled Shelby into his arms.

Robert stood on the shore, his weapon pointed at the boat behind them.

At the last minute, the motorboat whipped to the left and raced away, speeding across the water and around the point, out of sight.

Marcus brought his WaveRunner ashore and jumped off. "What the hell was that all about?"

With Shelby tucked in the crook of his arm, her body shaking and her face pale, Daniel had reached his boiling point. "Let's take this discussion inside."

Shelby was thankful for Daniel's support as she walked up the beach to the house. The fear of being chased by a motorboat full of thugs ranked right up there with being kidnapped and held hostage.

She and Daniel had come very close to being killed or drowning in the wake of their attacker's boat.

Mrs. Henderson came into the kitchen from another part of the house, took one look at her sons and Shelby and asked, "What happened?"

Daniel filled her and his father in on the attack and his mother's face blanched.

"Oh, my dear, sweet child." She wrapped Shelby in a tight hug and patted her hair, treating her as if she were a frightened little girl.

Tears welled in Shelby's eyes at the care and concern from a woman who'd only known her a day.

Daniel's father patted her back. "Are you okay?"

Shelby nodded, unable to speak around the tight knot constricting her vocal cords.

Robert was on his cell phone, giving details of the attack to what sounded like the police station where he worked.

Mrs. Henderson set her at arm's length and guided her to a chair. "Sit down before you collapse."

Grateful for the chair, Shelby sank onto the seat before her wobbly legs buckled.

A moment later, Mrs. Henderson planted a hot mug of tea in front of her. "Drink that. You're shaking like a leaf."

Shelby wrapped her hands around the warm mug, thankful for something to keep them from trembling.

Marcus charged into the room. "Holy smokes! That was insane. I didn't think you two were going to make it."

Mrs. Henderson frowned at her youngest son. "Marcus."

"Well, it's true. I thought that boat would run them right over."

Shelby forced a laugh she didn't feel. "You and me both."

Robert clicked the off button and turned toward Daniel and Shelby. "The station put out a report to the Maine marine patrol and the state police."

"Should we send everyone home?" Mrs. Henderson asked. "I'd hate for anyone else to get hurt."

"Not on my account." Shelby pushed to her feet, thankful her knees held. "I should leave. It was a bad idea to come here. The people after me seem to know where I'm going almost before I do."

"You're not going anywhere." Lea slipped an arm around her waist. "You're staying with us until we can figure this out."

She shook her head. "I can't get you all involved. It's too dangerous."

"We're not going anywhere until I check in with Kate and my boss," Daniel said.

"In the meantime, we have lobster for dinner." Mr. Henderson nodded toward Robert. "Or are they burning?"

"I'm on it." Robert spun and headed out the door at a jog.

"I'm keeping you all from your guests." Shelby smiled at the Hendersons. "I was really looking forward to the lobster bake."

"The guests know the routine. Sit on the beach, play music and eat lobster. We don't have to entertain them. And if you're surrounded by my big, strapping sons, there's no reason you still can't participate."

Daniel frowned. "It'll be dark outside soon."

"If we're all there," Marcus pointed out, "whoever is after her won't be able to get to her." He hooked Shelby's elbow. "What do you say, sister?" He followed with a playful wink.

"I'm game. Isn't Maine known for its lobster? It would be a crime to leave without trying some." She glanced at Daniel.

His face was set in stone, his brows dipped low. "I don't know if this is such a good idea."

"We won't go out on the water."

"What if they start shooting at you?"

"Then they could get me on the porch as easily as on the beach. And if I wear a hoodie, maybe they won't pick me out of the crowd."

"She has a point, dear." Daniel's mother touched his arm. "Let the girl enjoy her first lobster bake. We'll stay with her while she's outside. Won't we?" She glanced around at her two sons and her husband.

Daniel's frown eased slightly. "Okay, but we're not staying out all night."

"Agreed," Marcus said. He tugged on Shelby's arm. "Come on, the lobster won't last long with this hungry bunch. And I'd like to show up out there with the prettiest girl in a bikini."

Shelby glanced back at Daniel, hesitant to leave the house without him by her side.

"Beat it, Marcus." Daniel grabbed Shelby's arm from the other side. "You have your own date."

"Darn, I've always wanted to have two women to myself." Marcus winked.

"And how would Stacey feel about that?"

"Surely she'd understand. Most women would, right?"

"Marcus Henderson," his mother chastised. "Quit before you dig yourself into a hole."

"Yes, ma'am."

"Marcus?" Stacey entered through the back door. "Marcus? Are you in here?"

"There's my cue." Marcus hurried forward to take Stacey in his arms. "There you are. I've been searching all over for you."

Her brows wrinkled. "I was getting my things out of your car. Seems I missed all the excitement. What happened?"

He took her hand and led her out the back door. "Just a little fun and games on the WaveRunner, courtesy of my brother and his girlfriend."

Shelby opened her mouth to straighten them out about the girlfriend label. She wasn't Daniel's girlfriend. Lover, maybe, but girlfriend implied a level of commitment he wasn't willing to give.

But after running from a crazed motorboat driver, she didn't think it was worth the trouble to argue over something as minuscule as being called Daniel's girlfriend.

Instead of guiding her out the back door, he led her to his bedroom.

"I thought we were having lobster."

He rifled through his dresser and unearthed an old U2 T-shirt and held it open. "Much as I love you in that bikini, it's a moving target. Wear this." She took the shirt from him and put it on. The hem fell over her hips and halfway down her thighs, covering all her curves. So much for attracting Daniel's attention. He took out an old baseball cap from his closet and handed it to her. "I wore that to the junior varsity championships my freshman year in high school."

She held the hat in her hand, sensing another piece of Daniel's history in the item. He'd had a normal childhood, surrounded by a loving mother, father and siblings to keep him company.

Shelby would have loved being a part of a family like Daniel's. But she had her grandfather, and he was everything to her. The only times she'd missed her mother was at mother–daughter events in grade school and high school.

She pulled the cap over her head and stuffed her hair beneath it. "There. Am I a nondescript blob enough so that no one will suspect it's Shelby O'Hara beneath the brim?"

Daniel stood back, his eyes narrowing, the green so deep it reminded her of an evergreen forest at dusk, deep, mysterious and unfathomable. "I wouldn't say you were a blob. Even your legs are sexy sticking out from the hem of the T-shirt." He dragged her into his arms and held her close. "We don't have to go out if you don't want to."

"Your parents went to all the trouble of a lobster bake, we might as well make a showing. Besides, I wasn't kidding about the Maine lobster. I want the real thing, not some farm-raised lobsters."

Daniel kissed the tip of her nose, took her hand and walked to the door. "Come on. I have a lobster with your name on it."

With her hand in his, Shelby felt as if she could conquer the world, bad guys be damned.

She pushed to the back of her mind the reality that he would someday soon leave her. She'd gotten used to having him around. And the more she learned about him, the more there was to love.

She stumbled, her heart beating more wildly in her chest than when she'd been kidnapped or chased by a killer boat.

Could it be that she'd committed the ultimate mistake? Was she falling in love with Daniel?

If so, she was in for a whole lot of heartbreak.

Chapter 16

Daniel stayed attached to Shelby's side as family and friends gathered around the fire pit with plates of steaming lobster, corn on the cob and clams. If he wasn't so scared of someone taking a potshot at her, he'd relax and enjoy watching her experience her first lobster bake.

But every loud noise and every engine rev made him jump. With the sun beneath the horizon for the night, the air had chilled. He'd stuck his pistol in the pocket of his jacket and kept one hand on it at all times, the other arm around Shelby. Not only did he like holding Shelby, but it also kept her close and secure against his side.

Shelby dug into the lobster like a pro, her face covered in juice, her lips dripping with butter sauce.

Daniel couldn't resist. He leaned over and captured

a drop of butter, sucking her bottom lip into his mouth. "Mmm. Tasty."

"The butter?"

"No, you."

She leaned into him, staring at the fire. "I could stay like this forever."

"Not me."

She sat up straight. "I'm sorry. Was I making you uncomfortable?"

"Yes," he said. "In the best, worst way." He shifted, tugging his jeans to a looser position.

She smiled, her blue eyes shining. "In that case..." Leaning back against him, she took another piece of lobster, dipped it in a cup of butter, popped it into her mouth, chewed and swallowed.

Every movement she made looked incredibly sexy. She even made butter look desirable. When she started licking her fingers, he grabbed her hand, raised it to his lips and sucked her finger into his mouth. "Mmm. You're delicious."

She laughed. "Not me, the butter."

He sucked her finger into his mouth again. "No, it's you."

Shelby pulled her finger from his mouth and kissed his lips. "Do you kiss all your jobs like this?"

"Mostly when I'm undercover. You and Kate Winston are my only bodyguard gigs so far in the Secret Service."

"Really?" She stared at him for a moment. "You haven't kissed Kate, have you?" Her brows furrowed. "I mean that would be really weird, kissing my grandmother and all."

Daniel laughed. "No, I haven't kissed Kate. You are my only lapse in professionalism."

Her furrows deepened. "That doesn't sound romantic at all."

"It wasn't supposed to."

She clucked her tongue. "Here we are, on a beach with a fire warming our faces, the sound of the surf to give the place ambience and you ruin it by calling me a lapse in professionalism."

"It's a lapse I can't seem to shake."

"Then stop trying." She stood, held out her hand, looking a lot younger than her twenty-three years wearing the extralong T-shirt. She turned to his mother and father. "This was lovely. Thank you for including me."

His father and brothers stood. "Do you want us to follow you two to the house?"

Shelby glanced at Daniel. "I think we'll be okay."

Daniel took her hand and let her tug him to his feet. "Are you ready to go inside?" He glanced around, carefully searching the shadows for anyone lurking, waiting to pounce.

"Yes, I'm ready." Her lips quirked at the corners as they moved away from the people sprawled on the beach, finishing up the last of the clams and lobster. "I'm ready to show you that I'm not a lapse in professionalism." She tilted her head, a lift to her step. "I'm more of a rebellious streak you'll soon grow out of." She left him standing in the sand and ran up the path to the house.

Daniel's pulse kicked up and he ran after her. Catching her by the waist, he swung her around and set her on her feet. "A rebellious streak, huh?" Taking her hand, he climbed the steps slowly enough for her to keep up, when he'd rather be running through the door and down the hallway to his bedroom.

She paused on the porch and looked out over the bay where the moonlight glistened like diamonds on the water. "You grew up in a beautiful place."

He wrapped his arms around her waist and pulled her back against him, nibbling at her neck. "You wouldn't think so in the winter. It's brutally cold."

"I'm sure you find ways to keep warm." Shelby leaned her head to the side, allowing him better access to her neck.

He pulled her hat off, letting her hair down around her shoulders, loving the way it fell into place no matter how disturbed by a hat, wind or rain. Perfect in every way, and he was so very wrong for her.

She deserved a man who'd stick around, be there for her when she needed him. A man who'd share diaper duty when kids came along, who'd go to all the soccer games and T-ball practice. Not a man who'd be on assignment, away from home, out of contact for weeks at a time.

Shelby needed someone else. Not him. He stiffened and was about to pull away when her hands curled around his and brought them up beneath the T-shirt to cup her bikini-clad breasts.

"I can tell when you start thinking too much." She reached behind her and loosened the clasp on the bikini top, giving his hands free access to her. "Stop thinking and live in the moment. I don't expect anything from you past today."

He couldn't stop himself. Not now that she'd invited him to play. With his palms cupping her, he couldn't focus past the way her nipples tightened into little buds. He closed his fingers around the knobby tips and pinched, pulling softly.

Her back arched and her hands cupped his, encouraging him to continue. While one hand stayed firmly over one breast, she dragged the other downward and slipped it beneath the elastic of her bikini bottom.

As they stood on the porch in the moonlight, his fingers curled around her sex, one sliding up inside her.

She leaned into him, rubbing her bottom against the ridge beneath his shorts, letting her head drop back against his shoulder.

"Shouldn't we take this inside?" he whispered against her earlobe.

"I thought I was your rebellious streak. Are you telling me you're a lot tamer than that?"

His blood coursed through his veins. "I think I had you all wrong."

"How's that?" Her hand curved over the one in her bottoms, pressing another finger into her channel.

"You're not a goody-goody at all."

"I never claimed to be. However, I was a little more conservative until I met a Secret Service agent who lured me over to the dark side." She led his finger to her sweet spot, parting her folds for him to concentrate on the center. "You make me want to be bad."

"And you make me want to forget all the rules."

"Rules?" She snorted. "What rules?"

He flicked her nubbin and her body went rigid against him. "Like that?"

"Please, do it again," she said through gritted teeth.

He nipped her exposed throat and rubbed her with his thumb while thrusting two fingers into her slick entrance.

She dragged in a deep breath, which pushed her breasts out, the one in his hand swelling against his palm.

His shaft hardened to steel and he couldn't hold back any longer. He scooped her up in his arms, carried her to the French doors to his bedroom, flung them open and strode in. After he set her on her feet, he ripped the T-shirt up over her head and threw it across the room. Her bikini top hung by the strap around her neck, her breasts bobbing free of the fabric.

Daniel tugged the bow at the back and the top fell to the floor at his feet. She stood in the blue bikini bottoms, her back straight, her breasts perfect, her narrow waist flaring down to the gentle swell of her hips.

Her gaze locked with his as she slipped the bikini bottoms down her legs and stood naked in front of him. She held out her hand.

He took it and she walked backward, leading him toward the bed. Once there, she slid his polo shirt up and over his head, then hooked her hands in the elastic waistband of his swim trunks and slid them down over his hips. Together they climbed up onto the bed and began a slow, sexy exploration of each other's bodies, taking their time. Daniel left kisses all along the length of her torso, tasting her smooth skin with his tongue, nibbling on the turgid peaks of her nipples.

When he couldn't take any more, he reached into the drawer beside the bed and fished for a condom. When he found one, Shelby took it from him and slid it down over him, her hands lingering at the base.

Her expression was sad. "I don't know why, but I feel like this might be our last time together." She reached out, captured his face in her hands and pulled him down for a kiss, a single tear sliding from the corner of one eye.

As much as he wanted to refute her claim, Daniel didn't. He never knew what the next day would bring. If the men who were after her were miraculously caught, he'd be reassigned, maybe back to detective duties or bodyguard work for Kate Winston. In which case, he'd see Shelby, but not as much. Maybe not at all if she went back to her life on the Outer Banks.

"What was it you said? Let's make good use of the time we have together." He'd worry about tomorrow when it came.

Settling between her legs, he nudged her entrance with his thick, hard member, and then bent to claim her lips as he thrust into her in one long, swift push.

She gasped against his lips, her fingers digging into his hips, pushing back, then pulling him forward until he settled into a smooth, steady rhythm.

Shelby dug her heels into the mattress and met his every movement, driving him deeper. When at last he launched off the precipice, he held her close, buried deep inside her, wondering how he'd live without her.

This woman he'd pulled out of a fire had pulled him out of the rut he'd been in and reminded him that there was more to living life than a single-minded focus on his job.

He dropped down to lie beside her, gathered her in his arms and held her for a long time, his mind drifting back over the time they'd been together. Though short, it felt like a lifetime. She was the only woman he felt he really knew and who could touch his heart.

After a while, he slipped out of the bed and dressed.

"Where are you going?" Shelby sat up, the sheet falling around her waist. Moonlight shone in through the window, making her body glow a silvery-blue.

Daniel bent to kiss her.

"Come back to bed," she urged.

"I have to make a phone call."

"Then you'll come back?"

"I promise."

She slipped out of the bed.

"Where are you going?" he asked.

She slipped into a pair of jeans and threw the big T-shirt over her head, pushing her arms through. "The bathroom, to brush my teeth and wash my face."

"I'll go with you." He put his phone in his back pocket.

Shelby held up her hand. "No. Sometimes a girl needs her privacy."

He nodded, walked her to the door and watched as she crossed the hall. When he was certain she was inside and safe, he stepped back into the bedroom, grabbed the portable phone from the nightstand and stepped out through the French doors onto the porch. He punched in the numbers for Kate Winston's personal cell phone.

Debra answered on the first ring. "Good evening, this is Debra, Kate Winston's assistant. How can I help you?"

"Debra, this is Daniel Henderson. Is Kate available?"

"Sorry, Daniel. She's at a fund-raiser dinner. Can I take a message for her?"

He held the phone, thinking through his options. "Yes. Have her call me when she's free."

"Is it an emergency?"

"Yes."

"Should I take her out of the dinner to get her to return that call?"

"No. Have her call me when she'd normally come out."

"Yes, sir." Debra hesitated. "Is her granddaughter all right?"

"Yes. But there have been some incidents."

"Are you safe now?"

"We are, but I'm not certain for how long."

"I'll have her call as soon as she's out."

"Thank you."

Daniel hung up and dialed Jed Kincannon.

"Kincannon speaking."

"Mr. Kincannon, Daniel Henderson here."

"Daniel, what's happening in Maine?"

He filled the director in on the occurrences and finished by saying, "I think whoever is after Shelby has followed us up here. I'm for bringing her back to North Carolina, closer to home and family."

"I agree. Let me get with Kate and see if she feels the same. In the meantime, I'd wait until morning to head out."

"Yes, sir." Daniel hit the end button and was turning around when he heard footsteps on the porch beside him.

He turned to confront whoever it was, but before he knew what was happening, he was hit on the back of the head with something cold and hard.

Pain ripped through his skull and darkness engulfed him.

* * *

Shelby washed her face, finger combed her hair and brushed her teeth, taking longer than necessary to give Daniel time to check in with her grandmother without interrupting his report. When she'd done all she could to waste time, she crossed the hallway and entered the bedroom, closing and locking the door behind her. After the bright lights of the bathroom, the darkness of the bedroom left her blinded while her eyes adjusted.

A movement she caught in her peripheral vision made her turn with a smile on her face. "Well, what did Kate say?"

Two men grabbed her. One clamped his meaty hand over her mouth before she had a chance to scream. She struggled, kicking and bucking, desperate to break free. The second man grabbed for her feet.

Shelby slammed her heel into the nose of the guy holding her feet. He grunted as blood spurted out then he growled, his eyes blazing in the light from the window. He swung his arm and backhanded her in the face.

Her head whipped around and her vision blurred. For a moment she was too dizzy to fight, teetering on the verge of blacking out.

The man holding her from behind spun her around, slapped duct tape over her mouth and used it to bind her wrists and ankles. Then he tossed her over his shoulder.

With the bleeding man leading the way, they exited through the French doors and ran across the porch to the steps, leading out to the road. They clung to the shadows of trees as they hurried parallel to the pavement.

Shelby bounced against the man's back, wiggling

pitifully and fighting back the dark cloud of uncon-
sciousness threatening to overtake her.

When they emerged onto the road, they dumped her
in the trunk of a dark sedan and closed the lid.

Her heart racing and her head throbbing, Shelby
tried to scream. But no one would hear her, no one
could. The nightmare she thought she'd escaped had
come back to haunt her, and all she could think about
was Daniel. Where was he? Why hadn't he come to
her rescue?

Unless they had killed him before taking her.

Overwhelmed by fear, trapped in a small, dark, tight
space and dizzy from the blow to her face, Shelby suc-
cumbed to the darkness.

Chapter 17

"Daniel!"

Someone was shaking him, and every time they did, he felt as if he was being hit in the head with an electric prod.

Daniel fought back the black fog and emerged into a dull yellow light filled with shadows. He was lying facedown on the wooden planks of the porch, his head throbbing.

"Daniel, where's Shelby?" He focused on the voice, finally identifying it as his mother's.

"Shelby?" he muttered, afraid to worsen the pain splitting the back of his head.

"You know, the woman you were protecting?" his mother said. "James, call 911. We need an ambulance."

Memories of Shelby lying naked in the bed rushed back to Daniel, along with the shadowy movement before the crashing pain in the back of his head. "Shelby." He pushed to a sitting position, swayed and would have fallen if Marcus hadn't caught him.

"Stay down until the ambulance gets here," Marcus said.

"Can't." Daniel tried to get up, but his brother's hand on his shoulder kept him from rising. "Let me go. Where's Shelby?"

"Oh, baby, she's gone," his mother said, tears trickling down her cheeks. "Everyone started leaving the lobster bake and we came up to check on you and Shelby. We found you, but not her."

Daniel cursed and tried again to rise, finally knocking his brother's hand off his shoulder. "We have to find her." When he made it to his feet, he staggered, his shoulder slamming into the wall before he could right himself.

His father looped his arm over his shoulder. "If you're going to be stubborn about this, at least let me help you inside. We can call whomever you need to notify. Robert is already on the phone with local police and he'll put the word out to the state police."

"I failed her, Dad." Daniel squeezed shut his eyes as another stabbing pain ripped through his head.

"You did no such thing. You were overpowered. If anything, we failed her by not being here for you both."

"No, it was my responsibility. My promise to protect her." He straightened, his vision blurring for a moment before it cleared. "I have to find her."

"At least come into the house in the light." His father angled him toward the open French doors and stepped inside. The room didn't look much different, other than the fact that the lamp on the nightstand had been knocked over and the throw rug on the floor was bunched and dark red strains trailed toward the door. Someone had put up a fight, and Shelby was gone, leaving a gaping emptiness in the room and his chest. How could he have been so careless?

"The phone. Where's the phone?" He held out his hand and his mother slapped the portable phone into it. "I found it out on the porch. It's cracked, but it still works."

Daniel blinked to clear his vision and punched the numbers for Kate. He could barely focus as his father walked him into the kitchen and eased him into a chair.

The phone was answered on the first ring. Before Kate's assistant could say a word, Daniel spoke, "Shelby's been kidnapped."

"I'll notify Mrs. Winston at once and have her call you back immediately. I assume she can reach you at this number?"

"Yes."

"She'll be with you momentarily." Debra hung up.

Daniel laid his head on the kitchen table. "Who would have known to follow us here?"

"Everyone has been asking about the woman you brought home, but we gave them a different name," his mother said. "We called her Celia Townsend, like you asked us to."

"No," Daniel moaned, his head hurting so badly he couldn't think straight. "It had to be someone back in North Carolina. Can I get a bottle of painkillers?"

"You need to see a doctor," his mother insisted, but she dug in the medicine cabinet next to the stove and brought out a bottle. "Ibuprofen will have to do." She shook out two pills and handed them to Daniel with a glass of water.

"Who knew Shelby was here, besides you?" Robert asked.

Before he could answer, the phone rang, the sound splitting Daniel's head in half each time it chirped. He hit the talk button and said, "Kate?"

"What happened?" Kate's voice sounded calm but intense.

Daniel told her what he knew and then asked, "Who besides your sons, Patrick and Director Kincannon would have known where I was taking her?"

"No one. Patrick's been with me the entire time, and I'd trust my sons with my life and Shelby's. They wouldn't have given out that information to anyone."

A sinking feeling filled his gut, adding more pain to the ache in his head. "The only other person who knew we were coming up here was my boss, Jed Kincannon."

Kate was silent for a moment. "Do you think he had anything to do with Shelby's disappearance? Are you sure you didn't let it slip to anyone else?"

"Shelby and I didn't tell anyone we were coming here. We went to great lengths to make sure we didn't leave a trail that could be easily followed. Only someone who knew we were going to be here would have gotten men up here that fast."

"Why would the director of the Secret Service take my granddaughter?"

"I don't know, and it doesn't make sense." Daniel tried to shake his head, but the pain intensified with the movement. "I could be wrong. It had to be someone else. Could anyone have listened in? Have you had the house swept for bugs?"

"My security team sweeps every morning. No one could have listened to our conversation," Kate assured him.

"It doesn't change the fact that she's gone." Hopelessness filled him when he considered the vastness of the country. Shelby could be anywhere. "And I have no idea where to begin to look. Our only clue is not much more than a suspicion that the Cartel is involved." His elbow on the table, he rested his forehead against his palm.

"Then we start there. I'm sending my private jet to pick you up. I'll have Debra notify you when it takes off and give you an expected arrival time."

"I can't leave Bar Harbor. What if they're holding her close by?"

"If this is about me, they'll bring her closer to the source. I need you here." Kate paused. "But while you're waiting for the jet, have a doctor check you out for concussion."

"I feel fine," he lied, the pain pulsing in waves through his head.

"I don't care how you feel," she said, her tone clipped, no-nonsense. "Get checked. I don't want you on a plane if you're suffering from a concussion. And you're probably in no condition to drive back down here."

And it would take too long. The thought of the thirteen-hour drive made him cringe. "Okay, I'll have the doc check me out, but I'll be on that plane."

"Good. We need you here to lead the investigation. I want my granddaughter back, unharmed."

"Agreed." He wanted Shelby back, safe and in his arms.

Kate hung up about the time the ambulance showed up, sirens wailing, reigniting the pain in Daniel's head.

His mother stood with her hands on her hips, her diminutive form no less intimidating. "Now, don't you say one word about the ambulance. You're going to the hospital if I have to knock you out to take you."

Daniel grinned, the effort costing him another wave of agony. "Okay. I'll go, but you didn't have to send for the cavalry. You could have taken me in the truck."

"Not in my truck," his dad said. "It's wrecked, as you well know." He stared at Daniel, his eyes narrowing. "I think you got hit harder than you think."

Daniel tenderly felt the egg-size knot at the back of his head. "I remember the truck."

"Good, then let the EMTs check you over." His father nodded to his mother. "Show them in."

Daniel's mother hurried to the door as the bell rang.

"If they say you don't need to ride in the ambulance, I'll take you in my car," Robert offered.

Daniel closed his eyes, the bright lights making his head throb. How long did it take for ibuprofen to work? "I don't care as long as I'm at the airport when the jet gets there."

"We'll get you there, even if we have to give you a police escort," Robert reassured him.

"We can do that?" Marcus asked.

"Shh." Robert shook his head and winked at his brother. "Don't advertise it, but I have connections on the police force."

Marcus shook his head. "I work there, too."

His mother entered the kitchen, followed by two emergency medical technicians, one of whom carried a medical kit.

After taking his blood pressure, checking his pulse, examining the lump on the back of his head and shining a light into his eyes, the technicians asked if he wanted to ride in the ambulance to the hospital for further examination.

"No, thanks. I have to go." Daniel tried to stand.

Robert pressed a hand on his shoulder, keeping him down. "You're not going anywhere until the doctor clears you. You might as well see one before you fly."

"We'll get him there," his mother assured the paramedic and showed him out of the kitchen.

The phone rang as they were headed for the front door. Debra relayed the expected time of arrival of the jet and said that Kate would be at the airport to greet him on his return.

Daniel rode to the hospital with Robert, his mother and father in the backseat with him, Marcus and Stacey choosing to hold down the home front just in case someone called with a ransom demand.

Daniel didn't think it would happen. Not with his parents. They weren't wealthy in any sense of the word. Not like Kate Winston. If a ransom were demanded, it would be Kate's money they'd be after. The sooner he returned to Raleigh the better.

After the doctor on call at the emergency room checked him over and ran a few tests, he gave him some pain meds and told him to take it easy for a few days.

By the time he was done at the hospital, it was almost time for the jet to land at the Bar Harbor Airport.

The ibuprofen had taken the edge off his headache and he was almost feeling normal when he boarded the luxury jet. Once he was inside, a flight attendant served him a drink. He asked her to wake him if there were any communications from Mrs. Winston. Then he reclined in the leather seat and dozed fitfully, thinking about the people who knew of their plans to go to Maine, reviewing the attempts on Kate's life and those on her family members.

When he'd spun the possibilities every which way until his head ached, he thought about Shelby and what she must be going through. His heart broke for her, imagining her terror at being kidnapped for the second time in less than a week.

If it was the last thing he did, he'd free her and make her captors pay for what they'd done.

When the plane landed in Raleigh, the pain had subsided to a dull ache, and Daniel was more in control. The catnap he'd taken refreshed him and he was ready to find the bastards who'd taken Shelby and pound them into the ground.

As he stepped down from the plane, a limousine rolled to a stop beside it. The chauffeur got out and opened the rear door. Patrick O'Hara got out and turned to help Kate to her feet. She crossed the tarmac and hugged Daniel. "Patrick and I have been beside ourselves since we heard."

"I can't believe it's happened again." Patrick ran a hand through his hair. "I can't imagine what Shelby's going through."

Daniel didn't want to imagine it, either. Though he'd tried to sleep on the plane, he'd been plagued with scenario after scenario, each worse than the last.

"Have you received any calls, ransom notes, anything?" he asked.

Kate nodded. "I got this today. It arrived in the mailbox."

Daniel turned the envelope over. No return address, no stamp and only *Kate Winston* printed in block letters. He pulled the slip of paper out of the envelope, unfolded it and read the words aloud, "'Publicly renounce your candidacy for president or your granddaughter dies.'"

"This sounds like Cartel tactics." Daniel glanced up.

"I had already toyed with the idea of backing out. My family has been through enough without bearing the additional threats and scrutiny of running for the highest office in the nation."

"And now?" Daniel asked.

"After all that's happened, and with Shelby missing again, I'm positive the position of president is not for me. I was encouraged to run to keep Richard Nelson from being elected. My sources tell me he's heavily connected to the Cartel. So your statement that this is mafia tactics might not be too far from the truth. The last thing this nation needs is a Cartel-owned government." She shook her head. "It doesn't matter whether or not I'm running or why. What does matter is that we get Shelby back."

"What are you going to do?" Daniel asked.

She slipped an arm around Patrick's waist and he hugged her close.

Daniel could see the love in Patrick's eyes for the former vice president. Apparently that love hadn't waned over the forty years since they'd last seen each other. What would it feel like to love someone so much you couldn't see yourself with anyone else?

An image of Shelby popped into Daniel's head. Shelby walking along the land bridge. Shelby's face shining in the glow of the fire, her smile when she ran to get on the WaveRunner, hot-dogging out on the water. He could still feel the softness of her hand in his and smell the fragrance of her hair.

"I have a press conference scheduled for tomorrow morning. I'm planning to make the announcement and hope she's released. If anything happens to my grand-daughter because of me, I could never forgive myself."

Daniel nodded. "We're going to get her back."

"Damn right we are," Patrick agreed. "She means the world to me."

Kate smiled sadly. "I want to know her. She's all I have left of the daughter I never met." Kate's voice caught.

Patrick's arm tightened around her. "Let's get back to the house. Kate's boys are gathering there. If we all put our heads together, we'll come up with a plan to bring Shelby back."

The three of them climbed into the limousine and the driver took them to the Winston Estate.

Thad, Trey, and Samuel Winston waited in the con-ference room, sitting in the leather chairs around the large table. They all stood as Kate breezed in and took the seat at the head, Patrick at her side. She nodded to Daniel. "Please, fill them in."

Daniel remained standing. He told them how they'd been sideswiped by a vehicle in Bar Harbor and how a boat had almost run them over on the WaveRunner. When he spoke of how he'd been knocked out only to awaken and find Shelby missing, the three brothers leaned forward, their jaws tight, fists clenched.

Daniel held up the note demanding that Kate for-mally announce that she had no intention of running for president. "This is just one clue as to who might be at the bottom of this."

"Mom's potential opponent for the party nomination, Richard Nelson, has been linked to a group that likes to call itself the Cartel," Sam said. " This is just the kind of dirty dealing they like to do. Rather than let the public decide, they've gone so far as to kill off candidates to ensure their nominee wins."

Thad sat forward. "I can ask around. We might have an undercover operative from the police force working with the Cartel."

"Check on it." Daniel glanced around at all the people in the room. "The whole purpose of me taking Shelby to my parents' house in Maine was to get her as far away from potential kidnappers as possible and hide her. Since she was kidnapped anyway, we know someone leaked her location to the Cartel."

The brothers all frowned at once and started to rise.

"Are you accusing us of ratting out our own niece?" Thad asked.

"He's doing no such thing." Kate stood and gave her sons a stern look. "Sit. Daniel has a point. Let him speak."

"Thank you." Now that he was on the ground, Daniel's head was clear and he'd had time to think about the entire situation. A couple of things stood out in his mind. "Over the past few months, members of the Winston family have been the targets of attempted murder on a number of occasions."

Trey piped up, "The shooting at the fund-raiser. The one that landed Mother and you in the hospital."

Daniel nodded, the injuries still fresh in his mind and still causing him some pain. He glanced across the conference table at Kate. She'd been in physical therapy almost as long as he had.

Sam added, "Then there was the brainwashing of soldiers to work as assassins, including my army buddy who tried to shoot Mother at Trey and Debra's wedding."

"And when Sam pulled a gun on Trey." Thad shook his head.

"It leads me to think the Cartel has some connections in pretty high places." Daniel paced to the end of the table and turned to face the Winstons and Patrick. "Places that have the means and position to capture or incarcerate U.S. soldiers and manipulate their minds to do their bidding. So far, their attempts have been aimed at the Winston family. And then there was D'Angelis."

"A Secret Service agent—" Thad started.

"One of your organization," Sam interjected.

"And a mole in our mother's security team," Trey finished.

"Murdered in a seemingly secure facility," Patrick said.

In between stabbing pain and semiconsciousness, Daniel's mind had played over all the scenarios. "The way I see it, everything culminates with the attacks on Shelby and the demand for Kate to back out of running for president. Someone has been targeting Kate and her family to keep her from running."

"Seems like a whole lot of trouble to get her to quit," Thad observed. "Why not use the usual tactics of mudslinging?"

"Whoever is behind all the attempts is connected with the Cartel and in a position of power within our own government. Capable of brainwashing and using

U.S. soldiers as assassins to do his dirty work. And he had to have known I was taking Shelby to Maine."

Trey raised his hand. "None of us would want our mother dead, and we wouldn't hurt Shelby. Hell, we didn't know she existed until Patrick came knocking on the door."

"And none of us are in a high position of power," Sam said.

Patrick gripped Kate's hand. "I don't think any of the people in this room could have leaked the information about Shelby's whereabouts. But there was one other person who knew, who was there when we discussed the plan."

Kate's face hardened. "Jed Kincannon."

Daniel's jaw tightened and a knot formed in his gut. "I don't like the idea of accusing my own boss of kidnapping, attempted murder or anything else, but it's the only scenario that makes sense. I called him from Maine to inform him of the attack on the truck I was driving and the boat incident. I knew then we'd been compromised, but he told me to stay put a little longer."

"So that his men could get in place and steal the girl," Thad said.

The muscles in Daniel's jaw tightened. "The more I thought about it, the more it began to make sense. Why else would the director of the Secret Service spend so much time with Kate? He's a director—he should be running the organization at the highest level, not working in the trenches."

"Jed was there the day I mentioned running for president." Kate sighed. "I thought it was a good idea. But after holding the office of vice president, I have no real desire to be the president. I'd rather spend time with my grandchildren, getting to know them." Her eyes filled. "I want to get to know Shelby and be there any time she might need my help. I didn't get to know my daughter. I'll be damned if I miss out on my grand-daughter."

Patrick kissed her forehead. "You'll get that chance."

Daniel nodded. "So here's the deal. We need information on Jed Kincannon."

Thad stood. "I can run some checks, but I'm betting his record is clean. He wouldn't hold the office of director if he had any blemishes on his record. I'll notify the FBI and have them set up surveillance here in the house to monitor the phones. If the kidnappers make contact, they might be able to trace the call."

"My campaign managers are good at digging up dirt." Trey rose to stand beside Thad. "I can check old photographs of political events. Maybe something will turn up showing a connection between Kincannon and Nelson and any known members of the Cartel."

"An old friend of mine has contacts at the television station," Trey said. "Perhaps I can find video footage of Kincannon, Nelson and Cartel members."

Daniel's chest swelled. When the going got tough, the Winston family pulled together in a united front. "And I'll follow Kincannon and see if his movements shed light on his activities and possibly the location where they're keeping Shelby."

"What about us?" Patrick asked.

"You two have to be here with the FBI, or whoever sets up the communications surveillance, in case the kidnappers call." Daniel glanced around the room. "Keep in contact. If you find anything, even the most seemingly insignificant clue, let me know."

"It goes both ways," Thad reminded him.

Daniel nodded. "Everyone has their jobs to do. Let's get to it. I'm going now to report in to my boss."

Kate stared across at Daniel. "What are you going to say?"

"Just the facts, nothing about our suspicions. For now, I'd like to keep my return as under the radar as possible." He glanced around the room. "No one is to know I'm back. Please make that clear to the limousine driver and Maddie, the housekeeper. And it would be best if we all pretend this meeting never happened. I suggest you call Kincannon and let him know you got a note and want to know the status of your grand-daughter. Act as if it's the first time you've heard the news when he informs you she's been kidnapped."

"I will." Kate laid a hand on his arm. "Be careful, Daniel. If it really is Kincannon orchestrating all this violence, he's proved that he's dangerous."

"I know. But someone has to get close enough to him to follow him. Who better than his direct report?"

Chapter 18

The car carrying Shelby drove for an hour or more before it stopped and the two goons who'd attacked her got out, slamming the doors.

In the pitch-black interior of the trunk, she had no clue where she was or what they would do with her. Having been kidnapped before made her numb to fear for herself. She was more concerned about Daniel. What had they done to him in order to get to her? Had they killed him or left him injured and bleeding somewhere?

Shelby prayed Daniel's family found him in time to save him.

This time, she had a glimmer of hope. If Daniel was able to, he'd come after her. He'd found her once; surely he could find her again.

Lying in the dark, all she had were the images in her mind of growing up with her grandfather and, more recently, the days and nights she'd shared with Daniel both in North Carolina and in Maine. To keep from going insane, she replayed those images in her mind like video recordings, examining every scene, noting the details as if she was admiring beautiful flowers. When she felt a panic attack sneaking up on her, she remembered how great it felt to be in Daniel's arms.

She'd told herself she was satisfied with whatever time she could have with him. But she'd been lying to herself. Maybe she was greedy and selfish, but she wanted to spend a lifetime with Daniel Henderson. He made her come alive in his arms, and to not have him in her life would be like not being able to breathe.

The trunk popped open and the two men who'd kidnapped her leaned in and grabbed her beneath the arms and legs and hauled her out of the car, standing her on her feet.

They wore ski masks over their faces, so Shelby couldn't tell who they were. One of them tossed a dark pillowcase over her head and duct taped it around her neck. What little light was available was snuffed out by the dark fabric.

The larger of the two thugs tossed Shelby over his shoulder and carried her away from the car.

Her belly bounced against his shoulder and blood rushed to her head, making her dizzy.

Unable to see, Shelby concentrated on the sounds around her. An engine started up. Not like a car engine, more like that of a small aircraft. Then the ape was carrying her up steps and ducking as if to enter a small space.

At last, the man dropped her onto what she assumed was a floor.

The engine sound increased and whatever they were in started moving, the entire craft rumbling across the ground, the speed picking up, faster and faster, then the rumbling stopped and the vehicle floated.

She was in an airplane, bound for where, she didn't know. Fear found its way back into her psyche, knowing she was getting farther and farther away from Daniel.

In a country as vast as the United States, they could be taking her anywhere and no one would ever find her. For all she knew, they could be taking her anywhere in the world.

By the time Daniel showered and shaved, the sun had risen. Dressed and ready for the day, he placed a call to Jed Kincannon using a phone Thad had loaned him that would display "Blocked Sender" in the caller ID on the other end of the call.

When the director picked up, Daniel said, "Director Kincannon, Daniel Henderson here. I'm glad you picked up. My phone is dead and I'm using one I purchased until I can get mine replaced. Did I catch you at home?"

"I was just about to head out to the office. What's happening?" Kincannon asked.

If this man was truly behind all the attempts on the Winston family, he knew damn well what was happening. Daniel sucked in a deep breath to calm his anger. "They got past me. The O'Hara woman was kidnapped."

His boss cursed. "Did you see who took her? Can you identify her attackers?"

"No, they knocked me out before I could get a look at them."

"I'll notify Mrs. Winston as soon as possible and send agents to your parent's home to help in the investigation."

"I'd appreciate that. I know how heartbroken she will be and I… Well, I just can't face her. I've failed to do my job and protect the former vice president's granddaughter."

"We'll discuss your performance when you return. When will you be heading back?"

"I got hit pretty hard. The docs here want me to take it easy, not go far in case of concussion."

"Let me know when you get back to Raleigh. I'll find you a new assignment."

"Thank you, sir. Please tell Mrs. Winston how sorry I am."

"Got a call coming in now from her. I'll tell her."

Daniel hung up and hurried downstairs, wearing a gray hoodie and sunglasses. Staying in the shadows, he walked out the front gate and down the road where Samuel Winston had arranged to leave a nondescript rental car for him.

Climbing in, Daniel grinned. On the seat beside him sat a pair of binoculars and a listening device like those used by private detectives. Where Sam had come up with the device, Daniel didn't know and really didn't care. Armed with it, he'd have a better chance of staying out of sight while listening in on Kincannon's conversations.

Daniel drove to Director Kincannon's home and parked a couple houses away along the side of the road. He slumped down in the seat, the listening device switched on.

He didn't hear any conversations and presumed either Kincannon was in the shower or had already left for the office.

Twenty minutes later, he heard the man saying goodbye to what sounded like his wife, then the garage door opened and Kincannon left his house in a sleek and sporty Lexus.

He drove in the expected direction, toward the building in which the agency had rented offices, parked in his reserved parking space and carried a briefcase inside.

Daniel aimed the listening device at Kincannon's office window on the second floor and waited for the man to slip up and reveal information on Shelby's whereabouts.

Twice people came into his office talking about mundane papers that needed signing, and Kincannon answered the phone on his desk three times. None of the conversations sounded like coordination with kidnappers or the Cartel. The longer Daniel sat in the car, the more frustrated he became. Shelby was out there somewhere, possibly being tortured or mistreated by her captors. He had to find her soon. And if she had seen or recognized the people who were behind her abduction, even if Mrs. Winston backed out of the presidential race, Shelby could be murdered to keep her silence. Time was not on their side.

Kate was due to give her speech at eleven o'clock that morning in front of the Raleigh courthouse. She'd called a press conference and had Debra notify reporters across the nation of the speech Kate would make.

Daniel hoped the public announcement would keep Shelby alive long enough for them to find and release her.

The lump at the back of his head ached, and he needed sleep, but he couldn't let himself drift off. Not when Shelby's life was at stake.

As lunchtime approached, the cell phone in the car's cup holder rang.

Daniel hit the talk button and fumbled with the phone to get it to his ear, knocking his head on the back of the seat in the process.

"Henderson, it's Trey."

"Whatcha got?"

"My campaign manager is a miracle worker. If you ever want to run a dirty campaign, he's your man."

"What did he find?"

"Several images of Kincannon walking and talking with Richard Nelson. There's another shot of him playing golf with Nelson at a club in Bethesda, Maryland."

"So he meets with Nelson. What else?" Daniel asked, impatiently.

Someone had entered Kincannon's office and they were talking in lowered voices.

"There are also clips of Richard Nelson talking with Frank Chambliss at a charity ball, and of them arriving at a D.C. gala in the same limo."

"Frank Chambliss." Daniel rolled the name over in his mind. "Hasn't he been rumored to be in bed with the Cartel?"

"Not only in bed, but he might just be the lead. Nothing verified. But then no one gets inside the Cartel easily, and once in, they don't get out. Those who've attempted to get out or share information about the Cartel end up in the Potomac River."

"Nice. Sounds like Richard is living up to the rumors."

The conversation in Kincannon's office was getting a little heated, the voices almost loud enough Daniel could hear them.

"Look, Trey, this is good information. Good job. I have to go now."

"Are you following Kincannon?"

"I am."

"Just remember, we don't need more heroes. Call us if you need backup. I'm going to text you the photos."

"Thanks."

Daniel hit the end button and turned up the volume on the listening device.

"Shh. She's about to go on now."

Kincannon's office grew quiet and then the sound of a news reporter came across the device, announcing Kate Winston.

Kate's voice came through some static as she spoke to the crowd in front of the Wake County Courthouse.

Daniel turned on his radio and turned the dial until he found a local station with Kate's voice crisp and clear.

"I want to thank all the people of Raleigh and of the country for their support while I was vice president of the United States and for their continuing support as I navigated my responsibilities after my term expired.

"Now I'd like to discuss the race for president of the United States."

A roaring cheer rose from the crowd and Mrs. Winston had to wait until the din subsided before continuing.

"Much as I enjoy serving the country that I love with all my heart, I want to quell all the rumors with the following statement. I am no longer considering running for president of the United States. If my party leaders ask, I will politely decline.

"I've already done my civic duty. It's time for someone else to step up to the plate. I think it's a great honor and a privilege. However, I want to spend time with my family.

"Again, thank you for all of your support. It means a great deal to me and I wish you happiness and peace in the future. Thank you."

The news reporter went on with a recap of the speech and Daniel switched off the radio, his heart swelling with the emotion he felt for Kate Winston. She was one classy lady. And if anyone deserved to be president, it was her. She had her head on straight and she wasn't afraid to stand up to either side of the political fence. The country needed more leaders like Kate.

"You think she meant it?" the man in Kincannon's office asked.

"Sure she meant it. If there's one thing I've learned about Kate Winston, she doesn't lie." Kincannon paused. "Should I make that call?"

"No. I want you to take care of it in person. We won't want to leave any witnesses."

"Got it," Kincannon said.

A door clicked closed in the office and the room was silent. Then the sound of a second door closing was the last thing Daniel heard.

Daniel sat forward, his heart racing. What did the

men mean when they said they didn't want to leave any witnesses?

Not once had they mentioned Shelby or a woman being held hostage. What else could they be talking about?

If they were talking about Shelby, would they kill her even though they'd gotten what they'd demanded?

Daniel started the engine and waited for Kincannon to leave the building.

Several minutes passed, and he didn't come out the front door. A vehicle exited from the back parking area.

Daniel lifted the binoculars to his eyes and focused on the dark gray four-door sedan. He caught a glimpse of the driver. It wasn't Kincannon. He shifted his gaze to the passenger.

Kincannon.

The vehicle turned onto the road and sped away in the opposite direction.

Daniel floored the accelerator and yanked the steering wheel hard to the left, pulling a U-turn in the middle of the busy road. Tires squealed as other drivers hit their brakes, screeching to a stop, just short of crashing into Daniel.

Unfazed by the commotion he'd caused but thankful no one was hurt, Daniel kept his eye on the gray sedan as he broke speed limits to catch up. He stayed back far enough he wouldn't be noticed, but close enough that he'd see when they turned.

His cell phone buzzed, indicating an incoming text. He ignored it, keeping his gaze fixed on the vehicle that could possibly lead to Shelby. It *had* to lead to

Shelby. He didn't have any other clues, and his gut said this was it.

They turned off the main road and wove through some smaller roads, heading into a rundown residential neighborhood where men walked the streets and small children ran around with no adult supervision in unkempt yards. The deeper they went, the more rundown the houses became, some of them boarded up, others with roofs caving in.

It became impossible to follow close behind the sedan and not be noticed. Daniel had to wait at corners and drive past turns to keep the driver from noticing his vehicle trailing them. He thought he'd lost them once when he had to parallel their path one block over.

His heart pounded against his ribs as he sped to the end of the street and turned back in the direction he'd last seen them.

Then he saw them at a stop sign, turning his direction.

Keeping his cool when his insides were quaking, Daniel drove past and kept going, watching in his rearview mirror as they turned into an abandoned schoolyard, the chain-link fence falling down and the windows busted out in the classrooms. It appeared to be an old high school that had long since sunk into disrepair.

Kincannon's vehicle pulled around the back of the building.

Daniel drove past the next house until he was certain his car was out of sight. He pulled up in the driveway of a vacant house, the for-sale sign trampled in the knee-high grass. Shifting into Park, he jumped out and ran back the way he'd come, dodging between trees, bushes and derelict buildings.

He had to get to Shelby before Jed and his thugs did something terrible.

As he neared the old school, he paused in the shadows of the vacant house across the street. There were no bushes or anything to conceal him as he crossed the road. He'd be risking his life if Kincannon had guards positioned in or around the building, watching for intruders.

He pulled the pistol out of his shoulder holster tucked beneath his jacket, released the clip, checked to see that it was full and slapped it back into the grip. Then he stared down at his phone. The image that had been texted to him was of the man he'd seen driving Kincannon away from the office building. The caption attached to the picture read "Nelson and Chambliss." Damn. He'd suspected the man who'd been talking to Kincannon was bad, but now he was beginning to think he was worse than he'd originally thought. Frank Chambliss was possibly the head honcho of the most powerful and notorious Mafia group in the country.

If Chambliss was who they thought he was, he would be ruthless. If he meant leave no witnesses, he was there to kill Shelby.

Daniel keyed his location into the phone and hit Send, returning the text to Trey with the message, Send backup, ASAP.

Trouble was, he couldn't wait for backup. Shelby might not be alive long enough for the cavalry to arrive.

He pulled the hoodie up over his head and ducked his chin to keep his face in the shadows, then he stepped away from the building, his gun in his pocket, hand on the grip, finger ready to pull the trigger.

He strolled across the street as if he didn't care where he was going. If someone looked out the window, they'd see a young man walking along, kicking pebbles.

He passed the school and walked on to a gap in the broken chain-link fence. Bushes almost covered the gap. At the very least, no one would see him from the school when he slipped through the hole in the fence. Once through, he had to cross an old parking lot to get to the side entrance of the two-story building.

He paused in the leaves of the bush and stared up at the building. A shadow moved in one of the broken upper windows. The metal tip of a rifle poked out, a man wearing dark clothes positioned behind it. His gun was pointed toward the front, main entrance.

When Daniel was as sure as he could be, he hurried across the open space, trying to move as quietly as he could. Just as he reached the wall, his foot dislodged a small rock and sent it skittering across the broken pavement.

He plastered himself to the wall of the building, praying the shooter in the window above couldn't see over the edge of the broken glass without sticking his head through the jagged edges.

Daniel froze and carefully looked up. The nose of the rifle pointed toward the location where the rock had rolled, three feet away from where he stood. After several long, agonizing moments, the rifle turned toward the front entrance again.

Letting the air out of his lungs, Daniel waited a fraction of a second longer and then eased his way around to the side of the building and peered through the dirty window in the door. The hallway was empty and the chain around the door had been cut, the door hanging drunkenly on its hinges.

Daniel passed it and checked the back of the building. The gray sedan was parked between two rundown portable buildings, completely hidden to the casual observer. Nothing else stirred behind the building.

Daniel retraced his steps to the side door and eased it open enough he could slide through. He listened before stepping inside.

Voices and footsteps in the hallway made him pause, his back to the wall. He waited for the voices to fade before he slid through the gap and ducked into the first classroom. The once-polished tiles were yellow with age, and a stack of old student desks was bunched in the middle of the room, most of them broken.

With his gun out in front of him, Daniel moved low and fast down the hallway, checking every room for Shelby. When he reached the halfway point, he noticed a doorway marked Staff Only leading into a stairwell that only went down.

Voices echoed off the walls of the basement below.

"You'd be better off taking her to where you want to dispose of her," Kincannon was saying.

"We won't find a more perfect place than here." Chambliss said. "It's abandoned. No one will come near here for weeks."

The sound of someone moaning made rage bubble up inside Daniel. He fought the urge to charge down the stairs, shooting every one of the men holding Shelby hostage and talking about killing her as if she didn't count for anything.

She was everything. Bright, beautiful, independent and fun to be with, and just beginning her life as an adult. She deserved to live longer, have children of her own and be happy, damn it.

"Go ahead, Jed," Chambliss said. "This has been your project from the start. Finish it."

"Have one of your men do it. I didn't sign on to bloody my hands," Kincannon claimed.

Daniel eased down the metal stairs, carefully placing one foot after the other. When the stairs began to angle to the left, he could see the basement stretched out in front of him, Kincannon and Chambliss at the center, Shelby bound and gagged with duct tape, lying on her side on the floor. She was the only one facing him. Everyone else, including the three thugs with AR15s slung over their shoulders, were gazing down at her.

Daniel could tell the moment when she spotted him. Her eyes widened and she jerked her head as if to say no.

He lifted his finger to his lips.

Chambliss shoved a gun into Kincannon's hands. "Do it now, or I'll kill her. And then I'll kill you."

Kincannon pushed the gun toward the man. "Don't threaten me. You and Nelson need me to see him elected into office. You kill me and you lose your government connection."

"Seems you already ruined that when your assassins were caught. And now that the Winston woman isn't running for office, we really don't require your services anymore." Chambliss took the pistol Kincannon had pointed at him. Instead of aiming it at Shelby, he aimed it at Kincannon's head.

"What the hell are you doing?"

"What does it take to get through to you that we don't need you anymore? I told you I was getting rid of all the witnesses. Since we don't need you, you're nothing but a witness."

No matter how much Daniel hated Kincannon for his betrayal, he couldn't stand by and let Chambliss kill him. He aimed at Chambliss's arm and pulled the trigger.

Chambliss yelped and the gun flew from his hand and skidded across the floor.

The three men who'd had their rifles slung over their shoulder tilted them upward, all aiming at him.

Daniel leaped over the railing as they opened fire, landed on the concrete floor, rolled and dived behind a short wall of concrete blocks.

Once on the ground, he picked off the thugs one by one until all three lay writhing or dead on the ground.

"Don't move and I might spare your lives," Daniel called out. From where he huddled behind the concrete wall, he could see Kincannon standing, but he couldn't see where Shelby lay on the ground.

Chambliss threw himself down, reaching for his fallen gun. Daniel fired again, hitting Chambliss in the head, killing him instantly.

When he shifted his attention back to Kincannon, the man had disappeared.

Daniel rolled out from behind the concrete wall, pointing his gun at the spot where Shelby had been.

Kincannon yanked her to her feet by her hair and pointed a pistol at her temple. "One more step and I pull the trigger."

"It's over, Kincannon. It's only a matter of time

before the police arrive, and you won't have any way of escaping."

"You know as well as I do that hostages make great shields. Miss O'Hara is my ticket out of here. Kate won't let any harm come to her."

"You won't get far."

Kincannon sneered. "Oh, I think I will. I prepared for this. I have a backup plan."

"You won't get out of here."

Footsteps pounded down the hallway toward them.

Daniel knew it was too soon for the police or SWAT team, but Kincannon didn't know that.

"They're coming. Put the gun down or they'll shoot," Daniel said, praying Kincannon would do as he said before the shooter from the third floor burst into the basement.

"No way. I'm not giving up my—"

Shelby pitched sideways, slammed her head into Kincannon's. She pivoted and brought her knee up into his groin, and then dropped to the ground, landing on her side.

As Kincannon aimed his weapon at Shelby, the shooter from the third floor stormed down the staircase.

Daniel had to choose whether to shoot Kincannon or the man coming down the stairs.

Daniel pulled the trigger, aiming for Kincannon, and then threw himself to the floor, rolled to his feet and fired at the man on the stairs.

Kincannon jerked backward and fell flat on his back.

The shooter on the stairs jumped to the concrete floor and raised his rifle, getting off one round as Daniel pulled the trigger again, hitting the man square in the chest.

The shooter's bullet hit Daniel in the shoulder less than a second later, slamming him backward to land hard, the goose-egg–size bump on his head bouncing off the concrete.

Daniel's vision blurred and he struggled to stay conscious. Sirens blared in the distance as he pushed to his hands and knees.

Shelby sat up, tears streaming from her eyes.

Behind her, Kincannon lurched up, holding his gun.

"Get down!" Daniel yelled.

Chapter 19

Shelby dropped back flat on the ground as a shot blasted out behind her. She glanced back at Kincannon, who had fired his gun. She spun back toward Daniel, her heart banging against her chest. Apparently, the shot had gone wide, giving Daniel enough time to raise his uninjured arm and nail the bastard who'd become a traitor to his own country.

"Henderson! Shelby!" A voice echoed through the hallway above them.

"Down here!" Daniel called, hurrying over to Shelby, his arm hanging down by his side. He carefully peeled the tape off her mouth, the adhesive ripping at her skin. "Are you okay?"

She coughed, cleared her throat and breathed in through her mouth, then answered. "I'm okay, but you're bleeding. Get me out of this so I can help."

With her hands still bound in front of her, she could only nod at his shoulder.

"Just a flesh wound." He tried to raise the arm, winced and left it hanging at his side as he tore one-handed through the tape on her wrists.

She raised the tape to her teeth and tried to bite her way through the thick tape. She had to get loose and help him. "Daniel, forget about me. Do something to stop the bleeding."

"I'm fine, I tell you." He smiled and pulled her against him with his good arm. "I'm just happy that I got here in time."

She laughed. "You and me both."

"I didn't realize just how much I'd miss you until you were gone." He bent to kiss her gently on her raw lips. "You scared me more than I've ever been scared in my life."

She leaned her cheek against his. "I knew you'd find me."

"I don't see how. At first, I didn't have a clue who'd taken you. But damn it, I had to find you." He kissed her cheek and softly brushed her lips with his again. "I'd move heaven and earth for you."

She smiled. "I know."

Footsteps clanked down the metal stairs into the basement. Men in black uniforms and bulletproof vests with scary guns stormed into the basement.

"You're too late." Shelby chuckled. "Daniel took care of it all."

"I had help from one amazing, determined woman." He kissed her nose as a paramedic eased him to the side and ripped the shirt away from his shoulder wound.

Another paramedic cut the tape away from Shelby's

wrists and peeled it off her skin. When she was free, she went to Daniel and held his good hand while the paramedic applied a pressure bandage to his shoulder.

"We'll have to take him to the hospital. He's lost a lot of blood and there's no exit wound. The doc's gonna have to go fishing for that bullet."

"Great." Daniel smiled and winced as they pressed the bandage to his shoulder. "I don't care. Shelby's alive, we've found the person behind all of the attacks and, if I'm not mistaken, Chambliss there is the leader of the Cartel. With the head pinched off the snake, there won't be much trouble coming from them for a while."

The medic leaned over him. "Sir, we're going to load you on the stretcher now."

"I can walk," Daniel insisted.

"Sir, let us do our jobs. Your job is done here."

Shelby laughed at the glare on Daniel's face. "Do it, you hardheaded man."

"I just found you again. I don't want to let you out of my sight. You have a habit of disappearing."

"I'm not going anywhere." Shelby turned to the paramedics. "Can I ride with him in the ambulance?"

"Are you a relative?" the medic asked.

Before Shelby could respond, Daniel said, "Yes."

"Then you may."

The medics eased a disgruntled Daniel onto a stretcher and carried him out of the basement.

Thad, Trey and Sam arrived as Shelby emerged from the old schoolhouse, and joined her as the medics loaded Daniel into the ambulance.

"He's going to be okay," Sam said.

Trey curled an arm around her shoulder. "We'll

bring your grandmother and grandfather to the hospital and sit with you while Daniel's in surgery. They'll want to be there for him as well as you."

Shelby smiled. "Thank you." Then, on impulse, she leaned up and kissed Trey's cheek. "I think I'll like having uncles looking out for me."

"Hey, where's mine?" Thad turned his cheek and bent for her to give him a kiss, and Sam did the same.

"Gotta go now." The paramedic helped her up into the back of the ambulance and they closed the door.

She held Daniel's hand all the way to the hospital, filling him in on what had happened from the time she'd been kidnapped to his finding her in the basement of the abandoned school.

She'd never been happier to see anyone.

When they arrived at the hospital, Kate was there with her grandfather. He had his arm around Kate's waist, and not like a friendly hug, but an intimate one.

Too worried about Daniel to think about the progression of a relationship between her grandmother and her grandfather, Shelby pushed it to the back of her mind and followed the stretcher carrying Daniel into the hospital.

Before they took him to surgery, Daniel said, "Wait."

The orderlies stopped and let Daniel address Shelby.

She lifted his hand and brought it to her sore lips.

"Will you be here when I get out of surgery?" he asked.

"You bet."

Daniel stared around her at Thad, Trey, Samuel, Kate and Patrick. "You heard her. I'm counting on you to make it happen."

"We'll keep an eye on her," Trey said.

Thad chuckled. "You singlehandedly took care of the threat. I don't know what you're worried about."

They rolled him away and Shelby turned back to her grandfather and Kate, tears welling in her eyes. "He's going to be okay, isn't he?"

Kate and her grandfather wrapped their arms around her.

"Daniel is a fighter," Kate said.

Lucy joined Thad, slipped her arm around him and addressed the folks gathered. "From what the paramedics said, he'll be okay. It's a fairly clean wound to his shoulder. Once they dig the bullet out, he'll be back to normal in no time."

The tears fell faster. And Shelby couldn't stop them.

"What's wrong, dear?" Kate brushed the hair from Shelby's wet cheeks.

Shelby sniffed and tried to get a grip. "Now that the threat is taken care of, Daniel will be reassigned."

"Oh, Shelby, that's what Secret Service agents do."

"I know," she sniffed. "It's just that I've gotten used to him being around. I don't want him to leave."

"Don't you worry, dear. Things always work out," Kate said.

"Sometimes it takes forty years, but they work out." Patrick cupped Kate's cheek and gazed into her eyes.

The ever-handy Debra pulled a tissue from her pocket. As she reached out, she doubled over slightly. "Ow."

"What is it, sweetheart?" Trey asked, his arm going around Debra, his brow wrinkled in concern.

Debra straightened and smiled. "Nothing. Just a really strong Braxton Hicks contraction. I'm okay. The baby's not due for another two weeks." She handed Shelby the tissue. "Got this from the nurses' desk. Thought you could use it."

Shelby accepted it gladly, patted her eyes and cheeks dry and looked around the room at the people who were now her family. They stood strong in support of Daniel and her. She only ever dreamed of being part of a big family...and now she was.

Her eyes welled again.

"What's wrong, Shelby Raye?" Her grandfather pulled her into his arms. "Lucy said Daniel's gonna be all right."

"It's just that it's nice to have so much support from..."

"From all of us?" Kate asked.

"No, from my family." Shelby smiled through her tears.

Kate's eyes filled and she pulled Shelby into her arms. "I'd give anything to have known your mother. But I'm very happy that you're now in my life so that I can get to know and love you."

Shelby's grandfather hugged her, as well. Soon, Thad, Sam and Trey, Lucy and Debra joined the hug and they ended up laughing and smiling.

When the doctor finally emerged from surgery, he gave them the good news that Daniel would make a full recovery and be able to return to duty soon.

Surrounded by her family, Shelby was happy for Daniel, knowing he loved his job as a Secret Service agent, but sad for herself. In the short time that they'd known each other, she'd learned that he was special. A man she could trust. A man she could love with all her heart.

And now he would be leaving.

Her heart already aching, Shelby wondered how long would it take for her to get over him.

Shelby glanced at her grandmother and grandfather. As far as she could tell, her grandfather had never loved anyone else for forty long years.

Would that be her? Would she refuse to love another after loving Daniel?

Daniel arrived back in Raleigh two weeks after his surgery. Shelby had been at the hospital the entire time he'd been there, fetching him water, fluffing his pillow and sitting with him when he thought he'd go nuts from boredom. And he'd only been in the hospital two nights.

As soon as he was released from the hospital, the new director of the Secret Service had called him to the main offices in D.C. where he'd spent the next week and a half debriefing a panel of agents and the director on Kincannon's role in the attempts on the lives of Kate Winston and her family.

When the hearing was over, the director had commended him for his selfless acts and had given him a citation for heroism. He and the panel had been so impressed with his efforts, the director had offered him any position within the agency Daniel wanted, including the highly coveted position of guarding the president of the United States.

Daniel had told the director he'd think about it.

And he had. Until he'd gotten a better offer.

Kate Winston had asked him back to Raleigh where she'd offered him the position of head of security for Adair Enterprises. She'd told him not to decide right

away, but to come back for her official press conference where she had some announcements to make. At
that time, she hoped he'd give her his answer.

Samuel Winston and his fiancée, Olivia, picked him
up at the airport.

"Mother would have come with us to welcome you
home, but things have been pretty crazy over the past
couple weeks."

"Everyone is okay?" Daniel asked. He'd gotten close
to the Winstons during his time as their bodyguard and
had a lot of respect for Kate and her sons.

"If you're asking about Shelby," Olivia interjected,
leaning over the back of the seat, "she's doing fine.
She's fully recovered from her kidnapping ordeals and
has gotten back on track with her studies. She's due
to finish her coursework by the end of the semester."

Samuel grinned. "That woman is like a bulldog.
When she wants something she goes after it. It's still
hard to believe I'm an uncle twice over."

Daniel's brows drew together. "Twice?"

Samuel turned from the steering wheel. "You
haven't heard?" He laughed. "Debra went into labor
the day after you went to D.C. She had a baby boy.
She and Trey named him Adair Winston. After the
press conference, we're headed to the church for his
christening."

"I guess I have been out of the picture. That's great
news. What's the press conference about?"

"You'll see. Let Mother tell you all about it." Samuel glanced across at Daniel. "Have you thought about
Mother's offer?"

Daniel had, but he hadn't made a decision. "Some."

"Well, if it helps, I was a career soldier. I was so

focused on being a soldier, I lost sight of what I was fighting for. I forgot to live my life. Being that focused is great to help keep you alive, but doesn't necessarily allow you to live. When I came back from Afghanistan, I didn't know what to do with my life." He shot a smile over his shoulder at Olivia. "I know now. You need to really think about what you want out of life. Leaving the Secret Service isn't a betrayal to your country. It's a choice to allow yourself to live life to its fullest." Samuel shrugged. "Think about it."

Daniel already had.

Samuel pulled into the parking lot of the church the Winstons attended and parked in a reserved spot. The lot was full of vehicles and news vans. Reporters gathered around the steps of the church.

"Mother decided to make her announcement here, since the christening is to take place immediately following."

Daniel climbed out of the vehicle, his arm still in a sling. He searched the crowd for one face. The face that had haunted his dreams for the past two weeks.

The double doors to the church opened and Kate Winston emerged with Patrick O'Hara at her side. She was followed by her other two sons, along with Debra and Lucy.

"Come on, the party is about to begin." Samuel held Olivia's hand and led the way through the throng.

Daniel followed, unsure of his role in this press conference as he hadn't given Kate his response yet.

"Thank you all for coming this fine day," Kate began, smiling brightly. "I have a few announcements to make, and then you all should go enjoy this incredible sunshine.

"I'd like to begin by sharing my joy at welcoming my grandson Adair Winston into the world. I, my son Trey and my personal assistant who happens to be his wife, Debra, are over the moon with the addition to our family."

Trey held the baby in his arms, smiling for the cameras as they flashed.

Kate went on. "I'd also like to announce that I have another grandchild." She paused, her eyes misting. "When I was a young woman, not even out of my teens, I gave birth to a baby girl. Carrie." Kate reached for Patrick's hand. "I was very much in love with the baby's father, but due to complications of a breech birth, I was anesthetized. When I awoke, I was told the baby had died. My father kept the entire matter from the public and I mourned my baby's death in private.

"Not until forty years later did I learn my baby girl had not died in childbirth. She'd lived and had been raised by her father and went on to have a baby girl of her own. Sadly, my daughter died in an automobile accident."

Kate blinked back tears, biting down on her lip to keep it from trembling. When she had herself together again, she continued.

"I'd like to present my first grandchild, Shelby O'Hara. A very special young woman I hope to get to know and love as much as I love her grandfather."

Kate drew Shelby forward to the sound of applause and shouted words of congratulations.

Shelby blushed and her gaze found Daniel's, her eyes widening. The corners of her lips lifted into a dazzling smile.

Daniel's heart swelled to the point he thought he

might bust the buttons off the suit jacket he wore. He couldn't wait for the press conference to be over so that he could go to Shelby and hold her in his arms.

Beaming, Kate held up a hand. "I'd also like to announce my upcoming marriage to Shelby's grandfather, my first love, Patrick O'Hara." She laughed at her sons' surprised expressions. "That was a surprise to my sons. You all are the first to know. As you can see, I won't have the time to run for any further political offices as my hands will be quite full while we plan the wedding. Thank you for coming."

Cameras flashed and news reporters spoke in front of their cameras. Eventually the crowd of media dispersed.

Trey, Samuel and Thad crowded around to hug their mother and shake Patrick's hand.

Kate laughed. "I was afraid you all would be upset to see your mother remarry."

"Are you kidding?" Trey asked. "We're happy to see you so happy and in love."

"You deserve all the happiness in the world." Sam smiled at Patrick. "Congratulations. You must be special for Mother to choose you."

"I'm feeling pretty lucky right now. I've never stopped loving her." Patrick slipped his arm around Kate and held her close.

"Since we're all making announcements," Thad started, "I have news to share." He grinned like a kid with a new toy. "Lucy and I are moving our wedding date up."

Kate's brows rose. "To when?"

"Sometime in the next eight months." Thad hugged

Lucy so tight she yelped. "Our six-year-old is going to be a big sister."

The family converged on Lucy and Thad and the congratulations began anew.

Daniel took the opportunity to sidle up to Shelby. "Hi."

She smiled shyly at him. "Hi, yourself."

"I missed you."

Tears welled in her eyes. "I missed you, too. How did things go in D.C.?"

"I was offered any position I wanted in the Secret Service."

She gulped and looked down at where he held her hand. "Congratulations. Does that mean you'll be leaving?"

"That depends."

She glanced up, her eyes narrowing. "On what?"

"On you." He pulled her into his arms. "Is there any way a society debutante like you can be interested in a banged up ex-agent like me?"

Her brow puckered. "I'm not a society debutante—" Her breath caught as if his words sank in. "Ex-agent?"

He nodded. "I handed in my resignation."

"But you love your job." Shelby gripped his hand, shaking her head. "What will you do?"

"I'm accepting another job, with Adair Enterprises," he said loud enough Kate could hear.

"Daniel!" Kate exclaimed. "That's fabulous news!"

"So what's your answer?" Daniel smiled down into Shelby's eyes. "Would you be interested in a banged-up ex-agent like me?"

"Yes! Yes, of course!" She flung her arms around his neck and hugged him tightly for a moment, but then pushed him to arm's length. "But why give up being in the Secret Service?"

He lifted her chin and brushed his lips across hers. "I'd rather be in North Carolina working for the family I hope to marry into someday. So what do you say? Wanna date me and see if we can get along enough to tie the knot?" Daniel held his breath, waiting for her response. When her eyes lit up, his heart took flight.

"You bet I do," Shelby said. "I thought you'd never ask."

Daniel kissed her, holding her close and loving every minute of it.

"Hey, if you two are finished sucking face, we have a christening to go to," Trey said, bouncing baby Adair in his arms. "Hear that, Adair? Before you know it, you'll have a dozen cousins to run around with. And if you want to be in the Secret Service, the army or even a fry cook in restaurant, I'm okay with that. You can choose whatever path your heart desires."

Kate laughed. "That's right. It's our legacy."

Shelby slipped her arm around Daniel's waist and followed her family into the church. "Our children will grow up in a family that loves them, and they'll always be encouraged to follow their hearts."

Daniel kissed the tip of her nose. "That's right. Just like us."

* * * * *

BODYGUARD'S
BABY SURPRISE

LISA CHILDS

For my mother, Mary Lou Childs, who passed away while I was writing this book. She loved babies and dedicated her life to raising not just hers, but her grandchildren as well. She was an amazing, generous, loving woman who will be dearly missed.

Prologue

Hand shaking, Nicholas Rus pushed the door through the broken jamb. His other hand grasped his weapon. "Stay back," he told the woman who stood behind him—too close. Despite the chill November air, he could feel her warmth.

Annalise was always warm—in temperament and temperature. With her yellow blond hair and bright green eyes, she was like summer sunshine. No matter how many times he had pushed her away and called her a pest when they'd been kids, she had always come back with a smile and a hug. Her hugs were the only ones he'd known in his adolescence.

"I forgot you don't like people getting in your personal space," she murmured. But before she stepped back, she touched him—as if she couldn't help herself. Her fingers brushed across the back of his jacket. Despite the layers of leather and cloth separating them, he felt that touch.

"I don't want you getting hurt," Nick said. "Someone could be in there."

"There was," she said. "I was in there. Whoever did this—" she gestured with a shaking hand at the broken door "—was long gone then."

He wasn't so sure about that. What if the person had still been inside? What if that person had hurt Annalise? Nick shuddered.

"So they're longer gone now," she said.

"You shouldn't be here," he said. And neither should he. He hated this house. He had always hated this house. Not that there was anything wrong with the two-bedroom bungalow; it was the feeling that being inside it had always given him that he hated. His stomach muscles tightened into a tight knot of dread—the same miserable feeling he'd had every time he'd walked through the front door—and even when he'd been a kid, that had been as seldom as possible.

Drawing in a deep breath, he forced himself to cross the threshold. Despite what he said, he didn't protest when Annalise followed him—like she'd always followed him—and flipped on the lights.

"Why's the power on?" he asked. He hadn't paid a bill since *she* had died. He had done nothing with the house—except try to forget about it.

For once Annalise was quiet. But it didn't last long. She reluctantly admitted, "I've been paying the utilities."

"Why?"

"So the pipes won't freeze," she said matter-of-factly, "so it'll be ready when you want to come home."

He snorted. This house, in the lower middle-class area of Chicago, had never been home to him. "I left this place when I turned eighteen." And he had never looked back until his mother had died.

"That was when you joined the *Marines*..." Her voice cracked with emotion.

She had been upset when he'd joined. She'd been only twelve and hadn't understood how badly he'd needed to get away. But that wasn't why she was emotional.

"I'm sorry," he said. That was why he'd come back—not to deal with the house but because he'd known Annalise needed him. Actually, she didn't need him. She needed her brother, but nobody knew where Gage was. He had disappeared behind enemy lines.

"It's not your fault," she said.

Nick blamed himself. Annalise hadn't been the only Huxton who'd followed him around; Gage had, too. He was only three years younger than him, so he'd joined the Marines three years after Nick had. He'd also followed Nick's path after the corps—to college for a criminal justice degree and then into the FBI. The one thing Gage had done that Nick hadn't was reenlist. And that move had probably gotten him killed.

She touched him again, her hand reaching for his—for the one that didn't still grasp his weapon. She was right that he didn't need the gun. There was no one inside the house anymore. The intruders had done their damage—overturning furniture and even smashing holes in the drywall—and left.

"It's not your fault," Annalise said again, as if she somehow knew how guilty he felt about Gage.

She was also right when she'd said earlier that he

didn't like people getting in his personal space; he didn't like anyone getting too close to him. So he pulled his hand from hers to pick up an overturned chair.

"I had nothing to do with this mess," he agreed—though he had created one for himself in River City, Michigan—some three hours north of where he'd grown up.

"The house has been sitting vacant for too long," Annalise said.

She had been dead for almost a year now.

"You should let me either rent it or list it for you," she said. Annalise was a real estate agent and property manager. She'd done well for herself—probably because of her natural warmth. People trusted her.

Even Nick trusted her, and he'd never trusted easily.

She moved around the room, picking up things. The overhead can lights glinted off her pale blond hair and made her pale skin even more luminescent. She looked like an angel.

"Give it away," he said. "Maybe the fire department will take it and burn it down for practice." He liked the idea of burning up all those horrible childhood memories—of coming home from school to find his mother drunk or drugged out of her mind.

If not for the Huxtons living next door...

Annalise and Gage's parents had taken care of him like he was one of theirs. But they didn't live next door anymore. They had retired and left Chicago for a warmer city—in Alaska. They'd found a friendly little town they loved. With Gage gone, Annalise was all alone now.

She sighed. "If you don't want to keep it, let me sell it for you. I can make you some money."

"I don't want it," he said. "The house or the money." He had the only thing he'd ever wanted from his mother: the truth. She'd written it down in a letter he hadn't been given until after her death.

"I took some things out of the house that I thought were yours," she said.

He shook his head. "I didn't leave anything here that I wanted. I don't want any of it."

"Nick..." She obviously didn't understand his bitterness. She couldn't. She was too kindhearted to harbor resentment.

"I'll sign it over to you," he said. "You can do whatever you want with it." Maybe that would keep her busy enough to keep her mind off Gage.

The skin beneath her green eyes was dark—as if she hadn't been sleeping. And her full lips weren't curved into their usual smile. He missed her smile. He had missed her.

"Are you okay?" he asked.

She nodded—too quickly. "Of course. I told you no one was here when I found the house like this last week."

"I wasn't talking about the house."

Her lips lifted now, just slightly, as if she forced the smile. "You're talking about Gage."

He'd tried to bring Gage up earlier, but she hadn't let him. She'd changed the subject. He waited for her to do it again.

"You know he's fine," she said.

"I hope so."

"I know so," she said. And her smile widened as she summoned her faith. He'd never known anyone as optimistic as Annalise. "How about you?" she asked. "Are you okay?"

He was worried about Gage. But he wouldn't admit that to her.

"Tell me about them," she said. "About your family."

She'd been there when he'd read the letter his mother's lawyer had given him. Annalise had always been there. Maybe that was why he'd missed her so much the past several months.

"The Paynes are not my family," he said.

"You all have the same father," she said.

"And they resent me for that." Like she should have resented him for Gage joining the Marines.

"Then they're idiots," she said.

"They're not," he said. And his instant defense surprised even him. But the Paynes were good people who'd been hurt—whom he'd hurt with his mere existence. They had every reason to resent him—to look at him like they did—with anger.

Annalise looked at him now, and her green eyes filled with warmth and compassion and something else—something he'd seen in her gaze and no one else's. "Nick, I know you don't like it, but I have to..." And she hugged him like she always had, her arms sliding around his waist.

But it didn't feel like it used to. Annalise wasn't a child anymore. She hadn't been one for a long time. Her breasts were full and soft against his chest.

"It's not that I don't like it," he said. It was that he liked it too much. Maybe because it had been so long since anyone had showed him warmth. Or maybe because it was Annalise.

But he lifted his arms, and after holstering his

weapon, he slid them around her. She tensed in his embrace and glanced up at his face. "Nick...?"

Then he lowered his head and brushed his mouth across hers. And the chaos wasn't just in the house anymore. It was in his heart, his mind, his body. He knew he was about to make another mess, but he couldn't stop himself. He couldn't stop kissing Annalise.

Chapter 1

Six months later

The soft metallic click echoed in the eerie silence of the ransacked living room. FBI Special Agent Nick Rus tightened his grasp on his weapon, but he knew it was too late. Whoever had broken into his place had already cocked his gun, and the barrel of that gun was dangerously close to his head. Out of the corner of his eye, he could see the metal glinting in the faint light of the lamp overturned on the hardwood floor.

Was this it? He had lived most of his thirty-one years on the edge. As a Marine, he had been deployed to the most dangerous places in the world. As an FBI agent, he had taken on some of the most dangerous criminals in the world. But he was going out in the living room of some River City rental house?

Hell, no. He ducked and jammed his elbow back—
into the ribs of the intruder. Then he wrapped the fingers of one hand around the barrel of that gun and
shoved it up while he swung his own gun around and
jammed it hard into the other man's chest. "Who the
hell are you?"

"Your friend—I thought," Gage Huxton murmured
before uttering a low groan of pain.

"My friends don't pull guns on me." But then he remembered a few instances when they had. "Well, at
least they don't trash my place." He released Gage's
weapon and holstered his own. "I've had some bad
houseguests before, but you…"

Gage chuckled, but it was rusty-sounding. "Funny.
I walked in here just a few minutes ago and found this
mess."

Nick picked up the lamp from the floor and shone
the light around. The couch cushions and pillows had
been slashed, the stuffing pulled from them.

"Looks like somebody was looking for something,"
Gage remarked.

Nick shrugged. "I can't imagine what." He'd lived
such a nomadic life that he had few possessions. "More
likely someone is trying to send me a message."

"You piss someone off lately?"

"I've pissed off a lot of someones since I came to
River City," Nick admitted. His move to Michigan had
been tumultuous for him and for the people his presence had upset. Not just the Paynes but the criminals
he'd put away since his arrival in the city.

"Has this been going on that long?" Gage asked.
He'd been back in the US only a few weeks—back from

the dead, actually, since he'd gone missing on his last deployment and had been presumed dead for months.

Nick nodded. "Yeah. That's why this is my fourth place in just a little over a year." He'd kept moving around, but they always found him—whoever it was routinely trashing his place.

"That's why you're doing the short-term rentals," Gage said.

"I was supposed to be here short-term," Nick reminded him. The Bureau had sent Nick to River City to clean up the corrupt police department. After years of going undercover to expose corruption, he'd become an expert at handling it. But cleaning up the River City Police Department had taken longer than he'd thought it would. It had also made him some dangerous enemies.

"Why would you leave?" Gage asked. "You've got family here."

Nick snorted. "I don't think they consider me family." But he had begun to think of them that way. "Especially Nikki." She was the one who'd told Gage where to find Nick a few weeks ago. She was the one who could track down anyone. He glanced around at the destruction. Did she resent him enough to do this to his place?

"Nikki," Gage said with a wistful sigh.

Nick shoved him again.

"Don't worry," Gage said. "She's your sister, so she's off-limits. That would be like you going for Annalise."

Actually, that would be worse, because Annalise was really Gage's sister. Other than them both being named for their father, Nick had no connection to Nikki Payne. Gage apparently hadn't talked to his sister yet. He didn't know about Nick and Annalise. If he had, he might have pulled that trigger when he'd had the chance.

"You need to call her," Nick said. Sure, she might tell Gage how he'd treated her. But he didn't care about himself. He cared about her and how worried she'd been about her brother.

Gage sighed again—raggedly. "I can't. She can't hear me like this." His voice was raspier than it had once been, but Nick suspected that wasn't what his friend worried his sister would hear. He worried that she would hear his pain—whatever hell he'd endured all those months he'd been missing. "But I sent her an email. I let her know that I'm back—that I'm okay."

He was alive. Nick wasn't sure how okay he was. He wasn't sure if Annalise was okay, either—since he hadn't talked to her for the past six months. He hadn't known what to say. "Sorry" hadn't seemed adequate—although he had told her that, too. He'd made a mess of their friendship. And when Gage learned what he'd done, he would have made a mess of that friendship, too.

So maybe it was fitting that someone kept trashing his place—since Nick kept trashing his life.

Payne Protection Agency, Annalise read the sign and confirmed she'd found the correct address. The body-guard business occupied both floors of the brick build-ing in the industrial area of River City, Michigan. The email had come from here.

Gage.Huxton@PayneProtectionAgency.com

It had to be real. Her brother was alive. And it made sense that he would have come here. Not to the body-guard business per se, but here to River City—to Nick.

Even after whatever he'd been through in the past six months, he was still intent on following Nick around.

She had once been, too. But not anymore.

Nicholas Rus was the last person she wanted to see. Maybe she shouldn't have come here. But River City was nearly as big as Chicago. She was unlikely to run into him. She opened the door and stepped into the brick foyer of the building. Another door led to the lobby, but when she reached for the handle, it escaped her grasp as the door pulled open. A man stepped out, nearly colliding with her. Strong hands caught her shoulders and steadied her.

"Sorry," a deep voice murmured with concern.

She glanced up—into Nick's handsome face. The jaw, the cheekbones, the nose were chiseled, the eyes so bright a blue they were almost startling. But he was staring down at her as if she was a stranger—as if he had never seen her before.

"Are you okay?" he asked.

"Nick?" But it couldn't be. Even Nick couldn't be cold enough to pretend that he didn't recognize her. And she didn't feel the way she usually felt when she saw Nick. Maybe her heart had finally given up on him.

The man's brow furrowed. And he shook his head. "No. You know Special Agent Rus?"

She'd thought she knew him better than anyone else. But she'd been a fool. For so many reasons...

"He's not why I'm here," she said.

"Do you need a bodyguard?" the man asked. "I'm Logan Payne—CEO of Payne Protection."

"He never tires of saying that," another deep voice murmured as a second man stepped into the building from outside. Their faces were identical, but this man's blue eyes sparkled with amusement. "He used to be the sole owner, but our younger brother and I each bought our own franchise. If you want a bodyguard, come see me." He held out his hand. "I'm Parker Payne."

"Which one of you does Gage Huxton work for?" she asked.

"He should work for me." And then there were three. This man had come in behind the other brother. "I'm Cooper Payne, and my team has all the ex-Marines."

"Unless they're family," Logan said. "Then they work for me."

"Gage isn't your family," she said. He was hers. So why hadn't he come to see her since he'd been back? Why hadn't he at least called? Why had he only sent that short, impersonal email?

"He's Nick's family," Logan said. "So that makes him our family."

"Nick's not family," she said.

"Finally someone speaks the truth around here," a female voice remarked. The woman was small, but she shouldered the larger men aside and stepped closer to Annalise. She didn't look like them. Her hair was reddish-brown instead of black, her eyes brown instead of blue. But she was as much a Payne as they were. As Nick must be…

This was the family his mother's letter had told him about—the siblings he'd never known he had.

"Who are you?" the woman asked as she thrust out her hand.

"Annalise Huxton."

The woman's eyes widened. "Gage's wife?"

"Gage isn't married," Annalise said. While her brother hadn't been particularly forthcoming in his email, she doubted he'd met anyone and married her while he'd been missing. Before he'd reenlisted, he had been pretty serious about a woman, but she'd broken his heart, which had probably precipitated his reenlistment. "I'm his sister."

"I'm Nikki Payne," the woman said.

"Nice to meet you," Annalise said as she took Nikki's hand, which was small but callused. And her grip was surprisingly strong. Maybe having all older brothers had made her tough, whereas Gage had always tried to coddle and protect Annalise. Even Nick had, when he hadn't been ignoring her. But Nick wasn't her brother.

She'd always known that, but until six months ago, she'd thought Nick had considered her a pesky little sister. He hadn't ignored or coddled or protected her that night. Instead, he'd broken her heart.

But he'd done more than that...

Much more. She flinched as a little foot struck her ribs, and she pressed her hand over her stomach. That was probably why Nikki had assumed she was Gage's wife. Because she was pregnant.

Maybe coming here—even to see Gage—had been a mistake. He would want to know who the father was. And she couldn't tell him. She couldn't tell anyone.

"Gage isn't here," Logan said. "He left for an assignment this morning."

Even as disappointment flashed through her, she breathed a little sigh of relief. She wanted to see her brother—wanted to see for herself that he was all right. But she didn't want to have to answer his questions any more than he probably wanted to answer hers.

"When will he be back?" she asked. Eventually he would have to know that he was going to be an uncle in a few months. But that wasn't the reason she needed to see her brother. She wasn't even here to make sure he was all right. He was back. He was working. He was probably fine.

Annalise was the one who needed help.

Logan shrugged. "It's hard to say. Days. Maybe weeks. As long as the person he's protecting is in danger."

For her, it had been months. She'd been in danger since that night Nick had showed up in Chicago. That couldn't be a coincidence. He must have gotten her in trouble somehow—in more ways than one. Because someone had spent the past six months stalking her.

Logan Payne had been running Payne Protection long enough to recognize when someone was in trouble. Annalise Huxton was in trouble. The fear was in her pale face, her wide green eyes. She was scared.

He silently cursed himself for sending her brother away. He could pull Gage off the assignment, though. He could bring him back and send someone else.

A small hand squeezed his forearm. "Let me take Gage's place," Nikki said. She must have recognized what he'd seen. She was intuitive. But she was too little, too young, too fragile to do their job.

"You don't work for me anymore," he reminded her. "You went to work for Cooper."

She thought she could manipulate Cooper more easily than him or Parker. But he doubted Cooper would hand her any assignments more dangerous than the desk jobs Logan had given her.

His sister glared at him, and he was used to it. She hadn't been happy with him for a while. So he wasn't surprised that when he split up the protection agency, she'd chosen to leave the franchise he was keeping.

"Annalise needs to see her brother," Nikki said. "He was missing for months." She glanced at Cooper then—and there was no glare on her pretty face.

Maybe that was why she'd asked to work for him—because she'd missed him so much when he'd been deployed.

"It's fine," Annalise said. But the crack in her voice made it sound as if she was anything but fine. "I'll see him when he comes back."

"Will you stay in River City and wait for him?" Nikki asked.

"I—I could check into a hotel," Annalise said. "I haven't yet."

Logan wondered why. Had she worried about her reception from Gage? Or had something—or someone else—made her afraid of staying?

"I don't know how long he'll be gone," Logan reminded her.

"Maybe I could stay at Gage's place," Annalise murmured.

"He's been staying with Agent Rus," Nikki said.

Would his sister ever accept that Nick was their brother? Logan hadn't been happy, either, to learn their father had betrayed their mother. But he hadn't blamed Nick.

Annalise's face paled even more, and she quickly said, "I can't stay there."

From what Logan had been told, Gage had grown up next door to Nick in Chicago—making them as close as brothers. Obviously Annalise hadn't felt any more like a sister to Nick than Nikki did.

"You can stay with me," Nikki offered. She must have recognized what Logan had—Annalise was scared. Or maybe she just liked that Annalise wasn't a fan of Nick's, either.

But the blonde shook her head. "I couldn't impose."

"No imposition at all," Nikki assured her. "Did a cab drop you here?" She glanced around as if looking for bags.

Annalise shook her head again. "I drove my car. It's not that far a drive from Chicago."

"So you're parked out front?" Nikki asked. "I am, too. You can follow me back to my place and we'll get you settled in."

"And I'll see about sending a replacement for Gage so he can come back early," Logan offered. If Annalise was as scared as he suspected she was, she needed family. She needed her brother.

Nikki held open the door for her, and Annalise walked out with his sister. They were gone for only a moment when he heard the scream and the squeal of tires.

As usual, his instincts had been right—Annalise was in danger. And that danger had followed her to River City. He drew his weapon, just as his brothers had, and the three of them rushed out to the street. But they hadn't reacted quickly enough—because gunshots rang out.

They were too late.

Chapter 2

Nick's heart hammered against his ribs as fear and panic overwhelmed him. He flashed his shield and hurried past hospital security—into the ER waiting room. Logan and Cooper rushed up to him.

"Where is she?" he asked. "And how badly is she hurt?" She had to be hurt or they wouldn't have brought her here. His panic intensified and pressed on his lungs, stealing his breath.

Logan shook his head. Was it so bad that he couldn't answer him?

"We don't know yet," Logan said. "A doctor is checking her out."

"What happened?" he asked. What was she even doing in River City? Gage hadn't called her, and it sounded as if his email to her had been brief. Had she come to visit *Nick*?

Six months had passed since that night. Six months with no contact, which had been unusual for her. Before, she had always called or texted or emailed him to see how he was doing. But not this time.

Not after what he'd done…

No. She hadn't come to visit him.

Logan shrugged. "We didn't see it. She and Nikki had stepped outside…" He pushed his hand through his black hair. "But I knew she was in danger."

"How?" Nick asked.

"She looked scared," Logan said.

What the hell did Annalise have to fear? Then Nick remembered that house—his mother's house—and how badly it had been ransacked, like his place kept getting ransacked. He shook his head. It couldn't be related. His mother's house had sat vacant for months. That was why someone had broken into it.

"Thanks for calling me," Nick said.

"I was going to call Gage," Logan admitted. "But Cooper told me to call you instead."

Nick spared Cooper a glance of gratitude. Even though Gage hadn't spoken of it yet, Cooper, as a Marine himself, must have sensed what Gage had been through and understood that he hadn't been ready to see his sister. And how would he handle her being hurt? Even Nick couldn't handle it.

"I'm glad I'm the one you called," Nick said.

"Annalise won't be," Nikki said as she walked into the waiting room through a door marked No Admittance. She had come from inside the hospital, maybe inside the ER.

"Where is she?" he anxiously asked. He had to see her—had to make certain she was all right.

"She doesn't want to see you," his half sister said. Even though she couldn't stand him, she probably wasn't lying.

Because of what had happened—and his silence for the past six months—he could understand if she never wanted to see him again.

But she was Annalise, always so warm and affectionate. Surely she would forgive him...even if he would never be able to forgive himself.

Annalise's head pounded as images flashed through her mind. It had all happened so quickly. She had walked outside with Nikki, only to find two men breaking into her car.

Not again...

Frustrated and angry, she had reacted without thinking. She'd run across the street to stop them. The moment she'd crossed the road, she had realized her mistake. She had gotten too close. One of them had reached out, wrapped a huge hand around her arm and jerked her toward the open back door of her car.

She'd screamed then. And shots had rung out—fired from close range and also from across the street. She had struggled harder, fighting for herself and her baby. She had to get away. If she left with them...

The car started away from the curb, but she was half in and half out, her feet touching the road. She reached up and clawed at the face of the man holding her. He howled and released her, and she tumbled to the asphalt.

She pressed trembling hands over the mound of her belly. What had she done? She had been so stupid to run toward the car—so careless. What if her baby had been harmed?

Her belly shifted beneath her palms as her baby moved. At her last regular OB appointment, she'd had an ultrasound, but the doctor hadn't been able to determine the sex. Annalise didn't care what she was having— just that the baby was healthy. He or she had to be okay.

Annalise had been scared when she'd found out she was pregnant—scared that she wouldn't be able to handle raising a child alone. But she had never been as scared as she was now—not even when that man had grabbed her. Her heart pounded frantically, making the machine next to her bed beep faster. The curtain partitioning her bed off from the rest of the ER rustled. The doctor must have returned with the ultrasound results.

"Is my baby okay?" she asked.

"Baby?" a deep voice, gruff with emotion, repeated the word.

Her heart rate sped faster as she glanced up into Nick's handsome face. While he looked like every one of the male Paynes—with his chiseled features, thick black hair and startlingly blue eyes, she had no doubt that this man was Nick—for so many reasons.

First, that quickening of her pulse—that tingling of her skin. She reacted to Nick as she had no one else. Second, he was the most handsome man she had ever seen. His eyes were bluer than his brothers', his features sharper, his jaw squarer. Finally, the other men had all seen her and knew she was pregnant. It was clear that Nick had had no idea. Those bluer blue eyes were wide with shock as he stared down at her belly.

"You're pregnant?"

She splayed her hands across her belly, but she couldn't hide it from him. So she nodded.

"Is it mine?"

A gasp slipped through her lips—that he would ask, that he wouldn't just know. She didn't sleep around. She wouldn't have slept with him six months ago if she had been involved with anyone else at the time.

Or would she have?

She had wanted Nick for so long—even before she'd known what desire was. When he had finally returned that desire, she hadn't been able to resist and probably wouldn't have even if she'd been in a relationship at the time. But thanks to Nick—and always wanting him— she'd had few relationships. No ordinary man or high school boyfriend or college crush had been able to measure up to the hero she had made Nicholas Rus out to be in her girlish fantasies.

Nick was no hero, though. He was just a man—a man who'd always made it clear he didn't like anyone getting too close to him. And until that night six months ago, he had never let Annalise too close.

Before she could answer him, the curtain rustled again, and another man joined them. His light green scrubs hung on his tall, thin frame. The young ER doctor glanced at her and then at Nick as if trying to gauge the relationship.

"Is she all right?" Nick asked. And his gaze skimmed over more than her belly now. He looked at her face, and his breath audibly caught at the scrape on her cheek. He reached out, but his fingers fell just short of touching her.

"Is the baby all right?" she asked. The baby was all she cared about. She didn't care about her car. It wasn't the first one she'd had stolen.

She'd been so stupid to risk her pregnancy over a damn car...

The doctor glanced at Nick again—as if wondering if he could speak freely in front of him. Damn HIPAA laws. She didn't care about her privacy right now.

"Please," she implored him. "Tell me!"

The baby shifted again. He or she had to be okay, or he wouldn't move like he was. Right?

"Your baby is fine, Ms. Huxton," the doctor assured her. "It appears that when you fell out of the vehicle, you fell on your side."

Nick flinched as if he'd taken a blow.

"Your shoulder took the brunt of the force," he continued, "and it appears you've struck your head, as well. You have a slight concussion."

That explained why her head kept throbbing so painfully. She lifted her fingers to her temple. "But the baby... Is he or she..." They hadn't been able to determine the sex on this ultrasound screen, either. The tiny legs had been crossed again. " ...all right?" She needed that reassurance, needed to know that her recklessness hadn't put her pregnancy at risk.

The doctor reached out, and his fingers did touch her, squeezing her hand. "The baby is fine. Strong heartbeat. Active. All properly developed for twenty-four weeks."

She uttered a sigh of relief. "Then I can leave?"

The doctor pulled his hand away. "I'm not concerned about the baby," he said. "But I do have concerns about your concussion."

"There's no reason for concern." She shook her head but winced as pain reverberated inside her skull. Maybe she did have a concussion. "I'm fine."

"You're not fine," Nick said. "You've been hurt."

He would know. He had done it. But he wasn't referring to his breaking her heart. He probably wasn't even aware that he had.

"The address you provided for your intake paperwork says that you live in Chicago," the doctor said. "You definitely cannot drive that distance, or really at all, for at least twenty-four hours."

A giggle bubbled up inside her, but not wanting to sound or become hysterical, she suppressed it. "I have no car to drive," she said. "It was stolen."

"Is that what happened?" Nick asked. "You were carjacked?" He uttered a slight sigh, almost as if he was relieved.

Surprised by his reaction, she stared at him.

"Logan made it sound like something else," he explained. "Like it wasn't random."

She doubted it was random. After everything else that had happened, it would have been too much of a coincidence. But she wasn't sure how much she wanted to share with Nick. He had already proved to her that she shouldn't have trusted him—with her heart, and maybe not with anything else.

"You shouldn't drive," the doctor repeated as if they hadn't spoken. "And you should not be alone tonight."

"She won't be alone," Nick said. "She's going home with me."

She gasped. "No." But before she could finish her protest—that there was no way in hell she would go home with him—the doctor and Nick both turned to her.

"I'm sure you'd rather not stay in the hospital," Nick surmised—correctly. And of course, he knew the only way the doctor would release her was if he believed she would not be alone.

Damn him. He'd always had an uncanny ability to know what other people wanted or needed—except her. He had never known how much she'd wanted him—needed him—until that one night.

But that night had been an aberration. He hadn't realized how much she'd needed him after that—more than she ever had. Or maybe he'd known and hadn't cared.

What was different now?

The baby? He must have realized the child Annalise was carrying was his.

"She doesn't want to go home with you," Nikki said.

Special Agent Rus flinched as if she'd struck him. She had watched the man take a blow and even a bullet without ever betraying an ounce of fear. But this caused him pain. Annalise Huxton caused him pain.

"She doesn't," he agreed with a glance to the door of the bathroom where Annalise was changing from the hospital gown back into her clothes. They were torn and stained from her tussle with the men and the asphalt. And thanks to Nikki letting them get away with her vehicle, those clothes were all she had in River City.

Nikki flinched now. Maybe her brothers were right. Maybe she wasn't cut out to be a bodyguard. She hadn't reacted fast enough.

"I told her she could stay with me," she said. But now she wondered if that was a good idea—if she could keep the pregnant woman safe.

"I appreciate the offer," he said.

She opened her mouth to point out that she hadn't made the offer to him when he continued, "And I appreciate you saving her from the carjackers."

Her face heated now as it flushed with embarrassment. "I didn't," she said.

"But Logan said you exchanged gunfire with them."

"I did," she said. She had gotten off a couple of shots and might even have hit one of them. "But Annalise got free on her own. She's tougher than she looks." Just like Nikki had always tried to convince her brothers *she* was tougher than she looked. "Maybe that's why she ran toward them when she saw them stealing her car."

"She ran toward the carjackers?" he asked, his face paling with fear as he probably imagined all the horrible things that could have happened—that Nikki had almost let happen.

She nodded. "Just before she did, she mumbled something about *not again*. Her car has been stolen before. Once would be random. But twice?"

When Nikki had joined her brothers in the waiting room, Logan had said he'd sensed she was in danger. Logan was rarely ever wrong—except about Nikki. Or at least she'd like to think so?

"That's why she's going home with me," Nick said, his square jaw clenched with grim determination.

"You didn't know, did you?" she asked.

He arched a dark brow.

"That she's carrying your kid."

His face flushed now, and he shook his head.

"Maybe it's good that you were named after our father," she said. "Apparently you're the most like him." Of course, she had been named for him, too—something she resented nearly as much as she resented Nicholas Rus's existence.

Rus flinched again, and a twinge of regret struck Nikki. Giving him a hard time had become more of a habit to her than anything else. It wasn't like she hated him—like everyone else thought.

Sure, she wasn't happy with how he had come into their lives and turned them upside down—especially Mom's. But apparently Mom had always known that her husband had cheated on her. Was any man worthy of a woman's trust?

Annalise stepped out of the bathroom, and she looked up at Rus with mistrust. Then she gazed at Nikki, imploring. Nikki wanted to offer her hospitality again. But after the incident in the street, she wasn't certain she could keep the woman and her unborn baby safe.

"I want a full report about what happened and descriptions of the men," Agent Rus told her.

She would have bristled at his bossiness. But she understood why he was. He'd been running the police department since coming to River City to clean up the corruption. Apparently he thought she worked for him. But his demand wasn't unreasonable. She intended to do more than fill out a report. She intended to track down the men herself. They wouldn't get away from her again.

"I also want you to come down to the station and look through mug shots," he said, "if you think you would recognize the men if you saw them again."

She nodded in agreement. "Sure. I would."

"I could look at the mug shots, too," Annalise offered.

Nick shook his head. "You have a concussion. You need to rest. Once the doctor brings your release papers, I'm taking you home."

Annalise glanced at her again—with that imploring gaze. And Nikki's stomach knotted. She hated to disappoint Annalise, but she didn't want to endanger her, either. "I'd better get going," she said as she hurried out.

In case her brothers were still in the waiting room, she bypassed it and took the elevator to the underground parking garage. She didn't want to see her family again. She'd already spoken to them once— to assure them that Annalise was all right. They'd been so concerned about her that they hadn't questioned Nikki. And she hadn't looked at them. She didn't want to look at them now. She didn't want to see the *I told you so* on Logan's face, didn't want to see the doubt on Cooper's. She didn't want him second-guessing hiring her.

Tears stung her eyes, blurring the elevator doors. But then they slid open, and she stepped into the parking structure. She had been in such a rush to follow the ambulance to the hospital that she couldn't remember where she'd parked. Which floor had it been?

She walked through the structure, looking for her black coupe. Logan hadn't given her a black SUV like he had everyone else who worked for him—probably because he hadn't wanted bad guys blowing her up when they meant to blow up one of her brothers instead.

She uttered a regretful sigh as she remembered the men who'd lost their lives when one of their SUVs had exploded. Someone had been trying to kill Parker and had nearly succeeded. Tears stung her eyes again, and she blinked furiously. When her vision cleared, she realized what she'd found. Not her coupe but *them*.

Nikki had known she would recognize the men if she saw them again. Unfortunately they glanced up, furtively—from the black SUV they were trying to jimmy open—and saw her.

They clearly recognized her, as well. She reached for her weapon—realizing too late that she'd locked it in the glove box because she'd known she wouldn't make it past hospital security with it.

So she was unarmed and outnumbered.

Chapter 3

Nick cursed himself for not just leaving his SUV parked illegally outside the emergency room entrance. He should have exercised his authority, so that security wouldn't have dared to have his vehicle towed away. But he hadn't been thinking after Logan's call. He'd been so anxious to get to her—so anxious to see Annalise for himself. He'd pulled into the first available spot in the garage and run up the stairs to the ER. Now he struggled to remember where he'd parked.

He didn't want to leave Annalise alone long—waiting in a wheelchair in the lobby. She'd looked so pale sitting there, so fragile. Even pregnant, she was still slight because of her small frame, narrow shoulders, thin arms and long, slender legs. Dark circles rimmed her green eyes, as if she hadn't been sleeping well because she'd been afraid. Logan had noticed her fear.

Nick saw it now, the fear and the vulnerability. Nikki had told him Annalise was tougher than she looked— that she'd saved herself. Of course, she was a Huxton. Gage wouldn't have survived being missing in action for months if he wasn't tough, too.

At least Annalise wasn't alone in the lobby. Or just with hospital security, either. Logan and Cooper stood over her chair, offering more protection than Nick had thought she'd get from some nervous hospital security guard. She was safe.

He wasn't as certain about Logan and Cooper. Annalise was furious. She didn't want to go home with him. And she hadn't wanted to ride in the wheelchair, let alone having to wait in it until he pulled his vehicle up to the lobby doors. His half brothers probably had a fight on their hands to keep her in the chair and make her wait for him.

She might see this as her opportunity to call a cab to take her home to Chicago. Her home was in Chicago; his wasn't. He had never felt as if that house or anyplace else he'd lived was home. The only time he'd ever felt as if he was home was when he'd been with Annalise. When he'd given in to his desire to kiss her, he'd worried that it might have been awkward. They'd known each other so long.

But it hadn't felt awkward. It had felt right and passionate and thrilling. And he hadn't been able to stop. But he'd felt most at home buried deep inside her body.

Had they made a child that night? Twenty-four weeks ago. The doctor had said that was how far along her pregnancy was. However, Annalise had never confirmed her baby was his.

But he knew…

Annalise carried his child. And she hadn't called him. She hadn't told him about the pregnancy. Or that she was in danger.

She probably wouldn't be waiting for him to come back with his vehicle. She had no intention of staying with him. So he quickened his step, running toward his SUV just as he'd run toward the ER earlier.

That was when he heard it—the scream. It wasn't just a shrill cry. It was his name, full of terror and warning. "Nick!"

Someone was in trouble—someone he knew.

"You're in trouble," Logan Payne said.

Annalise laid her palms over her belly. "That sounds like something my grandmother would say."

His face, so similar to Nick's, reddened. "I wasn't talking about your pregnancy."

"Then how do you mean I'm in trouble?"

Did he know how deeply she loved Nick? And how unlikely it was that Nick would ever return her feelings? She had to get over him. If she was going to mend her broken heart, she could never trust him with it. He would only hurt her again.

"Those guys weren't stealing your car," he said.

"Really?" she asked. And his brother Cooper, who also stood beside her chair, furrowed his brow, mirroring her confusion. "Then why is my car gone?"

If she had it, she would have driven herself back to Chicago—doctor's orders be damned. Or better yet, she would have driven herself to Alaska. She had thought she'd needed Gage. But maybe she needed her mom and dad more.

She would have gone to them before, but she didn't

want to put them in danger. Gage could handle it. He could protect her. He had survived being missing in action when everyone else had given him up for dead. She hadn't. She knew her brother was tough. Trying to be like Nick had made him tough.

"You know what I'm talking about," Logan said.

Unable to hold his gaze, she glanced down at the terrazzo floor of the sun-filled glass lobby. "Have you called Gage?" she asked.

"No," Cooper answered for Logan.

"Why not?" she asked. She needed her brother— more than she ever had.

Cooper wouldn't meet her eyes.

And she realized why. Concern filled her. She had been so happy—so relieved—he had come back alive that she hadn't considered what condition he might be in. "He's not all right, is he?"

"Physically he's fine," Cooper assured her.

"And...?"

"Mentally and emotionally, he has some recovering to do yet," Cooper said. "He'll get there. It just takes time—more time for guys who've been through what he has."

"Thank you," she said.

Cooper shrugged off her gratitude. "I haven't gotten him to talk about it. I don't really know what he's been through. The only one who might know is Nick."

Gage had always gone to Nick—had always told him everything. If Nick knew, why hadn't he told her? Why hadn't he called her? Had he been so determined to avoid her after they'd made love that he hadn't even wanted to call to talk about Gage?

"Thank you for not calling him," she clarified. "I

wouldn't want to add to whatever he's going through."
She couldn't imagine the horrors her brother had endured while he'd been missing. Gage was tough, but
everyone had a limit.

"Then you'd better be honest with us about what's
been going on with you," Logan said. "Your getting
hurt might be more than your brother could handle."

He was right. It wasn't that she didn't want to share
her troubles with someone. But she wasn't certain whom
she could trust.

These were Nick's brothers. She couldn't trust Nick—
not after the way he'd treated her. So how could she
trust any of them?

"My sister told me what you said when you saw those
men jacking your car," Logan said. "This isn't the first
time that's happened."

"No," she admitted.

"And it's not the only thing that's happened to you."

Her head began to pound as other memories rushed
in, and she squeezed her eyes shut to block them out.

"Annalise?" Logan prodded her.

They hadn't been raised together, but he reminded
her of Nick. Even before he'd become an FBI agent,
Nick had always been good at asking questions and
finding out information. Perhaps Logan should have
been an FBI agent, too. He was a natural interrogator, as well.

And she had never been good at keeping secrets.
She parted her lips to speak, but someone shouted. She
opened her eyes to see a security guard running up to
Nick's brothers.

"You guys are with Payne Protection, right?" he asked.

Both men nodded. "What's wrong?" Logan asked.

Because it was clear that something was. The young man was flushed and breathing hard.

"There's a shoot-out in the parking garage! I called 911, but I don't think the police will get here in time. So I need to go down there." His throat moved as he swallowed hard, obviously afraid. "I need backup."

Annalise's heart hammered against her ribs. "Nick's in the parking garage." He'd gone down to get his vehicle to pick her up. Just like her car getting stolen again, it couldn't be a coincidence. Nick had to be involved in that shoot-out.

"I think Nikki's down there, too," Cooper said.

Logan's face paled, and his hand shook slightly as he reached beneath his jacket—probably for his weapon. But his holster hung empty from his arm. He glanced at her. "I told Nick…"

That he would protect her. She had heard him, and she'd thought it was ridiculous that they thought she needed protection inside the hospital. Obviously they'd been right.

"Go," she urged him.

He shook his head and turned to Cooper. "You go."

Cooper was already grabbing the arm of the security guard and pulling him across the lobby.

"Be careful!" Logan called after him. "And make sure they're okay!"

Cooper glanced back and nodded. But he could only do his best—if he arrived in time. Annalise worried that he and the security guard would be too late to help.

Nick couldn't be gone.

She pressed her hands over her belly again. And the baby shifted within her womb. Her child couldn't lose his father before she was even born.

* * *

As Cooper Payne shouldered open the door to the parking garage stairwell, shots reverberated inside the concrete structure. He kept the security guard behind him, shielding him as he would have a Payne Protection Agency client or a fellow serviceman. Fortunately he'd the foresight to leave his weapon with security, so he'd retrieved it before they'd left. He clasped the Glock in both hands, swinging the barrel in each direction he looked.

Where the hell were they? The noise faded to a faint echo as the shots stopped.

His heart stopped, too—for just a second. From his years in combat, he knew why the firing ceased. Because everyone was dead...

His blood chilled, and the hair lifted on his nape. He still kept his hair short, as he had when he'd been enlisted. His brothers wore theirs longer—except for Nick, who had also been a Marine. Nick looked the most like him, and they were nearly the same age.

His half brother was too young to die. Cooper bit the inside of his cheek, resisting the urge to call out to him. To Nikki...

Had she gone down to the parking garage? She hadn't said goodbye. She had simply disappeared from the hospital. Nikki always did that when Nick was around, though. She couldn't handle being near the evidence of their father's betrayal—couldn't stop blaming Nick for what their father had done.

He hoped she had left before Nick had come down for his SUV, and she was safe.

Cooper slowly moved forward, keeping low so he could duck for cover if the firing started again. Because he was staying down, he saw the blood—the droplets of it sprayed across the concrete. Someone had been hit.

How badly? And who?

Then he saw the SUV. Like the Payne Protection company vehicles, it was black, but this one had all the windows shot out, the glass scattered across the concrete like the blood. The government plate on the back confirmed his fears. It was Nick's.

But where the hell was Nick?

He lowered one knee to the ground as he leaned down farther, looking for bodies on the other side of the vehicle. He found more blood—small pools of it. Maybe more than one person had been hit since there was blood on both sides of the SUV.

As he looked around, he noticed a Payne Protection vehicle parked nearby—not one of the black SUVs but Nikki's small coupe. He recognized it from the furry pink dice hanging from the rearview mirror.

The former cops—Logan and Parker—gave her so much crap about those dice. They had warned she might get a ticket for obstructed vision. Nikki probably didn't even like them, but she was too stubborn to remove them now. She was too stubborn to give in.

Even if she'd had the chance to drive off, she would have stood her ground. She would have fought to prove herself. That was why Cooper had hired her for his team. He wanted to convince her to believe in herself.

"What the hell happened here?" the security guard wondered aloud, his voice unsteady with fear.

Cooper shook his head. He hadn't holstered his weapon. He gripped it tightly as he moved around the coupe to the passenger side. The door hung open, and so did the glove box. A box of ammo lay on the concrete next to some spent shells. And some more broken glass. The rear window was broken, and bullets had dented the trunk.

He looked again at the ground—looked for the blood he'd found around the SUV. The search must have distracted him, because he heard a gun cock—a gun too close to him. How the hell had someone gotten the jump on him?

He swung around, pointing his gun barrel behind him—into the pale face of his little sister. His breath shuddered out. "Are you all right?"

She nodded. But she was trembling. So badly that she nearly dropped her gun when she lowered it. "I'm sorry. I didn't know it was you."

He didn't care that she'd pointed the gun at him. "Were you hit?" he asked.

Her curly hair was usually messy, but it nearly stood on end now—almost as if someone had pulled it. There was a red mark on her cheek that would undoubtedly become a bruise, and her sleeve had nearly been torn free of her jacket. She'd been in a hell of a fight.

Concern and anger both gripped him. He wanted to make sure she was okay even while he wanted to rip someone apart—whoever had hurt her.

"We need to get you to the ER." He holstered his weapon now and reached for her. He would carry her there—like he'd carried other soldiers from combat. Nikki looked like she'd been to war.

She stepped back and shook her head. "I'm okay," she said. But her voice cracked on the claim, and her brown eyes glistened as tears pooled. "Thanks to Nick."

Cooper tensed. That might have been the first time she'd referred to their half brother by his first name.

"Where's Nick?" he asked, and his voice cracked now as he remembered all the blood he'd found. Had that been Nick's blood?

Nikki shook her head. "I don't know…but I think he got hit."

The blood had been Nick's—at least some of it.

A tear slipped between her furiously blinking lashes and trailed down the red mark on her cheek. "We need to find him."

Depending on where he had been hit, they might not have much time to find him and get him help before it was too late.

Before Nick couldn't be saved…

Chapter 4

He was a dead man.

Nick had learned long ago that there was no honor among thieves. His own mother had turned on her former boss and lover and testified against him—to save herself from a prison sentence.

Nick had just witnessed that lack of honor again as one of the gunmen, with no regard for his injured partner, had jumped into his vehicle. Or was it the one they had stolen from Annalise earlier that day? The little SUV wasn't the older model sedan she'd had six months ago. But the Honda had an Illinois license plate. Maybe the men were from Illinois, too. Maybe they had followed her to Michigan.

But why? Why would anyone want to harm sweet Annalise?

Nick intended to find out. But the man sped off in

the little SUV, leaving his partner behind. His concern was only for himself. Nick had pursued the vehicle first, running after it as it careened around the corners of the parking structure. He'd fired shots into the rear window, taking out the glass like the gunman had taken the glass out of his SUV, when they'd fired at him through it.

And Nikki...

Rage gripped him as he remembered what he'd stumbled upon when he had headed toward his vehicle. The fight. Those men had hurt Nikki. They had pulled her hair, punched her face. She'd fought. His sister was a hell of a fighter. She had punched back. She had kicked. She had pulled moves he hadn't known she knew. But she'd been outnumbered...

The rage kept him from reacting to his gunshot wound—from one of the bullets fired through the broken window of his SUV. He'd felt the sting of it and could feel the blood oozing from his torn flesh to soak his shirt. But he ignored the pain to pursue the vehicle—until it was clear he wouldn't catch it. The engine revved as it pulled out of the parking garage and onto the street. Horns honked as other vehicles nearly crashed into it. The Honda sped off. One of the gunmen had gotten away.

The other man couldn't.

He had been hit. Nick wasn't sure which one of them had fired the shot, him or Nikki. As well as a good fighter, she was a good shot. If she wasn't, the men might have abducted Annalise outside Payne Protection. Was that why they had come to the hospital parking garage? Had they been determined to try again?

But if they'd been after Annalise, why had they been attacking Nikki? Why had they been standing beside Nick's government-issue SUV?

Who the hell was their real target?

Nikki?

Her coupe had been parked near his SUV—near enough that she had been able to go for her gun. If she hadn't, he might not have survived the onslaught of ammunition the other men had fired at him. Sometimes she acted like she hated him, but she had helped him. Hell, she'd probably saved his life.

And instead of making certain she was okay, he had left her alone. Sure, the other gunman was injured. But he was still armed. He could hurt her.

Of course, the injured man had been running after his partner, too—until he'd seen Nick behind him. Then he had dived between some parked cars. Nick hurried back toward where he'd remembered losing him—between a Hummer and a Cadillac—in the reserved staff parking section.

It was easy to track him. All he had to do was follow the blood trail—the one that wasn't his. His blood was running down his arm and dripping from his fingertips. At least it was his right shoulder that had been hit, since he was left-handed.

He gripped his gun more tightly as he tracked the blood to where it turned from a trail to a pool. But he didn't need a weapon. He found the man leaning against the side of the Hummer. Deep gouges marred his face. Someone had scratched him. Nikki? Or Annalise? His eyes were open. So was his mouth.

But he wouldn't talk. He wouldn't answer any of Nick's many questions. He was dead.

Then Nick heard the telltale metallic click of another gun cocking—near his head. And he worried that he might be a dead man, too.

Annalise had loved Nick too long to lose him now. Not that she'd ever really had him. Even that one night…

They had made love. But he didn't love her. Not like she had always loved him. She couldn't remember a time that she hadn't been in love with Nicholas Rus.

"Where is he?" she asked Nikki.

Tears brimmed in her brown eyes. She shook her head and tousled her already tangled auburn curls around her pale face. "I don't know…"

Logan cursed.

Nikki flinched—either over his reaction or because she was in pain. She had obviously been roughed up. But she had refused medical attention for her injuries. She had rushed into the lobby instead—to fill in Logan on what had happened in the garage.

The men who'd stolen Annalise's car had come back. They had been waiting in the parking garage.

For her?

For Nikki?

For Nick?

Why? What did they want?

Annalise owned nothing of value to anyone but her. After all the times they'd broken into her home and her office and stolen her vehicle, they had to realize that she had nothing they wanted. So why wouldn't they leave her alone?

Unless it really wasn't her that they were after…

The trouble hadn't started for her until after Nick had

been to Chicago, until after that night they had made love in the house where he'd grown up.

"Nick chased them out of the parking garage. And I don't know how he could…" Nikki's voice cracked with emotion as she continued, "I think he was hit. I *know* he was hit."

"Hit?" Panic clenched Annalise's heart. "You think he was shot?"

Biting her lip, Nikki nodded. "He was bleeding. There was blood all over the cement." She shuddered. "But it didn't stop him."

Nothing stopped Nick from going after what he wanted. The son of a drug addict single mother—the odds had been against his making anything of his life. But he had accomplished everything he'd wanted. He'd joined the Marines, gone to college and earned a high position in the FBI. No, nothing stopped Nick.

"So he must not have been hurt badly," Nikki said as if she was trying to convince herself.

But his half sister didn't know Nick like Annalise did. She had no idea how determined—how single-minded—he could be.

"He needs medical attention," Annalise said. How long could he survive with a bullet in him? Even Nick had limits to what he could endure.

"Cooper will find him," Logan assured them.

Then he focused on his sister, and a muscle twitched in his cheek, above his tightly clenched jaw. Annalise recognized the telltale sign of stress and tension. She'd seen that same muscle twitch in Nick's cheek so many times. But she had seen him clench his jaw like that even when he hadn't been stressed or angry. She'd seen it when she'd hugged him. She had thought that was because he didn't like being touched.

But maybe her hugging him had stressed him out. Maybe he'd had to struggle for control of the passion she'd experienced the night they'd made a child together.

"And while Cooper is finding Nick," Logan said, "you're going to the emergency room to get checked out." When he took his sister's arm, she flinched. "Nikki, you are hurt!" And he swung her up in his arms as if she were a child.

Embarrassment flushed Nikki's face with color even brighter than the mark on her cheek. Annalise's heart swelled with concern and sympathy for the other woman. She understood what it was like to be underestimated—like Nikki's brothers obviously underestimated their little sister. She also understood what it was like to be hurt and need their comfort and protection. She could recognize that Nikki was torn between wanting to be a tough, independent woman and the little girl who needed her big brothers.

The wheelchair forgotten, Annalise hurried after the brother and sister as Logan carried Nikki back to the ER. Logan shouldered open the door marked No Admittance. There was no security guard to stop him. They were all in the parking garage—looking for Nick and the men who'd shot at Nikki and him.

Not just *at.*

Nick had taken a bullet. He was bleeding. He needed to be in the ER, too.

"I'm fine," Nikki said as she wriggled in Logan's arms. "I'm not the one who needs medical attention."

She was worried about Nick, too. But then, she'd been there. She knew how badly he'd been hurt.

"You shouldn't be back here," the doctor who'd treated Annalise agreed. "We have critically wounded coming in!"

"Critical?" Annalise uttered the word on a gasp of shock and pain.

A ding rang out, and doors to an elevator at the end of the hall opened. Two men—dressed in scrubs like the doctor—pushed out a gurney. A sheet covered the patient from head to toe.

She couldn't see the man's face. But his legs dangled from the end of the gurney. He was tall and broad. His shoulders hung over the sides.

Her heart pounded furiously with fear and dread. Nick was tall. Nick was broad. But it couldn't be Nick.

It couldn't be.

When he'd enlisted in the Marines, she had been so afraid that she would lose him. And when he'd joined the FBI…

He had been in so much danger so many times and had survived. Today he'd only been going down to the parking garage to retrieve his vehicle—for her. He shouldn't have been in danger there. Of course, she shouldn't have been in danger outside the Payne Protection Agency, either.

Her voice cracking, Nikki asked the question burning in Annalise's throat. "Is he dead?"

The medical professionals ignored her—until the doctor standing beside them asked, "Did you pronounce him?"

One of the doctors nodded.

"There was nothing we could do," the other one said. "He bled out before security cleared the parking garage for us to treat him."

Tears burned Annalise's eyes. Nick had bled to death while waiting for help?

She couldn't bear the thought that he had been alone and hurt. But then Nick was always alone. He insisted that was the way he'd wanted it. That was the reason he'd given for always pushing her away.

Nikki gasped, too, and the tears that had brimmed in her eyes spilled over. "No…"

They had been named for the same man. If they had anything else in common besides their names, they might not have pushed each other away. Now Nikki would never have the chance to connect with the brother she'd obviously resented.

And Annalise's baby would never get to meet his or her father—just as Nick had never had the chance to meet his. Horror and regret overwhelmed Annalise, making her legs tremble and threaten to fold beneath her. Before she could fall, though, strong arms closed around her, holding her up.

"Mrs. Payne?" a young woman asked. She stared across the desk at Penny, her dark eyes wide with concern. "Are you all right?"

She nodded and replied, "Of course."

She was anything but fine, though. Her heart had started pounding faster and harder, thumping inside her chest. She didn't want to betray her fear to the young bride, though. Megan Lynch was already too nervous about her pending nuptials. Too nervous to be getting married.

Penny held her tongue and her opinion. She had once been a nervous bride herself. Maybe, in the way that she somehow knew things, she'd known she would lose her husband too soon. There had been rewards for the pain she'd endured, though: her children.

Panic clenched her heart.

One of her children was hurt. She knew it. Even before the phone rang, she knew it. She had that tightness in her chest and that sick feeling in the pit of her stomach. She was often teased about being psychic. But she was no medium. She just had a very special connection with her children. Her feeling that one of them was hurt had never been wrong.

And it wasn't wrong now. Her hand shaking, she reached for the phone before it even started to ring. She skipped her usual greeting of "White Wedding Chapel. Penny Payne, wedding planner, speaking," and just said, "What is it?"

"Mom," Nikki spoke tentatively—almost fearfully.

"What is it?" Penny asked again.

"I'm fine," Nikki replied.

And Penny remembered the first long trip Nikki had taken with her new driver's license and the phone call she had received from her youngest and her only daughter shortly after Nikki had left. "Mom, I'm fine but…"

Then she'd dissolved into tears over the deer she'd struck and killed. That was partially why Logan had kept his sister behind a desk instead of assigning her fieldwork. She wasn't as tough as she acted. If she had to hurt anyone…

"But?" Penny asked. Nikki hadn't said the word this time, but she'd heard it in her voice.

"Mom…" And just as when she'd inadvertently killed the deer, Nikki broke into tears. Her sobs rattled the phone.

"You're fine," Penny reminded Nikki and herself. Her daughter wasn't hurt. But what about her sons?

Nikki drew in a deep breath. "Yeah, I'm fine. I'm fine." And now it sounded as if she was trying to convince herself.

"Who's not fine?" Penny asked.

Nikki's breath escaped in a ragged sigh. "Nick."

The panic already clenching her heart squeezed tighter. Nikki had never referred to her half brother by his first name. She usually never referred to him at all if she could help it. The fact that she was saying his name now—and with so much emotion...

Nicholas Rus wasn't one of Penny's children. She hadn't given birth to him like her sons and daughter. But she had that same connection with him that she had with every one of her biological children. Sometimes it felt even stronger than that connection—because of all her children, Nick was the most like her. Somehow they both instinctively knew what other people needed.

But about their own needs, they were clueless. Nick had no idea what he wanted or needed. And now he might never have the chance to figure it out.

Chapter 5

Nick's shoulder throbbed. Maybe he shouldn't have refused the painkillers the doctor had tried to push on him. But he needed a clear head now. He needed to focus. There were so many voices—all of them talking at the same time in the way that the Payne family conversed. Only he who spoke loudest was heard. Usually that was Logan—especially since they were in the dark-paneled conference room of the Payne Protection Agency and, as he was quick to remind the others, he was CEO.

But it was Penny Payne's soft voice that cut through the rest of them. "Quiet down," she said in that tone of hers that brooked no argument. That was how she had raised four kids on her own after her husband had been killed in the line of duty. "Nick is hurting."

"Then he should have stayed in the hospital like the doctor told him," Garek Kozminski said.

Nick snorted. "Like you ever followed a doctor's orders." A few months ago, Garek had checked himself out of the hospital with a hole in his leg. That was worse than a hole in the shoulder. At least Nick's gunshot wound had been a through-and-through.

"Like he ever follows anyone's orders," Logan murmured.

Garek flashed his brother-in-law-slash-boss a wide grin. That was how he and his brother Milek had become honorary Paynes; their sister had married Logan. "I get the job done."

Nick couldn't argue that. Garek had helped him bring down one of the most dangerous crime bosses in River City—hell, in the country.

"We need to get this job done now," Nick said. "We need to make sure Annalise is safe."

"And Nikki," Logan chimed in.

Garek's wife and fellow bodyguard—Candace—was still at the hospital with Annalise and Nikki. Annalise would have collapsed had Nick not caught her in the hallway of the ER. He hadn't even noticed his shoulder wound then. His concern had been only for her.

That concern clutched his heart now. But the doctor had convinced Annalise to let him monitor her for a while. And Candace was probably the best of the Payne Protection bodyguards. She wasn't alone, though. Because of the shooting in the parking garage, the police were involved. Nick had requested his best men—the ones he knew he could trust now—to back up Candace and make sure the man he'd let drive off didn't come back.

He silently cursed himself for letting him get away. That guy had been alive and able to talk—unlike his partner, the man Annalise had mistaken for Nick lying on the gurney. Was that why she'd collapsed? Or had that been because of the concussion she'd sustained during the carjacking?

She and Nikki were also giving their statements to Nick's best detective and their descriptions of the man who'd gotten away. With all of River City's finest working the case, they would find him.

But that wasn't enough for Nick. He had to make sure Annalise and his half sister were safe. That was why he'd called this Payne family meeting. While he hadn't been to many of their meetings, it wasn't the first one he had attended, either. But those other times he'd been on the sidelines, just offering his opinion or his warning.

His warnings were probably why he wasn't often asked to the meetings. This one he'd called himself. He wasn't asking their opinions, though. He already knew what he had to do.

He hadn't expected Penny to invite herself along. But since she had silenced the others, he appreciated her input.

Then she added, "We also need to make sure Nick stays safe."

He swallowed a groan and assured her, "I'm fine."

"You lost a lot of blood," she reminded him of what the doctor had said when he'd argued against Nick leaving the hospital. She stepped closer and gently patted the side of his face as she always did her sons'. "I was afraid that we were going to lose you."

They had never really had him. But he didn't point that out—because he didn't want to hurt her feelings. She had done nothing to deserve the pain his mere existence had already caused her.

"It's going to take a lot more than a bullet to bring down Nick," Parker Payne said. He should have known. He'd survived being blown up.

She ignored Logan's twin, leaned forward and kissed Nick's cheek. "Promise me you'll be careful," she implored him.

Her sons groaned in sympathy. They knew what she was asking. For Nick—with Annalise in danger—it was the impossible. He shook his head.

"Nicholas," she murmured.

Logan came to his rescue. "Mom, we need to strategize."

She arched a reddish-brown brow and asked, "Are you throwing me out?"

Logan probably wouldn't dare. But he gently guided her toward the door of the Payne Protection Agency conference room. Their heads close, they whispered together, shooting glances back at him.

Uneasiness lifted the short hairs on the nape of Nick's neck. They were obviously talking about him. He knew it wasn't the first time he'd been the topic of Payne family conversations. But he suspected he wasn't the only one about whom they talked. He didn't want them talking about Annalise, speculating about what their relationship was.

Nikki had already figured it out, though. She knew he'd gotten Annalise pregnant—just like his dad had gotten his mother pregnant. He had never met the man, but Nikki was right: he was the most like him.

Everyone else talked about Nick Payne like he'd been a hero. But he hadn't been any hero to Nick. He'd abandoned him to the care of a drug addict.

Nick wanted to be a hero for his kid. But mostly he

wanted to be a hero for Annalise. When they'd been growing up, she had always acted like he was one—always looked at him like he was one. He'd let her down once already. He didn't want to let her down again.

Logan swallowed the sigh burning in his lungs. He'd made the promise to their mother that Nick had refused to make. After she walked out, he closed the door of the conference room and turned back toward the others.

He would make sure Nick was careful—that he didn't get hurt again. A twinge of panic struck his chest as he remembered the fear that Nick had been the one lying on that gurney, a sheet covering his face. Even when Nick had appeared next to him, holding up a faint Annalise, Logan hadn't been sure the guy would survive. Blood had been dripping from him, running down his arm from his blood-soaked shirt and coat.

He wore a scrub shirt now. Blood had seeped through the bandage and the shirt, though. The damn fool should have stayed in the hospital. But he was stubborn—more stubborn than Logan had ever realized.

"We've got this. We'll make sure Annalise and Nikki stay safe," he assured Nick.

Nick snorted. "You're crazy if you think I'm going to sit back and do nothing."

Logan had to acknowledge that he probably *was* crazy if he thought he could keep Nick away from the action. But he'd made a promise to their mother, so he had to try. He pointed out, "You have your hands full with the River City PD."

"I'm done," Nick said.

After he'd brought down the biggest crime boss in

Michigan—hell, probably the US—he had every reason to believe that. But it hadn't stopped there.

"The corruption runs even deeper than you thought," Logan reminded him. "Every time you've thought you caught them all, you've found more corrupt officials."

Milek grunted in acknowledgment. Nick had just arrested his wife's former coworker, an assistant district attorney who'd taken bribes for dismissing charges.

"And that's probably what's put me in this situation," Nick said.

"What situation is that?" Garek asked the question. "What's been going on, Nick?"

He sighed. "Not long after I took the assignment to clean up River City PD, someone started breaking into my place and ransacking it."

"That's why you've moved so often," Parker said.

"But they always find me again."

Frustration gnawed at Logan. Why hadn't Nick told them what was going on? Because he hadn't been raised like them—with them—he was used to handling everything alone.

But apparently he hadn't been completely alone. He'd had the Huxtons.

"So you think whoever's going after you is going after Annalise now?" Logan asked.

Nick didn't reply. His jaw was clenched too tightly, so tightly that a muscle twitched in his cheek. But he gave a sharp nod.

Whoever it was must have suspected he cared about the young woman. She was Gage's sister. What was she to Nick? The mother of his unborn child?

He wanted to ask. "Nick—"

"I'm done," he said again with a finality that chilled Logan's blood. "I'm going to quit."

"You would really quit your assignment?"

"Not just my assignment," Nick said. "I'd quit the bureau."

For Annalise?

She obviously meant a lot to him. Why had Nick never mentioned her before? But then, Nick had never shared a lot with them. He'd put his life on the line for them in the past, but he hadn't told them much of anything about his life.

"You don't have to quit your job," Logan said. But he wasn't certain he could reason with Nick. He wasn't just determined; he was mad. And despite everything they'd been through together in the past year, Logan didn't think he had ever seen Nick mad before.

"After bringing down Chekov, you could take over the whole damn bureau," Garek said. "You can't quit— not after making the coup of your career." Garek had nearly lost his life and the woman who was now his wife when they'd helped Nick take down Chekov.

"I don't give a damn about my career," Nick said.

It was clear he cared about only one thing—one person, actually. Annalise.

Logan stepped closer and assured him again, "We'll keep her safe for you."

Nick shook his head. "*I* will keep her safe."

"You're not a bodyguard."

"I should be," Nick said.

Logan couldn't argue that. As good an FBI agent as Nick was, he would make an awesome bodyguard, with his intuition and his protective instincts.

"I want to be," Nick said.

"Are you asking for a job?"

"Would you give me one?"

Logan would have loved nothing more. "On one condition."

"I don't care what you say," Nick said. "I won't be too distracted to protect Annalise. I'll be more focused and dedicated than any other bodyguard you have."

No other bodyguard present attempted to argue. They didn't doubt Nick. Not in this situation.

"I know," Logan said. "That's why your first assignment will be protecting Annalise."

"Then what's your condition?" Nick asked.

"That you work for my franchise," Logan said.

Cooper and Parker both cursed him. Getting Nick on either of their teams would have been a triumph.

Nick hesitated. "But your team…"

"It's the family team." Or what was left of the family since Cooper and Parker had started their own franchises and Nikki had gone with Cooper. Logan felt a pang in his chest that the family was divided. He had the Kozminskis, though. And Gage. And if Nick was foolish enough to give up his career with the FBI, Logan wanted him, too.

"But, Logan—" Nick was going to argue, like he always did, that he wasn't really family. But he was.

So Logan interrupted him. "Can you work for me, though?" It was a valid question. "You've been running the whole River City PD since you came to town. Is being a bodyguard going to be enough for you?"

"Keeping Annalise safe is all I care about," he said. "That's why I'm heading back to the hospital now." When he stood, he swayed on his feet.

Garek caught his uninjured shoulder. "You should check yourself back in."

"He should," Logan agreed. But they all knew he wouldn't. It was clear that Nick's only concern was for Annalise—not himself.

It wasn't until he left that Logan realized Nick hadn't answered his question. Would being a bodyguard be enough for him? But then, Nick probably wasn't thinking about the future. Hell, if he ran into another shootout like the one in the parking garage, he would be damn lucky if he survived the present.

Annalise leaned back in the passenger's seat of the black SUV and drew in a deep breath. She'd felt suffocated earlier. She wasn't used to people fussing over her. She wasn't the one who'd been in the parking garage. She hadn't been in a fight like Nikki, whose cheek had gone from red to purple. She hadn't been shot like Nick.

She shuddered as she remembered the blood soaked into his shirt and coat. She'd felt the clamminess of the blood through her clothes when he'd caught her in his arms. Despite his gunshot wound, he had stopped her from falling.

To the ground.

She'd fallen long before that moment in the ER. She'd fallen for him so long ago that she couldn't remember the exact moment when it had happened.

But she knew why. Because he was Nick.

Because he was strong and honorable and heroic. For the past six months, she had been doubting that and cursing him. Then he'd risked his life to rescue his sister. And then, even injured, he'd caught Annalise.

She'd had only that moment—seeing the dead man

on the gurney—when her knees had weakened. There had been no reason for them to whisk her back into a bed. No reason for them to keep her for monitoring.

When she'd finally convinced them of that, Nick was already gone. He'd checked himself out against doctor's orders. He was gone, just like he'd been the morning after they had made love in his mother's house.

"Will you take me home?" Annalise asked the female bodyguard. Candace Baker-Kozminski was an Amazon—tall and strong and intimidating. But she had fussed, too. And so had Nikki and the River City detective who'd taken her statement about the carjacking. They were all so concerned about her—making sure that answering questions and looking at mug shots wasn't too much stress for her to handle.

Candace glanced away from the traffic for just a moment to meet Annalise's gaze across the console of the black SUV she was driving. "Home?"

"Chicago."

"You can't be alone right now," Candace said.

"I don't think I have a concussion," she protested. The pain in her head was only a dull ache now.

"You can't be alone. You're in danger."

She shivered. She had been afraid before—over the break-ins and the previous car theft. But after they'd tried to pull her into the car, she couldn't deny it or pretend it was all a misunderstanding anymore. She *was* in danger.

"I can bring you home with me," Candace said. "Garek and I have a great security setup. You'd be safe. But I need to check in at Payne Protection first. See what the plan is."

"I haven't hired Payne Protection," Annalise said.

Candace chuckled. "You don't hire family."

"I'm not a Payne." And neither was Nick—at least, not legally.

Candace glanced over again, but at Annalise's belly—like she suspected that she carried one of them. "Your last name doesn't have to be Payne to be part of the family."

Annalise opened her mouth to argue, but Candace continued, "Your brother works for Payne Protection. And every bodyguard becomes part of the family."

She needed her brother. But Cooper was right. She couldn't risk upsetting Gage now. He had already been through too much. And if she tried going home alone and something happened to her...

She shuddered. She couldn't risk that for Gage or for her baby. She had to accept help from the Paynes.

"Okay," she agreed. "But can we stop somewhere first so I can pick up some things? I need clothes and toiletries." Her overnight bag had been stolen with her car.

Candace glanced into the rearview mirror and nodded. "I haven't noticed anyone following us. It should be safe." A few miles farther, she pulled into the parking lot of a department store. "This should have everything you need."

It wouldn't have Nick. She'd once thought he was everything she needed. But Nick would never be there for her the way she needed him. He could be physically present even when he was injured, but she doubted he would ever be emotionally available. He'd shut off his emotions long ago, when he was a kid.

And now he wasn't even physically around. He'd run

off, leaving her to the protection of the Paynes. At least she could trust them.

As she reached for the door handle, Candace cursed.

Annalise's hand trembled. She recognized the frustration and fear in that one word. "What?"

"I was wrong. We *were* being followed." And she reached for her gun.

Chapter 6

What the hell had he agreed to? Sure, Nick wanted to work for Payne Protection. He had actually been thinking about it for a while—had been thinking about how bodyguards protected people. Nick usually just put them in danger.

Was that why someone was after Annalise? Was it his fault?

It had to be. Annalise was too sweet and honest to have angered anyone enough to go after her. But someone was after her.

He'd been too late getting back to the hospital. The Payne Protection SUV had already been pulling away from the lobby doors—with Annalise in the passenger seat and Candace driving. He'd pulled out behind them, but his hadn't been the only vehicle.

It wasn't Annalise's small SUV. That would have

been too conspicuous with its shot-out windows and bullet-ridden metal. That must have been ditched somewhere—for a rental with an Illinois plate. It was a nondescript sedan, something he might not have noticed if not for the plate and the fact that it stayed behind Candace's SUV.

Why hadn't she waited for him at the hospital?

Because Logan was giving the orders. *He* was the boss. Why the hell had Nick agreed to that?

He would do anything to keep Annalise safe...

He'd thought Candace would, too. But instead of heading toward the Payne Protection Agency, she pulled off into the parking lot of a busy department store. Maybe that was smart, though.

Whoever else was following her might not try anything here. But then, he and his partner hadn't hesitated to open fire in a hospital parking garage. What would stop him now?

Nick.

Maybe he was wrong. Maybe it was just a coincidence that it had an Illinois plate. But it wasn't a chance he was willing to take—not with Annalise's safety at stake. So he careened into the lot behind the car.

He'd had to ditch his shot-up SUV, too. It was probably good that Logan had hired him since he now had a Payne Protection company vehicle. It had more horsepower than even his government SUV had had. He pushed hard on the accelerator and headed toward the sedan.

Before he could ram it, shots rang out. But the bullets didn't strike his vehicle. They hit the glass of the SUV Candace drove, shattering the rear window.

Had Annalise been hit?

Rage coursing through him, he continued to drive straight toward the car. But as if the driver had finally noticed him, he gunned his engine. Nick could have chased the car as it sped from the lot. He didn't.

His heart was beating hard and fast with fear and dread. He had to make certain that Annalise was okay. She was his only focus—she and the child she carried.

Garek Kozminski's skin itched beneath his clothes that suddenly felt too tight, too constricting, like all the bars and bulletproof glass of the concrete fortress. He had been in prison before, a long time ago. And he'd vowed to his sister and to himself that he would never go back.

But he had been back—to visit his own father. And now he was visiting the man who'd tried to step into his father's place when Patek Kozminski had gone to prison. But like his father, Viktor Chekov had only wanted Garek to steal for him.

"Bring back memories?" Chekov asked as he settled onto a chair across the table from Garek in the visitor's area.

Too many memories. But Garek refused to admit that to the former crime boss—his former boss. He just grunted. "I didn't come here to get all sentimental with you," he said.

"Have you come to gloat?" Chekov asked. He looked older now than his fifty-five or sixty years. His hair was even grayer. His face was gray, too, and wrinkled. And he'd gotten thinner, his shoulders bowing as if he didn't have the strength to hold them straight anymore. Or as if he carried too heavy a weight on them.

Guilt?

He doubted Chekov had enough of a conscience to feel any guilt. To feel anything.

Except concern for his daughter. That was what had driven him to confess to all his crimes in order to reduce her sentence for the people she'd killed and had tried to kill.

"No gloating," Garek said. He couldn't believe he had once feared this man. But he'd been a kid then—afraid of what the crime boss would do to his younger brother and sister if he defied him. "No reason to gloat."

"You've gotten your revenge," Chekov said. "Doesn't it feel good?"

"Is that what this is about?" Garek asked. "Revenge?"

Viktor's dark eyes narrowed. "What are you talking about?"

"Revenge," Garek said. "You brought it up. Isn't that why you're going after Nicholas Rus?"

A gasp of surprise escaped Viktor's thin lips. "Nicholas? He's in danger?"

"It almost sounds like you care," Garek remarked. And the surprise was all his now.

"I like Nicholas," Chekov admitted. "He's one of the last honest lawmen."

"He's changed that," Garek said. "He's found other honest lawmen. He's cleaned up River City."

Chekov snorted. "I'd expect a naive remark like that from your brother, Milek. Not from you."

Milek was the sensitive one—the artist. No one had ever called Garek naive.

"Nicholas would never make such a naive remark," Chekov said. "*He* knows better. He knows there's no cleaning up corruption. Men will always be greedy for money. For power."

"What about revenge?" Garek asked, steering the conversation back where he wanted it. Motive. "Are men hungry for revenge?"

"Not just men," Chekov said.

Garek's pulse quickened. What was Viktor telling him? "Your daughter…"

"Is locked up in a psychiatric hospital where she can't hurt anyone," Chekov said.

Garek snorted now. "Just because people are locked up doesn't mean they don't have any ability to get things done on the outside."

Chekov uttered a dirty little chuckle. He was probably still ruling his crime empire from the inside despite Nick's best efforts to contain him. Then he shrugged. "*I* would not hurt Nicholas."

"There are plenty of other people who would like to, though," Garek surmised.

Chekov nodded. "I have no problem with Nicholas. He has kept his word to me. He's a man of honor."

That meant more to Chekov than anything else— that a man kept his word. If someone was after revenge against Nick, it wasn't Chekov.

"But some people don't respect honor like I do," he allowed.

"Who are these *some* people?" Garek asked. Not that he expected the mobster to give up names. Chekov was old-school. He would not narc on anyone else—even if he could have reduced his own sentence.

Predictably he shook his head. But then he added, "Tell Nicholas I hope that no harm comes to him."

"You know Nick," Garek said—because it was apparent that Chekov did. "He isn't worried about himself."

"I didn't think Nicholas had anyone else to worry about," Chekov said.

Neither had Garek...until he'd heard about Annalise Huxton. His wife had met the pregnant young woman. Was she carrying Nick's baby?

And even more important, was she in danger because of Nick?

Annalise studied the house. It had a stockade fence around it and bars on the windows. This was where Nick had been staying in River City? Where her brother had been staying with him?

Nick held open the front door for her to walk past him. He'd left Candace to file the police report at the department store parking lot while he'd brought Annalise back here.

She glanced around the stark living room. They had a leather couch and a chair, but both had been duct-taped back together. What had happened to them?

"Are you okay?" Nick asked the question again—just as he had when he'd pulled open the passenger side door of the shot-up SUV.

And just as then, she assured him, "Yes."

But that was only because Candace had pushed her down—below the windows. Otherwise she might have been hit. Glass from the back window had exploded throughout the vehicle and rained down onto the dash above Annalise's head.

She reached up to touch her hair. Nick's hand was already there, fingering through the tresses.

"There isn't any glass," he said as if he'd read her mind.

Sometimes she had wondered if he really *could* read minds. He seemed always to know what someone else was thinking or feeling. It was his own feelings that were hard to read—so hard that Annalise had occasionally wondered if he felt anything at all.

His hand moved from her hair to skim along her jaw. He tipped up her chin so that her gaze met his. He stared at her intently—as if he was trying really hard to read her mind now.

She shivered from his touch and because she knew he could see all. She had never been able to hide her thoughts or feelings. He had to have known that she loved him, that she had loved him for years. But she had finally realized love wasn't enough—not when it was on only one side.

"Were you going to tell me?" he asked.

Maybe he didn't know everything.

"About what?" she asked. Finally she summoned the willpower to step back, to step away from him. His hand fell to his side. But her face still tingled as if he was touching her yet. "My car being stolen before?"

"It wasn't just your car," he said.

She shook her head. "No, my office was broken into," she said. "My apartment, too."

That muscle twitched along his jaw. And he glanced around his place.

"Maybe if I had bars on the windows and a fence, it wouldn't have happened," she mused.

"Those don't keep everyone out," he murmured.

"Someone has broken in here, too?" she asked. And her pulse quickened even more than it already had from his touch. "Are we safe here?"

He nodded. "Gage put up the bars."

"So he didn't feel safe here?"

He sighed. "I don't know if Gage will feel safe anywhere ever again."

She shuddered. What had her brother been through? "Has he talked to you about what happened over there? Where he was those months he was missing?"

Nick sighed again. "He hasn't talked much."

Nick had been over there, too. He had never talked about it, either. But he was Nick. He rarely talked at all—at least, not about himself.

But Gage had once been so gregarious and charming. Even when he'd been missing, she hadn't believed she'd lost her brother. Now that he was back, she was worried that she might have lost the man she had known and loved.

"Seems like neither Huxton has been talking to me like they used to," Nick mused aloud.

"You haven't talked to me, either," she reminded him. Not since the night they'd made love. And he actually hadn't done much talking that night, either.

Kissing…

Touching…

Stroking…

She shivered again.

"You're cold." He picked up a plaid blanket from the duct-taped couch and wrapped it around her shoulders. But he didn't step back. His hands stayed, holding the blanket on her. "Or you're in shock." He peered into her eyes again. "Maybe you should go back to the hospital."

"I'm fine," she said irritably. "And I'm sick of everyone fussing."

"Good thing you didn't meet Mrs. Payne yet." A slight smile curved his lips, and affection warmed his blue eyes. "She fusses." But judging from his tone, he didn't seem to mind it.

Of course, Nick had never had anyone fuss over him except Annalise...

He'd hated it when she'd done it. He'd called her a nuisance and a pest. He'd told her to get a life. They had been kids at the time. But his words had still stung because she'd loved him so much—even then.

"I won't be here long enough to meet her," Annalise said. "I need to go home tomorrow." She had a closing on a home she'd sold and a property management business to run.

His grasp on her shoulders tightened. "You need to stay here where you can be protected."

She didn't feel safe. Staring up into his face, she felt scared. "Nick..."

"You should have called," he said. "Or come to me."

"About the break-ins?"

Finally his hands moved from her shoulders. But they only slipped lower—down her body—to her belly. He cupped it in his palms. "You should have called me about getting pregnant."

The baby shifted beneath his hands as if she felt her daddy's touch. Tears stung Annalise's eyes. This was what she wanted. Nick and their baby. But it wasn't what he wanted, or he would have called her after the night they'd made love. He would have come back to see her.

She was just a pest to him, just the nuisance she'd always been when they were kids. Even more so now that she carried his baby.

But maybe he didn't have to know it was his. "Why would I have called you about that?" she asked.

"Because it's my baby." He said it as if he had no

doubt, as if it was a foregone conclusion. He hadn't looked that certain back at the hospital.

"Why would you think that?" Because she didn't want him to think that. She didn't want him to assume he had to take care of her because of the baby. She didn't want to be a responsibility that he resented.

"The doctor said you're twenty-four weeks along," he said. "It was twenty-four weeks ago."

She closed her eyes as images tumbled through her mind: Nick's blue eyes darkening with desire as he stared down at her. His arms rippling as he dragged his shirt over his head, baring his chest but for a dusting of dark hair over his sculpted pecs. He was so muscular. So handsome, so sexy...

And the way he'd touched her...

The way he'd kissed her...

Her heart pounded, and it was hard to draw a deep breath, hard to focus on anything but her desire for him to touch her again, to kiss her again.

She opened her eyes and his face was close, his head lowered to hers. Anticipating his kiss, she drew in a quick gasp of air.

But he only stared at her—as if looking into her soul. "Are you telling me it's not mine?"

She flinched as the baby kicked her ribs, as if in protest. She couldn't lie to anyone, let alone Nick, and not about this. "I don't—"

The muscle twitched in his cheek as he tightly clenched his jaw. But somehow he managed to ask, "Is there someone else, Annalise?"

Because of him, there had never been anyone else. Even knowing now that he would never return her feelings, she doubted there would ever be anyone else. Like

Nick knew everything, he had to know that. So she began, "Of course—"

But then her cell phone rang. At least that hadn't been in her car when they'd stolen it. It was in her purse. She fumbled inside for it, mumbling, "That's him."

Nick tensed. "Him?"

She nearly laughed at the expression on his face— the utter shock. He thought another man was calling her and that man was the father of her unborn child. Maybe Nick didn't know her as well as she'd thought he did.

She held the phone out to him. "I can't answer it," she said. "I can't talk to him right now." Because Gage would hear it in her voice, the fear that hadn't left her since the man had tried to pull her into the backseat of her vehicle. And she didn't want him to worry.

He had enough problems of his own—more than she'd realized.

"What do you want me to do?" Nick asked.

"Talk to him." He was probably the only one who could. She pressed the green circle to accept the call.

But Nick just stared at her. Maybe she was imagining it, but she thought she saw more than shock in his blue eyes. She thought she saw disappointment. And maybe hurt...

Chapter 7

Did he know Annalise at all? She had grown up next door to him—from a chubby-cheeked little girl to an awkward adolescent. But when he'd left, he had still been a teen himself. He hadn't been there when she had matured from teenager to woman. He didn't know how many boyfriends she'd had or apparently still had.

He wasn't her boyfriend, though. He'd been only a one-night stand. And this guy...

He must be her boyfriend. So why had she handed Nick the phone? Why did she want him to talk to him?

Was this who'd been threatening her? A jealous boyfriend? An obsessed ex? Maybe this guy had found out about the night she'd spent with Nick, and he'd started stalking her.

If Annalise had been any other woman, he would have considered that option first. But she was Annalise. And he couldn't imagine her with anyone else. He couldn't imagine her with anyone but him.

And he kept imagining that.

Her silky blond hair spread across the pillow as she stared up at him, her face flushed with passion. Her already full lips swollen from his kisses. Her arms and legs clinging to his body as he moved inside her.

"Annalise!" a male voice shouted her name.

And Nick realized who'd called her. "Gage?"

"Nick? What the hell are you doing with Annalise's phone?" her brother asked.

He'd been wondering that himself—until now. Now he realized that Annalise hadn't wanted to worry her brother, and she'd thought she might give away something if she talked to him.

"She's here, of course," Nick replied.

"At our place?" Gage asked. Then his curse rattled the phone. "I thought she might show up after I sent that email. That's why I called."

"You've owed her a call for a while," Nick admonished him. But Gage hadn't wanted to worry Annalise any more than she wanted to worry him now. The Huxtons were like the Paynes in how unselfishly they loved each other.

"Then why did you answer the phone instead of her?" Gage asked, his voice even gruffer than usual with suspicion.

Annalise's face paled, and she shook her head. She wasn't a liar. So she couldn't come up with an excuse on the spot. That was why she'd handed Nick the phone: to lie.

"She's…"

What the hell would Annalise be doing if she'd come up for a regular visit?

"She's cooking," he said. She had made a habit of coming over to Gage's and cooking for him when he'd worked for the Bureau. Nick had always been invited over, as well. Maybe that was why he hadn't considered that she could have another guy. She'd always had time for her brother.

And him.

She'd never dragged a boyfriend along. Nick's stomach tensed at the thought of Annalise with another man—the way she'd been with him.

How she'd clung to him and moved beneath him.

The way she'd shuddered and screamed as she...

"What's she cooking?" Gage asked wistfully.

Sweat beaded on his upper lip. She was cooking him—scorching him with just the memory of her passion. "I don't know."

Gage chuckled, and his voice wasn't as rusty-sounding as it had been. "She won't let you in the kitchen?"

"You're the one she doesn't let in the kitchen," Nick reminded him. Gage had no domestic abilities whatsoever. Their mom had been a real mom—like Penny Payne—who'd enjoyed taking care of her family. Gage never had to fend for himself or starve like Nick had.

Nick knew his way around the kitchen. So Annalise used to let him help. But she'd always stood too close, always touched him too much.

Even her innocent touches—her hand on his back as she leaned around him to grab a utensil, her hip bumping his as she dried the dishes he'd washed—had affected him. Made his body tense and needy.

But he'd denied what he had been feeling for her, had denied that need—until six months ago.

"I wish I was there," Gage murmured. He missed his sister.

Nick could understand. He'd missed her, too, so badly, the past six months. His gaze moved down her body to the swell of her pregnant belly. He'd had no idea.

"I thought you weren't ready to see her," Nick said.

Annalise flinched.

Gage's sigh rattled the phone. "I didn't think I was."

But he was changing his mind. And Nick couldn't have that yet. He couldn't let Gage come home too soon, before he'd had a chance to explain what had happened that night when he'd lost all control.

Hell, it didn't matter what excuse he used. Gage wouldn't understand. He lived by a code, and Nick had violated that code when he'd crossed the line with Annalise.

"Be sure you're ready before you see her," Nick advised.

Gage sighed again. "You're right. I don't want to worry her."

And she didn't want to worry him. "So you don't want to talk to her?"

Annalise shook her head, tumbling her blond hair around her thin shoulders. As if worried that he might hand the phone to her, like she had him, she stepped back.

"Not yet," Gage said. "Just tell her I called, okay?"

"Of course." He clicked off the phone before Gage could say more—before he could inadvertently make Nick feel worse about keeping so much from him. He should already have told him about that night. And now there was so much more he didn't know—about the danger or the baby.

Nick wasn't sure he knew about the baby, either. So the minute he clicked off the phone, he asked, "Is it mine?"

Hurt flashed in her green eyes. "Of course…"

Of course. She was Annalise. She was too good-hearted, too sweet to have cheated on another man with him. Or was he being a fool, thinking only of the girl she had been instead of the woman she might have become?

He had to know. He had to ask. "Was or is there anyone else?"

Her face flushed, but it wasn't like that night—it wasn't with passion. Maybe embarrassment. Maybe anger. She didn't answer him. She only shook her head.

He reached out and skimmed his fingers over the side of her head, where she'd hit it on the asphalt. "All this—the break-ins, the car thefts—couldn't a jealous ex be behind it?"

He could understand a man not wanting to give her up once he'd had her. It had taken all Nick's willpower to stay away from her the past six months—to avoid going back to Chicago to be with her again.

And again…

She laughed as if the thought was ridiculous. But then, she'd never known how special she was—how beautiful.

Maybe when she looked in the mirror, she still saw that little girl with the chubby cheeks or the adolescent with the pimples. Maybe she didn't see herself the way Nick and every other red-blooded male saw her.

"You can't tell me there was no one else." Not as beautiful as she was, as sensual. The way she'd made love to him.

Her eyes narrowed. "You think I sleep around?"

"You were trying to make me think your baby might not be mine," he reminded her. "Why?"

"I—I didn't want to trap you into anything."

"So you were never going to tell me?" Maybe she wasn't the Annalise he'd thought she was. Maybe she was as selfish and deceptive as his mother had been when she hadn't told Officer Payne that she'd gotten pregnant with his child.

Pain gripped Nick, squeezing his heart in a tight vise. He'd thought Annalise was different. He couldn't trust her any more than he'd been able to trust anyone else.

Her mouth was open as if she was trying to form an answer to his question. Before she could say anything, he shook his head. "I need to check outside," he said, already heading toward the door, "and make sure nobody followed us."

Nobody had. He'd made damn certain of that. Being inside with her was more dangerous than anything he'd find outside. She had just hurt him more than anyone else could have.

Gage stared down at the dark screen of his cell phone. "What the hell's going on?"

He wouldn't have survived to twenty-eight—not with the life he'd led—if he couldn't trust his instincts. And his instincts were telling him something was wrong—really wrong.

It wasn't his current assignment. That couldn't have been any less dangerous than it was. The only threat to the client he had been assigned to protect was in the elderly lady's mind. Probably the onset of Alzheimer's disease. One of his grandmothers had had it. He remembered her paranoia that someone had been stealing her clothes—like anyone else would have wanted to wear the polyester pantsuits that had gone out of style decades before.

Like his grandmother, Mrs. Toliver could have used a nurse, not a bodyguard. He wasn't needed here.

But he suspected he was needed at home—with Annalise. He wasn't surprised that she'd come to see him. He was surprised she hadn't come earlier. And why hadn't she taken his call?

He couldn't believe she hadn't had her phone with her in the kitchen. As a real estate agent and property manager, she said she couldn't afford to miss any calls and lose a client. Why had she missed his call?

And Nick…

He'd been acting strange since Gage had come back. At first he'd just thought he'd surprised him—with being alive and all. Everyone had given Gage up for dead months before.

But Annalise…

She was too optimistic ever to let herself think the worst. Just like she'd always thought she would have a chance with Nick someday. Knowing Nick and how he would never see Annalise as anything but a pest, Gage had told her to give it up. He wished she had listened to him, because now he understood what it was like to love someone and not have that love returned. It hurt like hell. Worse than anything he'd suffered in Afghanistan.

No, it didn't matter where he was. He wasn't safe. Not from those feelings. And he certainly wasn't safe back at the place he was staying with Nick. Someone kept breaking in. Someone was after Nick besides Annalise, for once.

She shouldn't have been there. Shouldn't have been where she might get hurt because of Nick. Gage turned on his cell again and considered hitting Redial. Maybe this time she would answer. But knowing his sister, she wouldn't listen. She never listened to him when it came to Nick.

So he scrolled down to another number and hit that. It was after office hours, but Logan answered right away—almost as if he'd been waiting for Gage's call.

He updated his boss about Mrs. Toliver and concluded, "I'm not needed here."

"I'll let her family know," Logan said.

"So I can come home soon?"

"Are you ready?" Logan asked. There was something in his tone, something that had been in Nick's, too. A caution. Everyone had been cautious of him at first—like they thought he might lose it at any second. They had no idea the control he'd had to learn. He wasn't about to lose it. But now—along with the caution—there was an evasiveness. They were keeping something from him.

And he'd had it. He wasn't losing control; he was losing patience. He didn't need protecting.

"What's going on?" he asked. His instincts were right. He was needed at home.

Annalise's nerves were frayed, and as always when she was nervous, she talked too much. "I could have had someone else drive me."

She'd wanted to—but Nick had refused with just a

shake of his head. He had never been much of a talker, but he'd taken his reticence to another level. Since the night before—since Gage's call—he'd been giving her the silent treatment.

It was going to be a long three-hour drive to Chicago. "I really couldn't postpone the closing," she said. "It's already been postponed a couple of times because of issues with the property that had to be fixed before the bank would give my client financing."

He glanced away from the rearview mirror to meet her gaze. "Are you talking about Carla's house?"

"Your mom's?" He'd never called her Mom or Mother. Just Carla. The woman had never been much of a mother, though.

He nodded.

"If I'd sold hers, you would have to be at the closing, too," she said. That was why she hadn't listed it for sale. She hadn't wanted to see Nick again—unless he'd wanted to see her. But he hadn't even called.

A pang struck her heart, and a little foot struck her ribs. Their baby was active.

"Did you burn it down?" Nick asked—hopefully.

She shook her head. "I rented it." Which had been unusual.

The tenant had paid an entire year's rent in cash, but she didn't think he had even moved in. He hadn't switched any of the utilities to his name. And the number he'd given her was no longer connected.

Weird.

So many odd things had been happening. The strangest had been Nick making love with her that night six months ago. She had given up hope that he would ever be attracted to her. But she must have caught him in a weak moment.

She would have liked to give herself a similar excuse. But she never needed an excuse to want Nick. Even now.

She couldn't stop staring at him—at his strong hands gripping the steering wheel. She remembered how they had looked moving over her body, cupping her breasts...

Her nipples tightened as she remembered his thumbs sliding over them. His thigh shifted as he pressed on the accelerator, the muscles moving beneath his black pants. And she remembered how they had moved as he'd thrust his hips.

Her body began to throb as desire overwhelmed her. Before, she'd had only her girlish fantasies of what it would be like to make love with Nick, of how it would feel. Now she knew.

Nick wasn't looking at her, though. He was totally focused on the street as he weaved between cars. His attention was divided only when he glanced into the rearview mirror. And he kept doing that.

Annalise's stomach lurched—not from his driving but from fear. Even before he said the words, she knew.

"We're being followed."

Would the men never give up? Would they keep coming after her?

And why?

Chapter 8

Damn it...

Nick had been certain he hadn't been followed the night before. So where the hell had the tail come from?

How had they found them?

Or had they already known where he was?

With Annalise in the SUV, he didn't want to drive too fast—too recklessly. But he either had to lose the tail or...

But that would be even more dangerous—doubling back—catching him. He would be armed, as he'd been in the hospital parking garage and department store lot. He would fire more bullets. And maybe this time he wouldn't miss Annalise.

Nick's shoulder throbbed. The bandage, stiff with dried blood, pulled at the stitches beneath it. He would have blamed the wound for keeping him awake last night. Or the danger.

He'd sat up on the couch, his gun nearby, just in case he'd needed it. But he wouldn't have been able to sleep even if there was no threat. No injury. He wouldn't have been able to sleep because Annalise was in the house. And his body had throbbed in a place other than his shoulder. It had throbbed with desire, with need.

He couldn't be distracted, though, not with her safety at stake. Hers and their baby's. But would they ever be safe until whoever was after them was caught?

He jerked the wheel to do a quick lane switch. Then, at the last moment, he took a sharp turn. He hadn't lived in River City all of his life, but he'd been there long enough that he knew it well. He knew the back alleys and the side streets and the deserted areas of the city where the economy had yet to rebound.

Maybe that was his fault. He'd shut down so much of the corruption that some areas weren't doing the business they once had. There weren't as many street corner drug dealers or prostitutes. Whoever was after him might think it was his fault, too. They might blame him for their business not doing as well. And they wanted to shut him down.

Why go after Annalise?

Had they followed him that night to Chicago—to her? When he had spent the night with her, maybe they'd thought she meant more to him, more than he was willing to admit she did.

He focused again—on the street and the rearview mirror. The black vehicle was back there yet. And because it had nearly lost him, it was going faster, making the tail more conspicuous.

They were definitely being followed. He took another sharp turn and another.

Annalise gripped the passenger door and the console.

"Are you okay?" he asked. Was he endangering her? Or the baby?

She nodded. "Did you lose him yet?"

"No."

"He's that good?"

"He is." And realization dawned. He knew who was behind him. He pulled over into a dead-end alley and stopped the SUV.

Annalise glanced fearfully around. "What are you doing?" Her green eyes widened as the other vehicle pulled into the alley behind them. "We're trapped."

He shook his head, even as he drew his weapon. He didn't think he would need it, but he had learned to take no chances. Except for that night.

The night he'd gotten Annalise pregnant.

He reached for the driver's door handle. But before he could push it open, Annalise clutched his arm. "Nick!"

"It's okay," he told her. But it wasn't. He stepped out, walked back to the other vehicle and pounded on the driver's window.

It rolled down, and the blond-haired bodyguard leaned out. "How the hell did you make me?"

"You're not that good," he said.

Milek Kozminski chuckled. "I'm the best."

"I made you," he reminded him.

And color flushed Milek's face. "You wouldn't have if it hadn't been for the other car."

"Someone else was following me?" Panic clutched his heart, and he tightened his grasp on his gun and glanced around the alley. But there were only rusted dumpsters and their two vehicles.

Nobody else.

"You lost that tail easily," Milek said.

At least there was that. "That's good."

"You shouldn't have been trying to lose me," Milek admonished him.

"I didn't know for certain it was you." Not at first, anyway.

Milek sighed. "You know how this works."

"This?"

"Payne Protection," Milek said. "We have each other's backs. No man—or woman—is left alone in danger." Milek would know that. His family had protected him even when he hadn't wanted their protection.

Now Nick could understand Milek's irritation with his fellow bodyguards. "It's *my* job to protect Annalise."

"And it's my job to protect you," Milek said.

"I don't need any protection," Nick said.

Milek pointed toward his wounded shoulder. "You've already been shot. Of course you need protection."

"I've been taking care of myself for thirty-one years," he reminded Milek.

Milek pointed toward the SUV Nick had left idling. "Now you have someone else to worry about."

He couldn't deny that he was worried. "I'll protect her, too."

"How?" Milek asked. "By going off alone without letting anyone know you were leaving?"

Nick wasn't used to having to answer to anyone. For the past year, he'd been the boss. His bureau chief in Chicago had given him full autonomy. Chief Lynch trusted him; the Paynes should, too.

"Where were you going?" Milek asked.

"Chicago."

Milek shook his head. "No. It's too dangerous."

Nick had tried to tell Annalise that. But she'd been determined to go to her closing, to check in on the property management business she ran. And it was Annalise.

He'd always struggled to tell her no. But he had, until that night six months ago.

That night had changed so much.

"Logan won't approve it," Milek said. "And you agreed you're working for him."

Nick sighed and holstered his weapon. "Fine. I'll bring her back to my place."

But that was dangerous, too. Not because of someone finding them there. It was dangerous for Nick to be alone with her. He wanted her too much....

Something was going on with Nick—something that Milek recognized. The internal struggle.

It was more painful than a physical one. He wanted to help. But Nick had to conquer his inner demons on his own. Milek could help him fight only the outer ones. So he followed him again—back to his place.

He had trusted that Nick would go back to his rental house in River City. The FBI special agent had realized it was too dangerous to go to Chicago. So why had he been going? Had he been seeking out his contacts there—the agents he'd worked with out of the Chicago Bureau?

Milek had met most of them, had worked protection duty at a couple of their weddings. They were good guys. But they weren't Payne Protection bodyguards. No one would guard Nick more faithfully than family.

And to Milek, Nick was family. They didn't share blood like Nick did with the Paynes. But Milek owed Nick his life and, more important, the lives of his family. Nick had protected the woman Milek loved and their son. He would do the same for Nick now.

He pulled to the curb behind the black SUV as he had in the alley. But Nick didn't jump right out like he had back there. Instead, he idled at the curb for a while. Long enough that Milek exited his vehicle and hurried up to Nick's side.

The window was already down, Nick's weapon already drawn. Milek drew his as he glanced toward the house. Then he saw what Nick had; the front door stood open. They hadn't left that long ago—less than an hour. It was possible that whoever had broken in was still inside. If they had broken in to get to Nick and Annalise, it was probable they were still inside—waiting for their return.

"I'll check it out," he said.

Nick shook his head. "I will."

"We can't leave her out here alone," Milek said as he glanced around. Other vehicles were parked along the street. Someone could have been ducked down low in one of them, waiting for the opportunity to get Annalise.

"No, we can't," Nick readily agreed. "That's why you're staying with her."

"But I'm assigned to protect *you*," Milek reminded him.

Nick snorted. "Like you never disregarded Logan's orders before."

He had. But it had nearly cost him his life.

"It's too dangerous for you to go in alone," Milek said. He reached for the transmitter on his collar. Thanks to Nikki's computer savvy, they had the same high-tech gadgets the FBI had. "Let me call in backup."

Nick opened the door. "I already waited too long," he said. "If we wait any longer, they'll be gone."

Annalise leaned across the console, her hand extended toward Nick. "Don't go," she implored him. "It's too dangerous."

Milek heartily agreed. But he knew it was pointless to argue with Nicholas Rus. He'd never known a more determined or stubborn or fearless man.

Until Nick turned back to him.

There was fear in his eyes. But it wasn't for himself. Flinching as he lifted his right hand, he clasped Milek's shoulder. Despite the wound to his own shoulder, his grasp was tight—like that of his left hand on his gun. "Protect her," he ordered Milek.

It was an order he couldn't disobey. He nodded. Then he watched as Nick hurried off toward the house and that open door. It was all he could do not to follow him, simply to watch as he disappeared inside.

He lifted his hand and flipped the transmitter on his collar. "Nick's house has been broken into," he reported.

"Are he and the subject inside?" a voice asked. It wasn't Nikki. It was whoever Logan had hired to replace her as the computer guru for his division of Payne Protection.

"Annalise is with him. Nick went inside alone."

"What the hell is Nick doing?" Logan's voice emanated from the radio now.

"He's evaluating the threat," Milek said. But that was his job—the job Nick had refused to let him do.

"He's going to get himself killed," Logan said.

Milek hoped like hell that the boss wasn't right.

Annalise didn't know the man who now sat in Nick's place in the driver's seat. But she reached across the console and grasped his arm. "Please," she said. "Go in and help him!"

He shook his head. "I can't."

Because he thought he had to protect her. She was the subject, according to the first voice that had come through the radio on his collar. She was the client even though she had yet to pay anyone. In her business, the client was always right.

"You have to help him," she said as she stared through the windshield at the house.

Nick had left the door open, like he'd found it. Or maybe because it was broken. It swung strangely from the hinges as a breeze kicked up.

Despite that it was spring, that breeze blew through the open window and chilled her. She shivered.

Milek moved his hand toward the power button to roll it up. But she clutched his arm harder. "No," she said. "Leave it open."

Not that they could hear anything. The house sat back far enough from the street that they could hear no sounds emanating from it. The blinds were drawn, too, so they could see no movement inside.

"Logan's right." At least, she assumed it had been Logan whose voice had come second through the radio. "Nick's going to get himself killed."

He had already been shot. He was in no condition to take on—alone—whoever had broken into his house. There could have been one man or two or more.

She shivered again.

"He's armed," the blond bodyguard said. "And he's a damn good shot."

And just as he made that pronouncement, a shot rang

out. But they didn't know whether Nick had fired it. Instead it could have been fired at him.

She screamed and reached for the passenger door. But the man held her back.

"It's too dangerous."

That hadn't stopped Nick from going inside alone. And it wouldn't stop her. Tugging free of the man's grasp, she pushed open the door and ran for the house.

Ran for Nick…

Chapter 9

So much for the reinforced locks he'd bought. The door had been nearly ripped from the hinges. As he'd pushed past it, Nick had glanced around, but with all the blinds drawn inside, the house was dark.

So much for the bars on the windows and the stockade fence, too. They hadn't kept out his intruder. Who kept breaking in? And was he still there?

Grasping the Glock tightly, Nick moved through the house. Closets and cupboards stood open like the front door. Furniture had been tossed.

Too much destruction had been done for the intruder to be gone already. It would have taken too long to do all this and get away in the short time Nick and Annalise had been gone. The perpetrator had to be inside yet. And Nick heard the telltale thump of something moving.

Maybe it was only the back door. Maybe it had been

broken from the hinges like the front. But as he moved toward it, he located the noise—in the bedroom at the back. Gage had been staying in it, except for last night.

Last night Annalise had slept there while Nick had sat up tensely on the couch, his body aching for hers. She was outside now, safe with Milek. He had to believe that. Or he would be tempted to go back to check on her.

There could have been more men outside, waiting for him to leave her unprotected. But he hadn't left her unprotected. Milek might disobey Logan, but he wouldn't disobey Nick. He wouldn't endanger Annalise or the baby's safety.

So Nick reached for the door of that back bedroom. It wasn't closed tightly, so he only had to push it open slightly to see a dark clothed figure moving around in the shadows. Annalise's few things, the clothes Candace had gone inside the department store and purchased for her, had been thrown around the room. They lay across the hardwood floor and the unmade bed. It looked as if she hadn't slept any more than he had. But then, she was probably too afraid to rest.

And she had every reason to be.

He swung his gun barrel toward the figure and shouted, "Put your hands up! You're under arrest!"

He'd told Logan he was quitting the Bureau, but he hadn't given notice yet. So he still had his badge—his authority. His weapon…

And as the man catapulted toward him, he fired it. If a bullet struck the intruder, it didn't stop the huge guy. He kept coming at Nick and knocked him back against the hallway wall. His breath left his lungs at the force of the assault. And as his head struck the wall, black spots obscured his vision. He peered into the man's face, trying to get a good look so he could identify him.

Nick didn't think it was the guy from the parking garage. But it could have been. A big hand locked around his, fighting for the gun. He fired it again.

And finally the man loosened his grasp. Nick slid down the wall at his back. But he kept his weapon in his hand—waiting for the guy to come at him again. Instead the intruder turned and ran for the back door. Nick needed to get up—needed to chase him. To stop him.

To find out what the hell he wanted.

But he couldn't catch his breath, couldn't completely clear his vision yet. Then another shadow rushed toward him. He should have known the guy probably wasn't alone. There had been two in the parking garage. The one who'd died had probably been replaced with the man who'd just attacked him. This would be the second guy.

So Nick raised his gun. Just as his finger was about to squeeze the trigger, his vision cleared. He noticed the slight figure but for her belly. And the blond hair flowing behind her as she ran toward him.

"Annalise!" He shook in reaction—not from the fight but from the fact that he had pointed his weapon at the woman who carried his baby.

A shadow loomed behind her. He raised his gun higher and met Milek's gaze. "I'm sorry," his friend said. "She got away from me."

She hadn't been in danger outside. She'd been in danger with him. He could have shot her and their baby.

"Are you okay?" she asked. "We heard a shot!"

"No," he said as he finally regained his feet. "I'm not

okay." He was mad as hell. "What were you thinking to come running in here?"

The color drained from her face, leaving her pale but for the bright sheen of her green eyes. Her voice quavering, she murmured, "Nick…"

"Obviously you don't care about your life, or you wouldn't have tried to stop them from stealing your car yesterday, and you wouldn't have run toward the sound of a gunshot," he said. "At least care about the life of our baby!"

She flinched, and tears shimmered in her eyes. "I—I'm sorry."

He was the sorry one. He shouldn't have lashed out at her. He'd been scared. Scared that he'd nearly hurt her. And then he had.

Emotionally.

She was probably in more danger from him than from whoever had broken into his place. He was the one who kept hurting her. And he hated himself for it—probably as much as she was beginning to hate him.

She loved Nick. That was why she'd run toward the sound of the gunshot—because she had been scared that he was hurt. Or worse…

But he was right. She should have thought about their child—about the danger she was putting their baby in when she reacted without thinking. She would be more careful from now on. She wouldn't take any chances with her safety.

Or with her heart.

"You'll be safe here," Milek Kozminski assured her as he showed her into the master bedroom of the warehouse that had been converted into living space. It was all exposed brick and corrugated metal. "My brother and I installed the best security system we could find when I bought the place five years ago. We were barely able to crack it ourselves, so no one else will be able to."

"Is that part of your job?" she asked. "To make sure security systems are secure?"

His mouth curved into a slight grin. "It is now."

Apparently it hadn't always been his job. Was this his home or a property he rented out?

She glanced around. It was furnished yet somehow looked deserted, too, as if nobody had lived there for a while. "Are you going to stay here, too?" she asked.

He shook his head. "My wife and I moved out last month—when we got possession of the house we bought."

"Oh."

"We needed a yard for our son." He glanced down at her belly.

She didn't have to worry about a yard for a while. If Nick was right and she kept putting herself in danger, she wouldn't ever have to worry about a yard. She blinked back the sting of tears. She wouldn't cry. She hadn't back at Nick's place. And she wouldn't here. She was tougher than that.

But then Milek opened the bedroom door, and she heard Nick's deep voice, heard him telling Logan Payne, "You should give this assignment to someone else."

"You don't want to protect Annalise?" Logan asked him.

"I can't."

Milek whirled around as if his body could shield her from what she'd just heard. "You should lie down for a while," he said. "Rest."

She nodded although she knew she wouldn't be able to sleep. But she wanted him to leave her alone. She needed to be alone.

Actually, she needed her life back. She needed to be back at her job in Chicago—buying and selling houses, managing property. She knew what she was doing there. She didn't know what she was doing when people were trying to abduct her or shoot her.

She didn't know how to react—how to protect herself. It didn't even seem like it was really happening, like it was real at all. Why was *she* in danger?

Nick, she could understand. This was his life, the one she had been upset that he'd chosen when he joined the Marines and then the Bureau.

Milek had been gone only a few minutes when the doorknob rattled again. She quickly lay down on the king-size bed to pretend, at least, that she was resting. But she turned away from the door so he wouldn't see her face—her open eyes.

The mattress dipped as someone settled next to her. Surprised, she rolled over and discovered it was Nick who'd joined her. He was lying beside her as if they routinely shared a bed. They'd had only one night.

Her hand rubbed over her belly. One night had been enough, though.

"I thought you were leaving," she said.

"Why would you think that?"

"I heard you telling Logan to give this assignment to someone else," she said. To him, she would always be the pest he wanted to get rid of it. "You don't want to protect me."

He reached out, and his fingertips skimmed across her cheek, brushing back a lock of hair. "I can't."

"I'm sorry," she said. "It was stupid of me to run toward them when they were taking my car. And it was stupid of me to run into the house after we heard the shot."

His hand moved, his thumb sliding over her lower lip. "I'm sorry," he said. "I was too harsh with you."

"You were right, though," she acknowledged. "And I'll be more careful now. You won't have to worry about the baby."

"I'm worried about you," he said. "I almost shot you today." He shuddered, and the bed shook beneath his body.

She slid toward him until they touched. Her arm against his, her hip, her thigh.

Her breath caught as her pulse quickened. She hadn't been this close to him since that night. But that night, they had been even closer. No clothes had separated them. Nothing had as he'd filled her.

"That's why I don't think I can protect you," he said. "I'm so worried about you that I can't focus." He blinked as if he were struggling now. His lashes were so long and thick, so black like his hair. He kept that short, but it was soft. She remembered how soft it had felt that night beneath her fingers, against her breast and her thigh.

She shivered.

And as if he thought she was cold, he pulled her closer, wrapping his arm around her. Her body pressed tightly against his now. But they weren't close enough.

Not as close as she knew they could be.

"You're not just trying to get rid of me?" she asked. "Like you used to?"

He chuckled. "If I wanted to get rid of you, I would have pulled that trigger." But there was no amusement in his blue eyes—only something that looked like despair. "I came too close to doing that, to hurting you."

He had hurt her.

And as if he knew it, his arm tightened. "I'm sorry, Annalise."

"It was my fault," she said. "You were right. I keep putting myself and the baby in danger." Like now…

She should have been protecting herself—protecting her heart as it swelled in her chest, filling again with love for Nick. Love that he didn't want, just like he didn't want her.

"I think it's my fault you're in danger," he said. "Someone's after me, and they're using you to hurt me."

She must have been more tired than she'd realized. "How?"

"Hurting you would hurt me."

"Why?" she asked. "I don't mean anything to you."

His blue eyes widened in surprise. "You really believe that?"

She nodded. "I'm just a pest—"

Before she could say any more, his mouth covered hers. He kissed her gently at first, his lips just brushing across her lips. But then she gasped for the breath that had escaped her lungs. And he deepened the kiss.

What the hell was wrong with him?

Logan had no idea why he had refused Nick's resignation. Sure, he wanted the FBI special agent working for him. Nicholas Rus was one of the most brilliant men Logan had ever met; he was also strong, fearless and intense. And more intuitive than any other person Logan had met besides his mother. If Nick didn't think he could protect Annalise Huxton, Logan should have taken him at his word and removed him from the assignment.

"The condo is safe," Milek assured him.

Logan hadn't realized he'd been staring at it through the windshield of the SUV. From the passenger seat next to him, Milek studied it, too. Made of brick and metal and concrete, the place really was a fortress.

"Nobody can get in there unless Nick or Annalise lets him inside," Milek said, but it was as if he was trying to assure himself now.

The security system wasn't infallible. Logan's wife had breached it once. Sure, she'd set off the alarm, but she had made it inside. Stacy was a Kozminski, though.

"Well, nobody but Garek or I," Milek amended himself before adding, "And Stacy..."

Logan chuckled.

"And none of us poses a threat to Nick." The Kozminskis had once mistrusted lawmen and with good reason. A cop had framed their father for the murder of Logan's father. But they all trusted Nick. Because he was Nick.

None of them had met a more honest man. And Nick had said that he couldn't protect her.

Logan suspected his brother wasn't talking about physically. Even with a shoulder wound, Nick could take care of himself. It was in other ways that Nick thought he couldn't protect Annalise Huxton. The baby she carried had to be his.

He'd wanted to ask, but he worried that Nick would think he was prying. And he would shut them all out when he'd finally let them into his life.

Logan shook his head and focused on the real issue.

"Who does pose a threat to Nick?" he wondered

aloud. "Garek talked to Chekov. He doesn't think it's him."

"And Amber talked to Evelyn Reynolds," Milek said, his voice taking on the usual pride he had in his wife.

Nick had recently jailed the former district attorney for corruption. Evelyn Reynolds had every reason to want revenge against him.

"And?"

Milek shrugged. "Amber doesn't think Evelyn has the ability or resources anymore to go after anyone." He uttered a ragged sigh. "If she did, I think she'd go after Amber instead of Nick." Because Amber now had the job her former colleague had coveted.

Logan nodded. "So who is it?"

Milek shrugged again. "Nick made a lot of enemies in River City."

A lot of dangerous enemies.

"And who knows what he did in the FBI before he came here," Milek continued.

It must have been big to be given the assignment of cleaning up an entire police force. Finding who was after him could take a while.

Maybe even forever.

"I'll talk to his former colleagues," Milek offered.

"I already have a call in to Chief Lynch," Logan said. The Bureau boss would help—if he could.

Could anyone help Nick?

Maybe Nick was right. Maybe he couldn't protect Annalise. He was going to have his hands full protecting himself.

Chapter 10

Her lips were so soft, so silky beneath his. And her mouth…

He slipped his tongue into the heat and tasted the sweetness. Her tongue met his, shyly at first. And then she kissed him back. Her lips moved beneath his, and her teeth nipped, lightly grazing his tongue and his bottom lip.

Given her sweetness, her passion was a surprise. It had caught him off guard that night six months ago. It had severed his always tenuous hold on his control around her. And he'd forgotten who she was and who he was.

He'd acted only on the desire. That desire coursed through him now, heating his blood, making his heart pound furiously.

Making his body tense as need overwhelmed him. He slid his hands down her body, down the length of her back to the curve of her butt and hips. He wanted to bury himself inside her body—like he had that night. He had never felt anything as incredible as being inside Annalise.

Her hands were moving, too, from his hair down the nape of his neck to his shoulders. He flinched as she grazed over his wounded one.

She must have felt that flinch. "I'm sorry," she murmured. "I didn't mean to hurt you."

He knew that. Annalise would never deliberately hurt anyone. Or at least, he hadn't thought so. But she hadn't told him about the pregnancy. And that hurt.

It also worried him.

Could he trust her?

Or was she more like his mother than he ever would have guessed? He pulled back.

"Are you okay?" she asked anxiously. Her fingers touched the bandage on his shoulder. "Do you need to go to the hospital?"

He shook his head.

"The stitches might have gotten torn open when you fought with that man in your house," she said.

It hadn't been much of a fight. He hoped he had, at least, hit the son of a bitch with a bullet. He had his officers at the River City PD checking hospitals and clinics. When his cell vibrated, he hoped it was one of them. He pulled it from his pocket and glanced at the screen.

He didn't recognize the number, but he answered it anyway. It gave him an excuse to roll away from Annalise, to put some much needed distance between them. He sat up on the edge of the bed, his back to her.

"Special Agent Rus here," he murmured into the phone.

"Agent?" his sister remarked. He hadn't realized she'd had his number. But there wasn't anything Nikki Payne couldn't find out on her own. She was an expert computer hacker, probably because Logan had always kept her chained to a desk. "I didn't think you'd really quit."

He hadn't. Not yet. "I haven't had time to give my notice yet," he pointed out.

She actually chuckled. "And you don't want to give up the resources yet, either."

"No," he admitted. She was smart. Logan had probably lost his most valuable employee when she'd switched over to Cooper's team.

"Send your resources over to the alley behind Chekov's nightclub."

He cursed. "What will they find?" He hoped not another damn body. Even though the place had been shut down months ago, bad things continued to happen there. It continued to be a beacon for crime.

"Annalise's car," Nikki replied.

"How'd you find it?" Had she thought to look there, or had she been tipped off?

"Traffic cams."

"You hacked into them?"

She snorted. "What? You going to arrest me for hacking into River City PD?"

"I would have given you access if you'd asked," he said. "Thanks for finding the car."

"It's empty," she said with a weary-sounding sigh. "They must have taken her overnight bag. It's probably been wiped clean, too."

"I'll send over the crime lab to check," he said. "Just

in case." Ideally the men had missed something, like the seat lever or rearview mirror.

"Maybe the techs will find something," she said doubtfully.

She'd probably already checked those places for prints. She was resourceful. She was also stubborn.

"Does Logan know you're working the case?" he asked.

"I don't work for Logan anymore," she reminded him.

"He's still your brother," Nick said. "And he's not going to be happy if you put yourself in danger." Neither would Nick, especially if she was doing it for him. But why would she do that? She resented the hell out of him.

"I shouldn't have let them get away," she murmured.

He knew that feeling of guilt and responsibility. He deserved to feel like that, though. She didn't. "Nikki—"

"Call your crime lab," she said. And she clicked off before he could offer her any reassurances.

It wasn't as if she would listen to what he said, anyway—not when she never listened to Logan. And she actually loved that brother.

"She found my car?" Annalise asked.

He nodded but cautioned her, "It's probably a total loss. It got shot up in the hospital parking garage."

Her fingertips skimmed over his shoulder again. "So did you."

"Maybe I'm a total loss, too," he murmured.

"You weren't supposed to leave the hospital yet, not with all the blood you lost. And you could have been reinjured when that man attacked you in your house," she said. "You should go to the hospital to have them check your stitches."

"I can't leave you."

"The other bodyguards are here."

He shook his head. "They left." But knowing how Payne Protection worked, he doubted they had gone very far. He wasn't accustomed to or entirely comfortable with having all this support. Growing up an only child, he'd thought he would always be a loner. Sure, Gage had followed him around. And Annalise.

But he'd always known they weren't family, only neighbors who had pitied him. They'd had a loving, supportive family—unlike him.

But that was then. Everything had changed when his mother died and left him the letter telling him who his father was. Everything but him.

He was still a loner. He still didn't know how to let people in. Not even Annalise.

Except for that one night. That night she had gotten closer than anyone else ever had to him. She'd touched something Nick hadn't even realized he had: a heart.

He was a total loss. Annalise knew it. Like her car, she needed to write off Nick and finally let go of her hope that they would ever be together.

Again.

They'd had that one night. And in a few months, they would have a child. Did Nick want to be a part of their baby's life? He had never wanted to be a part of hers.

Moments after his sister's phone call, he had slipped out of the bed and walked into the other room. She'd heard the rumble of his deep voice as he made calls. Probably to the crime lab. Maybe to his brothers.

He was keeping them apprised. She was the one who

felt in the dark. Not just about why someone was after her but also about Nick.

Despite knowing him almost her entire life, she doubted she would ever understand him. So she focused on her life again. She had calls of her own to make—apologizing to the client whose closing she'd missed. Checking in with her subcontractors for the property management business.

She had so many responsibilities. Movement fluttered inside her belly, reminding her of the greatest responsibility of them all. Her baby.

Nick's baby.

She had to delegate. Her career wasn't as important as her child. She handed out some assignments to her employees. Then she turned off her phone. She wouldn't worry about what was happening in Chicago. But without work to focus on, her mind went back to Nick. Her lips tingled yet from his kisses. She'd thought he'd wanted her again. And maybe he had, until she'd touched his wounded shoulder.

She glanced at her phone again. If she had Logan's number or Nikki's or Milek's, she would have called them—would have convinced them to get medical help for Nick. But she didn't know how to reach them.

She didn't know how to reach Nick, either. Doubting he would return to the bedroom, she opened the door and ran into his chest.

His hands gripped her shoulders, steadying her. "Are you okay?"

She nodded. "I'm fine. I just didn't expect you to be standing outside the door. Is that what a bodyguard does?"

He shrugged. "I wouldn't know. I haven't been a bodyguard very long."

She remembered what she'd overheard of his conversation with Logan and his sister. "You're really going to quit the Bureau?"

He nodded.

Shock gripped her. He loved his job. His enthusiasm for it had been the reason Gage had decided to become an FBI agent, too. "Why would you do that?"

"To keep you safe."

"I won't be in danger forever," she said. At least, she hoped she wouldn't be. "What will you do when I'm safe again?"

"I'll keep working for Logan," he said.

She doubted that. "I know why you're doing this," she said. "You feel responsible, that you put me in danger."

"I'm sure I did."

She didn't believe that. But she couldn't imagine what she would have done to put herself in danger, either. Despite his doubts the night before, she had no crazy exes. No one obsessed with her or wanting vengeance.

"It's not your fault," she said.

"It is if they're after me and they're using you to get to me."

"Why would they use me?" she asked. "Why would they think you cared about what might happen to me?"

He reached out, and his fingers skimmed over her belly. "They must have followed me that night I went to Chicago."

She shivered as she realized what they had observed—him going inside a house with her and not leaving until morning, after they'd made love for hours and hours.

"Why?" she asked, wondering why he hadn't pushed her away that night like he had every other time she'd hugged him.

He shrugged. "I wish I knew."

She suspected he didn't know what she'd really asked when he continued, "I've put away a lot of people. Someone must be after revenge."

And they were using her to get it. Or so he believed. She wasn't convinced.

But she wanted her real question—the one that had bothered her for the past six months—answered. "Why did you make love to me that night?"

He sucked in an audible breath. "Annalise…"

"You've pushed me away for years," she reminded him. "You didn't want me following you, touching you."

"You were a kid," he said.

"I haven't been a kid for seven years…" An adult was considered eighteen. That was how old he and Gage had been when they'd joined the Marines. "You have acted more annoyed with me as we've gotten older, more insistent that you don't want me hugging you."

He caught her hand in his and brought it down to the front of his pants. "This is why," he said as he rubbed her knuckles down the erection pushing against his fly. "Because every time you touch me, I react like this."

Hope swelled in her heart. His hand dropped away from hers, but she kept rubbing her fingers along his fly. Until he groaned.

"You're killing me."

She wasn't trying to—someone else was doing that.

She didn't want to hurt him. She wanted the same thing she'd always wanted from Nick—his love.

That was probably the lost cause. But even if she couldn't have his love, maybe she could have his desire.

She stepped back, through the open door of the master bedroom. Then she reached for him. Linking their hands, she tried to tug him inside with her.

He hesitated at the threshold, his gaze skimming down her face to her belly. "I can't."

"Nobody will get in the condo," she reminded him of what Milek had told her. "The security system is too high-tech. You don't have to worry about keeping me safe."

"Yes," he said. "But I worry about more than just you now." He touched her belly again. "I don't want to hurt the baby."

"You won't." Her doctor had assured her it was safe to have sex. Annalise had nearly laughed when the obstetrician had told her that. She hadn't thought she would get this close to Nick again. But she wasn't close enough.

Not yet…

She had felt the effect she had on Nick. Knowledge was power. She remembered what had driven him crazy that night—how he'd reacted to things she'd done, the sounds she'd made.

She stepped back again, closer to the bed. And she lifted her shirt. Pulling it over her head, she dropped it onto the floor. Her breasts were fuller than they'd been six months ago. They nearly spilled out of her lacy bra.

Nick's gaze was focused on them—so focused that her nipples tightened and pushed against the lace. She needed his touch. She needed him.

She pushed her pants down her hips and stepped out of them. She wore lace panties that matched the bra. They were her regular size. Her hips hadn't spread yet. Only her belly had swelled. She wasn't huge yet—not like the women she'd seen in her OB's office.

Nerves fluttered in her stomach, along with the baby's kicks. She wasn't looking forward to getting that big, to being that uncomfortable.

Maybe she was already too big, though. Maybe Nick didn't find her attractive anymore. Heat rushed to her face. And she leaned over to pick up her shirt from the floor. But before she could tug it on, it was pulled from her hand.

Nick tossed it aside as he reached for her. "You are so damn beautiful," he murmured as if the words were wrenched from him.

He wasn't staring at her body, though. He was staring into her eyes. His hands cupped her face, and he leaned down to kiss her. His mouth covered hers, and he kissed her deeply, passionately. His tongue slipped between her lips.

She gasped at the sensations racing through her. She wanted him even more than she had the last time—because now she knew how incredible it could be between them. Her girlish fantasies hadn't even come close to the reality. To how incredible they were together.

He kept kissing her. But he touched her, too. One fingertip traced down her spine before his hands cupped her hips. He dragged her closer to him. And she could feel the hardness of his erection.

She reached between them for the button on his pants. But she fumbled with it. So he moved her hand aside and pulled the button free. Then he lowered his zipper. He kicked off his pants. Stepping back, he removed his holster and put it and the gun on the bedside table. He pulled his shirt up over his head.

Heat flushed her body at the sight of his chest and arms—all bare skin and rippling muscles. Her gaze lowered, tracing his washboard abs. His erection had pushed up out of the waistband of his boxers. The tip of it begged for her touch.

She obliged.

He groaned as her fingers closed around him. She pushed his shorts down and slid her hand up and down his shaft.

"Annalise..." That muscle twitched in his cheek again.

He pulled her hand from him and lifted her. He carried her to the bed as easily as if she didn't have extra weight now. As if he didn't have a wounded shoulder.

She reached for it but was careful not to touch his injury again. "Nick, you're going to tear your stitches open for certain."

"Don't worry about me," he said.

But she did. She always had. She'd worried about him living alone with that woman who had cared more about her next high than she had about her son. She'd worried about him when he'd joined the Marines and when he'd been recruited into the FBI. She had spent her life worrying about Nick.

And given their current situation, she wasn't about to stop anytime soon. Unless they could stop whoever was after them.

He kissed her forehead, where furrows of concern had formed for him. Then he kissed her nose and her lips and the end of her chin. His lips kept moving, down her throat, over her collarbone.

Finally he pushed her bra down, and his lips closed over the tip of one breast. She arched up as pleasure spiraled through her body. He tugged gently with his lips and then his teeth. A tension began to build inside her.

She squirmed on the bed. His hand was there, moving between her legs. He pushed aside her panties and stroked his fingers over her.

"Nick..."

The tension eased as pleasure coursed through her. But it wasn't enough. It wasn't nearly what she knew he could give her, what they could give each other.

She reached for him, stroking her hands over his back and butt. She pulled him toward her as she lifted her hips. She needed him inside her—needed to feel one with him as she'd felt that night.

He pulled off her panties and dropped his boxers. Then he was there—his erection nudging against her. She parted her legs as he pushed gently inside her. She arched her hips, taking him deeper, and locked her legs around his waist.

"Careful," he murmured, moving slowly as if he still feared he would hurt the baby.

But the baby was safe. Annalise was the one in danger—of falling even more deeply in love with Nick. "It's okay," she assured him.

He tensed. "Just okay?"

A smile tugged at her lips. "Well..."

He withdrew.

She clutched at him. "Nick!"

He pushed back inside her.

She gripped him with her inner muscles, holding him

deep inside her. But he pulled back again. And, teasing her, he stroked in and out.

The sensation built the tension, winding it so tightly that she couldn't get enough of him. She raked her nails lightly down his back and sank them into his butt.

And she rose up and nipped at his chin and his neck.

"Annalise…" He growled her name like a warning.

She didn't heed it. She couldn't listen to reason; she'd completely shut off the voice inside her head that had told her to be careful with Nick. She couldn't deny herself what she had always wanted: Nick.

As he continued to move inside her, the tension finally broke. Her body shuddered as she came. His name left her lips in a scream of pleasure.

He tensed, and then his body shuddered as he filled her. He rolled so that she sprawled across his chest. Her head settled between his neck and uninjured shoulder. Feeling at home and safe in his arms, her eyes immediately drifted closed.

She didn't know how long she slept. When she awakened, her head was on a pillow. Blankets had been pulled over her body, but she still felt cold without the heat of Nick's body. He was gone.

She tensed as she remembered how she had felt the last time she'd awakened alone after making love with him. Then, as now, she wondered if it had really happened at all or if she'd only dreamed it. But their baby shifted inside her, and she knew it had happened.

And when, like last time, she'd accepted that it had happened and he'd left before she awakened, humiliation washed over her. Why did she keep throwing herself at Nick only to have him run away?

He might have wanted her. One night. Now two…

But he didn't love her. And he probably never would.

Tears stung her eyes, but she blinked them back. She had to learn to protect herself. Not from the men trying to abduct her. She had to learn to protect herself from Nick. He was the one who would hurt her the most. Who already had.

But then she felt real pain. It shot through her stomach like a bullet or a knife—so sudden and sharp that she lost her breath at the intensity of it.

What was happening? What was wrong?

Her stomach tightened. As she placed her palms over it, she felt the hardness of it. Something was wrong—with her baby.

The pain came back—radiating throughout her. And she screamed. "Nick!"

There was no movement inside the condo. Where was he? Where had he gone?

She needed his help—needed him to help her save the baby before it was too late. Before they lost him or her…

Penny jerked awake as if someone had called her name. She'd done that when the kids were little. Even before they'd called out for her, she'd known they needed her. Somebody needed her now.

She flipped on the lamp beside the bed. It illuminated the darkness in a circle. On the pedestal table she'd painted a pale blue was her cell phone. She picked it up and stared at it. But the screen stayed dark.

No one was calling her. The kids were older now. They tried to handle things on their own. But ultimately they would reach out to her. They would call her.

Unless it was Nick who needed her. He hadn't yet learned to reach out, to trust that he would get assistance when he needed it. She could only hope that he would learn…before it was too late for anyone to help him.

Chapter 11

Nick had thought he'd heard something. Or at least, that was the excuse he'd given himself to leave Annalise lying alone in the bed in which they'd just made love. Like last time, their intimacy had humbled him and scared the hell out of him.

He'd never felt like that—as if he'd belonged anywhere—until he'd been inside her, their bodies joined. Her heart had beaten in sync with his until she'd fallen asleep. While hers had slowed, his had continued to beat fast.

And despite the release he'd found buried deep inside her, the tension hadn't left his body. So maybe he'd only imagined that he had heard something. But he'd eased her onto the pillow and covered her up.

Then he'd dressed quickly and grabbed up his weapon. He hadn't found anything amiss inside the condo. The

open living room, dining and kitchen area had been un-
disturbed. The bedrooms off the other side of the condo
had been empty. So maybe the noise had come from the
other side of the back door. It didn't open onto an alley. It
opened onto the unconverted part of the warehouse. Security back there wasn't as high-tech as inside the condo.

When he stepped inside, he didn't understand why it
wasn't wired with alarms, too. If someone was going to
break in, they probably would have wanted to get inside
Milek's studio. Penny had mentioned that the younger
Kozminski brother painted. She had even pointed out
the portrait he'd done years ago, which hung on the wall
of her office at the White Wedding Chapel.

But Nick didn't realize how talented or prolific Milek
was until he saw all the canvases. They leaned against
the walls, stacked upon each other. So many canvases.
Only one stood by itself. The canvas too big for an
easel, it leaned against a couple of metal barrels in the
middle of the room. Paint spattered the cement floor
all around it.

Intrigued, Nick walked up to it. And his breath
caught at the realism of it. It wasn't just the vibrancy
of the paint. It was the vibrancy of the people in the portrait. Milek had caught all of them as they were. Penny
sat in the middle like the matriarch she was. She ruled
her family with love, though, and it radiated from her—
from the warmth in her brown eyes.

The whole portrait radiated warmth and love. Love
among mother and sons and daughter. Love between
spouses like Logan and Stacy. Even Stacy's brothers
had been included in the portrait with their wives. And
Nick was there.

Why had she had Milek include him?

He had no doubt that the portrait was being painted at Penny's request. She would have wanted it because her family had expanded. Nick could understand her wanting her daughters-in-law and grandchildren in the portrait. He could even understand her including the Kozminskis; they had been part of her life for a long time—ever since their father had gone to prison for murdering his.

But him…

Nikki wouldn't be happy about his inclusion. Like him, she was alone in the portrait—at the other end of the family from where he was. Keeping them apart had been no accident. Despite being surrounded by all that family, Nick looked alone.

He looked like something was missing. Love.

And Annalise. She should have been in the portrait, too. And Gage. They were his family. They always had been. And now, with the baby she carried, Annalise and he were starting their own family.

Then he heard a noise. This time he had no doubt it was real. And he had no mistake about what it was: Annalise's scream.

He had left her alone in the condo and vulnerable to whoever might have broken in while he'd been distracted. He should have known—no place was impenetrable. And nowhere was safe enough for Annalise. Her scream chilled his blood. She sounded more terrified than he'd ever heard her.

In Afghanistan, Gage had learned to rely on his instincts. If he hadn't, he wouldn't have survived even the first time he'd been deployed. And he certainly wouldn't have survived the last.

His instincts had told him that something wasn't right with Nick and Annalise. He hadn't realized how serious the situation was until he learned she was at the hospital. Would Nick have even told him if Gage hadn't called him?

And the only damn reason Gage had called was that he'd come back to Nick's place and found it had been broken into—again. The door had hung from its damaged hinges. And it had looked as if there had been a struggle in the hallway. There was a body-sized dent in the drywall and droplets of blood on the floor.

Gage had called because he'd been worried.

And Nick had made him even more worried when he replied, "We're at River City Memorial…"

That had been just minutes ago. But those minutes had felt like hours while Gage had driven over to the hospital and parked in the underground garage. It hadn't helped that security had stopped him at the door. They'd frisked him like he would have searched a perp. Apparently, there'd been some trouble there recently and River City PD had advised the security staff to be extra vigilant.

Fortunately Gage had left his gun in his glove box, or they might not have let him into the ER waiting room. The minute he stepped inside, he looked for Nick. But he was probably hurt, too.

Because he wouldn't have let anyone get to Annalise without one hell of a fight. As much as he'd complained about her pestering him, Nick had always had a soft spot for her, something most people probably didn't even realize he had. He always acted so damn tough.

The waiting room overflowed with Paynes—all tall guys with black hair and blue eyes. He walked up to the one who looked the least surprised to see him and asked Logan, "Where are they?"

"I'm here," Nick said as he stepped away from the others.

Hell, even as long as he'd known him, Gage had still mistaken him for one of the others—for one of his half brothers. Nick looked that much like the others.

"Are you okay?" he asked.

Nick nodded. But he didn't look okay. He looked like hell, his jaw shadowed with stubble and what looked to be the beginning of a bruise. The corner of a ragged-looking bandage stuck out of the collar of his T-shirt.

But knowing Nick as well as he did, he understood those injuries were nothing to him.

"What about Annalise?" he asked.

"The doctor's checking her out," Nick replied.

"What the hell's going on?" Gage asked. "Your place has been ransacked again. Everything's all broken up. Was she hurt there?"

And if so, it was Gage's fault—because she had come to River City looking for him. The minute he'd gotten back to the US, he should have gone to see her, should have assured her that he was all right. Sure, he hadn't been, not totally. But at least he'd been alive.

And she wouldn't be in danger now.

Nick shook his head. "She wasn't hurt there."

"But she was hurt."

"Someone carjacked her yesterday," Cooper said. With his close-cropped hair, the former Marine looked the most like Nick. They were even about the same age. Their dad must have been some son of a bitch to get two women pregnant at nearly the same time.

Of course, they didn't talk about him like that. At

least, the Paynes didn't. They acted like the dead cop
had been a saint. But that was how people acted after
someone died; they remembered only the good things.

Was that how everyone had acted when they'd
thought he was dead? Had they remembered only his
good qualities? Had *she*? Not his sister but that other
woman, the one who'd ripped out his heart before he'd
reenlisted?

But at the moment, as anger coursed through him,
he couldn't recall any of his good qualities.

"Yesterday?" Clenching his fists, he stepped closer to
Nick. "She was hurt yesterday and you didn't tell me?"

"I didn't."

He slapped his palm against Nick's chest and pushed
him back. "You answered her phone and told me she
was in the kitchen cooking. And she was here—in the
emergency room. You lied to me!"

"She wasn't in the hospital yesterday," Nick said. "At
least, not when you called."

But she had been.

Gage's stomach churned. He felt sick, so sick at the
thought of his sweet sister injured. "What's wrong with
her?"

Cooper was the one who stepped up to answer again.
"She got a concussion during the carjacking."

Gage's head pounded as he thought of it—of the dan-
gers of a head injury. "She shouldn't have left the hospital, then." He pushed Nick back again. "You shouldn't
have let her leave!"

"You know Annalise."

Yes, he knew his sister. She was as stubborn as she
was sweet. And she was far stronger than he or Nick
had ever given her credit for being. So, yeah, she would

have put up a fight to leave. But if he'd been there, he would have made sure that she stayed—that she wasn't put in any danger.

"I want to see her!" Gage said. "I need to see her. Now!" He had to make certain his baby sister was all right. "Where is she?" He didn't wait for any of them to reply, though. He headed toward the doors marked No Admittance.

Before he could push open the doors, a strong hand caught his arm and yanked him back. "No, Gage."

He turned back to Nick, and his anger bubbled, threatening to boil over as his skin and even his blood heated from the intensity of it. He couldn't remember feeling like this—actually *feeling*—in a long time. "No?"

"You need to calm down," Nick said. "You're only going to upset her if you go in acting like this."

He wasn't acting. He was pissed. More pissed than he could remember being in a good long while.

"She's in the hospital," Gage said. "She must already be upset."

"Yes," Nick agreed. "And she can't get any more upset. It won't be good for her or for…"

There it was again in Nick's voice—that caution, that evasiveness. Gage narrowed his eyes and studied his old friend's face. "For *what*, Nick?"

That telltale muscle twitched in Nick's cheek. And it looked as if he made an effort to unclench his jaw before he finally replied, "For the baby."

Shock gripped Gage. He had seen and done things he'd never imagined he would see or do. But he had never been as shocked as he was now. "What baby?" he asked, his voice cracking with the emotions pummeling him. "What the hell are you talking about?"

"Your sister's pregnant," Nick said. "That's why she's here. She thought she was going into early labor."

"How early?" Gage asked. Then he added the better question. "How far along is she?"

"Twenty-four weeks," Nick replied with an almost ominous certainty. Maybe he knew because Annalise had told him or he'd overheard the doctor.

Or maybe…

He shook his head. No. Not Nick.

He wouldn't have crossed that line, not with Annalise.

No, some other guy had to have gotten her pregnant. Gage wasn't naive enough to think his sister was a total innocent. Once she'd hit her teens, she'd started dating. Yet she'd never gotten serious about anyone before—because of her stupid, stubborn crush on Nick.

But Gage had been gone a long time. She must have met someone while he was missing. He glanced around the waiting room. He still saw only Paynes. So where the hell was the baby's father? He had damn well better be next to her bed, holding her hand.

His gaze returned to Nick. And that sick feeling churned his stomach again.

The answer was on Nick's face: the guilt, the regret.

Gage shook his head. "No."

"It's my fault," Nick said. "It's all my fault…"

Since Gage heard she was in the hospital, he hadn't had much of a hold on his temper, but whatever control he had totally snapped. And he swung. His fist slammed right into Nick's clenched jaw. Pain coursed through Gage's hand from his knuckles to his wrist.

Nick—who had killer reflexes—hadn't even ducked. He barely stumbled back.

After shaking off the stinging in his hand, Gage clenched his fist again and wound up to swing once more. But before he could connect with Nick—who stood straight again and ready for another blow—someone stepped between them. Strong hands shoved Gage back.

"You want to fight?" a deep voice asked.

Gage blinked to clear his vision, but he was so angry he was literally seeing red. The man looked like Nick— enough like Nick that he swung. But his fist didn't connect. It was blocked. And he took a blow—to his stomach. He doubled over as pain radiated throughout his body. The pain wasn't from the blow itself but from the old injuries it aggravated: the broken ribs, the bruised organs.

He coughed and choked but came up swinging—for Nick. A hand caught his fist and held it. Again it wasn't Nick but Cooper, who'd stepped between them, who was trying to fight Nick's battle.

"What the hell are you doing?" Gage asked.

"Nick took a bullet to his shoulder yesterday," Cooper said. "He's in no shape to fight. You want to fight? You fight with me."

"I don't have a beef with you."

"Sometimes a soldier doesn't need a beef," Cooper said. "Sometimes he just needs to fight."

Was that Gage's issue? Had he just been itching for a fight?

No. His sister was in the hospital—pregnant and injured—and Nick had willingly taken the blame for her being in that situation.

No. He didn't want to fight just anyone; he wanted to fight Nick until his old friend was as hurt as Annalise was.

Annalise hurt, but it was only her pride. She had made such a fool of herself—with the screaming, with the hysteria—over Braxton Hicks contractions. Most pregnant women experienced them. They weren't even real contractions, just a dress rehearsal for the real thing.

"The baby is fine," the doctor assured her. He pointed toward the monitor showing her baby was curled up, sleeping. Annalise should have been, too. But she'd awoken in such a panic. That had had more to do with Nick being gone than the contractions, though.

Maybe she wouldn't have panicked so badly if he'd been with her. But she couldn't count on Nick being there for her. He would never stop running away from her.

The doctor reached for the belt to remove the monitor for her belly. But she caught his hand. "Can you leave it on?" she asked hopefully. "For just a little while longer."

She couldn't move her gaze from the monitor. She couldn't stop watching her baby—to make sure she or he was really all right. The baby wasn't doing anything now but sleeping. But the screen pulsed with every steady heartbeat. Annalise needed that reassurance—visually and audibly—that her baby was fine.

The doctor nodded. "Sure, I'll give you a few more minutes." He pulled the ER curtain aside and closed it behind him. But just seconds later, the curtain swept open again.

"No..." she murmured, her eyes filling with tears. She needed more time—more reassurance.

"It's all right, honey," a soft voice said.

She glanced up, expecting a nurse. But this woman wasn't dressed in scrubs. She wore jeans and a short-sleeve sweater. Her curls tumbled around her face, and her brown eyes radiated warmth.

"Nikki?"

The woman smiled, and lines crinkled her eyes and creased the skin around her mouth. She was older than Nikki.

"I'm Penny Payne," the woman introduced herself. "You're Nikki's mom?"

She smiled. "The boys', too."

"Of course." But that didn't explain why she was here—why she'd come to see Annalise.

The woman's gaze moved to the screen. She reached out and touched the baby on the monitor, her finger tracing over the image. As if the child could feel that touch, he moved inside Annalise—stretching and sprawling.

Annalise gasped as she realized what she'd just seen.

Penny chuckled. "Another boy—of course."

"Another?"

"Boys are prevalent in the Payne family."

Maybe Annalise really did have a concussion, because confusion muddled her mind. Nick didn't consider himself a Payne. But that wasn't even the issue. "How do you know my baby is Nick's?" she asked.

Penny's lips curved into a smile—an all-knowing smile. "I know."

Nick hadn't even been certain the first time he'd seen her in the ER.

"I don't think there has ever been anyone else for you," Penny added.

Annalise chuckled now. She hadn't been a virgin when she'd made love with Nick. "I think you have the wrong impression—"

"You don't love him?" Penny arched a reddish-brown brow.

"I love him," Annalise admitted. Tears stung her eyes, but she blinked them back to clear her vision. She couldn't stop staring at that screen—at her son. "Growing up next door to him, I can't remember a time that I didn't love Nick."

"I'm glad he had you," Penny said. Her hand touched Annalise's now with a comforting squeeze. "I have worried that Nick had no one who cared about him growing up."

Why would she care? What kind of person was Penny Payne that she had so much concern for her husband's child with another woman?

Loving. Amazing.

"Nick had me, too," a deep voice said. And the curtain was pushed aside again.

She hadn't seen him in so long that it took Annalise long seconds to recognize her brother. His hair was a darker blond than she remembered and cut so short she could see scars on his skull. Or were those just shadows? He was thinner, too, his jeans and shirt hanging on his long frame.

He was staring at her as if he didn't recognize her, either. And maybe he didn't. His gaze skimmed over her body—over her belly. Then he finally stepped forward and his arms closed around her, pulling her away from the pillow and against his chest.

She couldn't blink away the tears that stung her eyes now. They were too persistent—too numerous. They spilled over and trailed down her face. She had never lost hope—totally—that he was alive. But it had slipped sometimes.

She had wondered...

And she'd worried.

But he was alive. He was really alive.

The baby kicked, as if rejoicing in their reunion, too.

The only person who wasn't rejoicing was Penny. Annalise could see her face over Gage's shoulder. Her brow puckered with confusion and faint disapproval, she asked, "Who are you?"

She didn't just care about Nick's past. She cared about his present, too. She obviously worried that Annalise had another man.

Gage released Annalise and stepped back. His gaze went from one woman to the other. He had no idea who Penny was, either. He must not have met his boss's mother yet.

"This is Penny Payne," Annalise introduced them.

He held out his hand to the other woman. His knuckles were cracked and swollen, blood oozing from fresh wounds on them.

"I'm Annalise's brother—Gage."

"You're Gage Huxton?" Penny Payne asked. And she looked as if she'd seen a ghost. But then, Gage had been presumed dead for months—by everyone but Annalise. Despite the couple of doubts she'd let herself have in dark moments, she had known her brother was too tough to give up without one hell of a fight. He looked as if he'd just been in another one.

And she realized why. He hadn't been surprised to

see her pregnant. He'd known. Nick must have told him. And knowing Nick, he had admitted to being the father. How badly had Gage hurt him?

Chapter 12

Pain radiated throughout Nick's jaw. He cupped his chin and turned it from side to side. It wasn't broken. He was surprised, though not that Gage had hit him. He'd had that coming. He was surprised that Gage hadn't broken his jaw.

Gage wasn't as strong as he'd been before he'd gone missing. He hadn't yet recovered completely from all those months he'd been gone. At least, not physically.

Personality-wise, he was Gage again. He was the act-first, think-second hothead he had always been. A smile tugged at Nick's mouth, but he flinched as pain radiated through his jaw at the movement.

Something cold pressed against the side of his face. What the hell had happened to his reflexes? Usually he would have seen that coming—like Gage's fist. He had seen that, and he'd purposely resisted the urge to duck.

He'd deserved that punch and whatever other ones Gage might have landed.

Cooper shouldn't have stepped in. Nick glanced up, expecting that was who'd brought him the ice. But his gaze met Penny Payne's warm one.

"I didn't know you were here," he remarked. He hadn't called her. He wasn't sure if anyone had. She had probably just known she was needed.

Not that Nick needed her.

Nick had never needed anyone. But an image flickered through his mind, of Annalise lying naked beneath him.

And need gripped him, overwhelming him with its intensity. He'd needed her last night. And six months ago.

He needed to see her now. The doctor had already spoken to him, had assured him that she and the baby were fine. But he needed to see her for himself, needed to know that she wasn't screaming in pain like she'd been earlier at the condo. Panic clutched his heart as he remembered how terrified she'd sounded.

He needed to make sure that she wasn't afraid any longer.

But Gage had gone back with her. Brother and sister deserved some time alone—after all the months they had been apart.

"I met Annalise," Penny said.

Nick groaned, and it wasn't because of the pain in his jaw. It was because of the humiliation that washed over him. He didn't deserve to be included in the Payne family portrait. On the other hand, he probably fit in more now than he ever had. He was a chip off the old block.

"You must think I'm like my father now," Nick said, "getting a woman pregnant and walking away."

"You're not walking," Penny said as she settled onto the waiting room chair next to him. She patted his hand. Like Annalise, Penny couldn't *not* touch people. She overflowed with warmth and affection. "You just didn't know."

Would she have told him? She had gone six months without telling him. Of course, she might not have realized right away that she was pregnant. But it didn't matter when she'd found out. She should have told him the minute she had. He had a right to know.

Now he didn't know if he would ever be able to trust her. She was like Penny Payne in some ways. But not all ways.

"Your father didn't know about you, either," Penny reminded Nick. "He wouldn't have let your mother leave if he'd known she was pregnant."

The police officer who'd gone undercover to take down a drug kingpin wouldn't have had a choice in whether or not his mother had left. After she'd agreed to testify against that kingpin, she'd been put in witness protection. But even if Nicholas Payne had known…

Nick snorted. "He wouldn't have chosen her over you." No man in his right mind would have. He'd often wondered if his mother had drugged the undercover cop. How else could she have gotten him to cheat on his amazing wife?

But before the drugs had ravaged her, his mother had been attractive. She'd kept an album of old photos—even though she should have left them behind after testifying. Maybe she'd kept the pictures to remind her that she'd once been young and beautiful.

And happy…

He had never seen her happy except in those old photos.

"Your father would have chosen you," Penny said, and she squeezed the hand she held. "He would have chosen to be a part of your life—or he would have tried to talk her into giving up custody to us."

"Us?" He turned fully toward her—shocked at what she was insinuating. "You would have wanted to raise another woman's baby?"

Could anyone be as selfless as she seemed?

Because he was watching closely, he noticed the flicker of pain and resentment. She was careful to hide her true emotions from her family. She was used to being strong for them—ever since she'd become a single parent after Nicholas Payne had been killed in the line of duty.

Nick was glad he'd caught that glimpse of the real Penny. She was human. She hadn't entirely forgiven the man who'd cheated on her.

Her family thought she'd never remarried or even seriously dated because she had loved her husband so much and mourned his loss yet. Nick realized now that it was because her husband had betrayed her. He'd destroyed her trust. And she struggled to trust again— even all these years later.

He squeezed her hand back and murmured, "I'm sorry."

"It wasn't *your* fault," she said.

"That wasn't," he agreed—even though he still felt guilty over the pain Penny had suffered because of him. "But Annalise—that is my fault."

She lifted her free hand to his swollen jaw. "Is that why you let Gage hit you?"

"I deserved more." Cooper should have let Gage pound the hell out of him.

"You deserve happiness, Nick," she said. "You deserve Annalise."

Annalise was happiness—or she had been before he'd put her in danger. Now she was scared. And she must have been angry with him for making love with her six months ago and walking away. That had to be why she hadn't told him she was pregnant—because he'd hurt her. She hadn't even called him or texted him like she used to before he'd slept with her.

If only he hadn't been such a fool.

Penny lowered her hand from his face and glanced toward those no-admittance doors to the ER. "I thought Gage Huxton was dead."

"I didn't realize you knew anything about him and Annalise." It shouldn't have surprised him that she did, though. Penny always knew more than anyone else— even him. And he was the guy who knew more than anyone else, or so he'd thought. For the past six months, he'd been completely unaware that Annalise was pregnant and in danger because of him.

She turned back to Nick and released a weary-sounding sigh. "I'm planning the wedding for FBI Chief Lynch's daughter," she explained.

Nick knew Woodrow Lynch well. After his wife had died, he'd spoiled his daughters to make up for the pain of their loss. "Is she a bridezilla?"

"Megan?" Penny adamantly shook her head. "No."

"Then what's the issue?" He could tell there was one. Penny replied, "She thinks Gage is dead."

Nick had been so busy, he couldn't remember if he'd mentioned Gage's survival to his boss and Gage's former boss. Maybe he hadn't. Gage hadn't exactly left the Bureau on the best of terms—not after he'd acted like a hothead. "She hasn't heard he's alive?"

Penny shook her head. "I don't think she would be getting married if she knew."

"She would," a gruff voice said as Gage joined them.

Penny jumped and pressed her hand against her heart. "You keep sneaking up on me." And she obviously wasn't used to that.

Gage had gotten good at that, at the silent approach. He hadn't gotten good at hiding his emotions, though. Bitterness emanated from him. "Megan Lynch and I were done a long time ago."

Even if Penny wasn't almost clairvoyant, she couldn't have missed his pain. It was palpable. "I'm sorry," she said. "I didn't mean to interfere."

Of course she did. It was what she always did. But Gage didn't know that. He didn't know Penny.

She stood up as if getting ready to give up her chair to Gage. Nick wasn't certain his old friend would want to sit next to him, though. Or if he even considered him a friend any longer.

Gage caught Penny's arm. "Don't leave," he told her. "I need your help."

"My help?" Her face brightened with hope. "With Megan?"

He snorted. "Hell, no."

Penny cocked her head. "Then what?"

"I need you to plan another wedding," Gage said, "for him and my sister." He nearly shoved his finger into Nick's chest. "Nick and Annalise are going to get married as soon as possible."

Nick should have been horrified, or at least afraid. But he felt none of that. He felt like he did when he made love with Annalise.

Like it was right.

Like it was home...

"Nick and Annalise are going to get married as soon as possible." The words hung in the suddenly silent waiting room. Annalise wished she could grab them from the air and shove them back in her big brother's big mouth.

She had pulled off the baby monitor and dressed as quickly as she could because she'd been afraid of what Gage would do. She'd worried he might have already hurt Nick and that he'd gone back to hurt him some more.

She hadn't realized he was going to embarrass the hell out of her. Her face heated with embarrassment as everyone stared at her. Were they waiting to see if she would agree?

Maybe they thought it was her idea, that she'd gotten pregnant to trap Nick. She'd worried that was what he would think. That was partially why she hadn't told him when she'd found out she was pregnant a few months ago. She'd worried that he would think she'd done it on purpose.

The other reason she hadn't told him was that when she'd found out three months had already passed—in which he hadn't contacted her. No phone call. No email. No text. It was as if he'd forgotten about her completely, while he had never left her mind. Or her heart.

But as much as she loved him—or maybe because she loved him so much—Annalise didn't want to marry Nick because he'd been pushed to the altar at the end of a shotgun.

She forced herself to laugh, but it rang hollowly in the crowded but weirdly silent room. "Don't be ridiculous, Gage."

He turned back to her as if he was surprised she would protest. But then, after all the years he'd watched her chase Nick, he had to be surprised that she wouldn't take advantage of the situation to catch him.

Annalise knew that even though she'd caught Nick, she couldn't hold him. He would run away again. At the moment, she wanted to run first. Her overreaction to the Braxton Hicks contractions had been embarrassing enough, but Gage had mortified her.

"I'm being realistic," Gage said. "You two need to get married."

"Why?" she asked. "This is the twenty-first century. It's almost more common to be a single parent than to be a co-parent."

Nick hadn't had a father. After his father had died, his brothers and sister hadn't had one, either. Penny Payne had managed on her own; Annalise could, too.

As if disgusted with her denseness, Gage shook his head and turned back to Nick. "Tell her you're going to marry her."

Nick's face flushed now. He was apparently as embarrassed as she was. "Gage..."

"Do you want my nephew to be a bastard like you are?" Gage asked.

Annalise's gasp escaped into the silence left after Gage's obnoxious remark. Nick gasped, too. And now the color drained from his handsome face, leaving him pale and shaken. But he wasn't offended. He was in awe.

"Nephew?" he repeated. Then he turned toward her. His blue eyes intense and curiously bright, he asked, "Are we having a son?"

She couldn't speak. Too much emotion welled up, choking her. She could only nod.

Then one emotion overpowered her others: anger. She struck out at her brother, pushing him back. Gage, who was usually so solid and immovable, stumbled away from her. "The only bastard here," she told him, "is you! How dare you call my son that."

Or the man whom she loved.

As he finally came to his senses, Gage shook his head with regret and murmured, "I'm sorry. I shouldn't have said that."

"No, you shouldn't have." Penny Payne was the one who admonished him in that maternally disapproving way that made every child, no matter how old, squirm.

"He's right," Nick defended his oldest friend. He was still staring at Annalise with that strange look of hope and awe and shock.

From the fresh bruise on his jaw, she could tell he'd fought with Gage. Had he struck his head, as well? Did he have a concussion that had addled his brain? Because he couldn't seriously be proposing what she thought he was proposing.

To her.

Confirming it, he uttered the phrase she'd longed for most of her life to hear him say. "We should get married."

Nick didn't love her. And because he didn't love her,

there was no way Annalise could marry him. But she was too overwhelmed to speak again.

Everyone else was talking, offering congratulations and suggesting plans, as if her wedding was a foregone conclusion. She could only stand on the sidelines, watching the action of her own life, and shake her head.

No matter how much she wanted it—how much she'd always wanted it—there was no way she would ever be Nicholas Rus's bride.

Guns weren't allowed in the hospital—which was probably lucky for Nick. Cooper didn't believe Gage would have actually shot his friend and former idol. But he suspected he would have threatened him with it.

Threatened him in order to get Nick to marry his sister...

Not that Nick had put up much of a fight.

Annalise was the one who looked as if she wanted to fight. But no words of protest emanated from her mouth, either. She was probably exhausted. And so was Nick.

Payne Protection needed to get them safely back to the security of Milek's condo. Still talking about a wedding, the group moved through the hospital lobby.

Cooper's marriage had started as one of convenience. Because the real groom had disappeared, Cooper had stepped into his place. He hadn't given up that role—he was still Tanya's husband—because he was the one she'd really wanted to marry.

Did Annalise want to marry Nick? Sure, she carried his baby, but that didn't mean she loved him. The way she'd defended him to her own brother showed that she did.

But sometimes love wasn't enough.

His own parents had proved that to Cooper. Even as much as they had loved each other, his father had still betrayed his mother. He'd broken their vows.

So would it matter if Nick and Annalise married?

Cooper doubted either of them would get the chance, not with someone determined to take them out.

Gage wasn't the only one who posed a threat to Nick. Someone had shot at him. If the bullet had gone six inches or so lower and to the left, it could have killed him.

Nobody could get into the hospital with a weapon. So they were waiting outside. Since it was night yet, the glass doors of the lobby just reflected back the interior. Cooper couldn't see them.

But he knew they were out there—just as he'd known when insurgents were lying in wait for the convoy. He hadn't been wrong in Afghanistan, and he wasn't wrong now.

The minute Nick and Annalise—with Penny and Gage—stepped outside, gunfire erupted. The glass in the lobby doors shattered and sprayed inward, across the terrazzo floor and Cooper's face. He'd known they were out there, but he still hadn't been prepared.

Neither had Nick.

Chapter 13

Nick's head buzzed with the rapid retort of gunfire. Cooper had warned him, had shared his suspicion that someone might stage another attack outside the hospital. He hadn't needed the warning. His instincts had told him the same thing.

They could have tried to sneak out another way. Before they'd left the waiting room, they had studied the alternative exits. But walking into the parking garage or the back alley would have been more dangerous. They could have been trapped. The lobby entrance was along a four-lane street with plenty of room for escape.

The only trick was not to get hit. Ducking low and using his body as a shield to protect Annalise, as Gage used his as a shield to protect Penny, they ushered the women into the open door of the Payne Protection vehicle parked directly outside the lobby doors.

The vehicle—this one with bulletproof glass and metal—withstood the onslaught of bullets.

"Hurry up," Garek ordered from the driver's seat. But he didn't wait for Gage to pull the door closed behind them before he careened away from the curb and into the street. Gage struggled but managed to slam the door closed.

Outside the darkened glass, Nick watched the flashes of gunfire. How many shooters had lain in wait for them?

There had to be more than the one man who'd escaped him in the parking garage and the second man who'd escaped him in his ransacked house.

With all that gunfire, there were definitely more than two shooters. More than two people after him and Annalise. The threat kept increasing. Why?

Who the hell wanted him dead that badly?

Even though the doors were closed, and the distance between them and the shooters grew as Garek sped away from the hospital, Nick kept his arms wrapped protectively around Annalise. His head was even still bowed over hers, her face in his chest.

She trembled against him.

"Are you okay?" he asked her.

He felt her move but couldn't tell if she nodded or shook her head. He eased back slightly. She peered up at him, her green eyes wide with fear and her face pale. But she nodded and assured him, "I'm okay."

He leaned across Annalise to ask Penny. "Are you okay?"

She smiled and, reaching across Annalise, patted his hand and said, "Of course I am."

They hadn't wanted to put her in danger. But she

already was, as much as she looked like her daughter. If she'd gone out another door alone, a gunman might have mistaken her for Nikki and shot her.

Gage seemed okay. He was trying to twist his long body to ease over the console and into the passenger seat. But Garek turned the vehicle, and Gage struck his head on the roof and cursed.

He might have a concussion, but he wasn't shot. So he was safer in the SUV than he would have been in the lobby with the others.

Annalise turned around and peered toward the hospital disappearing in the distance. "Is everyone else okay?" she asked.

"Yes," Garek replied from the front seat as he tapped his radio earpiece. "Nobody got hit." He made a sharp turn, and Gage, settling into the passenger seat, hit his head on the bulletproof side window.

He cursed again.

"Drive it like you stole it," Garek remarked.

Instead of getting mad, Gage chuckled and said, "You'll need to teach me how."

Unlike some of the kids in their neighborhood, Nick and Gage had avoided joining gangs. But Nick hadn't resisted because he hadn't wanted to steal cars. He had resisted because the gangs around them had mostly sold drugs. And he hadn't been about to support his mother's addiction.

"Pay attention," Garek advised his passenger. "I'll show you how to make sure nobody's tailing us."

Garek's lesson took a while because he wanted to make extra certain that none of the gunmen had followed them from the hospital. He wanted to protect not just Penny, whom they all adored, but Nick and Annalise, as well.

Before he moved to River City, Nick would never have believed he would become friends with an ex-convict like Garek Kozminski. A man who'd served time for manslaughter and was rumored to be as renowned a thief as his infamous father. But Nick wasn't just friends with the man; he was family, too.

And when he married Annalise, she and Gage would also become family. Over Annalise's blond head, he met Penny's gaze and nodded.

He didn't need to say it aloud for her to understand his intentions. She would plan his wedding. And knowing Penny, she would have Milek add Annalise and Gage to that family portrait, as well.

The only thing Nick had to worry about was keeping Annalise and himself alive for their wedding day.

Annalise couldn't stop shaking, and it wasn't just because the spring night was unseasonably cold. Heat blasted from the vents in the condo, but her skin and her blood wouldn't warm. She had gotten so cold when those shots had been fired at the hospital, shattering the lobby doors and windows. It was a miracle no one had been hit.

She shivered.

"You need to get back in bed," Nick said as he led her toward the master bedroom. His arms had been around her from the moment they'd started across the hospital lobby. But for once, his closeness hadn't warmed her.

"It's almost dawn," she murmured as she noticed light beginning to filter through the skylights in the living room. They passed through it quickly, though, into the darkness of the bedroom where there were no skylights. Not even a lamp had been left burning.

She shivered again as she imagined men hiding in the darkness, like they had hidden outside the hospital. She turned back toward the light of the living room.

But Nick propelled her gently toward the bed and pushed her down onto the edge of the mattress. "You need your rest," he said. "You're exhausted and probably in shock."

As if she were a child, he undressed her, taking off her shoes and pulling down her pants. He left her in her shirt and panties, gently pushed her onto her back and covered her with blankets. The sheets were cold against her back, and she couldn't stop shivering.

Concern furrowed Nick's brow. "Maybe you should go back to the hospital."

"No!" she sharply protested. She wished she had never gone, that she hadn't overreacted to what nearly every other pregnant woman experienced. "I'm fine."

Calling her out on the lie, he said, "You're not fine." But instead of insisting she go back to the hospital, he kicked off his shoes, took off his holster and weapon and crawled under the blankets with her. He wrapped his arms around her as he had in the hospital lobby. Tucking her head beneath his chin, he held her closely.

She felt his heart beating against hers. It was pounding quickly. He hadn't been unaffected by the gunfire, either. Only one person really had seemed unaffected.

"I'm not Penny Payne," she said resentfully.

"What?"

"She was so calm," Annalise remarked. "Like getting shot at was no big deal."

Nick chuckled at her petulance. "She's had more experience with that than you have."

"She's been shot at before?"

He nodded, his chin bumping against her head. "She has, just like every other member of her family. They've been through a lot together. That's why she's so strong."

Annalise's brief flash of resentment gave way to admiration and envy. Like the rest of her family, Nick obviously thought very highly of the woman. "I wish I could be like her."

"You *are* like her," Nick said.

Annalise laughed. "Now you're just patronizing me."

He eased her away from him and tipped up her chin. Light filtered in from the living room and fell across his handsome face, highlighting his every chiseled feature and the seriousness in his blue eyes. "I thought that the first time I met her."

"What?"

"That she was like you."

Annalise smiled. If only...

She wished she had that kind of strength, that kind of composure under pressure. "Why did you think that?"

"Because she is so friendly and warm," he said. His mouth curved into a slight grimace. "And so affectionate. She radiates—" his grimace grew as he struggled to express himself "—like you radiate."

"I radiate?" she asked. "What do I radiate?"

"Love."

So he was aware that she loved him. Maybe that was why he had agreed to Gage's crazy idea. Because he felt sorry for her.

"You're so sweet and loving to everyone you meet," Nick continued.

So maybe he didn't take how she acted around him personally. Maybe he didn't know how she really felt about him.

"That's why it has to be my fault," he said. "That's why whoever has been terrorizing you with the break-ins and thefts must be doing it because of me."

She stroked her fingers along his swollen jaw. "It's not your fault."

"I am responsible."

"Why?" she asked. "Because you've taken criminals off the street? That's a good thing. You're doing good things, Nick." She had never doubted that he would. He had always been her hero.

His hand moved lower, over the swell of her belly. "This will be a good thing," he said. "Our son…"

Tears stung her eyes. "Of course."

"I should have protected you that night."

They'd gotten carried away with passion. Protection had been the last thing on both their minds.

"I will protect you from now on," he promised.

She shook her head.

"I will—"

That wasn't what she was protesting. "You don't need to marry me to protect me."

He needed to marry her only if he loved her. And she doubted that he did.

But he wanted her. She felt it in the tenseness of his body, in the erection straining against his fly to press against her hip. She wanted him, too. Making love with him would finally warm her up, would stop her shivering. Even now her blood was beginning to heat and pump faster in her veins.

He touched her, his hands moving over her bare

thighs to her hips. He slid his fingers beneath her panties and teased her. He stroked his thumb over her most sensitive spot until she squirmed and moaned.

So she teased him back. She stroked her fingers over the ridge of his erection until finally he undid his pants and pushed them down his legs. He pulled off his shirt, too, and hers. Within seconds nothing separated them. They were skin to skin.

He kissed her everywhere but her lips. He kissed her shoulder and her elbow. And the curve of her hip. Then he moved his mouth lower and made love to her with his lips and his tongue.

Her hands in his hair, she clasped him against her as she arched her hips and came. But it wasn't enough. He touched the tightened tips of her nipples, and the pressure wound inside her again. Only he could give her the release she needed, when he buried himself inside her. But he didn't lift her legs. He didn't push inside her.

Instead he flopped onto his back, his chest rising and falling as he breathed heavily, fighting for control. She wanted him out of control. So she leaned over and teased him as he had teased her. She licked her tongue down the pulsing length of him.

He groaned her name and tangled his fingers in her hair. She slid her lips around him and took him deep in her mouth. But it wasn't enough.

He bucked beneath her. But he didn't come like she had. So she eased back. Then she straddled him. Rising up, she guided him inside her. She was still wet and ready for him. He edged slowly inside until he filled her. But she wasn't able to take all of him.

She moved up and down, clutching at him with her inner muscles as he gripped her hips in his hands. He helped her move, helped her find the rhythm that drove them both to madness. He bucked beneath her as she rode him. Then he slid one hand between them and stroked her with a fingertip.

Her body tensed, then shuddered as an orgasm overwhelmed her. She screamed his name and collapsed on his chest. He gripped her hips and shoved up, driving deep, as he shouted his release.

He didn't pull out, just pressed her against him and pulled the blankets over them. And he held her as if he never intended to let her go.

But Annalise knew better now than to get her hopes up. She understood that when she awakened, he would probably be gone again. There was no way he would ever marry her because there was no way he would ever stop running away from her.

She wasn't the one he needed to outrun, though. He needed to outrun whoever was after them. Or getting married would be the least of their concerns.

The River City Psychiatric Facility for the Criminally Insane was every bit as scary as Candace Baker-Kozminski had imagined it would be. But she had convinced her husband, Garek, that she was the one who needed to pay this visit.

But even as tough as she was, she was unnerved. Patients yelled. They flailed. They beat themselves with their fists until men in white suits restrained them.

But far scarier than any of that behavior was the eerie stare of the woman sitting across from her. Tori Chekov studied her as she might study a cat she was about to torture cruelly. A small smile played around her mouth, and a gleam of insanity twinkled in her dark eyes.

"I have dreamed of seeing you again," Tori admitted.

Candace had, too: nightmares. Nightmares of this woman killing Garek. But she always awakened in the comfort of his embrace, his strong arms locked around her.

"Really?" she asked, as if she cared.

"I have imagined all the things I would do to you," Tori said, and her dark eyes hardened with hatred.

Candace forced a laugh. "Nice to see that expensive psychiatrist your dad hired has done you so much good."

Tori's smile widened. "Oh, you'd be surprised what she's done for me."

A chill chased over Candace's skin. This woman might be locked up, but she was still dangerous. And maybe she was using her psychiatrist to cause problems on the outside. Problems with Nick?

"You've done a lot for me, as well," Tori said.

"I have?" She sure as hell hoped not.

"Those self-defense moves you taught me when you were my bodyguard."

Candace felt a twinge of regret and embarrassment. Tori had used those moves against her. "Yes?"

"They've protected me in here—" she pitched her voice to a creepy whisper "—with all these crazies."

"I think you should be in prison," Candace honestly remarked. "It was your father and Special Agent Nicholas Rus's idea to commit you here."

For life. That was the only reason, as one of her victim's, that Candace had agreed to the sentence Nick had hammered out in exchange for Viktor Chekov's confession. He had owned up to all his crimes. So if he was going after Nick, he probably would have admitted it.

Would Tori?

"My father is a weak old man," Tori replied with disgust and hatred.

"And Agent Rus?"

Tori's lips curved, and that crazy glint sparkled in her dark eyes. "He is one beautiful man. I dream about him, too."

Candace didn't have to wait long before Tori added, "I dream of all the things I would do to him—" she uttered a wistful sigh of resignation "—if I wasn't in here."

Fortunately she was in there. But Candace wasn't certain that meant she and Nick were actually safe. If Tori really wanted to get to them, Candace suspected that she could. And she would.

Chapter 14

Nick understood where Milek had found the inspiration for his family portrait as he gazed around the condo living room at everyone gathered for the Payne Protection Agency meeting. Nikki wasn't there, but since he was, that wasn't unusual. And Logan usually excluded her from the bodyguard business meetings, anyway.

It wasn't a family meeting because the spouses weren't there, at least not the ones who weren't bodyguards. The children weren't there, either—just his baby, his *son*—inside Annalise's belly.

She had insisted on being included in the powwow. And since she was stuck in the condo, too, it would have been hard to exclude her, even though she had no real reason to be there. The attempts on their lives had nothing to do with her.

But Logan, who was always thorough, interrogated

her, anyway. "No disgruntled clients?" the former River City PD detective asked.

She shook her head.

"No jealous ex-boyfriends?"

She laughed—as she had when Nick had asked. She glanced at him before shaking her head.

Logan looked at him, too, as if considering that he was a jealous ex. When it came to Annalise, Nick was jealous and possessive. But he wasn't an ex, not yet.

He would marry her so his son's parents would be married when he was born. But Nick doubted Annalise would want to stay married to him. She deserved more. She deserved someone who could love her as she loved—freely and affectionately.

"This is stupid," Gage said. Since returning from his last bodyguard assignment, he had been sticking close to Annalise. And of course he had insisted on being included in the Payne Protection meeting. "You're wasting your time questioning my sister."

"He's right," Nick said.

Instead of looking grateful for the confirmation, Gage glared at him. He had not forgiven him for crossing the line with Annalise. Ignoring his remark, Gage continued, "She has no enemies—unlike Nick."

"They've only been going after Annalise to get to me," Nick agreed. Gage had no doubts about that, just as he didn't. The others had been more hesitant because they didn't know Annalise. They didn't understand how she was like Penny and could have no enemies.

"You have too many enemies," Garek said.

"We're narrowing it down," Nick reminded him. Garek had ruled out Chekov. And while Candace wasn't certain his daughter had nothing to do with it, Nick was.

The break-ins at his places and at Annalise's had started before he'd taken down the Chekovs. Until he had, they'd had no reason to want vengeance on him. They hadn't even been aware they had been in his sights.

He trusted few people. Only Garek Kozminski had been aware of that plan, and Nick had brought him in only because he'd needed his help. He needed all of their help now—for Annalise.

"We're narrowing it down to people you've pissed off more than six months ago," Gage said. "That's still a hell of a lot of people."

Nick couldn't agree more. He had compiled a list. And even to him, it was overwhelming. He had passed out copies to the others, and they riffled through the pages.

"Seriously?" Garek Kozminski asked. "You've pissed off more people than I have."

"And that's saying something," his brother Milek added.

"Are these all professional enemies?" Parker asked.

When someone had been trying to take him out, everyone had thought it was personal. That he had pissed off a lover's husband or something.

Nick had never been the playboy his half brother had been rumored to be. He nodded. "Of course."

"Why?" Logan asked. "You could have a jealous ex-lover, too."

Like Annalise had, he laughed at the far-fetched notion. "That's ridiculous."

"It makes sense," Candace said. "A jealous woman is more likely to go after a man's girlfriend than a professional enemy would."

"I'm not his girlfriend," Annalise said quickly, defensively.

She wasn't his girlfriend. What was she? Lover. Mother of his unborn child? Fiancée? He hadn't put a ring on her finger. Not yet.

But he had no doubt Penny was planning their wedding. The professional wedding planner had probably started planning it the moment she'd heard about Annalise showing up in River City. Pregnant with his child.

Hell, Penny had probably known before he had.

Would he know if Annalise hadn't been in danger? Would she have told him? That was why he'd trusted few people—because few people had proved worthy of his trust. Gage.

And as a reward, he had betrayed that trust when he'd crossed the line with Gage's sister. Why should he expect trust when he'd done nothing to earn it himself?

"We need a list of ex-girlfriends," Logan prodded him as he waved those pages around. "So this is complete."

"You don't think the list is long enough as it is?" Garek asked with a weary-sounding sigh. "There are already too many to check them all out."

"You need Nikki's help," Parker said.

"She doesn't work for me anymore," Logan reminded them.

And from their faces Nick could tell, they all doubted she would help. They didn't know how much she'd already assisted him. Not that the crime lab had found any prints in Annalise's stolen car. As Nikki had surmised, it had been wiped clean.

Cooper said, "I'll put her on the case."

Nick had already emailed her a copy of the list. He

suspected she was working on it—checking alibis, known associates, everything Nikki checked.

But even as good as Nikki was, he doubted they would be able to whittle down that list to the right suspect anytime soon. He could only hope that they stopped the person before it was too late, before he lost Annalise.

Annalise was lost. And it wasn't because they all spoke at once that she couldn't understand what they were saying. It was their reasoning she couldn't follow. They were brilliant bodyguards. Every one of them had been something else before creating or joining the Payne Protection Agency.

They'd been police officers or detectives, soldiers or FBI agents. Or thieves.

And all of these brilliant people believed someone was using her for revenge against Nick. Even Nick thought so.

But it made no sense to her. Why?

Nick would have to have feelings for her—beyond responsibility—for her situation to really affect him. And he didn't have feelings for her. He didn't love her.

He hadn't even made love to her again since that dawn they'd escaped the shoot-out at the hospital. As she'd suspected, she had awakened later that day alone. And he hadn't shared her bed since.

For the past couple of nights, he'd planted himself on the couch, as if anyone could bypass Milek Kozminski's security system. Nick was just running, as far away as he could while still being close enough to protect her.

And since that dawn, he hadn't mentioned marrying her again. He obviously had no intention of following through on a wedding despite her brother's proverbial shotgun threat.

So how would hurting her cause Nick any pain?

She was the one suffering. She was the one living with a man she loved but knew she could never really have. She was the one who'd put her career on hold while she lived in relative captivity. With a twinge of regret, she glanced at her brother.

He'd been through far worse than what she was going through. So she had no right to feel sorry for herself. No reason to sulk. Because she couldn't stand inaction, she moved to the kitchen. She would cook or bake, depending on the ingredients available. She would do anything but pine for Nicholas Rus. She'd spent too much of her life doing that.

Gage had spent most of his missing six months in pain. And it hadn't all had to do with his captivity. It had had to do with the kind of pain he saw on his sister's face.

Heartache.

It was worse by far than anything anyone could physically suffer. It left a gaping hole where a heart should be. And there was no filling that hole with anything but love.

So when that love wasn't returned, the hole just remained open and gaping and sore like an untreated wound.

He'd seen that pain on her face in a vulnerable moment. But she was doing her best to hide it now. She bustled around the room, offering food to everyone present. The house was warm from the heat of the oven and her personality. It was fragrant from the smells of the feast she had thrown together.

"She's so much like Mom," he heard Parker Payne murmur.

Logan nodded in agreement. "Nick's right. This is about him. Not her."

Gage had been telling them that, but they'd had to see for themselves the magic that was Annalise.

Nick had seen it. He'd tried turning a blind eye to it for years. He'd tried to ignore her. But she had been persistent. And if she had a flaw, Annalise's only one would be her stubbornness. She'd wanted Nick for so long.

Gage shouldn't have been surprised that she'd finally worn him down. But he was disappointed. Nick had always been his hero—the man he had hoped to become someday. Strong. Smart. Honorable.

This time, he'd crossed a line with Annalise that he would never be able to uncross. Marrying her wouldn't make him honorable. It would probably only put her in more danger.

All the Paynes looked alike, but he knew it was Nick who settled onto the couch next to him. "I was wrong," he said.

"No, you weren't," Nick said. "It's all my fault. You should have hit me harder."

Gage grunted. "Yeah, I should have."

"So you're not talking about hitting me?" Nick touched his jaw as if it still hurt.

But Gage knew he wasn't as strong as he'd once been. Before he'd gone missing, he would have broken Nick's jaw had he hit him like he had. But before he'd gone missing, he had never wanted to hit Nick.

"You know what I'm talking about," Gage murmured.

Because he was Nick, he always knew everything. That was why he had come to Nick when he'd gotten back to the States. Because he hadn't wanted to talk. He'd just wanted someone to know—without his having to say a word. But now he wanted to make sure Nick understood, so he said, "You can't marry her. It would put her in more danger. Then whoever's after you will know she's important to you."

Nick grunted his agreement. "You're right." He understood. He knew what he had to do—or actually *not* do.

He couldn't make Annalise his bride. Marrying her wouldn't just put her in more danger physically, though.

She would also be in more danger emotionally—because while she would have Nick's name, Gage doubted she would ever have his heart.

He suspected Nick had had that gaping hole in his chest for a long time.

Maybe he'd never even had a heart to lose.

Chapter 15

Annalise was safe in the condo, Nick assured himself. It was okay that he'd left her. Her brother was there. Gage would willingly give up his life for hers.

So would Nick.

But Annalise didn't want his life. She wanted something else from him. Something he had never been able to give her or anyone else.

Gage wasn't the only one protecting Annalise. Candace and Garek had stayed, as well. Nick wasn't sure who was following him; he just knew that someone was.

Since he hadn't picked up the tail, he guessed it was Milek. It would have been a point of pride with the younger Kozminski brother to go undetected this time. Nick probably could have made him—had he cared. But since Annalise wasn't with him, he didn't care. Her safety was his only concern.

Not his own.

He didn't want to endanger this woman, either, so he had been careful when he'd left the condo. He'd taken a circuitous route to the White Wedding Chapel. The only person who might have been able to follow—given the way he'd been driving—was Milek. Milek would protect Mrs. Payne, too, if Nick had brought danger to her like he had Annalise.

Before he could even reach for the door, though, someone burst through and slammed into his chest, nearly knocking him down the stairs he'd climbed. He gripped her shoulders to steady her.

And Megan Lynch glanced up at him through tear-filled eyes. "Nick? Nicholas Rus?"

He nodded.

Her face flushed bright red. "I'm sorry. I wasn't looking where I was going."

She was obviously upset and in a hurry.

He held her shoulders a little longer and asked, "Are you okay?"

She jerked her head in a sharp nod, and a few wisps of brown hair escaped the bun at the nape of her neck. By her father's own admission, he had doted on her and her sister after their mother died. But few other men had ever paid Megan Lynch attention. She was almost painfully shy, and maybe because her mother had died so young, she'd never learned how to wear makeup or flattering clothes. So she wasn't just shy. She was awkward, too.

For some reason, Gage had found that endearing. Everyone else, including Megan, had thought he was just doing the boss's daughter in order to get ahead in the Bureau. But Nick knew Gage better than that.

Unfortunately, Megan had not.

"I'm fine," she said. And because she'd been raised to be polite, she added, "And how are you?"

He touched his swollen jaw. "Could be better."

She sighed. "Me, too."

He squeezed her shoulders. "Is there anything I can do?"

She shrugged, and his hands fell away. "It'll be over soon."

She acted as if she was talking about a root canal or winter. Not her wedding.

He opened his mouth. He needed to tell her about Gage, if she didn't already know. But first he said, "I'll be talking to your dad soon." He would make sure that Chief Lynch knew Gage was alive and let him decide what to do with that information. The Marines had determined to keep his escape secret. Nick wasn't certain if that was to protect Gage from unwanted media attention or if there was a concern about the insurgents who'd held him somehow getting to him again.

She nodded. "Of course. He talks about you often, Nicholas. You're one of his favorites." The tears shimmered in her eyes.

Lynch had had another favorite: Gage. Until he'd left.

"Congratulations," he offered belatedly. "Penny will make sure you have a beautiful wedding."

She nodded, and the tears brimmed over and trailed down her face. Her voice quavering with emotion, she murmured, "I'm sure she will." Then she broke free of him and ran down the steps to her car parked at the curb in front of his SUV.

He continued up the steps and pushed open the door. He passed quickly through the foyer and descended the interior stairwell to Penny's office in the basement. Despite it having only one small window, the space was sunny and bright. And it wasn't because of the yellow paint or lighting. It was because of the woman who radiated sunshine and warmth.

"Good afternoon, Nicholas," she greeted him with a smile as she glanced up from her desk.

"Penny…"

"Did you run into Megan Lynch?" she asked.

He nodded. "Literally. She ran into me. I don't think she could see me through her tears."

Penny sighed. "She's the unhappiest bride for whom I've ever planned a wedding."

"Did you tell her Gage is alive?" Maybe that was why she'd been crying. But wouldn't those have been happy tears? Unless Gage was right, and she didn't care if he was alive. Or maybe she didn't want him alive.

Penny shook her head. "No. I didn't." She studied his face for a moment. "You didn't, either."

"No," he said. "Gage is already angry enough with me. I didn't want to make it worse."

"Marry his sister," she said. "That'll make it better."

Nick shook his head. "Gage has changed his mind about that. He knows what I know—being around me puts Annalise in more danger."

"That's a load of bull and you know it," Penny accused him.

He drew back in surprise. Penny had never said a sharp word to him before—even though she'd had every reason to be upset when he had turned up in River City looking exactly like her sons, like her dead husband. He must not have heard her correctly. "Excuse me?"

"I'm talking to you like I would talk to Logan or

Parker or Cooper," she said. "I call them on their nonsense, too. I never thought I would have to do that with
you."

"Because I'm not your son?"

"Because you're usually smarter than they are," she
said. "And you *are* my son."

"Penny—"

"I don't care that another woman gave birth to you,"
she said. "You're *my* son now."

"I saw the family portrait Milek is painting for you,"
he admitted.

"Then you know how I feel," she said.

"You may feel that way, but the rest of the family…"

"Feel the same way."

Logan had made it clear that he did. And Nick had
never picked up on any animosity from Parker or Cooper. But…

"Not Nikki," he said.

"She's coming around," Penny said.

He shook his head. "No, she's not."

Sure, she had called him about finding Annalise's
stolen car. And he'd emailed her the list of his enemies.
But he hadn't actually seen her since that horrible day
in the parking garage. She hadn't attended any of the
Payne Protection Agency meetings. Of course, Logan
never included her in anything he perceived as dangerous, and she had been in more danger that day than
any other in her life. But because of that, Nick had
expected her to insist on being involved. While she'd
found the car, she hadn't called him again. She hadn't
even emailed him back that she'd received his list. She
probably didn't want to help because she didn't care
that he was in danger.

Unfortunately, Annalise was in danger, too. So Nick needed his sister's help. He would have to call her, see if she'd checked out the list or added her own name to it.

"The portrait is missing someone," Penny said.

Nick tensed. "Did my father have another—"

Her glance as sharp as her tone had been earlier, Penny stopped him from saying the rest. *Bastard.* That was what he was—just like Gage had called him. And if he didn't marry Annalise, his child would be a bastard, too.

Of course she was right. It was the twenty-first century now. And there were probably more single-parent households than two-parent households. But he wanted his son to have his name, to know who he was.

Until his mother had died, Nick had never known who he was.

"The portrait is missing Annalise," Penny said.

He had thought the same thing when he'd seen it, that he looked so alone. Like Nikki on the other side of the portrait. But as much as he would have liked to, he couldn't bring Annalise into the family. He had already put her in enough danger.

"I can't marry her," Nick said.

"Now that's ridiculous," Penny said. "She was in danger in Chicago. She is in more danger alone than she is with you. No one will protect her like you will— because you love her."

Since the first moment Nick had met her, he had felt a connection with Penny Payne. He had more of a kinship with her than with the family with whom he actually shared DNA. So he admitted to her what he never had to anyone else. "I don't know what love is."

She flinched as if he'd slapped her. "Oh, Nick."

He shook his head. "I don't want your pity." But he had it; he could feel it even before he noticed the tears shimmering in her eyes.

"You don't have my pity," she insisted. "You have my love."

"Why?" Because he looked like the man she had loved and lost, the man who had betrayed her love?

"For the same reason that Annalise Huxton loves you. Because you're you."

Maybe they loved him. But he couldn't return that love. He didn't know how. So he only reiterated, "I can't marry Annalise because I can't give her what she deserves. I can't love her."

Annalise glanced across the SUV console at the man who looked the most like Nick of all the Paynes. Nick was gone, though. He'd been gone for a while. He was running again.

She knew why Nick was gone. She wasn't as certain about why her brother was gone. He'd been here when Nick had left, but he hadn't stayed long. So it was Cooper Payne who had to drive her to the Payne Protection Agency. She had put her career on hold as much as she could. But there were things she needed to handle. For one, she needed to use the office equipment at Payne Protection.

She asked the former Marine, "Why isn't Gage protecting me?"

Cooper glanced across the console at her and replied, "He doesn't trust himself yet."

A twinge of concern squeezed her heart. "He was on assignment when I arrived in River City," she said. "Is he worse now than he was?"

He looked bad, like he'd aged years instead of months since she'd seen him last. And he was so thin and haggard-looking.

Cooper shook his head. "No. He's actually doing quite a bit better."

"Then why wouldn't he trust himself?"

Cooper offered her a quick smile. "Because your safety is too important to him. He wants to make sure you have the best protection." But as he said it, his brow furrowed, and his focus turned to the rearview mirror.

"I hate that I need protection," she said.

Nick blamed himself, but she wasn't entirely convinced the men coming after her had anything to do with him. How could they think that she mattered that much to him when she didn't believe it herself?

"You do," Cooper said.

And she realized why his focus had turned to the rearview. "Someone's following us."

Dread knotted her stomach. She was so sick of the attacks, of the vehicle chases and the gunshots. She wanted her life back, her boring, unendangered life. But all of that had changed after the night she'd spent with Nick. Nothing had been boring since then.

Cooper cursed, then apologized.

"I grew up with Gage," she reminded him. She was used to swearing. She actually felt like swearing herself now. If not for her baby, she might have. But she didn't know how much her son could hear in her womb.

Or feel. She had to make sure he stayed safe. She slid her palms over her belly, but she couldn't protect him— if whoever was following them caught them.

Unless...

"Isn't it one of you?" she asked hopefully. "Another Payne Protection bodyguard?"

Like when Milek Kozminski had been following Nick.

But she could tell from the grim look on Cooper's face that it wasn't. He had no idea who was following them.

So if it wasn't a friend, wasn't it a foe?

One of the men who'd attacked her was dead. Nikki had seen him that day, lying on a gurney in the ER hallway. And she had been so relieved it wasn't Nick.

She had to make sure that it didn't wind up being Nick yet. The list he'd emailed was too long even for her to work and eliminate suspects before someone eliminated Nick. But besides that, she couldn't help but think that they were all missing something.

Nick assumed someone was after him and Annalise out of a quest for vengeance. While Nikki owed her half brother for saving her life in the parking garage, she still wasn't entirely ready to let go of her resentment of him. She would actually find it pretty sweet if she could prove Nick—who was usually right—wrong.

So she'd gotten out from behind the desk where Logan had always tried to put her. And she was doing fieldwork. Even though all of River City PD had been searching for it, she was the one who'd found Annalise's stolen car.

She might find something no one else had at Nick's place. Boards had been nailed across the front door to keep out intruders. And her.

The bars on the windows offered her no entrance, either. Using her skills as a former gymnast, she leapt onto the stockade fence and pulled herself up and over it so she could get into the backyard. That door hadn't been boarded up, and there were no bars on the windows in the rear of the house.

With a surge of excitement, she reached for the lock pick tools the Kozminskis had given her. She could finally test her newly learned tricks. But when she reached for the door handle, it turned easily.

It hadn't been locked.

With a sigh, she slipped the tools back into her pocket. She would be able to use them eventually now that she was working for Cooper. He wouldn't treat her as Logan always had. He would respect that she could take care of herself.

Like Nick did.

How was it that the brother who'd known her the least amount of time knew her the best?

Because he was Nick.

He had that same uncanny ability her mother had, which was so weird and gave Nikki another reason to resent him. She didn't care that he knew her so well. She cared that he had the gift of her mother's that she'd always wanted.

She always felt as if she were in the dark, like now. With all the blinds drawn, the house was pitch-black, as if it was night already. She stumbled over things that had been strewn across the floor.

She expelled a ragged breath. The place must have been trashed. She doubted Nick, who was always so controlled, was this much of a slob. Now, Parker...

She would believe that of Logan's twin. Not Nick.

The place had been destroyed, but it had also been

searched. Every closet and cupboard had been inspected, the contents of every drawer tossed out.

This wasn't about vengeance.

Triumph surged through her. Nick was wrong.

A sharp noise drew her attention to the front door. A board cracked. Wood splintered. Someone was breaking in.

Her hand trembling, she reached for her weapon. She could fire it. She had proved that in the hospital parking garage. It might have been her bullet that had killed the man.

She shuddered as she remembered him lying on that gurney. She had never killed anyone before. She'd felt no triumph in having done it. She'd felt only horror.

But if it came down to it again—her life or someone else's—she would pull the trigger. She moved her finger toward it as she pointed the gun barrel at the front door.

Chapter 16

The boards were flimsy. Nick broke them easily with his foot as he kicked in the door. It bounced back against the interior wall as light from outside streamed in. Like the beam of a flashlight, it illuminated a dark-clothed shadow standing in the hall. That light bounced off the metal of a gun.

He silently cursed himself for losing Milek. As he'd suspected earlier, Kozminski had been his bodyguard. He'd been testing himself when he'd lost him, and he seriously hadn't thought he would need protection.

He'd been wrong.

Just as the shot rang out, Nick ducked. Wood splintered the jamb near his head. He rushed forward, toward the shadow. He could have fired back, but he couldn't get answers from a dead man. He tackled his intruder instead, knocking him to the ground as he grabbed for the gun. He snapped it easily from the person's grasp.

Breath whooshed out of the suspect, followed by a very unladylike curse.

"Nikki?" He quickly rolled off his intruder.

She choked and gasped for the air he'd knocked out of her.

"Are you okay?" he asked anxiously as he helped her sit up. He hadn't expected to find her inside his house, shooting at him.

She leaned against the wall of the hallway where he'd been knocked down a few days before. She drew in a deep, unsteady breath. "And everybody wonders why I don't like you."

He chuckled as he held her gun aloft. "I'd better not hand this back to you yet. You almost hit me once."

"I didn't know it was you," she said.

"Or you would have hit me?"

She laughed now. "I wasn't aiming to kill," she said. "Or I would have hit you."

He didn't doubt that. She was a good shot. Logan had no idea the caliber of bodyguard he could have had if he'd given Nikki a chance.

"That was just a warning shot," she said.

"Warning shot?" he repeated.

"You were breaking down the door."

"I live here."

She laughed again. "So it's okay for you to break down your own door?"

"Seems like everybody else has done it whether they live here or not."

"I went over the fence," she said. "And the back door was unlocked."

She sounded almost disappointed. Then he noticed the tools that had fallen from her pocket when he'd knocked her down. He handed her the set. "Might not be a good idea to let a lawman see these."

"You're not a lawman anymore," she said. "You're a bodyguard."

When he said nothing, she narrowed her brown eyes and studied his face. "You haven't given your notice yet?"

He groaned. "I've been having my detectives keep me apprised of what's going on at the station while I take some time off."

"Have you changed your mind?"

It wasn't that he didn't want to be a bodyguard. But he didn't want to be Annalise's bodyguard. Being around her only seemed to put her in more danger. "Not about the job. I still intend to talk to the chief." Just like he'd told Megan. He needed to give his notice.

"Have you changed your mind about the assignment?"

He nodded.

"I think you're wrong about someone using Annalise to get back at you."

His heart swelled. He hoped he wasn't the reason she was in danger. "What did you figure out?"

She stood up and gestured around them. "Somebody was looking for something."

"Or just trashing the place."

She shook her head. "No. It's a search. Drawers. Closets. Cupboards."

"There were holes in the drywall at other places." He turned toward the living room. "Cushions ripped open."

"You thought it was vandalism."

"A message. Like the gunshots," he said. "That's not

someone looking for something. You were there in the parking garage—"

"I caught them around your SUV," she said. "They could have been trying to steal it—like they'd stolen Annalise's car. That had been searched, too."

He nodded. "But the gunfire outside the hospital the other night…" Nobody had been looking for anything that night but blood.

She shrugged. "You're probably pissing them off."

"You know the feeling," he teased.

A smile tugged up her lips, seemingly against her will. "Yeah, you piss me off all the time."

He held out her gun to her, but when she reached for it, he pulled it back. "Sure you're not going to shoot me with it?"

"I would have done that a long time ago if I wanted you dead."

And what she'd said finally clicked with him. "If someone wanted Annalise dead before now, she would already be dead." She had been on her own for the past six months.

Nikki nodded. "This isn't about killing her or you. It's about getting something from you."

"So the gunfire could have been warning shots."

She shrugged. "Or a distraction."

He glanced around his place. "What are they looking for?"

"You tell me," Nikki said.

He sighed. "I have no idea."

Nikki's dark eyes had narrowed with suspicion, the warmth and amusement all gone. "Really? No idea?"

"No."

"Somebody thinks you have something."

She did, too.

But he wasn't like the people he'd arrested for corruption. He had never confiscated a drug dealer's money or assets for himself instead of putting them into evidence. And he was offended that Nikki thought he could have. Hell, he was offended that anyone thought he could have.

"I don't have anything," he murmured.

"That's too bad," Nikki said.

"Why?"

"Because if you had something and gave it back, this could all be over," she explained. "You and Annalise would no longer be in danger."

Since he had nothing to return to whoever thought they were the rightful owner, he had no idea how to make sure that Annalise would be safe again.

Annalise didn't feel safe.

She knew that Cooper was a good bodyguard—good enough to head up his own franchise of the security business. But she didn't understand why he'd driven right past the Payne Protection Agency.

"You told me someone is following us," she said with a nervous glance in the side mirror. "Shouldn't we stop for help?" She would have felt safer in the security offices with the other bodyguards.

She would have felt safer with Nick. Why had he left the condo? He hadn't said. The others had assumed he was working the list of enemies he'd given them. And Milek had followed him, which had reassured her. He wouldn't be able to lose Milek.

Was Cooper as good?

He snorted. "You think I need help losing a tail?"

She was not reassured—until he reached up to the device on his collar. He touched a button and spoke into it. "Hey, guys, I picked up a shadow."

"I see him." Another voice emanated from the small radio on Cooper's collar.

Annalise looked in the side mirror again, but she noticed nothing out of the ordinary. "Someone else is behind us?" It was a Payne. All of their voices sounded so alike.

"Of course," Cooper replied. "When family is in danger, we work as a family." So he hadn't been protecting her alone.

She released a slight breath. She was safer than she'd realized. But still…

Remembering the barrage of bullets the other night, she pressed her palms over her belly. She wasn't worried about just her safety. She was worried about her baby.

"And because we aren't alone, maybe we should try trapping him," Cooper suggested.

"No!" The shout crackled through the radio. Since it was closer to his ear, Cooper flinched.

But Annalise heard it clearly, too. And she recognized the voice. Nick.

"Don't listen to him," Annalise said. She wanted this to be over. She wanted her life back. "You need to catch him. You need to find out what he wants with me."

Because she didn't believe it was vengeance over something Nick had done. Sure, she didn't think she'd made any enemies, but maybe she had. Maybe someone resented something she'd done. Maybe it wasn't Nick who had put her in danger but she who had put Nick in danger.

Because if the person knew her, he would know how she felt about Nick—how she had always felt about Nick. She loved him.

* * *

He was probably making a huge mistake. And if the plan failed, Nick would kill him. But Cooper understood Annalise's frustration over not knowing who was after her or why.

And the only way to make certain she stayed safe was to find out. The risk wasn't as great as Nick probably thought it was.

The entire Payne Protection Agency force—all the newly divided franchises reunited—was working this assignment. For Nick.

They wouldn't let anything happen to Annalise and the baby she carried. They wouldn't let the tail get close to her. They'd only let him think that he could.

So Cooper slowed down as he headed toward the part of the city that had yet to recover from the economic downturn. He headed toward the area that was all abandoned warehouses and factories. If whoever was following him intended to a make a move on the vehicle—on Annalise—he would do it here.

"Is everyone in place?" he asked, and he heard the telltale nervous break in his own voice. The plan was risky. But with everyone working together, there was no way someone could get hurt.

"No," Nick protested again. "It's too dangerous."

"We've got this." It was Logan who spoke—Logan who was the boss on this assignment. But they all knew who was really the boss: Nick. And he hadn't approved this plan.

"The vehicle is coming up too fast," Nick said. "It's going to ram you."

Cooper glanced in the rearview mirror and realized that Nick was right. The truck that had been following them had shot forward—past Parker's SUV. The former vice cop was a good driver, but he wasn't as good as he needed to be now.

Cooper pressed on the accelerator, trying to get farther ahead of the truck. If it rammed them at the speed it was coming...

Annalise would be hurt. So would the baby.

He cursed. An intersection was coming up, the light changing to red. This area wasn't as populated, so he could take the chance of blowing through it without being hit. So he did.

The vehicle behind him wasn't as lucky. As the truck hit the intersection, an SUV hit it, coming at it full force. Metal crunched. Tires squealed. And both vehicles spun around.

Annalise reached over the console and grasped Cooper's arm. "Who was that? Who hit the truck?"

She must have recognized the black SUV like he had. It was a Payne Protection company vehicle. He cranked the wheel to turn around, to head back toward the crash.

From the curious silence on the radio, he knew who'd been driving that SUV. And from the way Annalise's hand clutched his arm harder, it was obvious that she knew, too.

"Nick," he murmured.

Nick had been driving the SUV that took out their tail. But through the spider-webbed glass of the front window, Cooper could see that his half brother wasn't alone. The person slumped in the passenger seat had brown curls. Nikki was with him.

He braked and glanced over at his own passenger. Annalise's face was pale with fear, but not for herself. She was afraid for the others like he was.

Cooper saw no movement inside either crumpled vehicle. He saw nothing but smoke curling out from beneath the hoods. Then sparks ignited.

"Go!" Annalise shouted at him.

He flung open the driver's door and ran toward the crash. He had to get to Nick and Nikki before their vehicle blew.

Chapter 17

Gasoline fumes burned his nose, the scent heavy in the front seat of the SUV. Nick blinked and tried to focus. With the air bags pushed against the cracked windshield, it was hard to see. But the sparks were an unmistakable warning. He glanced toward the passenger seat. Nikki was slumped against the side window, blood trickling from her head onto the glass. Since they'd hit the other vehicle head-on, the side air bag hadn't deployed.

"Damn it!"

What if she was seriously hurt? Her head? Her neck? Dared he move her?

The sparks ignited with a hiss, and flames shot up from the engine. Heat instantly filled the front seat. He had no choice. He kicked open his crumpled door. Then he reached for Nikki. He couldn't wait. He had to get her out now. So he dragged her limp body over the console and out the driver's side. Despite her slight weight, his wounded shoulder ached in protest. But Nick ignored the pain. He clutched Nikki close as he ran from the SUV.

He'd only made it a few yards when the flames hissed again. A whoosh knocked him to the ground and the vehicles exploded. As he fell, he rolled so that he didn't crush Nikki. But he lost his grasp on her. She fell to the ground next to him.

Her face was so pale but for the blood trickling from the wound on her forehead. His gut twisted with guilt. He shouldn't have put her in danger. "Nikki?"

"Nikki!" another voice echoed his. "Nick!"

There were more voices shouting over the noise of the burning vehicles. Glass shattered. Flames hissed.

Suddenly, strong hands reached for him, helping him to his feet. They didn't touch Nikki, though. Her brothers stood over her, staring down in horror at her.

"Is she…" Logan asked, his face growing pale as his voice cracked with fear.

It had to seem like his worst nightmare come to fruition. He had tried so hard to keep her safe.

"Dead?" Nikki was the one who finished the question for him. Her eyes fluttered open and she stared up at them. "I sure as hell hope not. There's a lot I want to do with my life before that happens."

What? Nick wanted to ask her. But there was a more important question. "Are you all right?"

She sighed and reached out her hand. "I will be once you help me up."

Before he could close his hand around hers, someone shoved him back. "What the hell were you thinking?"

Logan shouted at him. "You could have killed her. You could have killed both of you!"

"I had to stop that truck."

He'd been thinking about Annalise and the baby. And with the speed with which that truck had been bearing down on them, they would have been hurt. Or worse.

He turned to Cooper. "Are they all right?"

He nodded. And he looked as guilty as Nick felt. They'd both taken chances they shouldn't have taken.

"You compromised the whole operation," Logan said. "And nearly got Nikki killed."

Nick had never seen the oldest Payne so angry. He stepped toward Nick, yelling in his face until small hands wedged between them, pushing Logan back.

"Shut up," Nikki yelled at Logan. Then she turned toward Nick and threw her arms around him, hugging him. "Thank you!"

"Saving you from the crash he caused is the least he could do," Logan said.

"No," she said with a glare at her oldest brother. He'd beat Parker from the womb by just a few minutes, but he'd never let anyone forget. "That's the least any of you could do. Nick did the most. He treated me as an equal. Now and that day in the parking garage. He trusts that I can take care of myself, unlike the rest of you."

Logan opened his mouth, probably to argue. And there was plenty to argue about in that statement since Nick had wound up saving her both times. But for once, the oldest Payne didn't have to have the last word. He closed his lips and just nodded.

Nikki was okay—that was all that mattered now. But Nick turned with frustration toward the burning vehicles. The other driver hadn't made it out of the crash. And as badly as his body was burning, they might never learn who he was.

Annalise had never been so afraid as she'd watched the vehicles explode. She would have pushed open the passenger door—would have run toward the wreckage as everyone else had. But the SUV must have been equipped with some special security system, and Cooper had locked her inside. She hadn't been able to open her door. And she hadn't been able to see anything but the flames rising from the blackened metal.

She'd thought for certain that Nick was dead…until, long moments later, she'd seen him and his family walk around the burning vehicles. He and Nikki had survived. The driver of the truck hadn't been as lucky.

She grimaced as she remembered what she'd seen, what she'd wished she had never witnessed.

"Are you having more of those contractions?" Nick asked with concern.

Everyone else had left an hour ago. But he sat up— as he had the past few nights—on the couch.

She shook her head. "No. I'm fine."

"It's late," Nick said. "You should get some sleep."

She was afraid that if she closed her eyes, she would see that crash again. But instead of the other man burning, she would see Nick.

"What about you?" she asked. "You must be exhausted." He had spent night after night on the couch— watching the door.

Exhaustion darkened the skin beneath his bright blue eyes, and that muscle twitched again in his cheek, above his tightly clenched jaw. He hadn't changed. He still wore his jeans and a black shirt. Blood stained the shirt. She wasn't certain if it was his—seeping through from his shoulder wound—or if it was Nikki's.

He shrugged off her concern. "I'm fine."

He wasn't. He had been shot. And he'd been in a car accident.

"You should have gone to the hospital with Nikki," she said.

"I didn't need to."

"She said the same thing."

"She'd lost consciousness for a little while," Nick said. And that muscle twitched in his cheek as tension filled him. He must have been reliving the accident, too. "She needed to be checked for a concussion. And she probably needed stitches."

She heard the guilt in his voice, the regret. "I'm sorry," she said. "I shouldn't have left the condo earlier."

"Why did you?" he asked.

"I—I had all this work I needed to do," she said. "I needed a fax machine and a way to telecommute—"

"And Logan offered his office," he surmised.

She nodded. "But I shouldn't have risked it." She ran her palms over the baby. She shouldn't have risked his life for her career.

He sighed. "I'm the one who shouldn't have left."

"Where did you go?" she asked.

"To see Penny."

She suspected it hadn't been to discuss wedding plans. Probably to end them.

"That's fine," she said. She hadn't agreed to marry him, anyway, even though it was what she'd wanted

as long as she could remember. "I had plenty of protection."

"But you were still in danger," Nick said.

Tears stung her eyes. "Will I always be?" she wondered aloud. "Will I ever be safe again?"

"Of course," he said. "We'll get to the bottom of this.
We'll figure out who's after me."

"That vehicle was tailing me," she reminded him.

"Because of me."

"You don't know that."

He sighed. "No. But Nikki and I have come up with
another theory."

So had she. "I think it could have more to do with me
than I realized. Maybe another real estate agent wants
to eliminate me as competition." It was possible. The
Chicago real estate business could be quite cutthroat.
"Or maybe I do have a stalker."

He narrowed his eyes. "I thought you didn't have
any crazy exes."

"I don't," she said. "But a stalker can be anyone. I
could have smiled at someone on the street and given
him the wrong impression."

He nodded slowly as if considering it. "You do have
a very friendly smile."

She didn't know if he was complimenting or teasing her.

"I really don't think this has anything to do with
you," he said.

"You and Nikki talked it over," she prompted him.

He nodded more quickly now. "We would have presented our theory to everyone tonight, but it was more
important that Nikki go to the hospital and get checked
out."

More important than his getting checked out. Nick had always been such a loner that he'd acted as if he could barely tolerate her and Gage following him around. But it sounded as if he was beginning to care about this family he hadn't known he had until his mother had died.

And if he cared about them, could he someday come to care about her, as well? She'd spent years trying and had never reached his heart. It had taken them only months. She had to accept that it just wasn't meant to be.

"We'll have a meeting about it tomorrow."

"That's good," she said. The danger needed to end. She wanted her life back.

"And in the meantime, you're safe here," Nick said. "Nobody can get inside this place."

"I don't feel safe," she said. That was why she couldn't sleep. She had felt safe only one place—in his arms.

As if he'd read her mind—as he always did—he wrapped his arms around her and pulled her against his chest. His heart beat fast and heavily. Maybe it was residual adrenaline from the crash.

Or maybe it was...

She stared up into his face and saw the way his blue eyes darkened, his pupils dilating. He wanted her, too.

"You need to go to bed," he said. And he lifted her easily in his arms—despite his wounded shoulder and her extra weight—and carried her into the master bedroom.

She locked her arms around his neck so that when he laid her down, she pulled him down with her. "I'm not tired," she said.

"Oh, I didn't say you were going to sleep," he murmured. Then his mouth covered hers. He kissed her passionately, as if he'd been starving for a taste of her lips.

She had been starving for him. Her body ached with desire. She had felt so empty—so hollow—without him. She pulled at his clothes, trying to tug off his shirt, his belt. But she was too anxious—too inept.

He stepped back and pulled off his holster and gun. His shirt followed, and his jeans. He was so damn sexy.

She reached for her clothes. She wanted to be as naked as he was, wanted nothing between them but skin. But she fumbled with the buttons.

He undid them. And as he parted her blouse, he pressed kisses against the skin he exposed—on her throat, then the curve of her breast and her belly. The baby shifted beneath his lips.

And a smile spread across Nick's face. Was he happy about the baby? She hadn't thought so. She'd seen only his shock. Until now...

She wanted to ask him how he felt. But then his mouth was on hers again. He kissed her, his lips sliding over hers. She gasped at the delicious sensation, and his tongue slipped inside her mouth. It stroked back and forth between her lips.

Desire overwhelmed her.

He unclasped her bra and pushed it and her blouse from her shoulders. Then he touched her breasts. Cupping them in his palms, he teased the nipples with his thumbs.

She moaned and pressed against him, wanting more. His erection pushed against her hip, so she wrapped her fingers around it. She stroked him.

He groaned, and his control snapped—like it had that night they'd made love the first time. He lifted her so that she straddled his lap. Then he eased inside her and filled the emptiness.

She felt whole again. Safe.

But she felt so much more than that. As he moved inside her, the tension built. She clutched at his shoulders and his back as she moved frantically. She rocked and bounced and arched, desperate for the release only he could give her.

He clutched her hips in his hands and helped her match his rhythm. They moved together as one. And they came as one, shouting as pleasure overwhelmed them.

He dropped onto his back on the mattress and pulled her down on top of him. He wrapped his arms tightly around her, as if he never intended to let her go.

But Annalise knew better.

She knew he wouldn't stay.

He cursed as he watched the news footage of the crash. Another lackey dead.

He'd lost one man in the hospital parking garage. And now another...

Nicholas Rus was good. Too good. The FBI special agent had made so many enemies that it hadn't been hard to find more men to take him on. The only problem was that they didn't want what *he* wanted. They wanted vengeance. Because Rus had shut down so much crime in River City and Chicago, they wanted him to pay—with his life. They were imbeciles. The shoot-out at the hospital wasn't going to get *him* what he wanted.

What was *his*...

But he had been looking—as discreetly as possible—for months. And his patience had worn out. Where the hell was it? What had Nicholas Rus or that woman done with it?

One of them had it. They had to.

They probably just didn't realize what they had. He had to get it before they did. Or maybe he would make Nicholas Rus bring it to him. He just needed to make sure he had something Nick wanted as desperately as he wanted his property.

The woman was the key. Annalise Huxton was the key to him reclaiming what was rightfully his.

Chapter 18

Nikki looked like death. She'd already had the bruise on her left cheek. Now she had another on the right side of her face along with a short line of stitches near her temple.

Nick's heart contracted with regret that she'd been hurt—because of him. "I'm sorry," he murmured as she stepped inside the condo.

Her brown eyes twinkled. "Sorry? You're the first one to make sure I'm included in a Payne Protection meeting."

Nick was sympathetic. He knew what it was like to be on the outside looking in on a family. He had felt like that with the Huxtons. He'd understood he wasn't one of them, but at least Gage and Annalise had tried to include him. Nikki had known she was a Payne, but her brothers had never included her like they should have.

Until now…

Everyone else fell silent as she walked into the condo. They were probably staring at the bruises. Nikki tensed as if she thought they were going to throw her out.

Nick said, "Now that Nikki is here, she's going to run the meeting."

Predictably, Logan bristled. "She's not up to speed on this assignment."

"She's more up to speed than you think," Nick said. "She's been working this assignment all along. She found Annalise's stolen car for me when the whole River City Police Department couldn't find it."

"You had no right to put her on this assignment," Logan said.

It wasn't the first time Nick had heard that. He'd put Garek Kozminski on assignment for the FBI and had nearly gotten him and Candace killed. He'd made mistakes. So he wasn't going to argue with his half brother, especially now that Logan was his boss.

Logan's face flushed with anger as he continued, "You've put her in danger over and over again."

And Nick didn't feel good about it. But he felt compelled to point out, in Nikki's defense more than his own, "And she survived it. She is tougher than you all have given her credit for being."

Nikki didn't just smile. She beamed.

And Nick's heart swelled with pride in her. He finally understood Gage's connection with Annalise. He glanced over to his friend sitting next to Annalise. Right now, Gage looked better than Nikki did. Whatever physical injuries he had sustained while he'd been missing were healing. Nick hoped his other injuries were healing, too.

"Suck-up," Parker called him.

Unabashed, Nick grinned. Maybe he should have sucked up to his sister a while ago. "She's smart, too."

"We never disputed that," Logan said. "That's why she's best behind a desk."

Nikki snorted derisively.

"She figured out what no one else has," Nick said. "This isn't about revenge."

"What is it about?" Annalise asked the question. She'd been worried that it was about her, that she had made someone jealous or obsessed. She could have. Her smiles were powerful enough to make a stranger on the street fall in love with her. But Nick doubted it had anything to do with her.

Everybody looked at Nick, but he turned toward his sister.

Nikki shrugged.

"I thought you figured it out," Logan said, frustration joining his earlier irritation.

"We don't know *what* it's about," she said. Her suspicion from the day before was gone.

The tightness in Nick's chest eased. Nikki didn't think the worst of him anymore. She didn't think he was corrupt, like all the cops and public officials he had busted in River City. Maybe she was even beginning to trust him.

Logan's brow furrowed with confusion, and he began, "I thought—"

"It's about *something*," Nikki said. "But we don't know what."

Nick could see the others were still confused, so he explained, "People think either Annalise or I have something they want."

A ragged sigh of relief slipped from Annalise's lips. "Of course."

"The break-ins," Gage said. "I thought it looked like someone was searching for something."

Nikki nodded. "That's what I thought when I checked out the scene of the last break-in."

The scene where she'd nearly shot him. But he kept that to himself. He didn't need the others to think she'd overreacted. Her quick reflexes were what would keep her alive when she was a true bodyguard.

"And that's probably the reason for the car thefts, too," Nikki continued. "They think Annalise or Nick has something."

"What?" Logan asked.

"I have no idea," Nick said. But he glanced at Annalise, who had fallen curiously silent after her sigh.

"I had some idea," Nikki sheepishly admitted.

Logan groaned.

"What?" Annalise and Gage asked the question together.

Explaining for his sister again, Nick said, "She thought I was dirty. That I stole drug money or something that should have been entered into evidence."

Gage uttered that rusty-sounding laugh of his. "You, dirty? That's hilarious!"

Nick hadn't found it amusing at all.

And realizing that he had been offended, Gage laughed again. Then he turned toward Nikki, whose face had grown red with embarrassment. "You really don't know squeaky-clean Nick. He's the only one Chief Lynch considered sending up to handle the corruption in River City because the chief knows for certain he's beyond corruption."

And that tightness in Nick's chest eased even more. Despite his crossing the line with Annalise, Nick hadn't completely lost Gage's respect.

But the tightness only eased. It didn't disappear entirely. It wouldn't until they figured out what someone wanted so desperately from him that they kept going after Annalise. Maybe they had figured out that if they wanted to work an exchange, the only things Nick cared enough about to barter were Annalise and their unborn baby.

Garek waited until the team had returned to Payne Protection Agency before he spoke. He shut the door behind them and settled into the chair across from his boss's desk. Most of the team—including his beautiful bride—had stayed outside the condo for added security for Nick.

Even if Cooper would have assigned her fieldwork, Nikki was in no condition to work at the moment. So she settled carefully into the chair next to him. She looked like hell, but she was also happier than he'd ever seen her before.

The irony was that the guy who'd made her unhappy—by merely existing—had made her happy again. Or maybe that wasn't ironic but appropriate. Nick had given her the respect her other brothers hadn't.

She'd earned that respect, though. He believed her theory was right. Maybe she'd been right about everything.

He began, "Just playing devil's advocate here."

Logan snorted. "You enjoy that role too much."

"But what if we've been wrong about Nick?" he wondered aloud. "What if he *is* dirty?"

Logan shook his head. "Not possible."

Garek didn't think so, either. But he trusted that Nikki was right. It made sense that someone had been breaking into Nick's and Annalise's places and vehicles because they were looking for something. But Nick had to have something they actually wanted badly enough to kill to get.

So how could he not know that he had it? And it had to belong to someone desperate, someone dangerous.

"I agree," Nikki said, which shocked Garek for a couple of reasons. First, she was actually concurring with something Logan had said. Second, she trusted Nick. Of course, he had saved her life more than once.

But perhaps the fact that Nick had rushed to everyone's rescue multiple times had blinded them to his true nature. Maybe he wasn't as squeaky-clean as the Huxtons believed. Actually, Gage had been the only one to speak up on his behalf. Annalise had remained curiously silent.

Did she know something the others didn't? She was obviously closer to Nick than anyone else. Garek suspected that nobody understood him better than she did.

"You've been quiet," Nick said after the others had left. She was sitting on the couch, and he knelt in front of her and studied her face. "Are you feeling all right?"

Annalise felt sick. But it had nothing to do with her pregnancy and everything to do with what she had done. It was all her fault. It had to be. "No…"

His handsome face tensed with concern. "I'll take you to the hospital."

She shook her head. "No, I don't need to go to the hospital." Even if she was having medical issues, she wouldn't risk it, not after what had happened the last time they had gone.

"Is it the contractions again?" he asked. He put his hands over her stomach as if he could feel them, too. Or as if he could make them stop.

He was so protective. But that was just his nature. She couldn't read more into it than that. She couldn't convince herself that he actually cared about her.

"No," she replied. "It's not the baby."

He leaned closer, his blue gaze intense as he studied her face. "But I can tell you're not feeling well."

Tears stung her eyes—tears of regret. "That's because of what I've done," she admitted.

He tensed and eased away from her. "Annalise…"

"It's my fault." It had to be.

"What did you do?"

She'd realized it when Nikki had been talking. She'd realized then what a huge mistake she'd made. "You're going to be furious with me."

Chapter 19

Dread settled heavily on Nick, pulling his shoulders down. He flinched at the pain. His gunshot wound had barely begun to heal. But his physical pain was milder than what he was feeling emotionally.

He got back to his feet and paced the length of the living room before turning back to her to ask, "What did you do?"

What could Annalise have done that had put them in danger? Gage had called him squeaky-clean, but Annalise was more honest than he was. Or so Nick had always believed.

She'd been just a kid when he'd lived next door to her. And he hadn't stayed in touch with her throughout the years like she had tried to stay in touch with him. He had no idea what kind of men she'd dated. She might have fallen for a bad boy who'd gotten her into trouble.

"I know what you told me to do."

He'd told her a lot of things over the years. To stop following him around.

To stop hugging him.

He hadn't really meant those things.

"What did I tell you?" he asked for clarification.

"You asked me to get rid of your mom's house."

"You said you rented it." He wished she'd burned it down instead. Or sold it.

She nodded. "The tenant paid the whole year's rent in cash."

A chill raced down his spine. "Someone paid for the year up front? Is that normal?"

She shrugged. "I've had it happen before, when someone has sold a house and wants to rent."

"Had this guy sold a house?"

"Maybe," she said. "But I didn't handle the sale. I probably wouldn't have rented to him if he hadn't been able to pay the cash up front."

The short hairs lifted on Nick's nape. "Why not?"

"He had no credit history. No job history."

"But he had a year's rent money?"

"In cash."

Criminals had cash. Who the hell had she rented to? "Annalise…"

"I'm sorry," she said.

"There's more?" he asked.

She nodded. "You told me to get rid of all of her possessions, too."

"And you didn't."

She had never believed he'd meant the other things he'd told her—or she would have stayed away. She would have stopped hugging him. But she hadn't. So she must not have thought he'd meant what he'd told her about his mother's estate, either.

"Did you rent the place furnished?" he asked. That would have made sense and explained why she hadn't gotten rid of anything.

She shook her head. "The tenant wanted me to," she said. "He even offered to pay me extra. But I didn't want to leave her possessions there."

"She had nothing of value," he said. "You could have left everything. Or given it all away."

"I kept her belongings," Annalise admitted.

"But I told you to get rid of everything."

"I thought you might change your mind," she said. "I didn't want you to have any regrets."

"I regret that you didn't get rid of her crap," he said. Especially if having it had put her in danger. "Did you bring it home with you?"

She shook her head. "I have a few storage units. I either put stuff in them when I'm staging houses or store the stuff I use for staging in them."

"I don't think my…" He hated calling her Mom. In the short time he'd known her, Penny Payne had already been more of a mother to him than the woman who'd given birth to him had ever been. "… I don't think Carla had anything you could use to stage a house."

"No," Annalise admitted. "But I thought you might want something of hers, something to remember her by. And I didn't want to have given it all away."

He had something to remember her by: the letter she'd left telling him who his father really was. She had given him the family he'd never thought he would have. She had given him a real mother. And she had allayed the fear he'd always had that his father was some drug dealer.

What else had she given him? Had she left him something that had put his—and worse, Annalise's—lives in danger? She had given him one family. But if he lost Annalise and their unborn baby, he'd lost the family he could have made for himself.

"What do you think you're doing?"

Annalise dropped her sweater into her open suitcase, turned around and found Nick leaning against the doorjamb. "I'm packing."

"Why?"

After she'd admitted to ignoring his command to get rid of all of his mother's things, she'd thought he would be happy to get rid of her.

"Because we're going back to Chicago," she said.

"Why would we do that?" he asked.

How could he not know? He was the lawman. She was just a real estate agent. "Because we need to go through the storage units and find what they're looking for."

"Did you see a wad of money?"

She shook her head.

"Of course not," Nick said. "Because anytime Carla got her hands on money, she used it to buy drugs."

She ached for Nick, for the sad little boy who'd grown up too quickly next door to her family.

"So it must be something else," she agreed.

He shook his head. "What? If it was anything of value, she would have pawned it for money for drugs. There's nothing."

"Then why did someone break into her house and

mine and yours?" she asked. "Just hours ago you said somebody thinks you have something they want."

"Thinks," Nick said. "We don't actually have it."

He was probably right. But that only increased her frustration. "How do we convince whoever is after us that we don't have it?"

She wanted her life back. She'd worked hard to build her career. And as a single mom-to-be, she needed it more than ever.

"We find him."

"How do we do that?" she asked.

He shook his head. "Not you. You've already been in too much danger because of this."

And she heard the anger again. He was mad that she hadn't done as he'd asked, that she hadn't gotten rid of everything. Hell, he was right. If she'd known what was going to happen to her life, she would have burned down his mother's house herself. But she'd done what she'd thought would be best for him, like she always had.

She'd thought *she* would be best for him. That was why she'd been so persistent in loving him. She'd thought she could make him happy. But all she had done was create more problems for him.

He would be better off without her. She tossed another sweater in the suitcase. Candace had been sweet to buy her more things. But now she had too much.

"Why are you still packing?" he asked.

"I have a job, too," she said. "I have a life that I can't stay away from any longer."

"You still want to go back to Chicago?"

She nodded. She needed to go back, needed to get away from him before she fell any deeper in love with him. Before she began to imagine that they could actually have a life together. It was clear that Nick didn't want that. She wasn't even certain that he wanted to have a baby together. Or if she really would be raising their child alone.

"Give us more time," he implored her.

"Us?" Her heart swelled with hope.

"The Payne Protection Agency," he said. "Give us more time to figure out what you and I might have that someone wants. We'll check out the renter in Carla's house. We'll find out if he's involved in all of this."

"Of course."

He was talking about his family. They were the *us*. Not her and him. They had never been an *us*. And maybe it was time that she accepted that they never would be.

"Annalise?" he called her name as if he'd said it more than once.

She raised her gaze from the suitcase to his handsome face. "Will you give us time?" he asked.

She'd already given Nick her whole life. She couldn't give him any more time.

Penny had a wedding to plan. But it wasn't the one she wanted to plan. She wanted to plan Nick's to Annalise. As if thinking about him had summoned him, he appeared in the doorway to her office.

She caught a glimpse of what he must have been like as a boy, longing for love. She'd worried that he hadn't had any in his life. But after meeting Annalise Huxton, she knew he had. The girl next door had loved him her whole life.

Before she could even greet him, he said, "She's leaving." And his voice was full of frustration and pain.

Penny pressed a hand to her heart as it leaped with fear—for the young woman and her unborn baby. "But she's in danger."

"She's not leaving right now," he said. "I talked her out of that. But she'll leave soon."

"Not if you stop her."

"I can't," he said. "She has a great career in Chicago. She has to go back."

Penny shook her head. "Give her a reason to stay."

"What reason can I give her?"

"You know what reason, Nick," she said. The most important reason. "Give her your love."

His handsome face—so like her sons' faces—twisted into a grimace. "I don't know how."

Her heart ached for him, for the love he'd never known. "Nick…"

He shook his head, brushing off her sympathy. "I don't know how to love someone," he said. "You can't give what you've never received."

"Hasn't that changed?" she asked. "Haven't we changed that for you?"

He sighed. "I think it's too late."

"It's never too late to love someone," she insisted.

He looked at her, his blue eyes steely, his gaze intense.

"What?" she asked uneasily. Nick could see through her like no one else ever had. Even his father had never understood her like this son of his.

"You talk about love," he said, "but I don't think you're an expert, either. I don't think you know how to love any more than I do."

"I know how to love," she insisted. "I love my kids. I love you."

"What about a man?"

"Nicholas died so many years ago."

"Exactly," he said. "He died years ago. You should have moved on. You should have had another relationship."

She shivered at the thought. "I didn't need another one. I had my great love."

"I don't think so," he said.

"Because he cheated on me?"

"Exactly. He didn't deserve you, Penny. He betrayed your love and your trust, and I think you never had another relationship because you're afraid you'd get hurt again. You're afraid to trust again." He stepped closer, and for once he took her hand instead of the other way around. He squeezed it gently. "I think you're afraid to love."

She couldn't argue with him. She couldn't even stop him as he walked out of her office. But she followed him and watched as he pulled away from the chapel. She wasn't the only one. Another vehicle pulled away from the curb and trailed after his.

Was it someone from Payne Protection? She shivered and knew that it wasn't. Someone else followed Nick. He wasn't in danger of losing just his heart. He was in danger of losing his life, too.

Chapter 20

Nick was being followed. But he was alone, so he didn't care. He wasn't putting Annalise or Nikki in danger. His life was the only one at risk.

He couldn't give Annalise his heart. He didn't have one to offer her. But he could give her back her life—the one she'd worked so hard to build for herself. That was the least he could do for her, for all she had endured because she'd thought she was helping him.

She didn't realize he'd made peace with his mother long ago, before she'd died. He'd realized she had a disease, an addiction she couldn't beat. He hadn't been able to help her because she hadn't wanted help.

So he'd dedicated his life to the people he could help. He could help Annalise.

He could stop the person who was after them. He spoke into his phone. But he wasn't talking to anyone at the Payne Protection Agency. He asked for directions to the nearest storage facility. Whoever was following him thought he was going to get whatever the hell he thought he had.

Maybe he could lure him out in the open. Maybe he could end this now. He turned in the direction the phone had told him. He was sure whoever was following him wasn't alone. There had to be someone else back there.

A Payne Protection bodyguard…

Milek. Garek.

The only person he was certain it wasn't was Nikki. Her brothers weren't going to let her anywhere near him until this was over. And maybe not even after that.

As he thought of her, his phone lit up with her number. He touched the speaker button. "That was quick," he said. He'd called her on his way to the White Wedding Chapel.

"It was easy," she replied. "He gave Annalise a fake name on the rental application."

"That was why she couldn't find any credit or work history for him," he surmised. "But if all you have is a fake name…"

"Fake name," she said. "Real person. Ralph Adams died over thirty years ago."

"Ralph Adams…" The name sounded vaguely familiar.

"Your mom testified in his murder trial," she said. "Her testimony helped put away the drug dealer who killed Ralph. Darren Snow. His nickname was—"

"The Iceman," Nick said. After her death—after he'd found that letter—Nick had checked out everything his mother had claimed in it. He'd learned about the Iceman.

"Who was just paroled," Nikki said, "six months ago."

Nick glanced into his rearview mirror, trying to catch a glimpse of the driver in the vehicle tailing him. "It has to be him."

"But what does he want?" Nikki asked. "What could your mom have that he thinks is his?"

The car was bearing down on him quickly. The driver was not even trying to hide the fact that he was following Nick.

"We'll have to talk about that later," Nick said. "I have to go now."

He clicked off the phone and returned to his directions to that storage facility. It had to be close—the facility and the end of the danger in which he and Annalise had been living.

Annalise shivered. And it wasn't just because of the conversation she'd overheard Nikki having with Nick about a killer drug dealer named the Iceman. It was because of the abrupt way that conversation had ended.

"What's going on with him?" she asked.

Nikki's face had paled beneath the bruises, and she shook her head. "I don't know. He seemed like he was in a hurry."

"To get back here?" Annalise asked and hoped.

Instead of answering her, Nikki clicked another button on her cell phone. "Hey? Who's on Nick?"

She hadn't put the call on speaker, so Annalise couldn't hear the name that Nikki heard. But from the look of doubt and concern on her face, she suspected she knew.

Gage. And apparently Nikki didn't think Annalise's

brother was ready for the assignment. Unfortunately, neither did Annalise.

"Does he know where Nick is going?" Nikki asked whomever she'd called—probably her brother Logan. She grunted. "Of course not."

Nikki turned her focus back to the computer she'd brought to investigate the person to whom Annalise had rented Nick's mother's house. Because Annalise had been giving her information, she'd been sitting next to Nikki and could easily see the screen. After tapping the keyboard a few seconds, Nikki pulled up Nick's phone record.

"Yeah, I'm hacking," she told her brother—with no shame. "Last thing Nick did was get directions to the nearest storage facility." She gave Logan the name and address.

Even though he wasn't on speaker, Annalise could hear Logan's curse. He knew what Nick was doing.

"Is anyone else close enough?" Nikki asked. She really didn't trust Gage as Nick's only backup. And she cursed at Logan's reply.

Annalise's stomach churned with concern and with the baby's restless kicks. It was as if he knew, too, that his father was in danger. She waited until Nikki clicked off the phone before she said, "He's risking his life."

Nikki shrugged. "Just leaving the condo puts his life in danger."

Hers, too. Annalise had learned that the hard way. But she wanted to leave now. She wanted to be with Nick—to make certain that he was all right.

"What's going on?" Annalise asked.

"He picked up a tail after he left Mom's chapel." There was more unsaid in Nikki's tone.

"And…?" Annalise prodded her.

"He's leading the tail to that storage facility."

"He's using himself as bait," Annalise realized. "To catch whoever's after us." And he was out there with only her brother as backup—a man who hadn't trusted himself to protect her. Why had he trusted himself to protect Nick?

He obviously wasn't ready. And if Nick died, would Gage ever be able to forgive himself? Would she?

It was Annalise's fault that Nick was in danger in the first place. She should have sold the place the way he'd told her to—totally furnished. Then his mother's possessions would all have been gone. Nobody would be looking for something he was so desperate to retrieve that he was willing to kill.

But then, according to what Nikki had said, the Iceman had killed before. He would have no compunction about killing again.

Gage had heard the doubt in everyone else's voices. They'd thought him ready to protect an elderly woman from her own paranoia. They hadn't thought he was ready to protect Nick. Just a couple of days ago, he wouldn't have thought he was ready, either. He hadn't trusted himself to protect Annalise. But he'd been feeling better—stronger.

He hadn't been having the nightmares like he had before. He hadn't been sleeping much, so the nightmares weren't really an issue.

Maybe what he'd been through wasn't the reason the others hadn't trusted him to protect Nick. Maybe it was because of what Nick had done to Annalise.

He'd gotten her pregnant.

Gage waited for the betrayal and anger to rush over him again. But instead, he felt an odd surge of happiness. He was going to have a nephew, a child that would be equal parts of the two people Gage loved most in the world. Now.

He had loved someone else more before. But that seemed like a lifetime ago. He wasn't the man he'd been back then. That man was still missing.

Gage doubted he would ever be found. That was fine, though. Maybe it would make it easier for him to move on—at last.

What about Nick?

When they caught whoever was after him and Annalise, would Nick move on? Or would he want to be part of his son's life? Part of Annalise's?

She loved him. She had always loved him.

But what about Nick?

He touched the radio on his collar and asked, "What the hell are you doing?"

"Gage?"

"Yeah."

"You're my tail?"

"I don't know who the hell your tail is," Gage said. But he'd been following him since Nick had left the chapel. "He's driving a rental. And all I can see through the back window is a bald head."

"So there's just one of them?" Nick asked.

"As far as I can tell…" Inside that vehicle. But there could have been other ones—ones that had stayed farther back so neither he nor Nick had made them.

Nick's sigh of relief rattled the phone. "That's good. We've got him outnumbered. We can catch him."

Gage worried that Nick was giving him too much

credit. "This is risky," he said. "We haven't had time to plan. We need more backup."

"They're on their way." Nick was certain, probably because the Paynes seemed to travel in a pack. There would be other bodyguards close.

But Gage didn't think they would make it in time. The gate to the storage facility came into view. Nick must have broken the lock and jimmied open the gate, because that rental vehicle passed easily through. Not wanting to tip the man off, Gage hesitated a moment before driving through the broken gate himself.

The storage units were tall and deep enough for motor homes and boats. There were also—so many rows that he had no idea which alley Nick had driven down. Or the man who'd been following him.

"Nick?" he called into the radio. "Where the hell are you?"

Nick must have shut off the radio so he wouldn't give away his location to other man. But Gage needed to know where he was in order to protect him.

As he passed another row, he noticed a car parked far down the alley, its taillights burning holes in the gathering darkness. The sun was just beginning to set, but here between the tall buildings, it looked like night already.

Gage stopped his vehicle and called out his location into the radio. Nick might not be able to hear him, but the others hadn't shut off their radios. And they were on their way. But as Gage opened his car door, he heard the gunshots.

And he knew no one else would get there in time to help. It was up to him. He was Nick's only backup. His heart pounding frantically, he drew his weapon from his holster and headed around the front of his SUV. He'd parked it to block off that alley—to trap the car inside it with no escape.

The taillights turned to backup lights. Tires squealing, the car reversed—heading right toward him. Now he was the one trapped between his vehicle and the one bearing down on him. He lifted his weapon and squeezed the trigger. He had no idea if his shots struck anything but metal and glass.

He heard the metal ping. The glass shatter. But the car kept coming. Feeling the whoosh of air as it neared, he jumped, launching himself at the side of the one of the units. Metal crunched, and he waited for the pain.

But the car missed him. It didn't miss the SUV. It struck it hard, hard enough to push it back. But it didn't leave a space big enough for the car to get through. Brakes squealed again as the car lurched to a stop.

The driver's door opened. The man was just a shadow. The only thing Gage saw was the gun he held, the barrel pointed directly at him. He lifted his own weapon and flinched as shots rang out.

The sound of gunfire had memories rushing over him—of other firefights. Of losing friends...

Where was Nick?

What had happened to him?

Would Gage find him as he had the others? His body bloodied, staring up at him through lifeless eyes...

Chapter 21

Nick cursed. He'd fired shot after shot. But from how easily the man ran away—around his wrecked vehicle and Gage's—he doubted he'd hit him.

At the moment, he was the least of Nick's concerns, though. "Gage!"

If anyone had been hit, it was Gage. The man had struck him either with his vehicle or with his bullets. Nick's stomach lurched as he relived seeing Gage trapped between his SUV and the car bearing down on him.

Gage couldn't have survived hell only to die at home—because of Nick. Nick would never forgive himself. And neither would Annalise.

He rushed over to where Gage's body was slumped against the metal door of one of the storage units. Dropping to his knees, he leaned over him. He couldn't see any blood but Gage's jeans were torn and so was the sleeve of his shirt. His short golden hair was mussed, too. "Are you okay?"

Since night had begun to fall, the light above the door of the unit kicked on and shone down on his friend like a spotlight.

Gage's eyes—the same clear green as Annalise's—were open but unfocused, as if he couldn't see. Or as if he could see something Nick couldn't, something only inside Gage's mind.

"I'm sorry," he murmured. "Sorry I didn't save you."

"I'm fine," Nick said.

Gage just shook his head as if he didn't believe him. But Nick wasn't sure he'd even heard him.

"Are you hit?" Nick asked. Maybe he just couldn't see the blood. He didn't want to move Gage, didn't want to risk injuring him more like he could have Nikki had she been hurt more seriously. Nothing was going to blow up here. The only risk was the gunman returning to shoot at them again.

He kept his weapon in his hand, ready to fire if he needed to. He could check Gage for injuries only with one hand. His wounded shoulder ached in protest, but he moved his arm, running his hand along Gage's ribs.

The other man flinched. He was hurt. But Nick didn't know if the injuries were new or old ones that had been aggravated. What the hell had Gage gone through all those months he'd been missing?

Nick touched the radio on his collar, turning it back on. "I need an ambulance."

"You're hurt?" Logan asked.

"Not me," Nick said.

"Gage?"

A strong hand clasped his. "No," Gage murmured. "I'm fine."

He wasn't fine. His eyes were still unfocused. And he kept flinching even though Nick wasn't touching him. He was reliving the nightmare he'd endured.

Then Nick's nightmare returned as he heard footsteps moving across the concrete behind him. He had his gun, but he wouldn't be able to fire it fast enough to save both him and Gage.

Had she lost one of them? Or both?

Candace and Nikki claimed everyone was fine. But they drove her to the hospital, both their usually beautiful faces grim with worry. If everyone was fine, they wouldn't have brought her here. Annalise was frantic.

She had nearly lost both men before. Gage all those months he had been missing in Afghanistan…

And Nick in the very hospital garage in which Candace parked the Payne Protection SUV. He'd been shot. He could have been killed then. It could have been his body she and Nikki had seen on that gurney.

Nikki reached for her hand and squeezed it. "He's fine."

Which *he*?

They wouldn't have brought her to the hospital if at least one of the men she loved hadn't been hurt. More Payne Protection bodyguards joined them. Garek and Milek helped escort her to the elevator and up to the emergency room.

The doors slid open to Logan and Parker pacing the lobby. They looked as grim as Candace and Nikki. "What's wrong?" she asked. "Who's hurt?"

She turned toward those doors marked No Admittance and thought about forcing her way through them—just as someone stepped out.

Nick glanced at her before looking at the others. "You shouldn't have brought her here."

"Why not?" she asked. "What's wrong?"

Oh, God, it was Gage.

"It's too dangerous," Nick said. "You remember what happened last time."

The gunfire in the lobby. She would never forget. But that didn't matter now.

"What's wrong with Gage?" She reached out and clasped Nick's forearms, gripping them for support.

"He's fine," he replied, too quickly.

"He wouldn't be here if he was fine," she pointed out. "Why did you bring him here if he wasn't physically hurt?"

Nick's face was as grim as everyone else's had been. And that muscle twitched in his cheek, his telltale sign of stress. "I don't think he was physically injured."

"What happened?" she asked.

"There was gunfire—"

She gasped as panic overwhelmed her, stealing her breath away. She gripped Nick more tightly and ran her gaze over him. He didn't look as if he had been hit. "But you would know if he'd been shot..." He would know for certain whether or not her brother was physically injured.

"A car nearly hit him, though."

"Nearly?"

"It missed him. But he'd had to move quickly to get out of the way."

He'd gotten out of the way, and he hadn't been shot.

"Why did you bring him here?" she asked.

Nick released a ragged sigh. "He wasn't…he wasn't… right. Something was wrong."

Cooper walked up. "He was probably having flash-backs," he said. "The gunfire probably triggered it."

"He kept thinking I was hurt," Nick said. "That I'd been hit." He shuddered.

And Annalise's heart ached for what both men she loved had endured. "Will he be okay?" she asked.

Nick nodded. "We brought in a doctor who gets it, who's been there and knows how to help him."

Annalise wished she could help her brother. But he hadn't come to her when he'd finally come home. He had come to Nick. And Nick had gotten him help.

"Can I see him?" She wanted to make certain he was all right. That he was still the Gage she had known and loved their whole lives.

Nick didn't argue with her like he had when she'd first arrived. He slid his arm around her and brought her back to the emergency room. For once, Annalise wasn't the one being treated. But she felt no relief.

Nick paused outside a curtain and warned her, "He's sleeping."

He announced it as if it was monumental that her brother was asleep. She didn't understand, but she had no intention of disturbing him. She only wanted to make certain he was all right.

Nick pulled back the curtain. Gage lay on a gurney, his eyes closed. There was no tension in his body. He looked completely relaxed. He looked like Gage again.

She stepped closer and slid her hand over her brother's.

"In all the nights he spent at my place," Nick said, "he hadn't slept."

Now she understood why it was so monumental that he was sleeping at last.

"I'm sorry," Nick said.

She glanced back at him, confused. "Why?"

"If I'd known it was Gage on my protection duty..." He moved forward, too, so that he stood behind her, the heat of his body warming the chill from hers.

"You shouldn't have risked your life, either," she admonished him. In a few months, he was going to be a father—unless he had no intention of being involved in his son's life.

"I had to try to end this."

"Did you catch him?" she asked. She doubted that they had, though, or everyone wouldn't have looked so grim.

He sighed, and this time the breath was ragged with frustration. "No."

Her shoulders sagged. It felt like her burden grew. A burden of guilt and regret. She should have done what Nick had asked. He'd wanted nothing of his mother's. If she'd gotten rid of it all like he'd wanted, nobody would think he had something he didn't.

His hands covered her shoulders and squeezed. "We're getting closer," he said. "We'll get him."

But the Iceman was getting closer, too. He'd nearly run down Gage tonight—nearly shot him and probably Nick, too, although he hadn't admitted it.

Two men had already died. She worried that more men would before it was all over. She worried that the men she loved would die.

Darren had almost had him, could have killed him. A dead man couldn't lead him to what was his. But once he'd recovered his property, Nicholas Rus was a dead man.

The FBI special agent had tried to trick him, leading him to that storage facility. If what he wanted was in storage, it was probably in Chicago. Near the place the US Marshals had relocated Carla to after she'd testified against him in River City.

But it was small enough that it could have easily been transported to River City. Nicholas Rus could have found it the last time he'd been at his mother's six months ago. He could have brought it back with him then. Or even before.

When she had died...

Too bad her death had been of natural causes—or as natural as years of drug abuse could be on a body. If Darren had known where she was, if he'd had a clue...

But he hadn't known where she was or that she was even still alive until after she'd died. Then the bitch had had some lawyer send him a letter taunting him. He'd gotten it before he'd been granted parole.

He'd been damn lucky that whoever read prison mail hadn't realized what she'd been talking about, about the evidence she would have used against him had he ever found her.

She was damn lucky that he'd never been able to find her. Evidence be damned, she would have died a long time ago—that traitorous whore. And it would not have been as painless as an overdose. He would have made her suffer for all the years he'd spent behind bars because of her.

While he couldn't make her suffer anymore, he could make her son suffer. But he wasn't sure if what would hurt Nicholas Rus the most was killing him or killing the woman and the baby she carried.

It had to be Rus's kid. In all the months Darren had followed her around, he hadn't seen her with any other man.

Annalise Huxton was a good woman.

Too bad she would wind up dying because of her love and devotion to Nicholas Rus. Yes, she was the key, the way to get back his property and to get back at the man who'd kept him from it.

Chapter 22

Nick had worked hard so he would never make the mistakes his mother had. He had never gotten involved with the wrong people. He'd never tried drugs. Hell, he rarely ever drank, because he hated the thought of losing control.

The only time he had ever lost control had been with Annalise. He'd wanted her so badly that he hadn't thought about how it would complicate their relationship and potentially destroy his friendship with her brother. He hadn't thought about protection, either. And now she was pregnant with his son.

What kind of father would he be when he'd never had one? Hell, he hadn't had a real mother, either. Hadn't had love…

Would he be able to love their son like he deserved to be loved? Like Annalise deserved to be loved?

Penny thought he was capable. But she was like Annalise, always so optimistic and hopeful. Except when it came to her own life. After Nicholas Payne had broken her heart, she hadn't trusted it to anyone else.

She didn't know or trust love much more than Nick did.

"Don't worry about this." Nikki's voice emanated from the cell phone sitting on the coffee table in front of the couch on which Nick had sprawled. "I'm working it."

"You shouldn't be working it alone," he said. "I ordered the transcripts of the Iceman's trial." Maybe they would find a clue in them to what his mother had taken from her former drug dealer and lover.

"And I'll have hacked into the court records before you get them," Nikki said.

He chuckled because she was right. And a little scary...

He was glad she was on his team now. Well, technically she was on Cooper's. But they were all working together now because they were family. His heart swelled at the thought. Despite what he'd said to Penny, he had one. He had a heart; he just had never learned how to use it, how to open it to receive and express love.

"Get some rest, Nick," his sister advised him. "We're getting close."

She was as optimistic as her mother when it came to work. Nick doubted she would ever trust anyone with her heart, either, not after learning the man she had respected most had betrayed her mother.

"You need some rest, too," he said.

"I need some respect," Nikki grumbled.

"You have it." She had his. And she was earning the

respect of her other brothers. They would see her for the capable woman that she'd become.

She said nothing for a long moment. He must have flustered her. Finally she spoke again. "I'll let you know what I find out. Good night."

"Good night." He clicked off the phone. With the light pouring through the skylights, though, it was probably closer to dawn. He'd spent too much of the night at the hospital with Annalise, watching Gage sleep.

He was all right, though. It was Annalise whom Nick worried about more. She was blaming herself for not getting rid of his mother's things. But even if she had, the Iceman might have thought they still had whatever it was.

What the hell was it?

What had his mother done?

Annalise could feel Nick's pain and frustration—just like she'd heard it in his voice when he had talked to his sister. From the bedroom doorway, she watched him. He was lying down, but he wasn't trying to sleep. His eyes were open as he stared up at the skylights.

"You're not going to take your own advice?" she asked.

He tensed as if she'd startled him. Then he sat up and stared at her. "What advice?"

"To get some rest." She'd heard him tell Nikki—after he'd already sent her to bed.

"You didn't take it," he pointed out.

She shrugged. "I can't sleep."

"Don't worry about Gage," he said. "I think he's getting better. Finally getting some sleep should help him a lot."

She suspected Gage had bigger issues than sleep,

maybe even bigger than what had happened when he'd been missing. Because he'd already been hurting before he'd reenlisted. His heart had already been broken.

Like Nick would undoubtedly break Annalise's.

"I'm not worried about Gage," she said. And at the moment, she wasn't.

He stood up then and walked toward her. "Are you worried about the baby?"

"Always," she admitted. "I worry that I won't be able to take care of him."

Nick reached out and skimmed his fingertips along her jaw. "That's ridiculous," he said. "You take care of everyone. You're a natural mother." The fingertips of his other hand skimmed over her belly. "This little guy is very lucky to have *you*."

"What about you?" she asked.

Nick uttered a ragged sigh. "You're more than enough."

A twinge of pain struck her heart. "You don't want to be involved at all?" she asked. She'd known that Nick didn't love her, but she thought he at least *cared*—about her, but also about their baby.

"I don't know how to be involved," he said. "I never had a father."

And he hadn't had much of a mother, either. Annalise had been taking the blame for not getting rid of the woman's things. But it was Carla who'd stolen something from a drug dealer. What had she taken?

"Do you want to be involved?" she asked. That was the important question.

Her belly shifted beneath his hand, which he'd pressed against it. And his blue eyes widened with surprise and wonder as they had every time he'd felt the baby move. He reacted like it was a miracle.

Maybe it was. She had never expected that Nick—who had always griped at her for touching him—would make love to her with such passion that they made a child together.

He was looking at her now—and the surprise and wonder was still in his gaze. Along with something else...

But she was probably only imagining it. Nick didn't love her. As he'd said a million times, he didn't even know how to love.

Nick didn't love her. But he wanted her. His hands moved from her belly to her breasts. She wore only a light nightgown. Her nipples puckered through the thin material. He brushed his thumbs across them.

She bit her bottom lip to hold in the moan that burned the back of her throat. But then his mouth was there, his teeth nipping lightly at her bottom lip, too. She gasped at the delicious sensation, and his tongue stroked soothingly over her bottom lip before sliding inside her mouth.

He kissed her deeply, passionately—so passionately that her knees weakened and she trembled. He swung her up in his arms and carried her to the master bedroom.

"What are you doing?" she asked. He hadn't answered her last question, hadn't told her whether or not he wanted to be involved in their son's life.

Or was this his answer?

"You told me to get some rest," he reminded her. He laid her on the bed, then stripped off his clothes.

Somehow she doubted he was going to get any rest. And neither would she. But she would rather have Nick than sleep any day.

She held out her arms, reaching for him, tugging

him down onto the bed with her. His erection prodded her hip. But he held back, held on to control, and made love to her. He touched her everywhere, his fingertips gliding over her skin. And he kissed everywhere he touched.

He made love to her with his mouth. She squirmed against the mattress, clutching at him as she sought the release she needed from the tension he'd built inside her body. Finally it broke, and she cried out his name.

Nick tensed. She knew he needed it, too. He needed her love. She showed it in her touch, in her kiss.

She made love to him with her mouth. But he pulled back and pulled her down on top of him. He helped her straddle him and take him deep inside her. His hands on her hips guided her, teased her.

Until she felt that unbearable pressure building again. She needed it to break. Needed Nick…

She rocked against him, and her body shuddered as the orgasm overwhelmed her. She'd never felt the pleasure Nick gave her. She'd never felt that soul-deep connection with anyone else.

Only Nick…

Could all of that be only her imagination—like the love she'd thought she'd glimpsed in the depths of his blue eyes? Or was it possible that Nick loved her but didn't know how to express it? Or maybe he didn't think that he could express it right now because he didn't know if either of them would survive the danger they were in.

The ding of an incoming email jerked Nikki awake. Not that she'd been sleeping on purpose. She must have nodded off at her computer. She straightened up from slumping over her desk at the Payne Protection Agency.

She had come back to Logan's offices because it was where she'd worked the longest. She didn't have her desk set up yet at Cooper's—because she didn't want a desk job anymore. She wanted fieldwork, wanted to be a real bodyguard. Not a computer nerd.

But being a computer nerd had its perks, too. She opened her email with a cry of triumph. She'd told Nick she would get the transcript before him, and she had, but probably only because she'd hacked his email and stayed awake until it came in.

She felt a momentary flash of guilt. But it wasn't as if she wasn't going to tell him what she learned. It wasn't as if she didn't trust that he would have told her what he'd found out.

He would have.

Probably.

But then again, he was Nick, and he was used to being a loner. Used to making his own plan and carrying it out like he'd tried to at the storage unit.

Everyone else had been upset with him for going rogue. But Nikki had understood. He'd had an opportunity, and he'd taken it. He would have been a fool if he hadn't at least tried to take down the man who'd been terrorizing Annalise.

He loved her. He looked at her the same besotted way her other brothers looked at their wives. The way the Kozminskis looked at theirs.

Did Nick know it, though?

From what she'd found out about his biological mother, Nikki suspected he'd had very little love in his life. Just Annalise…

She reminded Nikki of her mom. She was that affectionate, that nurturing. So Annalise's love would have been enough.

Why hadn't Penny been enough for Nikki's dad? Why had he betrayed her with a woman like Nick's mom? She flipped through the transcripts that painted a vivid picture of Carla Monelli. Rus had been the last name of the US Marshal who'd relocated her after she'd testified against Darren Snow.

She had probably seduced him, as well. She'd been beautiful with that kind of waiflike vulnerability a lot of men found irresistible. Nikki was petite like her mom, but she had never been vulnerable and never would be. Not physically and sure as hell not emotionally.

Penny was tough, too. She'd had to be or she wouldn't have survived all the pain she had suffered because of a man. Even before he'd been killed in the line of duty, Penny had lost Nicholas Payne.

To Carla...

A woman who would have done anything to feed her addiction. But that addiction might have been men as well as drugs. Nikki's heart ached for the childhood—or lack thereof—that Nick must have had. With a woman like Carla, he would have had to be the responsible one. The adult.

No wonder he was as independent as he was. He was used to having to take care of himself. And her...

But Carla had done something to take care of herself. She'd taken something for insurance. Testifying against the drug dealer had gotten her away from the abusive man as well as setting her up in a new life, in a new city, with a new name and a house and a job.

Maybe she'd thought she would have a man with her,

maybe Nikki's dad. But he had stayed with his wife. She hadn't entered the witness protection program alone, though. She'd been carrying Nick and whatever she had stolen from the Iceman.

Money?

Nick had doubted it. He'd said she would have used it for drugs. He'd said she would have pawned anything of value, as well. So what was it?

She had testified against Darren for witnessing one murder. But he'd been suspected of several others. What if the gun that he'd used was found?

Nikki snapped her fingers. That was what she'd taken. Hell, Nick should have figured that out. Not long ago, he'd sent Garek Kozminski undercover to find a gun to link Viktor Chekov to a murder.

That gun had implicated another killer entirely, though. But Nick had still brought down Chekov. If he found this gun before Darren Snow found it, he could send the recently paroled killer back to prison. No wonder the Iceman was so desperate to get it away from Nick.

As Nikki had learned over the years, desperate men were incredibly dangerous. Nick had to be careful. But he wasn't the only one. Anyone helping Nick was in danger, too. Nikki had already been hurt. She touched the bruises on her face. Her skin was tender and swollen. And the stitches pulled at the cut on her temple. Pulled and itched.

She resisted the urge to scratch them. Barely.

A few bruises and a little cut were no big deal. Annalise had gotten a concussion, and Nick had been shot. The Iceman was definitely dangerous.

To all of them…

She had no more than considered the thought when she heard it—the sound of someone rattling the outside door, trying to get in. It was too early for anyone else to be arriving at work. Even Logan didn't come in this early—at least, not since he'd married Stacy Kozminski.

No. It had to be someone else breaking in.

Maybe someone who had realized that she'd been helping Nick—that she had the answers he wanted. She reached for her weapon. This time her hand shook less than it had before. She was getting used to pointing the barrel at someone, getting used to firing.

Because she knew with a killer like the Iceman, she would get only one chance to protect herself.

Chapter 23

Nick must have been given an old key when he'd hired on to Payne Protection, because it had stuck in the lock. He'd had to wiggle it to get it to turn. He'd thought he had seen Nikki's coupe in the lot, but the door had been locked.

She might have locked it for protection, though. With a killer like the Iceman on the loose again, they were all in danger. Maybe it was that anticipation of danger that had him ducking the second he heard the cock of a gun. But the bullet had already been fired, so he was too late to avoid a hit.

If Nikki hadn't jerked the barrel at the last moment and sent the bullet into the wall above his head, he would have been hit.

"Damn it!" she cursed. "You need to stop sneaking up on me!"

"Agreed," Nick said. "You're too damn trigger-happy."

"I am now," she agreed. "Getting shot at tends to make you that way."

He chuckled. "I can't argue with that."

"What are you doing here?" she asked. "I thought you were going to get some rest."

"Thought you were, too," he said.

He had known she wouldn't rest, though. That was why he was there. He'd figured she wouldn't have been able to stop working the case. And he hadn't wanted her to be alone and vulnerable.

He had left Annalise alone, but only in the bed they'd shared. Parker had taken over the couch in the living room. He would make sure nobody got past him to get to her.

"You knew I'd be here," she said. "You're just like Mom." She snorted. "Which is weird and impossible but totally true."

He wished he was like Penny Payne. She had no problem showing her affection and warmth for others. But that was for her family. She hadn't given her heart to another man.

"I knew you'd be here," he said. "And I figured you hacked my email."

Her face blushed a bright pink, which highlighted the darkness of her bruises. He felt too bad about her injuries to get mad at her for invading his privacy.

"You got the transcript," she said. "I found some other stuff."

"Like…?"

She had two computer monitors. One held the trial transcripts from his email. Another displayed a montage of old photos. She pointed first to the transcripts, to the part she'd highlighted about the missing murder weapon.

He cursed. How had he not realized it?

And of course his mother wouldn't have dared to pawn a murder weapon. She wouldn't have wanted to be implicated in those crimes. It would have blown her new identity and the arrangement she'd had with the River City district attorney.

"Ironic, huh?" Nikki asked. "You were looking for a gun to nail Chekov, and your mother had one this whole time."

"But where?" he wondered. Growing up, he'd never seen a gun in their house. She must have hidden it somewhere and hidden it well.

"We'll figure it out," Nikki said. "The good news is that the Iceman hasn't found it yet or he wouldn't still be looking."

That was good news. But they had to find the murder weapon before he did. If he got to it first, he would destroy it, and if they couldn't tie him to any of the destruction at his or Annalise's homes or to the attempts on their lives...

Then he would remain a free man.

The transcripts had nothing else to reveal, so Nick turned to the photos. Carla had once been beautiful, with huge, vulnerable dark eyes. The other photo could have been Nicholas Payne. It was a mug shot, though. Of course Payne had been undercover when he'd met Carla, when he'd turned her against her lover. How complete had his cover been?

But he leaned closer and read the name on the book-ing. Darren Snow. His breath hissed out. "Damn…he looks like…"

"My dad," Nikki said.

"He looks like I did at that age," Nick admitted. "Maybe your dad didn't cheat on your mom. Maybe Darren Snow is my dad." The thought filled him with dread, but he knew it would make Nikki happy.

She shook her head and dismissed the idea. "You're my dad's son," she said. "After you showed up in town, Mom told me that she'd always known he had cheated on her with your mom. He told her about it right after it happened."

"Why?" Nick wondered. "Did he think it was honorable to tell her the truth?" He could find no honor in a man who'd cheated on a good woman.

Nikki shrugged. "Maybe he couldn't live with what he'd done."

Or he had been looking for an excuse to leave. Maybe he'd thought that Penny would throw him out once she learned the truth. But instead, she'd forgiven him.

"I don't know how she forgave him," he said.

Nikki sighed. "Me neither. I want to think it's because she loved him."

"You don't think she did?"

"Times were different back then," Nikki said. "She was pregnant with Cooper. She already had twin sons less than two years old. Maybe she stayed with him because she didn't know if she could handle raising kids alone."

"She handled it after he died," Nick reminded her. "I think she loved him." Even though he hadn't deserved her or her love—kind of like he didn't deserve Annalise or her love.

But Annalise loved him. He couldn't deny her feelings. She'd always made them blatantly clear, and never more so than when they made love and she gave herself so generously to him. No. He didn't deserve her.

Nikki touched her computer screen and pulled up a picture of their father in his River City police department uniform. His black hair was cut short in the photo, like Nick's and Cooper's, and his eyes were the brilliant blue Nick saw every time he looked in the mirror or met one of his brothers' gazes.

"You're his son," she said. "The same as Logan and Parker and Cooper. He wouldn't have lied to her about cheating. He wouldn't have hurt her like that for no reason."

"But he hurt her."

"*He* did," she said. And she glanced up from the monitor. "Not *you*."

Since he had showed up in River City a year ago, he'd had a heavy pressure on his heart. He had regretted how his appearance had affected the Paynes. Mostly he'd regretted how much he had upset Nikki. And he'd never thought she would get over her resentment of him.

Had she? It felt as if she had finally let it go.

She looked at the picture of their father again. "You're his son. You're my brother." She didn't glance up at him now, and her bruised face had reddened with embarrassment over getting emotional.

Poor Nikki. She always thought she had to be as tough as her brothers, that she couldn't show any of her emotions. She had probably mistaken having emotions for weakness.

Nick thought it was a strength, one he didn't possess

himself. He cut her a break and teased, "Wow. You must really want to go with me to find the gun."

She looked at him then and laughed. But her laughter quickly faded. "Of course I'm going. You wouldn't even have known what you were searching for if it wasn't for me."

Actually, he would have once he'd read the transcript she'd hacked from his email. He didn't point that out, though. He liked this new relationship with his sister. He liked that they finally had one.

"I have a more important assignment for you," he said. "I want you to protect Annalise. She's going to want to go along as badly as you do."

Nikki opened her mouth as if she was about to argue. Then she smiled instead, as if she knew something he didn't. But he knew...

Annalise was sweet and loving, but she was stubborn as hell. She'd had to be, or she would have given up on him years ago. She was going to insist on going.

Annalise had awakened alone hours ago. Maybe that was why she was so angry. Nick would let her close physically but never emotionally. He kept running away from her.

Now he was trying to run even farther.

Back to Chicago.

"I have to go," Annalise insisted.

They were all there in the living room of Milek's condo. There was no mistaking this meeting for a family one. The Payne Protection Agency meant business today. Guns were spread across the coffee table and the granite counter along with surveillance equipment.

Intent on getting their gear ready, they were all pretty much ignoring her, just as Nick always had.

Just as she always had, she pestered him. She clasped her fingers around his forearm and turned him toward her so he had to look at her. So he had to listen.

"I put your mother's stuff wherever I could find room," she said. "It's spread between three storage units along with all kinds of other things I use for staging houses. You're going to waste too much time looking at the wrong things. I can tell you what's mine and what was hers."

That muscle twitching in his cheek, Nick shook his head. "It doesn't matter how much time we waste," he said. "I'm not putting you at risk."

"With all of you there—" she gestured at the room crowded with bodyguards "—I won't be at risk. I'll be safer there than I would be here."

"She's right," Nikki said.

"You're just saying that because you want to go, too," Logan accused her. He glared at Nick. "I told you that you could work for me only as long as you respected that I'm the boss. You can't hand out assignments."

"Nikki works for me," Cooper said. "And I'm fine with Nick giving her a job."

Logan cursed, but they all ignored him. Annalise was glad she wasn't the only one they were ignoring.

Nikki spoke again. "Annalise is right about needing to be there. We can't risk the Iceman finding that gun before we do. We can't waste any time getting to it."

Annalise reached out and grabbed the other woman's hand. From the first moment they'd met, they had bonded. That hadn't been just because they'd fought off armed carjackers together. It was because they understood each other so well.

Nikki smiled and squeezed her hand. And they both turned toward Nick.

Annalise couldn't get through to him, but Nikki had. He released a ragged sigh and nodded. "Okay, but the priority is making sure that Annalise is never in any danger."

She had gotten what she'd wanted. She was being included. But Annalise didn't feel any triumph. Only trepidation.

Had she done the right thing?

Or had she put her life and her baby's at risk?

Cooper spared a glance at Gage, who sat in the passenger seat of the SUV Cooper was driving. They were behind the one carrying Nick, Annalise, Nikki and Candace. Logan and Parker were in the front. Milek and Garek brought up the rear. He wasn't certain which one of them was driving. They'd been arguing about it up until the moment they had all left the condo.

And as heavily as rain had begun to fall, he couldn't see them clearly in his rearview mirror.

The convoy to Chicago brought back memories for Cooper. He could imagine the memories it brought back for the soldier who'd just recently returned from hell. But Gage was back now. Even before the Kozminskis had radioed about the tail, Gage had spotted it.

He glanced over at Cooper now. And there was fear in his eyes. But it was the healthy kind of fear. The kind of fear that was for the present, not for the past that couldn't be changed. Gage was worried about his sister—not about the soldiers he hadn't been able to save.

At the time, it had sounded like a good idea to bring Annalise along to search the storage units. But now...

Now she could wind up a civilian casualty. Cooper felt that worry himself and saw it in her brother's eyes. But Gage was 100 percent again, which was a damn good thing, because they would need every team member fighting at full capacity.

They were being followed from River City to Chicago, but it wasn't just one vehicle. There were several.

They were going into war.

Chapter 24

Nick had spent so much of his life pushing Annalise Huxton away from him. He should have been an expert at it by now. But when it had mattered most, he hadn't pushed her away. Now she was in danger.

"What's the plan?" Logan asked *him*, his voice emanating from the radio. Despite all his bluster about being the boss, he was willingly handing over the responsibility to Nick now.

Her brown eyes wide with shock, Nikki stared at him. Logan had surprised her.

But he hadn't surprised Nick. Logan knew that this was Nick's call. The woman he cared about—the woman who carried his unborn baby—was in danger. It was Nick's responsibility to keep them safe.

If only he hadn't put them at risk.

Now that he had, he needed to figure out how to mitigate that risk and keep them safe.

Annalise sat in the backseat with Candace. The female bodyguard had her weapon out, ready to fire, but Annalise didn't look reassured. She'd heard everything that had come through the radio. She knew they were being followed. She knew she was in danger. Her fear was apparent in how shallowly she breathed, in how pale her face had become.

She should never have experienced the kind of fear she was feeling. She wasn't like him or Gage. She hadn't chosen a life of risk.

But she had chosen him. He wanted to ask her why. It was something he'd never asked her before. Why did she love him? He'd never given her any encouragement— until that night they'd made love. He'd never given her any hope that his feelings would change, that he could actually have feelings.

Why had she persisted?

Why hadn't she given up on him?

He had—long ago. He'd given up the hope of ever having a family, of ever feeling as if he belonged somewhere. Now he had a family. They might not have embraced him at first, but they were there for him now. When it counted...

When it would keep Annalise safe.

"Do we separate and divide them?" Logan asked.

That would divide them, as well. Nick was used to going it alone. Even as an FBI special agent, he hadn't often worked as part of a team. He'd gone undercover on his own to sniff out corruption in police departments across the nation. That was how he'd wound up with the assignment to clean up River City PD—because he'd been doing it for years.

Alone.

That was how he'd lived his life. Or had tried.

But Annalise had always been there. No matter how much he had complained, he hadn't really minded. He'd actually appreciated her attention—her love.

He couldn't lose her now.

"No," Nick replied. "There's safety in our numbers. We stick together."

Nikki smiled her approval. She was in danger, too—just like her other brothers had feared she would be. But there was no fear on Nikki's face. Like Candace, she had her gun out, grasped in a steady hand. She was ready.

Nick wasn't. He didn't want to lose Annalise. He didn't want to lose anyone else, either. And if there were as many men following them as Milek and Garek had warned, there was a very good chance there would be a confrontation.

A shoot-out.

With that much gunfire, there were bound to be casualties—on both sides.

The bulletproof vest weighed heavily on Annalise's shoulders—along with the burden of guilt. If only she had listened to Nick.

If only she had gotten rid of all of his mother's things.

No one would be in danger. Now everyone was—everyone Nick cared about—because of her. She could tell that he cared for them. Maybe he hadn't wanted to. After all, he was Nick, always so determined to be a loner.

But there were no loners in the Payne family. They all stuck together. Like Nick had said, there was safety in their numbers.

Yet Annalise didn't feel safe—even with the bullet-proof vest. It hung low, covering her belly. The baby would be safe from a bullet. But if Annalise took one in the head... The baby might not survive without her. The risks of his being born this early were too great. He moved restlessly inside her as if he felt her fear.

She was scared, not just for herself but also for everyone else. Milek and Garek were posted at the storage unit gate so the vehicles following them couldn't get inside. Logan and Parker were nearby to back them up. Gage and Cooper stayed in front of the storage units Annalise searched with Nick and Nikki and Candace.

The rain was falling even harder now, beating down on the metal roof of the unit. Would they be able to hear if someone snuck up on them?

"There's so much stuff," Nikki murmured.

Annalise felt compelled to apologize again. "I shouldn't have kept everything." But she hadn't known what Nick might want, what could have meant enough to his mother that it would help him remember her.

She'd wanted him to have some fond memories of the woman who'd given birth to him. But she realized now that there were few fond memories to be had of Carla.

"What could she have hidden a gun inside?" Nikki asked the question.

Annalise had no idea. She knew what would stage a house, not what would hide a weapon.

"A book. A statue. A canister," Nick replied. "Something out of character for Carla to own."

"How is owning a book out of character?" Nikki asked.

"The woman never read," Nick replied. "And she

wouldn't have kept anything that could possibly have been of value."

"Are you sure she didn't pawn the gun?" Candace asked. She stood at the door to the unit, staring outside as if looking for any sign of danger.

Maybe that was why no one had been able to find the gun—because it was gone.

"No," Nick and Nikki answered in unison.

"It would have showed up in the system again," Nick said. "The kind of people who buy guns from pawnshops use them, usually in the commission of a crime."

Nikki snorted. "Yeah. And I checked records. Nothing matching its ballistics has been used in over thirty years."

"So where would she have hidden something for thirty years?" Annalise wondered.

A book. Like Nick said, Carla had never read. But there had been a collection of books. A whole series about famous criminals. Annalise had thought they were Nick's, something he might have had to read when he was in Quantico. But he had never returned home after leaving for the Marines. So she realized now the books wouldn't have been his.

What had she done with them? She'd taken them out of the house shortly after Carla had died because she'd thought they were Nick's and she hadn't wanted them to go into probate in case Carla hadn't had a will.

And yet Carla had had a will. Her lawyer had been holding that letter for Nick to be read after her death. That letter had given him a family.

There had been another letter, too—one they'd learned had been sent to the prison where Darren Snow had been serving out the last of his sentence. Maybe that letter would take away Nick's family since it had sent the Iceman after Nick. And the Paynes had risked their lives for him and her.

She heard the gunfire…

It was even louder than the rain hitting the roof. It sounded as if it was near the gates.

"We have to get out of here," Nick said. He grabbed her arm with one hand. His weapon was out in the other.

But Annalise resisted. "I know where it is," she said. "I can find it."

She'd put those books in the storage unit that contained her personal things. Her condo was so small that she had no place in it to store her holiday decorations and out-of-season clothes. She used one of the units for all that. It had given her a little spark of hope to see what she'd thought were Nick's possessions among hers, as if they would one day be together.

Now she doubted that would ever happen, even if they survived. Nick would never stop running from her. He was trying to run now toward the SUV parked outside the unit. But once they cleared the door, Annalise jerked from his grasp. If it hadn't been raining, she probably wouldn't have been able to slip free of his hold.

She had the keys to all the units in her hand. She had to find the one that opened the unit on the end. Her hand was shaking badly, and the keys were getting wet like her hair and her skin and her clothes. She dropped the keys on the pavement. "I need to open—"

"There's no time," Nick said.

The gunfire grew closer now. The men had made it past Milek and Garek. Beneath the bulletproof vest, her heart pounded wildly with fear.

Nick was right. There was no time.

Then Candace and Nikki began to fire their weapons. Where were Gage and Cooper? Their SUV was still parked at the end of the row. The back door opened.

Nick swung Annalise up in his arms and rushed toward it. "We need to get you out of here." But when he neared the SUV, it wasn't Gage or Cooper who leaned out to grab her.

The man's head was bald, his blue eyes icy with hatred. "Where's the gun?" he asked.

Nick held up his own barrel pointed toward the Iceman.

But the killer laughed and pressed the barrel of his weapon against Annalise's temple. "Try it," he dared Nick. "And she's dead before she and her baby hit the ground."

That muscle twitched in Nick's cheek. "We didn't find it."

The Iceman's gun cocked. The sound echoed inside Annalise's head. "That's too bad."

"I know where it is," Annalise said. She wasn't fighting just for her life. She was fighting for her son's. He deserved a chance.

He deserved a life.

She couldn't fight like she had the day the men had stolen her car. If she tried to claw at this man's face, he would just kill her. He was that cold. She had to reason with him instead. "Let me get it for you."

He didn't loosen his grasp on her. Despite how wet her clothes and hair were, he held her easily. He was strong, so strong that he jerked her fully inside the SUV with him, onto the backseat. Now her body blocked his. He was using her as a shield as more bodyguards closed in behind Nick. Shots continued to ring out—bullets pinging off metal, shattering glass.

"No, he'll get it for you," the Iceman said. "He'll get me the gun in exchange for your life."

"I don't know where it is," Nick said.

"My unit," she told him. "Number fifteen."

"Find the gun," the Iceman said. "And call me once you have it."

"I don't have your phone number," Nick said.

"You have hers." He reached for the passenger door to pull it closed.

"You won't get out of here alive," Nick threatened him.

"Then neither will she," he said.

Tears stung Annalise's eyes. But she refused to shed them. She refused to let either this man or Nick see her fear. She had to send Nick a message about where to find the gun without telling him exactly where it was.

If she blurted out that it was in the books, the Iceman might just kill them all right there and find it himself. He had brought enough men with him to outgun the bodyguards. But if it would take a little longer for him to find it, he wouldn't risk it. Even now she could hear sirens in the distance.

The police were on their way. He wouldn't risk sticking around for them to arrive.

"He's a killer," she told Nick, hoping he'd get the message. That he would look in those books about serial killers for the gun. "He won't hesitate to pull the trigger."

The Iceman chuckled. "Listen to your girlfriend," he advised Nick as he pulled the door shut.

"Drive!" he ordered the man in the front seat.

Where was Cooper? Where was Gage?

Had she gotten her brother back just to lose him here, when he'd been trying to protect her? She closed her eyes as grief threatened to overwhelm her. There had been too many shots fired. Someone had gotten hurt.

Or worse...

Darren clasped her phone in his hand. Why hadn't it rung yet?

"What the hell is taking him so long?" he asked.

"Maybe he couldn't find it," the woman suggested, her voice quavering with fear.

She was smart to be afraid. She probably knew that even if Nicholas Rus brought him the gun, there was no way she was going to live. He couldn't leave a witness like he had before.

He should have killed Carla thirty-two years ago. Then he wouldn't have spent half his life behind bars. He wasn't going back.

There was no way in hell he would return to hell.

"You told him what unit it was in," Darren said. "He should have found it by now." And he probably had. The guy had a reputation for being squeaky-clean. He'd probably turned the damn gun over to the FBI.

Once they ran ballistics and DNA and whatever the hell else they could get off evidence nowadays, they would be able to link him to more murders. A lot of murders...

It wasn't like the old days when all it had taken to convict someone was an eyewitness. A jury wanted solid evidence. The gun was it. "I've got to get out of here," he told the driver. And he wasn't talking about the alley where they'd parked the stolen SUV. He wasn't talking about Chicago.

He needed to get the hell out of the country—to somewhere without extradition.

"What about her?" the driver asked.

He lifted the gun to her head again. She flinched as he pressed the barrel against her temple. "I'm going to kill her."

And once she was dead, he would kill the driver, too. He couldn't leave behind any witnesses anymore.

Chapter 25

Why the hell wasn't the Iceman answering Annalise's phone? She'd had it on her. She always had it on her. While she'd left her purse in the SUV, the phone hadn't been inside. She must have put it in her pocket while they'd been searching the units.

Had Darren Snow given up waiting for him? It had taken Nick too long to get rid of the police, who'd showed up to investigate the gunfire, and find the gun. He should have realized what Annalise was telling him about the killer—about the trigger.

The gun was inside the books he'd found in her storage unit. The series of serial killer books had been out of place among her cheerful assortment of decorations and clothes. But it had taken him a few minutes to realize that was where she'd meant him to look.

Hell, she could have just told him. But she'd probably

been worried that the Iceman would kill him then and just find the gun himself. She would have been more concerned about Nick's life than her own.

She was probably concerned about everyone else, as well. She couldn't know that they had all survived the gunfight. Everyone was okay.

But her...

Panic pressed on his lungs, stealing his breath away as his heart raced. "Answer the damn phone!" he yelled.

Nikki jumped; his outburst had startled her. The others were too shell-shocked to react. If they hadn't been wearing vests...

The shots that had hit them would have killed them. The vests had stopped the bullets but not the impact. Ribs were bruised or broken. But no one had sought medical treatment.

Gage paced the storage unit. "You shouldn't have made us stand down," he said. "You shouldn't have."

"He had his gun pressed to her head," Nick said, his heart aching as he remembered the fear on her face. "He would have killed her." And the damn vest he'd put on her wouldn't have saved her.

Nothing would have.

Maybe nothing had.

He could see the thought on the faces of the others. They thought she was dead. Even Gage...

"She never gave up hope on you," he told him. "Everybody else thought you were dead, but Annalise wouldn't consider it. She knew you were too damn stubborn to give up."

Gage released a shaky breath. "And I've got nothing on her. She's a helluva lot more stubborn than I am."

Or she would have given up on Nick years ago. He

saw that on Gage's face, too. She hadn't given up on him, and he wouldn't give up on her. He hit redial.

And finally someone picked up the call. "Special Agent Rus," Darren Snow greeted him.

"No," Nick replied. "I'm not an FBI agent anymore. I'm a bodyguard." But he had failed to protect the person who mattered most to him.

The Iceman chuckled. "So you haven't brought that gun to the FBI evidence locker yet?"

"I haven't," Nick said. "And I won't. I'm bringing it to you—in exchange for Annalise. Just like we agreed."

"I had heard you're a man of your word," the Iceman replied.

"What about you?" Nick asked. "Are you a man of your word?" He'd read those trial transcripts. Darren Snow was no Viktor Chekov. While Chekov was a killer, he lived by a certain code. The Iceman had no code—no moral compass whatsoever.

"I was beginning to think that you'd turned on me, Nicholas," Darren said, "just like your whore of a mother did."

"I'm nothing like my mother," Nick said. At least, he wasn't like the one who'd given birth to him. He'd rather be like Penny Payne—the woman who wanted to assume the role of his mother.

"I've heard that," Darren said. "I've heard you're all about law and order. It's hard for me to believe that you'd turn over evidence to me."

"We made a deal," Nick said—although he hadn't been given much choice in the matter, not with that gun barrel pressed against Annalise's head. "I'm holding up my end of it. Are you going to hold up yours?"

The Iceman chuckled again. But Nick didn't know what had amused him. His uneasiness grew.

"I want to talk to her." Nick hadn't given up, and yet he needed to be certain that she was all right. He needed to hear her voice.

The Iceman's silence unnerved him and the others. They all glanced at each other, as if wondering…

Worrying. That Nick had taken too long, that he'd called too late.

"Nick?" Annalise's voice emanated from the speaker on his phone and echoed hollowly throughout the storage unit in which they all stood.

He uttered a ragged sigh, and the pressure on his heart eased. She was alive. "Annalise, are you all right? Has he hurt you?"

"You heard her," the Iceman said. "She's alive. For now. But she and your kid she's carrying don't have much longer if I don't get that gun in my hands."

"Where do you want to meet?" Nick asked.

"You're not going to try to lay a trap for me, Nicholas?" the Iceman asked.

"Of course not." He would take no chances with Annalise's life.

"We'll meet out in the open, Nicholas, so I can be certain that you've come alone." And he named a park not far from the storage facility. "Near the basketball courts."

Logan was shaking his head, but Nick ignored him. "Agreed. But you won't see me or the gun until I see Annalise. Alive."

The Iceman chuckled again—like he had a secret joke. Before he clicked off the phone, Nick heard Annalise shouting out a warning, "Don't trust him, Nick!"

Gage cursed. He had probably guessed what her outburst would cost Annalise. Pain.

The Iceman would hurt her. But he wouldn't kill her. He wanted the gun.

"You need to listen to her," Logan said. "You can't trust him. You can't go alone, and you can't bring that gun with you."

Nick shook his head. "I'm going to do exactly what he says."

"That's evidence, Nick," Logan reminded him. "You can't turn it over to a criminal. You know better."

Nick shrugged. He knew the law, probably better than anyone else present. But for the first time in his life, the law didn't matter to him. He didn't care about right or wrong. He cared only about Annalise.

"We could switch the gun," Logan suggested. "Get one that looks like it."

"There's no time," Nick said. "And he would know."

"It's been over thirty years since he saw it last," Logan argued.

"He would know," Nick said because of his face. If the Iceman was going to believe Nick had brought the real gun, he'd need to see the struggle on his face, the guilt he'd feel for handing over evidence. While he'd feel some guilt, it wasn't the moral struggle he'd thought it might be. It was no struggle at all.

It didn't matter what the law said was right or wrong. All that mattered was Annalise.

Had Nick heard her? Had he heeded her warning? Annalise's heart pounded quickly and frantically. She knew Darren Snow had no intention of letting her or

Nick live. He'd called up the men he'd hired, the ones who'd survived the gun battle at the storage unit.

There had been fatalities. She hoped only on the Iceman's side. Her brother had to have survived. He was tough—tough enough to make it through whatever hell he'd endured in Afghanistan. It would take more than a bullet to end his life.

She hoped the same for Nick. Because the Iceman had set up the park. He had shooters positioned on rooftops—ready to take head shots once the gun had exchanged hands. If Nick showed up at the park, he wouldn't leave alive.

And neither would she.

"I'm sorry," Darren told her. But his apology lacked sincerity. "You seem like a sweet girl. But I can't risk going back to prison."

She nodded as if she commiserated with him. But she could never understand a human taking another human's life, unless it was in self-defense or defense of someone else.

"You really should have rented the place to me furnished," he said. "Then we could have avoided all of this nasty business."

"It is my fault," she agreed. And there was no way she could remedy it now. Nick had been right to push her away all these years. If she hadn't been so stubborn…

If she'd given up on him years ago, he wouldn't be in danger now. And neither would she.

The rain continued to fall, beating down on the roof of the stolen SUV—flooding the parking lot near the basketball court. No one played on the courts. Thanks to the rain and the encroaching darkness, it was deserted.

But for the man who stood with his back against one of the buildings near the court. Even through the rain, she could tell it was Nick. His black hair was wet and slicked to his head, but his eyes shone brightly in his handsome face.

The Iceman wasn't as certain, though. He peered at him. "Is it him or one of those bodyguards…?"

The driver shrugged. "Looks like him. And you told him to come alone."

The Paynes wouldn't have allowed that, though. Would they? The family stuck together, protected each other. They had to be out there, ready to protect Nick. But she peered around and could see no one else.

From inside the SUV, she couldn't see the men Darren Snow had positioned on the rooftops, either. She didn't doubt they were there. He'd offered to pay them well.

Would Nick see them? He wasn't looking up. He was staring instead at the SUV.

"There's no one else around," the driver said. "It has to be him."

The Iceman hesitated yet, looking uncertain.

"It is," she said. "It's Nick." She'd loved him too long to mistake him for anyone else.

The Iceman released a breath. He believed her. Finally he opened the back door and pulled her across the seat and out the door with him. She stepped into a puddle, the water rushing over her shoe to soak her foot. Within seconds, her clothes were soaked, too, down to her skin.

The Iceman had taken the bulletproof vest from her. It wouldn't have mattered if she'd worn it, though, not when he'd ordered his snipers to take head shots. He wore it himself under his coat.

He didn't expect Nick to honor their deal any more than he intended to honor it. But he didn't know Nick.

He didn't know that he was a man of his word.

He gestured for Nick to come forward. Nick stepped away from the wall and crossed the basketball court. And Annalise held her breath.

They weren't supposed to shoot yet, though. Not until Nick handed over the gun.

Wait for my signal, the Iceman had told them. *Once I know it's my gun, I'll raise my hand. That's when you open fire.*

"Don't give it to him!" she shouted at Nick. "He's going to kill us."

Nick didn't react. He wasn't surprised by her warning. He'd known. But he'd come alone, anyway.

For her? Or for their baby?

Where was everyone else?

It was just the two of them—against a killer.

The Iceman jerked her arm behind her back until she cried out at the pain. "Stop it!" he told her. "Or you won't die quickly. You'll just die painfully." In his other hand he held a gun, pressed against her face.

"Let her go," Nick said as he rushed forward. "She has nothing to do with this!"

The Iceman chuckled. "She has everything to do with it, Nicholas. You wouldn't have brought the gun if I hadn't taken her." He used the barrel to gesture at Nick. "Did you bring it?"

"Of course."

The Iceman's pale eyes narrowed skeptically. "I find

it hard to believe that a man of your high moral values would have compromised his principles like this."

Nick held up a velvet bag—one in which a fifth of whiskey usually came. His mother had liked to drink, too. "It's in here." He tossed it over.

But with the Iceman's grip on her and his gun, he couldn't grab it before it hit the ground. He let her go so abruptly that she fell to the wet pavement.

Gunfire erupted. And Nick lunged toward her, as if to cover her body with his. But before he reached her, a bullet struck him. She didn't know if it came from above or from Darren Snow.

His gun was pointed at Nick. Nick kept coming.

He fired again.

Annalise screamed and, desperate to help, she grabbed up the bag. Knowing Nick, it could have been a decoy, a fake weapon. But she pulled out a real gun, the metal heavy and cold. It probably wasn't loaded.

Snow had forgotten about her lying on the ground. His focus was on Nick now. He stepped forward and pointed his gun at Nick, who was sprawled on the ground, rain falling on his face. His eyes were closed.

Was he already dead?

Darren must have wanted to make certain, because he cocked his gun and lowered the barrel close to Nick's head. Annalise lurched to her feet and squeezed the trigger of the gun she held—the gun that had already been used to kill.

Her wrist snapped at the recoil, and the weapon fell from her suddenly weak grasp. Pain radiated up her arm.

Darren Snow spun toward her, his eyes open with surprise. Then he dropped to his knees on the pavement and fell forward. She screamed as she saw the wound in the back of his head. Had she done that?

Had she killed a man?

She didn't care at the moment. All she cared about was Nick. She dropped to the ground next to him. "Are you all right? Nick?"

But his eyes—his beautiful eyes, usually so bright—remained closed. She'd killed a man to save him. But she might have been too late.

She had known, as Penny always did, that her children were in danger. This time it had been all of them. Panic constricted her heart, squeezing it painfully. She didn't know how she'd managed the drive to Chicago or how she'd found the hospital where they were.

But she'd managed somehow to get to them. Was she too late, though? Had she lost one of them?

She hurried to the waiting room.

"Mom," Logan gasped as she walked in. Instead of protesting her being there, he hugged her tightly. As if he was a little boy who needed comfort.

Since his father had died, he'd been the one who'd given the comfort—even to her. Tears stung her eyes. It was bad. Even worse than she'd feared...

"Who is it?" she asked. Who had she lost?

She pulled free of Logan's embrace and peered around the crowded room. Other people might have been there, but she saw only her family.

Milek and Garek Kozminski stood close together, almost as if they were holding each other up. "Are you all right?" she asked them.

Milek nodded.

"Gonna take more than an SUV to wipe us out," Garek assured her as he pulled her into a hug.

But as she hugged him back, he flinched. He'd been hurt.

They all looked the worse for wear. Gage Huxton had blood smeared on the side of his face, but she wasn't certain if it was his. He would have done anything to protect his sister. Just like her boys would have Nikki.

Nikki—dear sweet Nikki—had already been bruised and stitched. But she wore those wounds like badges of honor. Stubborn girl.

A smile tugged at Penny's lips. She loved her baby girl so much. And she worried about her nearly as much as she worried about Nick.

"Nick?" she gasped his name as she realized who wasn't present. "Where's Nick?"

"Surgery…" The voice came from behind the others. They stepped aside to let Penny through to the chair where a frail-looking Annalise sat. "They took him back right away…"

They must have been at the hospital a while—long enough for Penny to make the nearly three-hour drive. But Annalise's clothes still looked damp from the rain. Or perhaps it was from the blood that stained them.

Penny dropped to her knees in front of her chair. "Are you okay? Has someone checked you out?" She glanced around at the others. Hadn't anyone helped her?

"She refused," Gage said. And from his tone, it was obvious that he'd given up arguing with his sister.

Penny touched the young woman's hands where they covered her belly. Her skin was as cold as ice. "You need to let someone look at you," she said. "You need to make sure your baby is all right."

Her green eyes brimming with tears, Annalise shook her head.

And panic gripped Penny. Had she lost the child? Was that why she had blood on her clothes?

"Get help," Penny yelled at the others. "She needs a doctor." Penny worried that it was already too late for the baby.

What about Nick? He'd been in surgery such a long time. Was it too late for him, too?

Chapter 26

Nick fought his way to consciousness. He'd been out too long. He knew it. Something bad had happened. He could feel it in the heaviness of his heart, which beat slowly with dread. The last thing he remembered was lunging toward Annalise, but he hadn't reached her before the shot had taken him down.

Had she been hit?

Was she safe?

"Annalise!" He jerked awake with her name on his lips.

"Are you okay?" a soft voice asked.

He struggled to keep his eyes open—to focus on the face above his. Penny Payne stared down at him, her brown eyes warm with concern.

His throat was dry, and he tried to swallow, tried to clear it. But his voice sounded gruff when he said again, "Annalise…"

Penny took his hand in hers. Was she offering comfort? Or was she the one who needed it?

He squeezed her hand and urged her, "Tell me. Was she shot?"

Penny shook her head. "No. She wasn't shot. But you were."

He remembered the flash of pain he'd felt. He didn't feel it now. His body was actually numb. It was his mind that was reeling. And his heart—it hurt, too.

"The surgeon is worried because the bullet was close to the spine," she said, "too close."

Nick tensed, his muscles tightening.

She spoke softly and gently as she must have to her kids when they'd had nightmares or missed their dad. "He's concerned that you could have some paralysis."

Nick squeezed her hand again, and then he kicked at the sheet covering him. "I'm not paralyzed," he said.

Not anymore.

He'd been paralyzed most of his life—afraid to let himself feel love. But not anymore.

"I'm getting out of this bed," he said, "and I'm going to find Annalise."

He needed to make sure she was all right. But more important, he needed to make certain she knew that he loved her. That he had always loved her—he'd just been too scared to admit how much she had meant to him: everything.

Penny pushed him back against the bed. "You need to rest, Nick. You were in surgery for hours."

So where was Annalise? Had she given up on him?

After all these years of loving him, had she finally changed her mind? Had he waited too long to tell her he loved her, too?

"If she wasn't shot," he said, "why isn't she here?" Images flashed through his mind. He remembered the way Darren Snow had shoved her to the ground. Had it been hard enough to hurt her? To hurt the baby?

Dread washed over him. "It's the baby, isn't it?"

Penny squeezed his hand again. "Nick..."

He kicked at the sheet again, and this time he managed to swing his legs out of the bed. "I have to be with her. Have to make sure she's okay."

If she'd lost the baby, she would be devastated. Hell, he would be, too. But he was more worried about her.

"Why, Nick?" Penny asked. "Why do you have to be with her?"

Had the woman lost her touch? Usually she understood what was going on with people before they understood it themselves. How could she not know what he had just realized?

"Because I love her," he said. "I love her!"

"You could sound a little happier about it," a soft voice remarked.

Penny didn't look surprised at the sound of Annalise's voice. She must have known she had come into the room. She smiled and stepped back from the bed. "I'll leave you two alone," she said. "You need to talk."

But Nick couldn't talk. Maybe he *was* paralyzed— because all he could do was stare at the woman he loved. She looked so beautiful, more beautiful than he had ever seen her.

The way he was staring at her made Annalise uneasy. "Are you okay?" she asked. Maybe she needed to call his doctor. He didn't look right, more like dazed. Maybe it was the drugs.

Maybe that was why he'd said what he had. That he loved her.

Dare she believe him?

"Nick?" Instead of going for a doctor, she stepped closer to the bed. She had been so worried that she'd lost him. That he wouldn't survive the shots he'd taken.

He blinked as if snapping out of a trance. And now he looked at her as if he were truly focusing. His gaze ran over her tangled hair and down her bloodied clothes. And he reached out for her, pulling her into his arms.

She tried to hold back. She didn't want to hurt him.

"It's okay, sweetheart," he said, his voice gruff with emotion. "We can have another baby."

Another one? What was he talking about?

"I know you're upset, but we have each other. We'll get married—"

"What?" The doctor had said she was in shock—that was why she'd been so cold, so out of it in the waiting room. It must not have worn off yet. "Why are you talking about getting married?"

He must have known it didn't matter to her what Gage had said. Annalise wouldn't have let her brother force him to marry her.

"I love you," he said.

And she was as shocked as the first time she'd heard him say it. Was she dreaming? Had she fallen asleep in the waiting room and she was only imagining that she was here—in his arms? She slid her arms around his neck. He felt real to her. Warm and strong despite having been shot.

He tightened his arms around her, pulling her closer yet. "I want to marry you because I love you. So it doesn't matter that you lost the baby. We'll have another—"

Finally realization dawned, and she pressed her fingers over his lips. They were dry beneath her touch. He'd been through so much. No wonder he was confused. "I didn't lose the baby." And as if to prove it, their son kicked.

Amazement and relief brightened Nick's eyes as he felt it. "You didn't." He pulled back and stared down at her clothes. "But the blood."

"It's yours," she said. "From the park..." And it might have been Darren Snow's, too.

"I don't know what happened," he said. "You fell and the gunfire began. Is everyone okay?"

She nodded. "Your family took out the snipers Darren Snow had on the rooftops. He was the one who shot you."

"What happened to him?" he asked.

"He's dead." She shuddered as she remembered how he'd stared up at her with such surprise.

Nick pulled her close again. And he noticed her wrist. The doctor had wrapped the sprain. That—and the shock—had been her only injury. Now his eyes widened with shock as he realized how she'd hurt her wrist—from the recoil from the old gun. "You shot him?"

She shrugged. "I shot that gun. But I don't know if it was my shot that hit him." Gage claimed that he'd done it—from one of the rooftops. But she didn't know if he was telling the truth or only trying to make her feel better. He understood her well enough to know that she would struggle with having killed a man.

But she wasn't sure that she would. Nick was alive.

That was all that mattered. That and the fact that he loved her.

"And now I love you even more," he remarked. "There's something I want to ask you."

He had already said they were getting married. But if he wanted to propose properly, she wasn't going to stop him. Smiling she asked, "Yes?"

"Why do you love me?"

And she laughed.

"I'm serious," he said.

Realizing why he was asking, pain constricted her heart. Now she knew why he had pushed her away, why he had never accepted her love. He hadn't believed anyone could love him.

"You are the most amazing man," she told him. "You were amazing even when you were just a boy. You have such honor and integrity. You always want to do the right thing. You always want to protect everyone else."

And maybe that was why he'd spent so many years pushing her away. He'd wanted to protect her.

"I didn't think I deserved your love," he said. "I didn't think I was worthy of it."

"Nick…"

"My own mother couldn't love me," he said.

"She was an addict," she reminded him.

"She was all I had."

Annalise shook her head. "You had me."

He clasped her closer. "I'm so sorry I didn't realize how I felt sooner. I didn't recognize it."

He didn't recognize love because he'd never felt it before. Her heart ached for all he had missed. "I'm not the only one who loves you, Nick," she assured him.

"You have a family out there who is frantically worrying about you."

He smiled. "I'm sure Penny has assured them that I'm fine. Right now she's probably getting them all fitted for tuxes for the wedding."

"It's too soon to worry about fittings," she said.

"I'm marrying you as soon as I get out of the bed, Annalise." And he tried to stand again.

"I've spent my life waiting to marry you, Nicholas Rus," she told him. "I think I can wait a little longer."

"I can't. I want to marry you right away. I don't want to waste another minute of time that I can be with you."

Tears stung Annalise's eyes. She'd always known she'd loved Nick. But she hadn't known Nick could love like this—as completely as she loved him.

"Shh…" he murmured. "I don't want you to cry."

"I've shed a lot of tears over you," she admitted.

He grimaced. "I don't ever want to make you cry again."

She leaned forward and pressed her lips to his. They kissed softly, tenderly. He lifted his fingers to her face and wiped away her tears.

"You'll make me cry again," she said. "Because these are happy tears. And you've made me so happy…"

She'd thought all she'd wanted was for Nick to survive his gunshot wounds. She hadn't realized how badly she'd wanted him to love her—until finally she had her wish. Her dream was realized.

Nicholas Rus loved her as much as she loved him.

"Make me happy," he said.

She tensed. "You're not?" she asked. Of course, he was probably in pain. He'd just had surgery. She tried to pull back, but he held her tightly.

"I will be," he said, "when you finally agree to become my wife. Marry me, Annalise. Right now."

She laughed. "I guess I'm the one who will need to
teach our son patience."

"You have been patient with me," he said. "For so
many years. That's why I don't want to wait. I don't
want you finally to give up on me."

"Never," she assured him. "I will love you for the
rest of our lives, Nicholas Payne."

"And I will spend the rest of our lives loving you."

Nikki smiled with pride. Even though she worked
for Cooper, Nick had given her another assignment. She
would have thought it would have gone to Gage—who'd
known him longest. Or to the FBI agent he'd roomed
with in Chicago—Jared Bell. Or even to one of the
brothers he'd just recently discovered. But she was the
one he'd asked to be his best man.

After all the times she had been a bridesmaid, it felt
good finally to wear a tux instead of a damn dress. Her
mother had been sad, though.

Not about the marriage. She had been thrilled to
throw together Nick and Annalise's wedding. She had
even been happy that Nikki was his best man.

But she'd admitted that she wanted for Nikki what
Nick had with Annalise. She wanted her daughter to
be as happy as all her sons were.

From her place at Nick's side at the altar, Nikki stared
out at everyone gathered in the church. It was good to
see her brothers so happy—with women they'd made
as happy as they were.

But her mother stood alone—as she had for so many
years. And Nikki realized that Penny needed to worry

about herself instead of her. She was the one who needed to find someone to make her happy, someone who finally and truly deserved her.

Nikki was happy. Her brothers were finally taking her seriously. She wasn't going to be strapped to a desk anymore. She was going to do fieldwork.

Probably.

As soon as she was fully healed.

It had been only a couple of days since the shoot-out at the storage units. She was surprised that Nick could even stand after the surgery on his back.

But he stood tall and proud beside her, staring at the doors of the church. Music began to play, and everyone stood and turned toward the back—to Annalise starting down the aisle, holding on to her brother's arm.

Her parents hadn't been able to get a flight out of Alaska in time for the service. But they would make the reception later.

Annalise wore the same wedding dress so many other Payne brides had worn. Penny's dress.

It was lace and satin, very vintage and graceful. If Nikki ever married—and she doubted that would happen—she wouldn't wear that dress. But Annalise looked beautiful in it. The empire waist hid the swell of her belly.

Beside her, Nick gasped. And Nikki grabbed his arm in case he toppled over. He wasn't in pain, though. He was in awe. "She's so beautiful," he murmured.

"She is."

The kind of beautiful that radiated from the inside out. As she drew closer, it was clear to see that love radiated from Annalise, as well.

She loved Nick with all her heart—the same way he loved her.

Nikki felt a flash of envy for that kind of happiness. But she didn't need love. All she wanted was to be taken seriously. She had that now—thanks to Nick.

So she pushed aside that momentary lapse and focused on being the best man. She handed over the rings with a steady hand.

Nick slid a diamond band on Annalise's finger. She slid a silver band on his. They repeated their vows in strong, certain voices. They had no doubts—only love. They would love and honor each other forever.

Epilogue

Hours had passed since their wedding. It was all a blur to Annalise, a kaleidoscope of color and music and voices. But she remembered staring up into Nick's handsome face as he pledged his love and devotion.

She would never forget that. She would never doubt his love. He had given her his heart—like she had given him hers so many years before.

Fingertips trailed over her naked skin. He hadn't left her alone in bed this time. He lay next to her, staring at her in the moonlight. "I am the luckiest man in the world."

She laughed. "That's the same thing your surgeon said."

A fraction of an inch to the left and the bullet would have paralyzed him. He had been so lucky.

"You're the reason I'm so blessed," he said. His fingertips trailed over her belly now—where their son moved beneath his father's touch.

She smiled. "We both are." She was so happy she felt almost guilty.

Now Nick touched the furrow that had formed between her brows. "What? What are you worried about?"

"Not us," she assured him. She had no doubts they would be happy. "About Gage…"

"He made it back," Nick said. "Both physically and mentally. He's doing great."

He was better. But he still wasn't whole. It was as if a part of him was still missing. He'd lost something. And she suspected it wasn't in Afghanistan. He'd lost something before he'd left: his heart.

"I want him to be as happy as we are," she said.

Nick sighed and pulled her into his arms. Holding her close, he murmured, "Me, too…"

* * * * *

MOUNTAIN BODYGUARD

CASSIE MILES

To Khloe Adams and her brilliant advice.
And, as always, to Rick.

Chapter One

The hotel was a bodyguard's nightmare. Mason Steele fidgeted beside French doors that opened onto a flagstone terrace. With extreme impatience, he watched while Admiral Edgar Prescott, tonight's honoree, made his way through the stragglers who were toasting the crimson glow of a June sunset and finishing off their complementary glass of Colorado merlot.

Number one security problem: isolated mountain location. This seven-story structure was surrounded by national forest with only two viable access roads. Never mind that Aspen was less than forty minutes away, this site was remote. An attacker could assault the hotel, dash across the ninth green and vanish into the forest before Mason and his colleagues figured out where they were hit. To prevent such an ambush, his firm, TST Security, had stationed their own snipers on the roof.

This charity banquet was all hands on deck for TST. They were using five regulars and six part-timers, plus had a helicopter pilot on standby.

Security issue number two: though the styling of the hotel was meant to resemble a hunting lodge from the early 1900s, the interior of the banquet hall featured a wall of windows and another of French doors. The design was an open invitation to long-distance shooters.

Issue number three: the people. Too many had been invited. The circular tables reached almost to the walls, which meant a sure pileup if they had to evacuate quickly. The well-dressed guests had all passed through metal detectors, but that was no guarantee of safety in this era of plastic firearms. Potential weapons were everywhere. Prime rib was on the menu; steak knives were on the tables. The centerpieces blocked sight lines, and the tall Art Deco arrangements on either side of the dais were large enough to hide a couple of AK-47s.

As soon as the admiral stepped over the threshold from the terrace, Mason signaled to one of his men to round up the last few people that were outside and lock the French doors. As for himself, he took a position against the wall where he could watch the crowd. Most of them had settled into their assigned seats. Some had already been served. Others table hopped, chatted and chuckled and showed off photos on cell phones.

A woman in a sleeveless blue jumpsuit approached him. He'd been introduced to her before, had noticed her thoroughly and had paid particular attention to the way the clingy blue fabric hugged her curves. She was part of the entourage for the admiral, his movie star wife and their several children. When the lady in blue sidled up next to him, the top of her head was only as high as his shoulder. Lights from the chandeliers glistened on her curly auburn ponytail.

She nudged his elbow. "Whose body are you guarding?"

"The admiral's." He dropped a glance in her direction, expecting to quickly look away. Instead, she seized his attention with her big brown eyes and the constellation of freckles that spread across her nose and cheeks. The corners of her mouth naturally turned upward as though caught on the edge of laughter.

"Your friend across the room," she said with a nod toward Sean Timmons, who was the first *T* in TST Security, "must be in charge of watching Helena Christie Prescott's body. How did he get the good assignment?"

"Seniority." The admiral's glamorous dark-haired wife showed a lot of cleavage, and the slit on her skirt was thigh high. Watching her was kind of a treat.

"You're Mason, right?"

"Yes, ma'am." Mason Steele was the *S* in TST Security. "And you're Francine Alexandra DeMille."

"Call me Lexie."

"Why not Francine?" he asked. "Or Franny?"

"Because of my job. I take care of the Prescott kids."

Which made her Franny the nanny? He stifled a chuckle. "There are six of them, right?"

"Two teenagers from the admiral's first marriage. The ten-year-old twin boys come from Helena's union with the hunk who's in that stripper movie—a deadbeat dad, but, oh, those abs."

"I know who you mean."

She stared intently at him. "You look a little bit like him. With the buzz haircut and the cool blue eyes and those big, muscular...arms." She squeezed one of his biceps and immediately yanked her hand away. A pink blush colored her cheeks. "And the six- and four-year-old are from this marriage."

When he forced his gaze away from her and checked out the children's table, the littlest girl stood up on the seat of her chair and waved at him with a golden magic wand. He fought the urge to laugh. On the job, he couldn't afford to be distracted by cuteness, but this little golden-haired girl was irresistible. He grinned back at her and winked.

Mason had always thought a big family would be fun.

He was his parents' only surviving child. Thanksgiving was no picnic. And Christmas? Forget about it.

"Here's my problem," Lexie said. "The younger kiddos are restless and on the verge of turning into a nuisance. The older ones are bored. And we're at least a half hour away from the speeches. Do you have any security issues if I whisk them out of here in a few minutes?"

He was glad she'd asked before dashing out the door. TST provided extra security when children were part of the scene. Mason looked around the banquet room, trying to spot the bodyguard who was responsible for keeping an eye on the Prescott offspring.

"Strange," he muttered. "I don't see Carlos."

"Nope." Lexie shook her head, and her curly pony-tail bounced. "He introduced himself earlier, and I would have gone to him, but I lost track of where he was, which is kind of hard to do, since good old Carlos is the size of a side-by-side refrigerator-freezer combo."

A former pro football linebacker, Carlos was six feet five inches—only a little taller than Mason, but Carlos outweighed him by nearly seventy-five pounds. The big man was good at his job and wasn't the type to wander off.

Where the hell was he? A twang of apprehension jangled Mason's nerves. "It might be a good idea to get the kids out of here."

Immediately, Lexie picked up on his mood. Her grin disappeared. "Is it dangerous?"

Always. There was always danger. He didn't want to tell her that; didn't want to point out the obvious fact that his security firm had been hired to protect the admiral and his family from an imminent threat, which meant a threat existed.

"Let's see what I can find out." He gave her a light pat on the shoulder. His intention had been to reassure her, but when he touched her bare skin, a spark ignited. Like wild-fire, an unexpected heat crackled though his nerve endings and turned his blood to lava. For an instant, he was struck dumb. He had to drag his focus away from Lexie before he spoke into his headset to Sean.

After a quick, quiet conversation with his partner, Mason regained his self-control. There was no room for further distraction; tonight was important. TST was there to protect Admiral Prescott, a man he respected and admired. Though the admiral had been retired for three years and wasn't in uniform tonight, his posture bespoke military discipline. Mason's brother, an expert in naval intelligence, had known the admiral personally.

Lexie cleared her throat. She looked to him for an all-clear signal. He wanted to give her a thumbs-up so she'd reward him with that cute upturned smile of hers. When she lifted her hand to brush back a wisp of russet hair, he noticed her delicate charm bracelet. The silver chain shone brightly against her tanned forearm. One of the charms resembled a ninja throwing star.

Sean's voice came through his earbud. "I found Carlos. I knew I'd seen the big guy headed this way. He's in the bathroom, puking his guts out."

"What's wrong with him?"

"Might have the flu," Sean said. "One of his kids is sick."

Or he could have been drugged, could have been poisoned. Several scenarios flipped through Mason's mind, ranging from an attempted abduction of the children to a full-on assault with fiery explosive devices. In every possible circumstance, he needed to get the children to safety.

Keeping his voice calm, he spoke to Lexie. "Tell the kids we're leaving. We'll go out through the terrace. It's the closest exit."

"Should I be worried?"

Not wanting to alarm her, he didn't offer an explanation. "I thought you wanted to get the kids away."

"True, and I don't mind missing those speeches myself."

With a toss of her head, she pivoted and returned to the circular table where the Prescott brood was sitting. The teenagers were texting, the younger kids were playing with their food and the princess with the magic wand was waving to everyone.

In a hushed tone, Mason informed Sean that he'd take over Carlos's job, guarding the children and moving them upstairs to their bedrooms. The hotel had provided extra security guards on the seventh floor, where the entourage was staying. "While I'm gone, you watch the admiral."

"I'm worried," Sean said. "What if Carlos was drugged?"

Mason was about to ask if Carlos had eaten anything or had anything to drink. Before he spoke, he realized that it was a dumb question. Carlos was always eating and drinking. "Let's hope it's just the flu."

He scanned the crowd. As more people were served, the sound of conversation was replaced by the clink of silverware against china. The situation was under control. Earlier today, they'd come up with several possible evacuation plans. But what if the attackers had outthought them and were already waiting outside? Mason contacted his snipers on the roof, letting them know that he intended to exit with the kids.

He seriously doubted that the bad guys had gained entrance to the banquet hall. The guests, cooks and servers had all been vetted and the TST Security computers were a foolproof system, protected by something Dylan Timmons, who was the second *T* in TST Security, called the mother of all firewalls.

Mason's gaze flicked around the room. Could he

trust computer clearances? Doubt assailed his judgment. "Maybe we should shut this operation down."

A voice in his head—which was actually Sean—advised, "It's your call, Mason."

At TST Security, the three partners had their areas of expertise. Dylan specialized in computer security. Sean was former FBI, more of a detective and a profiler—a deductive genius. And Mason was the muscle—the man in charge of action and strategy. "First, I'll get the kids to safety."

As if he needed another complication, the admiral had left his banquet seat and was coming toward him. Smiling and genial, the admiral picked his way through the crowd and stood beside Mason. "What's the problem?"

"The bodyguard protecting the children has a suspicious case of the flu." He kept his voice low so the other guests wouldn't take notice. "It's probably nothing, but I recommend escorting the kids to their rooms on the seventh floor."

"Agreed. I don't take chances with my children's safety." He beckoned to Lexie, who began moving the kids in their direction. "I'll help."

"My men can handle the situation, Admiral. It's not necessary for you to leave the banquet."

"I'm retired, Mr. Steele. You can drop the admiral and call me Prescott. But make no mistake—I still give the orders."

The expression on Mason's face didn't change a bit. Inside, he was cheering for the old warrior who was still man enough to take care of his children, marry a movie star and lead the charge into battle. Still, he said, "Sir, let me do my job. If you come, I need to pull other security. Please, stay here."

Their gazes locked. Each man took the measure of the other.

Prescott grinned. "I worked with your brother."

"I know."

"Carry on, Mr. Steele."

While Prescott returned to his seat, Mason signaled his man who had earlier locked the terrace door and instructed him to accompany them, bringing up the rear. When the children and Lexie had gathered, Mason opened the door onto the flagstone terrace and stepped outside into a rose-colored dusk.

He led the way down a wide set of stone stairs to a wooden door. Like the rest of the hotel, this entrance was less than a decade old, but had been aged to look antique. What did they call it? Distressed. The wood had been distressed to make it seem as though this door and the stone wall were part of a hundred-year-old hunting lodge. In contrast, the door was opened by a computer pad that required Mason to enter a code. He opened the door and led them into the parking lot under the hotel.

The sound of their footsteps made a hollow echo in the concrete structure filled with vehicles. Many of the guests at the banquet were also staying at the hotel. Tomorrow, some of them would play golf with Admiral Prescott, which was another complicated scenario for TST Security.

Mason had already checked out the parking garage. With four separate exits on each level and six elevators, it was a good place to bring the kids for an escape. He hustled his little crew toward the elevators.

The teenagers were mature enough to know that something wasn't exactly copacetic. The oldest girl held the youngest boy's hand. These were military kids; they knew how to behave. Not so much for the Hollywood twins—handsome ten-year-olds with shaggy blond hair and dark eyebrows. They were punching each other, whining about how they wanted pizza and making growling noises interspersed with high-pitched squeaks.

Lexie hustled the gruesome twosome forward. Throughout this whole process she'd kept her cool and followed instructions. Mason noticed that she was carrying the emergency alert equipment Carlos had given her. If she ran into a threat, she was supposed to hit the red button and all TST Security personnel would respond.

He wondered if she'd had any specialized training to protect the kids. She was in good shape, had an athletic stride and her arms were well toned. But did Franny the nanny do kung fu?

He wanted to know more about her. Maybe tonight after the kids were in bed, they could get together. Maybe they'd talk, maybe laugh, maybe she'd allow him to glide his fingers down her smooth, tanned shoulders and arms. At the elevators, she shot him an over-the-shoulder glance before turning her full attention to the twins, who were trying to expand their obnoxious behavior to include the other kids. She moved quickly to separate the twins from the rest of the herd.

But one of the twins shoved into the teenage boy, Eddy Jr., who was at the age when he was almost manly. In a voice that was significantly deeper than that of the twins, he muttered, "Watch what you're doing, dork face."

"You're not the boss of me."

"But he's bigger than you." His twin poked him in the back. "He could kick your—"

"Enough," Lexie said.

She stepped between the twins and Eddy Jr. Both elevators dinged as the doors opened simultaneously. Lexie entered one elevator and dragged the twins with her. "The three of us will take this one. We'll meet the rest of you on the seventh floor."

"Wait!" Mason said. This wasn't procedure. The kids should be accompanied by a bodyguard at all times.

She flashed him a wide grin. "Don't worry. I've got this."

The elevator door snapped closed, and he was left with a vision of her dark eyes sparkling. Her expression was full of mischief and something more. There was something mysterious about her, and he wondered what she knew that he didn't. She seemed to be laughing inside as though she had the punch line to an untold joke.

Chapter Two

In the elevator, Lexie stood between the twins and glared at the wood-paneled walls. The boutique hotel's impersonation of an old-time hunting lodge was beginning to annoy her. She didn't mind the elk and moose heads mounted on the walls in the lobby. After all, her dad and three older brothers had taken her on her first hunting trip when she was eight years old, and she understood their desire for occasional taxidermy.

But a real hunter would never stay at a place like this. Not with the golf course, the fake Persian rugs, the ornate imitation antique furniture and the kitschy Old West touches, like brass spittoons. Spittoons? This pricey hotel didn't allow smoking, much less chewing tobacco.

"You ticked off that bodyguard," said the twin named Caine.

"He'll get over it."

The other twin—who she always thought should have been named Abel but was actually Shane—tilted his head to one side and gave her a freakishly mature look. "I think you like that bodyguard."

How could he possibly know that? The kid was right, of course. She was drawn to Mason like a spinster moth to a muscular flame, but she didn't intend to discuss her personal feelings with the kids. "Mr. Steele seems like a nice man."

Caine tugged her right arm. "You really like him."

Shane snickered. "You want to marry him."

Ignoring the twins, she stared at the lighted numbers for the floors as they passed the fourth. An interruption would be most welcome, but she wasn't having any such luck. The twin monsters prattled back and forth about how she wanted to kiss Mason and "do it" with him, about how she was in love with him.

Though tempted to respond with a childish and extra loud "am not," she kept her voice trained to a calm level. "That's enough."

"But we got more, lots more."

"If I hear another word from either of you, there will be no pizza tonight, no ice cream, no TV, no computer games, no nothing. We clear?"

They went silent, nodded and stood up straight. Though the boys were only ten, they'd had a growth spurt and were almost as tall as she was at five feet three inches. Like golden retriever puppies, their feet and hands were too large for their gangly bodies. Someday they'd be huge, handsome dudes like their matinee idol father.

She liked big men, but not big babies like the twins' irresponsible daddy. She preferred a guy like Mason who was physically fit and in the business of protecting other people. A steady, stable guy, someone she could count on, a man she could trust.

Rein it in, Lexie. Sure, Mason was handsome with his buzz haircut and his square jaw and his butane-blue eyes. But she knew nothing about his character. He might be a cheat or a liar. Being drawn to him wouldn't be the first time she'd been fooled by a man with a pretty face and muscular shoulders.

With a scowl, she reminded herself that she had no proof that Anton Karpov had betrayed her. He'd disappeared while doing a job that might be connected with the admiral. That was what he'd told her. Most likely, he'd been lying. The admiral had never heard of Anton and didn't recognize him from photos.

At the seventh floor, the elevator dinged and the doors swept open. A man in a security guard uniform assigned by the hotel stood waiting, but she didn't recognize him. He didn't look like an employee, not with that stubble on his face.

She sensed a threat. She could smell it. Spreading her arms, she kept the twins on the elevator. Down the hall on the left, she glimpsed a body on the floor.

Backing into the elevator again, she said to the phony security man, "Oops, I forgot something."

When she reached back and hit the elevator button for the lobby, he reacted. His arm blocked the door from closing. He grabbed her shoulder. "You ain't going nowhere."

Lexie hit the red alert button for TST Security and said to the twins, "Go to the lobby."

She shoved the guard in the chest, keeping him away from the twins. Lexie went on the offensive. Her first flying kick was aimed at the guard's midsection. He bent double. She fired another kick at his right kneecap.

Behind her back, she heard the elevator doors snap shut. The twins were safe. Good, she'd do anything to keep these kids from harm.

The fake guard clutched at his gut. His knee bent sideways as he made a gurgling noise in the back of his throat. Then he collapsed onto the fancy Persian carpet and rolled around while grabbing his injured leg.

She had to move fast. Where there was one thug, there would be others, and she didn't want to take on the whole gang with no other weapon than her karate skills. Lexie delivered another sharp kick to the head of the first thug. He went limp, unconscious. Since she'd chosen flats instead of pointy-toe stiletto heels for tonight's event, this fake guard might survive.

She dropped to her knees beside him and yanked his gun from the holster. Aiming high, she fired at two other men who were running toward her.

Her warning shots had the desired effect. The phony hotel guards sought cover, which gave her a few seconds to locate a better position.

MIDWAY THROUGH HIS elevator ascent with the children, Mason heard the warning squawk from Lexie's emergency alert button. What the hell? Had she run into trouble on the seventh floor? The sound of gunfire overhead was his answer.

He jabbed the elevator button, stopping the car on the sixth instead of the seventh floor. When the doors opened, he spoke to the other bodyguard. "Take the children to the lobby."

"What about you?"

"I'm going up."

Leaving the elevator, he listened to the babble of confused voices coming through his headset. They had all gotten the alert from Lexie. He heard Sean take control inside the banquet hall. Following procedure, Sean ordered most of the other TST guards to the front lobby, where Dylan—who was stationed at the reservation desk—would organize their operation.

The gunfire from above had not abated. What the hell was going on up there? He gave Sean an update. "It's Mason. I'm going up to the seventh floor where shots are being fired."

"Copy that," Dylan responded from the lobby. "I have the twins and the other kids. All secure."

The children were safe. Good. "What about Lexie, the nanny?"

"The twins say she's on the seventh floor."

Mason's gut clenched. If anything had happened to her because he'd let her take the elevator alone, he would never forgive himself. He spoke into the headset. "I'll be out of touch for a few minutes."

He unscrewed the earbud and welcomed the attending silence. His entire focus needed to be on Lexie.

Drawing his gun from the shoulder holster, he sprinted down the hotel corridor and through the door below the red Exit sign. He rushed up the concrete staircase to the seventh floor and eased his way through, moving carefully until he got his bearings.

The difference in decor on each floor was as subtle as the varying shades of beige on the wallpaper above the waist-high wood wainscoting. Antique-looking picture frames held sepia photos from the early 1900s, including many of Theodore Roosevelt, who was known for hunting in the Colorado Rockies and for establishing the National Park Service. Against the wall opposite the elevators was a claw-foot table with a floral arrangement and a teddy bear with the stuffing blown out of its chest. An unconscious man in a hotel uniform lay on the floor. Good guy or bad?

There was no sure way of telling. Down the hall was another unconscious man wearing only his underwear. Quick conclusion: the men who had been stripped were the real guards. The uniforms were being worn by impostors.

The *rat-a-tat* of automatic gunfire came from his left.

There were only fourteen rooms on this deluxe level, including a massive suite for the admiral and his wife. The floor plan was a B-shape with the elevators in the middle.

Peering around the corner, he spotted the backsides of two uniformed men. When they tried to advance, a single shot repelled them. Lexie? Where did she get the gun?

Mason fired twice and got two hits. Both men reacted but neither went down. They must be wearing Kevlar vests under their uniform shirts. When they turned toward him, he saw Lexie dash across the end of the hallway. He hoped she'd run to the relative safety of her room.

No such luck.

While he and the impostor guards exchanged fire, she circled all the way around and came up behind him. "Mason, do you have another gun?"

"Not for you."

"Don't be a jerk. I've only got one bullet left."

"Where's your room?" he asked.

She pointed behind them and waved her key card. "It's over here. I'm not sure it's safe. There are two other thugs who aren't wearing uniforms. They could be hiding inside."

They were outnumbered, and the bad guys had more firepower. The best option was to retreat. "Take me to your room, unlock the door and I'll enter first to make sure it's safe. Then you follow me in."

"You and me in the bedroom? Well, that's the best offer I've had in a long time."

He didn't take his eyes off the two men who were laying down a steady barrage of gunfire; he didn't need to look at her to know she was grinning. Calm under pressure, he liked that. What he didn't like was the way she squatted down and tugged at his pant leg. "What are you doing?"

"Looking for your ankle holster. Aha!" She undid the snap and took his second weapon. "Thanks, I need this."

She hustled down the hallway, and he followed. At her room, she unlocked the door and stepped aside. He entered, holding his gun with both hands as he searched the bath-room, the closet and under the beds. "All clear."

Instead of obeying his instructions to follow him in-side and lock the door, she braced herself in the doorway and dropped to one knee as she fired down the hallway. It was obvious that she knew what she was doing. Earlier, he'd been wondering if she had self-defense instruction. The answer to that question was a resounding yes. Lexie was dangerous.

When he pulled her inside and closed the door, he no-ticed the slash of red across her upper arm. "You're bleed-ing."

"Just a graze, but it really stings." She looked down at the angled cut that dripped blood down to her elbow. "That's going to leave a scar."

He dragged a heavy silk-upholstered chair and posi-tioned it in front of the doorway. He added a desk. The barricade would slow down any attacker long enough for him to get off a couple of accurate shots.

From the bathroom, he grabbed a fluffy white hand towel and brought it to where she was sitting on a carved wooden bench in front of a mirrored dressing table. He wrapped the towel around her wounded arm and brushed escaped curls off her forehead. Under her freckles, her complexion had faded to a waxy pale.

"Are you all right?" he asked.

"Sure. Fine."

When the energizing effect of adrenaline wore off, he expected her to crash like a rock slide. And he wanted to be there when she unwound, to catch her before she fell, to hold her and tell her that life was going to get better. There was something about her that awakened his protec-tive instincts.

As a rule, he kept his distance from other people and

avoided committed relationships. Losing his brother had torn a hole in his heart and made him wary of deep connections. But Lexie's grin repaired his pain. He wanted to be close to her.

He held her hand, marveling at her slender fingers and the delicate turn of her wrist. His gaze lifted to her dark eyes. "I won't let anything bad happen to you."

"I know you'll do your best." She shrugged. "Sometimes there's no way to prevent the bad stuff."

Though she was acting nonchalant, the hollow echo in her voice surprised him. He could tell that this woman had experienced more than her fair share of tragedy. Immediately curious, he wanted to hear more about her life, her dreams and her plans for the future.

But this wasn't the right time. Gently, he removed his gun from her clenched fingers. Her vulnerability touched him, but he also appreciated her strength. When she'd needed to be tough, she held off four bad guys—five including the unconscious one outside the elevator. Now she could relax.

He didn't have that respite. An aggressive burst of gunfire echoed in the corridor like a call to duty. He stuck his earbud back in. Sean was screaming his name, demanding an update and informing Mason that they had a group ready to storm the seventh floor.

Gun in hand, he turned his attention to TST Security business.

Chapter Three

Leaving Mason to growl orders on his intercom, Lexie slipped into the bathroom, locked the door and leaned against it. Stillness wrapped around her. Inside this pristine tile and marble cubicle, the gunfire seemed far away.

Exhaling a sigh, she slid down the wall. *Sanctuary!* Not that she was truly safe. This peaceful feeling was akin to being in the eye of a tornado while danger continued to swirl, but she was glad for the momentary respite—especially glad she'd made it into the bathroom before she swooned like some kind of whimpering Southern belle.

Mason didn't need to know she was scared. She liked him and wanted him to like her. And something told her that he wasn't the kind of guy who enjoyed being around girlie girls. She'd seen the gleam in his eye when he watched her taking aim and when he tended to her bullet wound. As if on cue, the red-stained towel fell from her arm. Oozing blood smeared and saturated the blue fabric of her jumpsuit.

"Bummer." This was one of her favorite outfits.

It didn't hurt. Not much, anyway. But her body was having a reaction that was out of proportion to the injury. Was this some kind of panic attack? She was acutely tense. Her muscles twisted into knots. Her gut clenched. Other symptoms slammed into her, one after the other. She was light-headed. Her breathing was labored, and she smelled the odor of rotting meat. The inside of her mouth tasted like ash. Shivers twitched across her shoulders.

Her spine buckled, and she ratcheted down to the floor. She lay on her side with her wounded arm up, the white marble cooling her cheek. She tried to breathe deeply and calm herself. But she was too tense…and too cold, ice-cold. Her fists clenched between her breasts. Her pulse pounded. She pinched her eyes closed, hoping to blot out the terrible fear that threatened to overwhelm her.

She had to get control. *I'm going to be all right.* No matter how many times her conscious mind repeated those words, a deeper place in her soul didn't believe it. *I won't die.* Post-traumatic stress squeezed her in a grip so tight that her bones rattled. *Everything is going to be all right.* She wasn't in mortal danger, not this time. *This isn't like the accident.*

Her memory jolted. Flung backward in time, she heard a fierce metallic crunch and the explosion of the air bag from the steering wheel. Her brother's little bronze sedan had been thrown onto its side and was skidding toward the edge of the cliff near Buena Vista. Cringing, she heard the grinding screech of her car door against the pavement. *Should have taken the truck.* Jake was going to kill her for wrecking his car. *Not my fault.* The other car—black with tinted windows—had crossed the center line and hit her front fender.

Her mouth opened wide as she desperately tried to scream. The air bag had stolen her breath. She could only gasp. And then her brother's car was falling, crashing end over end, down the steep hillside and into the trees.

Other people had told her that they couldn't recall a single moment of their accidents. In the midst of their traumatic events, they experienced amnesia. Not her. She felt every twist and turn as the car plummeted. Fully conscious, she braced herself for what would surely come next: the gas explosion that would tear her limbs apart and the flames that would sear her flesh.

That wasn't the way it turned out. Though the driver who had hit her fled the scene, there was a witness in another vehicle. She was rescued, taken to the hospital and stitched back together. The doctors fixed as much as they could.

Replaying the accident—the worst moments of her life—lessened her current panic. The terror that had threatened to smother her receded into the shadows of her mind. She forced her thoughts back to the present reality and focused on what had just happened. She'd been attacked by five armed men.

Instead of sliding deeper into fear, she chuckled to herself. This definitely wasn't like the horrible feeling of helplessness in the car accident. When it came to self-defense, she did okay. Not a big surprise, as she'd been trained by her three older brothers, who ran a karate dojo. And her dad, a Marine Corps sergeant, had insisted that she know how to handle rifles, pistols, handguns and other weaponry.

Thinking of the DeMille men calmed her. Even though they were a thousand miles away in Austin, Texas, they were watching over her. They'd made her into what she was today: an independent, stubborn, kick-ass tomboy. A survivor.

When she'd encountered the first man outside the elevator, she knew—without the slightest doubt—that she could take him down. Lexie had earned her brown belt in karate when she was fifteen.

Shooting at people was more difficult; she didn't want to kill anybody. If Mason hadn't shown up, she had no idea what she would have done. He'd taken a risk by charging onto this floor to help her. Of course, security was his job…but still, she was grateful.

There was a tap on the door. "Lexie, are you all right?"

She scrambled to get her legs under her. "I'm fine."

"Are you sure? It's quiet in there."

"I'm fine," she repeated.

She should have turned on the shower. Mason wouldn't have knocked if he'd heard water running. Struggling, she lunged to her feet and hit the faucet in the sink. There! Was that enough proof enough that she was fine and dandy?

Her reflection in the mirror confronted her. Not a pretty sight! Her arm dripped blood, her makeup was smudged and her ponytail was tangled like a bird's nest. What she needed was a shower, but stripping off her clothes while bad guys were on the prowl seemed like an invitation to more trouble—naked trouble.

She went to the bathroom door, pressed her ear against it and listened for the sounds of battle from the outer corridor. There were distant pops. This wasn't the kind of cheesy motel where you heard every cough and sputter from the neighboring room, but gunfire was loud. She expected to hear somethi—

"Lexie?" Mason knocked again.

She jumped backward with a yelp. Off balance, she stumbled into the wall beside the huge Plexiglas shower with four separate spray nozzles. "Fine," she shouted. "I'm perfectly fine."

He opened the door.

"I locked that," she said.

"And I picked the lock." He strode toward her.

Whether she wanted his protection or not, Mason was here. He guided her across the marble floor and lifted her onto the counter with double sinks. "Do you want the outfit on or off?"

"On, of course." She pushed at his chest, accidentally staining his light blue shirt with blood. "Jeez Louise, I'm sorry."

"Jeez Louise?" He lifted an eyebrow.

"I don't swear. It's a nanny thing."

"Did you used to?"

"Hell, yes." She felt a grin spread across her face, and she was amazed by how swiftly her mood had transformed. Mason was magic. "I have three brothers."

He nodded. "Every other word was obscene."

"Not as much as you'd think. Dad didn't tolerate bad language."

"Was he a religious man?"

"Worse. A marine sergeant. Discipline was his middle name."

"My older brother was in the corps. He worked with the admiral in the Middle East." His shoulders flexed in a tense shrug. "I'd like to think that one of the reasons TST Security was hired was the admiral's good opinion of my brother."

Being from a military family, she was sensitive to the fact that he spoke of his brother in the past tense. "I wonder if your brother knew my dad, Daniel DeMille? He was stationed in the Middle East, too. He retired five years ago."

"My brother was killed six years ago in Afghanistan."

"I'm sorry."

"So am I." He peeled off his suit jacket, tossed it into the bedroom and started rolling up his shirtsleeves. "Now I'm going to clean your wound."

She pointed toward the open bathroom door. "What about those thugs in the hallway?"

"My partners have it under control. The local police and

sheriff are on the way." He tapped the listening device in his ear. "TST Security has rounded up all but one of the bad guys. He locked himself in a room down the hall and thinks he's safe."

His full lips quirked in a wry smile that told her the criminal hiding in one of the rooms was making a big mistake. She asked, "What's going to happen to him?"

"While he's watching the door to the hallway, one of the snipers on the roof is going to bust through a window."

"And you'd like to watch," she said.

"Oh, yeah."

His tone reminded her of the DeMille men, but there was nothing brotherly about the tingling she felt when he touched her arm. He moistened a washcloth under the hot water she'd been running in the sink. Holding her arm below the elbow, he cautiously wiped away the blood.

"The cut isn't too deep," he said. "I don't think you'll need stitches, but you should have a doc take a look."

"Sure." While he focused on taking care of her, she studied him. Her father would approve of his buzz cut and no-nonsense attitude, but she was more impressed by his deep-set dark blue eyes and high cheekbones. His tanned forearms showed that he spent time outdoors, but her thoughts about him required an indoor setting… A bedroom scenario, to be specific.

He lifted his gaze. What would it be like to wake up and see those eyes looking back at her? He was almost too handsome, too good to be true. *Please, Mason, don't be a liar or a cheat.*

Using a clean towel, he patted her arm dry. When he reached behind her head, unfastened her ponytail and let her curly hair fall to her shoulders, his face was near hers. If she tilted her head and leaned in, their lips would touch.

Impulsively, her fingers snatched his striped silk necktie, and she held him in place. He was mere inches away from her, so very close that she felt the heat radiating from his body. She smelled his aftershave, a citrus and nutmeg flavor with a hint of something else…the indefinable scent of a man.

"You smell good." She hadn't intended her voice to become a purr, but that was what happened.

"So do you."

Her gaze twined with his, and she tugged at his necktie to pull him a half inch closer. She wanted to kiss him, but the situation was messy. She was sitting on the countertop at a weird angle. If she pressed her body against his chest, she'd smear the blood all over his shirt. More important, she barely knew this man and could be setting herself up for a world of embarrassment.

He ended her indecision. She should have known that he would. Mason was a take-charge kind of guy. He buried his fingers in her untamed hair and held the back of her skull so that he was supporting her. Then he kissed her.

Crazy, wild sensations bloomed inside her. He kissed the same way he seemed to do everything else: with skill and finesse. His lips were firm, and he exerted exactly the right amount of pressure.

His tongue traced the line of her mouth, slipped inside and probed against her teeth. She opened wider for him. Her tongue joined with his and—

There was a hammering noise from the door to the hallway. A deep voice shouted, "Mason, you in there?"

They broke apart so quickly that she bit the inside of her cheek. "Bad timing," she muttered.

"I have to go."

Twenty questions popped inside her head. *Can I see you again? Will there be another kiss? Can I give you my phone number?* She said only one word aloud. "Thanks."

"For what?"

"Saving my life."

He dropped a light kiss on her forehead. "My pleasure."

As she watched him walk out the door, she whispered, "The pleasure was all mine."

PEERING THROUGH THE infrared scope of his rifle, Anton Karpov scanned the windows on the seventh floor of the mountain hotel, trying to catch a glimpse of Franny. Earlier tonight, he had watched her through the crosshairs on his scope. She'd been outside on the terrace, meeting and greeting, laughing and smiling. She looked good— damn good. Until tonight, he hadn't paid any attention to the nanny.

But now he knew. Anton had positively identified Franny DeMille, the chick he'd almost moved in with. Why was she calling herself Lexie? How the hell did she get to be a nanny?

The Franny he knew was a kick-ass daredevil who couldn't care less about kids and didn't know a damn thing about taking care of them. When he was dating her, she'd told him—flat out—that she didn't want babies. Hey, great news for him. He wasn't meant to play daddy. He wasn't serious about her, either. Still, it made him mad when she dumped him. It was supposed to be the other way around. He made sure she knew that.

His cell phone vibrated in his pocket, and he answered.

The voice on the other end was the leader himself. There had been a lot of talk at meetings about how no single person was more important than another. They were equals. Some had special skills or areas of expertise, but their group didn't operate within the structure of a hierarchy.

Anton didn't buy in to any of that phony, mealy-mouthed philosophy. While others talked about all for one and "the greater good," he held his silence. There was only one truth he believed in: dollars and cents. He'd been associated with the leader for almost ten years, performing special tasks for decent pay.

Quietly, the leader said, "Move out. I'll contact you later, Tony."

Long ago, Anton had Americanized his name to Tony Curtis after the old-time movie star. He even looked kind of like that Tony, with his curly black hair and blue eyes. The real Tony Curtis was usually cast as a pretty boy hero, and that didn't suit Anton Karpov, not at all. He only changed his mind when he saw the movie star play the role of Albert DeSalvo, widely believed to be the Boston Strangler.

"Are you sure I should go, sir?" He was one of the few who knew the leader's real name, but he seldom spoke it. "I have a couple of angles for a clear shot."

"I'm tempted, Tony. I'd like to kill those idiots who got caught."

"Is there any chance they won't spill their guts?"

"Oh, they'll talk. The admiral's men are skilled interrogators."

"Is that a problem?"

"They don't know enough to worry about. They're unimportant."

The leader didn't seem concerned about losing five men. The less influential members of Anti-Conspiracy Committee for Democracy, also known as AC-CD, had access to a limited amount of information. They were assigned simple jobs. Tonight, the only thing they'd been required to do was disable the hotel security and fill in for them, leaving the way open for more experienced operatives. The trained, experienced staff, led by Anton/Tony, would have kidnapped the admiral.

Anton/Tony slung his rifle over his shoulder and rose to his feet. "It was the nanny who messed up the plan."

"How could a little girl like that be such a big problem?"

The leader didn't know her. For a couple of seconds, Tony felt superior to the man who usually gave the orders. For a change, it was Tony who had the ace up his sleeve, information the leader wasn't privy to, and he was tempted to hold back.

But he didn't care about showing how smart he was and gaining power in AC-CD. He was after a quick payday, and the best way to separate the leader from his cash was to show him something he might want to buy. Franny was a prize he could set before the leader.

"She says her name is Lexie, but I recognized her tonight. The nanny is a karate expert. It's Franny DeMille, my old girlfriend."

"You don't say." The leader's voice dropped to a low, thoughtful level. "If you asked her to help you, would she?"

"We didn't break up on good terms, but I could always get her to do what I wanted." Not exactly true, but he wished it so. When he'd been with her, he was a better man. "She'll do what I say."

"I'll be in touch."

Before leaving his sniper nest, Tony pulled up his balaclava to cover the lower part of his face. Silently and stealthily, he made his way through the forest. His experience as a hunting guide was why he'd been pegged for this assignment. He could be trusted to blend with nature and not be seen. And his skill at marksmanship was worthy of a world-class assassin.

Chapter Four

In the rustic-style foyer outside the banquet hall, Mason
conferred quietly with his partner Dylan, whose tall, wiry
frame had been transformed from nerdy to sophisticated
by a tailored black suit and a striped silk tie. Likewise, his
messy brown hair had been tamed in a ponytail at the nape
of his neck. They were waiting for the admiral's wife to
leave the hall and join them. Prescott had asked them to
escort her to the conference room, where he and several
branches of law enforcement and the military had gathered.

"NSA, CIA, Interpol, army and navy intelligence,"
Dylan said. He pushed his horn-rimmed glasses up on
his nose. "The gang's all here."

"How do you know their affiliations?"

"They were all at the banquet." As part of security procedure, he had vetted the invited guests and used facial rec-
ognition software to make sure they matched their stated
identity. "Some of these guys are high-ranking hotshots.
On six of them, I got an 'access denied' message when I
searched for further info."

"Did you?" Mason asked. "Tell me the truth. Did you
dig deeper?"

"Not yet."

But he could if the need arose. Dylan was a skilled
hacker, capable of breaching NSA or CIA security with-

out leaving a trace. He'd already patched Admiral Prescott through to the offices of the Secretary of the Navy on a video server so that SecNav could join the meeting in the conference room.

The sound of laughter erupted from inside the banquet hall. For the past hour, the guests had been watching a PowerPoint presentation that outlined the medical and sanitation needs of children in sub-Saharan Africa.

Mason glanced over at his partner. "We did good."

"How do you figure?"

"All five bad guys have been taken into custody."

"Have they?" Dylan arched an eyebrow in a skeptical expression that irritated Mason to no end. "The so-called baddies are still in the hotel."

The local sheriff, Colorado law enforcement and NSA were all fighting over who would take possession of these low-level thugs. "Arresting them isn't our problem."

"What if there are others?"

"We'll handle it. This assignment still counts as a success for TST Security." And for him, personally. Not only had he shown Admiral Prescott, a man he admired, that he was competent, but he'd also met Lexie. Her grin lifted his spirits. Their kiss elevated the evening into noteworthy; he'd remember that short, sweet contact for a very long time.

Dylan slouched and jammed his fists into his pockets, distorting the crisp line of his suit. "I don't like this, Mace. Too many questions. Not enough answers. We don't know why those guys invaded the seventh floor or what they were after."

"Whatever it was, they didn't get it. We stopped them. We met our objectives." Mason ticked off their achievements on his fingers. "The admiral and his family are safe. None of the good guys, not even the hotel guards, were seriously injured. And the people who came here for a banquet are still having their coffee and chocolate mousse dessert."

"I'd approximate that eighty-five percent of the guests are oblivious of the attack."

Though he had no idea where Dylan got his percentage, Mason assumed that his computer-geek partner was correct. Most of the guests had remained in their chairs while the servers cleared away their plates and refilled their wineglasses. Some of them might have looked around when they heard the sound of approaching police sirens, but the flashing red-and-blue lights weren't visible from the banquet hall, and the hotel management people were doing everything in their power to make sure their guests weren't aware of the mayhem on the seventh floor.

The door swept open and Helena Christie Prescott charged toward them. She was a classic beauty with long raven hair and a killer body, but all Mason saw were her flared nostrils and the flames shooting from her green eyes as she demanded, "What the hell is going on?"

"Your husband asked that I bring you—"

"Edgar is all right, isn't he?"

"Yes, ma'am."

"That's good, because I'm going to hurt him, hurt him bad." She had morphed from fiery dragon into sinister assassin, a role she'd played in a movie Mason saw. The assassin might even have used that line about hurting him bad. "And the children?"

"Everybody's okay." Mason gestured toward the hallway. "Come with us to the conference room, where your husband can brief you."

"Lead on." She strode along beside him, leaving Dylan in their wake. In her five-inch heels, she almost matched

Mason's six-foot-three-inch height, and she hiked up the side of her gown opposite the slit so she could move faster.

Dylan—the coward—had cleverly fallen back, leaving Mason to deal with Helena. He was certain that any comment from him about not worrying or calming down would not be prudent.

"We're almost there," he said. "It's on this floor."

She came to a sudden halt. "I'm not being the least bit unreasonable. But what am I to think? My husband gets called away by his assistant, then the military guys and four agents—two CIA and two from some weird NSA department—slide out the door. What the hell is happening? Has Aspen been invaded by terrorists?"

Mason couldn't have been happier to see Lexie step out of the elevator and come toward them. A short while ago, he'd saved the nanny's life. Now it was her turn to save him.

She'd changed into casual clothes: sneakers, jeans and a long forest-green sweatshirt. Her wild auburn hair was held back from her face by a yellow band.

Helena spotted her and flung both arms around Lexie in a dramatic hug. "Thank God you're here."

Though jolted back on her heels, Lexie recovered her balance and spoke calmly. "Everything is going to be fine."

"Is it? Is it really?"

"Sure," Lexie said. "The kids are okay. They're all together in your suite. I left the hotel babysitter to keep an eye on them. Plus two of the TST bodyguards." She glanced at Mason and mouthed, *Is Carlos all right?*

He gave her a thumbs-up. The big guy had recovered and was sheepish about being sick. Since there didn't seem to be a connection between his stomach flu and the ambush on the seventh floor, he doubted that poison was involved. Carlos was once again in charge of guarding the children.

"Why wouldn't the kids be fine?" Helena asked. "Has there been a threat?"

Lexie turned to him. "You haven't told her?"

"The admiral wanted to explain himself."

A ringtone—a song from *Mary Poppins*—sounded, and Lexie retrieved her cell phone from a sweatshirt pocket. After a glance at the caller ID, she looked back at the admiral's wife. Her eyes narrowed. "Your husband has some serious explaining to do. Where is he?"

Mason opened the door to the conference room and stepped out of the way as the two women marched inside. Most of the people seated around the long table were men. One of the two women wore US Marine Corps dress blues, while the other was super chic, probably a higher-up in the CIA who shopped in Paris. In keeping with the early-1900s hunting lodge theme, the conference room was wood-paneled with elk, deer and bear heads on the walls. The snarling grizzly over the stone fireplace matched Helena's fierce expression.

Prescott leaped to his feet. "I believe you all know my wife, Helena Christie Prescott. And this is our nanny, Lexie DeMille."

The chic older woman applauded Lexie. "Impressive job, young lady. If you're ever looking for a job, contact me."

"She's not looking," Helena said curtly. "Edgar Prescott, step outside with me, please."

Without saying a word, Mason sent the admiral a mental warning. *Do what she says, man. Your wife is ticked off enough to play an assassin in real life. And you're her target.*

Apparently, Prescott's antennae were working well enough to pick up on the message. He excused himself, stepped away from the table and went into the hallway. As soon as the door to the conference room closed, he apologized to his wife.

Though this was a private conversation, Mason and his partner had to be there. It was their job to guard these two bodies. They were far less uncomfortable than Lexie who shuffled her feet and stared into the distance, pretending to be somewhere else.

"I didn't want to upset you," the admiral said to his wife. "There were gunshots fired on the seventh floor."

"Our floor?"

"Lexie was involved," he continued, "and, as you can plainly see, she's fine. TST Security rounded up the bad guys and took care of the threat. We're safe. There's nothing to worry about."

Not quite true. Mason found the situation worrisome, but that might just be his naturally vigilant nature. Overall, he was satisfied that they were safe. Choppers were airborne and searching. Local law enforcement had set up a perimeter around the hotel and would be escorting those who were leaving to their cars. There were enough armed officers patrolling in the hotel that Mason and TST Security were almost redundant.

"Very well," Helena said as she linked her arm with her husband's. "Come back to the banquet hall with me and give your speech."

"I should stay here." He looked over his shoulder at the closed door to the conference room, and then he turned to his wife. "Is there any way I can convince you to give my speech for me?"

"My dah-ling, don't be absurd. These people want to hear from you. I've only visited Africa a few times. You lived there. You know what this charity is all about."

He lifted her hand to his lips and kissed her manicured fingertips. "On our last trip to Madagascar, I remember how you took over the school and taught the kids how to sing."

Mason made eye contact with Dylan, who was being so unobtrusive that he was nearly invisible. He and his partner, both of them single, could take lessons from the admiral as he wove a charmed web around his formerly furious wife.

Helena rubbed against his arm like a slinky panther wanting to be stroked. "I had fun with my little friends, my little *marafiki*. And I loved the midnight spice market in Madagascar. But the people at this banquet have contributed a great deal of money, and they deserve the full package."

"I'm playing golf with the big investors tomorrow."

"Everybody else expects to hear a talk from you."

"Fine." He kissed her hand again. "I'll come in with you and give a brief hello. Then I'm heading back to the conference room and you can talk."

"About what?"

"I think you know," he said. "These people are educated, philanthropic, intelligent and discerning. They'll want to know about Hollywood."

"They always do," she said as she adjusted his necktie and patted his bottom.

Before they went into the banquet room, the admiral turned toward him and said, "Mason, wait for me out here."

Applause sounded as the door closed behind them. Dylan dodged around him, grabbed Lexie's hand and gave a firm shake. "From what I hear, you kicked butt. Martial arts?"

"My brothers run a karate dojo in Austin. I was starting to teach a couple of classes of my own before I became a nanny."

Mason liked the way her eyes crinkled at the corners

and her mouth turned up at the edges. He didn't so much like to see her grinning at his partner. "Dylan, I thought you were anxious to return to the front desk."

"I am?"

Mason wanted her all to himself, even though they only had a few moments and limited privacy. He tapped Dylan's arm a little bit harder than necessary to drive home the point. "Don't you need to be somewhere else?"

"Actually, I do." When he nodded, his glasses slid to the tip of his nose. "I have an audio and video recorder set on the conference room and it needs monitoring. So, I should go." Suiting the action to the words, he started walking backward while waving goodbye and mumbling about how busy he was.

Lexie turned that pretty smile on Mason, which was where it belonged. "Your partner is kind of a goofball."

"That's what happens with these genius types. They trip over their shoelaces because their brains are occupied with complicated problems."

Her gaze flicked toward the doors to the banquet room and then focused on him. "I need to talk to Prescott. Do you think I'll get a chance? I just need a few minutes."

"It shouldn't be a problem." He gently took her left arm—the one that wasn't injured—and escorted her across the open space outside the banquet hall to an antique-looking red leather love seat. "How's the bullet wound?"

"Just a graze," she said. "I'm fine. The hotel doctor patched me up and slapped on a bandage."

She perched nervously on the edge of the small sofa. On duty, Mason seldom allowed himself to sit; he needed to be on his feet and ready to move at the first sign of a threat. But the man he was guarding was inside another room where there were at least three other TST Security men. He sat beside Lexie, thigh to thigh. It would have been easy to rest his arm on the back of the love seat, but he exercised restraint.

"Prescott will talk to you," he assured her. "He's got to be grateful to you for keeping his kids safe."

"I hate to bother him with my problems. He put up with a lot of mistakes from me when I was learning the ropes. Being a nanny is more than babysitting, you know, especially when you're working with smart kids."

When she spoke, she gestured with her hands, but most of her animation came from her face. She punctuated her sentences with lifts of her eyebrows, scowls and grins and even a twitch of her freckled nose. The light makeup she'd worn at dinner had been wiped away, but she still looked good. He could watch her for hours and not get bored. "Did you get training on how to be a nanny? Did you go to nanny school?"

"I have a degree in psychology. Not that my studies help when Shane and Caine are punching each other. Or little Stella loses her magic wand." She grimaced and smirked at the same time. "I could probably use some instruction. I kind of lucked into this job, just showed up on Admiral Prescott's doorstep with no expectations. I didn't know they needed a nanny and didn't know I could be one."

"Tell me more."

"It was about a year ago. I was twenty-four, finished with college, living with my dad and working at the dojo. I didn't know what I wanted to do next. It needed to be something where I helped people, but I didn't know how or where. I liked the idea of working for something like the admiral's charity in sub-Saharan Africa." She tossed her head, setting her reddish curls into motion. "Or maybe not."

Somehow she'd gotten distracted. He pulled her back to the main topic. "Why were you on the admiral's doorstep?"

"There was this guy…" She paused and laughed. "How many wild stories have started off with those words? Anyway, this guy—his name was Anton—was kind of my boyfriend and he wanted to move in with me. Did I mention that I lived with my dad? Being the only girl in the family meant I did most of the cooking and shopping and laundry. In exchange, I didn't pay rent."

Once again, she'd gone skipping off on a tangent. He could feel her tension. Nervous energy had her running on high speed, making it hard to rein in her thoughts. He wanted to hold her and calm her down. Even though they had kissed, he had the feeling that this wasn't the right time. "When you were with your dad, did you like the arrangement?"

"I love my family. Living with Dad was comfortable. I'd work at the dojo, come home, cook dinner and handle a couple of chores. Then I'd do pretty much whatever I pleased. My biggest worry was that I'd get too cozy. On some fine day, I'd wake up and find out that I was seventy years old and never left home."

"Did you move in with Anton?"

"It was the other way around. He wanted to move in with me, with my family, which was a little creepy. And I couldn't imagine asking my dad. No. Way."

"Glad to hear it."

"Don't get me wrong," she said. "My dad liked my boyfriend. The two of them bonded over their guns. Anton worked as a hunting guide and had some high-profile positions. He'd even worked for the admiral, which impressed my dad because he knew the Admiral Prescott, too. Anyway, I wanted to—"

"Wait."

He held up a palm, signaling her to stop. Lexie seemed to be bounding over the relevant portions of this story.

She'd already mentioned that her father was stationed in the Middle East but never said he knew Prescott…and now her former boyfriend?

"Problem?" she asked.

"Your father, my brother and your boyfriend were all buddies with the admiral. That's an unbelievable coincidence."

"In the first place," she said, "I wouldn't exactly say they were buddies. More like acquaintances."

"You're right," he admitted.

"As for your brother and my dad, they were both in the Marine Corps, and both were stationed in the Middle East, where Admiral Prescott was one of the top guys running the show."

"What about the boyfriend?"

"He came looking for us because Prescott mentioned that he knew my dad and my dad lived in Austin. I met Anton through my father. I remember when I walked into the house and he saw me for the first time. His jaw dropped…literally. He thought I was something special."

Though Mason had never met the guy and probably never would, he didn't like this Anton character. What kind of man tries to move in with the father of his girlfriend? "When he asked to move in with you, did he propose?"

"I wouldn't let him. He hinted and I shut him down. I wasn't looking to settle down and get married. I told him he couldn't move into my dad's house and he should think again about our relationship." She gave another one of her adorable shrugs. "He left me without saying goodbye. He left a note that told me to kiss off."

When she met his gaze, Mason saw anger and determination in her chocolate-brown eyes. Her expression was similar to when she was shooting at the fake security guys.

Apparently, nobody told Lexie to kiss off and got away with it.

Now he understood how this twisted little story fit together. "You went looking for Anton."

"I wanted him to know that I broke up with him. Not the other way around. And I also wanted to get out of Austin for a while."

"You came to Colorado. To the admiral's doorstep."

"No sign of Anton. Prescott didn't remember him very well at all. Still, he invited me to stay for as long as I wanted, because of my dad." Her gaze drifted as she recalled. "I was surprised. I didn't think my dad was a big deal in the military, but I guess he was important enough for the admiral to think of him as a friend."

"And while you were there," Mason said, "you became the nanny."

"The nanny who was there when I arrived decided to quit. And I stepped in. I've never regretted it."

Her cell phone rang again.

She pulled it out and stared at the caller ID before she leaped to her feet. "Hi, Dad."

Chapter Five

Lexie's dad spoke in tough, uncompromising tones. Sure, he was retired, but he still hadn't stopped being the ultimate hard-ass Sergeant Major Daniel DeMille. "You listen to me, Franny, and you listen good."

"I'm not going by Franny anymore." She walked a few paces on the patterned hallway carpeting. "Call me Lexie."

"Your mother and I named you, and I'll call you whatever I damn well please, Miss Francine Alexandra DeMille."

The use of her full name was not a positive sign. Nor was the mention of her mother, who had divorced Daniel when Lexie was twelve. After Mom left, Dad didn't often link them together. In doing so, he seemed to be summoning up the ghost of a past that no longer existed. Perhaps it never had. Perhaps they had always been a dysfunctional family. With Mom gone, Grandma took over. And Dad was usually stationed on the other side of the world.

He growled. "You haven't returned my phone calls."

"I talked to you once and gave you my answer." She paced farther down the hall, noting that Mason kept a discreet distance but stayed with her.

"That answer, your answer, is unsatisfactory."

"I'm not going to change my mind," she said. "I won't quit my job and run home because you're worried about me."

"Either you get your rear end back to Texas or I'm coming to get you."

"I'm putting you on hold."

"Why?"

Because I'm furious and don't want to say something I'll regret later. "Excuse me, Dad."

She clicked him to silence and shook her fist at the cell phone. Her lips pinched together in a tight knot. Then she exhaled in a whoosh, blowing through her pursed lips like air coming out of a balloon.

She whirled around and looked at Mason. "My dad is treating me like I'm five years old. He's ticked off about what happened on the seventh floor."

"Did Prescott call him?"

"It was his assistant, Josh Laurent. You've probably met him. Long, pointy nose. Beady eyes. Stooped shoulders. He looks like a woodpecker."

"Yeah." Mason wiped the smile off his face. "We've met."

"Good old Josh didn't do a very good job of telling my dad what happened." She stopped beside a tiny desk with carved legs and a brass spittoon to one side. "He made that stupid ambush sound terrible and dangerous."

"It was dangerous. Those were real bullets. The blood on your arm? That was real, too."

"Really real," she muttered under her breath.

"What?"

"There's real life, which is what life is supposed to be. And really real life, which is how it actually is. Okay, for example, I'm a nanny in real life. In really real, I'm also an assistant, a nurse, a secretary and a teacher."

"In these real and extra real worlds of yours, where do you put the bullets?"

"Whose side are you on?"

"Yours," he said without hesitation. "But if you were my daughter, I'd be worried about you."

Men! They were all alike, thinking that women were helpless creatures who couldn't survive without one of them standing at her side and flexing his biceps. She was an adult. Not daddy's baby girl. Lexie could take care of herself.

She hadn't always been so independent and strong. When she came home from the hospital after her accident, she'd had serious nerve damage. Some docs had predicted that she'd never walk again. Her internal injuries had resulted in life-altering surgeries. She was scared, so deeply scared that she'd prayed to go to sleep and never wake up. It had seemed that life was too much to handle.

That was when her father stepped up and faced the challenge. Whether she needed him or not, he was there. Day and night, he watched over her and nursed her back to health. His gentle manner kept her spirits up. His firm encouragement reinforced her progress in physical therapy, where she literally started with baby steps.

After four weeks of recovery, when she'd been able to walk with crutches, she found out that he'd retired so he could take the time to be with her. Though he'd put in enough years with the military to qualify for a very nice pension and had plans for his retirement, she felt guilty about taking him away from a career he loved. The very last thing she wanted was to be a burden to her family.

She looked into Mason's steady blue eyes. "Why do you think my dad should worry about me?"

"Because he loves you."

Her tears sloshed and threatened to spill over her lower eyelids. Though the male of the species could be overbearing and pushy and demanding, they could also be achybreaky sweet. All that blustering and flexing was the way they showed that they cared.

Once again, she was stabbed in the gut by guilt. She didn't want to upset her dad. "In your professional opinion, do you think it's dangerous for me to stay with the Prescott family?"

"I can only assess one situation at a time. Right now I'm pretty sure that everybody's safe. Do you want me to talk to your father?"

"Not a good idea. Right at the moment, he doesn't think much of your abilities, even though I mentioned that you saved my life. And I explained how I ignored your advice to ride up on the elevator by myself."

He pointed to the phone. "You can't keep him on hold forever."

"I'm going back to my original plan." She tapped on the cell phone screen. "Dad, I'm going to have you talk to Admiral Prescott. He can explain why it won't be dangerous."

"I'll be waiting for that call."

She rolled her eyes at the phone. "I know you will."

PRESCOTT EMERGED FROM the banquet hall in full sail, leaving cheers and applause in his wake. There wasn't time for Lexie to ask him to talk to her father or to do anything else. With long determined strides, the admiral charged down the hall toward the conference room with the animal heads on the walls.

Before entering, he paused and straightened his necktie. "Be ready to move, Mason. I intend to get out of here ASAP."

"I understand," Mason said.

"Do you?" Prescott lifted an eyebrow.

"I'm not a police officer, but I'm sure there hasn't been enough time for thorough questioning and investigation.

Since you made the decision to stay at the hotel tonight, it seems wise to wait until morning, when you have enough information to know what needs to be done."

"My thoughts exactly."

Lexie felt like cheering. Mason's rational assessment made the crazy situation seem manageable. Not like her father, who was probably out by the barn shooting tin cans off the fence.

Mason said, "Lexie has something she needs to talk to you about."

"Of course." He pivoted to face her, held her at arm's length and peered into her eyes. "How are you holding up?"

"Good." She gave him what she hoped was a confident smile. "The problem is my dad."

"Danny-boy DeMille? He's a problem solver, not the other way around." He dropped his arms and raised his eyebrows. "Is he worried about you?"

"He's overreacting, right? I'm better equipped than most people to take care of myself. I'm good with a gun and an expert in karate and other martial arts."

"Sorry, kiddo, logic doesn't apply when it comes to family." He rubbed his chin. "On the off chance we might have some clear intel that your dad would want to hear, I want you to come into this meeting with me and Mason. After that, I'll make the call."

"Thank you."

"This is as much for my benefit as yours. I don't want to lose you as the kids' nanny."

The compliment was nice to hear. She followed Prescott inside and took a seat near the end of the table beside Josh. What a jerk he was! She felt like punching him but held back. Instead, she smiled and nodded to several of the people at the table whom she'd met before when they visited the Prescotts' home in Aspen.

Sitting to the admiral's left was Hank Grossman—a slouchy, sloppy, middle-aged man with hair that looked like steel wool. Instead of waving, he pointed at her as though his fingers were a gun—a gesture that was particularly inappropriate given the circumstances. Did he mean to threaten her? Was she working with the bad guys? Lexie copied his gesture and pretended to shoot back at him. *Take that, Grossman.*

He was with the NSA. She knew his job was top secret but had no idea what he did or what his title was or anything else about him, other than he couldn't get through a meal without dribbling a smear on his necktie.

Beside Grossman was Sam Bertinelli, also NSA, who was dark with classic features and much more pleasant. He gave her a nod and a wink. His buttoned-down appearance was well suited for a junior executive, but Bertinelli was a little too old to be a junior anything. Certainly too old for her, which was basically what she'd told him when he'd asked her out on a date a few months ago. They had both been polite, but she'd seen the flare of hostility in his hazel eyes. The two NSA dudes were a little scary.

Josh's pointy woodpecker nose jabbed in her direction. "I spoke to your father."

"I'm aware," she said in a low voice oozing with sarcasm. "You made it sound like we were under assault from terrorist madmen. He's freaked."

"Odd. He's a marine. I didn't think he'd get upset."

She hated the insinuation. Her dad was tougher than nails; he could handle anything. "Are you saying that my dad is a wimp?"

"Hush, now."

"Take it back."

"Fine."

His head swiveled so he faced the head of the table.

Again, he reminded her of a bird with virtually no neck and a round, soft body. Why did Prescott keep him around as an assistant? Josh was neither smart nor funny nor pleasant. He did, however, fulfill whatever he was ordered to do without question or hesitation. She supposed there was something to be said for blind obedience.

Including Josh, there were seven men seated around the table and two women, one in uniform and one in a body-hugging cocktail dress with one shoulder bare.

At the head of the table, next to the bared shoulder, was a slick, good-looking guy. He rose to his feet and buttoned the front of his tux. He wasn't as tall as Mason, who was standing behind the admiral, and he wasn't as muscular. But a lot of women would have found his sweep of glistening blond hair and brilliant blue eyes appealing. The tux helped.

She leaned toward Josh. "Who's that?"

"Robert Collier, CIA."

His voice was a bit higher than she expected and had an interesting accent. Maybe French? Lexie had gotten accustomed to these suave, international men who came to visit at the Prescott home in Aspen. She suspected Collier would be a hand kisser.

"The woman next to him," she whispered to Josh, "is also CIA?"

Josh nodded.

Apparently, Collier had been waiting for the admiral to return. He addressed the group. "In my interrogation of the four men in custody, I have learned that they are part of a group called the Anti-Conspiracy Committee for Democracy, or the AC-CD."

The name of the group didn't sound dangerous. Nobody in this room was against democracy. And who wasn't anti-conspiracy? Resting her elbow on the table, she leaned forward and focused on Collier.

He pointed to the flat screen mounted on the wall behind where she was sitting. She turned to look over her shoulder. The screen was blank. Mounted on the wall near the door was an elk head with an impressive ten-point rack. On the other side of the screen was a seriously ugly boar with curly tusks.

"I would usually have photos and a logo," he said in his lilting accent, "but the members of the very loosely organized AC-CD pride themselves on being anonymous. They meet in groups of no more than five. The head of AC-CD is referred to as the leader, and sometimes different people take that responsibility."

Bertinelli nudged the shoulder of his NSA boss as he pointed out the obvious. "For a group opposed to conspiracy, they have a lot of secrets."

"That is why," Collier said with a cold glance toward the NSA contingent, "it is complicated to compile facts and information about the AC-CD."

"How did you get them to talk?" Bertinelli asked.

"They would hardly shut up. I have never had an interrogation like this. They were eager to tell me that their job was vitally important on a global level. They all used the same words—'vital importance' and 'international repercussions' and more of those catchphrases."

He swore in French and stuck out his jaw. His icy blond hair shimmered under the overhead lights.

"Excuse me," said the uniformed woman, "but what was the job they were assigned to do?"

"To kidnap the admiral."

All eyes focused on Prescott. Unperturbed, he shrugged and said, "Then they weren't after my children. Is that correct?"

"Correct, sir."

"Or my wife."

"Just you," Collier said. "Their plan was to drug your wife's bedtime drink so she would sleep soundly. When everything was quiet, they would slip into your bedroom and abduct you. Under no circumstances were they supposed to hurt you."

"Why?" Prescott asked.

"They are searching for the Damascus Cache, and they believe you have knowledge of its whereabouts."

Prescott scoffed. "The Damascus Cache was destroyed years ago."

Beside her, Josh wriggled in his chair like a schoolboy who had the right answer to the teacher's question. She gave him a nudge. "Go ahead and speak up."

"I better not." That was why he was a woodpecker and not an eagle. To her, he whispered, "I've heard chatter. People talking about the cache."

Her cell phone buzzed. A text was coming through from Megan, the oldest Prescott kid. It said, Hurry back. The brats won't go to bed.

It was kind of amazing that Lexie had been away for as long as she had without a minor crisis or two from the children. It looked as though she'd have to wait until later to get Prescott to talk to her dad.

She stood and pointed to her phone. "Please excuse me. Duty calls. I need to go upstairs and tell some bedtime stories."

"I'll be up soon," Prescott said. "Mason, accompany her."

He was at her side so quickly that he was turning the doorknob before she could touch it. In the hallway, he closed the door and spoke into his headset.

When he was beside her, she asked, "Who were you talking to?"

"Dylan. He has cameras in the conference room so he can keep an eye on things until I get back."

"Do you need to go back?"

"Prescott asked me to stay close."

She didn't like the way that sounded. "He doesn't trust the people around him."

"Do you blame him?"

"Not really."

The men and women in that conference room were spies, spooks and feds—high-ranking members of the intelligence community. It dawned on her that she'd met several of these people. "Do you think my dad is right? Am I in danger?"

"Not right now."

As they strolled to the elevators, his vigilant attitude relaxed, and he seemed to shed his bodyguard persona. She liked being with him. And he must like her, too. He'd kissed her, after all.

She pushed the elevator button. "Should I stay with the Prescotts or should I quit?"

"Do you like your job?"

"I do. It's not a career I want for the rest of my life, but I like it."

"Are you scared?"

She thought for a moment before answering. In the bathroom upstairs, she'd had a few moments of intense panic when she'd fallen through a time warp to relive her accident. But her fear had dissipated. "I'm cautious but not frightened."

"Cautious is good," he said as they boarded the elevator. "There's no glory in taking risks."

"I don't know what to do."

The elevator doors closed. They were wrapped together in a wood-paneled cocoon. She caught a whiff of his citrusy aftershave. She slowly blinked. In her imagination, their clothes melted away. In another long blink, they twined in each other's arms. A gush of passion swept through her.

An elevator bell dinged when they hit the seventh floor, and she focused on him. He was watching her with a wary but bemused expression. "You checked out. What were you thinking?"

She stepped into the hallway outside the elevator. The teddy bear on the side table that had been gunned down earlier had already been replaced by a new stuffed animal. No way would she tell him that she'd fantasized about him. Instead, she switched direction. "You haven't answered me. Stay or go back to Texas?"

"I don't think there's a logical solution," he said. "What does your heart tell you?"

Lexie didn't usually think of things in touchy-feely terms; she wasn't raised that way. But she did have feelings about her job. Going back to her father's house felt like admitting defeat. Along that line, she wasn't one to be scared off.

Her heart also told her that she liked being part of the Prescott clan. With them, she shared intimate family moments that had never been possible with her brothers and father.

And there was one more heartfelt reason. She thought of it as she watched the two littlest Prescott kids dashing down the hallway toward her with the huge Carlos in pursuit. If she left Colorado, she would probably never see Mason again.

She turned to him and gave a decisive nod. "I'm staying."

Chapter Six

The next morning at nine o'clock, Mason climbed into the passenger side of a golf cart beside Admiral Prescott. Following an asphalt path, Prescott drove from the practice putting green toward the first tee. In normal circumstances, Mason enjoyed the game and was a couple of notches under par. From a bodyguard's perspective, he hated golf. Everybody on the course was carrying a bag filled with metal implements, providing a handy hiding place for a gun or rifle. Though Mason would be sticking tight to the admiral for close-in protection, they were surrounded by forested hills where an army of bad guys could be lurking.

The local sheriff had his deputies combing through the trees and rocks, and helicopters made occasional swoops, but there was no effective way to shield against an assault from a sniper with a long-range precision rifle. Those babies were accurate at a thousand yards.

Mason took comfort in the knowledge that the Anti-Conspiracy Committee for Democracy plan was for kidnapping and not assassination. Also, if the guys they picked up last night were any sample, the AC-CD was a committee of numskulls.

Last night he'd heard more details from CIA Agent Collier's interrogation. The AC-CD thugs had broken into the admiral's room and downloaded the contents of his computer and his wife's computer onto memory sticks. They'd readily admitted to Collier that they didn't think the admiral was careless enough to transport the Damascus Cache on his personal computer, but they needed to look everywhere.

Their kidnapping plot was foiled when Lexie showed up too early on the seventh floor. Her appearance caught them unprepared; they'd only had time to get changed and drag a couple of the real guards into a vacant room to hide their unconscious bodies. The real guards had been zapped by stun guns and none of them were seriously injured. The only person to require an ambulance was the guy Lexie had karate kicked into dreamland.

The thought of the petite, auburn-haired nanny beating up an armed bad guy brought a smile to Mason's face. This mental image of Lexie was a pleasant distraction. Behind his sunglasses, he kept his eyes in motion, scanning the hillsides, anticipating threats before they became real.

"I'm glad you and your men are here," Prescott said.

"You're the boss. We'll stay as long as you want."

"Good to know." He checked his wristwatch. "In about an hour, I'll need to pull away from the rest of the foursome and take a meeting on the computer."

"A face-to-face meeting?"

"Yes, your partner Dylan set it up for me. He says all I have to do is turn on the laptop and push one button."

"I'll make sure the meeting stays private." Mason glanced over at Prescott. His close-cropped white hair was covered by a dark blue cap with *NAVY* written in gold. He was tanned and looked healthy in khakis and a lightweight gray sweater. "Lexie said you were keeping TST around because you don't trust these other guys."

"She's a very perceptive young woman—her father's

daughter." Prescott frowned. "My conversation with him last night could have gone better. I get it. The man is concerned. Hell, I'd feel the same way if one of my kids had been attacked. But I believe these idiots were after me, not the nanny or Helena or the children. They should all be safe."

"What did her father say to her?"

"He was willing to have Lexie stay."

And that was fortunate, because she'd already made up her mind about what she intended to do. "Do you mind if I ask a personal question?"

"Go ahead."

Mason cleared his throat. "Is Lexie dating anyone?"

"When she first came to us, she asked about a boyfriend by the name of Anton. But she's forgotten him. And she's only gone out on a couple of dates." He gave a sly grin. "Any other questions?"

"When is her next day off?"

MASON ACCOMPANIED THE FOURSOME: Prescott, Collier and the two NSA guys—Hank Grossman and Sam Bertinelli. Predictably, Collier was a superb golfer with picture-perfect form. Bertinelli wasn't half bad, but took way too long to set up each shot, testing the wind direction and picking bits of grass out of the way. The admiral played solid, par-level golf. And Grossman cheated.

Since they were zipping around in golf carts, the only chance for conversation was on the green. Collier, Prescott and Bertinelli followed golf etiquette and kept their voices low so they wouldn't disturb the putter. Grossman wasn't so polite.

"Listen up, boys," Grossman growled. Mason guessed that the gray-haired, stoop-shouldered man was older than the admiral, definitely north of sixty. "Let's take advantage of this time alone to talk about the Damascus Cache. We all know what it is. Don't pretend that you don't."

"I've heard talk," Prescott said, "about a comprehensive list of personnel and weapons in the Middle East and sub-Saharan Africa. A cache of information, compiled several years ago at the end of the Bush administration."

"More valuable than a cache of gold," Grossman said.

"Not all of it." Prescott's ball was in a bunker, farthest from the hole. Therefore, he was first to shoot. After selecting a wedge club, he positioned his feet in the sand, straightened his shoulders, glanced at the flag and hit a perfect chip shot. The ball stopped a mere six inches from the hole.

As he tapped his ball into the cup, he continued, "There were lists of supplies, locations of arsenals and maps of supply lines. At least, I'd guess the cache included that information—details that are now worthless."

"It is about the people," Collier said.

The next to putt was Bertinelli. His ball was about thirty-five feet from the hole, and Mason guessed it was going to take five minutes for Bertinelli to test the wind and tamp down divots. A waste of time—this average golfer wasn't going to make such a long putt.

"I agree about the danger posed to the people on this list," said Prescott. "I'm not saying that I've ever seen the cache or that I even know it exists, but I'd guess that it would give details about intelligence operatives for the military, the CIA, NSA and Interpol. Many were undercover."

"Many still are," Collier said. "These are people who may or may not still be involved in espionage. Some have dropped off the grid and are leading normal lives. They are married. They have children."

"Ha!" Grossman exploded with a loud, humorless laugh.

"I'm guessing that these former spies sure as hell don't want their names made public."

"Exposure would be a death warrant."

Finally in position over the ball, Bertinelli looked confused. "Why would AC-CD want the list?"

"Hurry up and putt," Grossman said. "As for the AC-CD, they claim to be anti-conspiracy. So they might think they're doing the world a favor by causing trouble for spies."

"An altruistic motive," Prescott said.

"Yeah, yeah, they're shining a light on the truth. That kind of phony-baloney."

Mason pinched his lips together to keep from blurting out his ideas and opinions. His college degree was in international relations. Because his brother had been stationed in the Middle East, he'd focused on that area and on Africa. These were lands where espionage ran rampant, lands where bribes were more common than taxes, lands of genocide. Heinous battles were motivated by politics, religion, ethnicity and plain old greed. He seriously doubted that AC-CD wanted the Damascus Cache to expose the truth.

Bertinelli tapped his ball. It traveled slowly but steadily and...plink! He sank the putt and gave a victorious arm pump. This guy wasn't the sharpest tool in the shed, but he shouldn't be counted out.

"I got the answer," Grossman said. "Destroy the damn list. Delete it from all servers. Encrypt the hell out of it."

While he babbled about how they could destroy the cache, he misfired on a four-foot putt. His ball was about as far from the hole as Collier's, which was good enough for Grossman. He scooped it off the green and into his pocket. "That's a gimme."

Collier spoke in his smooth, lightly accented voice as he lined up his putt. "We cannot destroy something that we do not have. The Damascus Cache, whether it exists or not, is nowhere to be found."

The stroke of his putter was as elegant as his tailored black trousers and cashmere sweater. When the ball dropped into the hole, he casually removed his sunglasses. His blue-eyed gaze zeroed in on Prescott. "I wonder, Admiral, why do these people believe that you are in possession of the cache?"

"A damned good question," Grossman bellowed. "I know you worked in intelligence with the navy SEALs, but you're retired."

Not to be left out, Bertinelli added his two cents. "You're a surprising target, sir. You have a reputation for not being comfortable with computer technology."

"True," Prescott said. "I still have trouble figuring out how to make my phone send texts."

"Why you?" Collier repeated.

The admiral didn't even attempt to answer. He shrugged, checked his wristwatch and started walking toward their cart. "Play the next hole without me. I'll catch up after I take a meeting."

"We're going to miss you," Grossman called after him.

"I'll bet."

The admiral drove the cart toward a grove of aspens that were several yards off the fairway. Apparently, he wanted privacy for this meeting. Not only did he put distance between them and the others in the foursome, but the outdoor location made it difficult for anyone else to overhear. Mason knew that his buddy Dylan would have set up a computerized meeting that was nearly impossible to hack.

"I need you to keep time," Prescott said as he handed Mason the Luminox wristwatch preferred by the SEALs. "I need to log on at precisely 10:44 and log off at 10:59."

Mason took the watch. Three minutes until log-on. The

admiral had the computer open on his lap. He flexed his fingers and cleared his throat. And then...

"Trouble approaching," Mason said.

A golf cart with a distinctive pink top bounced across the fairway toward them. In the driver's seat, Helena hunched over the steering wheel like a speed racer and squealed wildly on every bump. Riding shotgun, Lexie clung to the fringed pink top and laughed.

The admiral shook his head and grinned. "That's my woman."

A lot of men, especially those in positions of authority, would have been annoyed by Helena's wild driving, but Prescott was amused, even a little bit proud of his flamboyant wife.

"Sir." Mason tapped the face of the watch. "It's time."

Prescott touched the correct computer key, and the laptop screen showed a broad-shouldered man sitting at a desk. His face was easily recognizable from television talk shows—a lantern jaw, heavy brows and thick black hair with silver streaks at the temple. He was the Secretary of the Navy, Thomas Benson.

"Good morning," Prescott said.

"Maybe where you are it's morning." Benson's jaw lifted, and he scowled into the screen. "Here at the Pentagon it's past my feeding time. What's happening, Prescott? Tell me about these anti-conspiracy whack jobs."

"Not much to tell," he replied. "My concern is the Damascus Cache. I thought we'd destroyed every copy."

Mason took note of the change in Prescott's attitude. With the other golfers, he'd been cagey about whether or not the Damascus Cache even existed. While he was talking to the SecNav, a veteran officer who was a peer and an equal, there was a total lack of pretense. These two spoke truth to each other.

The SecNav shook his head. "I can't be certain that one copy didn't get away from us."

"Who was responsible for getting rid of this intelligence?"

"Your old buddy, Al Ackerman."

"I was afraid you'd say that."

With one last squeal, Helena parked next to them in the shadow of the aspens. She bounded from the cart and came around so she could see over her husband's shoulder. The instant she recognized the man on the screen, she fluttered her fingertips in a wave. "Hello there, Tommy."

"Helena." His smile was so broad it looked as if his jaw would unhinge. "Lovely as ever, and who's that with you?"

"Our nanny, Lexie DeMille," she said as she dragged Lexie into the camera range.

Mason noticed how Lexie's posture went from relaxed to as stiff as steel rebar, almost as though she was standing at attention. He understood why she straightened up. No matter where she went or what she became, Lexie was a military brat. SecNav was a man of the highest rank and authority.

"It's a pleasure to meet you, sir," she said with a slight quaver in her voice.

Prescott said, "She's Danny DeMille's daughter. As long as I'm making introductions, my bodyguard is Mason Steele. His brother was Matthew."

To his amazement, the SecNav saluted him. "Matthew Steele was a hero. His quick thinking saved thirty-seven children. My condolences to you and to your parents."

"Thank you, sir."

Mason was reeling. The SecNav knew his brother. More than that, he knew something about the circumstances of Matthew's death. He had posthumously been awarded a Purple Heart, his second such award, so his family had known that he'd died honorably. Still, hearing the details would mean a great deal to Mason's parents.

With a start, he realized that Prescott was talking to him, telling him to move the ladies out of the way while he finished his conversation. Mason herded Lexie and Helena deeper into the aspen grove while leaving a clear route back to the admiral in case he needed to get back there in a hurry.

"Wow," Lexie said. "Thomas Benson knows who my dad is. I can't believe it! And I met him, too."

"He's just good old Tommy," Helena said. "The man is a sweetheart and a ham. Did you know that he was a pilot?"

Both Mason and Lexie nodded. Though he was interested in her story, he kept one eye on Prescott. Mason was curious about the "old buddy" named Ackerman. Why had the admiral expressed concern when the SecNav mentioned him?

"At a karaoke bar in DC," Helena continued, "Tommy and Prescott serenaded me. Can you guess what they sang?"

Lexie nodded. "The SecNav was a top gun. I'm guessing they sang 'You've Lost That Lovin' Feelin'.'"

"Of course, you're right."

Helena started singing, and Lexie backed her up. Damn, they were cheerful. If he hadn't known better, he wouldn't have believed that Lexie had recently been in a firefight and Helena's husband was under threat of abduction. Was the singing and smiling a front? Showing a brave face so the kids wouldn't be scared?

He took a long moment to study Lexie. Her black jeans fit smoothly. On the top, she wore a white shirt with an eyelet trim under an embroidered denim jacket. Once again, her curly hair was yanked up in a high ponytail.

He liked the casual version of Lexie. If she was faking this carefree attitude, he'd have to nominate her for an award.

Prescott motioned for them to join him as he powered down the laptop and closed it. Still singing and snapping her fingers, Helena approached him and kissed both cheeks, leaving a scarlet imprint of lipstick.

"Are we okay?" she asked.

"We're fine," he assured her. "But I'm going to need to spend another day or two at the Pentagon next week."

"Next week is the start of our summer schedule. We're all taking off in different directions, and I want to get packed and organized."

Prescott looked around her shoulder to make eye contact with Lexie. "How about it—are you ready to organize the Prescott troops?"

"Ready to try," she said.

"How's the arm?"

"Doesn't hurt a bit. At the worst, I'll have another scar to add to my collection."

Mason had wanted to ask the same thing. What did she mean about a collection of scars? There was so much more he wanted to know about her.

Prescott took on a serious expression. "I want to promise you, Lexie, that we will find and destroy any existing copies of the Damascus Cache. But I know better than to make guarantees that cannot be fulfilled with certainty."

"I'm sure you'll do your best." Her lips twisted in a confused smile. "But I'm not sure why this would be important to me."

"The cache is a list of undercover operatives in the Middle East. It was generated several years ago." He took her hand and squeezed. "Your father's name is on it."

Chapter Seven

Tony Curtis blended in with the valets handling parking at the boutique hotel. He'd grabbed a uniform—a black vest and a bolo tie—from the garage, and he found a name tag in the top drawer of a beat-up desk by the lockers. The name was Andy. Not entirely accurate, but close enough. He sidled up the drive to the desk at the front entrance, where guests were checking out and demanding their vehicles.

Though he was probably fifteen years older than the other valets, his build was as lean and wiry as an eighteen-year-old's, and he'd plucked the few gray hairs from his thick black mane. It was no problem for him to pass himself off as a young dude with a hard-luck story.

Along with the rest of the crew, he hustled back and forth to the underground parking to retrieve the Escalades, Bimmers and Hummers. He let the other guys do most of the work. They didn't care. This was a job that ran on tips.

Tony made no effort to be secretive or to hide. Instead, he acted as if he belonged. He played his role as a guy who was too old to be making a living as a valet…doing it anyway but not even trying to do it well.

A job like this might have been his really real life. He smirked at the thought, acknowledging that the person who had babbled about really real life was Franny, who now wanted to be called Lexie. Hell, why not? Lexie rhymed with sexy, and that suited her. She was hot, sexier now than when he'd known her. He was almost glad he hadn't killed her.

What set him apart from the other valets was his intense training with firearms and his instinct for murder. In the past few moments, he'd been tempted to lash out. Taking gratuities made him feel like a servant. When a pompous, red-faced rich man dribbled a one-dollar bill into Tony's outstretched hand and stood waiting for a "thank you, sir," a homicidal urge boiled up inside the not-really-a-valet.

Since metal detectors were all over the hotel, he hadn't hidden a gun up his sleeve. Nor was he carrying the well-honed hunting knife he used to gut and clean a deer in five minutes. Tony had two weapons strapped to his chest under his vest. One was a stun gun. The other was a razor-sharp plastic chef's blade.

He locked gazes with the pompous hotel guest. Tony could kill this fool in ways that didn't require a weapon. With a deft twist, he could snap the rich man's neck. Eye gouging was an option. Or a quick, lethal chop to the trachea.

The rich man must have recognized Tony's deeper nature, because he peeled off a ten to accompany the one-dollar bill, quickly dived behind the steering wheel of his shiny SUV and drove away.

Nobody paid any attention when Tony edged around to the side of the hotel and pulled out a cigarette. From this vantage point, he could see the admiral and his buddies playing golf. Life would have been so much easier if he could have just killed the admiral. The kidnapping scheme meant the admiral had to be incapacitated and then removed from the scene. Neither would happen while the bodyguard protected him.

Tony traced the edge of the leather knife sheath fastened to his chest. He came to the conclusion that the only way to abduct the admiral required killing the bodyguard.

THOUGH THE DAY was sunny and clear, Lexie felt cold shadows closing around her, tweaking her shoulders and sending shivers down her spine. Standing on the balcony outside her hotel room, she stared into the warm blue Colorado sky and thought about Texas, the closest place she had to a home. Like most military families, the DeMilles had moved from base to base around the country while her parents were together. After the split, she and her brothers had been raised by her grandma in Austin while her dad was stationed far away. And working as a spy?

She hadn't even known that the marines had spies, but of course they did. Every branch of the military had intelligence officers, and the SEALs were totally involved in undercover ops. Still, she didn't think of her dad as a secret agent. How could that be? Suave wasn't part of his vocabulary. He was loud, demanding and straightforward… just about as subtle as a charging Brahman bull.

But the SecNav and Admiral Prescott wouldn't lie to her. According to those two, Danny DeMille was not only a spy, but in danger of being outed by something called the Damascus Cache. What could she do? How was she going to keep her dad safe?

The smartest move would be to rush home, throw a fence around him and shoot anybody who got too close. As if he'd put up with that? His lifestyle didn't exactly lend itself to the efforts of a bodyguard. Why couldn't he be a typical retired dad who stayed at home and puttered and watched football on TV?

When he'd left the marines and come home to nurse her back to health, she felt bad about making him change his whole life. He confided that being a soldier hadn't been his number one choice, anyway. His cherished goal in life was to be a cowboy. After she was mostly recovered, he made his dream become really real when he found a job with a buddy who owned a dude ranch. The work suited him. Her dad was the Marlboro Man without the cigarettes.

She heard a rap on the door and turned. "Come in."

Mason pushed open the door. She hadn't expected to see him again but was glad he'd shown up. Last night, she'd experienced a wonderful, luscious sleep filled with X-rated fantasies about this tall, muscular man with the sky blue eyes and the buzz-cut hair. Whether her dreams were a result of the pain pills the hotel doctor had given her or came from a deeper need, she hadn't wanted to wake up this morning.

With his hand on the knob, he stood framed in her doorway like a cover photo. He looked great in his khaki trousers, collared shirt and the dark blue sports jacket he wore to cover his gun holster. And what would she call this portrait? Casual stud? Golfing bodyguard? Husky, handsome hunk?

She cleared her throat. "Are you done with your golf round?"

"Prescott only played the front nine. He wanted to come back here and talk to Helena before she took off with you and the kids."

"So you left the two of them—the admiral and his wife—alone in their bedroom suite," she said. "Is that proper bodyguard procedure?"

"Not really." With the door to Lexie's room still open, he turned his head and looked down the hall toward the suite. "I should be right outside his door, but I wanted to catch you before you left."

She truly enjoyed hearing those words. The chill of fear

that had been poking at her melted a bit. Mason warmed her in many different ways. She floated across the room, stood beside him and whispered, "What did you want to say to me?"

"Prescott said you'd talked to your dad. Are you going back to Austin?"

The apprehensions that had been momentarily swept aside surged to the forefront of her mind. "Do you think I should?"

"If you're scared, my answer is yes." Parallel lines creased his forehead as he considered. "However, I don't think you need to feel nervous or afraid. The AC-CD is after the admiral, and he's planning to fly straight to the Pentagon after one more round of golf with big donors."

"Hold on there. He's supposed to return to the house with us." She followed Mason's glance toward the suite. "Oh, I see. He's trying to explain. I don't think Helena expected him to go to the Pentagon so soon. He's retired, supposedly."

"He mentioned that I might want to protect him from her."

"Indeed," she said.

Helena had a temper, and she'd be plenty angry that her husband was escaping the hectic hassle of getting ready for the summer season. During the next few days, the kids would be taking off in different directions for different projects. Even Helena was busy—scheduled to be filming in Toronto.

"The admiral has to fend for himself when it comes to his wild and crazy wife," Mason said. "I'm worried about you."

"Me?" She pulled one fist to her waist and thrust the other forward in a karate pose. "I can take care of myself."

"You are wise, Lexie-*san*. Not going back to Texas?"

"I didn't say that." She dropped the pose. "I'm nervous about my father being named in the Damascus Cache. He's done so much for me. He stayed with me when I thought I was going to die. At the very least, I should run home and watch his back."

"I thought you had brothers in Austin."

"I do." Unfortunately, contacting her brothers and telling them about the threat wasn't possible. The admiral had made her promise not to tell anyone else. "The Damascus Cache is top secret."

"Right."

"I could try to convince my dad to go into hiding. Maybe he'd qualify for witness protection."

She seriously doubted that he'd agree to any form of protection, even if it made sense. Whether he was wearing his dress blue uniform or riding the range in his favorite Stetson, her dad was a manly man. He believed in uncommon valor and never ran from a fight.

"Best-case scenario," Mason said, "Prescott locates the existing copy of the cache—if there is such a thing—and he destroys it."

She didn't understand why it should be the admiral's job to deal with the cache. He was retired. Why didn't the AC-CD understand that? Why had they come after Prescott? And why wasn't she taking this conversation with Mason to a more interesting place? "Enough about my dad."

"Talking about him is important. If you leave to watch over him, I have to drive over nine hundred miles to take you out to dinner."

"And if I don't go?"

"It's a mere two hundred miles from Denver to Aspen. When's your next day off?"

"Thursday," she said quickly. In her mind, that date was

lit up in neon party colors. Five days from now on Thursday, the Prescott family would be pursuing their summer adventures. She'd have the house to herself.

"I'll pick you up at five." With most guys, hand kisses were smarmy. Not Mason. He lifted her hand and lightly pressed his full lips against her knuckles. The resulting angle of her arm was a bit uncomfortable. She winced.

"Does it hurt?" he asked. "The bullet wound?"

"I hardly feel it." There were light twinges when she moved her arm a certain way, and she intended to baby herself for a couple of days—not lifting children or carrying luggage.

"What did you mean when you said it was another scar for your collection?"

"I was in a car accident. Operations on both legs left some interesting marks, and I've got a couple of surgical scars on my abdomen."

"That sounds serious."

"A hit-and-run," she said dismissively. Her accident was definitely *not* something she wanted to talk about. Instead, she concentrated on the fun she'd have going out with Mason. "Where should we eat?"

"Do you like German?"

"Ja, ich liebe Strudel."

"You love strudel. Me, too." He chuckled. "Tell me more about this car accident. How old were you?"

"Fresh out of college." She shook her head. No more about the accident. "Five o'clock is an early start for a date."

"We'll have a couple of German beers before we eat." He cocked his head to one side. "I want to hear more about this accident."

"There's not much to say. Another car clipped my fender. I lost control and drove my brother's car over a cliff. While I was crashing, I was more scared about how mad he'd be that I broke his car."

"And was he?"

The familiar ache crept over her. Her brothers had been only concerned about her. In fact, the one whose car she'd been driving blamed himself for not having a safer vehicle. "You know, Mason, I don't want to talk about the accident. I should have died, but I didn't. That's all."

He gently glided his hand down her uninjured arm and held her hand. "You don't mind having another scar?"

"Not from a bullet wound." She lifted her chin and looked up at him. "It's kinda cool. That's what the kids say."

"The twins caught a glimpse of you doing a flying kick on the armed man outside the elevator. Impressive move!"

"Yeah, they think I'm awesome until the next time I tell them they can't drink a gallon of their favorite high-octane energy drink before bed." She knew it wouldn't take long for the kids to slot her back into the boring-nanny category.

"Kids keep you grounded. The Prescott gang doesn't care that their father is an international consultant. Mom is a movie star? So what?"

Those were perceptive observations for a guy who was essentially an only child and didn't have regular contact with children. "How come you're not a daddy?"

"I haven't found the right mommy." Still holding her hand, he pivoted slightly to face her. His gaze bored into hers. "I wouldn't mind settling down and having a family. Not that I'm looking…"

But he was, she could tell. She felt him peering into her eyes, trying to discover a sign that she was the one he was looking for. Could she be the right mommy for his children?

Part of her wanted to fling herself into his arms and tell

him that she was the one. *Yes, pick me.* But motherhood wasn't in her future. It was cruel to lead him on. Dating her would be a waste of his time.

Before she could say anything, the door to the Prescott suite opened and the admiral stepped out. His gray sweater was askew. He was carrying his hat and his shoes. Helena appeared in the doorway behind him, wearing a sultry smile and a filmy black negligee with a feather trim that made it over-the-top.

Mason whispered, "Looks like they're done fighting."

"And have moved on to makeup sex." Lexie was familiar with this pattern. Passionate arguments followed by what she could only assume was equally passionate lovemaking was typical. "Here's what's strange about the movie star/love goddess. She's kind of a prude."

"Hmm." Mason wasn't actually drooling, but was clearly mesmerized by the voluptuous body under the sheer black fabric. "You don't say."

"But I do." She pulled her hand back and punched his arm. "Here's how Helena rolls. After marriage, anything goes. But she won't allow unmarried couples to sleep in the same bedroom in her house. That might explain why she's been married five times."

"Probably," he agreed.

Prescott waved to him as he stuck his toe into his right shoe. "Let's go, Mason."

"Apparently, we're done playing golf. The admiral isn't wearing his spiked golf shoes, just sneakers." He took a step away from her. "There's another alternative—something else you could do about your dad."

She followed him, taking two steps in his direction. "What is it?"

"Do you remember how I said this could all be over

if the admiral found copies of the cache and destroyed them?"

"Yes." Of course she remembered. It had only been a few minutes ago.

"Admiral Prescott isn't the only one who has access. I'll bet you've overheard more top secret intelligence than most high-clearance agents are told."

"Me?" Her voice was a squeak. "You think I could figure this out?"

"It's better than sitting around doing nothing."

As Mason hustled down the hall to the admiral's side, she watched his retreating form. She liked the breadth of his shoulders and his athletic stride. If she'd had a clear view of his bottom under his jacket, she probably would have liked that, too. More than anything, she appreciated the way his mind worked.

Someone had to locate the mysterious Damascus Cache. Why not her? Mason was correct when he said that she'd overheard a lot of high-level intelligence. Most people didn't pay much attention to the nanny. She'd have to put it all together and figure it out. She was good at puzzles. The solution couldn't be that complicated. She could do it.

Her father had devoted much of his life to protecting his home and country. He had always kept her safe. Now it was her turn.

Find the cache. Save her dad.

Chapter Eight

Given her new agenda about searching for and ultimately destroying the Damascus Cache, Lexie looked forward to the fifty-minute drive from the hotel to the family's home near Aspen. She'd have a chance to talk with Helena and get the inside scoop. No matter how much Lexie had overheard during the last couple of days, those meetings, discussions and consultations weren't the same as private conversations.

The admiral often chose to confide the most important details to his wife. He didn't blab about troop movements or spy craft or undercover operations, but he told her the human stories—the incidents that affected his heart.

More than once this morning, Lexie had noticed Helena studying her with a goopy, sympathetic expression on her beautiful face. Neither of the Prescotts was the sort of person who treated the nanny like a piece of furniture, but they weren't all buddy-buddy. Lexie's wild ride across the golf course with Helena was an exception to the rule. They were always friendly, but didn't hug each other every five minutes, which was exactly the way Lexie liked it.

How come Helena kept looking at her and exhaling a massive, dramatic sigh? What did she know? And how could Lexie get the admiral's wife to open up? There were a lot of distractions, but that was inescapable with six children.

At the front of the hotel, the kids fought about who got to sit where. Lexie moved closer to Helena, watching as the hotel porters loaded suitcases into the back of the second SUV.

"Ridiculous," Helena murmured. "We have too much stuff."

"No way around the baggage," Lexie said. "Including me, there are suitcases for ten people. Six kids, you and the admiral, plus me and Josh."

"Some days, it feels like all we do is pack and unpack."

"So true." Impatiently, Lexie waited for the right moment when she could change the topic from luggage to espionage.

"I told Josh he couldn't ride with us."

"Good." Let the woodpecker use his own car. "What about the admiral?"

"Edgar will be taking a chopper. Top Gun Tommy decided that my husband needs military protection, so he has a couple of stiff-neck men in uniform tromping along behind him."

Lexie didn't bother correcting her about the top gun status; the SecNav ranked way higher than that. But she had another concern. If Prescott had military bodyguards, he didn't need TST Security, which meant that Mason wouldn't be coming back to the house with them. Damn it, she missed him already. "What are the driving arrangements for you and me?"

"You drive the car in front with the older kids, and I'll take this one with the twins and the babies, and I'll use a driver from the hotel."

Lexie had wanted time alone with Helena, but that wasn't going to happen on this ride with only the two of them to handle all the kids. Later she'd find a time for a private talk with Helena.

The twins positioned themselves on either side of Lexie. Caine rested his shaggy blond head against her shoulder. "I want to ride with you."

Shane did the same with the opposite shoulder. "I want you to protect us."

"What about me?" their mother asked. "I'm a straight shooter, and I'm great at hand-to-hand combat."

"In the movies," the twins said together.

The oldest boy, Edgar Jr., popped into the conversation. "I'm almost old enough to drive. I could use the practice."

"I don't think so," Helena said.

Lexie knew what was going on with the kids. They were swarming, taking advantage of their mom being tired and a little bit frazzled. It was time for Lexie to turn into Bossy Nanny and take charge. She shook off the clingy twins.

Her first order was directed at them. "Shane and Caine, take your little brother and sister and put them in the car seats in the back SUV. You will also ride in that car."

"With you?"

"With your mom and a driver from the hotel." She made a quick pivot and pointed to the oldest girl. "Meggie, you ride with me and Eddy in the second car."

Eddy beamed, and she could see the beginning of a resemblance between the teenager and his father. "I get to drive."

"If you're really good, I'll take you out later. For practice."

"No fair. Meg gets to drive all the time."

"She's a year and a half older than you."

"But I need to drive."

Meggie said, "And I want to ride with Justin."

"Who?"

"The driver from the hotel."

Lexie was sympathetic when it came to Meggie and her potential boyfriends. The young man in question seemed polite, clean and he was a local with a job. She nodded to Meggie. "I think I can change the seating arrangements."

"You're the best."

She took over the rest of the preparations for departure, instructing the hotel staff on where to put the suitcases and herding the kids and their mother into the cars. She went to the head valet to get the keys.

There was no need to tip; Helena had given the concierge a huge gratuity to cover their departure. Lexie could tell from the giant grin on the valet's face that he was aware of the bonanza tip that would be his. He gushed over his goodbye and added, "Hope you enjoyed your stay."

She was about to make a snarky comment about how it was hard to enjoy herself when she was being shot at. Then she caught a glimpse of another one of the valets. Tall and lean with curly black hair, he was walking away from her. There was something familiar about the way he moved. Before she could ask his name, Mason rushed up beside her.

He spun her around to face him. "Thursday night at five."

"If there's a problem, I have your phone number."

"No problems." His blue eyes commanded her attention. "I'm not going to let you slip out of my life."

Her defenses went up, and the smile froze on her lips. She wanted to tell him that she wasn't part of his life, they weren't in a relationship and she was the one who decided whether she was staying or slipping. But the kids were bouncing in the cars. Little faces pressed against the windows. She had to go.

"Thursday," she said.

He ran back into the hotel, and she trotted around the two SUVs. Her mind flashed back to that valet. Someone she knew? Surely not one of the guests. But he might have been a server at the banquet. She shrugged off the vague impression.

The final arrangement in the cars put Meggie and Eddy, Jr. and the twins in the second vehicle. Lexie was driving the lead car with Helena in the passenger seat, which was exactly what she'd wanted. The two youngest were in the rear in their car seats. She started up the engine and turned to Helena.

Her gleaming black hair tumbled loosely to her shoulders as she covered her green eyes with sunglasses. Lexie knew for a fact that Helena had gotten up with the kids, had breakfast, chased after her husband with a golf cart and made love. But she still managed to look like a movie star in her leopard-patterned Windbreaker and skinny black jeans with strappy platform heels. Considering her gorgeous appearance, Helena spent remarkably little time fussing with her hair and makeup.

"It's hard to believe," Helena said, "that you don't have special training as a nanny. You're quite effective at getting everyone organized."

"That's how I was brought up. I had three older brothers and we were a handful. Organization was essential. I learned spit and polish from my Marine Corps dad."

Helena exhaled another dramatic sigh. "Your dear, sweet father."

"Clearly, you don't know my dad." He was seldom described as "dear" or "sweet."

"Edgar told me all about him. He's a good man. When you were hurt in that terrible car crash, your father came home to take care of you. He taught you to walk again."

Though she could have argued that it was her own

strength of character and—as her dad readily admitted—her own damned cussedness that got her back on her feet, she agreed. Her father was a truly good man. Sometimes he was overprotective with "Daddy's baby girl," and other times he was a total hard-ass. But he was a decent human being who had done right by her. Her question was: Why were the admiral and Helena talking about Danny DeMille?

She gazed through the windshield at the beautiful spring day. The gleaming white cap of snow on Mount Sopris stood out against the clear blue sky. Fresh green buffalo grass and bright wildflowers in red, blue and yellow covered the fields. She'd miss the mountains if she had to go back to Texas.

Lexie asked, "What else did your husband say about my dad?"

"They worked together in the Middle East. They were both in attendance at Al Ackerman's wedding to that Saudi princess."

Her dad never mentioned a Saudi wedding. She was beginning to think she didn't know the man at all. "Anything else?"

"I know what you're doing, Lexie." Helena adjusted her seat belt across her breasts and glanced into the back, checking on the kids. The two little ones would quickly fall asleep in their car seats. "You're probing me to get information about the Damascus Cache."

"You got me. There's no way I can trick you into telling me everything you know. You're an actress, a good one. If you decided to stonewall or fake me out, you could easily play those roles." And Lexie couldn't compete. She was a terrible liar, incapable of manipulating. "If you don't want to talk to me, you don't have to. But I'm going to lay my cards on the table."

"Go ahead."

"Before yesterday, I'd never heard of the Damascus Cache. Then your husband was targeted for kidnapping because of it. And then I find out that my dad's name is on it. He's in danger." She caught Helena's gaze and stared hard for a second before turning back to the road. "I want to do whatever I can to find the list and destroy it."

"How can I help?"

"Tell me what you know."

"Oh, dear, where should I start?" Helena twisted a strand of ebony hair around her finger and stared out the window.

"At the beginning."

"The first time I met Edgar was in Paris. He wore a tuxedo, not a uniform, and he seemed to know everyone. He spoke fluent French, German and Japanese. And when he took me in his arms to dance the tango…"

Her voice took on a resonant, lilting tone. Helena made her real life sound like a romantic movie with perfect moonlight and fragrant gardens and a beautiful couple falling deeply and passionately in love at first sight. Lexie had heard this story before and didn't mind hearing it again.

In this retelling, Helena ended her story with an unexpected twist. "To summarize, I knew Edgar was a spy before I realized he was an admiral."

"Wow." Lexie stared through the windshield at the two-lane road that stretched before them. She knew that Prescott had worked with navy intelligence in the Middle East and western Africa, but she'd never thought of him as a spy. "Why haven't I heard this before?"

"My dah-ling Edgar wouldn't be much of a spy if everybody knew about it. And he doesn't participate in an active way. Not anymore."

"Not until this stuff with the Damascus Cache."

"Ah, the cache," Helena said. "I don't have many details."

"That's fine. Simplified works best for me."

"At one time, years ago, Edgar was one of the authors of the Damascus Cache. It contained information about supply lines, weapons, contractors and undercover contacts. The names listed represented all the various groups from the military to the CIA to MI6 to Mossad and Interpol."

"It sounds like a large document. Did they reduce it down to a flash drive?"

"Indeed, there were several copies. Here's what Sec-Nav told Edgar." She leaned across the console and whispered, "These crazy anti-conspiracy people think Edgar has hidden the cache."

"Where? At the house?"

"Apparently."

The Prescott home was twelve bedrooms on seven acres. Though the setting was secluded, the house was a hive of activity. For the past two weeks, the entire family had been in residence, which was an unusual synchronizing of schedules for a movie star, an international consultant and six active children.

The idea of searching that sprawling house for something as tiny as a flash drive was daunting. Not to mention the barn for the horses and the outbuildings. Lexie had lost pairs of shoes and pillows and notebooks that had never been found.

"Here's what I don't understand," she said. "If the cache is at the house, why come after him at this event?"

Helena shrugged. "This is where it starts getting complicated. They might have already searched the house. Probably they have. There's evidence that someone sneaked into Edgar's office and the town house in DC."

"Wait a sec. Are you saying that these AC-CD people

have broken into the house in Aspen? Where we have intense electronic security and lots of people milling around?"

In addition to the family, there was a cook, a house-keeper and a couple of assistants like Josh. Also, the Prescotts did a lot of entertaining and had frequent house-guests. Lexie thought of all the people who came and went: groundskeepers, wranglers for weekends when they had horses, maids, delivery guys who handled groceries, fire-wood, dry cleaning and late-night pizza. Then there was Helena's staff, including a personal trainer and her hair and makeup people.

"Maybe they joined the parade of people who are al-ways coming through." She chuckled.

"Their search of the house failed," Lexie said. "Then, their plan was to kidnap your husband. Not a clever scheme. Admiral Prescott would never give up classified information."

"Of course not. Nor would you."

"Not a chance."

"You're very brave, Lexie. That's something else you learned from your father."

Why did Helena bring up her father again? She'd deliv-ered an important nugget of information by telling Lexie that the cache might be hidden at the house. But what else? "Is there something I'm missing? Something about my dad?"

"As an actress, I like to observe characters and charac-ter traits. Your father fascinates me. What happens when a dedicated military man is faced with trouble at home?"

"You mean when he came home to take care of me." She'd wondered about that, too. "I never understood why he retired. He could have taken a leave and then returned to active duty."

"Guilt stopped him. Your father blamed himself for what happened to you. He would never leave you unprotected again." She smiled and gently patted Lexie's arm. "When you came to work for us, he made Edgar promise on his life that he'd take care of you."

"Why would Dad feel guilty? It was my fault. I should have done more to avoid the car that hit me."

"It wasn't an accident, Lexie. The car that hit you was sending a message to the entire espionage community. If your father and my husband didn't cooperate and turn over the information they wanted, people would die."

Starting with me. Lexie's sense of what was really real had just adjusted a few notches. Someone had tried to kill her and had almost succeeded.

Helena continued, "We'll understand if you want to go back to Texas."

She'd never give up. "I'm staying."

Chapter Nine

Alone, at last! On Thursday at noon, Lexie perched on a stool at the marble-topped counter in the kitchen and savored a mug of free-trade coffee from Colombia. The stillness was pure luxury. Her eyelids lowered and lifted in a slow blink as her breathing regulated to a less frantic pace. Ever since the Prescotts had returned from the hotel on Sunday afternoon, she'd been running in high gear, racing madly to prepare the family for their summer activities.

Her lazy gaze slid around the huge French country-style kitchen with quaint white cabinets, double-sized stainless steel appliances and gobs of gadgets neatly arrayed on marble countertops. The curtains and trim were slate blue. French doors opened onto a huge cedar deck, which was perfect for entertaining and offered a wide view of Henscratch Valley, where three small rivulets combined into one wide creek that flowed into the Roaring Fork River. From a bird's-eye view, the joining of the rivulets resembled a hen's claw. Hence, the name Henscratch.

Though the Prescotts employed a cook for entertaining, grocery shopping and those occasions when Helena was on a special diet, Lexie or one of the other adults usually cooked for the family. Lexie was teaching the older kids how to make basic survival food, not that these youngsters would ever need to survive on omelets and ramen noodles.

At present, the kitchen was well stocked, thanks to a massive shopping trip by the cook, who was taking a month off...as was the housekeeper.

Lexie swung around on her stool and gazed into the huge family room. On the wall above the shelves and storage for toys was a large flat screen that served as a calendar to outline the various activities of each member of the family for the next six weeks. Each person had a horizontal line. The weeks were broken into seven vertical days. This screen synced with her handheld tablet and contained all contact information, locations and names. All she had to do to find the details for one of the kids was tap the appropriate space on the screen and the information popped up.

The first row was dedicated to Edgar. Currently, the admiral was in DC, staying at the town house he'd owned for years.

Helena had taken the twins for a weeklong visit to her ex-husband in California. Afterward, she'd drop the kids off at a horseback riding camp on Catalina Island. She would then proceed to a movie set in Toronto for six weeks of filming.

The two littlest kids were at summer camp for eight weeks. Though the family could easily afford the finest camping experience available for the munchkins, Prescott had convinced Helena that the kids could use a dose of reality in the woods. They were at a camp run by former SEALs where they would learn survival skills. *For four-and six-year-olds? Really?* The side benefit to this camp was that the entire staff were trained bodyguards. If there was danger, the little Prescotts were safe.

Thinking of safety reminded Lexie that being alone in a house that bad guys wanted to search might not be the smartest plan in the world. A shiver prickled her spine. She looked down at the coffee mug and saw that her hand was trembling. Ever since Helena had told her that her accident wasn't accidental, fear had been creeping around the edges of her consciousness. She kept looking over her shoulder. Remembered pain tensed her muscles.

Over and over, she told herself that there was nothing to worry about. This house had been searched by the CIA, the NSA and the admiral's assistant, Josh. They'd used an array of equipment designed to locate miniaturized circuits or magnets or whatever went into a flash drive. Josh had attempted to explain the technology before Stella grabbed the search probe and waved the long rod like a magic princess wand.

The thought of adorable blonde Stella brought a smile to Lexie's face. That was what she needed. Confidence and cool detachment were essential if she was going to figure out a way to use her special perspective to find the Damascus Cache. Mason might help. He'd be here by five o'clock, fewer than five hours. She could last until then.

The alarm on her watch went off, reminding her that she needed to make a phone call to check on the two oldest kids, who were staying with their mother in Seattle and taking a sailing trip on the Strait of Juan de Fuca. Taking her phone from the pocket of her jean shorts, she hit the speed dial for Meggie. The girl was far more likely to answer than Eddy Jr., who didn't like to be monitored.

The young woman's voice took on the chilly, whiny tone she used when adults were being annoying. She reported, "Our plane got in okay, but Mom's running late to pick us up. You'd almost think she wasn't thrilled to see us."

"Sarcasm?"

"What do you think?"

"More sarcasm."

"We only see her for an extended time twice a year. You'd think she'd make an effort. Oh, wait." Her voice lightened; she almost sounded happy. "Here she is. It's Mommy. 'Bye, Lexie."

"Have fun."

Her words were lost in Meggie's haste to get off the phone, and she wondered if Edgar had warned his former wife about the potential danger to the kids. Meggie was old enough to date, to be out on her own. The experts thought no one was in danger except for the admiral, but her experience had been different.

The image of her own car crash appeared in her mind. She mentally replayed those few seconds before impact. Could she have pumped the brakes or cranked the steering wheel harder? Had that bastard deliberately targeted her?

She didn't know. The perpetrators had never been identified, mostly because her dad had done what they wanted and quit the military. According to Helena, the car crash had nothing to do with the Damascus Cache. Nor was the anti-conspiracy group involved. The leader of AC-CD might have been using a different name at that time or she might even have been attacked by some other hater.

The attack was meant as a warning to men like her dad who dabbled in secrets. By hurting her, the bad guys were showing that their evil could reach all the way across the ocean and hurt loved ones in the States. She was a pawn to them. She meant nothing.

Yet that crash had changed her life and destroyed her future. In addition to the broken bones and torn muscles in her legs, the internal injuries were devastating. A collapsed lung, a punctured spleen and there had been nerve damage. She had required a hysterectomy.

The fragile dreams she'd had of a husband and family had been shattered. It wasn't fair for her to date or form a serious relationship. Maybe she should call Mason and tell him not to come. Clearly, he was a man looking for a settled-down relationship with the standard wife and kids. That was something she could never do.

A burst of rage spread from her belly to her chest. A flush crawled up her throat. Her cheeks flamed.

When she was taking care of the kids, she couldn't allow her emotions to get the better of her. She'd been holding back this outburst since Sunday. Now she was alone. So. Very. Alone.

She leaped from the stool onto the wood parquet floor. Her red sneakers thudded as she ran to the spacious entryway with its two-story ceiling and modern silver chandelier. A sweeping staircase going up led to the master suite and four other guest bedrooms, along with another suite for special guests. The kids had a wing of their own at the northern end of the house. Lexie slept there, but that wasn't where she was headed.

In the hallway beyond the foyer, she took the staircase to the lower level of the house. Tension kept building inside her. And the heat—she was on fire as she darted down a long hallway, passing storage spaces and the twenty-four-seat home theater. The southern-most room in the house was the home gym.

Too bad the swimming pool was empty! It would have been a relief to dive into the long narrow lap pool that stretched along the farthest edge of the room. The pool was surrounded on three sides by triple-pane bulletproof windows and had a fitted cover that matched the empty hot tub. With two young kids running around, the open water was too dangerous.

But the kids weren't here. Lexie was free to play rough. On the admiral's side of the gym were gray metal weights, a heavy punching bag, dumbbells, mats and a speed bag. Helena's side focused on movie-star exercises, like yoga and stretching. She had mirrors and a ballet barre and sometimes worked out to the music from Tchaikovsky's *Nutcracker* Suite. The admiral preferred Sousa marches played by the Marine Corps band.

Lexie took her cell phone from her pocket and placed it out of the way, then kicked off her sneakers and went through her karate warm-ups, starting by bouncing on the balls of her feet and progressing to stretches, squats and light kicks. Ever since she first started training with her brothers, she'd done this routine, and the repetition of familiar motions helped her get centered. Her tension wasn't gone; that would be far too simple. But she was beginning to loosen up. She added shouts to her kicks. "Ha. Ha. No fear. Ha."

She bounced over to the sound system. Amid the marches and the operas, there was a sound track of mixed selections that both the admiral and Helena liked. Lexie picked one. The first song: "Sweet Caroline." With the music cranked up loud, she sauntered toward the heavy punching bag suspended from the ceiling. With a fierce yell, she unleashed a series of kicks first with one leg, then the other. She expanded her attack to include a freestanding kick bag that popped back up when she knocked it down. She rolled down onto the mats and up again. Now she was singing along with the music. "Good times never seemed so good…"

Whirling and leaping and kicking, she made a circuit around the gym, practicing her poses—*Kihon Waza*—building her adrenaline, working off fear and dread. She came to a halt in front of Helena's wall of mirrors and stared at herself.

Under her freckles, her skin was flushed. She tore off her light sweatshirt. The T-shirt she wore underneath had sleeves too short to cover the puckered pink scar left by the bullet graze. She studied it. "What does one more matter?"

In the mirror, she had a full view of her legs. Her tan was marred by a faint patchwork of scars. The broken bones in her ankle had required surgery and both knees had had arthroscopic work done. More than once, she'd tried to tell herself that they were like tattoos. The difference was that she hadn't asked for these marks. It didn't matter that they weren't all that noticeable; she didn't want them.

"Those bastards," she muttered. How dare they come after her? She almost wished that her dad hadn't given in to them. If he'd kept up the fight, what would have happened to her? Would they have come after her in the hospital? After racing around the gym, she was pumped, energized, feeling no fear. She threw a couple of karate jabs and high kicks at her reflection in the mirror.

On the other side of the gym, she heard her cell phone ring. She dashed across and answered. It wasn't a number she recognized.

The voice on the other end of the call was patchy. "Are... surprise...ready."

"I can't hear you," she yelled. The loud background music didn't help. "Let me turn this down."

Quiet descended.

"There," Lexie said. "What did you say?"

"Are you alone?"

"What did you say?" Her breath froze in her lungs. "Who is this? What do you want?"

The call disconnected.

In spite of the static, she knew what he'd said. *Are you alone?* Anticipation of danger was often worse than the actual threat. She didn't scare easily. If somebody was coming for her, she would be prepared to take them on.

She peered through the wall of windows on the other side of the lap pool. Outside, there were trees and boulders, leafy bushes and shrubs. A stand of pine obscured the view down the slope to Henscratch Valley. When she saw movement, she jumped. A scrawny black squirrel darted across the top of a flat granite boulder.

Though certain that she'd locked the doors and set all the alarms, Lexie left the exercise room and went down the hallway to an unmarked door. Inside was a small room that the admiral called Command Central, which contained an impressive and extensive array of surveillance equipment. Monitors on sensors showed that none of the doors or windows had been opened or broken or compromised in any way. Outdoor cameras covered seven different angles. She studied each of these approaches to see if anything was out of place.

Nothing. She stared more closely. It all looked fine. That weird phone call was a fluke. Then she saw it. A rope dangled against the wall at the far north end of the house. Was it left over from a game the kids had been playing? *The roof?*

If an intruder intended to break into the house through the roof, he'd have to go through a window, which would set off an alarm. She'd heard nothing. The cameras didn't show anyone creeping through the surrounding forest. But there was that phone call…

She needed to go outside and take a look at the rope, and that meant she needed to be armed. Her karate skills were useful for surprise attacks, but she needed a gun for protection. She headed up the stairs to the main floor, where there was a locked gun cabinet.

In the front foyer, sunlight from high windows splashed against cream stucco walls and the gray tile floor. The overall style of the house was clean and modern with high ceilings and windows, so many windows. The branches of trees always seemed to be moving. Shadows changed and shifted.

Her ringtone sounded. She heard the breathiness in her voice. "Hello?"

"Are you alone?"

"Who is this?"

Chapter Ten

"If you're by yourself, I'll come to the front door." Mason heard the tension in her voice through the phone. "If somebody else is in the house, meet me by the garage."

"Come to the front," she said.

"I'll be there in five minutes."

When he'd gotten the call that morning from the admiral, hiring him to stay at the mansion in Aspen with Lexie for the next few weeks, Mason hadn't asked for much information. There was no need to question the best stroke of luck he'd had in years. He'd pounced on the chance to stay at a mansion in Aspen. Oh, and would he object if an attractive auburn-haired woman stayed with him? Mason couldn't say yes fast enough. He'd just won the lottery!

The edginess he'd heard in her voice gave him second thoughts...not enough to make him drop the assignment. No way would he back out. This job was fate, kismet, the way things were meant to be. Ever since he saw Lexie, he'd been thinking about her, trying to figure her out. The woman was a wealth of contradictions. She was optimistic and quick with a smile. But she was equally speedy with a karate kick to the groin and had done serious damage to that guy who attacked her outside the elevator. She was smart and had a degree in psychology. She kissed like an angel. But she had secrets—dark secrets—that gave her depth and complicated his job as a bodyguard.

He drove his Land Rover past a long building that had to be a garage designed to house a fleet of vehicles and ascended a sloping driveway toward a large structure with clean, bold architectural lines. It butted up to the granite hillside. Two stories in most places and three in others, the house was made of light cedar planks and accented with rectangular walls of concrete or natural stone. The angle of the entryway made him think of a boat, and the doorbell played a familiar sea chantey: "Yo ho ho, and a bottle of rum."

The door swung inward. Barefoot, Lexie dashed to the wall pad and punched in the code to deactivate the alarm. He noticed that she'd gathered a stockpile of weapons on the stairs: a rifle, two handguns and a hunting knife.

He glanced from the arsenal to her and back again. It was a little bit disconcerting. "Is there something I should know?"

"Never call a woman who might be alone and ask if she's alone."

"And why is that?"

"It's scary. You sound like a stalker." A smile played at the edges of her lips, but her dark eyes held a shimmer of real fear. "Or a pervert whose next question is going to be, 'And what are you wearing?' You should have explained."

"It was a bad connection."

"That's no excuse," she snapped. "Do I have to teach you phone manners? Like I do with the kids?"

I've been a naughty boy, nanny. Spank me. But she wasn't joking around. What had happened to the cute, funny, teasing Lexie? "You've made your point."

"Why did you want to know if I was alone?"

Her accusatory tone bugged him. Maybe he hadn't handled that phone call the right way, but it was time to let it go. She liked him, he knew it. Why else would she agree to a date? He pushed the door closed and dropped his backpack on the foyer floor. "The admiral suggested that—"

"The admiral? Why are you talking to him?"

"This morning he contacted TST Security and hired me for two weeks. It was his suggestion that I call ahead and see if you could meet me at the garage to open the door. I wanted to know if you were alone. If you were, I didn't want you running around outside."

"Why? Is there some kind of danger?"

Their earlier meetings had been natural, pleasant and encouraging. Now every word that came out of his mouth ticked her off. He didn't know how to approach her. If he told her to settle down or take a few deep breaths, she'd be insulted and then angrier. If he hid behind a fake smile and told her that there was nothing to worry about, she'd know he was lying.

There was only one approach that worked for him. "I'm going to tell you the truth."

She took a backward step. "Oh, my God, there is danger."

"I don't know," he said. "I need to do an assessment of the real and potential threat. That's what I always do when I come to a house as a bodyguard."

"You're guarding my body?"

Guarding wasn't the only thing he'd like to do to that slender, athletic body. He glanced at the scar from the bullet wound on her upper arm, which seemed to be healing well. Her snug coral T-shirt outlined her high, round breasts. Her cutoffs were frayed at the edges and short enough to display muscular legs with fading traces of scars that stood out against her tan.

It said something about her that she didn't try to hide the

scars. Lexie was comfortable with who she was. Unapologetic and tough, she was the sort of woman he liked. She didn't take herself too seriously, as evidenced by the fact that each of her ten toenails was painted a different hue.

"I like your feet," he murmured.

"For a guy who wants to tell me the truth, you're very slow to say anything."

"Is there danger?" He repeated her question. "The admiral doesn't expect an attack on the house. Apparently they've done a lot of searching. Correct?"

She nodded and her curls bounced. "Mobs of technicians with special instruments have poked in every corner and crevice."

"So the house is clean. The Damascus Cache isn't here," he said. "But Prescott didn't want to take any chances in case the bad guys didn't get the word and tried to break in. It's better to be safe than sorry."

She pinned him with a gaze. "Did he say that?"

"As a matter of fact, those are his exact words."

"My dad says that all the time. Better to be safe, better to be safe, it's better to be safe than sorry."

The last time Mason saw her at the hotel, she'd had an issue with her dad being overprotective. Did that explain her current hostility? "Have you talked to him?"

"Not yet. It's kind of a big deal between us. I'm not sure whether I'm mad at him or whether I feel guilty or what..." Her voice trailed off. "You haven't heard the latest development between me and my dad, right?"

"I haven't."

She pivoted and marched down a hallway. "Do you want something cold to drink? We have soda, water, lemonade and beer."

Mason didn't follow obediently behind her like one of

the Prescott kids. "You can't leave these weapons lying here."

"I'll clean up later."

Not good enough. He went to the staircase and picked up the rifle, handguns, ammo and knife. Even if no one else was in the house and the weapons weren't loaded, they needed to be returned to where they belonged. Taking a guess, he went down the hall behind the staircase. A light wood door stood open to his right, and he entered a very masculine office with an ornate, antique wood desk that looked as though it was seldom used for actual paperwork. The walls were lined with bookshelves. He spotted the gun cabinet behind the desk. The glass door stood unlocked and wide open. After he returned the guns to their places, he found the key in the middle desk drawer.

When he turned, he saw her leaning against the door frame with her arms folded below her breasts. She asked, "How did you know the key would be there?"

"It's the most logical place. Also the most obvious. I suggest hiding the key somewhere else. Better yet, put the gun cabinet in a room that isn't so easily accessible."

She exhaled in a huff. "You're right, of course. I've said the same thing to Prescott myself. With the kids getting into everything, we need to practice extreme gun safety."

"For now, I'll put the key back in the middle drawer. Tomorrow, we'll make adjustments."

"So you're going to be here two whole weeks."

He closed the middle drawer and came around the desk to stand before her. He was tired of her evasions. "Is that a problem?"

"Let's get you a drink."

When she turned, he grasped her uninjured arm above the elbow and held her gently but firmly. "Don't run away from me."

"I'm not." But she avoided looking at him.

It wasn't easy to protect anyone, much less a woman who was treating him like—what had she called him?— a stalker or a pervert. "If this is going to work, you have to trust me."

"It's not you, Mason. It's me."

"That's the oldest line in the book."

"Give me some time." Her gaze lifted, and he saw the pained vulnerability in her dark brown eyes. "I need to relax."

He released his hold. "Ten minutes."

"Fine."

This time, he followed her when she went down the hall and across the foyer to the kitchen. She still hadn't put on shoes. Her hips twitched in a way that was both athletic and sexy. Though she wasn't any taller than five feet three or four inches, her proportions were perfect and her legs were both slender and shapely.

In the kitchen she pointed to the stools at the counter. "Sit there. Now, what can I get you?"

"You mentioned lemonade."

She went to the side-by-side refrigerator, found the pitcher and poured a glass for each of them. She slid his across the marble-topped counter. It didn't escape his attention that she stayed on the opposite side rather than taking the stool next to him. She was keeping a distance between them.

He checked his wristwatch. He had promised ten minutes for her to relax. Only four minutes had passed, but he was too impatient to wait. "You said there was a development with your dad. I'd like to hear more."

"I have a question for you first."

When she took a sip of her lemonade, a bit of pulp stuck to her lip. She delicately removed it with the tip of her pink tongue…like a cat. An apt comparison, he thought. Like a cat, she captivated him with her graceful, clever moves. Like a cat, she turned her back without showing the least bit of interest in his response.

"Okay," she said. "You had arranged to pick me up for a date. But that's not why you're here right now. This is a job. Which is it?"

"A valid question." He translated her concern. "You want to know if it's unprofessional for me to agree to act as bodyguard for a woman I'm attracted to."

"Are you?" She brightened.

"Attracted?" He regretted the use of that word. "You're a good-looking woman. I'm a single man."

"And you're my bodyguard. If we're dating, isn't that a professional conflict?"

"I considered asking somebody else at TST to take this assignment." For about three and a half seconds, he'd considered. "It's not a problem. I can control my personal feelings. At five o'clock, I can quit being a bodyguard, and we'll have our date. Or not."

"How do you decide?"

"We'll know," he said. "Now it's my turn to ask you a question. Why did they leave you at the house alone?"

She pointed to a flat screen mounted on the wall in the room behind the kitchen. Unlike the rest of the sleek, stylish house, the family room had a more lived-in appearance. Toys were pulled off their shelves. A gang of stuffed animals sat side by side on the sofa facing the regular television. The blue and green colors with an occasional splash of yellow were cozy and welcoming.

He looked at the display on the flat screen. "A schedule?"

"It lists summer activities for all the kids and the admiral and Helena. There are camps and training programs.

Helena will be filming in Canada. And the older kids are visiting their mom."

The closest Mason had ever come to a summer activity was when his brother, who was seven years older, took him camping in the mountains for a weekend with borrowed sleeping bags and beat-up cooking gear. The total cost for one of these weekends was almost nothing, but he had loved every moment. He wondered if these rich kids appreciated what they had. "Do the kids enjoy their activities?"

"Last summer, they seemed to like it a lot. Couldn't stop talking about it." Her gaze narrowed. She could see his attitude, his judgment. "You think the kids are over-privileged and spoiled."

"These kinds of activities are costly."

"I won't lie to you. It's a difficult balancing act to keep them grounded. The admiral makes sure that the older kids understand that they've received a lot and need to give back. They're involved in charity work."

Mason expected the admiral to raise responsible children. He also knew that it was easy for him to criticize someone else's child-rearing tactics when he didn't have kids of his own. Someday that would change, and he'd become a father. Someday soon, he hoped. He was ready for that challenge. "If everybody else is busy with activities, why do you need to stay at the house?"

"Two reasons. First, somebody needs to watch the house. Second, these schedules don't fit together seamlessly. I'm here to cover the downtime after one activity ends and the next begins. Sometimes Helena will fly in with some movie friends for an impromptu party. Or her husband will hold a weekend conference with movers and shakers."

"But mostly you're at the house alone."

"Poor me," she said with a melodramatic rolling of the

eyes. "Here I am…all alone in a multimillion-dollar mansion amid some of the most spectacular scenery in the world."

He tried to find something objectionable. "What about housework? Or special projects that the family wants you to do?"

"The maid service comes in once a week. If there's a special project, the housekeeper has already hired someone to do it. For cooking, all I need to do is make a phone call. The chef lives in town and is happy to come out and prepare a single meal or a whole regimen for any of Helena's crazy diets."

"Why doesn't the housekeeper live here in the summer?"

"The summer house-sitting used to be her job," she said. "But she's sixty years old and likes to travel. I wanted to do it, and the housekeeper gets much-deserved time off. She's taking two of her grandchildren to Australia for the month."

He looked down at his watch, and then held it so she could read the dial. "Time's up. You said that you needed ten minutes to relax before you could talk. Ready?"

Resolutely, she lifted her chin. "What do you want to know?"

"You're different." He could tell that she was scared, but mentioning her fear seemed confrontational. "Something has changed from the last time I saw you."

"I learned that somebody tried to kill me." Her voice was eerily flat, as though she'd repeated those words a hundred times. "And they very nearly succeeded."

Chapter Eleven

When Mason showed up on the doorstep and said he'd been hired to be her bodyguard, Lexie had been relieved. The possibility of another attack had made her nervous. A deeper fear arose when Helena told her that the car crash hadn't been a random event. She'd been targeted. For the first time in her life, she'd felt like a victim.

Her life had been irreparably damaged. She'd never have kids. Every time she thought of that gaping hole in her life, she'd remember the black car with the tinted windows coming at her. Terror and rage would rise in her, again and again.

No way could she tell Mason about her hysterectomy. He was a family man, through and through. Solid, steady and stable, he was suited for a long-term relationship. That didn't work for her, but she was fairly sure that he'd be happy with a no-strings-attached affair. Most men were.

It wasn't her nature to have casual relationships, but her only other choice was to shove him out the door and insist on a less charming bodyguard. She didn't want to do that. She and Mason were most definitely attracted to each other. The moment he walked through the door, the air in the room had changed. The pheromones were flying. The snug fit of his jeans and the black T-shirt under his plaid shirt made her heart beat faster. Her fingers longed to embrace the breadth of his shoulders and slide down his muscular chest and abs. The timbre of his voice drew her closer.

He sat at the counter, sipping his lemonade and waiting for her to explain what she'd meant when she said that someone had tried to kill her. It was her turn to speak, and she knew it. But her throat had become a rusty hinge, holding back the words she needed to say.

"I'm not ready to talk about it," she creaked.

"Let's start with something easy," he said. "Why did you take out all those weapons?"

That, she could talk about. "I was in the gym when I got this creepy phone call."

"Ha-ha," he said.

"A really nasty voice," she teased, "ugly and evil. Then I went to Command Central, and I saw a rope dangling. I needed to check it out and didn't want to go in unarmed."

"You lost me. Let's go back to the gym."

"I'd love to."

"Can I see it? The admiral sent me blueprints of the security system and the house. The gym is huge, and I know Prescott would have the best equipment."

"Let's go. This way." She led to the staircase leading down. "I need to get my shoes, anyway."

Mason was a big man, several inches over six feet, but his hiking boots hardly made a sound when he walked across the wood parquet floor. Silence accompanied his movements. Not stealth. He had nothing to hide. But there was a stillness that came from his sheer, unshakable confidence.

At the foot of the stairs, he made a detour, turning right and opening the door to Command Central. Apparently, he already knew his way around the house. As he stood in the doorway, his gaze flicked from screen to screen, taking in all the dials and knobs. Again, he seemed to know how everything worked without having her explain. Why shouldn't he? Security was his job, after all.

"Show me where you saw this dangling rope."

Taking a seat at one of the consoles, she flipped though several views from cameras outside the house. She paused and pointed. "There it is. That's the north end of the house near the kids' bedrooms."

"It goes up to the roof," he said.

"But there haven't been any break-ins. If any of the windows or openings onto the roof were tampered with, an alarm would go off."

"I'm familiar with this system." He leaned over her shoulder to tap the keyboard, and the warmth of his body wrapped around her. His citrus and nutmeg aftershave teased her nostrils.

"What are you doing?" *Other than smelling good and driving me crazy.* "The screen went dark."

"I'm doing a rewind," he said. "I programmed it to go backward in twelve-hour jumps. Good eye, by the way. I never would have noticed the rope."

A picture on the screen came back into focus. The shadows and light were different, but nothing else had changed. The rope still dangled.

There was another picture and another and another. He leaned even closer. His cheek was even with hers. If she swiveled her head, she'd be looking directly into his ear.

He pointed to a time stamp in the corner of the screen. "This is Tuesday morning."

The next picture filled the screen. Together, they said, "No rope."

Using the keyboard, Mason had both arms around her, though the low back of the office chair separated them. It would have made sense for her to move, but he hadn't suggested it, and she liked being nestled in his arms. He played forward on the screen until he found Tuesday at four o'clock. The long shadow from the house almost obscured the appearance of a man dressed in jeans and a black Windbreaker. He wore a cap with the visor pulled down. His features were hidden.

Mason put the image on pause while he juggled dials to improve the resolution on the screen. "His jacket says CIA across the back."

"Tuesday was when Agent Collier and his men from the CIA were at the house, searching for the Damascus Cache. This guy could have been any one of them."

"To your knowledge, were they outside the house?"

"No, but I wasn't keeping track of what they were doing. You need to talk to Collier for verification."

As she watched the intruder, her muscles began to tense. The dangling rope indicated that someone had been there, but she was hoping for an innocent explanation. The intruder had a hook attached to the rope. He tossed it onto the roof three times before it caught. Then he used the rope to scale the wall.

"He's fast," Mason said. "That didn't even take five minutes."

"And we still haven't gotten a clear look at his face."

Mason straightened and stepped back from the console. His demeanor had changed; he'd gone from light to dark. "Do you want to know the worst thing about a risk assessment?"

"I think I know," she said. "Sometimes you find danger."

He nodded, then hit a button to pause the playback on the screen. "I'd like to see the gym before we finish the assessment."

She padded barefoot down the hall to the keypad outside the gym. "The code is B-U-N-S and never changes.

We have the room locked to keep little Todd and Stella away from the heavy equipment."

He trooped inside behind her. Helena's Pilates equipment, mirror and ballet barre were of little interest to him. His eyes lit up when he saw the array of weights and punching bags.

"Beautiful," he murmured with undisguised lust. He rubbed his palm across his close-cropped blond hair and turned toward the sunlit forest outside the wall of windows. He inhaled a deep breath, and his muscular chest expanded inside the black T-shirt. A wide smile stretched across his face.

It would have felt good to have him look at her with such naked longing. She huffed. "Do you love it?"

"I could live here."

"A gym rat, I knew it."

"I haven't always been that way." Bouncing on the balls of his feet, he went to the speed bag and punched it a couple of times with his bare knuckles. "When my brother was killed, I needed something to get rid of the tension, know what I mean?"

She did, indeed. Lexie relied on her karate exercises to relieve stress. She crossed the gym to the more feminine side and slipped into her red sneakers.

He shucked off his plaid shirt, picked up a ten-pound dumbbell and did a few curls. "I used to exercise until I could barely stand up. I'd stagger home, fall into the sack and my eyes would pop open. Couldn't sleep. My brain wouldn't shut down. I kept thinking that Matt wasn't really dead. It must be a case of mistaken identity. I couldn't let him go... Still can't."

She'd been so caught up in the tragedies of her life that she'd forgotten about him. When the SecNav had commended his brother's heroic action, she'd seen the pained and haunted look on Mason's face. A Purple Heart was a great honor, but he'd rather have his brother back.

Not that Mason was the type to indulge in a pity party. Automatically, he transferred the weight to his other hand to balance the exercise as he strolled toward the covered lap pool and hot tub. "Do you ever use these?"

"Yes for the tub. Not often for the pool. It takes thousands of gallons of water to fill and when the little ones are around, it's not safe." She wasn't ready to drop the subject of his brother. "How old were you when he died?"

"He was killed," Mason said. "Saying he died implies that there was something natural about it. Murder is an unnatural act. Six years ago, he was murdered in Afghanistan. I was finishing up college, deciding if I should go for my master's."

She hadn't pictured him as a college student. "What was your major?"

"International studies." He continued to pump the dumbbell as he walked the perimeter of the long lap pool. "Back then, I was young and innocent and thought I could make sense of the world. I learned that no single country can take credit for being the worst mess. They're all bad, even us."

"I could've figured that out." She wanted to know more about him, more details. "How did you get into security?"

Standing in front of her, he stopped pacing and dug into his jeans pocket. In his hand, he held a key chain. The brass fob was a four-leaf clover with TST Security written in a half circle across the top. Three of the leaves were a lucky-Irish green. One was red.

"I don't remember who came up with the idea," Mason said. "Me and Matt were buddies with Sean and Dylan, and we thought we'd be outstanding crime fighters. Just before Matt was killed, we sat down and talked about the possibilities. Sean's the oldest, and he had done a stint in the FBI. Dylan is a computer whiz, which is necessary for security work. Matt had top-notch military training. And I was a political wonk who could get by in seven languages."

"Seven? I'm impressed."

"Don't be. With language, you've got to use it or lose it, and I haven't kept it up. I turned into a gym rat. Now I'm the muscle in the group."

He was so much more than muscle. Not that she had any complaints about his body. But she found herself being drawn to his mind and the unique way he saw the world. For sure, he was cynical. But there was a redeeming ray of hope that kept him from being bitter.

With her forefinger, she pointed to the three green leaves. "These stand for you, Sean and Dylan."

He raised the red leaf to his lips and kissed it. "This stands for Matt. He's always watching over us."

If he was trying to seduce her, he was sticking to an extremely low-key approach. And yet she wanted him. She wanted him desperately. Maybe because she hadn't been dating much for the past year and a half, Lexie was ready to pounce, to drag him off to her bedroom and get sexy. Better yet, they could strip down right here in front of the mirror. Practically panting, she asked, "What comes next?"

"I'm not finished with my risk assessment."

Inwardly, she groaned.

He continued, "The dangling rope indicates that somebody might have tried to break in. But I need to talk to Agent Collier and find out if he sent one of his men up onto the roof."

"Then what?"

"I should familiarize myself with the house and make sure all security functions are working properly."

Following someone around and watching while he did

his job wasn't her idea of a great time. Besides, she seriously doubted that she'd be able to trail him all the way around the massive house without tearing off his clothes. "I'll leave you to your work."

As she went down the hall toward the staircase, she heard him call after her, "We have a date at five."

"How should I dress?"

"You decide."

She had a few ideas for her outfit. Maybe she'd go casually seductive with shorts and a bare midriff. She had a fancier outfit with a plunging neckline. Maybe she should go for a wraparound dress that could be removed with one light tug on the sash. Or she might decide to wear nothing at all.

Chapter Twelve

While he was exploring the main floor of the house, Mason's call to Agent Collier finally went through. He went into the formal office with the locked gun cabinet and sat at the massive, carved desk. Being in a classy office/library like this made him feel like a high-ranking officer. Tilting back in the swivel chair, he stretched out his legs and rested the heels of his hiking boots on the desk blotter.

"I'm at Admiral Prescott's house," Mason said. "Lexie told me that you and your men were here on Tuesday."

"Yes, I brought four agents." Collier's accent sounded thicker over the phone. "We discovered evidence that we weren't the first to go through the house."

"What did you find?"

"An infestation of bugs." He chuckled at his pun. "There were twelve listening devices planted throughout the house. Also, we found three cameras that weren't part of the Prescott security system."

The blueprints showed three cameras inside the house: one in the hallway outside the children's bedrooms, one in the kitchen where there were French doors and one in the lobby. "Are there more than three cameras inside the house?"

"That is all," he said. "While we were there, we made a thorough search, except for one room."

"Which room? And why not?"

"In the lower level, there is a safe room with a combination lock and a key. According to the magnificent Helena Christie Prescott, her husband possesses the only key. He was still at the Pentagon."

Keeping it locked was counterintuitive. A safe room was supposed to be entered easily by the people who lived in the house. Once they were safely locked inside away from any threat, the room should be impregnable to outsiders.

He jolted forward to sit upright in the chair and spread the blueprints for the house across the desktop. "I'm assuming they don't actually use that room as it was intended. Is it storage?"

"Helena says yes." Collier mumbled a few words that might have been curses. "Extreme valuables are kept there—artworks, statues, antiques."

"What about deeds and paperwork?" The safe room seemed like the ideal place to hide the Damascus Cache. The admiral was from an older generation where papers and documentation were all carefully stored in locked boxes in banks or in safes.

"Helena would not say more. But I suspect she has a key. Among the valuables, there must have been jewelry. *Her* jewelry."

"She stonewalled you."

"It was disturbing," Collier said, "to come all the way to Aspen only to be denied full access to the premises."

"It's not a bad trip."

"Marvelous scenery," he agreed, "and the gym is among the best home facilities I have ever seen."

Tracing with his forefinger, Mason found the safe room on the blueprint. It was located on the lower level at the opposite end of the hallway from the gym. The house butted up against a cliff with one floor stacked on top of another. At the northern end, the safe room would be underground. The level on top of it was the wing with the children's bedrooms, where the rope had been left dangling. Mason wondered if there was any connection.

"In your search," he said, "did any of your men go outside?"

"No, nor did we search the outbuildings, including the horse barn or the garage or anywhere that an outsider could approach without help from someone inside the house. We operated under the theory that the AC-CD believed the admiral had hidden the cache, and it was probably smaller than a matchbox—the size of a computer flash drive."

"Can you think of a reason why anyone wearing a CIA Windbreaker would want access to the roof?"

There was a moment's silence. In a moment like this, Mason wished he had Sean's training with the FBI. Sean had studied criminal psychology and profiling; he knew the various techniques of questioning. Sean would have known if Agent Collier's moment of hesitation had any significance. It seemed logical that he was hiding something. Was it guilt? Was Collier after the cache for his own nefarious purposes? Or was he embarrassed about his men breaking protocol?

"I require an explanation," Collier finally said. "Why do you think my men were on the roof?"

"One man." Mason leaned forward, resting his elbows on the desk. He wished he could see Collier. It was easier to catch someone in a lie when you were face-to-face with the liar. "An outdoor surveillance camera shows a man in a CIA Windbreaker throwing a grappling hook onto the roof and climbing up a rope attached to the hook."

"Not one of my men. Did the camera show this man coming down?"

"I haven't bothered to look," Mason admitted. "None of the alarms for the windows or the rooftop openings were activated."

"Of course they weren't. We shut them down."

"What? You turned off the security system?"

"Not all day. Occasionally." His voice was faster, his accent heavier. "We accidentally set it off twice. Then we made the decision to turn it off when we were searching."

Panic shot through Mason. He surged to his feet so quickly that his head whirled. How could he have been so careless? He should have known that the CIA would turn the system off. The intruder might have entered the house through the attic. *He might still be here.* "I've got to go. Thanks, Collier."

He dashed out of the office, down the hall and into the foyer. Lexie's bedroom was somewhere on the second floor, north end, but he didn't know which one was hers. He flew up the staircase, taking the steps two at a time. The landing stretched into a balcony that overlooked the foyer. Leaded glass windows above the front door admitted a splash of natural sunlight.

He called her name. "Lexie, are you here? Lexie?"

Skylights overhead kept the long hallway from being too dark, but he flicked a switch that lit sconces along the wall. Afternoon light poured through the window at the end of the hall, which was where they'd spotted the rope dangling.

His fingers drew into fists. He wasn't sharp enough to handle this job. Sean's deductive skills would have been more useful. Or Dylan's cleverness with computers. If anything happened to Lexie because of him, Mason would never forgive himself.

"Lexie?" Where was she? Did she step outside for a

walk? She would have told him, wouldn't she? He should have laid down ground rules. "Lexie?"

He took out his phone and punched in her number. It rang six times and went to voice mail. He charged down the hall and back again. Maybe she'd gone to the gym.

He hit redial for her phone. As he stalked down the hallway, he heard her ringtone, a song from *Mary Poppins*. The cheerful, perky music was coming from inside a room. He paused outside the first door to the right of the staircase and listened. "Just a spoonful of sugar…"

"Lexie!"

Without waiting for her to answer, he shoved open the door. She was nowhere in sight. Her phone in the center of the bed gave a final chirp and went quiet. The little red sneakers she'd been wearing peeked out from the edge of her comforter beside her neatly made bed. Her room was a good size, with a large window and a view of distant snow-capped peaks.

Where was she? He wanted to tear apart the bed and fling open the closet door. Then he heard the rumble of the shower from the adjoining bathroom. In a whoosh, he exhaled the tense breath he'd been holding. *She's fine. In the shower. Perfectly fine.* The classy thing for him to do would be to exit, close the door and knock on it until she answered.

Shower steam rushed from the bathroom door when she opened it a crack and poked her head through. "Mason? What's up?"

He strode across her bedroom. Without saying a word, he pulled her close against his chest and nuzzled her wet hair.

"Is something wrong?" She wriggled in his grasp.

"It's okay now." He held her closer. Obviously, he owed her an explanation, but all he wanted right now was to feel her energy and know that she hadn't been hurt. There was nothing between them but a bath towel, and his behavior was totally inappropriate. He didn't care.

Her arms wrapped around his torso and her wiggling subsided as she settled into a comfortable stance. In spite of the twelve-inch difference in their heights, their bodies fit together nicely. Her soft curves molded to his hard edges.

After a final squeeze, he took a step back. She managed to grab her towel before it fell, but not quickly enough that he didn't catch a glimpse of her left breast and the dusky rose of her nipple. As wardrobe malfunctions went, this was modest.

Still, she blushed. "Have you lost your mind?"

If he stood here and tried to make sense of his tension, panic and guilt for having failed her and failed at his job, Mason was fairly sure that he'd dissolve into an incoherent, babbling mess. All he could do was stare at the towel and wish for it to be gone.

"In the hall," he managed to choke out. "You get dressed. I'll be in the hall."

He made a crisp pivot and went out the door. In the long hallway, he was unable to make himself stand still. He paced up and down, trying to burn off the emotional shock he'd felt when he realized that the intruder could still be in the house. Though it was extremely unlikely, he and Lexie had to go downstairs to Command Central and play through the tape until they found him climbing down. Mason cursed himself. Why hadn't he done that in the first place? *What goes up must come down.* It was child's play to recall that simple formula.

Sean would have told him that you should never trust the security system. People relied too much on electronics. On the other hand, Dylan would have put his faith in the computerized security and pointed out that if it weren't for the outdoor surveillance camera, they wouldn't have seen anything.

Lexie joined him in the hall. She had on her cutoffs and a fresh T-shirt with hummingbirds on the front. She'd stuck her feet into flip-flops that displayed her multicolored toenails. Her damp hair was tucked behind her ears. She smelled like a garden of lilies, lilacs, roses and honeyed flowers.

She cleared her throat. "The last thing I remember you saying is that you were going to call the CIA."

"Agent Collier was helpful." He gestured for her to come with him as he descended the grand staircase into the foyer and the less grand set of stairs into the lower level. "Collier didn't send any of his men onto the roof, so our intruder must have swiped a Windbreaker so he could walk around unnoticed. A simple disguise."

"Or not," she said. "One of his agents could be a traitor."

"Correct." He liked that she was smart and saw all the possibilities. "The worst part is that Collier had the security turned off at various times during the day while he was searching. We never saw the man on the roof climb down."

"And you thought he might have gotten into the house?" Her tone was incredulous. "That he was hiding out in the attic?"

"It's possible."

"Since the weekend, there have been more than thirty people coming into and going out of this house. Managing to hide out from that mob would take some fancy footwork."

"Humor me, okay? Let's just see if he left."

They were in Command Central. He sat in front of the screen where they had watched the intruder climbing onto the roof. As Mason started running the images in fast-forward, she peeked over his shoulder, bringing that delightful fragrance with her. He inhaled deeply, trying to identify all the scents. The rose was from a soap from a hotel he knew in Grand Junction. Lilies and lilacs—the purple tones—were from a shampoo a former girlfriend had used. The honey sweetness emanated from Lexie herself. "Honey," he murmured.

"What?"

"You smell like honey."

"Honeysuckle," she corrected. "It's the fragrance of a moisturizing cream I use on my arms and legs. Is it too strong?"

"I like it."

"Colorado is the worst for dryness. I'm always smearing on moisturizer and guzzling water."

Whatever beauty regime she was using, it worked. Fresh from the shower, her clean skin glistened. The freckles across her cheeks were more obvious than those on her tanned arms and legs. She hadn't hidden any of those polka dots under layers of makeup.

"There." She pointed to the screen. "The guy in the CIA jacket is climbing down the rope."

Mason verified the time stamps on the footage and mentally calculated. "Our intruder was on the roof for less than an hour. We should go up there and see what he was doing."

"Do you need me to help you?"

To help him? Not really. But he wanted her to be with him until he was one hundred percent certain that the house was secure. "You're coming with me."

With her fists on hips and her legs slightly akimbo, she planted her feet as though taking a stand. "You want my help, right?"

"Sure." He didn't want to argue. When he'd thought she might be in danger, he used up his adrenaline spurt of panic tracking her down to the shower. His current energy level was more laid-back, less intense. "I'm not letting you out of my sight until I'm certain that it's safe."

"That's not fair. I'm—"

"Coming with me," he said, finishing her sentence. "What's the fastest, easiest way to get to where the rope is dangling?"

Her slender shoulders twitched in a shrug. She went to the door and turned left. "This way."

She marched down the hallway in the lower level toward the north end of the house. He could track their depth by the shape of the windows. At the southern point of the lower level—the gym—the windows were floor to ceiling. Heading toward the staircase, the windows were garden level. Then they were near the ceiling. In the last forty feet, there were no windows at all.

"We're underground," he said. "Is the safe room down here?"

"How did you know about the safe room?"

"I have blueprints," he reminded her.

The hallway ended in a T-shape. To his right was an open archway leading to what appeared to be storage. Lexie went past him and closed it. "This isn't supposed to be open. Not a good place for the little ones to play."

The door directly in front of him was matte black and mounted in a metal frame. There was a dial on the front and a door handle. "Have you ever been inside there?"

"When I first took the nanny job, Helena showed me how to get inside. It's really safe but scary. Going in there is a last resort."

"They don't call it a panic room for nothing."

"The Prescotts use it as a safe for their important papers, the furs, jewelry and a couple of paintings and sculptures." Her eyes darted nervously. "You know, stuff like that."

Lexie's furtive behavior made him think she was hiding something. Maybe the artworks hadn't been purchased legitimately. If so, it made sense that Helena didn't want Agent Collier and his men poking around in there. "Can you show me how to open it?"

She eyed him suspiciously. "Planning to steal a mink and a tiara?"

"I was thinking it might be useful to have a safe room. In case the bad guys show up."

She reached over and twirled the dial on the front of the door. "The entry code is different from the rest of the house, and it resets after every time it's opened. I can track the number down by accessing household computer files."

Access to the panic room was meant to discourage anyone from going inside. If there had been any reason to suspect Helena of hiding the Damascus Cache, Mason would look in this room first.

At the left end of the T-shape at the end of the hall, she punched numbers into a keypad and opened the door. She skipped up a flight of stairs, and he followed. They were in the forest.

Sunlight dappled the leaves of chokecherry shrubs and grasses while the breeze whispered through the high branches of surrounding pines. He loved being in the mountains. The air tasted fresher here. The light was clearer.

He hiked up the slope to where the rope was dangling. Though it was only a one-story climb to the roof, Mason stayed below Lexie. If she slipped, he'd catch her. Using the rope, she ascended quickly.

Standing on the rooftop, she spread her arms to take in the wide vista. "Great view. The admiral is thinking about putting in solar panels."

Far below the high cliff where the house perched, the

relatively flat land of Henscratch Valley stretched to another jagged ridge. A small herd of cattle grazed. A hawk
swooped across clear blue skies. He inhaled and exhaled
slowly. This was a king of the world moment. He was
overwhelmed by the spacious grandeur and would have
preferred sitting and soaking in all this natural beauty.

But he had a job to do. His footing on the thermal asphalt shingles felt solid. The landscape of the roof was
slants, slopes, gables and skylights, which Lexie scrambled over like a mountain goat in flip-flops.

Mason concentrated on figuring out why the intruder
had climbed up here. As far as he could tell, the wiring on
the windows hadn't been tampered with. The alarm system appeared to be intact.

About halfway down the north wing—an area that was
directly above the children's bedrooms—he noticed a small
but potentially lethal device tucked against the edge of a
skylight.

It was a bomb.

FROM HIS PERCH fifteen feet off the ground, Tony dropped
his binoculars into his lap and leaned back against the thick
trunk of the tall pine tree he'd chosen for his surveillance
point when he followed them outside. While they were in
the house, he was able to keep track of them using a heat-
sensing infrared camera that showed their images in red
outlined against the cooler green of their surroundings.
He'd been watching when Lexie and the bodyguard went
in different directions...and when they came together for
a steaming-hot embrace.

Tony almost felt sorry for the guy. He was falling for
Lexie, which meant she'd wait until she had him wrapped
around her little finger, and then she'd dump him. That was

what she did. He wasn't the only guy in Texas to get booted from his relationship by little Miss Francine Alexandra.

On the rooftop, she scooted toward the escape rope. The bodyguard warned her to get away; he'd located one of the tiny, cell-phone-activated bombs Tony had planted.

This guy didn't know much about explosives. These bomb charges weren't big enough to do serious damage. They were meant to be used as a distraction.

Tony wasn't going to blow up the house. Directives from the leader were clear: no one was to be harmed, especially not the kids. *And isn't that too bad?* Tony would have enjoyed inflicting harm on those spoiled brats, enough harm that they'd understand that they couldn't have everything they wanted. Sometimes your mama promises a kiss but you get a slap in the face.

He'd leave a few scars behind to remind them…like the scars on Lexie's legs.

Life wasn't all sunshine and butterflies. Why was the leader protecting these people, treating them as if they were special? Tony was sick and tired of pussyfooting around.

Being cautious wasn't getting the job done. If they didn't get their hands on the Damascus Cache soon, they'd miss out on a big payday. And there were other ways than kidnapping the admiral and trying to get him to talk. Tony had presented an idea about using Lexie as a hostage to leverage the admiral into giving up the cache.

Getting his hands on her would be easy. All he had to do was get that damn bodyguard out of the way. He closed his eyes and imagined Lexie all trussed up, naked and helpless. He'd take his time getting to know her body again, seeing her quiver when he squeezed her soft breasts, hearing her moan when he traced the folds between her legs.

She'd cry when he slapped her face. She'd fall to her knees and beg for his mercy.

Tony was tempted to put his plan to kidnap Lexie into effect. The leader could deal with the consequences. That would be his problem.

Chapter Thirteen

The Aspen fire department had done such an excellent job that Lexie wished the kids were home to watch. Less than twenty minutes after she'd called in to report the bomb, the shiny red truck pulled up to the front door with sirens blaring. Fortunately, she and Mason had been standing by to open the door, because the local firemen and one woman were armed with axes and ready to hack their way through to the nonexistent flames.

Their search of the roof had been eventful. They found six small cell-phone-activated charges, none of which would result in a major explosion. "More like fireworks than a bomb" was how the chief explained the devices. "More like a bomblet." But those nasty little bomblets were a fire danger and needed to be removed.

The fire department crew had used a long, basket-like tool to scoop up the bomblets and then deposit them in a shiny metal sphere called a blast chamber. This marked the first time they'd used the blast chamber. When all the devices had been collected and the chamber had been locked up tight, the threat was contained.

The crew seemed happy to have a new piece of equipment to play with. They were cheerfully discussing procedure for setting off the explosives when the chief pulled Lexie to one side and gave her a report sheet to fill in and sign. Out of respect for the admiral, he wouldn't conduct a formal investigation, but he would appreciate being kept in the loop. He was concerned because of the attack at the hotel, but the fire chief didn't have a beef about jurisdiction. He'd rather not be in charge.

Before he and the crew drove away in their shiny red truck, he'd consulted with Mason. As she watched the two men, Lexie realized that her bodyguard hadn't changed from the clothes he wore when he arrived, minus the plaid shirt. Not that there was anything wrong with the way he was dressed. She liked the simple, masculine look of his black T-shirt and jeans and hiking boots. But was it date appropriate?

The sun slipped lower in the sky, and Lexie checked her phone for the time. It was 4:35 p.m. Mason hadn't mentioned their date. Nor had she.

It seemed that the idea had simply faded away. Why bother dating when they had a mansion to themselves? If they wanted, they could fill the hot tub or watch a movie in the downstairs theater or make themselves a gourmet dinner. There was no need to go out, and he hadn't said a word about where they'd be going. She exhaled a disappointed sigh. It wasn't important.

She entered the house, climbed the staircase and went to her bedroom, where she sprawled facedown on the queen-size bed with the pale blue striped comforter. Lazily, she dragged her fingers through her shoulder-length hair that had dried in messy tangles. She should have done a quick blow-dry, but Mason had been in such a frantic hurry when he pulled her from the shower. He'd been afraid that something bad had happened to her. In his eyes, she had seen the glimmer of real fear.

In spite of the muscles, he had a sensitive streak. If he needed to kick ass, he could. But he was smart—smart enough to know that not all problems could be solved with his fists or by running away. Mason didn't fit the stereotype of a muscle head with a great bod and no brain. That was as unfair as the myth of the dumb blonde or the fiery redhead.

There was a rap on her door.

She sat up on the bed. "Come in."

Smoothly, Mason stepped into the room and closed the door. "I wanted to let you know that I'm going to be a few minutes late for our date."

"Is it still on?"

"I didn't cancel."

"If you don't want to go out, we don't have to bother."

"Not a bother." He crossed the room and lowered himself on the bed beside her. "It's my pleasure."

"Why?"

And why was she looking this gift horse in the mouth? If a man wanted to be nice to her, she ought to let him. She was always quick to throw up her defenses, maybe too quick.

"I like you," he said. "Dating is what happens when a man likes a woman. It's a great American ritual. Part of our culture."

"Our culture?" That description seemed a bit too grand. "You might be overstating."

"As an international studies major, I'd argue that American dating habits are one of our biggest exports. Going out with one boy, one girl and one car—it's the American style. No chaperones. No arranged courtships. And we definitely don't require dowries or bride tokens."

"What's a token?"

"A payment I'd make to your father for your hand. You know, a golden goblet and six goats."

"Only six?"

"You're sort of skinny."

"You pig." She smacked him on the arm. His easy conversation was relaxing her. The defenses were falling. "It's terrible that families used to do that to their women, selling them off for livestock. It shows no respect."

"Or is it the other way around? Their daughters are so precious that they demand payment for them."

"If it was acceptable, my dad would be like that. He'd ask such a ridiculously high price that nobody could pay it, and I'd never leave home."

"Did you get a chance this week to talk to him?"

"Not really." She collapsed backward on the bed. She'd talked to her dad but hadn't told him everything. She hadn't confronted him about the crash, about how it was his damned fault. It didn't seem that there was anything positive to be gained from that confrontation.

Mason stretched out beside her on the bed. Lying side by side should have felt intimate, but she was doing her best not to put him in that category. She wanted Mason to be a friend, someone she might know two years from now. Not a boyfriend. Her lovers came and went as fast as a revolving door.

"Did you tell him everything?" he asked.

"What do you mean?" Had Helena blabbed to him, too? "What do you know?"

"Only what you've told me," he said. "He was treating you like a child, saying that you had to come home at the first sign of danger."

"Right." Now she understood why her dad had been so concerned about her safety. "I kept a few things to myself."

"Like what?"

"He's so anxious to interfere in my life now, but there was a time when he should have protected me but didn't."

"That doesn't sound like a marine."

Though her bed was queen-size, the space seemed to shrink around them until it was as small as a camping cot. If she and Mason were going to have any sort of relationship, she needed to trust him and tell him the whole story. She scooted around until she was sitting cross-legged beside him, looking down at his handsome face.

There was something she'd wanted to do from the first time she saw him, and now seemed like the right time. She reached out and rubbed her palm back and forth over his buzz cut. His short, razor-cut blond hair tickled.

He caught hold of her wrist. "Is there a reason you're petting my head like a dog?"

The bristly haircut actually did remind her of a sleek-coated dog, like a Great Dane. "I wanted to see how the buzz felt."

"This is your one and only warning. If you treat me like a dog again, I will get you good." He released her wrist and lay back on the bed, staring up at the ceiling. "This thing with your dad, did it happen a long time ago?"

"It was the car crash when I was twenty. I told you about it." His teasing kept her from sinking into depression when she talked about the worst trauma of her life. "I always thought it was an accident, even though they never found the guy who ran into me. A hit-and-run accident. And I was lucky that another driver came along to help me and to call for assistance."

She shook away the dark, terrifying images. She'd seen the car coming at her. Through the dark-tinted glass, she couldn't make out the features of the driver.

Mason's large hand rested on her knee. Again, he wasn't trying to be sexy. His touch was meant to soothe her and offer comfort. When she gazed into his blue eyes, they seemed to absorb and reflect her pain at the same time.

"The driver," she said without a tremble, "was sent by

enemies of my father. He attacked me as a warning for my dad, a warning for the whole CIA, MI6 secret-agent community. They struck at me. I paid the price for all the other families."

"Finally," he whispered.

"Finally what?" she snapped irritably. "What are you talking about?"

"One of the first things you said to me was someone tried to kill you and very nearly did. Then you made a hundred and one excuses not to tell me. Now you trust me enough to tell me."

"Maybe I trust you. Maybe a little."

"Did your father know that you were the intended target of a hit?"

"No." At least, she didn't think so. "He couldn't have known. If he had, my brothers would be protecting me."

"When he was informed, what did your dad do?"

"The bad guys wanted him to quit the exercise he was involved with. He did. Then he took early retirement, left the marines and came home to take care of me."

So many emotions swirled inside her that she couldn't tell her anger from her fear from her guilt. Had she ruined her father's life, causing him to leave the work he loved? Or had he ruined hers by placing her in the line of fire?

"We never talked about it," she said. "He doesn't know that I know about the terrorist and how he quit to protect me."

Mason sat up on the bed. Gently, he stroked her hair off her cheek and tucked it behind her ear. "It's not your fault that your father chose to leave the marines and put you first. And it's not his fault that you were in the crash."

"Then who do I blame?"

"The hit-and-run driver. He's the one who directly hurt you. But you could also blame the larger organization that sent him. Blame the war. Blame the ongoing struggles. Blame humanity."

"It's not fair."

"And there's nothing you can do to change it. It's in the past."

With a frustrated little sigh, she leaned into him and rested her cheek against his broad chest. Holding her, he slid back into a reclining position. They were crosswise on the bed with one of his legs halfway off and his foot on the floor. She snuggled into the nook below his chin, rubbing her cheek against his soft T-shirt.

"I want the past to be different," she said.

"Good luck with that."

She wanted to be whole and complete. If he wanted children, she wasn't the right woman for him. *Keep your distance, Lexie.* It was smarter to end this relationship right now, before she got too wrapped up in him, before he became a part of her and dumping him was as painful as tearing off a limb.

She disentangled away from his embrace and got off the bed. Straightening her shoulders, she asked, "What should I wear for our date?"

LEXIE WAS GLAD she'd paid no attention to his suggestion of an outfit with a very short skirt and a casual but very low-cut top. Her choice for their date was skinny jeans with cowgirl boots and a turquoise blouse under a short, light-weight leather jacket. She'd be warm and comfy and looked pretty good with her hair held back by a thin gold band.

Mason had showered but hadn't shaved. The stubble on his chin was darker than the hair on his head and made him look a full five years older. Adding five years balanced out his youthful buzz cut, which made him look younger. She had calculated his age at twenty-seven or twenty-eight, which was a good match for her at twenty-five. On the drive to the restaurant in the hills outside Aspen, she'd been studying his profile. He had a classic Roman nose, but otherwise his features were Scandinavian, like a Viking's.

It was half past six when he pulled out her chair and tucked her into her seat at the table. After his lecture about the proper rituals of dating, he'd better be sharp about performing all those jacket-holding, door-opening jobs. No surprise, he was skilled at acting the role of a gentleman, which made her feel so ladylike that she crooked her pinkie when she lifted her water goblet, took a sip and looked at him over the rim.

"Did you ever complete your risk assessment of the house?" she asked.

"If I hadn't completed it, we wouldn't be here. In spite of the bomblets on the roof, the security system is intact and effective. Between the electronic surveillance, the alarms and Command Central, nobody is getting into that house without announcing their presence. The admiral told me his system was state of the art, and he didn't lie."

"Which makes me wonder." She set down her glass and smoothed the linen tablecloth. Since this was a nice dining establishment that was geared toward adults, not children, she hadn't been here. "If he's not really worried about security, why hire you?"

"Ever heard the phrase 'CYA'?"

"Cover your ass."

"I'm thinking the admiral wanted to settle his conscience, especially since you were attacked and targeted as a young woman. He wants to be sure you're protected. Just like your dad, the admiral carries his share of guilt."

"It's not necessary. Feeling bad never does any good."

He raised an eyebrow. "That sounds like something they teach in nanny school."

"Oh, my God, you're right. I sound like Mary Poppins."

"At least you get to fly."

"But I don't want to be a turn-of-the-century spinster who takes care of other people's kids." Those words were truer than he would ever know. "I'm changing my ringtone."

The waiter appeared and rattled off a list of special dishes ranging from chicken paprika to schnitzel and kraut. Without having to worry about watching the kids, she could choose adventurous foods. She selected something with potatoes and something with venison that she'd never before heard of. And they both ordered beer from a huge selection.

"This dating ritual is a little bit fantastic," she said. "I usually don't drink."

"Glad to oblige."

"I have an idea." She was still thinking about security and the cache. "We should do some crime solving. We're sitting in the middle of this great big web of intrigue and spies."

"So you're not Mary Poppins anymore."

"I never was."

"Now you're Nancy Drew."

"We might as well try to figure it out."

"It's not the worst idea I've ever heard," he said. "The anti-conspiracy people think the cache is in Prescott's house, and we're the only ones with access."

She hadn't forgotten that her father's name might be included in the cache. When it was located, he might be in danger. She wanted to find it, to end this threat. "The problem is that we're not cops. We don't have the authority to make people talk to us."

"But we hear a lot."

His knowing glance sparked her enthusiasm. In her role as nanny, nobody paid much attention to her. She never ever eavesdropped, but she couldn't help overhearing things. She knew that the handsome Agent Collier was having an affair with his fifteen-years-older CIA boss with the sexy shoulder-baring dress. She'd heard a couple of captains talking about someone else who had been fired. His name was Ackerman. Where had she heard that name before?

Their waiter returned with a basket of warm, fragrant bread and two frosted mugs filled with the restaurant's brand of beer brewed with local hops. "These drinks are from the two gentlemen sitting by the window."

She looked over and saw Hank Grossman and Sam Bertinelli. What were the NSA agents doing here?

Chapter Fourteen

Mason noticed that Grossman and Bertinelli had only a couple of beers on their table—no leftover plates from dinner—and their silverware sat neatly on their linen napkins. They hadn't been in the restaurant for long, had probably arrived within minutes of when he and Lexie got here. Had the NSA agents been following them?

Lexie waved to them across the dining room and smiled. "Should we go over and talk to them?"

"If we don't," he said, "they'll come to us, plant themselves in chairs and refuse to leave."

"I don't want to spend my date with Grossman." She popped to her feet. "Also, this is an opportunity to investigate."

Mason wasn't the sort of guy who leaped before he looked. Jumping feetfirst into an investigation without considering the information they needed might be dangerous. "Be careful."

She shrugged. "It's just Grossman and Bertinelli."

Her cavalier attitude came from having high-ranking officers and federal agents passing through the Prescott home. Most people would be plenty scared if confronted with two men who worked for the National Security Agency. A little fear was smart. Either of these agents could be involved with the AC-CD group. They might know more about the Damascus Cache than they admitted in the meetings. Mason considered it likely that they had information they hadn't shared. The NSA had more covert ops than any other US intelligence service, both at home and abroad.

He followed Lexie across the half-full dining room and waited while she gave each of the NSA agents a hug. Mason shook hands. He nodded to Grossman and saved his comment for Bertinelli, who was by far the less offensive of the two. "I'm surprised to see you gentlemen here. This place has a reputation for being romantic."

"German food?" Grossman answered for his partner, pulling a frown and holding his nose in a not-so-subtle indication that he wasn't a fan of the cuisine. "There's nothing sexy about kraut."

"We came for the beer," Bertinelli said. He seemed nervous, as though he'd been caught in a lie. It pleased Mason to have that effect. "This place has a great selection of beer."

"I wasn't aware that you were staying in the area," Mason said. "What are you working on?"

Grossman slouched down in his chair. Though the waiter had poured some of his beer into a glass, he drank from the bottle. "I could ask the same question, Mason. What made you come back to town?"

He rested his hand on Lexie's shoulder. "We're on a date."

"That's real sweet," Grossman said in the exasperated tone he might use to say *I've got a flat tire.* His patience for civil conversation was just about spent, which was sad because it hadn't taken much to wear him down. Pretty soon they'd be hearing the full-out, probably obnoxious truth about why the NSA was in town and why they'd been following Mason's car. Good old sloppy Hank wouldn't be able to keep his mouth shut.

Bertinelli straightened his posture. He was more corporate in his attitudes, more economical with his words. But it was obvious that he didn't like playing a cat-and-mouse game, trying to figure out what the other guy was doing without asking a direct question. He reached up to his throat to adjust his necktie, but he wasn't wearing one. He had on a pullover sweater and a shirt with a button-down collar.

He fiddled with the buttons. "We heard you had some excitement at the house this afternoon."

"We did," Lexie said with the sweetest of smiles. "Who did you hear that from?"

"I can't remember. Maybe the guy at the gas station. Was there an accident at the house?"

"It's all taken care of," she said.

"Perhaps we could help," Bertinelli returned.

"The fire department was terrific," she said.

"It sounds dangerous," he said.

"We have things under control."

"Never hurts to have someone else check it out."

The two of them were lobbing comments back and forth like a tennis match. Mason was pretty sure that Bertinelli wanted to wangle an invitation to the house so he could take a look around for himself. Mason didn't know what motivated Lexie, but she appeared to be enjoying herself. Her cheeks were pink, and her dark eyes glistened.

"That's enough," Grossman grumbled. "We all know what's going on here. We've been running surveillance on the house."

"Shocking," Lexie said.

"We saw the fire department and followed them back

into town to observe their use of the blast chamber, which was very groovy."

Mason had figured the detonation would be fun; watching stuff blow up usually was. He wouldn't have used the word *groovy*, though. "You followed us here tonight."

Grossman looked over at his junior partner. "I told you he picked up on the tail."

"I don't think so. I was careful." Bertinelli looked hopefully toward Mason. "Did you see me?"

Mason didn't want to squash this last grasp at competence. "I didn't see you following, but I knew you were surveilling. Your arrival here is too coincidental."

Lexie stamped her foot. In her little cowgirl boots, she was adorable. "Why were you watching us and following us?"

"We've got no leads," Bertinelli said. "The CIA team didn't find anything that would lead us to the cache. None of our informants know anything, which isn't surprising, because most of them are in the Middle East."

"Yeah, it's a problem." Grossman took a long glug of his beer. "There aren't many spies or snitches in the high Rocky Mountains."

"You don't have to creep around the house," Lexie said.

"No?" Bertinelli's brows went up.

"I'll check with Helena and the admiral to make sure it's okay, and you can come over tomorrow around two in the afternoon. You can poke around to your heart's content."

As they returned to their table, he wished she hadn't been so generous with her hospitality. He didn't trust those two. From what Mason understood, the Damascus Cache was worth a lot of money to the right people—enough money to tempt someone like Grossman, who didn't have many years left as an active agent. Bertinelli might opt for a big payoff so he wouldn't have to be under Grossman's thumb.

Mason held Lexie's chair for her again. She turned her head to look up at him, and her grin widened. "That was fun."

He sat opposite her and sipped his beer from the frosted mug. "How was it fun?"

"For one thing, we were just too cool for school. We were, like, good cop and bad cop."

"Which one were you?"

"I'd like to say I was the bad cop, but I kind of invited them over to the house."

The idea of this cheerful, open-faced woman being a stern interrogator tickled him. "And you'll probably feed them cookies and milk."

"I'd like to point out that my method worked. Grossman admitted everything. I'm a little peeved that they've been snooping near the house with binoculars."

"If I were you, I'd make certain my curtains were always closed."

"What about you?"

If somebody was spying on him, Mason would stand at the window naked, waving and making rude gestures. "It's different with guys."

"I grew up with three brothers." She cocked her head to one side. Her gaze softened as she took a sip. The dark beer left a trace of froth on her lips. They seemed to be moving into the dating part of their evening, when the conversation turned more personal. "You just had the one brother, right?"

Matt was several years older, and Mason sometimes felt like an only child. He remembered when he was seven and saw the sign at Elitch Amusement Park that said you couldn't ride until you were a certain height.

"You must be this high." He held out his hand beside the table. "That's what I felt like as a kid. Matt was on the roller coaster, and I was on the sidelines waiting to grow. Then I did. And the age difference didn't matter."

"Did your family always live in Denver?"

"We spent a couple of years near San Francisco in Silicon Valley." His dad was a computer guy and had brushed up his skills with a stint at one of the big software companies. "How about you? Where have you lived?"

"Everywhere." She stretched her arms wide apart. "When you're a military brat, you get accustomed to shuffling from one place to another. Mostly, I've been in Texas. I'm a countrified woman. I grew up knowing how to ride, shoot and hunt. I'm not scared of snakes or spiders. And I love beef."

He liked her résumé, even though their childhoods didn't have much in common. He'd been a city kid who shot hoops, played sports, jogged and spent every Saturday morning with the chess club before discovering the gym. "I always wished I'd lived in the mountains. I'd have a whole different skill set."

"Like snowboarding and skiing."

"Rock climbing and kayaking."

She flashed one of her upturned smiles. "I'd like to learn how to do those things, but it's impossible while I'm being a nanny and need to watch out for the kids."

"Maybe while I'm here," he said, "we could learn together."

"I'd love to."

Their dinner was served. He couldn't argue with the portions. With the side dishes, including a container of pickles, the plates covered the whole surface of the table. He hadn't realized how hungry he was until he dug in. The beef was so tender it could be cut with a fork, and everything else—even the sauerkraut—was perfectly seasoned.

As their official date progressed, he learned more about her. Almost all her fond memories about her mother were from when she was a little girl. With her dad being deployed, her mom was lonely and her daughter was her only company. Her mom cried a lot, and Lexie tried to make her happy. She'd dance around with a goofy smile on her face or tell a joke or make up a nonsense song.

The two NSA agents came over and said goodbye before they left the restaurant. If they had the okay from the admiral and his wife, they'd come to the house tomorrow and make their own search for the cache.

"I should warn you," Lexie said to Bertinelli, "there's no way that Helena will let you go into the safe room, and I don't know how to open that door."

"Nobody has ever searched in there," he said.

"And nobody ever will unless Helena gives the okay." Big smile. "I don't think any judge will issue a search warrant for Admiral Prescott's private papers."

"Is that what's in there?"

She shrugged. "Could be."

As soon as the agents left, he reached across the table and took her hand. "We're going to search in the safe room tomorrow morning, aren't we?"

"Absolutely. It feels sneaky to do that to Bertinelli. He's not a bad guy."

"We don't know that. Don't know hardly anything about him."

"I do." She squeezed his fingers and reclaimed her hand. "Sam Bertinelli with his neat black hair and pretty hazel eyes wanted to go out with me, and I got curious about him. He's from Chicago, was an accountant for an oil exploration company before he joined the NSA and is twice divorced, no kids. He's also forty-seven, which is old enough to be my father. He was annoyed when I told him no. Then he pushed, and I hinted very subtly that the age difference bothered me. And then he was seriously angry."

"Gee, I wonder why."

Her cute smile twisted into an evil smirk. Sweet little Lexie wasn't a wide-eyed innocent. "Age isn't the only reason I didn't want to date him. There was a whole list of problems."

"I hope you're not holding any of those nasty bomblets for me. Maybe you hate men with blond hair. Or you never date guys whose first names start with *M*."

"I don't *enjoy* rejecting guys." There was a dark undertone to her voice, a mixture of anger and sadness. "But I don't see any point in getting started with a relationship that can never work."

"Not every relationship is going to end in marriage."

"I know." She scowled. "There are a million different kinds of relationships. Friends. Colleagues. Coworkers. You and I could be partner detectives."

"A lot of possibilities," he said. But there was one relationship he wanted with her. Pure and simple, one word, he wanted to be her lover.

EVER SINCE THE CRASH, Lexie had preferred vehicles with substance. Mason's ten-year-old Land Rover fit the bill. Leaning back in the passenger's seat, she felt a pleasant sense of security that wasn't entirely due to the muscular SUV wrapped around her. Mason would keep her safe. He was her protector.

She noticed that he was taking a different route back to the house and wasn't using his GPS device. "Do you think Grossman and Bertinelli are trying to follow us again?"

"Probably not."

"Why are you going this way? It's longer."

"Since I'm going to be here for a couple of weeks, it's useful for me to know my way around."

She gazed through the window at the twinkling lights of Aspen to her left in the distance. Though it was just after nine o'clock, there wasn't much traffic outside town. An occasional car or truck zipped past the Rover on the two-lane road. A truck had been following them for a few miles, but when Mason made a left, the truck stayed on the main road.

He drove into a wide, rocky canyon with cute little cabins on either side. She lowered her window so she could hear the burble of the narrow creek that had dictated the winding path of this road.

"What's this creek called?" he asked.

"It's the Little Wapiti. That's the Shawnee word for elk." She felt another grin coming on. "Actually, it means white rump."

"So if you told the kids you were going to spank them on their little wapitis…"

"Oh, I've told them that before. I never could bring myself to hit them. The threat is usually enough. You know what's crazy? I kind of miss the little beasties."

"That's not crazy. You love those kids, even the twins."

"I guess I do."

Casually chatting, they drove out of the canyon into the open expanse of Henscratch Valley. In the distance, the looming hills, dark pines and jagged rocks seemed alive in the shifting shadows and moonlight. It was a beautiful night, and she realized that she was having a good time. This date was a success. The food was good. The conversation was interesting. Would it end with a kiss? Should she invite him into her bedroom?

The Rover glided onto a section of road that zigzagged

up the side of a cliff in sharp hairpin turns. Mason checked his rearview mirror. "Damn."

A ripple of fear went through her. "What is it?"

"The truck behind us. It's the third time I've seen him."

"Are you sure?" She turned and stared out the back window. A filthy truck was two car lengths behind them. "Lots of people drive trucks around here."

"Look at the license plate."

She wriggled around in her seat as much as she could without unfastening the seat belt. "I can't see it."

"Because he's covered the number with mud. On the front and back. Unidentifiable, he's just another beat-up old truck."

And the driver wants to kill us.

Chapter Fifteen

Remembered terror from her first devastating car crash sluiced through her veins and joined with a newer version of fear. Not again, not another crash.

Mason pushed the accelerator, and the Rover responded, leaping forward in a burst of speed. Though the narrow asphalt road ascended on a steep incline, their vehicle seemed to be going faster. They gained traction. The rear end fishtailed as they took the first of three tight curves.

The landscape whirled past her like a kaleidoscope. Her mouth was open to scream, but she couldn't make a sound. Her throat constricted, strangled by fear. Her heart thumped hard against her rib cage.

Even faster than the first curve, Mason swiveled the Rover around the second. The tires skidded but only a bit. He had control. He was a better driver than she'd ever been. With Mason at the wheel, they might survive.

If she had a choice, she might want to die rather than going through the physical agony of another bone-wrenching crash with injuries on top of injuries and days of constant surgeries. They said what didn't kill you made you stronger. Not true. Not for her.

It had taken every shred of her willpower to get through her painful physical therapy. She'd used up her lifetime allotment of courage battling the naysayers who told her she'd never walk again. But she would never choose death. She couldn't do that to her father.

There was only one more hairpin on this stretch. The vehicle behind them was so close that his headlights flashed in the Rover's rearview mirror and blinded her. Her hands flew up to cover her eyes. She couldn't bear to watch.

The Rover took the final curve at a fearsome speed. At the same time, the truck bumped the fender. They skidded and drifted across the center line. She heard gravel from the shoulder kick up and batter the undercarriage. Then the Rover straightened out.

Mason was driving so fast that she didn't dare peek at the speedometer, but she dropped her hands to her lap. "Is he gone?"

"Not yet."

The upper ridge of this cliff was above timberline; there were no trees blocking her view when she turned to look for the truck. He'd fallen back quite a distance. "Is something wrong with his truck?"

"It'd be a damn shame," Mason said, "if he damaged his vehicle while he was trying to kill us."

Her pulse was still racing, and she was breathing in frantic gasps. But they'd made it this far. She had reason to hope.

"What happens on the road ahead?" he asked. "It looks like we're headed into a forest."

"The trees are close on both sides of the road. It's a gradual descent, not a lot of huge drop-offs."

"I don't want to get trapped in there."

"No?"

"Hell, no. We're taking the fight to him."

But she didn't want to fight. She was happy to see the truck falling even farther back. "It looks like he's given up."

"Brace yourself."

The Rover rounded a gentle curve. For a moment, their vehicle was hidden from the truck behind a rocky mound. Mason tap-danced between the accelerator and brake, throwing them into a spin in the middle of the road. The Rover came around one hundred and eighty degrees. He killed the headlights. They sat and waited for the truck to approach.

She had no trouble screaming, "Are you insane?"

"This time, we'll get him."

"'This time'? What do you mean 'this time'? It's not the same guy who hit me before."

It couldn't be. That was in a different area, at a different time. The first attack was for different reasons. Why was Mason putting the two together?

She saw the headlights approaching.

Mason revved the engine.

She couldn't believe he'd try to take out a truck with his SUV. Land Rovers were sturdy, but this wasn't a Hummer. On the hopeful side, it was possible that Mason knew exactly where to strike the truck to disable it. His one-hundred-and-eighty-degree turn had been impressive.

He stopped revving and sat back in his seat as his hands dropped from the steering wheel. "It's not him," he said.

A Volkswagen bug chugged around the curve and kept on going. She asked. "How did you know?"

"The beams from the headlights were too low for a truck." He turned toward her. "We need to go after him. Keep your eyes open. He might have pulled off on a side road."

"No." She reached over and grabbed his arm as though restraining him could stop the car. "This is where we need to remember that we aren't federal agents or detectives. Here is where people like you and me have to back down and let the police take over."

"The guy who attacked us—the guy in the truck—is a lead. We can't let him get away."

"What if he's waiting for us? What if he's armed?"

Mason patted the shoulder holster he wore under his sports jacket. "So am I."

Turning her head away from him, she folded her arms below her breasts and stared straight ahead through the windshield. Arguing wouldn't do a bit of good. Mason was as stubborn as the men in her family. Once they got a course of action set in their minds, they couldn't be stopped.

He tapped the accelerator, and the Rover rolled slowly forward. The car eased around the edge of the mound. The high mountain road stretched before them. There wasn't another vehicle or human being in sight. Nothing but grasses and junipers and a single lodgepole pine that reached up toward the Big Dipper.

Instead of taking up the chase, Mason made a three-point turn. The Rover was headed back toward the house. "You're right. I have no business chasing after that guy."

She was grateful that he'd changed his mind. "Thank you for listening to me, for hearing me."

"I'm not a cop. It's wrong for me to put you in danger. My job is to keep you safe."

He activated his hands-free phone and called the chief investigating officer from the Aspen police, whom he'd met at the hotel.

She sat in silence, chewing her lower lip and wishing that she didn't like Mason as much as she did. *I don't want to hurt you. Don't make me hurt you.* The near crash reminded her of the past and made many things clear to her. After dinner, she'd been pleased with their date, thinking about their relationship and wondering if this evening should end with a kiss…or something more interesting. But that was wrong. Intimacy wasn't an option.

A committed connection with Mason would never work. She couldn't provide him with a family, and she knew he wanted kids. A bright energy emanated from him when he talked about his brother and growing up with his buddies Dylan and Sean. Mason was comfortable with the Prescott kids. He couldn't help chuckling when he was around little Princess Stella, and he was cool with the older boys. A natural-born family man.

She glanced over at him. He was watching the road and talking on the phone, describing the truck that looked like hundreds of other trucks in this area. There'd be a dent in the truck's front fender, passenger side and in the grille. He gave their location with pinpoint precision.

He would have made a good cop, but TST Security probably paid better and he had more freedom. The downside of TST was getting stuck with a prickly client like her. She needed to end this budding whatever-it-was right now. It was the smart thing to do.

WHEN THEY ARRIVED at the Prescott house, Mason was glad he'd insisted on parking in one of the four spaces attached to the house. Climbing the hill from the larger parking garage would have meant unnecessary exposure. The guy in the truck might have a cohort watching the house, a sniper.

But it seemed unlikely, because none of the attacks had been lethal. The charge on the bomblets had been too small to cause serious damage. The truck had given up too easily. The only thing accomplished by the chase on the mountain roads was scaring Lexie half to death. He'd watched as her fear rose up and overwhelmed her. He'd seen her pain.

When he parked in the garage and the lights came on,

she had her seat belt off in seconds. She reached for the door handle.

"Wait," he said.

"What for?" The harsh overhead light made the freckles stand out on her face. Her usually sparkling eyes were dull and tired.

"Just wait."

"Fine."

He came around to her side of the Rover and opened the door for her. "I won't pretend this date is ending the way I'd hoped, but it doesn't have to be all bad."

"I agree." Her forehead pinched in an unfamiliar scowl. "We're going to be together for a while, like it or not. Might as well try to get along."

"I wanted to say…" This wasn't an apology. He wasn't sorry that his first impulse had been to go after the bad guys. "I can't begin to understand the pain you suffered in that first crash. You're a brave woman, a strong woman. I respect you and your opinions. And I never should have suggested chasing down that truck."

Her features softened a bit. "I know why you were tempted. I'm as anxious as you to have this threat over with."

She left his car and walked toward the house. At the entry, Mason punched in the numerical code that was synced with all the other security systems. Feedback indicated that nothing had been disturbed, but he would make a visual sweep before they went to bed. The attack on the road meant he needed to step up his regular procedures. "Lieutenant Hough from the Aspen police is going to stop by tonight to take our statements."

"Can't it wait until morning?"

"He wants to get the details while they're fresh in mind. My car insurance company can wait."

After they moved from the garage to the house, he rearmed the alarm and followed her on a winding trek through the huge house to the kitchen.

She tossed a comment over her shoulder. "How are you going to explain to the insurance people that you couldn't exchange information at the scene of the accident?"

"Maybe they have a box I can check for lunatic psycho." He shrugged. "The Rover has been battered worse than this. She's a tough little car."

"She?"

"Rhonda," he said, "as in 'Rhonda, you look so fine.'"

She went to the fridge, got waters for both of them and placed the plastic bottles on the counter. Some of the tension had left her shoulders. Her posture was more relaxed.

He hated to do anything that would upset her again, but he couldn't let this slide. "I'm going to have to notify the admiral about this."

"I suppose."

"You know what that means."

"My dad."

"You have to call him, Lexie. He nearly went berserk the last time he thought you were in danger. A car chase seems even more directed, more personal."

She pinned him with a sharp gaze. "Is that what you think?"

"There's something weird about it." He pulled a stool up to the counter and sat. "How does running us off the road connect with the admiral and the Damascus Cache?"

"It might have been a warning. Like the first time I got crashed."

"But there's no clear message. What kind of threat is it to attack the nanny and a bodyguard?"

As her scowl deepened, her freckled nose twitched.

The woman couldn't help being adorable, even when she was deeply worried. "I don't suppose the admiral would be convinced to talk because you and I were hostages."

"He's got six kids. Any one of them would be a better hostage."

"Maybe not the twins." She tried to grin, but the attempt failed.

"Your dad might have some ideas," he said. "I'm sure he knows more about your first crash than anyone else."

"You can forget that line of questioning. I will call my dad and inform him that someone bumped your fender, but I'm not going into any details about the cache."

"Didn't you say his name was in it?"

"Yes, but…"

"Do you want me to call him?"

Her face lit up with pure, beautiful relief. The veil lifted from her eyes. Her smile came back. "I should be able to take care of this myself. Let me think about it."

"Think fast," he said. "It's ten o'clock here and an hour later in Austin."

Taking his water bottle, he went down the hall to the richly furnished office and sat behind the desk. It wasn't so much that he needed privacy, but he wanted Lexie to have some space to think. The call to her father was going to be difficult, no matter who made it.

He took out his phone. He wasn't pleased to be sending separate text messages to the admiral and Helena. This was his second message in one day—his first day on the job. The way he saw his security position was to keep the house and Lexie protected and not to bother the people who hired him. The Prescotts shouldn't have to worry, and he felt like an alarmist when he texted them about every little thing. But when emergency personnel, like cops and firemen, came to the house, the Prescotts needed to be informed.

He sent the texts, leaned back in the swivel chair and put his feet on the desk blotter. He waited.

Lexie appeared in the open doorway. "Make the call."

Chapter Sixteen

"Sergeant Major DeMille, this is Mason Steele from TST Security. We've never met, but you might have known my brother. He was a marine, stationed in Afghanistan. His name was Matthew Steele."

"Sorry, I don't recall the name." Lexie's dad cleared his throat. "I'll tell you what, young man. I'm giving you ten seconds to explain why you called in the middle of the night."

"I work for Admiral Edgar Prescott as a bodyguard." He put the call on speakerphone so Lexie could hear. "I'm at the Prescott home in Aspen with your daughter."

"Is she all right?" The anxiety was evident.

Mason imagined DeMille jolting forward, fully awake. "Yes, but there was an incident earlier tonight."

"Put her on the phone. What did you say your name was? Mason Steele? Listen up, Mason Steele, you put my daughter on the phone right now."

No doubt about it, Sergeant Major Danny DeMille was an intimidating person, a real hard-ass. But Mason had already backed down for Lexie and wasn't in the mood to do the same for her dad. "Your daughter asked me to explain."

"Did she, now?"

Mason started right in. "After dinner, we were driving back to the Prescott home in my Land Rover."

"What year is your Rover?"

"It's a 2003 Land Rover Discovery with the square top."

"Nice, that's a car that looks like a car."

Why was DeMille being chatty about vehicles? Trying to be friendly? No way. He might be trying to distract Mason. Or he might be nervous. This conversation about his daughter had been a long time coming.

Mason looked over at Lexie. At the far end of the tan leather sofa, she was curled up in a ball with her knees pulled up to her chin. Her eyes were squeezed shut, but she was still listening.

"Driving back to the house," Mason continued, "we came to a series of hairpin curves. A truck pulled up behind us."

"Had you noticed being followed before that?"

"Yes, sir, but the truck was maintaining a safe distance. This was a narrow mountain road with no exits. Evasive driving tactics were not possible."

"Anything's possible," he growled, "if you've got the guts to do it."

"The truck was on my bumper, going too fast. At the curve, he smacked my rear fender. I recovered and we reached an open stretch of road. I pulled far ahead."

"The truck didn't keep up?"

"No, sir, he fell back. When I got to a place where I could turn, I did a one-eighty and got ready to ambush this guy. But he was gone."

"Did you pursue?"

"My job is to keep your daughter and the Prescott home safe." He nodded to Lexie, acknowledging that the retreat was her idea. She didn't see him. Her eyes were still closed. "We immediately came back to the house, where the security system is fully activated. The police will come here to take our statements."

"Well, Mason, it sounds like you're doing a fine job. Put my Franny on. She's listening to this call, isn't she? Francine Alexandra DeMille, you pick up the phone."

Mason didn't give her the chance. He wasn't letting this guy off the hook until he got some answers. "What can you tell me about the Damascus Cache?"

"Sorry, son, that information is above your pay grade. It's none of your business."

"When somebody tries to run me off the road, it becomes my business. Why would somebody who's interested in the cache come after Lexie? Could there be a connection to her earlier accident?"

"Whoa, there. I never said these two incidents were connected. You're jumping to conclusions."

"She knows." He paused for a moment, allowing those words to sink in. "Lexie knows that the first accident was a warning to the intelligence community in the Middle East. She knows that she was hurt to prove a point. Helena Prescott sat her down and had a heart-to-heart talk."

"Damn it, Helena had no right to shoot off her mouth."

"Your daughter has a right to know." Her eyes were open, staring at him. He couldn't tell if she was angry or on the verge of tears.

"It was my fault," DeMille said. "My baby girl was almost killed because of my job."

"Like father, like daughter. Lexie blames herself for taking you away from the work that you love." He could have been angry with these two. They were so busy trying to protect each other that they didn't realize how much they were hurting themselves. "I've never known a family so anxious to take responsibility. You and your daughter must love each other very much."

"She's the light of my life." His voice caught, and he exhaled a ragged breath. "Tell me the truth, Mason. Is there any way I could help if I came to Aspen?"

"The investigation has run into one snafu after another. Prescott has no idea where the cache might be, and the Anti-Conspiracy Committee for Democracy thinks he's lying and has the cache hidden in the house. The CIA has made a search. The NSA is coming tomorrow." He decided not to mention the bomblets on the roof. "There's a serious lack of evidence."

"You're grasping at straws, young man. That's why you asked me about connections between Lexie's accident and this truck that bumped your fender."

"The truck was in serious pursuit. But he quit after one tap. Why?"

"The real question is, why do you think I'd know?"

"Because you probably know more about Lexie's first accident than anyone."

"You're right about that. I researched the hell out of the accident, got real serious about forensics and watched every interview with every suspect," he rambled on, describing a desperate yet futile investigation where he was riding the detectives every step of the way. "As you know, they never caught the bastard who did it."

"Did you work up a profile?"

"You know I did."

"Will you fax it to me?"

"I'll do better than that, Mason. I'll make a copy of the whole file and ship it express. There might be some detail that helps your investigating."

"Technically, I'm not an investigator."

"But you're in this up to your elbows." He chuckled. "Now will you put my daughter on the phone?"

Mason handed over the phone and left the room. As he closed the door, he heard her say, "I love you, too."

AFTER THE BEST talk she'd ever had with her dad, Lexie came out of the office to find Mason. She checked the time on her phone. She and her dad had only spoken for fifteen minutes, but she felt deeply loved by a man whose gruff manner couldn't completely conceal his open heart.

Not in the kitchen. "Mason? Where are you?"

"Upstairs."

She skipped down the hall and across the foyer toward the sweeping staircase that climbed to the second floor. Mason was unpacking the few belongings he'd brought with him in the best, largest bedroom suite in the house. Twice the size of the other bedrooms, this guest suite also had a sitting room with a huge sofa and chairs. There was even a desk by the window. The decor was a classic southwestern style. Two woven rugs with deep blues, sienna and turquoise decorated the floor. The rough-hewn coffee table held a round, fat cactus.

"Nice room," she said.

"I thought so."

"You think you're pretty hot stuff."

"There's a reason I'm taking this room. We're both going to sleep in here."

"Me? With you?" She didn't dare! Being that close to him would be too tempting, and she was determined to keep their relationship at the friend level. "I don't think so."

"It's not a choice," he said. "I can't protect you if we're sleeping in separate rooms."

"Oh, please. Do you really think somebody is going to get past all this security and sneak up on me?"

"After talking to your dad, I'm not going to take that chance."

Her father had that effect. "Yeah, if anything happens to me, you're a dead man."

He pointed to the extra-long king-size bed. "There's

plenty of room. You could fit all the Prescott kids and a small pony in that bed."

On this issue, she had to put her foot down. No way were they sleeping in the same bed. "There's the sofa. If you insist on being in the same room, you can sleep there."

"I suppose you know there's a tub with massaging water jets in the bathroom."

"On occasion, I've been known to take a nice, long soak in there. It uses less water than the hot tub."

"And you can be naked." He wiggled his eyebrows. "How did the rest of the conversation with your dad go?"

"Great! I forgave him and vice versa. He's still worried about me, but not so much with you being here. He's already looked up TST Security on his computer, and he believes you're qualified."

"Good to know."

"He checked out your photo. Likes your buzz cut."

"I don't wear it this way to impress retired marines," he said. "I like it short in the summer because it's efficient and cool when I'm outside."

"Apparently, there's a photo of you and your Land Rover on the TST website. He said to tell you it was a good vehicle."

"Ha!" He sank onto the sofa that would be his bed. "Your dad is a sneaky old codger. That's why he was asking about my car. First thing he did when we started talking was to look me up."

"'Sneaky old codger'?" She nodded. "That would be accurate."

From downstairs, she heard the familiar doorbell chime: "Yo ho ho, and a bottle of rum." She left the room. "That must be the cops."

"Lieutenant Hough," he reminded her. "Be nice to the guy. He's going out of his way for us."

"Don't go into the house," the leader said. "That is a direct order, Tony."

"What if I could slip in there for a few minutes and plant some bugs?" He'd had listening devices all over the house before the CIA came through and cleaned them out like a bunch of high-tech maids. "Or a camera."

"I don't want you to take the risk of getting caught. I need you. You're my best man."

"Damn right, I am."

"But if you ever pull a stunt like you did earlier, I'll get rid of you. No more easy paydays. No more fun."

"But there was no harm done."

"You ignored my orders. Never do that again."

Tony ended the call and dropped his glowing cell phone on the seat of the used sedan he'd bought in Denver when he knew he'd be spending time in the mountains. He didn't want to lose his easy paycheck.

Chasing down the bodyguard's Land Rover wasn't the first time Tony had disobeyed a direct order from the leader. There had been the incident in Montreal when he was supposed to grab a Russian drug lord off the street and rough him up. The guy was a loudmouth jerk. Tony had shut him up for good.

Ultimately, it turned out to be a good thing that he'd eliminated the threat from the Russian, but the leader had been angry when it happened. The same way he was mad at Tony for crashing into the Land Rover when he was only supposed to keep an eye on Lexie.

Tony hadn't set out to break the rules, hadn't planned it. He just couldn't stop himself.

When she and the bodyguard left the house, he'd been surprised. If Tony had been locked inside that mansion with a sexy little babe like Lexie, he wouldn't go anywhere. They had plenty of food, booze, a pool table, video games and a swimming pool. Hell, they even had their own movie theater in the basement.

He had watched them drive away. He didn't have to tail them because he'd already attached a GPS tracer to the bodyguard's car, but he followed, anyway. And he noticed another car watching. They were forming a damn parade.

That was when he got the idea of running them off the road. It'd be ironic. Five years ago, he'd almost killed Lexie with a car crash. It was one of his first assignments from the leader. At first, he thought the crash was a dumb idea. He'd told the leader that a bullet was more efficient, and he'd been right. She survived the accident. Apparently, that was the best outcome, after all. A bunch of the undercover ops and agents came to visit the sick little girl, and they could all imagine their family members going through a struggle like hers.

A year and a half ago, he'd arranged to meet her. He'd been expecting an invalid. At the very least, she'd be wheelchair bound or limping around on a cane. Instead, he found this energetic little fireball. She was hot. She was tough. And she owed her life to him.

He was ready to collect that debt. His first car accident failed to kill her. This one would succeed. If not, he had his rifle. He'd stolen a truck and waited. By the time they left the restaurant, he was pumped.

Making sure they didn't have another tail, he followed at a distance. At times, he let them get out of his sight and tracked them on the GPS. They wouldn't suspect a thing until…

Tony closed in at the first of the hairpin curves. That damn bodyguard was a good driver. His car was in control. When the first hit failed to even slow them down, Tony fell back. His plan was to wait for them to come to him.

He would have shot the bodyguard and kidnapped Lexie. But they never showed. Cowards.

The way he figured, she owed him one.

Chapter Seventeen

The detective from the Aspen police was cordial and efficient and offered very little hope of finding the driver who ran into them. The truck might have been stolen. Or the dirt obscuring the license plate might be legitimate grime. It could be local teens messing around.

It was frustrating not to get answers, but she understood. Everything about this case was baffling. Top agents in the CIA and NSA were stumped. Why should she expect local law enforcement to figure it out? It was clear that the Aspen police chief was backing away from this mess as quickly as possible. The five guys who were arrested at the hotel had already been transferred to federal custody and were being charged with attempted terrorism…or something like that.

After the lieutenant had recorded her statement, her interest waned to a mere sliver. Mason and the cop went into the garage to look at his crumpled fender, and she didn't bother to tag along. Though this hadn't been a physically taxing day, not compared with her usual chasing around with the kids, which kept her on her feet, she was tired. Today weighed heavily on her emotions.

From her first trickle of fear when Mason arrived to finding the bomblets to the car chase that had been horribly reminiscent of what happened to her five years ago.

She recalled what Mason had said. *This time, we'll get him.* What did he mean by that? It couldn't be the same driver, it couldn't be.

After they'd said good-night to the lieutenant, she trudged upstairs. Mason followed, making sure that she was going to bed in the large guest suite instead of her own cozy room.

As he watched, she dropped her nightshirt—a gift from Princess Stella that was covered in pink unicorns—at the lower end of the king-size bed and pulled back the gazillion-thread-count mauve duvet. "You know, movie stars have slept on this mattress. Famous people, fabulous people."

"Anybody I'd know?"

"I don't know. What kind of movies do you like?"

"I like when stuff blows up." He gave her a sheepish grin. "And zombies, yeah, I like zombies."

She named two older actors who starred in a zombie franchise. "And we've had vampires. And aliens."

"That must be fun."

"Not so much," she said. "These people are Helena's friends. They like visiting here because of the skiing. Since I'm not much of a skier or snowboarder, they have more in common with the guy who drives them to the slopes."

"Skiing is one of those things you never learned in Texas," he said. "I'm not great, but I could show you a couple of moves."

"Too bad there's no snow."

"But there will be in a couple of months," he said. "Winter always comes around too fast."

"I hope you're not planning to stay here as my bodyguard for the changing of the seasons."

"Maybe I wouldn't be your bodyguard."

"Stop!" She threw up a palm. "I don't make long-range plans. Leave the future to take care of itself."

She snatched up her nightshirt and stomped into the bathroom. Too bad she'd forgotten her toothpaste and brush from her bathroom down the hall. Her dramatic exit was ruined when she stomped past him again.

When she returned with her bathroom supplies, he was sprawled out on the sofa with his long legs stretched out straight in front of him. "I have an idea for our investigation, Nancy Drew. You want to hear it?"

"Toothpaste first."

"It's always something," he grumbled.

She returned to the room, went to the desk by the window and closed the laptop computer she'd placed there earlier. Then she perched on the desk chair, which just happened to be the farthest spot away from his sofa. "Okay, what's this big idea?"

"Let's agree that we can trust the admiral. That means he's not hiding the cache and hasn't seen it in years."

"Okay." She liked the way he laid things out logically.

"But the AC-CD group is certain the cache is in this house. That means someone else brought it to the house. And there's an informant who talked to AC-CD."

"This all makes sense," she said. "So we have to figure out who planted it and find the mole. When you break the problem down, the solution seems easy."

"Then you add in the dozens of people who have visited this house recently. You estimated that there were thirty in the past four days."

She started taking a tally on her fingers. The admiral and his entourage, including Josh and bodyguards, had flitted through on their way to the Pentagon. Helena's hairdresser and stylist came by before she left for California, because there was no way she intended to face her hunky ex-husband without looking fabulous. The older kids had had friends over. There had been a playdate for the little ones with three friends and their parents. The cook and her assistant received food and wine deliveries. The maids came through on Wednesday. The housekeeper had an appointment with an accountant. "At least thirty."

"We need a chart like the one downstairs that you made to keep track of the family's vacations. It'd show who came to visit, how long they stayed and if there was overlapping timing."

"I can use records from the housekeeper and the cook to put that together." His idea was proactive, and she'd much rather be working on that than sitting and waiting for the next weird assault. "I see only one problem with this. After we have everybody listed, how do we know who's guilty?"

"One step at a time." He hopped off the sofa and crossed the room to the desk where she was sitting. He leaned down and lightly kissed her forehead. "We'll take it one step at a time."

She wasn't sure if he was still talking about crime solving or their possible relationship.

Both, she hoped.

LEXIE WAS IN the middle of a nightmare, but she wasn't really scared because she knew she was asleep. The scenario was too obvious. A faceless driver dodged through a thick forest to chase her. He kept gunning the engine of his truck. *Vroom, vroom, vroom.* He was coming closer, and she was running but not really hard, not struggling. Then the scenery changed.

She was on a beach with the surf crashing and receding on hard sand. When she looked over her shoulder, the car was gone. A man was running toward her.

Even though he was far away, she recognized Mason's muscular shoulders and buzz haircut. He was running hard and wearing red trunks like the guys on *Baywatch*. *Vroom, vroom, vroom.* As Mason got closer, he was joined by members of the old cast, tanned men and gorgeous women in red suits. Over the sound of the surf, she could still hear the revving of the truck. *Vroom...*

She blinked and was awake. What did that dream mean? She was afraid of the car coming after her. That much was clear. But was she also afraid of having Mason pursue her? Or maybe her nightmare was about crime. Maybe it was telling her that David Hasselhoff was the faceless driver in the truck.

Squinting, she could see across the large room to the sofa where Mason curled on his side, unable to stretch out all the way. In contrast, her body barely made a ripple under the duvet on the huge bed. It really wasn't fair for her to have all this wonderful space to spread out while he was cramped. She ought to offer to trade for the rest of the night.

She slipped from the covers. The big room was cool at night, which was good for sleeping but not running around. She padded across the woven Navajo rugs to his sofa. If he was sound asleep, it meant he wasn't uncomfortable, and she'd leave him there. *Let sleeping dogs lie.* His eyes were closed.

On tiptoe, she approached and leaned over him, hardly daring to breathe in case she woke him. His dark eyelashes made crescents above his heavy cheekbones. His jaw and mouth were relaxed, making his lips appear fuller and softer. Glancing down, she noticed that he wasn't wearing a shirt.

A shiver of awareness went through her. She wanted him, wanted to feel his warm flesh against hers. It had been over a year since she'd been intimate with a man, and she felt a familiar need.

Lexie had never been a prude. Maybe because she grew up around men, she'd never learned to play flirty games like other girls. She enjoyed sex, and she was surprised when others complained about how they never got satisfaction from the act. She did, multiple times. A low groan escaped her lips. She missed it.

His eyes popped open. Even in the darkness of the bedroom, that flash of blue was startling. Before she could do or say anything, he grabbed her and pulled her on top of him.

He kissed her. His arm encircled her. His large hand cradled the back of her skull, holding her so she couldn't move, couldn't escape while his mouth ravaged hers. Usually, she didn't think in those terms. *Ravage* wasn't a word she used, but there was nothing else she could call it when he was so demanding and so dominant.

It was purely impossible for her to hold back. She flung herself against his bare chest. He was so toasty warm. She kissed the hard column of his neck and the hollow of his throat while his musky scent coiled around her. She glided her fingers down his arm, tracing the ridges of his thick, hard muscles under his supple skin.

She groaned again, arched her back. His hands were all over her, pulling up her unicorn nightshirt. He almost reached her breast. She stopped breathing, waiting at the peak of anticipation.

Then…he stopped.

He opened his arms wide.

She scooted away from him so quickly that her bottom landed with a thud on the floor. She pushed her hair off her face and glared into the darkness. "What?"

"I didn't mean to grab you like that," he mumbled as he sat up on the sofa. "I thought I was dreaming."

If they had both been asleep, sex would have been appropriate. There would be no messiness, no strings attached and no thoughts of their potential for a future life together. "But we're not sleeping."

"What are you doing all the way over here?" he asked.

"I felt sorry for you, all squished up on the sofa."

"Thank you." Before she could say that she no longer had any qualms about making him sleep here, he was on the move. He threw off the sheets and blankets. She was glad to see that he wasn't sleeping naked, but had on gray jersey boxer shorts. He shivered once, acknowledging that it was chilly in here, and then he charged across the room. In seconds, he was under the duvet on the opposite side of the bed from hers.

He exhaled a huge sigh as he snuggled into the pillows. "Oh, yeah. This is heaven."

Though she couldn't see his face, she knew he was smiling. She couldn't interpret the meaning of a sigh, but she knew he was happy. And she didn't have the heart to throw him out.

As she got under her covers, she said, "You have to stay over there."

"Not a problem."

"I mean it, Mason. Don't come sneaking across the bed in the middle of the night."

To emphasize her words, she constructed a wall of pillows using the ones on the bed and running back and forth to the sofa.

When she had them all piled up, he peeked over the top. "Is this supposed to stop me?"

"It's supposed to get your attention," she said. "Then

you'll notice that you're not sleeping and you'll stop yourself. Because you're a gentleman."

"Right," he drawled. "How is it that you don't have a custom-made chastity belt?"

She delivered a serious karate chop to the pillows. "I never needed one."

"Good night, Lexie."

She rearranged the duvet. With Mason in the bed—on the other side of the pillow wall—she fell asleep quickly and wasn't aware of any other bad dreams. When she woke, sunlight was streaming around the edges of the drapes. The digital clock showed the time as 7:22 a.m. She heard the thrum from the shower in the attached bathroom.

He'd interrupted her shower yesterday. Turnabout was fair play. She ought to sneak in there and steal all the towels. But no, she didn't want to encourage him.

Last night, their kiss had been accidental. At least, she could pretend that she'd never meant for it to happen, that she'd somehow been sleepwalking and had fallen on top of him. And all her groaning and groping was part of a nightmare where she was wrestling an octopus.

There was no excuse for that very hot, sexy kiss and embrace. She couldn't deny that she had wanted him. But she didn't need to mention it, either.

They were going to be spending a lot of time together over the next few weeks. She had to make sure their friendship didn't turn into anything more serious.

A romantic relationship would never work. Not only was there the whole issue of her not being able to have kids, but they were set on different paths in their lives. He was determined to make TST Security a success. She liked being a nanny.

There couldn't be anything between them.

Chapter Eighteen

Lexie marched resolutely to her bedroom, avoiding the temptation of lolling around in the king-size bed and watching Mason emerge from the shower with a towel slung around his hips. Nothing was going to happen between them. They were working together to find the cache. Other than that? *Nada.*

In her own small bathroom, she splashed water on her face, brushed her teeth using an extra brush she found in her cabinet and applied the tiniest bit of makeup. Just because she wasn't trying to seduce him, she didn't need to look like an escapee from one of those zombie movies he liked.

She made a mental note to tell him about the unique feature of the movie theater downstairs. Helena had wanted it to show films, but the admiral wanted a privacy room where no technology could reach him. He could flip a switch in the theater and create white noise so no one could listen with a bug. An invisible-to-the-naked-eye spectrum of light masked the presence of anyone in that room, and it could even fool infrared technology. Being able to disappear might come in handy.

She dragged a brush through her hair and pulled it up in a ponytail. For clothes, she put on sweats, a long-sleeve T-shirt and a fleece vest to ward off the morning coolness.

Nothing sexy or cute about this outfit. Then she bounded downstairs to make coffee.

Mason beat her to it. He stood over the coffeemaker and muttered, "Come on, how long does it take? Come on."

She took a mug from the shelf and joined him at the counter. "I heard you in the shower. How'd you get dressed so fast?"

"I air dried."

That would have been fun to watch. It seemed that he was one of those people who took a while to wake up. One of her brothers was like that—half conscious for the first hour of the day, totally unaware and funny without knowing it. "You must really need your coffee."

He rubbed his hand against his jaw. "Didn't shave."

His stubble came in fast. She guessed that he could sprout a full beard in a week or so. Apparently, he'd gotten the memo about not dressing up. On top, he wore a University of Denver sweatshirt that had been red about ten years ago. The sleeves stopped above his elbow and looked as if they'd been torn off by a grizzly bear. He wore baggy gray shorts on the bottom. No socks. Beat-up black moccasins.

Though he appeared to be inches away from homeless, there was still something appealing about him. The blond fur on his forearms and calves was probably longer than his buzz-cut hair, and she had a crazy urge to stroke him like a hound.

The coffeemaker was done, and she poured cups for both of them. He stumbled around the counter to a stool, sat and took a long sip. He scowled. "You're wide awake."

"Almost eight o'clock, it's time to get started. I should call the admiral and tell him about Grossman and Bertinelli coming here to search. Plus I'll report about the chase."

"Be sure to tell him that we talked to your dad."

"I will." That was her main reason for calling. Her talk with her dad had been great, and she didn't want Prescott calling him and saying anything that would make him worry.

"I texted both the admiral and Helena last night. You're aware of that, aren't you?"

"That was *your* business—bodyguard business. When I talk to them, it's more about family." She sipped her coffee. "And I want to get started on the charts we talked about."

His expression was blank. "Charts?"

She pointed to the listing on the wall that he'd used as an example last night. "We talked about this. The chart would show people who have been to the house, when they came, how long they stayed, et cetera. Then we can figure out who brought the cache here and hid it."

As she continued, he seemed to remember. He nodded, drank coffee and nodded faster.

"A spreadsheet for suspects," she said.

"And the room," he said. "You're going to open the safe room for me."

She wished he'd forget that little promise. To access the safe room, she needed to use Helena's personal computer. It felt like prying, and she was afraid of running across something private and secretive, like the time she'd accidentally opened the diary Helena had written when she and Prescott were dating. All doodled with hearts, everything was sweet and sexy and it was none of Lexie's business. But once she'd taken that first peek, she couldn't look away.

Mason finished his coffee and went down to the gym for a morning workout. Two hours later, she found him back in the kitchen, eating a bowl of granola cereal with a banana and, of course, more coffee. He looked like a new man. The stubble was gone, and he was dressed in layers for a spring day in Aspen with cargo shorts and hiking boots, a T-shirt on top and a plaid flannel over that.

"Wow," she said drily. "You look like the centerfold for an L.L.Bean catalog."

"Hey, this is how I dress. I've lived in Colorado for a very long time. I'm outdoorsy."

"Just keep telling yourself that, city boy."

His grin brightened the whole room. Then he shoveled in another spoonful of granola. "What have you got there?"

She flipped open her laptop. "I transferred records from the cook and the housekeeper to make a list of visitors for the past year. Taken one day at a time, it doesn't seem like much. But over a twelve-month period, there have been over three hundred people in the house."

"Can you break it down?"

"Already did. I eliminated locals, like delivery people and repairmen. Then I took out friends of the kids and social groups, like a charity board who met here to discuss their event."

"Did you keep those people on a separate list?"

"As a matter of fact, I did." It had taken some effort to compile these names, and she didn't want to dump them until they were sure they didn't need them. "Why?"

"A delivery person who appears innocent might be your faceless driver who tried to crash into us. Or might have planted the bomblets on the roof. Or could be searching for the cache."

She hadn't considered that possibility. Randy, the local florist who could whip up a centerpiece at a moment's notice, took on a more sinister aspect. How did he know Helena's favorite flowers were white roses?

She scrolled through the pages. "The last two groups are the movie people and the government types."

"Helena's friends." He turned his right palm up as

though he could hold these directors, actors and the starving writers as one group. "And Edgar's associates."

"I've been concentrating on the government types," she said. "There's not much I know about their backgrounds. It might be helpful to figure out who knows who."

"No problem. The computer guy at TST can take care of the research."

"Dylan," she said, recalling the lanky guy with the ponytail at the hotel. "He seems decent."

"A real peach."

He scraped the last nibble of cereal into his mouth, took his bowl to the sink, rinsed it and put it in the dishwasher. The easy way he went through these motions made her think that he was in the habit of cleaning up after himself. Mason was good at planning ahead, a trait that suited him well as a bodyguard. And he was tidy, almost obsessively.

The man was perfect husband material. Too bad she wasn't looking for a spouse.

"Okay," he said, "let's do the safe room."

MASON FOLLOWED HER up the stairs to the bedroom suite that belonged to the admiral and his lady. It wasn't any bigger than the bedroom they'd slept in last night, but the Prescotts' room had a sultry, sexy aura. The colors were deeper, richer, and there were lots of subtle personal touches. Helena's fancy bottles of lotions and perfumes mingled with his clothing brushes, aftershave and an opened bottle of single malt. There were chocolates in a container that looked like the Eiffel Tower and a cigar humidor with a couple of Cubans. She had a book on her side of the bed. From the steamy cover, it had to be a romance.

That was what the guest room lacked: romance. It was clean and attractively furnished, but there was no passion. By contrast, the Prescotts' suite was loaded with character. There were two desks by windows on either side of the bed. Helena's desk was strewn with knickknacks, including three acting awards, and her computer. Her husband had a filing cabinet on wheels. Mason went over and flipped the lid open. It was jam-packed with paperwork.

"It looks like the admiral hangs on to everything."

"This is a huge improvement," she said. "His assistant convinced him to do a monthly sweep to dump the junk. Last month, Josh found a warranty for a Betamax player from 1977."

"I guess it makes sense that Prescott would be in possession of the last remaining copy of the Damascus Cache. It's strange that his office downstairs is so neat."

"You love that office," she said.

"I do. I like to put my feet on the desk and pretend that I'm ruling the world."

"Yeah, well, the people who really rule the world don't operate like that." She crooked a finger at him. "You've got to see this."

"Where are we going?"

"Not far." In the hall, they took a sharp right turn. She pushed open a door, turned on the light and stepped aside so he could enter first. "The office downstairs is just for show. This is where the admiral does his real work."

Chaos reigned. The working office held dozens of cabinets and a huge scarred and battered wooden desk. Every flat surface was covered with papers and weird objects, like model cars and navy caps. The walls were hung with photos; unlike the posed shots downstairs, these were mostly snapshots.

Lexie slipped inside behind him. "I think this represents what's going on inside his head. It looks like a wild jumble, but the admiral knows where everything is. He can walk in the door and lay his hand on whatever he's looking for."

"What did Collier and the CIA guys say when they knew they had to search this room?"

"I wasn't close enough to hear the exact words. Helena told me there were a lot of French curses being thrown around." She gazed directly into his eyes. "An office like this would drive you crazy."

"I like to see the surface of my desk," he admitted. "But there's something I've always wanted to do with an office like this."

"Set fire to it?" she sweetly suggested.

"I'd like to do one of those one-armed sweeps and knock everything onto the floor. Then I'd grab the girl." He suited the action to the word. He cleared a space, took hold of her arm and spun her around. "Then I'd put her on the desk."

He leaned her backward on the wood surface. Though she hadn't resisted him, he saw the fire in her eyes. Her lips pulled back from her teeth.

"That's enough," she snarled.

"Then I'd take off her glasses."

"I don't wear glasses."

"You're beautiful, Lexie." He wasn't playing anymore. Looking down at her, he was struck by a realization so sudden that it had to be true. She was everything he had ever wanted. She was the woman he'd been waiting for. "You're so damn beautiful."

She sat up quickly. "The admiral isn't going to like that you touched his stuff."

"He won't mind when I tell him what I was doing."

"You wouldn't!"

"Don't worry. I'll claim it was an accident. Better yet, I'll blame Collier."

As she stomped from the room, he wondered at her reaction. She liked him, he knew she did. When they were on their date, they were enjoying each other. Why was she constantly pushing him away?

Carrying Helena's computer, Lexie returned to the office and set it down on the counter. After fiddling around on a couple of different sites, she wrote down a six-digit combination to open the safe room. She carefully tucked the note into her pocket and headed for the stairs. "I can't share this with you, Mason."

She wasn't sharing much. The atmosphere between them grew colder and colder. They'd be together for a couple of weeks, at least. There was time enough for him to be patient with her. But he didn't understand. Had he done something to make her mad?

At the door to the safe room, he stayed all the way down the hall so she wouldn't think he was sneaking a peek at the supersecret combination. Carefully, she turned the dial in the middle of the door. When the last tumbler clicked into place, she grabbed the door handle and pulled. The heavy door slowly swung open.

This time, she went first. At the flick of a switch, a cool overhead light came on. The rectangular concrete room was as carefully packed as a shopping boutique. The free-standing wardrobe hangers held several see-through bags, some of gowns and others of fur. Metal lockboxes were stacked on shelves. Three wooden crates marked "Fragile" lined the far wall. Storage racks covered with muslin or plastic held several paintings.

"It's cold," he said.

"The temperature is steady between fifty-five degrees and sixty, which is optimum for the furs. The humidity is set at twenty percent, which is best for the oil paintings."

"If the family ever had to use this room for an extended time, their combined body heat would throw off the storage temp and humidity."

"Here's hoping that Helena never needs to choose between her children and her furs."

He pushed the door closed. A chill intimacy surrounded them. It was just the two of them, tucked away from the rest of the world. Mason had never been a guy who worried about his relationships and dating. But here she was…the girl of his dreams. Getting close to Lexie meant opening himself to the possibility of losing her. She'd made it real clear that she didn't want anything long term.

But he did.

There was trouble ahead. He sensed the impending explosion. The fuse had been lit and the bomb was ticking down to zero hour. He wanted time to duck for cover.

"Is something wrong," he asked, "between you and me?"

"Why? Because I wouldn't have sex with you last night?"

"I wasn't even thinking of that." He paused. It was best to be honest. "Well, yeah, I was thinking about you in bed and how cute you looked in the morning with all those pillows around you. But that's not what I'm talking about. You seem angry."

"I told you before, Mason."

"Got it," he said. "No long-term commitments or relationships. I don't want that, either."

"You don't?"

Now she sounded hurt. He couldn't win! "Are we going to search in here or what?"

She went to the shelves and took down a metal box. Sitting at a small table, she unfastened the latch. Inside, she found an incredible brooch in the shape of a flamingo, a tiara with a huge blue stone, a diamond bracelet and a couple of rings.

When she looked up at him, a tear slipped down her cheek. She quickly dashed it away. "I never thought my life could be like this. I'm juggling diamonds and rubies, and I think the blue one is tanzanite. This is a good job, it pays well and I like the kids. I don't want anything to change."

"Never?"

She carefully returned the jewels to their box. "I'm not going to be a nanny forever. But I'm definitely not leaving a job I really like because some man wants me to."

Not making any sense. She'd gone back to angry. Now she was referring to him as "some man," and her tone implied that man was a jerk. "Fine."

"You bet it's fine."

He took down a box and opened it. More jewels.

Another was marked "Important Papers." Inside were legal documents, deeds, car titles and other stuff. He sat at the table to sort through it.

Lexie was far from calm. She flipped through the paintings in the storage racks. "I suppose I should take each of these paintings out and feel around the edges for a flash drive."

"Not necessary," he said.

"I want to be thorough."

He placed another metal box on the table and lifted the lid. It was filled with cash—mostly hundreds. With relish, he plunged his hands into it and felt around. "I can see why the Prescotts didn't want the CIA searching down here."

"And not the NSA, either." She went to a wooden crate that was taller than she was. "Should we break these down and see what's inside?"

"I don't think so." He closed the money box and put it on the shelf. "We're done in here."

"Why?"

"Reason number one—the Prescotts aren't deliberately hiding the cache, and this safe room is always closed.

Number two—the Damascus Cache is not a flash drive or a microdot."

"Hold on." She waved her arms. "That's what everybody has been looking for, a drive that plugs into a computer."

"Do you think the admiral knows how to use a flash drive?" He asked the rhetorical question and didn't wait for an answer. "From everything I've seen, this is a man who loves documents and disdains technology. If someone wanted to give him a copy of the cache, they'd bring a paper copy of the original."

Her eyes got wide. "You're on to something."

Finally, an acknowledgment. He bowed from the waist. "Thank you, Nancy Drew."

Mason might not be a detective and might not have the right stuff for a long-term relationship, but he was smarter than people expected.

Now he knew what to look for.

Chapter Nineteen

At two o'clock in the afternoon, Grossman and Bertinelli rang the sea chantey doorbell at the Prescott house. Instead of taking them into the cozy kitchen, Lexie escorted them to the huge, sprawling front room with the magnificent furniture that Helena brought to the marriage. There were two Degas paintings on the wall, perfectly maintained and perfectly lit, but the artwork was nothing compared to the view through the arched windows.

This was a breathtaking room; very impressive. She'd purposely brought the NSA agents here so they wouldn't dismiss her as the nanny or a pesky Nancy Drew. She wanted them to take her seriously, and she had learned—by watching Helena—that a display of wealth almost always got respect.

"Gentlemen, please sit. Have some lemonade. Before we get started, I want to set parameters for your search. And I have a few questions."

"This isn't a quid pro quo," Bertinelli said. "You don't get to ask. Our work is classified."

She'd expected a prissy-pants response from him. For one thing, he didn't like her. For another, he was frustrated by having to answer to Grossman, who was sort of a moron. She smiled and said, "I'd never expect you to betray classified secrets."

She sat on a Scandinavian-style chair beside the sofa. On the coffee table was a tray holding a pitcher of iced lemonade, alongside bowls of strawberries, cream and scones. Though Bertinelli held back, Grossman didn't hesitate before digging in. He sloshed the lemonade on the tray when he poured and loaded a delicate china plate with scones and one strawberry.

"I'm guessing," Grossman said, "there are places the admiral doesn't want us to search. I'm sure he's got private stuff. We all do."

"You have permission to go anywhere," she said, "but Mason and I will accompany you."

Mason came forward and shook hands with both men. Before the NSA agents arrived, she and Mason had decided not to be friendly. He had told her repeatedly that he didn't trust them.

"I should mention," he said, "that the CIA swept for bugs and cameras after their search. And I've gone through the house again. If I find any electronic devices after you leave, I'll have to assume they came from the NSA."

"Why would I bug you?" Grossman asked.

"Doesn't make sense to me," Mason said. "But you boys staked out the house. And you followed us to the restaurant. We must be doing something that you find interesting."

Ignoring the napkin, Grossman wiped his mouth on the sleeve of his beat-up sweatshirt. With his messy steel-wool hair and sloppy clothes, he was dressed for searching in dark corners of the garage and going through crawl spaces. He looked toward his neatly dressed partner.

"I forget," Grossman said. "Why are we watching them?"

"I thought it was your idea."

Lexie got the sense that Bertinelli was more in charge

than the senior agent. She cleared her throat. "The admiral asked me to put together a list of all the people who have been in and out of the house in the past year."

"That's got to be a significant list," Bertinelli said as he finally sat down. "How many names?"

"Over three hundred."

"I want a copy," Bertinelli said.

She pinched her lips together so she wouldn't blurt out what a jerk he was. Why should it be okay for him to get information from her but not the other way around? "Of course, after I get the okay from Admiral Prescott."

"Why do you want it?" Mason asked.

"You never know what might be useful in an investigation," Bertinelli said. "Information is power."

She centered her laptop on the coffee table in front of her. "I'm hoping you can give me details about the people whose photos I'm going to show you. The kind of thing I wouldn't find in a casual search on the internet."

"The dirt," Grossman said. He popped another scone in his mouth.

"I don't mean to gossip," she said.

"Sure you do. When you come right down to it, that's what we do as federal agents. Track down rumors and mine for gossip. Show me the pictures."

She started popping up the pictures on the laptop screen. Mason's computer genius partner had already found ID photos and provided minibiographies. She wanted the gossip. Among all these people, many of whom were tied to the intelligence community, who would have access to the Damascus Cache? Why would they drop it off with the admiral?

Grossman had a lot to say about the handsome Agent Collier, who was sleeping with his supervisor, Margaret Gray, and had bedded three or four other undercover agents.

"Under the cover of his sheets," Grossman said with a laugh.

She'd slipped in Josh Laurent's photo to see if she'd get a reaction. Grossman pointed at the screen. "Isn't that Prescott's assistant?"

She faked surprise. "Oh, you're right. That must have gotten in there by mistake."

"Or maybe not," Bertinelli said. "We've been looking far and wide for suspects. Maybe we should stick to our own backyard. Josh does a lot of whining about why he hasn't been promoted. He's a fan of conspiracy theories."

"Good to know."

It would be ironic if this AC-CD scheme had been engineered by the admiral's pointy-nosed assistant. Josh had the intelligence to create a complicated plot, but she didn't see him as someone who could organize other people. AC-CD was run by a mysterious figure called the leader. Josh? She doubted he could inspire followers.

One of the faces on her laptop belonged to Al Ackerman. Lexie didn't remember him from his visit. The housekeeper had made a note about special food requirements for his Saudi princess bride, but the new wife canceled and didn't make the trip. In her eyes, Al Ackerman became only another one of a group of spies. He had passed away this year.

"Murdered," Grossman said darkly.

She corrected him. "His bio says he died from complications after a heart attack."

"Sure, if those complications included a bullet. Everybody knew Ackerman, especially after he married the princess. In our business, that's dangerous."

Lexie had obtained all the information she wanted from

these two agents. She closed up her laptop and resigned herself to spending the rest of the day shepherding Grossman and Bertinelli around the house. No big deal.

She glanced over at Mason and winked. They were handling their investigation like a couple of ace detectives.

AFTER DINNER, MASON followed Lexie into the dramatic front room. It was easy to imagine this house filled with classy, cosmopolitan guests, from Helena's Hollywood contacts to the admiral's acquaintances from the world of international diplomacy. The Prescotts lived large.

Not a lifestyle he envied. Mason didn't need or want all that bustle and noise. The machinations of big money and international business fascinated him, but he was a behind-the-scenes guy. He liked to see how things worked.

He stood behind Lexie by one of the arched windows. Through the glass, a spectacular mountain sunset was unfolding with intense shades of crimson and gold. "So this is how the top one percent lives."

"It is," she said. "I've learned a lot in the past year."

Though he wanted to stroke her shoulders, he kept his hands to himself. "Is this what you want for yourself?"

"No." Her response was fast. "Living like this is way too high maintenance. The best part of the Prescotts' life doesn't have anything to do with money. They're a kind, caring family. And, best of all, Edgar and Helena are truly in love."

He didn't know them well, but he saw signs of their romance throughout the house and also when they were together. "Is that what you're looking for?"

She spun around to face him. "Are you sure I can't go for a walk outside?"

Her lightning-swift change of subject didn't escape him. Lexie would not be drawn into anything resembling a talk about relationships. He answered her question, "Until I'm sure there's no threat aimed at you, you're housebound."

"When will you be sure?"

"The Aspen police haven't found the truck that hit us. Basically, they've got no clue. If my back fender wasn't crumpled, they wouldn't believe it happened."

She paced in front of the window as though trying to simulate a walk in the forest. "Maybe tomorrow?"

"Maybe." There was no need for her to feel trapped. This house was like a very high-class amusement park. He selected the toy he'd most like to play with. "How about a soak in the hot tub?"

She beamed. "You're on."

Upstairs in the giant bedroom, he changed into olive green board shorts. If it had been up to him, he would have gone in the hot tub naked, but he was pretty sure Lexie wouldn't go for it. Before he dashed down to the workout room, he grabbed his shoulder holster. Even though he downplayed the danger, he kept in mind their suspects as well as the person driving the truck. Somebody wanted her dead. It was his job to make sure that didn't happen.

They went downstairs to the gym together. Her coral-colored one-piece bathing suit was just about the sexiest thing he'd ever seen. It wasn't skimpy, but the color was close to her skin tone. When she dropped the towel she'd wrapped around her waist, she appeared to be naked.

He had used this type of hot tub before and got the water started. Before he could play around with adjustments to the temperature, Lexie informed him that the maintenance for the hot tub and the pool was taken care of by the maid service.

A nice perk. There were some things about living large that he could get accustomed to.

The tub was designed for six, so there was plenty of room for him and Lexie to bob around while it filled. It would have been nice to use the lap pool as well, but he understood her concern with wasting water. Drought was a consistent problem in the West. This house had its own well and septic system, but the water table was only so large. Conservation was necessary.

Lexie backed up to a water jet and moaned with pleasure as the water massaged her back. "I can never get enough of this. When I was recovering after the first crash, my dad bought a hot tub. I scolded him about wasting all that money. He laughed and said, 'What makes you think I bought it for you?'"

"Did he use it?"

"Constantly. And so did I."

She ducked her head under the frothy water and then popped up like a cork. She laughed and giggled and splashed as she bounced through the hot liquid. At one point, she burst from the water and darted across the floor to the light switch.

The gym went dark. There was enough glow from the tall windows beside the hot tub and pool to see what they were doing, and he knew when Lexie came back into the water. The great thing about the darkness was being able to look into the forest. The vertical trunks of pine trees formed a backdrop for the leafy thickets and occasional wildflower. Far away, he saw the shadow of the mountains.

"Ackerman," she said.

"What?"

"The guy who married the Saudi princess and was murdered this year. Ackerman. My dad mentioned him."

It was another connection between the past and the

present, between the first attack on her and the recent crash. Were they related? He had plenty to think about. For right now, he was content to relax with Lexie and to keep her safe.

Chapter Twenty

Three days had passed, and Lexie hadn't seen anyone but Mason. She'd talked on the phone to other people, but no one had come by the house, and she hadn't been allowed to leave. Not while the truck driver who tried to kill them was still on the loose.

When she considered her enforced alone time with Mason, she should have been bored, but they'd found plenty to do. This house offered a number of amusements. They'd spent time in the gym, watched movies in the theater and taken baths in the hot tub. Last night, she'd baked a pie from scratch. He'd trounced her on all the computer games, and she'd defeated him in chess.

Even more surprising, they hadn't run out of things to talk about. The investigating and her suspect spreadsheet took up some of their conversation, but mostly they talked about themselves, their families and friends, their hopes and dreams. Mason was the most comfortable man she'd ever known, except for one thing.

She missed sex.

He had respected her repeated statement about not wanting a relationship. They could be friends but nothing more. Ha! She wanted a lot more. His muscular body was a constant temptation, and the magnetism was about more than the way he looked. It was his easygoing smile. The way he moved when they did tai chi together. His laughter made her happy, and his rich baritone tickled her desires.

In the middle of the afternoon, she got off the phone in the kitchen and went in search of Mason. He was hanging out in the fancy downstairs office. On the desktop in front of him, he had three framed snapshots that he'd rescued from the chaotic upstairs office.

"Take a look at this," he said. "Here's our suspect, Agent Collier, with his arm around another suspect, his supervisor, whose name is Margaret. They're standing by the fireplace downstairs. I can't tell for sure, but it looks like he's patting her bottom. Grossman thought this was gossip, but they're out front about the attraction."

"That was at a luncheon on New Year's Day," she said. "I was just in the kitchen and—"

"This picture is five agents from NSA. They're a chummy group, but notice this. Bertinelli is glaring at Grossman like he wants to slit his throat."

She really didn't want to talk about suspects. "I had a phone call from Josh."

"One more photo. It's another group scene." He pushed it toward her. "Over on the right side is Ackerman. It looks like he's presenting something to the admiral. Can you tell what it is?"

She peered at the photo. "It's an Arabian vase made of brass that looks like Aladdin's lamp, only it's bigger and taller. I know exactly where it is."

He glanced up at her. His eyes were an unreal shade of blue. His lips moved and her attention shifted to his mouth. She heard him say, "Why do you know where the vase is?"

"I made it disappear." As she spoke, she gathered her self-control so she wouldn't fly across the desk and attach herself to him like a limpet on steroids. "The admiral had it downstairs in a place of honor because it was a gift from his buddy and the princess. Helena hated it. I've got to say, I'm on Helena's side. The vase is cheesy. She asked me to get it out of her sight. So I moved it to the admiral's office."

"Then it's nothing important?"

"Probably not."

Mason shrugged. "Did you say something about a phone call?"

"It was Josh. He told me that Helena was stopping by the outdoor camp in Oregon to check on Stella."

"What's wrong with the munchkin?"

"She's feeling sick," she said. "Then Josh told me that he's coming back to Aspen and staying at the house. His arrival is tomorrow at eleven thirty."

Mason's grin faltered. "We won't have the place to ourselves anymore."

She hadn't been planning to make a decision so quickly. For the past three nights, she'd spent many sleepless hours on her side of the pillows, trying to make up her mind. But now it hit her: a sudden, certain revelation. Nothing had ever been so clear. They needed to have sex before the house was invaded by Josh and others. They needed to have sex now.

She reached across the desk and took his hand. Her voice dropped to a husky whisper. "We should take advantage of our time alone. There's not much left. Come upstairs and help me move some pillows."

He vaulted out from behind the desk. "It's about time." He pulled her out to the hallway and into the foyer. "I've been obsessed with your pillow wall. I want to destroy it." He started on the staircase, taking two at a time. When she couldn't keep up, he yanked her off her feet and carried her. "Let's set all these damn pillows on fire."

He dropped her in the middle of the bed.

She grabbed a pillow with each hand and flung them onto the floor. "Down, wall, down."

Leaping up beside her, he got rid of more pillows.

In seconds the bed was cleared. They were standing on top of the mattress where famous people had slept, staring at each other and breathing hard. Mason unclipped his holster from his belt and carefully placed the gun on the bedside table. With an evil grin, he turned toward her. He lunged and tackled her and they crashed down together.

Lexie was not inexperienced when it came to sex, but Mason's kisses made her feel as if this were the first time. He was so eager, nearly desperate. His mouth was everywhere. His hands roamed wildly over her body. And she was the same way, unbuckling his belt and groping until she touched his hard erection. Her self-imposed drought was over. *Let it rain.*

Gradually, they slowed to a less frantic, more sensual pace. His long fingers combed her hair back from her face until he reached her ponytail. With a deft twist, he unfastened the band she used to hold her hair back.

Her curls tumbled free, and he paused, rising over her on the bed and gazing down. "You're a beautiful woman, Lexie."

How could she respond to that? To say yes would be arrogant. No was a sure indication of poor self-esteem.

"Same to you," she said. "I mean, not a woman. And *beautiful* probably isn't the right word."

"I know what you mean."

"I thought you might."

They had much in common, but they weren't a perfect fit. And there were still reasons why they shouldn't take this relationship to the next level. But she wasn't going to stop.

She stroked down his chest to the edge of his T-shirt,

and then she slipped her hand under the fabric and pulled it up, baring his torso and his rock-hard abs. She stroked and fondled and tweaked, and before she knew it, his shirt was off.

When she got dressed this morning, she hadn't consciously thought about having sex, but she'd worn the perfect outfit for a simple strip: a striped blue blouse with buttons and a front-fastening bra.

He pushed her back on the bed and went to work on the buttons. In a few practiced moves, he had unhooked her bra and pushed the flimsy lace aside. Slowly, he lowered his head and suckled at her breasts. With every lash of his tongue against her tight nipples, an electric surge shot through her body.

"The rest of these clothes need to be gone," she said. "Right now."

"You think?"

She looked down the length of his body. His belt was unfastened and his jeans were pushed down to show a glimpse of black jersey boxers and a very large bulge. Farther down… "You still have your boots on."

"And an ankle holster."

Going to bed with an armed man was never a good idea. Was this a warning? Was she making a big mistake?

Removing the rest of their clothing wasn't graceful, but when their bodies came together, she felt as beautiful as he'd said she was. Having sex with Mason felt like a dance with different rhythms and textures than she'd ever felt before. Smoothly, he guided her through the steps, and she was happy to let him lead, right up until the moment when he rose above her and parted her thighs.

"Wait," he whispered.

She knew what was coming, knew what he would say.

She knew she wasn't going to like this. Still, she asked, "Why?"

"I have a condom in my wallet."

She didn't need one, would never need one again. There were other health protection reasons, but she never needed to worry about getting pregnant. She stiffened in anger. The dance was over. Reality had intruded.

Though he had been ready to mount her, he had changed positions. On the bed beside her, he cuddled her against his chest as though he could protect her by absorbing her sadness and rage.

"Something's wrong," he said.

"I'm okay."

She'd come this far and it had been amazing. She refused to turn around and go back, not even if she was leading him into a lie. Couldn't she pretend, just for a moment, that they were a normal couple? Couldn't she have this pleasure, just a thin slice of happiness to cut through the darkness?

She turned so she was facing him. It wasn't a lie. As long as she didn't do something stupid and tell him that she loved him, she wasn't making a promise.

Her frustration channeled into passion. As she threw herself into sex, every muscle in her body tensed. Her breasts flattened against his chest. She clenched her legs around him.

"Easy, now," he whispered.

"I don't want to go easy."

But he was much stronger, and he was in total control. He soothed her, cajoled her with slow caresses. So patient, so sweet, he entered her slowly, almost cautiously, as though she might shatter. His kisses were soft and gentle as he eased into a simple tempo.

Again, she was trembling. Goose bumps prickled her

arms. This time, the earthquake that rattled her body came from pure satisfaction and relief. When she fell back onto the bed, her smile was real.

A happy sound—sort of like a meow—came through her lips. It wasn't anything she'd heard from herself before. "You know, Mason, I wouldn't mind having a pillow."

"Only one," he said.

He pulled up a pillow, set it against the headboard and arranged the duvet so they could lie comfortably in each other's arms. In this cozy position, with an orgasm still resonating inside her, she wondered why on earth she kept pushing him away.

"It'd be nice to have servants," she said.

"Is there something you want?"

"Dinner."

The cook had left the freezer filled with prepared meals that only needed to be microwaved to be ready, but Lexie felt too blissfully lazy to even turn the microwave dial. She hadn't been so utterly relaxed in ages.

There was a noise from downstairs. Mason heard it, too. In two seconds, he pulled on his black boxers, grabbed his gun and went to the door. He eased it open and slipped into the hallway.

She fumbled from one side of the huge bed to the other, trying to find her clothes. She didn't hear gunfire from downstairs. *A good sign.*

She'd just zipped her jeans when the bedroom door flew open and Stella dashed inside. Lexie managed to get two buttons fastened before she wrapped her arms around the little girl and scooped her off the floor.

"Hey, cutie pie. What are you doing here?"

Stella poked out her lower lip. "I'm sick."

Helena charged through the door with Mason following. "I don't know what she has, but I wanted her to see her regular doctor, so I pulled her out of camp."

Lexie nodded. "Okay."

Stella pointed at Mason and giggled. "He's got no shirt."

"Pretty funny," Lexie said.

"Hysterical," Helena said as she glanced between them. Lexie wasn't sure if her boss approved or disapproved. Probably the latter.

Stella hopped down and went toward the messy bed. "Lexie, were you taking a nap?"

"You caught me."

"I don't like naps," Stella said as she meandered around the room. "I'm too old for nap time. Lexie, does Mason take naps with you?"

She swallowed hard. This would be complicated to explain.

"Let me," Helena said as she made a dramatic swoop toward her daughter. "Sometimes, when a boy and a girl like each other a great deal, they sleep together."

"In the middle of the day?" Stella wrinkled her nose at the ridiculous idea.

"And at night, too."

Helena cast a radiant smile at all of them. The actress actually believed that her quick thinking had averted the crisis, and she wouldn't have to explain to Stella in more detail. Lexie knew better. This little girl asked question after question. She wouldn't give up so easily.

Hoping to create a diversion, Lexie charged through the bedroom door into the hallway. "Let's bring your luggage inside."

Standing behind Lexie at the top of the staircase, Stella asked, "Lexie, do you like Mason?"

"Sure I do."

"Do you love him? Are you going to marry him?"

And there they were: the two sentences she wanted most to avoid. Sometimes she just couldn't catch a break.

Chapter Twenty-One

The explanations to Helena weren't difficult. While Lexie thawed dinner, tossed a salad and chatted to Stella, who was playing in the family room, Mason told Helena about the threats to the house and possibly to Lexie.

"The only way I could be sure she was safe all night was to sleep in the same room," he said. "That's why we took the larger suite."

Helena nodded and sipped the vodka martini with two olives that he'd made for her. Mason and Lexie weren't drinking.

"I'm too tall for the sofa," he said. "Lexie graciously allowed me to join her in the bed. She set up a wall of pillows between us."

"Then the wall came tumbling down," Helena said. "It's all right, Mason. If the other children were here, we might have to come up with another explanation so we wouldn't give the impression that we approve of or condone pre-marital relationships. The older boys would be quick to use that as ammunition when they bring girls home."

He remembered what it was like to be a teenage boy. Eddy Jr. was nearly ready to start driving. The twins were sneaking up on puberty. He didn't envy the situations Helena and the admiral would soon face. "Stella seems to accept that Lexie and I like each other and take naps together."

Helena cast a worried glanced in her daughter's direction. "She was running a temperature yesterday. When it continued into today, I felt like she needed to see the doctor. Stella is usually such a healthy child."

In the family room, the little princess sat at a kid-size table and colored in a book about Cinderella. Lexie peeked over her shoulder. Subtly, she felt Stella's forehead and frowned.

"What did your doc say?" Lexie asked.

"His office is running tests. If she's all right, I'll take her back to camp tomorrow. If not, she'll have to stay here." She confronted him directly. "Is this threat real?"

"As real as the dent in my bumper."

"We'll need to find somewhere else for Stella to stay. And for Lexie, as well. I had no idea how dangerous this was."

"We'll be all right tonight," he said firmly. "I'll contact my office and have another two guards sent for tomorrow."

She finished off her martini and asked for another. In his brief acquaintance with Helena, he hadn't seen her as a drinker. This was a different side of the actress's personality. She seemed a hundred times more subdued. Her voice was deeper. She looked tired.

That night in their bedroom, he asked Lexie about the change in Helena. "Is this a case of maternal concern?"

Lexie stuck her head through the open door and looked down the hallway toward the Prescotts' suite, where Helena would be sharing her bed with her youngest daughter. Talking in a low voice, Lexie said, "Yes, she's worried about Stella. Helena is a busy woman with her fingers in a lot of pies, but the kids are important to her. She told me that the drinking and the bummed-out mood are for the role she's playing. She's also trying to drop ten pounds in three days."

"By drinking martinis?"

"I don't ask," Lexie said.

She threw back the duvet and got into bed wearing one of her child-appropriate nightshirts. This one had row upon row of flamingos. She had left the door to their bedroom open so he could hear any disturbance and do his bodyguard thing.

His gaze devoured her. "How am I going to lie beside you and not make love?"

"Helena locked the door to her suite. Maybe they won't hear us."

Their first act of passion had been loud and energetic, involving the throwing of pillows and moans of pleasure and tackling and grabbing. The memory made him smile broadly. "We might be able to tone it down."

"Stella is only six. But I think she'll know the difference between napping and what we were doing before."

"I'm going to take that as a challenge. Silent sex." Now that he'd had a taste of the incredible passion that had been growing between them, he wasn't going to stop. "Aren't there religious sects that do that?"

"We can try."

That was all he needed to hear. They would be very quiet and very, very hot.

THE NEXT MORNING, Lexie was annoyed to find Josh standing at the front door before nine o'clock. He pushed a pair of horn-rimmed glasses up his nose and gave her a terse smile. "I caught an earlier flight."

"I didn't know you wore glasses."

"There wasn't time this morning to put in my contacts."

He dragged his suitcase across the threshold. "Did Helena get here with Stella?"

"I didn't know she was coming yesterday," Lexie said. "A heads-up would have been nice."

"When I talked to her she hadn't made firm plans about pulling Stella out of camp. I hope she didn't catch you in the middle of a wild party or anything."

You little beaky pervert! That was exactly what he'd been hoping—that Lexie would get caught. She'd come within minutes of having that be true. Helena wasn't upset now, but if she'd walked in on them while they were... It would have been bad.

"Where are you going to sleep?" she asked him.

"If Helena stays, I'll take the basement."

There was a small, plain, windowless bedroom in the basement near the safe room. Josh preferred it to the second- and third-floor guest rooms when the kids were at the house, because he liked the privacy. She'd never asked why he needed to be private, just assumed it was something creepy.

"Put your suitcase in the hall closet," she said. "We'll figure it out later. Right now I need to get breakfast."

In the kitchen, Mason sat at the counter. He saluted their entrance with a mug of coffee, which she figured must be his second, because he seemed wide awake.

"Good to see you, Josh. How are things at the Pentagon?"

"Every time the admiral goes there, he gets pulled into more meetings, totally unrelated to his main concerns. Our only solid information on the Damascus Cache is that all copies were destroyed years ago in a computer purge."

Mason exchanged a look with her. "What if there was a hard copy?"

"On paper? Nope, no way." Josh had noticed their sly

glance. His head swiveled like a woodpecker's as he looked from her to Mason and back again. "What did you find out?"

"We were speculating," Mason said. "We didn't locate the cache. Neither did a team from the CIA or two agents from NSA."

Wrapped in a silky robe, Helena joined them, pouring herself a mug of coffee. "Stella's still running a fever. I thought I'd let her stay in bed as long as possible."

"Good plan," Lexie said.

Since they were all at the counter, she decided to do breakfast like a short-order cook, with a menu of any-style eggs, toast and bacon. Helena and Mason both wanted scrambled with cheese melted on top. Josh wanted over easy, which meant he'd get served last.

Josh pointed to the chart on the flat screen on the wall in the family room. "What's that?"

Lexie winced. She hadn't changed the screen back to the usual display of family schedules. "It's a spreadsheet for suspects."

Mason took over the explanation, detailing that these were all the people who had been through the house and why they were there.

"Amazing," Helena said. "I didn't realize we did so much entertaining."

"Why is my name up there?" Josh asked. "Am I a suspect?"

Lexie wanted to tell him that he was their number one suspicious person and would, no doubt, spend the rest of his miserable, pointy-nosed life in a federal prison cell. But she opted for honesty. "We're just being thorough."

"I'm impressed," he said. "Can you run me off a copy?"

"I'll send the list to your email."

"Me, too," Helena said. "What else have you been doing?"

While Lexie served them breakfast and made up a plate for herself, Mason used the remote control to scroll through photos of their various suspects. Every time Helena made a comment, he slowed to study the person. He paused on Ackerman.

Helena exhaled a melodramatic sigh. "That poor, sad man. Lexie, do you remember that dreadful vase he gave us?"

"I made it disappear into the admiral's upstairs office."

"Perfect. Ackerman wanted Edgar to have it. And I don't have to look at it."

She also had a comment for Collier. "A ladies' man. He has women crawling all over him."

Josh finished eating, shoved his empty plate toward Lexie and dashed to the front closet, where he'd left his computer along with his suitcase. He returned to the kitchen, laptop in hand. "I'll need all this information. All the photos."

"Not so fast," she said, remembering her conversation with Bertinelli. "Let's try a bit of quid pro quo. What have you got that I might find interesting?"

"This isn't a game," he said with a haughty air of entitlement. "You should give the information to someone who can use it."

"And I could say the same to you."

"Fine." He tapped a few keys on his computer. "I just sent you a couple of my files. One of them is a brochure for AC-CD."

She really didn't care what it was. She just wanted to win. If this international incident involving the Damascus Cache was going to be solved because of work she and

Mason had done, she wanted credit. Maybe even a raise. Maybe she should have a change in status. She could be a nanny/investigator.

Chapter Twenty-Two

While Josh stormed off to parts unknown in the huge house, Helena's cell phone rang. She squinted at the caller identification. "It's the doctor's office."

Helena strode away from the counter, holding the phone to her ear, and Lexie looked toward Mason. "Multiply this by six kids and you have a typical morning at the Prescott home."

"With one major difference," he said. "All the kids are more mature than Josh. He's so damn whiny."

"He's supposed to be real smart," she said, "but you and I were the ones who made up the spreadsheet of suspects."

Mason took out his phone—which was synced with hers—and pulled up the files that Josh had transferred. "He's got basically nothing here. Places where AC-CD has been active, members of the group who are in prison. Here's their brochure."

He held his phone so she could read the sheet that was put together in a simple format. The first thing that struck her eye was the motto under the logo for Anti-Conspiracy Committee for Democracy: Information Is Power. It was attributed to Thomas Jefferson, but she'd heard the words recently. "Did you see this? That's what Bertinelli said."

"He could be the AC-CD leader," Mason said. "Under

his snotty, obsessive-compulsive exterior, he's a smart guy."

Had he been purposely giving them a clue? Or was he setting Lexie and Mason up to look foolish? "I don't like these games of one-upmanship. Why can't people just say what they mean?"

"Everybody lies," he said.

"Is that something you learned in international studies?"

"As a matter of fact, it is. But I also learned it in life."

"How?"

"Whether it's a fib about remembering somebody's name or a fake alibi for murder, we all dabble in misdirection. Even you."

She couldn't argue.

WHEN HELENA STRODE back into the room, her eyes were red-rimmed and bloodshot. Mason thought she'd been crying, but he couldn't be sure that she wasn't practicing for her upcoming role. The actress was hard to read.

"I'm a terrible mother," she said.

"You're not," Lexie said as she hugged Helena tightly. "What did the doctor say?"

"My darling little Stella has a strange variety of measles that's running rampant in Europe. She must have been exposed when we were in New York for a fashion show."

"Is it serious?" Lexie asked.

"No, she's been vaccinated so the case will be mild, and the doctor will contact the pharmacy and have meds delivered. He gave me the okay to leave." She gave a loud sob. "When I heard the doctor say that, I was relieved. That's why I'm a bad mother. I was glad that I didn't have to worry about my child and I could carry on with this movie role."

"That doesn't make you bad," Lexie said.

"I should cancel the movie."

While Lexie escorted Helena into the family room and they put their heads together, he had his own reaction to the news. If Stella had measles, the family surely wouldn't want Lexie to take care of her. He'd always heard that young women were supposed to avoid measles, mumps and rubella. She'd probably already been vaccinated, but he wanted to know for sure. Before he could pry her away from Helena, the house alarm went off. It gave one blast, then another, and then it went silent.

He ripped his gun from the holster and dashed to the foyer entrance. Inside the code box that disarmed the alarm was a schematic. He checked the blinking light. The alarm had originated from downstairs—from the door near the safe room.

Lexie and Helena appeared in the foyer. "Upstairs," he ordered them. "Make sure Stella is okay. Stay in Helena's room. Door locked."

He raced down the staircase.

Josh was coming down the hall toward him, waving both hands in front of his face. "Sorry, sorry, I set it off by accident."

Mason didn't put his gun away. "Why did you open that door?"

"I wanted to go outside and catch my breath. Lexie got me all flustered with her quid pro quo. I forgot the code for a moment, but then I remembered."

"I'll be making a thorough search of the house." Mason watched Josh to see if he had a guilty reaction. There was nothing. "I need to be certain we're secure."

"Like I said, sorry."

Mason pivoted and ran upstairs to tell the ladies that all was clear and Josh was an idiot. At the door to the Prescotts' suite, he tapped on the door. Helena opened it.

"False alarm," he said. "Josh wanted to go outside and accidentally set it off."

"I don't know which is more incredible—Josh being outside or Josh being sloppy enough to forget the code."

Beyond her shoulder, he saw Stella leaping across the bed toward Lexie. The kid didn't look sick at all. He waved to her. "Hey, princess."

"Mason is a basin," she yelled to him.

"Stelly is made of jelly."

"I'm not Stelly."

"Grant me some poetic license, kiddo. You're sweet like jelly."

She flopped on the bed. "Okay."

He took Lexie's hand and directed her away from the room and the germs in it. "We need to talk. Ladies, will you excuse us?"

As soon as they were in the hall, she asked, "What's wrong?"

He took her into their bedroom, closed and locked the door. "Stella has measles. I'm not sure what happens with the variety she has. According to Helena, it's some new variety from Europe. In any case, you should check it out before you expose yourself."

She shook her head. "I don't understand."

"This might be an old wives' tale, but I heard verification when we studied international pandemics in college. Measles can cause infertility in adults."

Realization hit her like a splash of cold water to the face. She gasped. Then she burst into tears. Her legs crumpled and she was on the floor, sobbing.

"I'm sure you're okay," he said. "We can go to the doctor right now."

"It doesn't matter."

"If it didn't you wouldn't be so upset."

She raised her tearstained face. "Fertility isn't an issue for me. After my first car crash, I had a hysterectomy. Mason, I can't have children."

"Then we don't have to worry about exposure."

"Did you hear what I said? I will never have kids. If you and I have a relationship, it'll never be what you want. I can't give you a family."

"I don't care."

"But I do."

LEXIE FLED FROM the bedroom and rushed down the staircase, not knowing where she was going. Her world was falling apart. She'd finally found the right guy, the man her dad would have wanted her to settle down and raise a family with. Mason was a partner, a friend and the best lover she'd ever known. He deserved children.

In the foyer, she blindly lurched toward the lower level. She needed to be alone, locked in the safe room where no one could hear her sobs. Could she remember that combination from yesterday? Doubtful. Instead, she went into the movie theater—the room the admiral had made soundproof and invisible to electronic searches.

She flung the door open and ran inside. The curtained room resembled an actual theater with well-padded seats that had footrests and separate snack tables. Four risers went all the way to the back wall. At the front there was a stage the kids used for performances. There were two screens, one that lowered and one huge flat screen.

She spotted Josh's head in one of the front row seats. He was just sitting there, motionless and in the way.

"Get out!"

He didn't move.

"Get out, get out, get out."

She ran toward him, ready to forcibly eject him if necessary. She wanted privacy for her breakdown. When she stood in front of him, she stopped. The handle of a hunting knife protruded from Josh's scrawny chest. The front of his shirt was covered in blood.

"Hello, Franny."

She whirled at the sound of his voice. "Anton Karpov."

"I go by Tony now—Tony Curtis, like the actor." He held his hands wide, gesturing to the stage he stood on. In his right hand, he had a Glock. "And you go by Lexie."

"Why are you here? How did you get in?"

"You can figure it out. You always were a smarty-pants. One plus one."

"Josh let you in."

She noticed the blood on the sleeve of his denim jacket. "Why did you kill him?"

"He's not dead, not yet. Wiggle your fingers, Josh. Show her that you're okay."

She noticed the slightest bit of movement. "He's lost a lot of blood. We have to get him to a hospital."

"Not until he gives me what I want." He strode across the stage as though he were lecturing her, schooling her on how to be a violent psychopath. "Our little Josh found the Damascus Cache. And the first thing he did was call the leader of AC-CD and tell him. It seems Josh has been blackmailing our leader for quite some time, and he forgot how to show the proper respect, the proper amount of fear."

Was it only a year ago that she'd dated Anton? How could she have been so blind? Yes, he was good-looking, with his blue eyes and his thick Tony Curtis hair. But his inner ugliness made him grotesque.

At the time, she hadn't thought she could do better than Anton, hadn't thought she deserved better. Mason had shown her a different way. He could care about her. But there was no future for them.

Anton said, "As soon as Josh gives me the cache, I'm gone. And you can take him to a hospital. What do you say, Josh? Do you want to live?"

His lips twitched. "Vase."

"I know what he's talking about." The Arabian vase from Ackerman, hidden in the admiral's office. "I know where it is. Should I take you there?"

"As soon as I get within karate range, you'll attack."

It was gratifying to know that he was still scared of her, but it was inconvenient. "Then you have to let me go and get it."

"So you can bring reinforcements? I don't think so."

"Rock and a hard place, Anton. What are you going to do?"

Muttering to himself, he paced back and forth on the stage. She watched him carefully, measuring his stride, plotting a possible move. If he hadn't been armed, she could have taken him. But she knew Anton, and he was an ace marksman.

"I should have killed you before," he said.

"Were you driving the truck that smashed Mason's fender?"

His smile was ice-cold. "That was my second try at vehicular homicide. The first time, I was in a black car, and you were on the road near Buena Vista. In that little bronze sedan you crashed off the cliff."

Her heart stopped. "You're lying."

"It was me, Franny. I've been working for the leader for years. He was disappointed that you didn't die." He bent at the waist and stared at her. "When you think about it, I did you a favor. The person you really want to hurt is the leader."

"Sam Bertinelli," she said. Bertinelli had quoted the motto of AC-CD. He had been spying on her. He was stronger and smarter than he acted while hiding behind his junior agent pose.

"Good guess," Anton said. "But not a smart guess. I want Bertinelli to keep paying for these jobs, and if you accuse him, he'll be out of business."

He lowered his gun and took aim. "I'm afraid you're going to have to die."

"No way, psycho."

She dived across the row of chairs and flattened herself on the floor while he fired three shots. She heard him moving and dodged to a different place. He fired again.

Her hope was that Mason would hear the gunfire. Not even the best soundproofing could muffle the concussive explosion of a bullet being fired, which was why Anton had used a knife on Josh.

Reaching the top row, she ducked underneath the risers. And there it was. The brass vase holding the Damascus Cache was right there on the floor at the back of the room. She wouldn't let Anton have it.

He dropped to the floor opposite her. His hard, cruel eyes peered through the scaffolding under the risers. "I see you, Franny."

She vaulted up and onto the risers again. Holding the handle of the brass vase, she dashed across the row of seats.

He'd taken too long to climb back up. She was close enough to fight him. Her flying kick hit him in the arm, but he didn't lose his gun.

She heard the door to the room open. Mason stood there, aiming his weapon with both hands. "Drop it."

She looked down at Anton. "Do as he says."

When he hesitated, she swung hard with the vase and connected with the side of his skull. Anton hit the floor, unconscious.

Mason had her in his arms. "Are you okay?" He kissed her forehead. "Were you shot?" Another kiss and another.

"I'm okay. But Josh is at death's door. We should call 911."

"Already did. As soon as I heard gunfire, I told Helena to get the cops and the EMTs."

"How did you know we'd need an ambulance?"

"I know you, Lexie." He smoothed the hair off her forehead. "If there's ever a confrontation, you'll kick somebody's butt hard enough that they need a doctor."

"I guess that's true."

"It's one of the things that make you special. I love you, Lexie."

"I'm not the right woman for you, remember? We can be friends, maybe even lovers. But we can't ever have a family."

He took his wallet from his pocket. "Have I ever shown you a picture of my brother?"

She took the official Marine Corps photograph from him. His brother was handsome in his uniform and his cap. "He's African-American."

"We were adopted, both of us. That was the family I grew up in, and it's the kind of family I want."

She knew how much he adored his brother. Adopted? "You don't care if the kids aren't your own?"

"But they are," he said. "If I raise them, they're my kids. I'm their dad. You're their mom. You don't need to have a baby to be a good mother."

She held him close. "I love you, Mason. And I always will."

"Let's clean up these scumbags and get out of here."

"Were you planning to go somewhere?"

He picked up the brass vase. "I think our first stop

should be the Pentagon, where we can drop this off with the admiral. And maybe we'll drop off Stella, as well."

"What about us?"

He suggested an elopement followed by a honeymoon in Paris, but she wanted her dad to meet the man she married before the ceremony. They were off to Texas and on their way to happily ever after.

* * * * *

LET'S TALK
Romance

For exclusive extracts, competitions
and special offers, find us online:

f facebook.com/millsandboon

🐦 @MillsandBoon

📷 @MillsandBoonUK

Get in touch on 01413 063232

For all the latest titles coming soon, visit
millsandboon.co.uk/nextmonth